UNIVERSAL CLASSICS LIBRARY

ILLVSTRATED
WITH PHOTOGRAVVRES ON
JAPAN VELLVM, ETCHINGS
HAND PAINTED INDIA-PLATE
REPRODVCTIONS, AND
FVLL PAGE PORTRAITS
OF AVTHORS.

WILDSIDE PRESS

MEMOIRS OF THE EMPEROR NAPOLEON

FROM AJACCIO TO WATERLOO,
AS SOLDIER, EMPEROR, HUSBAND

BY

MADAME JUNOT
DUCHESSE DE D'ABRANTÈS

IN THREE VOLUMES

VOL. III

WITH SPECIAL INTRODUCTION BY

S. M. HAMILTON
EDITOR OF "LETTERS TO WASHINGTON"

M. WALTER DUNNE, PUBLISHER
WASHINGTON & LONDON

ILLUSTRATIONS

(vii)

CONTENTS

VOL. III.

PAGE

(ix)

MEMOIRS OF MADAME JUNOT

DUCHESS OF ABRANTÈS

CHAPTER I.

Letter from Duroc — The Princess of Wirtemberg Expected at Raincy — Consternation — Preparations for the Reception of Her Royal Highness — Her Arrival — Her Portrait — Dismissal of Her German Attendants — The Royal Breakfast — M. de Winzingerode — Stag Hunt in the Park — The Princess's Dress — The Dinner at Raincy — Her Royal Highness's Request — Arrival of Prince Jerome — Recollections of Baltimore — Interview of Jerome Bonaparte with the Princess Catherine — Departure for Paris, and Arrival at the Tuileries — Junot's Distress — The Faubourg Saint Germain — Invitation to a Ball at the Hôtel de Luynes — My Dress — Madame de Chevreuse — Madame de Balby.

IT WAS the 20th of August; Junot had made all his preparations for his journey, and was gone to dine with M. Lalligant, one of his friends, to whose child he and Madame de Caraman were to stand sponsors. The house was encumbered with chests and portmanteaus, the courtyard with baggage wagons and carriages; everything announced the approaching departure of the master of the mansion: in fact, in two days Junot was about to set out for Bordeaux, the place of his immediate destination.

I had superintended all that was to make the journey agreeable, and I was fatigued; but at nine o'clock, just as I was going to bed, my *valet de chambre* informed me that one of the Emperor's footmen was in waiting to deliver a letter to Junot from the Grand Marshal. I took the letter, which was indorsed, THE GRAND MARSHAL OF THE PALACE; and beside this signature, in scarcely legible writing, were the words IN GREAT HASTE; the whole address was in Duroc's hand. I made two men mount on horseback, wrote a few words for each of them, and sent them in different directions to find Junot; but while they were in search of him he arrived. He had been to a certain hotel, where he had learned the purport of Duroc's letter, which was to the following effect:

"The Princess Royal of Wirtemberg, my dear Junot, will arrive at Raincy with her suite to-morrow morning at nine o'clock, and will rest there till seven in the evening. His Majesty has made this arrangement. Will you have the goodness to give orders that everything should be in readiness to receive her? I will send whatever you think requisite for her proper accommodation, and for the kitchen service.

"I renew my assurances of attachment to you.

"DUROC.

"20th — at six in the evening."

"Well!" said I to Junot, after reading it, "a pretty task they are setting us! it is much like one of the orders given to the Princess Graciosa by her tyrannical step-mother; but the misfortune is, we have no Prince Percinet with his wand." Junot walked about with an anxious look. I saw that I had done wrong in complaining, which would but increase his ill-humor, and, going up to him with a smile, I said:

"But standing there like the god Terminus will not forward this business that I am complaining of, and which, after all, is not worth talking about. It appears that her Royal Highness is to spend the whole day with us at Raincy; it will be your affair to dispose matters so that she shall not be weary of us; which is just possible, because neither the dogs nor the stags are packed up, so that you will be able to show her a hunt; and if it should not be quite so agreeable to you as your chase by the light of flambeaux, the Princess will understand that, with the best intentions in the world, it is only possible to give what one has. Come, answer Duroc; or do you wish me to do it." And I went to my desk. Junot looked at me, listened, and seemed to wake up by degrees; his fine countenance, to which gloom was not at all becoming, cleared up, and at last became even cheerful. "Yes, answer him," he replied, embracing me slightly.

I wrote to Duroc that we were about to give the necessary orders for the reception of her Royal Highness, and that Junot and I returned thanks to the Emperor for giving us this new opportunity of proving our devotedness to him. I thanked Duroc for his offer of sending us all things necessary for the service, but added: "This would inconvenience rather than assist us; and I engage to be perfectly prepared for the reception of the Princess at the hour appointed."

I then sent for Rechaud. This Rechaud was a clever, and, in our present dilemma, a most important, personage; he was, moreover, a thoroughly honest man, a qualification not often to be found combined with skill in his profession. He and his brother had been brought up in the kitchen of the Prince of Condé, and afterward became so expert in cookery that they attained great celebrity in the gastronomic world. Rechaud had previously given me a specimen of his ability in the direction in which it was now wanted, by preparing in a few hours for the reception of the Marquis de la Romana at Raincy in great form. I explained the state of the case, and he instantly understood all that was to be done. "Madame may set out for Raincy," he said with a *sang-froid* worthy of Vatel; "everything shall be ready at the time mentioned."

I knew Rechaud, and, getting into my carriage, set out for Raincy without any anxiety, at ten o'clock at night, and in delightful weather. On reaching the mansion I found carts already arrived with provisions for the morrow. All night the road to Raincy was traveled over by goers and comers transporting thither whatever was needful, not simply for food, but for luxury. The next morning, before I was up, Rechaud tapped at the door of the bathroom, where I had slept to leave my apartment for the use of the Princess of Wirtemberg, in case she should wish to retire to it upon her arrival; he came to tell me that everything was quite ready.

Neither had I been idle in the department which fell under my superintendence; all the apartments were in perfect order for the reception of the Princess and suite, even to the superb bathroom, which was prepared in case the Princess should choose to leave the dust of her journey in one of its fine marble basins. One thing teased me sadly: it was my curiosity to know why the Princess, on arriving within four leagues of Paris, should be detained there a visitor to the Governor of the City without daring to proceed.

My husband pretty well understood both the Emperor's orders in this matter and his reasons for them. He did not choose that the Princess Royal of Wirtemberg should make such an entrance into Paris as the Duchess of Bur-

gundy and her sister the fair Gabrielle of Savoy might
have made; and when he found that the march of the
Princess had been so stupidly calculated that she would
arrive within sight of the Barriers at ten o'clock in the
morning, he determined that she should not pass them
till eight in the evening, and that she should remain in
the interim at some private villa which might be hired for
the occasion.

The Emperor was going to dismiss Duroc after having
given him these orders, when he cried out suddenly:
" Oh! *parbleu!* — Junot — Junot has Raincy — the Princess
must spend the day at Raincy. It is a charming place,
and I hope she will think it a great deal more beautiful
than the huge demi-Gothic castles of Suabia and Bavaria.
Besides, Madame Junot knows how to speak to crowned
heads. Then write to Junot that the Princess Catherine
of Wirtemberg will pass to-morrow with him and his
wife. »

The Princess arrived at Raincy exactly at nine o'clock,
as had been announced. She possessed the German pre-
ciseness, even in its minutest details. I was impatient to
become acquainted with her. Jerome's fate could not be
indifferent to me, for I had loved him from childhood,
and though he only had treated me with coldness at the
death of my mother, I still continued very much attached
to him. He had sworn to me, when we met at breakfast
in Estremadura, that he should never forget the mother
of his son, her who had given him a paradise in a strange
country. I involuntarily thought of that young victim,
who was said to be so beautiful, and who was so affectionate! who had had a child! but was that child to become an orphan?

It was therefore with a strong prepossession against her
that I approached the Princess of Wirtemberg with my
welcome. She received me with perfect grace, and assured
me that if she had known my situation she would have
sent me a courier early in the morning to desire me not
to rise to receive her.

The Princess of Wirtemberg, at the time I am speaking
of, was about nineteen or twenty years of age; she was
handsome; the turn of her head gave her an expression
of dignified pride which became her noble brow, and which
would have been still more graceful had her neck, and

indeed her whole figure, been something less short. She was not pretty in the general acceptation of the word, though all her features were good, for she seldom smiled, and the expression of her countenance wanted urbanity; it was, if not disagreeable, at least exceedingly haughty, and was dignified and serious, rather than pleasing and gracious; her head was too much sunk between her shoulders, though she held it as high as possible to lose nothing of her stature, which was low. At the moment I first saw her this characteristic haughtiness was more than usually conspicuous.

At first this expression struck me as very disagreeable, notwithstanding her extreme politeness to myself; but in a few minutes I understood her feelings, and, far from blaming them, felt myself much interested in her situation. It was really a very painful one, and it was not for me, A WOMAN, to be insensible to it. Two days previously the Princess had been separated from all her German attendants. The Emperor, though he did not like Louis XIV., chose him for a model in matters of etiquette; and as he had isolated the foreign princesses who came into France, whether from the North, as in the case of the wife of his brother, or from the South, as the Duchess of Burgundy, so the Princess of Wirtemberg was separated from her German Household, notwithstanding a reluctance very natural to one in her situation. This situation was not similar to that of all princesses quitting their own country to share a foreign throne; she was obliged at the same time to surmount the national prejudice so strongly rooted among the Germans against unequal alliances (and if the Emperor, surrounded by the halo of his glory, that dominating spell which commands admiration, might be excepted from the ban, it was not so with his brothers); and the bitter consideration that she was about to give her hand to a man who had already contracted a marriage, which gave to another woman still living the rights of wife and mother.

This knowledge, sufficiently distressing to anyone, must have been doubly so to a princess condemned to silence, constraint, and dissimulation, and to the concealment of her tears from new servants, whose presence thus made the hours of retirement more heavy than those of public ceremonial. The Princess of Wirtemberg, then, was re-

ceived on her entrance into the French territory by the
Court of Honor which the Emperor had sent to meet her,
and which was wholly taken from that of the Empress,
and Marshal Bessières had espoused the Princess as proxy
for the Prince.

On the arrival of the Princess at Raincy she was offered
a bath in the elegant bathroom, but refused it, and seemed
desirous to have an early breakfast. As I did not know
what she might like, I had prepared two breakfast services, that she might take hers in her own apartment if
she preferred it; but she declined, and even expressed a
wish that all my inmates should breakfast with her, desiring me to invite them in her name.

She seemed uneasy, as far as the impassibility of her
countenance allowed me to judge, at the delay of her
father's Minister, M. de Winzingerode, who did not arrive until ten o'clock: he was a young man, tall, fair,
without the smallest degree of expression in his eye,
smile, or attitude; a perfect god Terminus: his wife, who
was also expected, did not come, for some reason which I
do not now recollect. The countenance of the Princess,
upon seeing the Ambassador, immediately changed, which
further convinced me that my former observation of the
constraint she had imposed upon herself was correct: it
was clear she was in a state of great suffering; the unexpected removal of her German suite had depressed her,
even to the injury of her health, which was manifestly
affected.

Breakfast was over by half-past eleven o'clock; I asked
the Princess whether she would like to witness a stag
hunt in the park, and whether she would ride on horseback or in an open carriage. She chose the carriage,
and having ordered two of that sort of basket sociables
which are used by the ladies who follow the chase at
Fontainebleau and Rambouillet, we set out to make the
round of the forest of Bondy; then re-entering the park
by the gate of Chelles, we were met by the huntsmen
and hounds, and a young buck was turned out, which was
almost immediately taken and very much maltreated by
the dogs. The Princess, who at first was serious, if not
melancholy, became more cheerful as we rode, and at
length seemed very well pleased. The heat being excessive, we returned to the house as the clock struck three,

leaving, indeed, not more than time enough for the party to dress for dinner.

When the Princess came into the drawing-room half an hour before dinner time I felt some regret that no one had had the courage to recommend her a different style of dress. She was about to have a first interview with a man on whom was to depend the happiness of her future life, and whose youthful imagination, poetical as is natural to the natives of the South, could adorn an absent object with additional charms, while Madame Jerome Bonaparte, without the aid of imagination, was really a charming woman.

As the Princess Catherine had made up her mind to give her hand to Prince Jerome, it was the more desirable that she should please him, as, notwithstanding his too ready submission to the will of Napoleon, it was certain he regretted his divorced wife, for Miss Patterson really was his wife, and it would have been politic to appear before him with all the advantages dress could bestow, while, on the contrary, hers was in inconceivably bad taste for the year 1807.

The gown was of white moiré, but of a bluish white, which was out of fashion at the time, and trimmed in front with a very badly-worked silver embroidery, in a style which had also been forgotten: then the cut of the dress itself corresponded exactly with its trimming in point of novelty; it was a very tight frock, with a little train exactly resembling the round tail of the beaver, and tight flat sleeves, compressing the arm above the elbow like a bandage after blood-letting. Her shoes were so pointed that they seemed to belong to the era of King John. The hair was dressed in a similarly old-fashioned style, and was particularly unbecoming to a countenance of which not only the features were good, but the expression very striking.

Her complexion was very fair and fresh, her hair light, her eyes blue, her teeth very white; all which, with a turn of the head at once gracious and dignified, gave her personal advantages which she seemed to despise by the total indifference with which she permitted those about her to take the entire management of her dress. She wore round her neck two rows of very fine pearls, to which was suspended the portrait of the Prince set in diamonds; the size of the medallion having probably been left to the taste of the jeweler, he had made it of dimensions capable of carrying the greatest possible number of jewels, but certainly much too large to be ornamental, as it dangled from the neck of the Princess, and inflicted heavy blows at every movement.

Rank, however, goes for much in all cases, for her Royal Highness, in this tasteless attire, entered the drawing-room of Raincy with the same majestic air which distinguished her at Saint Cloud two months after, when she walked the gallery in a full Court suit, embroidered by Lenormand, and made by Leroy, her hair dressed by Frederic or Charbonnier, and her neck ornamented by a magnificent necklace admirably set by Foncier or Nitot. Then her apparent indifference to such trifles proved what widely different subjects occupied her really superior mind in this, perhaps, the most important moment of her life.

By her own desire, the ladies only were to dine with her, and in consequence I ordered the dinner in the library, a large rotunda in the left wing of the mansion looking upon the park. We were six, including the Princess and her three ladies, for her Royal Highness was good enough to permit my friend Madame Lallemand to join our party, though she had not yet been presented.

A few moments before the dinner was announced I remarked that the Princess was much agitated. I concluded that she had some wish which she felt unwilling to express to the strangers who surrounded her, and who, in a moment when above all others she stood in need of sympathy, would probably answer her only by a respectful smile or with perfect indifference. I therefore approached her, and, without abruptly putting the question, I led her on to speak to me with more confidence than she had yet done to any of the persons in her service. "Would it be possible," said she, "for me to have some minutes' notice previous to the Prince's arrival?" She colored highly as she finished these words.

This emotion, which was certainly not the effect of love, must have been very painful; I appeared not to remark it, and congratulated myself on the facility with which I could gratify her Royal Highness's wishes. Raincy is, perhaps, the only county seat in the neighborhood of Paris which would afford this convenience. Its avenue of poplars leading from the highroad nearly to the grand entrance of the mansion is almost three furlongs in length.

I mentioned the Princess's wish to Junot, who thought with me that she was desirous of preparing her mind for an interview of which she had probably a painful anticipation. He immediately gave orders to M. de Grandsaigne to take his station at the end of the avenue nearest to the house, and the moment the Prince's carriages should appear to bring me word. I informed the Princess that her wishes should be attended to, and we sat down to table, while Junot entertained Marshal Bessières and the rest of her Royal Highness's suite in the dining room.

The dinner was dull. I watched the movements of the Princess, which were more restless than in the morning; her cheeks were highly flushed, and her absent manner betrayed an inward agitation, disguised by the dignity which she had been taught. We remained but a short time at table; when I had twice asked whether her Royal Highness would like to take her coffee and ice in the park or in the great *salon*, she looked at me with the air of a person who hears without understanding, and said: "Eh ? whichever you please."

At half-past six we retired to the *salon*, and the Princess having asked me whether I had thought of her wishes, I went to inquire if Junot had taken care that his *vidette* was at his post. But finding that Junot, Bessières, and the rest of the gentlemen, relieved from their attendance by the wish of the Princess, thought only of lengthening out the pleasures of a good dinner, and that the dining room was sending out loud evidences of their joviality, I went myself to the Russian cottage, where poor M. de Grandsaigne was dining all alone, and pointing his opera glass down the avenue.

"Sister Anne, Sister Anne!" I cried out to him from the lawn, for I was not in a condition to be very active — "Sister Anne, Sister Anne! do you see anything coming ?" "I see, my Castellaine, only the grass that's growing and the dust that's blowing," replied my gallant warder, with all the courtesy of one of Louis XV.'s musketeers, which had been taught by his father, who had belonged to that venerable troop. I also looked down the avenue and saw nothing.

But at the moment I was about to return into the house a cloud of dust arose on the road to Paris, and presently several carriages entered the avenue. I then immediately went to give notice to the Princess, who thanked me with a half smile which was painful to witness. Her face assumed a deep scarlet hue, and her agitation for a moment was alarming; but it subsided, at least outwardly, and she quickly regained her self-command.

She called Madame de Luçay to her, and probably gave her orders that her departure should immediately follow the interview; she then took her station in the *salon* where it was to take place. This *salon*, as previously described, is divided into three parts, the music room being at one extremity, the billiard room at the other, and the reception or drawing-room in the middle. In this center division the Princess seated herself beside the chimney, having an armchair near her which was intended for the Prince. We were all in the billiard room, from whence we could see all that passed in the drawing-room, being separated from it only by a range of pillars with statues in the intercolumniations. The Prince was to enter by the music room.

Already the rolling of the carriage wheels in the avenue was heard, when Madame Lallemand, catching hold of my dress, exclaimed: "Do you know it has just crossed my mind that the sight of me at this moment may make an awkward impression upon the Prince. I had better retire." "Why?" "Because the last time he saw me was at Baltimore with Miss Patterson, with whom I was very intimate. Do you not think that seeing me again, on such an occasion as the present, might recall a great deal that has passed?" "Indeed I do!" I exclaimed, thrusting her into the adjoining room, for at this moment a noise in the hall announced the Prince's arrival, and in a few seconds the door was opened and Marshal Bessières introduced him.

Prince Jerome was accompanied by the officers of his household, among whom were Cardinal Maury, the Chief Almoner, and M. Alexandre le Camus, who already possessed great influence over him, and who felt it advisable not to lose sight of him on an occasion to which his advice had given rise, and which might prove important to his future career. I do not believe that Jerome would ever have abandoned Miss Patterson if he had not been urged to it by counsels which he had not strength of mind enough to resist.

The *salon* of Raincy seemed to be made expressly for the interview which was now to take place. The Princess was seated near the chimney, though there was no fire. The Prince's attendants remained in the music room during the interview. On the Prince's entrance she rose, advanced two steps toward him, and greeted him with equal grace and dignity. Jerome bowed neither well nor ill, but somewhat mechanically, and he seemed to be there because he had been told, " You must go there." He approached the Princess, who seemed at this moment to have recovered all her presence of mind, and all the calm dignity of the woman and the princess. After the exchange of a few words she offered to the Prince the armchair, which had been placed near her, and a conversation was opened upon the subject of her journey. It was short, and closed by Jerome's rising and saying, " My brother is waiting for us; I will not longer deprive him of the pleasure of making acquaintance with the new sister I am about to give him."

The Princess smiled, and accompanied the Prince as far as the entrance of the music room, whence he retired with his attendants. As soon as she had lost sight of him, the color in her cheeks increased so violently that I feared the bursting of a blood vessel. She admitted indisposition; we gave her air and *eau de Cologne;* in a few minutes she recovered her self-possession. This fainting fit, though laid to the account of heat and fatigue, was certainly occasioned by the violent restraint the Princess had for some hours put upon herself.

I have heard the devotedness of the Queen of Westphalia very highly eulogized, and in fact it was truly noble in her peculiar situation. She was ready to set out when Junot came to inform her that her carriages were drawn up. I stayed at Raincy, for the day had been so fatiguing that I was unable to undergo another Court ceremonial. The Princess at the moment of her departure approached me, and said with a gracious smile: " Madame Junot, I shall never forget Raincy and the hospitality I have experienced here. This place will always recall some of the most pleasing moments of my life." Here was a speech worthy of the King, her father, an adept in diplomacy; for, honestly, the moments which had preceded its utterance were certainly sufficiently bitter.

She set out accompanied by Junot and Bessières. I afterward learned that on her arrival at the Tuileries the Emperor went to the top of the great staircase to meet her. On approaching him she made an effort to kneel and kiss his hand, but the Emperor, stooping immediately, constrained her to rise, and conducted her to the throne room, where all the Imperial Family were assembled, and where he presented her to them as a daughter and sister. She was surrounded, caressed, and received with every mark of satisfaction into the family circle.

When I returned to Paris I found Junot in a state of distress which gave me extreme pain. Every effort had been used to erect between the Emperor and his old aid-de-camp, his old friend, a kind of barrier, of the nature of which Junot himself was not aware, because his frank nature kept him a stranger to all mysterious manœuvers.

" You visit none but my enemies," said the Emperor one day to Junot, who was thunderstruck. Up to this time, this speech, a very common one, had been addressed only to me, and so little consequence did I attach to it that I had begun to take no notice of it whatever. But Junot was more astonished than I was in the habit of being at the strange reproach that was addressed to him, and he made no answer. " Yes," repeated the Emperor, " you visit only my enemies; what is the meaning of this whist party which you have drawn together, and which is composed of persons all objectionable to me ? " " This whist party, Sire, is composed of the same persons who played at M. de Talleyrand's, and I never heard of your Majesty having addressed such reproaches to him. I suppose they were all reserved for me."

" But," said Napoleon, " can you explain to me why you visit at a certain house in the Faubourg Saint Germain, where I am so much detested, to speak plainly, that I wonder why I allow such people to remain in Paris ? " " I visit at no house in the Faubourg Saint Germain, Sire. There was once in Paris a person in whom I had a warm interest, and at whose house I was in the habit of often meeting individuals whom your Majesty might consider your enemies, but of whom you have probably changed your opinion, as many of them are now about your person." " It is not MY actions that are in question," replied the Emperor, knitting his brow, as having evidently the

worst of the argument. "Why do you visit at Madame
de Luynes's, where you pass your day, and where you
allow yourself to be made game of by giddy girls, who
think themselves privileged by their sex to play with im-
punity with the sword of one of my bravest soldiers?
How long may they have thought this possible? Ah! ah!
Monsieur Junot! . . . you see that I know all. . . .
I am thoroughly well informed."

On hearing the name of Madame de Luynes, Junot did
not at first know what to think of it; but his surprise
soon gave way to so painful a feeling that he drew a
deep sigh, putting his hands before his eyes. The Emperor, believing him self-convicted, and that he was at a
loss for a defense, repeated:

"Yes, yes; I am perfectly well informed; you cannot
deny it." "Sire," said Junot at length, with great solemnity of manner, "I feel myself obliged to tender my
resignation to your Majesty; for it is impossible I can
continue my services about your person when you will
give credit to all the absurd falsehoods which are reported to you respecting my wife and myself. You would
believe me in a conspiracy against you if they were to
bring you a report to that effect!"

Junot's expression in making this last remark affected
Napoleon, who answered mildly: "That is a very different affair." "By no means, Sire, as your Majesty will
probably understand when I tell you that my wife and I
have been but once to the Hôtel de Luynes. My wife,
it is true, was well acquainted with Madame de Chevreuse
before her marriage, but her political opposition has been
so public that Madame Junot has not sought a renewal
of the connection. With respect to allowing myself to be
played upon by giddy girls, I am not aware of having
hitherto given much cause for supposing that I should
submit to disrespect from any individual whatsoever. But
I will prove to your Majesty how much you should be on
your guard against reports brought to you by other than
the constituted authorities, Dubois, Fouché, Duroc, or myself." And hereupon Junot succinctly related to the Emperor the circumstances which had given rise to these
calumnies; and I afterward described to him more at
length the history of the evening we had spent at the
Hôtel de Luynes.

I have already said that, during the Emperor's absence
at Warsaw, Junot, to console himself in his widowhood,
had renewed the whist parties of M. de Talleyrand. M.
de Narbonne belonged to them, and, being already our
friend, became a constant member of these meetings, and,
indeed, from this time took up the habit of coming to my
house every morning and evening. He once said to me:
"You were acquainted with Madame de Chevreuse when
she was Mademoiselle de Narbonne; then why are you
strangers now? I am sure you would suit each other."

I objected that, having never been intimate with Madame de Chevreuse, I could not choose a moment when
her opposition to the existing state of things was so
marked, to open a new acquaintance with her, although
otherwise nothing would be more agreeable to me.

"But she is a Lady of the Palace," said the Count.

"That," replied I, "is precisely my objection."

"But why? Is it a part of your protocol of Imperial
etiquette that the Ladies of the Palace are to comply with
his Majesty's will, even when he says to them : 'Come
and embrace me'? Did not you refuse?"

"Yes, certainly," said I, laughing; "but that is not the
present question."

"I beg your pardon, Madame la Gouvernante, Erme-
sinde does not even conspire against the Emperor's peace,
but is content, with many others, to admire him at a distance; for when this lion of yours yawns and stretches
out his paw, I am always afraid of coming within his reach.
Come, let us seduce you to the Hôtel de Luynes."

I wished to go for old friendship's sake, but made no
agreement to do so, and was some days afterward much
surprised by receiving an invitation to a ball there.

"Shall you go?" asked Junot.

"Undoubtedly, if you have no objection."

He acquiesced, and as I was still in mourning for my
mother-in-law, I ordered a dress entirely white and without silver; I intended to wear a great many diamonds,
but the dress itself was to be perfectly simple, and Madame Germon — who was then, as she always has been,
the best workwoman in Paris — made me a dress of crape
over white satin.

My particular friend Madame Zayoncheck was invited
to this ball, and it was arranged that she should go with

me: in relating this history to the Emperor, I remarked to him that so far was I from intimacy at the Hôtel de Luynes, that I did not feel myself privileged even to ask admission for Madame de Lallemand, who was then a part of my family. Madame Zayoncheck was to call upon me at ten o'clock; she was punctual, and found me promenading my room in great discontent, my hair dressed, my feet in full trim, and waiting for my gown, which had not arrived.

Who does not know the annoyance of waiting? but there is one much more serious, even alarming to think of — that of having your husband before you, full dressed, ready to set off, and laughing at you. Madame Zayoncheck found me in that state which just precedes tears. "Oh, pray!" she exclaimed, "do not cry; they must see you in your best looks."

But when she heard the subject of my chagrin, away flew her sympathy at once, and she joined in Junot's raillery. "*Parbleu!*" said the Emperor, interrupting me; "I should have done the same thing: what possessed you that you could only go out in this one new gown? But the women are all alike. You had perhaps a hundred in your wardrobe, for you pass for the most expensive woman at Court in matters of dress."

"But, Sire, I had not one that was all white; and I have already had the honor of telling your Majesty that I would not so much as admit a green leaf among the flowers that were to trim it."

"Why not? you were not going to make your First Communion?"

"But I was in mourning for my mother-in-law, and I would not throw it off; neither would I give this reason to Junot, or his good-tempered raillery and all his gayety would have been changed to melancholy."

The Emperor looked at me in silence for several seconds, and then said with a significant nod of the head: "It is well; go on."

"Well, Sire, I continued my promenade in my worked silk stockings and white satin shoes."

"Ah, ah! you like that way of adorning your feet, it appears; happily you did not wear a saber that day — hey, Madame Laurette?"

He was thinking of my unfortunate adventure in "Lovers' Follies."

« No, Sire, I had no saber; but your Majesty will remember that I was in presence of a two-edged sword, and
that I had some difficulty in defending myself from its
attacks; and it seems to me that you are willing to join
them; this is not generous . . . three against one.»

He laughed in that suppressed tone, resembling the laugh
of a ventriloquist, which he assumed sometimes when he
was in high good-humor, and at length said: « Well, the
white shoes, let me hear all.»

« Well, Sire, I had them on; and I walked about in a
little cambric petticoat, my head garlanded with white
violets and diamond ears of corn.»

All this time Junot, who was outwardly making profession of patience, but actually getting into a passion, whistled
a waltz or the « Grandfather »; and time, which waits for
nothing, pursued its course, till the clock struck eleven.
Junot yawned, stretched himself, and declared he should
go to bed. The weather was dreadful, the rain falling in
torrents and beating violently against the windows. I
desired Mademoiselle Reidler to take the carriage which
was waiting in the courtyard and go directly to Madame
Germon's. Junot wished me good night.

« You would do better,» said Madame Zayoncheck, to go
to the Hôtel de Luynes, announce Madame Junot's approaching arrival, and make her excuses on the plea of indisposition.»

« No, no,» replied Junot, « that might do in a house
where we were more intimate, but at that of Madame de
Luynes, whom I scarcely know at all, it would not be
right. If Laura thinks with me, we shall not go to-
night.»

While he was speaking we heard hasty steps approaching, and Madame Germon's workwoman came in; my valet
had been to fetch her in a hackney coach. I was very
angry, but when I saw the green taffety parcel laid upon
a chair, I no longer felt an inclination to scold; but
throwing off my shawl and placing myself before a glass,
I desired the young woman to put on my dress directly.
It was done in a moment, as I was quite ready, even my
necklace, bracelets, and earrings being all put on, and I
said triumphantly to Junot: « Now I hope you do not
want to go to bed, for in ten minutes we shall be at the
Hôtel de Luynes.»

"Brurrrr! . . . *Altro, figlia mia!* Can we ever be sure of anything with a woman? Good night, Laura; I am going to bed."

My look of consternation, I suppose, put him into a better humor, for he burst into a great fit of laughing. Then, resuming his serious look, he turned me round, took me by the arm, and, placing me again before the glass, pointed to a large green spot as big as my two hands, at one side of the skirt of my gown, upon the handsome point flounce. Let the men who chance to read this imagine it as much as they please, it is impossible for them to understand the excess of my distress; none but a woman, and a young woman, too, for the impressions of a ball night may be forgotten, can conceive the effect this vile spot produced upon me. It was so great that I had not even power to be angry, and I asked Mademoiselle Augustine, with apparent composure, how she came to do this piece of mischief.

She said that in coming out from Madame Germon's house she had to take twenty steps in the street to fetch a coach, and as it rained in torrents the unfortunate green taffety had stained the crape. But while in the act of speaking she was at work; and in ten minutes the stained point was taken off and replaced, and the quick trot of two of the most mettlesome carriage horses in Paris was rolling us toward the Rue Saint Dominique.

The balls were so very numerous this year that to come at so late an hour was not a matter of any surprise; and M. de Narbonne, in quality of relation to Madame de Chevreuse, and my very intimate friend, undertook to introduce me to Madame de Luynes. " MADAME LA GOUVERNANTE DE PARIS," said he to the Duchess, in the most serious tone possible.

Madame de Luynes, whom I had often seen at the Hôtel de Perigord and at Madame de Caseaux's without even speaking to her, received me in the most polite and engaging manner. M. de Luynes, who had one day been struck by the possibility of a reversal of the decree against the Marshal d'Ancre and the confiscation of his property, was very willing to be equally polite to Junot; he spoke to him between two naps, for every one knows that the worthy Duke slept wherever he was at rest even for a

2

minute.   The young Duc de Chevreuse passed unnoticed in the house, though by no means invisible.

The Duchesse de Chevreuse became immediately after her marriage the most remarkable person of the Faubourg Saint Germain, and the true mistress of the Hôtel de Luynes; for her mother-in-law had eyes and ears but for her, and wished to please her only.

The Duchesse de Luynes was herself a singular character; she was Mademoiselle de Laval-Montmorency, sister of the Duc de Laval so thoroughly accomplished in all games, and had been beautiful as an angel till she caught the smallpox after coming out of the convent where she had received her education.   From that hour so great was the change in her face that she considered the part of a woman to be no longer worth performing, and in its stead took to horses and dogs, leaping, hunting, narrowly escaping a broken neck, and recommencing her wild freaks the next day.   " I am glad to hear it," said the Duc de Laval, when made acquainted with her first pregnancy, " as it proves that my sister is a woman." Her heart was, however, always a woman's, a faithful friend, and loving all whom it was her duty to love with an excess of tenderness.

Madame de Chevreuse was one of those persons whose name belongs to the history of her era; but the true dignity of female character is scarcely compatible with the ridiculous scenes of which she was every day the heroine, and of which her own brothers disapproved so highly as even to reprove her in public, as on the occasion of her betting that she would stop her brother Alberic at eleven o'clock at night in the midst of the Palais Royal.   She did so, but he reprimanded her so roughly that she burst into tears.

Once, having heard that a retired grocer was expecting his niece by the diligence from Rouen, she presented herself to him the night before, gave some reason for her premature arrival, and so turned the old man's head that he was on the point of sending a petition to Rome for leave to marry so charming a niece.   Another time she introduced to her father-in-law a Swede covered with ribbons and stars; he was of the first rank in his own country.   He was courted and received with distinction everywhere, till it was discovered that he was the identical beggar to whom everyone was in the habit of giving a penny on Sunday at the door of the Church of Sainte Roche.

A volume might be made of the adventures, the mysti-fications of all kinds, contrived and carried out by Ma-dame de Chevreuse; it is inconceivable that she should not have destroyed her reputation a thousand times over! I know that these amusements are not criminal; but they show a complete contempt for the opinion of the world. Then Madame de Chevreuse was impertinent; rather, probably, as a habit than from any real intention of be-ing so; but an impertinent woman I consider to be quite out of her place in the creation. The protection of Ma-dame de Luynes was of immense weight in the balance in which the world measures the worth of women. With-out Madame de Luynes, Madame de Chevreuse had been lost!

On the evening of this ball at the Hôtel de Luynes, Madame de Chevreuse was in the midst of an intoxicat-ing incense of flattery, which might well have affected a stronger head than hers. In Paris fashion governs all things; and at this moment it was the pleasure of the society of the Faubourg Saint Germain to elect Madame de Chevreuse as the standard bearer of fashion. Thus, for example, as her head was dressed in a very peculiar style to conceal a wig which she had substituted for very red hair, all the ladies of the Faubourg Saint Germain, even Madame de Montmorency herself, adopted the same unbecoming headdress.

The make of their dresses also differed much from ours of the Court circle: the sleeves were larger and the waists longer. On this evening Madame de Chevreuse wore a dress of white blond over white satin. An immense comb ornamented with a single row of large pearls held her hair; her earrings and necklace were of pearls, not a sin-gle diamond. She was perfectly well dressed, and her appearance was graceful.

" But why," said I to M. de Narbonne, " is she also all in white ? "

" She has made a vow to wear only white," answered he in a laughably serious tone.

" She! Madame de Chevreuse! has made a vow to wear only white! It is perfectly ridiculous at her age."

"I did not say it was not; I have told her the same thing myself long ago."

"And what is the object of this resolution?"

"To have a child—and for the same reason she has abjured the theaters."

I remembered that for a long time I had not seen her at the *Comédie Française;* and this famous vow soon after prevented her attending the Empress to the opera.

She was very polite to me, though not quite so friendly as Madame de Luynes, who in recommending me to the attentions of M. de Narbonne, added: "You will meet here, Madame, many old faces who will remind you of the traditions of your cradle."

M. de Narbonne led me into a room devoted entirely to cards, and placing me opposite one of the tables, "Look," said he, "at the lady who sits next to M. de Saint Foix, and is at this moment speaking to him in rather a masculine voice."

"What am I to make of her?" said I; "she is the most comical figure in the room, and, morever, very ugly."

Her dress was singularly different from that of any other person present, and her face was excessively ugly, with the exception of a pair of very fine eyes. She was playing with a degree of interest almost amounting to passion at the game of *vingt et un.* "What a strange figure!" I continued; "I cannot describe to you the impression she makes upon me. Is she a good woman?"

"As wicked as five hundred devils, and she has as much spirit as they."

"So I should think. But tell me who she is."

"Guess; she has been loved, adored, because she has been charming."

"I am the stupidest creature imaginable at solving such enigmas; so if you wish me to know her name you may as well tell me."

"Madame de Balby."

"Impossible!"

"It is true."

"But she is horrible!"

"Not so much so as you think. Draw a little nearer, and look at her more attentively."

I contemplated the former *chère amie* of MONSIEUR, and still thought her face not only ugly, but very disagreeable.

At this moment she caught the eye of M. de Narbonne and smiled. A ray of intelligence passed over all her features, and embellished them at once. Then, observing that I was holding his arm, and knowing that I was expected at the Hôtel de Luynes, she surveyed me from head to foot with such an expression of impertinent mockery that I thought her ten times more ugly than ever. " Do, pray, let us go away," said I to M. de Narbonne; " I am frightened at this woman."

" She has frightened a great many other people more courageous than you," said Comte Louis; " but, then, if you knew the sense that is in that head! and its effrontery, and talent for amusing! There belonged to the society she frequented in London a beautiful young woman as stupid as a cabbage. Madame de Balby does not like silly people, and there I am quite of her mind. Happily for the simpleton, all the world was not; for, after all, everybody must live; one of my friends, who was not himself of the brightest, attached himself to the young woman; and as these sorts of attachments do not furnish matter for everlasting conversation, one day, for want of something better to say, he told her that Madame de Balby was calling her a simpleton everywhere, and as this was not right, he thought it better to warn her of it.

" ' It is terrible,' said she, ' I AM SURE I NEVER CALLED HER SO; what must I do ? ' For two such heads to hold council about Madame de Balby was too good; and the result soon appeared. The Beauty meeting Madame de Balby two days afterward at a dinner at the Prince of Wales's, called out to her across the table, in a voice which she intended should be very touching: ' How have I offended you, Madame ? ' Madame de Balby looked at her with astonishment, and all the company were silent. ' Yes,' continued the young woman, ' I must have offended you, for you tell everyone that I am a simpleton.' ' Madame,' replied Madame de Balby, inclining toward her, ' I hear everyone say so, but I assure you *I* do not.' Now you have an idea of the person, I think ? "

" Yes, truly. But was the Comte de Lille very fond of her ? "

Instead of answering, Comte Louis de Narbonne said with a smile: " I guess you would not have called him so ten years ago."

"Who?"

"The Comte de Lille."

"Perhaps not. But that is no answer to my question: was he fond of her?"

"He loved nothing. His heart was the coldest, and his conversation the most wearisome of any man I ever met with. He had a mistress for *ton*, for whom he cared nothing. However, having been informed that his Montespan was amusing herself by laying traps for hearts at Hamburg, Monsieur, who has a mania for writing, and whose compositions are the dullest and most prolix that can be imagined, wrote her a letter of twelve pages, in which he descanted upon the commerce of Hamburg, not in the first instance on that which she was carrying on, but, like a good and wise Prince, upon that of sugar and coffee, till, winding by degrees to the delicate subject, he told her that he had heard with much pain reports which he had no doubt were false relative to her association with Ar—— de Pe——, and finished his strange letter with this eloquent sentence: 'You are innocent, I know; but, my dear Countess, remember that Cæsar's wife must not even be suspected.' You will have seen by the story of *La Belle et Le Bête* that my old friend is sufficiently sharp in her answers; this time her letter contained but three lines; it ran thus: 'I understand nothing of what your letter contains; for you are not Cæsar, and you know very well that I have never been your wife.' Eh! Madame la Gouvernante, how do you like this retort?"

"So well that, in spite of her frightful little cap and wicked air, I am about to become very partial to Madame de Balby."

This ball at the Hôtel de Luynes afforded me an opportunity for much observation, but it did not give me pleasure; for the Faubourg Saint Germain had not then rallied under the Imperial banner as it afterward did. The society of Paris was then composed of two parties, I might almost say of two camps. Madame de Zayoncheck, always so witty, was unusually so that night, and the conversation of the friends who immediately surrounded me served to occupy the time very agreeably till four o'clock in the morning, when we went away. Then it was that the event occurred about which the Emperor had been so well informed.

We were to take M. de Narbonne home; he had left our party, and when we were going away was not to be found. We were on the point of leaving him behind, when we caught sight of him with a young person leaning upon his arm, of a very tall and remarkably fine figure, and a face which, without being regularly handsome, was strikingly prepossessing. I do not know from what accidental cause, but she no sooner saw Junot than she complained to M. de Narbonne of his having offended her.

M. de Narbonne having given her into the care of his sister, the Duchesse de Fitz·James, came to join us and taxed Junot on the subject, who was not a little astonished, as he had very much admired this tall and fine young woman, who proved to be Miss Dillon, now the Comtesse Bertrand, to whom, as well as to her husband, all France owes its love and veneration, as the only beings who, besides Marchand, gave ease to the Emperor's last moments. Junot not only admired Miss Dillon, but he had an interest in her as being then the affianced bride of our friend Alphonzo Pignatelli, brother of the Comte de Fuentes; this was a claim upon his regard, and Junot, who was always something more than polite toward the ladies, was as much so to her as propriety would admit.

The next day notes were written on both sides. The whole affair proved to have been an accident. Miss Dillon did not even know Junot when M. de Narbonne named him, and as she was thoroughly amiable, everything was amicably explained. She turned Junot's head. "That young friend of yours is a charming woman," said he to Count Louis.

I have related all the particulars of this little history to found upon it the just observation that the Emperor was surrounded by men who, without consideration for him, misinterpreted all the actions of his friends and reported them to him in a false light. What passed on this occasion was so very trifling that, speaking of it afterward to Madame Bertrand, she did not, any more than myself, remember the origin of it.

"And have you really been but once to the Hôtel de Luynes?" said the Emperor. fixing his eyes attentively upon me as he walked.

"But once, Sire."

"And the history of Miss Dillon is exactly as you have told it ? "

" Exactly, Sire. "

" It is very extraordinary. "

And the Emperor, I afterward learned from Duroc, sharply reprimanded his faithless correspondent.

CHAPTER II.

Junot's Departure for Bordeaux, and Subsequently for Portugal — Secret
Instructions Relative to the Portuguese Campaign — General Loison
— His Accusations against Junot — Colonel Napier — Predilections
in Favor of England — Charles X. at the Exhibition of National
Industry — Convention of Cintra — Fêtes at Fontainebleau — The
Emperor's New Amours — His Solitary Rides in the Forest — His
Dislike to Attendance — Melancholy Presentiments of the Empress
— Duroc's Hostility to Her — Interview at Mantua between Napo-
leon and Lucien — The Imperial Brother and the Republican Brother
— Lucien's Ideas of Kingly Duties — The Parting — Scene at Mal-
maison in 1804 — Lucien's Prediction.

JUNOT at length set out, on the 28th of August, 1807,
for Bordeaux.   He received secret instructions at
great length from the Emperor before his departure,
and further orders were to be sent to him at Bordeaux,
on the receipt of which he set out for Portugal, and his
army had already passed Alcantara before the people of
Paris were aware of its destination. Not only were the
ministerial orders precise, but the private letters of the
Emperor were peremptory in requiring the utmost possible celerity in his march upon Lisbon, and that he
should make great sacrifices to obtain the predominant
object of the expedition, which was to prevent the fleet
and ports of Lisbon being surrendered to the English.

"Grant nothing to the Prince of Brazil, even though he
should promise to make war on England; enter Lisbon
and take possession of the shipping and the dockyards. "
Such were Napoleon's secret instructions, written at his
dictation by M. de Menneval.

This campaign, one of the most remarkable in which
our armies had been engaged since that of 1790 (I mean

the first campaign of Portugal, for there were three, and, as Junot's wife, I must protest against either the second or third being attributed to him), offered nothing but discouragement and annoyance to my husband. Jealousy and envy erected a barrier to prevent his glory penetrating to the land of his cradle. There were generals in his army whose names were on the laurel leaves which composed the triumphal garland of France; these brave and talented men were true brethren-in-arms to their Commander-in-Chief.

At their head was the Duc de Valmy, the valiant and loyal General Kellerman, who, conscious of his own assured glory, dreaded not that of others. To him I may add the Generals Laborde, Thiébault, Quesnel, Taviel, and many others. But General Loison and another who shall be nameless were so lost to all generous sentiments as to become the accusers of a man who had loaded them with favors and honors; that other, whose perfidy to Junot was without cause, without even the slightest pretext, and who professed gratitude to him for the gift of a considerable sum of money, which now constitutes the greater part of his fortune, materially injured not Junot only, but also Ney in Masséna's campaign, when I was present and detected his intrigues.

When, some years afterward, arranging my notes relative to this campaign, anxious to render my narrative impartial, especially as regards one of the great names of our military history, and being unable to reconcile the various conflicting rumors respecting Marshal Soult and his desire to possess himself of the Portuguese crown, which had reached me while with the army, I called one day on La Maréchale, as I always prefer the most direct course, and related to her, and also to that loyal and frank soldier Colonel Bory de St. Vincent, attached to the Marshal's person, my wish to have the Marshal's own answer to the accusations of Loison, who would have accused his own mother if it had suited his purpose.

Marshal Soult received my request with more good-will than I expected, but since his accession to the Ministry he has made a point of refusing all my little demands upon him.

" Have the goodness to send me your notes," said the Marshal, " leaving sufficient margin for me to write the answers to your queries. Will that suit you?" I gladly assented; but Madame Soult objected that he might spare both himself and me the trouble by giving me the work of Colonel Napier and General Matthieu Dumas, the accuracy of which might be depended upon, and I should have but to copy what was already printed. I accepted the book, though not without regret that the Marshal's offer had failed of its accomplishment.*

On my road home I racked my brain to discover whence this Colonel Napier could come, of whom I had never heard; it was not till I arrived and opened the first of the four volumes, which as a former comrade, the Duchess of Dalmatia had been kind enough to lend me, that the marvelous truth was explained; he was an Englishman! Having been referred to this work for information, I made it a duty to read it attentively. On the principal object of my inquiry it was silent, or at least contained but two or three chance observations respecting the contested question of the Portuguese royalty.

But I was not a little astonished to find in the work to which I had been thus officially referred, an account of the campaign written in a spirit most inimical to the French, and especially to Junot. That campaign, the glory of which is recognized not only throughout Europe, but across the Atlantic, was acknowledged even by the rage of our enemies, who granted AN INQUIRY as their only recompense to Sir Arthur Wellesley. General Thiébault, the Chief of Junot's Staff, and son of that friend of the great Frederick who has left us so admirable a work upon the miraculous days of Prussia's exaltation, knew more, I imagine, of this expedition and of its commander than M. Napier, and when such a man as Thiébault, with a heart truly French, a noble mind, and talents as remarkable in the cabinet as was his valor in the field, preserved his attachment and esteem for his former commander, now

*If anything can nowadays excite surprise, it might be to find emanating from the national archives of the French Minister of War a book written by an Englishman in the English service, and animated by all the national animosity which has so constantly subsisted between the two countries. And one of our most distinguished generals translated this precious work! I flatter myself that in his younger days General Matthieu Dumas would have recoiled from such an undertaking; but he is in the case which must happen to us all — he is growing old.

laid in the earth, it may well be believed that the man
who was worthy of such attachment and of the affections
of all who belonged to him was not what Colonel Napier
has represented him.

In 1814 the Comte d'Artois uttered the memorable
words: "I AM ONLY ONE FRENCHMAN THE MORE"—an expression worthy of Bayard or of Francis I. But at the
Exhibition of NATIONAL INDUSTRY in 1827, Charles X., then
many years older, replied with a smile to one of our most
skillful armorers, who presented him with a new gun:
"I THANK YOU, BUT I SELDOM USE ANY BUT ENGLISH
ARMS."

And further on, when a Lyons shawl manufacturer was
displaying to him some admirable specimens: "Oh! our
neighbors far surpass us. We cannot contend with them."
"I have the honor to beg your Majesty's pardon, Sire,"
answered the manufacturer with spirit, deeply sensible of
this unjust reproach; "for more than six years past every
factory in Lyons sends to England five hundred thousand
francs' worth of these very manufactures which your Majesty considers so inferior to the English."

This incident may serve to show that there was a time
when the Court weathercock pointed northwest, and when
courtiers were obliged to sing "God Save the King," and
even "Rule Britannia"; it was natural enough that can-
ticles to the supremacy of England should then be found
in the library of the War Minister; but that matters
should remain the same after the Revolution of 1830 is a
little too bad.

When Junot had once accepted the command he resolved to justify the Emperor's confidence; and, although
his health was seriously impaired, he did not suffer indisposition to interfere with the most minute attention to all
the concerns of his army. But with Napoleon conquest
was indispensable. He had yet experienced no reverse,
nor would he endure that his lieutenants should; and
glorious as was the Convention of Cintra, admirable as
must have been that character which could obtain it from
the esteem of an enemy of five times his own strength,
this single act in which England ever treated with the
Empire was not sufficient; victory alone could satisfy Napoleon. With conscripts only; without supplies either of
arms or money, still he must have victory: nor can I

blame him, rigid as was the requisition; it was upon such principles he made the world his Empire.

The *fêtes* in celebration of the King of Westphalia's marriage still continued, and the Court of Fontainebleau was more brilliant than during the reign of Louis XIV., each successive day exceeding the past in magnificence. I was patiently awaiting my confinement at Raincy when I received an invitation, or rather an order, to repair to Fontainebleau for a few days. I obeyed; but not choosing to be an inmate of the *château*, I hired a small house close adjoining, and went every day to the Palace in a sedan chair; although Duroc had told me in confidence that the Emperor, whom I certainly feared the most, was about to set out on a journey.

No language can convey a clear idea of the magnificence, the magical luxury, which now surrounded the Emperor; the diamonds, jewels, and flowers, that gave splendor to his *fêtes;* the loves and joys that spread enchantment around, and the intrigues which the actors in them fancied quite impenetrable, whereas they were perhaps even more easily discernible than at the Tuileries. When the mornings were fine, and in October and November of that year the weather was superb, we went out hunting and breakfasted in the forest. The ladies wore a uniform of chamois cashmere, with collars and trimmings of green cloth, embroidered with silver, and a hat of black velvet, with a large plume of white feathers.

Nothing could be more exhilarating than the sight of seven or eight open carriages whirling rapidly through the alleys of that magnificent forest, filled with ladies in this elegant costume, their waving plumes blending harmoniously with the autumnal foliage; the Emperor and his numerous suite darting like a flight of arrows past them in pursuit of a stag which, exhibiting at one moment its proud antlers from the summit of a mossy rock, in the next was flying with the fleetness of the wind to escape from its persecutors. The gentlemen's hunting uniform was of green cloth, turned up with amaranth velvet, and laced *à la* Brandenbourg on the breast and pockets with gold and silver; it was gay, but I preferred the more unpretending shooting uniform.

Much gossip was at this time passing at Fontainebleau respecting both the present and the future, but all in whispers. The present was the very important subject of the Emperor's new amours. The beautiful Genoese, then at the acme of favor, had demanded to be presented at Court, which no other favorite had ever dared to think of; and the Emperor, though usually very little susceptible of influence from such connections, had on this occasion the weakness to accede.

But the future presented a far more serious consideration in the Imperial divorce, which occupied all minds, and was the subject of our conversation in the retirement of our own apartments. The designated Heir of the Empire was no more; and, though he had left a brother, Napoleon's hopes did not rest equally on him. He became thoughtful and abstracted, and would often ride into the forest in the morning, attended only by Jardin (his favorite pricker, who was much devoted to him), probably that he might meditate undisturbed upon the course he should adopt.

" How can you suffer the Emperor to ride almost alone in that forest? " said I one day to Duroc; "once in a way it would be immaterial, but if it is known to be habitual he may be watched for, and how easily may a mischance occur! " " I cannot hinder his going out unaccompanied," replied Duroc. " I have several times remonstrated, but he will not listen. I am, however, informed the moment he leaves the Palace, and do my best to watch over his safety. But the forest is large, and there is no ascertaining what direction he may choose, so that these solitary rides often cause me uneasiness. "

This may serve as an answer to the assertions in some biographies as to the extreme vigilance with which it was the Emperor's pleasure to be uniformly guarded. He had always the greatest repugnance to attendance; even in seasons of real danger I have seen him going out continually accompanied by Bourrienne, Junot, or Rapp, never more than one at a time. If such was his antipathy to attendance in France, how great must have been his annoyance when at Saint Helena English sentinels were instructed to escort him wherever he went!

The Princess Pauline and the Grand-Duchess of Berg were pre-eminent in the numerous train of young and pretty women who that year adorned the Imperial Court at Fontainebleau. Notwithstanding Napoleon's recent

attachment to Madame G—— he had also a great fancy for
Madame B——, who, as a lady in waiting on one of the
princesses, attended all the hunting parties, and frequently
breakfasted at the rendezvous. I know the whole of that
affair, and can assert, in opposition to the reports of scandal, that the Emperor never succeeded; though so powerful was the impression made upon him that he committed
it to writing, a circumstance very rare with him in his
transient entanglements, for such this would have been,
had not Madame B—— had the good sense to withstand
the infatuation of that halo of glory, that cloud of dazzling light which surrounded Napoleon.

The Empress, in spite of all her efforts to appear gay
and happy, was overpowered with melancholy. The
rumors of a divorce seemed to acquire more and more
consistency, and were all repeated to her; the frequent
exchange of couriers between Paris and Petersburg inspired a fear that the consummation of the peace of Tilsit
might be sought in a family alliance between the new
friends; and, to complete her uneasiness upon the subject, she dared not mention it to the Emperor.

Once when I had been paying my respects to her, she
did me the honor to say to me: "Madame Junot, they
will never be satisfied till they have driven me from the
throne of France—they are inveterate against me." She
meant the Emperor's family. And in fact her two sisters-
in-law, Jerome, and all to whom, as they said, the glory
of the Empire was dear, desired a separation. The Emperor himself said nothing, but his silence was perhaps
more alarming to his unfortunate consort than words
would have been. The death of the young Prince of
Holland had evidently overthrown all his projects.

The Empress burst into tears as she contemplated a
lock of the child's beautiful yellow hair, which she had
put under a glass on a ground of black velvet. The poor
mother's despair no language can express: that Queen
Hortense survived is satisfactory evidence that grief does
not kill. But the sufferings of the Empress were scarcely
less severe; her maternal affliction was enhanced by
incessantly renewed anxieties about the divorce.

As I had the highest esteem and tenderest friendship
for Duroc, whose memory is enshrined in my heart next
to that of my brother, I shall not be suspected of injus-

tice in blaming him for the revenge he took for the Empress's former opposition to his intended marriage. One day, as the Empress entered the throne room, her mournful and disconsolate looks seemed to be bidding adieu to every object on which they turned. I asked Duroc: "How can you avoid pitying her?" He looked at me for some time, as if in reproach; then taking me by the hand, directed my attention to the extremity of the *salon*, where a lady was seated, another standing by her side.

"Look there," whispered he; "that one is Heaven — the other is Hell! Whose doing is that? Is it not hers? No, no! I have no compassion for her!" I have adverted to Duroc's sentiments because, with his prodigious influence over the Emperor, he had much power of befriending the Empress; his hostility, I am certain, was not active; but there are circumstances in which silence is the most deadly injury.

We were informed one morning that the Emperor had set out at four o'clock on a journey, the object and destination of which were alike impenetrable. Yet Italy was the only direction he could have taken; and, in fact, the principal though latent motive of this journey was a reconciliation with Lucien. The Emperor was at length convinced, or rather he had never doubted, that of all his brothers, Lucien alone could understand and act in concert with him. But Lucien was far from yielding, and the Emperor, who knew his character, resolved himself to see and converse with him; the brothers consequently gave each other a rendezvous at Mantua. Lucien arrived about nine at night in a traveling carriage with M. Boyer, cousin-german of his first wife, and the Comte de Chatillon, a friend who resided with him. "Do not put up; I shall probably return to-night!" said Lucien, as he alighted to join his brother.

I have heard the particulars of this extraordinary interview from two quarters, both in perfect accordance. Napoleon was walking in a long gallery with Prince Eugène, Murat, and Marshal Duroc; he advanced to meet his brother, and held out his hand with every appearance of cordiality. Lucien was affected. He had not seen the Emperor since the day of Austerlitz; and far from being jealous of the resplendent blaze of his brother's glory, as it now passed before his mental vision, his noble heart beat responsively.

For some moments he was incapable of speaking; at length, having expressed to Napoleon his pleasure in this meeting, the Emperor made a signal and the rest of the party withdrew. " Well, Lucien," said Napoleon, "what are your projects? Will you at last go hand in hand with me?" Lucien regarded him with astonishment; for inquiries into his projects, addressed to him who never indulged in any, appeared most strange. "I form no projects," replied he at length. "As for going hand in hand with your Majesty, what am I to understand by it?"

An immense map of Europe lay rolled up on a table before them; the Emperor seized it by one end, and throwing it open with a graceful action, said to Lucien: "Choose any kingdom you please, and I pledge you my word, as a brother and an Emperor, to give it you, and to maintain you in it . . . for I now ride over the head of every king in Europe. Do you understand me?" He stopped and looked expressively at Lucien.

" Lucien, you may share with me that sway which I exercise over inferior minds; you have only to pursue the course I shall open to you for the establishment and maintenance of my system, the happiest and most magnificent ever conceived by man; but to insure its execution I must be seconded, and I can only be seconded by my own family; of all my brothers only yourself and Joseph can efficiently serve me. Louis is an obstinate fool,* and Jerome a mere child without capacity. . . . My hopes, then, rest chiefly on you; will you realize them?" "Before this explanation is carried further," answered Lucien, "I ought to inform you that I am not changed; my principles are still the same as in 1799 and 1803. What I was in my curule chair on the 18th Brumaire, I am at this moment beside the Emperor Napoleon. Now, brother, it is for you to consider whether you will proceed."

" You talk foolishly," said Napoleon, shrugging his shoulders. " New times should give a new direction to our ideas. You have chosen a proper opportunity, truly, to

---

* Louis was a constitutional monarch who endeavored to study the interests of Holland instead of merely subordinating his kingdom to the needs of France.

come here and theorize about your Utopian Republic! You must embrace my system, I tell you; follow my path, and to-morrow I make you the chief of a great people. I will acknowledge your wife as my sister; I will crown her as well as you. I will make you the greatest man in Europe, next to myself, and I restore you my entire friendship, my brother," added he, lowering the emphatic tone in which he had just uttered the preceding sentences to that soft and caressing accent I have never heard but from his lips, and which makes the heart vibrate. The man was altogether fascinating. Lucien loved him; he started as he listened, and grew pale.

"I will not sell myself," said he in an agitated voice. "Hear me, my brother, listen to me; for this is an important hour to both of us. I will never be your prefect. If you give me a kingdom, I must rule it according to my own notions, and, above all, in conformity with its wants. The people whose chief I may be shall have no cause to execrate my name. They shall be happy and respected; not slaves, as the Tuscans and all the Italians are. You yourself cannot desire to find in your brother a pliant sycophant, who for a few soft words would sell you the blood of his children; for a people is after all but one large family, whose governor will be held responsible by the King of kings for the welfare of all its members."

The Emperor frowned, and his whole aspect proclaimed extreme dissatisfaction. "Why, then, come to me?" said he at last angrily; "for if you are obstinate, so am I, and you know it; at least as obstinate as you can be. Humph! Republic! You are no more thinking of that than I am; and besides, what should you desire it for? You are like Joseph, who bethought himself the other day of writing me an inconceivable letter, coolly desiring I would allow him to enter upon Kingly duties. Truly nothing more would be wanting than the re-establishment of the Papal tribute." And shrugging his shoulders he smiled contemptuously. "And why not," said Lucien, "if it conduced to the national interests? It is an absurdity, I grant; but if it were beneficial to Naples, Joseph would be quite right in insisting upon it."

A variety of emotions rapidly succeeded each other on Napoleon's countenance. He paced the gallery with a hurried step, repeating in an accent that evinced strong

3

internal perturbation: "Always the same! Always the same!" Then turning suddenly to his brother and stamping on the marble floor, he exclaimed with a thundering voice: "But once more, sir — why, then, did you come to meet me? Why these endless contentions? You ought to obey me as your father, the Head of your Family; and by Heaven you shall do as I please."

Lucien was now growing warm, and all the discretion he had summoned to his aid was beginning to evaporate. "I am no subject of yours," cried he in his turn, "and if you think to impose your iron yoke upon me you are mistaken; never will I bow my head to it; and remember — hearken to my words — remember what I once told you at Malmaison."

A long, alarming, almost sinister silence succeeded this burst of generous indignation. The two brothers faced each other, and were separated only by the table on which lay that Europe, the sport of Napoleon's infatuated ambition. He was very pale, his lips compressed, the almost livid hue of his cheeks revealing the tempest within, and his eyes darting glances of fury upon Lucien, whose handsome countenance must have shown to great advantage in this stormy interview, which was to decide his future fate; nor his alone, but perhaps that of Europe; for who shall conjecture what might have happened had this really superior man been King of Spain, of Prussia, or of Poland?

The Emperor was the first to break silence; he had mastered his passion, and addressed his brother with calmness: "You will reflect on all that I have told you, Lucien; night brings counsel. To-morrow I hope to find you more reasonable as to the interests of Europe at least, if not your own. Good-bye, and a good night to you, my brother." He held out his hand.

Lucien, whose heart was susceptible to every kindly impression, and whose reflections at that moment were of a nature powerfully to awaken them, took his brother's offered hand, and affectionately grasped it between both of his as he reiterated: "Good-bye, and a good night to you, my brother. Adieu." "Till to-morrow!" said the Emperor. Lucien shook his head, and would have spoken, but was unable; then opening the door, he rushed from the apartment, re-entered the carriage where his friends awaited him, and immediately quitted Mantua.

The brothers met no more until the hour of Napoleon's adversity.

The scene at Malmaison, to which Lucien alluded in this interview, took place shortly before the Empire was proclaimed, when Napoleon's intentions were already known to his family, and disappointment on finding himself deceived in his calculations of making Lucien one of his most powerful lieutenants served to widen the breach which the marriage of the latter had produced. Lucien, who had hoped to see the happy days of the Forum restored, and could now only look for those of Augustus, was vehement in his reproaches, accused the Emperor of being faithless to him, and of violating his word; in short, the discussion ended in an open quarrel.

"You are determined to destroy the Republic!" exclaimed the enraged Lucien. "Well, assassinate her then; erect your Throne over her murdered remains and those of her children — but mark well what one of those children predicts: This Empire which you are erecting by force, and will maintain by violence, will be overthrown by violence and force, and you yourself will be crushed thus!" and seizing a screen from the mantelpiece he crushed it impetuously in his hand, which trembled with rage. Then, as if still more distinctly to mark his resentment, he took out his watch, dashed it on the ground, and stamped upon it with the heel of his boot, repeating: "Yes; crushed, ground to powder — thus!"

CHAPTER III.

Junot at Lisbon — My Accouchement — The Empress Josephine as Godmother — Imperial Magnificence — The Grand-Duchess of Berg — Queen Hortense — Commotions in Spain — Balls Given by Princess Caroline and Her Sister — My Daughter's Birthday Party — Adventure of Mademoiselle Poidevin and My Daughters — M. de Grancourt.

JUNOT had no sooner set foot in Lisbon than he found a detachment of the Legion of Police under the command of my old friend Comte de Novion. This corps consisted but of twelve hundred men, but these sufficed to maintain order in Lisbon.

It continued raining as it generally does in Lisbon at
that period of the year (November); Junot was suffering
from a nervous complaint arising from his wounds, which
was always increased when inquietude of mind was super-
added to fatigue of body. The pain of his wounds sometimes made him start from his seat.* He would not,
however, allow any personal considerations to impede the
accomplishment of his design. He entered Lisbon by the
Saccaven gate, viz, by the road opposite the Tower of
Belem. He addressed a few private instructions to two
grenadier officers who stood near him, directing them to
convey his orders to the troops.†

Junot's first object was to take possession of the Tower
of Belem. He entered the fort, and, espying a vessel
leaving the harbor under a press of sail, he conjectured
she had on board the Prince of Brazil or some of his
suite. Without losing a moment he loaded, with his own
hands, one of the guns of the fort, and directed M. Tas-
cher, his aid-de-camp, to point it. This was done with
such precision that the shot passed through the rigging,
and compelled the vessel to strike. She, however, had on
board no person connected with the Royal Family of
Portugal. On his return from Belem, Junot took a survey of
the principal parts of Lisbon, and walked for nearly six hours.

When Junot left France for Portugal I was staying at
Raincy. My condition afforded me a sufficient excuse for
not paying my respects to Madame, and I am bound to say
that in this, as in all other circumstances, she behaved with
great consideration and kindness toward me. I passed
two months at Raincy, and only returned to Paris a few
days previous to my accouchement.

I had already given birth to five daughters, and Junot
anxiously wished to have a son. The day therefore on
which I wrote to him, " You ARE THE FATHER OF A BOY!" was
one of the happiest of my life. The intelligence reached
him shortly after his arrival at Lisbon. He was in a
transport of joy.

" I thank you," he wrote me in reply, " for having presented me with a son; I can now leave the Emperor another

* One of these wounds, which crossed the top of his head, was of
frightful length and depth, and was, I believe, one of the principal
causes of his death.

† He had with him 1,200 men.

Junot, whose blood, like his father's, may flow for his Sovereign and his country."

Junot wished the Emperor to be godfather to his son, though he had already stood godfather to our eldest daughter, but he disliked being sponsor for two in the same family. However, as Junot urged me to prefer the request, I did so. The Emperor granted it with the best possible grace, observing: "I will do as Junot wishes; but who is to be godmother?"

This question was rather embarrassing. The divorce was at this time publicly talked of — at least, as publicly as people dared to talk, under Napoleon's government, of his domestic affairs. However, my embarrassment was not of long duration, and I replied:

"If agreeable to your Majesty, I should wish her Majesty the Empress to stand godmother."

The Emperor fixed upon me for a few moments his keen and penetrating glance, and rejoined:

"Would you not like Signora Lætitia to be godmother?"

"Your Majesty never did me the honor to speak of Madame Mère."

"Well, should you like her to stand?"

"I am," answered I, "ready to obey your Majesty's wishes."

"But this is no reply to my question. Who, I ask again, do you wish to stand godmother to your son?"

"Does your Majesty deign to allow me the choice?"

"I told you so," he replied, "an hour ago."

"Then," said I, "I request her Majesty the Empress to stand godmother to my son."

"Ah!" he responded, and gazed on me steadily for some time; at length he said:

"You wish the Empress to stand? Well, be it so."

The divorce took place in the following year. I have dwelt on the above circumstance because it has reference to a fact which gave a humorous turn to my child's christening, as already described.

The numerous Memoirs which detail the magnificence of Marly and Versailles convey no idea of the splendor which surrounded Napoleon's Court during the winter of 1808. One of its greatest attractions, and that which no other Court in Europe could equal, was the collection of beautiful women by whom it was graced. This may easily be accounted for when it is recollected that almost all the French generals and the superior officers of the Imperial Guard had married for love, either in France or in other countries, during their campaigns.

I have already spoken of the elegance which embellished the Consular Court; but we have now arrived at the period of the Empire, when that elegance was doubled, nay tripled, in refinement and magnificence. The Emperor's desire was that his Court should be brilliant; and this wish, being agreeable to everyone's taste, was implicitly fulfilled. The revolutionary law which prohibited embroidered coats was now forgotten, and the gentlemen rivaled the ladies in the richness of their dress and the splendor of their jewels.

I well recollect the truly fairy-like or magical appearance of the *Salle des Maréchaux* on the night of a grand concert, when it was lined on either side by three rows of ladies, radiant in youth and beauty, and all covered with flowers, jewels, and waving plumes. Behind the ladies were ranged the officers of the Imperial Household, and lastly the Generals, the Senators, the Councilors of State, and the Foreign Ministers, clothed in rich costumes and wearing on their breasts the decorations and orders which Europe offered to us on bended knee. At the upper end of the Hall sat the Emperor with the Empress, his brothers, sisters, and sisters-in-law. From that point, he with his keen glance surveyed the plumed and glittering circle.

Paris was unusually brilliant this winter. The various Princes of the Confederation of the Rhine; Germany, Russia, Austria, Poland, Italy, Denmark, and Spain — in a word, all Europe, with the single exception of England, had sent to Paris the *élite* of their Courts to pay their respects to the Emperor, and to fill up the magnificent retinue which followed him on a grand presentation day from the Salle du Trône to the play in the Tuileries.

The Grand-Duchess of Berg was the youngest and prettiest of the Princesses of the Imperial Family. The Princess Borghèse, languishing and seemingly feeble, never produced so great an effect as her sister in a ballroom. Besides, the Grand-Duchess danced, while the Princess Borghèse remained fixed to her sofa like an idol, of which, to say the truth she loved to act the part. The Princess

Caroline was the planet around which all the youth of the Court used to be grouped, without, however, encroaching upon the gentle and gracious empire of Queen Hortense, who, beloved by all, and adored by those more immediately connected with her, seemed to have formed the subject of M. de la Maisonfort's lively couplet:

« *A chacun elle voulait plaire,*
 Elle plaisait,
 Chacun l'aimait,» etc.

The affairs of Spain now began to assume a troubled aspect. The thunder which roared over the beauteous plains of Aranjuez resounded even to the courtyards of the Tuileries. The Emperor dispatched the Grand-Duke of Berg to take the command of the troops assembled on the frontiers of Spain.

This departure was by no means agreeable to the Duke. He had contracted habits of gallantry which he was foolish enough to believe were those of a man of fashion, while his connections were really of the lowest and most vulgar kind. He, moreover, made himself an object of ridicule by his affected manners and dress, his curls, his feathers, his furs, and all the wardrobe of a strolling player. The Grand-Duke and the Princess Caroline then occupied the Palais de l'Elysée. At the time of the marriage of the King of Westphalia the Princess Caroline had been in the habit of giving entertainments on a most magnificent scale. The winter which succeeded the marriage was distinguished by less brilliant, though equally agreeable festivities.

The princesses received orders from the Emperor that each severally should give a ball once every week, not that Napoleon was himself fond of dancing, but he liked to see others take part in the amusement. These assemblies were usually composed of from a hundred and fifty to two hundred visitors; and the ladies, who generally numbered above fifty, were almost all young and handsome, and attired with elegance and magnificence.

The Princess Caroline gave her balls on Fridays, Queen Hortense on Mondays, and the Princess Pauline on Wednesdays. The eternal indisposition of Pauline, whether real or pretended, formed no excuse for evading the Emperor's command. These balls were truly delightful! What excitement they occasioned! What business for the toilet!

We also admitted our children to a share of the pleasure we ourselves enjoyed. I set this example, being the mother of the eldest of the Emperor's goddaughters. My daughter's birthday was the 6th of January (Twelfth Day), and I invited in her name the children of Junot's brother officers, the families of the public authorities, and of my own private friends. On this occasion from 120 to 140 children were brought together, and we engaged for their entertainment General Jacquot, the learned ape, the performing canary birds who fired off a pistol, Fitz-James the ventriloquist, Oliver the juggler, etc. How shall I describe the joy which pervaded this young assembly? What exclamations of delight! what ecstasy! Then we gave them a supper, or, rather, a collation of ices, pastry, and the most exquisite *sucreries* which could be procured. It was a scene of fairy enchantment!

Sometimes these little parties assembled in masks. One of the most conspicuous figures in the juvenile groups was the young Prince Achille Murat. He was a very fine boy, but a most mischievous little imp, whose boisterous romping manners formed a striking contrast to those of his cousins, the Princes Louis and Napoleon, who were exceedingly sedate. The second, who survived his elder brother, died even in a more distressing manner, at the age of seven-and-twenty. He was a remarkably fine boy. His younger brother,* who is now in Switzerland with his mother, was likewise a very lovely child. We used to call him the PRINCESSE LOUIS, on account of his profusion of fine light hair, which gave him a strong resemblance to his beautiful and amiable mother.

On the occasion of one of our juvenile masquerades my daughters encountered a comical adventure, which I will relate.

At the time referred to here, Marshal Ney occupied a house in the Rue de Lille, having on one side the Hôtel of the Legion of Honor, and on the other the Hôtel of Prince Eugène. The Prince was then at Milan, and his house was occupied by the Prince Primate, a worthy man, but the most inveterate observer of forms and ceremonies I ever met with. On one of the carnival days Madame Ney

*Afterward Napoleon III.

invited our children to a masquerade to be given by her sons. Great was the joy of the little folks, and great the occupation of their mothers in preparing their various costumes, all endeavoring to excel one another in taste and fancy.

I had just returned from Spain, and the picturesque costume of that country being still familiar to me, I prepared for my daughters complete Spanish dresses. Nothing could be prettier. Their curled hair was confined in nets of silver and pink chenille, they had petticoats of white satin trimmed with pink and silver, and bodices with long sleeves ornamented with points and braiding. Thus equipped, they set off at seven in the evening, it being arranged that their parents should not join the party till nine, that we might not interfere with the amusement of the little guests.

Mademoiselle Poidevin, my daughters' governess, was directed to escort them to Marshal Ney's. The coachman and footman who attended the children's carriage had never been accustomed to drive them anywhere but to the Bois de Boulogne, or to the *Assomption*, when the weather was unfavorable. They inquired of the other servants the address of Madame Ney, and were informed that it was the Rue de Lille.

To the Rue de Lille they accordingly drove. On arriving there, the coachman, espying a large *port-cochère* with two posts, and a pair of blazing lamps, never doubted that this was the scene of festivity. He drew up at the flight of steps, the door of the coach was opened, and Mademoiselle Poidevin alighted with her two pupils, and inquired whether that was the residence of the Marshal.

" I suppose you mean HIS HIGHNESS ? " replied the valet, eying with astonishment the singular group before him.

Mademoiselle Poidevin had never heard the appellation " Highness " applied to Marshal Ney, yet believed it might possibly be the style of addressing him, so apologetically answered without hesitation:

" Oh yes, certainly, his Highness." And, somewhat embarrassed, she advanced toward the *salon* conducting her pupils by the hands.

" It is singular," thought she to herself, as she traversed several badly-lighted and gloomy-looking rooms — " it is singular that no noise, no sounds of mirth are audible. This is very strange ! "

"Is his Highness aware of your visit, Madame?" said the valet, suddenly turning round to Mademoiselle Poidevin and the young masqueraders.

"Certainly," replied she, "we have been invited here for this fortnight past."

The valet still hesitated for a moment, and then motioning with his head as much as to say, "*Ma foi!* let him settle the affair himself," he opened the door of the *salon* and announced in a loud voice, "Mademoiselle Poidevin," for in her confusion she had forgotten to give the servant the names of the children.

The door was no sooner opened than Mademoiselle Poidevin started back with astonishment, and the children instinctively clung to her from alarm.

The room into which the servant was about to usher them was very large and badly lighted. In the middle was an immense round table covered with papers, and round it were seated several solemn-looking gentlemen in black. Among them was an old man, bent down with age. He wore a small black silk mantle, in front of which was an immense silver medal.

The other individuals present seemed neither gayer nor more youthful than the gentleman just described, except perhaps one little man, distinguished by rather an obliquity of vision, and a sort of sarcastic smile, and who, as if regretting that he had only turned his thirtieth year, wore his hair cut *en vergette* and powdered, quite in the fashion of the last century. All this made a strange impression on my little girls, who had entered the house of Prince Eugène, which, as I before mentioned, was occupied by his Highness the Grand-Duke of Frankfurt, the Prince Primate.

The gentleman with his hair *en vergette* and powdered was no other than the Duke Dalberg, who was that very evening affianced to the beautiful and accomplished Mademoiselle de Brignolé. No traces of the happy event were observable in the house, where, on the contrary, everything wore so gloomy an air that my little girls, who thought themselves disappointed of their *fête*, began to cry. The Prince, who was a most ceremonious man, made at least half a dozen bows as he advanced toward Mademoiselle Poidevin, who on her part was utterly confounded.

At length, however, she summoned sufficient presence of mind to explain by what accident she and her pupils had so unexpectedly interrupted the drawing up of the Duke Dalberg's marriage contract. The Prince Primate was much amused by the mistake, and seemed almost inclined to ask my little Josephine and Constance to dance a fandango. Mademoiselle Poidevin, however, retired with her pupils, being politely bowed out by the Prince and the Duke Dalberg.

Some days after this adventure, Comte Louis de Narbonne said to me:

"Do you know, Madame Junot, that your daughters caused terrible consternation the other evening at the Prince Primate's? It was supposed that some forsaken mistress of the Duke Dalberg had come with her young family to oppose the marriage."

I laughed heartily at the strange mistake. "Well," said I, "his Highness must have been not a little puzzled by the fantastic costume of the two LITTLE ORPHANS."

On my arrival at Madame Ney's I found the juvenile party in the height of gayety: charades and dancing were kept up till one o'clock, and when the younger portion of the company had retired, M. de Grancourt dropped in and amused us for another hour or two.

M. de Grancourt was then a conspicuous character in the *beau-monde* of Paris, and one of the most curious relics of the last century. He was a native of Switzerland, a man of fortune, and generally known in the best society of Europe. In spite of these advantages, he was, both in appearance and manner, one of the most burlesque personages imaginable. His little legs supporting an immense body, and his head surmounted by a large wig, profusely powdered and frizzed, like that worn by Fleury in the *Ecole de Bourgeois*, were not, after all, half so droll as his amusing self-conceit and his mania of fancying himself irresistibly fascinating.

M. de Grancourt had traveled much, and had mingled in the best society in Russia, Germany, and England. He was an original type of the period anterior to the Revolution. He was the intimate friend of M. d'Espinchal, with whom he had frequent disputes to settle the question of which of the two was best versed in the science of knowing everybody who ought to be known in Paris. One evening M. de Grancourt was bustling about the lobbies of the Opera, in company with a friend just arrived from the country. M. d'Espinchal met them, and asked Grancourt why he was peeping so eagerly through the panes of the boxes.

"It is I, sir," said the country gentleman, "who am giving M. de Grancourt all this trouble. I arranged to meet my wife at the Opera this evening; but I have lost the ticket of the box and forgotten the number, so I am at a loss where to find her."

"Has Madame been long in Paris?" inquired D'Espinchal.

"Only two days."

"On what tier is her box?"

"On the first."

"I will tell you in a few minutes whether she is in the house or not."

M. d'Espinchal opened an empty box, and looked round the theater with his lorgnette. He then went to the opposite side of the theater and did the same. In a few minutes he returned to the gentleman, requested he would follow him, and pointed to a box.

"Ah!" exclaimed the gentleman, "here is my wife!"

"I was sure of it," said M. d'Espinchal.

"But how, sir? you do not know her!"

"That was the very reason I found her out."

The country gentleman stared with astonishment.

"To be sure," added M. d'Espinchal, "your wife is the only lady I do not know among the hundred who are seated in the first tier. Therefore I could not be wrong."

"Well," observed M. de Grancourt, shrugging his shoulders, "this is beyond me!"

CHAPTER IV.

The Romantic School in Literature — Napoleon as President of the Institute at Saint Cloud — Discussion between Cardinal Maury and the Emperor — Napoleon's Opinion of the Morals of the Present Age Compared with Those of Former Times — His Remarks on the Doctrine of Phrenology.

THE romantic school in literature at this period was in its infancy, and was not sanctioned by the great names now attached to it. Nevertheless, all the young generation of the reading portion of society — that is to say, those from the age of twenty to thirty — were passionate admirers of that fertile branch of literature, which opened so many roads to information, and diffused a light over objects hitherto concealed beneath the shade of prejudices called RULES.

Goethe, Schiller, Shakespeare — in short, all the eminent writers of Germany and England — were translated into French, and they imparted a powerful weight to the opinions of Rousseau, Voltaire, Bernardin de Saint Pierre, and André Chenier. Then came a torrent of new literary works, many of them monstrosities, it is true, but which nevertheless served to open a path to those men of real genius whose names will be handed down with honor to posterity. At the head of these may be placed Victor Hugo and his friend Alphonse de Lamartine.

The memories which I have just called up present to me many details in which Napoleon is concerned, which bear reference to literary subjects. Among these recollections there is one in particular which forcibly strikes me. It is an evening I spent at Saint Cloud, on which occasion Napoleon may be said to have played the part of President of the Institute; for he spoke for upward of three hours on literature, and the various resolutions it had undergone. Napoleon was quite a lover of the romantic school, and Ossian was his favorite poet.

It was Sunday, and there was a party at Saint Cloud. All the Emperor's favorite *savants* were present, and many other individuals whose talent and information eminently qualified them to bear a brilliant part in conversation. Among the company were M. Rœderer, M. de la Place, Monge, and Cardinal Maury. M. Chaptal had brought with him the first plates of his "*Vovage d'Egypte.*" M. de Lacépède was also one of the company, and I have some recollection that Cuvier was there too.

The object of this extraordinary convocation of talent was the discussion of some questions relating to chemistry and natural philosophy, respecting which some of our correspondents in Germany had sent reports. These reports referred particularly to the discoveries made in Bavaria by Baron d'Aretin. After the Emperor had heard the opinions of Berthollet and other members of the Institute, the conversation changed from the scientific subjects to which attention had been first directed, and took a very curious turn.

When I entered the *salon* the Emperor was speaking with great warmth; he was addressing himself to Cardinal Maury, who was always very much disposed to controversy, and who was not more courteous to the Emperor than he was to M. Brockhausen, the Prussian Ambassador, to whom he once said: "Monsieur, the fact is, Racine cannot be understood in Prussia for a century to come." His abruptness of manner and loud thundering voice always made me dread a literary or political discussion in which he took part, notwithstanding his talent for conversation.

The discussion had fallen, I cannot tell how, on the moral corruption of the French language. Napoleon by instinct could speak correctly on such a subject, but he was not competent to maintain an argument with a man like the Cardinal. Every voice was hushed except those of the two interlocutors, and not a word that fell from either of them was lost. Napoleon maintained that the change which had taken place in our language was an inevitable consequence of the influence of morals. The Cardinal replied that the question was not to determine the effect produced, but to inquire into the causes which had led to that effect.

"Probity, virtue, filial respect," said he — "in short, all that forms the basis of every well-constructed social edifice has been destroyed, never to be recovered; and I am of opinion that this destruction has exercised a powerful influence on the corruption of language, for I presume that your Majesty does not regard the change that has taken place as a defect tending merely to strip the language of its primitive and original character?"

This question seemed to be a sort of challenge addressed to the *Roi législateur*. Napoleon looked steadfastly at the Cardinal, and, with an expression which I cannot describe, exclaimed: "Surely, Cardinal, you do not imagine that I, the head of a great Empire, who am daily doomed to observe the most revolting examples of human turpitude, would think of defending the morals of the time of the Regency. There exist now, as there always have existed, corrupters and corruption, vice and atheism. We see religion forgotten by its ministers, and laws observed from fear, and not from respect. All this is the result of the subversion of order that has so long prevailed. Cardinal," he added with a smile, " I would have you be less severe upon the present generation. For my part, I think that people in a certain class are better now than they were a hundred, aye, even fifty or five-and-twenty years ago." Here he walked about the room, taking several pinches of snuff.

" Will your Majesty permit me to observe," resumed the Cardinal, " that two classes at least, the citizens and the peasantry, are very different with respect to purity of morals from what they were fifty years ago? — and those classes make up the bulk of the population." " You are wrong, Cardinal, you are wrong," observed the Emperor sharply. " But what do you mean when you talk of purity of morals in the class of citizens ? Do you allude to the period when Madame du Barry was *demoiselle de boutique?* " " Or per-haps," said Monge, " the Cardinal alludes to the time when the citizens went to mass and the peasantry paid tithes." I shall never forget the glance which Napoleon cast upon Monge at this moment — it was as eloquent as a whole speech.

Monge, who, like Volney, Dolomieu, and other *savants* of the day, was a decided atheist, had mistaken the Empe-ror's drift, and had made a remark that was anything but appropriate. He ought not to have forgotten the sharp remonstrance he received from the Emperor for the in-decorous *bonmot* which fell from him in reference to the dispute between the Curé of Saint Roche and the per-formers of the Opera on the occasion of the death of Mademoiselle Chameroi. " AFTER ALL," said Monge, " IT IS BUT A QUARREL BETWEEN ACTOR AND ACTOR.

Napoleon was offended at Monge's levity. His object was to restore moral and useful institutions — in short, all the good which preceding events had subverted. For the furtherance of these views he naturally directed his atten-tion to religion. He created PRIESTS, but not a CLERGY, and he said: " I restore priests in order that they may teach the Word of God, and not cause it to be forgot-ten."

Monge's observation on the subject of the tithes greatly displeased Napoleon, and, turning toward Cardinal Maury, he said: " Well, Cardinal, if you please, we will re-establish tithes for this night only, and they shall be paid by those who talk too fast." In justice to Napoleon, I must add that though he occasionally expressed his disapproval of

the opinions entertained by Monge on certain points, yet
he sincerely loved and esteemed that celebrated man.

The reader has seen how the scientific and literary conversation of the *soirée* at Saint Cloud insensibly became
political. The little storm which the remark of Monge
had produced suddenly interrupted it, and for several
minutes nothing was heard in the *salon bleu* but the voice
of the Empress — who was conversing in a low tone with
some of the ladies — and the footsteps of the Emperor,
who paced up and down, taking his eternal pinches of snuff.

At length he suddenly turned to the Cardinal, and said,
with an inexplicable mixture of severity and raillery: "You
maintain, Cardinal, that the morals of the people have become more corrupt during the last fifty years; but if I
were to prove to you positively the reverse, what would
you say?" "Sire, I should say nothing," replied the
Cardinal, resuming his confidence; "for to resist proof
would be a mark of the most perverse spirit. If I should
be convinced by your Majesty, I shall have nothing to say
in reply; but let us see the proof." "Well, I would first
ask whether, when you speak of the whole French people,
you mean only the population of Paris? That population
may, it is true, be counted as ten to one on the day of an
insurrection; but, apart from that, you must grant that
the civic and commercial population of the capital amounts
only to two hundred thousand individuals, men, women,
and children. Among this number there may certainly be
exceptions. The old customs that were hidden beneath
the triple spider webs which the Revolution swept away,
the old customs destroyed in certain families of the Rue
Saint Denis or the Rue du Marais, are no doubt regretted
by those families. But enlarge the circle around you;
go into the country and the neighborhood of the convents
and ask the village elders how the Benedictines and the
Four Mendicant Orders used to teach morality to females."

"Man is not infallible," replied the Cardinal pointedly.
"But look at the benefits which those men diffused around
them! What treasures those very Benedictines, whom your
Majesty mentioned, have bequeathed to literature! Their
works will be —" "You are wandering from the question, Cardinal, you are wandering afar. Because the Benedictines wrote "*L'Art de vérifier les Dates*," it does not
follow that they have not done a great many things be-

sides. But I will not exclusively attack the monks and priests in speaking of the morality of the *tiers-état* at the period we are referring to. I will ask you how that class raised its voice to defend itself when attacked by the *noblesse*, and commanded like slaves, to bow down before their superiors. Nothing was secure against the wild caprice of a libertine, and at that time every young noble-man was a libertine of the most lawless kind. Take, for example, the Duc de Richelieu, burning a whole district for an hour's amusement! Who is it says—

« '*Pour les plaisirs d'un jour, que tout Paris périsse*'?

Is it not Rousseau ? »

« No, Sire, it is Gilbert. » « When did he live ? » « He was contemporary with La Harpe, D'Alembert, and Di-derot. In that same satire which your Majesty has just quoted he alludes to La Harpe in the line which has been so often repeated—

« '*Tomba de chute en chute au trône académique.*' »

«*Pardieu !* » exclaimed the Emperor. « La Harpe may truly be said to have usurped his reputation. He was a greater atheist than any of the *coterie* of Baron d'Holbach and the Encyclopædists. He was the mean and servile flatterer of Voltaire; and he afterward made abjurations which were absurd and contemptible, for they were not the result of conviction. Did you know him ? »

The Cardinal replied in the affirmative; and, being an experienced courtier, he began to pronounce a sort of funeral oration on La Harpe, which was characterized by anything but Christian charity. I could not help smiling, for in his "*Cours de Littérature*" La Harpe speaks in high terms of the panegyrics of Cardinal Maury, when, being only an Abbé, he delivered them on Saint Louis and Saint Vincent de Paul before the King. The Cardinal would certainly have defended La Harpe against any other than the Emperor. But he had already *tenu tête à Napo-léon*, to quote the phrase which he himself always em-ployed, when he disputed with the Emperor an inch of ground on any question whatever. He thought he had done enough for one evening.

The conversation was kept up with spirit. The Emperor was in one of his most talkative humors. After this long

4

digression, the scientific subjects, for the discussion of which the party had been assembled, were again touched upon. Incompetent as I was to speak on such learned topics, I was obliged to answer a question put to me by the Emperor respecting M. de Fenaigle, the professor of mnemonics. I had repeated to the Empress a number of absurd things which I had heard from Fenaigle, whom Napoleon did not like.

As to Dr. Gall, he despised him, and had no faith in his system. He was just then beginning in France to acquire the great reputation which he has left behind him. I had received Dr. Gall on his arrival in France; for, as the wife of the Governor of Paris, I thought it my duty to show attention to a man who was reputed to have made great and useful discoveries in science. One day, when he was dining at my house, I requested him to examine the head of my little son, who was then six weeks old. The child was brought in, his cap was taken off, and the doctor, after an attentive examination of his head, said, in a solemn tone: "This child will be a great mathematician." This prediction has certainly not been verified. My eldest son, on the contrary, possesses a brilliant and poetic imagination. It is possible that he might have been a mathematician had he been forced to that study; but certainly the natural bent of his mind would never have led him to calculations and the solution of problems.

Monge and the Cardinal, knowing my intimacy with Dr. Gall, asked me some questions respecting him. I was aware of the Emperor's opinion of the Doctor and his system, and therefore I was not surprised when, turning to me, he said in a tone of disapproval: "So, Madame Junot, you patronize Dr. Gall. Well, you are *Gouvernante* of Paris, and I suppose you must show attention to MEN OF SCIENCE, even though they be fools. And what has the doctor told you?" I knew by experience that the way to deal with the Emperor was never to appear intimidated, but to answer his questions with confidence and presence of mind. I told him the result of Dr. Gall's examination of my son's bumps.

"Ah! he said that, did he? Then we will not make my godson a bishop, nor even a cardinal" — here he cast a glance at Cardinal Maury — "but he shall be a good artillery or engineer officer. A man like Dr. Gall is good for something, at least. I think I shall establish for him a professor's chair, so that he may teach his system to all the *accoucheurs* and *sages femmes* of Paris. It may then be ascertained as soon as a child comes into the world what he is destined to be, and if he should have the organs of murder or theft very strongly marked, he may be immediately drowned, as the Greeks used to drown the crooked-legged and the hunch-backed."

The Emperor considered the system of Dr. Gall as destructive of all order and of all law. Soon after the doctor's return from Germany he inquired of the members of the Institute if there was not one among them sufficiently courageous to refute " the foolish doctrine of Dr. Gall."

CHAPTER V.

I Am Summoned to the Tuileries by the Emperor — Kindness of Madame Mère — My Conversation with Napoleon — Raincy — M. Ouvrard — M. Destillières — Hunting — The Duc d'Orléans and the Comte d'Artois in Miniature — Junot King of Portugal — Napoleon Recommends Me to Go to Lisbon — The Interference of Women in Affairs of Importance — The Emperor's Opinion on That Subject — The Heart and the Head — Madame des Ursins and Madame de Maintenon — My Mother — The Invitation to Breakfast.

ONE day the Emperor sent me word, by Duroc, that he wished to speak to me, and that I must go to the Tuileries at half-past four. I looked at Duroc, and questioned him with my eyes. He smiled, and told me to fear nothing. " It is, I believe," said he, " about a business which does not concern Junot's interests in the least."

" The Emperor is highly pleased with Junot," he again repeated; " and you may go in all confidence." Notwithstanding this assurance given me by the Grand Marshal, I was not perfectly easy. It was now eleven o'clock. I was on duty, and I could excuse my absence only by a personal interview with Madame. This I sought, and I asked permission to leave her at four o'clock to go to the Tuileries.

"I was thinking of taking a drive," replied the Princess; "but I will postpone it, and stay at home. The conversation which the Emperor wishes to have with you renders me anxious on Junot's account. Be sure to return immediately, and tell me the result. If there should be any need of my influence, you know I am always ready to employ it in favor of you and your excellent husband."

Having given Madame my promise to return and render her an account of my conference, I left the palace at a quarter past four for the Tuileries.

The Emperor was engaged at a Council of State, which did not break up until six o'clock. This unexpected delay afforded me ample time to revolve in my mind every probable cause for which I had been summoned. At length M. de Merey came to tell me the Emperor would receive me.

His Majesty was evidently out of humor, but this circumstance had no reference either to me or to Junot. My acquaintance with his physiognomy enabled me to ascertain in a moment whether he were likely to be agreeable or the contrary. He smiled, and was going to pull my ear, but, missing it, he caught a lock of my hair, and pulled it till he almost made me cry out. In fine, he showed me all his *grâces*, as M. de Narbonne used to express it, and entering immediately on the subject of his message, he said to me:

"Does Junot write regularly to you?"

"Yes, Sire," answered I.

"What do you call regularly?"

"Once or twice a week—at all events, once a week."

"What does he write about?"

I looked at the Emperor without answering. My silence probably displeased him, as much as the almost imperceptible smile which played upon my lips; for his Jupiterian eyebrow began to assume a frown, and he repeated:

"What does he write about?"

"Does your Majesty," inquired I, "wish to peruse his letters? If so, I will do myself the honor of bringing them to you whenever you please."

"Madame Junot," said he, "I sent for you this evening to speak with you on a subject which will cause Junot some pain; for I know that trifling circumstances of the nature

I am about to allude to affect him seriously, because he thinks they are inconsistent with my friendship for him. But, on the contrary, it is a proof of friendship that I act toward him as I do."

He walked a few paces rather slowly, and then said: "I am going to take Raincy from you."

He stopped, and darted at me one of his penetrating glances. He seemed to wish that I should inform him not only of my own thoughts, but also of what Ouvrard, Junot, Destillières, in short, everyone concerned in the affair, was likely to think. All who knew the Emperor are aware of the excessive importance he attached to the veriest trifles, in which either his own name or that of his relations had been mingled.

"Has Duroc said nothing to you?" he continued, still eyeing me with his magnetic glance.

I shook my head, and replied in a very low tone: "No, Sire."

"Oh, oh!" said the Emperor, with a peculiar expression of countenance; "is it thus you show your attachment for Raincy? What! you pout like a child at the loss of a plaything! Well, to say the truth, I shall take it from you without regret, were it only for the sake of that fool Junot. Raincy has entailed a great expense upon him."

I made no reply, but thought of Junot. I knew how happy he was to be possessed of Raincy. He was a great sportsman, and the Forest of Bondy was contiguous to the Park of Raincy. The Emperor was not a huntsman, and the hares and deer which had superseded the robbers of the Forest of Bondy had no attractions for him. However, the tongue of envy and detraction had been busy; and I know it had been said of Junot that at Raincy he was playing the Duc d'Orléans in miniature, after having aped the Comte d'Artois at Longchamp.

"Well," continued the Emperor, "I will take Raincy off your hands. Write to your husband, Madame Junot, and inform him of this. What! are you fond of hunting, too? What is the matter? You seemed discomposed!"

The fact was, I knew how much Junot would be vexed by the loss, and I ventured to tell the Emperor so.

"Nonsense — nonsense! he can hunt as well in the Forest of Saint Germain as in the Forest of Bondy. I really think I am rendering him a service in depriving him of

Raincy; and since I have given Neuilly to the Princess
Pauline, it is necessary that I should have an estate myself near Paris.   Raincy is just the thing — I will take
that, and there the matter ends.   Come now, Madame
Junot, you know I am not in the habit of wasting my
time in explaining my motives to women."

I knew that well enough.   It was nothing, in fact, but
the trouble the Emperor had given himself to speak to
me on the subject that impressed me with the idea of its
importance.   The truth was, M. Ouvrard had been busying
himself in the matter, and wished once more to become
possessor of Raincy.   It was well known that the Emperor entertained for Ouvrard a feeling bordering on hatred.
His wish, therefore, to supply Junot's place at Raincy was
better explained by motives of personal pique toward
Ouvrard than by the reasons which he had advanced, and
which, with all respect for his excellent judgment, I could
not consider valid.

"Do you know why I just now asked you what Junot
wrote to you about?" said he, stopping in his eternal
promenade, and sitting down, while he pointed to a chair
for me.

"If your Majesty will explain your meaning to me, I
shall be able to understand it — not otherwise."

"I wish, then, to know whether he is happy and content.   Do you know all that I have done for him, Madame
Junot?   Do you know that he is now at Lisbon as powerful as a king?   He writes to inform me that the interest of the country requires that the French authority
should not be counterbalanced by any other; and the last
estafet I sent him conveys, along with the power he asked
for, another mark of my regard for him, for certainly I
should not have granted that favor to Portugal except at
his urgent solicitation.   It is as well that they should
know this at Lisbon.   Have you not friends there?   Write
them that they are greatly indebted to their GOVERNOR
GENERAL, for that is Junot's title there."

"Junot," he continued, "is in a fair way to reap a rich
harvest.   His Government in Portugal is organized in a
way which has never been known in that country since
the days of Pombal.   He is now installed as HEAD OF THE
STATE — he has HIS MINISTERS; and, in fact, everything is
going on well for him.   I am much pleased with the

speech he has delivered — very much pleased. It is full of good sense and dignity."

During all this explanation the Emperor smiled with complacency. Junot, in fact, was the child of his creation, and every meritorious action on Junot's part seemed to him but the consequence and effect of his own able instruction.

The Emperor was not the man to commence a conversation without a motive, or to prolong it because he did not know how to conclude it. For the last few moments I had been endeavoring to penetrate the motive which had induced him to send for me. Was it the affair of Raincy? Impossible! Was it to speak about Junot as he had done for the last quarter of an hour? That could never be. There must, I was convinced, be some other reason which escaped my penetration. The fact was evident; but how was I to unravel the mystery? He looked at me for a moment, and guessed what was passing in my mind; for he said to me, smiling:

"Do not trouble yourself to consider what you should do. Go! . . . The thing is clear enough."

Extraordinary man! I reddened, and was all confusion at finding my own thoughts discovered when I was endeavoring to ascertain his.

"So, then," continued he, with a tone that betrayed some dissatisfaction, "Junot has not told you of the good fortune which has befallen him? I did not think him so insensible to honors. He is a droll fellow."

Then turning suddenly round — for he was sitting before a window, and beating time upon the glass with his finger to the air of "*La Montferrine*," which was then a favorite in the streets of Paris — he added:

"And you, Madame Junot, who have a taste for all the fine things of this world, have you no wish to go and play the Queen with Junot? I do assure you that he is now in Portugal what Albuquerque and Fernando Cortez were in Brazil and Mexico."

I answered by a courtesy. I was afraid of giving a direct answer, lest I should say anything injurious to the interests of Junot.

"Well, adieu, Madame Junot," added Napoleon; "and I tell you again that if you have any wish to go to Portugal and play the Queen, I will answer for it you will find your husband there enjoying all the power and splendor you could wish. When will you write to him?»

"I think, Sire, of writing to him to-morrow, unless your Majesty commands me to do so this evening."

At first he made no reply, and appeared rather annoyed at the pointed manner in which I pronounced the word "command." He frowned, and at length said:

"Write when you please, and what you please; and perhaps the sooner the better. It is best for domestic happiness that the correspondence between husbands and wives should never be long suspended, whether they be near or far from each other."

This moral remark came so unexpectedly that I could scarcely refrain from smiling.

As the Emperor seemed to have dismissed me, I began to move toward the door, when he motioned me back with his hand, and said, as if a new idea had just struck him:

"Apropos, when you write to Junot, remind him of that aid-de-camp business about which Duroc has already spoken to him. It is an *enfantillage*, and for that reason I tell you to write about it. The affair is sufficiently unimportant for a woman to take part in it," added he, laughing.

"I thank your Majesty," replied I.

"Oh, you know I never like women to interfere in serious matters, because they are sure to be always intriguing!"

"Will your Majesty," said I, "permit me to deliver my opinion on that point?"

He made a sign in the affirmative.

"Women, then," said I, "seldom interfere of their own accord in serious business. Their natural indolence and love of pleasure incapacitate them from great exertions of mind; and whenever they are found mixed up in grave and important matters, it is only when they are the instruments of men who are worse intriguers than themselves. . . . You know it is alleged that the reigns of females are remarkable only because favorites have governed for them."

The Emperor laughed so heartily that I was astonished at having provoked so much merriment.

"Not that I think," continued I, "that women are incapable of holding the reins of government, and of holding them with vigorous hands, for I have a favorable, nay, a high, opinion of my sex; and I am inclined to believe that the solid education we have received, for the last twenty years especially, has placed us upon a level with most, if not with all, of the other sex. But there is one thing which must always disable us from exercising paramount authority."

"Oh, you concede so much, do you? And pray what may that obstacle be?"

"The heart," replied I.

"The heart! You surely mean the head?"

"I must beg permission to differ from your Majesty. What I allude to, Sire, is the feeling which impels a woman to devote herself for the well-being of her children, of her husband, of her friend! I do not say her lover, because I imagine the devotion I have just mentioned comprehends that negation of self which a woman possesses and exercises, though love may have no place in her heart."

"And wherefore, I should wish to inquire, do you deny this feeling to men?"

I answered by shaking my head, and I made some further remarks in support of my opinions. I may mention that this was the first time I ever recollect having been honored by so long a conversation with the Emperor.

"Do you not observe, Sire," I resumed, "the reason which at times makes us appear intriguers? It is because you men dispose of us; you compel us to move like the pieces on a chessboard; you, in short, make mere machines of us."

"How?" answered he. "What say you to Madame des Ursins and Madame de Maintenon? What say you to them? Will you assert they were not intriguers? Or need I mention a hundred other similar examples?"

"I confess, Sire," replied I, "I cannot defend the ladies you have just named against the imputation of being intriguers; but I contend that they form exceptions to the general rule, which serve to prove its correctness. Those women lived in an age whose moving principle was intrigue and turbulence; and I am sure I have heard your Majesty speak of Cardinal de Retz, and of M. de la Rochefoucauld, who flourished at the same period, as of men peculiarly formed for intriguers and shufflers."

The Emperor smiled again, and then abruptly said: "How old are you, Madame Junot?" I answered him by smiling in my turn, for he knew my age as well as I did myself. But he gave a wrong interpretation to my silence, and said:

"How! have you already begun to conceal your age?"

"I do not desire to conceal my age, Sire—if, indeed, it were possible, as it certainly is not, especially from your Majesty, who, I may almost say, knew me at my birth. I am twenty-two."

The Emperor took a pinch of snuff, and, counting the years on his fingers, thus proceeded:

"Yes! you are right; in 1795 you were eleven years old—right; and your mother? How old would she have now been? Ah, she never liked to tell her age! How absurd that was! What matters age to a woman so beautiful as she! She was indeed handsome. Have you her portrait?"

"We have her bust, Sire—a perfect likeness; at least, as she appeared at the time at which it was taken."

"She was," he resumed, "a singular woman! Amiable —excellent. But such a spirit! The spirit of a devil!"

As he spoke these words, he alternately took snuff and tapped his fingers on the arm of his chair; while I, with the door in my hand (which I had been holding for a full quarter of an hour), was waiting only to be dismissed. At the mention of my mother's name, however, I began to turn the handle, in order to make my way out at the first offensive word he might utter. This he perceived, and immediately said:

"Did she often speak to you of me?"

"Never, Sire," I replied.

"Impossible!" cried he, rising from his chair, with an air of displeasure—"Impossible!"

"Why so, Sire?" I asked.

Probably my imperturbability made him perceive the absurdity of his impetuosity, for he immediately resumed his seat, and remarked with some degree of bitterness:

"It is true, she had no kindly feeling toward me! Lucien was her favorite, and it is very certain that my severity to him eradicated from her heart any little regard she might before have entertained for me."

"My poor mother, Sire," I replied, "died long before your Majesty decreed the exile of your brother."

It is impossible to describe the emotion I excited in him by this seemingly innocent remark. He rose, endeavored to speak, and then sat down again. The color flew to his cheek, and as quickly deserted it. He rose a second time, pushed his chair from him with violence, and fixing on me a look, which, to say the least, was stern, seemed struggling to restrain his passion. At length, suddenly assuming the most gracious tone and manner, he said:

"Well, good evening; and when you write to Junot, give my remembrances to him."

I courtesied and left him, after a conversation which had lasted more than three-quarters of an hour. But I had no sooner reached the end of the gallery than the door of the cabinet opened, and the Emperor, in a loud voice, called after me, "Madame Junot!"

I turned, and perceived him at the door, beckoning me to return. I did so.

"Did you not tell me," said he, as soon as I approached him, "that you were in attendance on Signora Lætitia?"

"Yes, Sire," I answered; "and I am now going to her."

"Tell her, then, that I wish she would come and breakfast with me to-morrow."

The Emperor again bade me farewell with a gracious motion of his hand, and retired into his closet.

I found Madame impatiently expecting me. That excellent Princess evinced for me the utmost kindness and benevolence. I related to her the conversation I had had with the Emperor, and she seemed not at all displeased, for, to say the truth, the loss of Raincy was, in her opinion, rather a benefit than an evil. She appeared pleased to hear how angry I had made him by my remarks respecting Lucien. But when I delivered the message the Emperor had sent to her, she seemed vexed. I pretended not to observe this, and it was not till some time afterward that I learned the reason of her displeasure

CHAPTER VI.

The Emperor's Family — Negotiations between Napoleon and Lucien — M. Campi — His Mission to Canino — Madame Lucien Bonaparte — The Duchy of Parma and the Throne of Naples — Lucien's Magnanimous Conduct — His Daughter Charlotte — Her Projected Marriage with Ferdinand VII. — Her Departure for Spain Countermanded — Affairs of Spain — M. de Talleyrand.

THE interior of the Emperor's family presented a curious picture. There were circumstances connected with it which, though concealed from the world, had a strong influence on important public questions, as well as upon private interests. This was the case, for instance, on the occasion of the long negotiations which passed between the Emperor and his brother Lucien from the year 1807 to 1809. About this time the Emperor wished to establish a universal monarchy through the medium of the members of his family; and notwithstanding the scene which had occurred at Mantua, a new chance seemed now to offer itself of a reconciliation between the two brothers.

The pretext for opening this new negotiation was the demand made by the Prince of the Asturias to Napoleon for espousing a daughter of the Bonaparte family. The Emperor was perfectly convinced that Lucien would not be inclined to give, or rather to sacrifice, his daughter, by consenting to her marriage with a man who had acted a most unnatural part toward his father and mother. He therefore saw the necessity of managing the business skillfully, and he accordingly engaged M. Campi to be the bearer of the propositions to Canino, where Lucien then resided. M. Campi was a devoted friend of the Bonaparte family. He was a Corsican, and his talents were conspicuous enough to justify Napoleon's choice, without reference to favor or family connections. When Lucien was Minister of the Interior, he had employed M. Campi as his private secretary, and he entertained a high opinion of him.

The Emperor had two subjects equally difficult and delicate to propose to Lucien. The first was the marriage of Charlotte Bonaparte with the Prince of the Asturias. In this affair the Emperor behaved with a degree of duplicity which cannot be excused. It is evident that at that very moment he was revolving in his mind a plan with regard to Ferdinand which seemed utterly at variance with his communication to Lucien. M. Campi was the bearer of a letter, inviting Lucien, on the part of the Emperor, to repair to Paris in order to hear and discuss personally a new proposition which would be made to him: this was that Lucien should accept the Kingdom of Naples.

Joseph was to have another sovereignty, though its name was not specified; but Holland being the only one to give away, as Louis intended soon to renounce his throne, it might be presumed that the exchange was to be between Naples and the Hague. However, it was not so; for the throne of Spain was the point to which the Emperor's views were directed. He wished at the same time to have Italy at his disposal; and Lucien, whose courage, both moral and physical, he well knew, was the man suited to his purpose. On this occasion Napoleon proved how a determination once formed in his mind became stronger instead of weaker in time. He had said once in the Council of State: " I never will acknowledge the wife of my brother Lucien to be my sister-in-law."

These words having been emphatically uttered in the sanctuary of the laws, he regarded them as a solemn bond. But this was, in fact, only another proof of that despotic power which the Emperor was always eager to exercise whenever any member of his family attempted to become a free agent. In proportion as Lucien's conduct was noble and honorable in asserting his political independence, the more was the Emperor resolved to force him to give up another point, which he could not relinquish without a sacrifice of honor. Napoleon entertained for Madame Lucien a feeling closely bordering on hatred. I have frequently heard him speak of her with such bitterness that Josephine, who certainly owed no kindness either to Lucien or to any of his family, one day said to the Emperor, in her soft tone of remonstrance: " Recollect, my dear, that she is a woman."

That title to consideration might have sufficed, even had Madame Lucien not been, as she really was, the type of a Roman matron — such a one as we may conceive the mothers and wives of the celebrated Romans to have been. She lived in a style of magnificence which accorded with her husband's station; but seldom stirred from her home, where she was surrounded by a numerous family, which formed a sufficient defense against the tongue of slander. Her conduct was irreproachable, and she rendered Lucien completely happy.

Like him, she possessed a taste for literature, and her society served to alleviate the chagrin and irritation which occasionally resulted from the Emperor's treatment of his brother. Indeed, if it were true, as the Emperor used to say, that Lucien had contracted this union only to vex him, he at all events found in it a source of happiness which possibly might not have resulted from a marriage concluded under more favorable auspices.

Napoleon instructed M. Campi to convey to his brother the investiture of the Duchy of Parma; but it was not FOR Lucien, but for his wife ALONE. As to Lucien, he was to be King of Naples. Madame Lucien was to proceed from Rome to Parma in quality of Duchess, taking with her two of her children; that is to say, two of her daughters, for she was not to take either of her sons. When once beyond the walls of Rome, it was Napoleon's wish that she should be separated from Lucien as completely and finally as death could have separated her. On condition of her making this sacrifice, the Emperor was willing to acknowledge her as his sister-in-law, and to behave toward her as a kind relation. But she was to break every tie which attached her to life, and to be separated from all she held dear!

On receiving Campi's communication Lucien instantly refused, not merely the crown of Naples, with permission to be a free agent, but also the Duchy of Parma, which he conceived he could purchase only by base and dishonorable complaisance. The situation in which Madame Lucien was placed was totally different from that of her husband. What it was his duty to reject it was hers to comply with. She had only to follow the path which Fate had traced out for woman! In short, after a night passed in the most painful reflections, she declared to Lucien that she had determined to be no obstacle in the way of his elevation, that she had prepared an answer to that effect, and was about to send it to the Emperor.

"Where is the letter?" said Lucien with apparent composure. Madame Lucien gave it to him. He immediately tore it to pieces, and threw it on the ground. Madame Lucien insisted on conciliating the Emperor, and securing the advantage of her husband and children at any personal sacrifice to herself. But Lucien was firmly fixed in his resolution, and it was finally agreed that the Emperor's offers should be rejected. The carriage designed to convey Madame Lucien to Parma was in attendance; everything had been prepared for the journey; but all was instantly countermanded.

As to the proposed marriage of Lucien's daughter with the Prince of the Asturias, the refusal was not so immediate. On the contrary, Lucien directed preparations to be made for her departure to Spain. His daughter Charlotte was a beautiful and accomplished girl of fourteen or fifteen years of age.* Indeed, she would have formed a most desirable match for any prince in the world, and Ferdinand might have been most happy in possessing her.

The preparations for her departure were carried on with so much secrecy that the good people of Rome knew nothing of the matter, and probably I am now the first to give publicity to the affair. Madame Letiers, the wife of the Director of the French Academy, was selected to accompany the young Princess to Spain. Everything was ready, when one morning Lucien sent to request that Comte de Chatillon would come and speak to him. The Count, who was an intimate friend of Lucien Bonaparte, had been reduced by the events of the Revolution to the necessity of exercising professionally his talent in the fine arts. This gentleman had followed Lucien in his banishment to Italy. He resided in his house at Canino, and assisted in the education of his children.

Lucien, on sending for the Count, unexpectedly directed him to countermand all the preparations made for Charlotte's departure. "I cannot," said he, "resolve to separate from my beloved child! and, above all, I will never consent to her connection with a Court the vice and profligacy of which no one knows better than I. There is only one man who could protect her there, and that is Charles IV.; but though he might have the will, he

* She was afterward the Princess Gabrielli.

possesses not the power. Therefore it is better that my poor child should be under the protection of her father.» The Princess Charlotte accordingly remained at home.

Such is the history of the first negotiation for the marriage of Prince Ferdinand with a relative of Napoleon — a marriage which the former had solicited. M. Campi returned to France in order to report the result of his mission to Napoleon, and this affair contributed not a little to heighten the feeling of animosity which the Emperor entertained toward Madame Lucien.

A great deal has been said relative to Napoleon's project of giving to the surviving members of the Bourbon family a crown in Europe. It would be perhaps a difficult question to decide whether this project was the result of a sudden or a deliberate determination on his part. Be this as it may, I can assert, without the fear of contradiction, that the designs which the Emperor entertained with regard to Spain did not originate long before the time when Ferdinand wrote him the letter from the Escurial. At that period the weakness exhibited by the Court of Madrid led him to believe that it would be more favorable to the interests of Spain that he should give her a Sovereign than that she should be governed by an unprincipled favorite, a profligate Queen, and an imbecile King.

It has been alleged that M. de Talleyrand powerfully influenced the Emperor in the part he took after the affairs of Aranjuez. I do not deny that such may be the fact; but I must remark that Napoleon was not the man to allow himself to be greatly INFLUENCED by anyone. I know, for instance, that M. de Talleyrand advised him to go to Spain to consummate the work which had been begun by that good and trusty Castilian, Izquierdo; but I am inclined to believe that M. de Talleyrand, with all his finesse, was in this matter rather the instrument than the director, and that, in this Spanish business, Napoleon outwitted him.

CHAPTER VII.

The Grand-Duchess of Berg's Masquerade — A Quadrille of Sixteen Ladies — The Tyrolean Peasant Girls — Prince Camille Borghèse — His Extraordinary Disguise — The Blue Mask — Isabey Personating the Emperor — His Large Hands — The Dance Interrupted — Mademoiselle Gu——t and the Grand-Duchess — The New Nobility — The Duc de Rovigo — General Rapp — The Salute — The Duchesse de Montebello — The Pope's Bull and the Ass Laden with Relics.

ONE of the most remarkable entertainments in Paris was a masquerade given by the Grand-Duchess of Berg. In the course of the evening a quadrille was danced; this was really the first one which deserved the name; for those introduced at the marriage of the Princess of Baden had none of the characteristics of a quadrille, except that of being danced by four couples, dressed in red, green, and blue.

The costume which the Grand-Duchess of Berg selected was that of the Tyrolese peasantry, and her Highness had arranged that the quadrille should be exclusively danced by females. We made a party of sixteen Tyrolean peasant girls, and we were headed by our *bailli*. This venerable personage was represented by Mademoiselle Adelaide de Lagrange. The Grand-Duchess, for some reason or other, did not wish the quadrille dancers to assemble at her residence in the Elysée Napoleon. She requested that they might meet at my house, and proceed altogether to the Elysée. Her Highness gave orders to this effect to Despreaux, the director of the Court ballets. About nine o'clock I had a rehearsal of the quadrille in the grand gallery of my Hôtel. Several of my friends who were not included in the Grand-Duchess's invitation came to see the dance, and we were unexpectedly enlivened by an incident which I will here relate.

It was half-past ten o'clock; the moment for our departure to the Palace was fast approaching. I counted my masks. There were fourteen, the right number. There were the Comtesse du Châtel, the Comtesse Regnault de Saint Jean d'Angely, the Princess of Wagram (who was not then married), Madame de Colbert, Mademoiselle de la

5

Vauguyon, and her sister, the Princesse de Beauffremont. Then there was the Baronne de Montmorency, and some others whose names I forget. I believe the Duchesse de Rovigo was one of them. We were engaged in adjusting our masks, when M. Cavagnari* entered and whispered me that a lady who was included in the quadrille was waiting in the next room; but as she had come too late she wished me to go and conduct her in.

I cast my eyes over the list sent me by the Grand-Duchess. I found my number was complete; but as the Princesse de Ponte-Corvo, one of the masks, was not in my list, I concluded that she must be the lady who had just arrived. I therefore proceeded to the *salon*, which formed a sort of anteroom to the gallery. There I perceived, in the further corner of the apartment, a lady, whose short and bulky person was so ludicrous that at first I could not help starting back with astonishment. Imagine a figure about five feet some inches in height, but incredibly stout, and dressed in the Tyrolean costume. I approached this singular apparition; as I advanced, I became more and more amazed at the grotesque figure before me. " *Mon Dieu!* what an extraordinary person! " thought I to myself. " To whom have I the honor to address myself ? " inquired I.

The mask answered only by a deep sigh. I now found it impossible to contain my laughter. A second sigh succeeded, much more profound than the first, and it was breathed with such force as to blow up the lace trimming of the mask. Being anxious to terminate this embarrassing sort of conversation, I extended my hand to the lady, and proposed to conduct her to the gallery; when she suddenly seized me by the waist, and, raising her mask, attempted to kiss me. I screamed, and, disengaging myself, flew to the bell, and pulled it with all my might. Truly, my precipitation might well be excused, for I felt a rough beard in contact with my chin. M. Cavagnari entered, and immediately burst into a fit of laughter. The stout lady laughed with him; and, to say the truth, I laughed too, though half inclined to be angry; for I now saw before me the unmasked face of his Royal Highness the Prince Camille Borghèse.

At length I proposed to conduct his Highness to the gallery, where the ladies were not a little astonished and

* M. Cavagnari was a confidential domestic of the Duc d'Abrantès.

amused by the extraordinary *travestie*. It would be difficult to convey an idea of the burlesque figure he presented,
especially when, having removed his mask, he exhibited his
bluish beard, black whiskers, and bushy hair, some stubborn
locks of which escaped from beneath the Indian muslin
veil. The whimsical effect of all this was heightened by
the contrast of the young and elegant females who were
grouped around him, and whose costume he had closely
imitated. It was alternately amusing and provoking to
find our Sosio reflecting us so admirably in caricature.

It was now time to proceed to the Palace, and it was
agreed that the Prince should go with us. We found the
Grand-Duchess of Berg waiting to receive us in her private apartment, attended by the Princesse de Ponte-Corvo,
both dressed exactly in the same style as ourselves.
Great merriment was excited by the introduction of our
newly-recruited Tyrolese peasant girl. We entered the
ball-room headed by our venerable *bailli*, holding in her
hand her little white staff, and wearing her wig most
magisterially. As we were proceeding from the inner apartment to the gallery, a little mask in blue ran against me
on his way to the closet, where the dominoes were changed.
I was pushed aside with so much force that I almost felt
inclined to be angry. But the little blue mask was no
other than the Emperor!

Napoleon liked to divert himself, as he used to say, in
these saturnalia. He loved to disguise himself completely,
and allow some individual to assume his character. On
the evening in question Isabey was to personate him.
The humor of that celebrated artist was admirably calculated to enliven a masked ball, while the Emperor made
but a poor figure in such an entertainment. In personating
Napoleon, Isabey found it most difficult to disguise his hands,
which were exceedingly large, while the Emperor's were
small and beautifully formed. With the exception, however, of his hands, Isabey personated the Emperor to perfection.

The masquerade was kept up with great spirit; the
costumes were elegant, and the entertainment was altogether one of the most delightful that had been given
during that winter. In the course of the evening a little
incident occurred which had well-nigh interrupted the
general good humor that prevailed: Suddenly the cheerful

strains of the orchestra and the gay buzz of conversation were interrupted by the tones of a loud female voice, which exclaimed in an imperious tone: "I desire that she shall instantly quit my house!" This was the voice of the Grand-Duchess herself.

Those who were connected with the Imperial Court at the time will recollect that a very pretty girl named Mademoiselle Gu——t had been in the service of the Empress before the appointment of Madame Gazani. Mademoiselle Gu——t was a most beautiful creature, and Queen Hortense, who to every other proof of good taste joined that of loving to see agreeable faces about her, had been very kind to Mademoiselle Gu——t. She took the young lady to the Grand-Duchess's ball, where she was to be one of the characters in a quadrille. Whether the Grand-Duchess was really ignorant of the presence of Mademoiselle Gu——t until the moment of the exclamation above cited, or whether she maliciously wished to place the young lady in a painful situation, I pretend not to decide; but certain it is that she seemed to evince great astonishment at learning that Mademoiselle Gu——t was in the room, and instantly gave vent to her indignation in the words I have recorded.

Poor Mademoiselle Gu——t, in tears, declared that the conduct of the Grand-Duchess was most unjust and cruel, and could not be excused, even by the jealousy of an offended wife. The truth is, it was the love of the Grand-Duchess for the Grand-Duke which had given rise to this angry scene. Mademoiselle Gu——t had attracted the notice of his Highness, and that was sin enough to be thus visited by a public censure.

Queen Hortense, however, warmly espoused the cause of the young lady, and with some success. But it may easily be conceived that the whole scene had a very ludicrous effect. I might myself have quarreled with Mademoiselle Gu——t on the same grounds, but I restrained my feelings. I consoled myself with the idea that the Grand-Duchess, from the recollection of our early friendship, had taken up my cause along with her own.

Be this as it may, Mademoiselle Gu——t was amply indemnified for the painful situation in which she had been placed. The Empress took her into her service.

However, it is but just to all parties to mention that very shortly after the Empress's arrival at Bayonne it was found necessary to furnish Mademoiselle Gu——t with a passport to return to Paris to her mother.

I have not yet spoken of a most important circumstance in the political life of the Emperor, viz, the creation of his new Nobility. The institution of the Order of the Legion of Honor had already paved the way for this, but the work was not consummated until the creation of hereditary titles, with endowments. It was indeed expected that the Emperor would earlier have directed his attention to this matter, for the creation of the Duchy of Dantzic on the 28th of May, 1807, sufficiently revealed his intention.

I was on duty with Madame at the Tuileries, and used to accompany her to the family dinners which took place every Sunday. On one of these occasions, while I was waiting in the *salon de service* in the Pavilion of Flora, I perceived Savary approaching me. "Embrace me!" cried he; "I have good news." "Tell me the news first," said I, "and then I shall see whether it be worth the reward." "Well, then, I am a Duke." "That is news indeed," said I; "but why should I embrace you for that?" "My title is the Duke of Rovigo," continued he, marching up and down the room in an ecstasy of joy. "And what do I care for your ridiculous title?" said I in a tone of impatience.

"Had he told you that you are a Duchess," said Rapp, stepping up to me and taking both my hands in his, "I am sure you would have embraced him, as you will embrace me for bringing you the intelligence." "That I will," said I, presenting my cheek to my old friend Rapp, whose frank and cordial manner quite delighted me. "And another for Junot," said he, smiling. "Well, be it so," answered I, "and I promise you I will inform him that you were the first to tell me this good news." "And, moreover," said Rapp, "you have the best title of the whole batch of Duchesses. You are the DUCHESSE D'ABRANTÈS." I perceived that the Emperor had given Junot the title of the Duc d'Abrantès as a particular compliment to him. I therefore was doubly gratified, and Junot was deeply impressed with the Emperor's kindness.

We descended to the *salon* at the foot of the staircase of the Pavilion of Flora for dinner. At the head of our table usually sat the Empress's Lady of Honor (then the Comtesse de la Rochefoucauld) or the *Dame d'atours*. Sometimes, in the absence of both these ladies, the lady in waiting at the Palace would preside. On the day I allude to, Madame de la Rochefoucauld was at her post — an honor, by the bye, which she seldom conferred upon us. I found myself quite solitary in the midst of the company. The party was composed of individuals whose manners and conversation did not suit my taste.

Thus I was very glad when I saw Madame Lannes enter the *salon*. Her company was always welcome to me, but now it was especially so. We immediately drew near each other, and sat down together at the table. "Well," said I, "here are great changes, but I am sure they will work none in you." I was right. She might subsequently have conceived a taste for these pomps and vanities, but at that time she was a simple, kind, and perfectly natural creature. "You may, indeed, be sure that I care but little for them," replied Madame Lannes; "and I am sure Lannes will not feel himself elevated by them. You know his turn of mind; he is still unchanged; but there are many who surround the Emperor who entertain diametrically opposite opinions. Look around you."

I looked up, and beheld opposite to me the Duc de Rovigo, whose countenance was radiant with self-complacency. The Duchesse de Rovigo sat at some distance from us. "I'll wager," said I to Madame Lannes, "that she is not so vain of her elevation. She is an amiable woman, and not likely to assume any of these ridiculous airs." Madame Lannes smiled.

"And what title have you got?" said I, after some further conversation. "Oh, a charming one!" replied she: "Duchesse de Montebello! Mine and yours are the prettiest titles on the list." Here she drew from her girdle a small card, on which were inscribed the names of all the Dukes the Emperor had created, as also the *major-ats** appertaining to the titles. The Palace of the Tuileries had never been the scene of more ambitious agitation. From the Marshal to the lowest *employé*, all were eager to obtain at least a feather of the nobiliary plume.

* The pecuniary allowance attached to the title.

Our Sunday evenings at the Tuileries were not like others; for on that day we were not permitted to enter the Emperor's *salon* to wait for the Princess. Sometimes, when the Emperor was in a good humor, he would invite the *Dames de Palais*, or other ladies who accompanied Madame, to enter. It happened so on the day I here allude to.

"Well, *Madame la Duchesse Gouverneuse*," said the Emperor to me as soon as I entered, "are you satisfied with your title of Abrantès? Junot, too, ought to be pleased with it, for I intend it as a proof of my satisfaction with his conduct.* And what do they say of it in your *salons* of the Faubourg Saint Germain? They must be a little mortified at the reinforcement I have sent them."

Then, turning to the Arch-Chancellor, he said: "Well, Monsieur, after all, nothing that I have done is more in unison with the true spirit of the French Revolution than the re-establishment of high dignities. The French people fought for only one thing: equality in the eye of the law, and the power of controlling the acts of their Government. Now, my Nobility, as they style it, is in reality no nobility at all, because it is without prerogatives or hereditary succession. The only prerogative it enjoys, if prerogative it can be called, is the fortune conferred by way of recompense for civil or military services; while its hereditary succession depends on the will of the Sovereign in confirming the title on the son or nephew of the deceased holder. My Nobility is, after all, one of my finest creations."

About this time a curious circumstance happened to me, which affords an example of the accuracy with which the Emperor gained information of everybody's affairs and actions. I always entertained a sort of religious veneration for old family connections, in spite of my altered circumstances. Thus, whenever it lay in my power, I endeavored to show kind attention to the good nuns of

---

* I have already mentioned that the Emperor had directed Junot to enter Lisbon at all hazards; and it was Junot's bold entrance into Abrantès which decided the success of the expedition. "I wished to give him the title of Duke of Nazareth," said the Emperor to me, "but I was afraid that he might get the nickname of Junot of Nazareth."

La Croix, who had educated my sister, Madame Geouffre,
and to the Abbé Remy, who had been her confessor.
The Abbé, whom I have not seen more than five or six
times in the course of my life, was an honest man, but
perfectly null with respect to talent, and certainly quite
incapable of being the leader of a conspiracy.

When the Abbé Remy came to Paris he brought me a
letter of introduction from my brother Albert, from which
I learned that the good priest, who had been formerly
my sister's tutor, had escaped the massacres of September.
I received him as I would receive an old friend, and, had
Junot been in Paris, I am sure I could have convinced
him that it would have been wrong to do otherwise.
But Junot was then in Lisbon; and I did not write to
him on the subject, conceiving it to be quite unimportant. What was my surprise when Duroc, who was always
sent on missions of this sort, called one day to inform me
that I had received in my house a factious priest, who
had brought to France copies of the Comminatory Bull
addressed to the Emperor by Pope Pius VII.!

I stared at Duroc as though he had been addressing me
in Greek. A Bull of Excommunication appeared to me a
thing so perfectly fabulous, that I never dreamed it could
have existence in the year 1808. It was no less extraordinary that I should be accused of having any knowledge
of it. I said this to Duroc, and he pressed the matter
no further. He informed me of what I was very sorry
to hear, viz, that the Abbé Remy, like the ass laden with
relics (I ask his pardon for the comparison), had actually
brought, in a letter of six or seven envelopes, the famous
Comminatory Bull.

The Emperor was in a rage. " I had seen this man, I
had known him long. How happened it that I was always
— always — in league with his enemies?" I was angry
with Duroc for being the bearer of such an absurd charge.
I was weary of this eternal repetition of unfounded suspicion, and for the first time during our long acquaintance
Duroc and I quarreled. The Emperor, blinded by the reports of his police and counter-police, might have lost
himself in the labyrinths of his own creating; but that
Duroc, who knew me as well as he knew his own sister,
should be so far misled, was a thing I could not pardon.
Duroc was a warm-hearted friend; but he, too, had his

faults; he was not more gifted with patience than I was. He spoke to me sharply; I replied to him still more sharply. He rose and took his departure, and the result of this fine scene was that I burst into a flood of tears. M. de Narbonne, who called on me almost every day, happened at this moment to enter.

On learning the cause of my distress, he told me that he had a week before heard the whole history of the Bull. He very well knew, he said, the man who had brought this document into France — a document which, he observed, was very stupidly drawn up, and was likely to make the Pope lose St. Peter's chair; and that if the Abbé Remy had brought a copy of the Bull, it was only a duplicate.

I confess I did not very well understand the matter, even after this explanation. A Bull of Excommunication was to me a sort of miracle. The learned word COMMINATORY, which M. de Narbonne was also obliged to explain, appeared to me more calculated than all the rest to rouse the Emperor's anger. " But what," said I to M. de Narbonne, " is the cause of this sudden misunderstanding between his Majesty and his Holiness ? " The circumstances attending the removal of the Pope were but little known then in Paris,* and yet what a noise that event and the Excommunication of Napoleon were making in other parts of the world!

One day while we were in Spain (at Ledesma) and I was sitting at my window admiring the enchanting beauty of the surrounding landscape, Junot suddenly entered the apartment. He was gloomy and disturbed. I read in his countenance that some serious event had occurred. " What is the matter ? " inquired I eagerly. " Look," said Junot, throwing into my lap a paper printed in the Spanish language; " read that."

It was a copy of the political catechism which was then circulated in Spain. To it was appended a proclamation of the famous Don Julian, exhorting all good Spaniards to assassinate the French, because, being the subjects of an Excommunicated Sovereign, they were themselves excom-

* The Emperor interdicted their publication in France and Italy. In Spain they were suppressed, as a matter of course. It was, therefore, only in England and a part of Germany that any such intelligence could see the light.

municated. I mention this fact in conjunction with the Comminatory Bull. I have not yet come to the Spanish war. I merely wish to point attention to the importance which was attached to the Pope's Bull, even in the perfumed valleys of Castille and Estremadura. The following is a fragment of this curious document:

"For some time past the Holy See has been obliged to support the enormous burden of your troops. Since 1807 they have cost more than five millions of piasters.* You have taken from Us the Duchies of Benevento and Ponte-Corvo! and you have constituted Us a prisoner in Our Apostolic residence. We appeal to all nations, and, above all, we appeal to you yourself, as to a SON CONSECRATED and VOWED, to repair the injury to, and maintain the rights of, the Catholic Church."†

Napoleon replied to this by immediately taking possession of the provinces of Ancona, Macerata, Urbino, and Camerino, and annexing them to the kingdom of Italy. The Pope's Legate quitted Paris. M. de Champagny, who was then Minister for Foreign Affairs, but who, like the rest of Napoleon's Ministers, was only a kind of chief clerk, published a sort of apology for the conduct of France.

The Pope replied through Cardinal Gabrielli, his Secretary of State (and uncle to Prince Gabrielli, who afterward married Lucien's daughter). The answer of his Holiness was couched in those terms of peace and conciliation which became the Chief of the Christian Church — the Vicar of Christ. But if ever circumstances can justify the Sovereign Pontiff for entering upon a war, Pius VII. may honorably claim that justification.

* About one million sterling.
† The whole of this document may be found in the "Memoirs of the Cardinal Pacca," with many curious particulars relating to this rupture.

CHAPTER VIII.

Letters from Junot and Duroc — Junot Proposes to Resign All His Appointments — My Visit to Princess Caroline — The Emperor's Kindness to Junot — He Promises to Write to Him Himself — An Old Recollection Revived — The Audience Prolonged till Half-past Eleven at Night — My Conversation with the Grand-Duchess of Berg — Duroc's Letter to Junot.

ONE morning when my *femme de chambre* entered my apartment to call me up, she told me with a joyous air that news had arrived from Lisbon, and she laid on my bed a packet which she said had been brought by M. Prevost, Junot's aid-de-camp. I immediately opened the packet. It contained two letters, one from Junot, which was as follows:

« As soon as you receive this letter, my dear Laura, make every preparation for leaving Paris, so that on my arrival nothing may retard us. I know how great will be your astonishment; and I will explain myself.

« I received by the last *estafette* a letter from Duroc. He wrote, on the part of the Emperor, informing me that I must choose between the post of first aid-de-camp and that of Governor of Paris, because the two appointments were incompatible one with another. His Majesty cannot suppose that I would hesitate for a single instant in the choice he offers to me. To live for him, and for him only, has long been the dearest wish of my heart. When I again appear before him, he shall find me just what I was in the glorious days of the Army of Italy. Let him lavish his favors on the men who surround him — all of whom are eager for favors and honors. For my part, I relinquish them. Let the Emperor press my hand at parting, or, rather, let him say that I am never again to quit him, and I shall be happier than I have been with all the splendor with which he has loaded me. . . . Besides, I am at present ill in health. My old disorder is returning, and the wound I received in Egypt is threatening to open again. I shall demand a definite *congé*, which his Majesty cannot refuse me. I will go to Baréges and try the baths, and then I shall be in a condition to serve the Emperor wheresoever he may be pleased to send me. If he decline my services I will retire to my relations in Burgundy, with my Laura and my children. . . . There we shall yet be happy, in spite of the malevolence of mankind, for I shall enjoy the blessings of a pure conscience, and a mind free from remorse.

« I send you Duroc's letter. . . . He was not the man who should have executed such a commission. . . . You may tell him so from me.

"Adieu, my dear Laura. I know that this letter will render you uneasy; but I cannot refrain from making you the confidant of all my troubles. You know that, next to you, the Emperor has, of all persons in the world, the most power to make me either miserable or happy! . . . It is because you know my heart that I thus unfold it to you. . . . Adieu, my beloved Laura . . . embrace our children — above all, our son. In the retirement in which I shall henceforth live, I must owe to you the only happiness to which I shall henceforth aspire."

" THE DUKE D'ABRANTÈS."

The following is a copy of Duroc's letter, the original of which is in my possession:

"MY DEAR JUNOT: — I am directed by his Majesty to acquaint you that he considers the two posts of aid-de-camp and Governor of Paris incompatible the one with the other. I presume your choice cannot be doubtful, one of the appointments being merely an empty honor. However, it is not for me to tell you what you ought to do. But I recommend you to reflect maturely before you write your answer; and, above all, look upon the communication which I now make to you on the part of the Emperor AS A PROOF OF HIS ATTACHMENT TO YOU. These are his own words. As to me, my dear Junot, you can never doubt my regard for you; and I hope you do me the justice to place me foremost in the list of your best friends.

"Adieu, my dear General. Rely on my friendship.

" DUROC.
" Paris, February 10th."

For a few moments after the perusal of these letters, I was plunged into a sort of stupor. At length, when I had somewhat recovered from my bewilderment, I began to feel uneasy about the impression which might be produced on the Emperor by Junot's intended letter. He might possibly accept the proffered resignation; and if Junot should seriously have thought of retiring to Montbard, I confess I had not sufficient philosophy for that. I was aware that it was necessary to act in this juncture with caution and promptitude. I looked at my watch; it was a quarter past ten. A thought suddenly came across my mind, and I hastily rang my bell.

Josephine, my *femme de chambre*, immediately entered. " Inquire whether M. Prevost is gone," said I.

" Oh, Madame, he set off immediately to the Tuileries when he heard that you were not up!"

" Well, assist me to dress immediately, and order the carriage to be got ready."

In ten minutes I was seated in my carriage.

" To the Elysée," said I to the chasseur.

About half-past ten I entered the courtyard of the palace, where I saw a plain carriage with the Emperor's livery.

"Can it be he?" thought I to myself; and, without entering the *salon de service*, I inquired whether I could for one moment see Madame Dupont, the Princess Caroline's principal *femme de chambre*. I was right in my conjecture. The Emperor was with his sister. For me this was a most fortunate accident; but how was I to disturb the fraternal *tête-à-tête?*

"They are walking together in the garden," said Madame Dupont; "but if you will write a few words to her Highness, I will go and deliver them."

Madame Dupont gave me pen, ink, and paper, and I wrote to the Princess Caroline that I begged the favor of a few minutes' conversation with her on a subject of the utmost importance to me. The billet was immediately carried to the Princess.

"Oh, oh!" said the Emperor; "you receive letters betimes! What is that?"

Without further ceremony, he took the note out of his sister's hand, and read it at a single glance, for it contained but three lines.

"Diable!" he exclaimed; "is Madame Junot up already? Well, I will leave you to chat together, and I will go back to the Tuileries to breakfast. Adieu, Madame Caroline!"

He embraced his sister, and took leave of her very good-humoredly, for I could see him perfectly well from the little apartment in which I was waiting.

The Princess sent immediately to request that I would come to her. She received me with the kindness of an old and cordial friend.

"Mon Dieu!" she said, taking me by the hand; "what is the matter? How pale you are! Has any misfortune befallen Junot?"

I could reply only by tears, and I presented my husband's letter to the Princess. She read it attentively, and then said:

"What a hot-headed man that is! Who knows how the Emperor may take this!"

"I fear he will be very much displeased," observed I. "But, Madame, has not Junot written to acquaint you with this affair?"

At that moment a *valet de chambre* stepped up to the Princess, and delivered to her a large packet, on the back of which I recognized Junot's handwriting. M. Prevost had not come to the Elysée until after he left the Tuileries, and finding that the Emperor was at the Elysée, he thought it best not to deliver the packet until the Princess was alone. Junot's letter to the Princess was almost the same as that which he had written to me.

"What had I best do?" said I.

"It is evident," replied the Princess, "that the Emperor is not out of humor. He was joking and laughing during the whole of his visit to me, which was a tolerably long one. If he had been offended by Junot's letter, I should have discovered it in his manner. Besides, he would have mentioned it to me; and he said not a word about it."

"But what shall I do?" I again repeated.

"Ask the Emperor for an audience."

"I should wish to do so. But do you think he will grant it?"

"That will be the touchstone," observed the Princess. "If he grant the audience, it is clear he is not offended. If he refuse it——"

"Do you think it likely he will refuse it?" inquired I, pressing her pretty little hands in mine.

"No," replied she, "I do not think so; and even though he should, rely on my friendship — rely on that of Madame. But how hasty Junot is!"

When I left the Princess, I was somewhat more at ease, though I had no particular reason to be so. I returned home, and immediately wrote to the Chamberlain on duty, soliciting an audience of his Majesty. At two o'clock I received a letter from the Chamberlain, announcing that the Emperor would receive me that same evening at nine.

I was in a transport of joy. The audience was not only granted, but it was granted with a readiness which boded favorably. I sent for M. Prevost, and questioned him about what I presumed he might know. But I found he was utterly ignorant of the business about which I was so anxious. The Duke had received an *estafette*, as he did every week; and on the day after the arrival of that *estafette*, he, M. Prevost, left Lisbon, and in fifteen days reached Paris. He, however, informed me — for his attachment to the General rendered him observant — that Junot appeared much depressed in spirits.

I spent the remainder of the day in reflecting on the interview of the evening. It was evident that the Emperor knew why I had solicited the audience, and that he did not disapprove my motives. But what would he say to me? Perhaps he would approve of Junot's retirement without withdrawing from him his friendship. " Princes are as chary of their favors as they are of their friendship," thought I, as my carriage rolled rapidly toward the Tuileries. " If — but no; that is impossible."

As the palace clock struck three-quarters past eight, I alighted; for I knew the Emperor to be extremely punctual in all his appointments — at least, when they did not happen to interfere with a review or with the Council of State.

This interview with Napoleon formed a memorable epoch in my life. It had an important effect on the subsequent life of Junot, which was henceforth deprived of the radiant prism which had before illumined it. His happiness was separated from that of the man who disposed of our destinies as a magician rules those of the beings subject to the power of his wand.

On arriving in the *salon de service*, where the aids-de-camp and civil officers of the Emperor's Household were assembled, I asked the first person I saw whether the Emperor was alone. I was informed that he was. I was so agitated that I cannot (and, indeed, I could not the very next day) recollect who were the individuals in the *salon de service*, with the exception of one only. I seated myself in the great red armchair which stood beside the fireplace, and there I remained absorbed in a profound reverie until I heard someone address me by name in a low tone of voice. I looked up, and saw Duroc standing before me.

" Are you still angry with me ? " said he, smiling.

I had quite forgotten the quarrel which we had had a few days before, and, stretching out my hand to him, I asked him why he thought I was angry.

" Well, all the better if you have forgotten it," said he. " You will be the better able to bend your thoughts to the conversation you are about to have with the Emperor."

"Do you think," said I, "that I have anything to fear?"
"Nothing whatever," replied he. "The Emperor has
said not a word to me of the letter which he has received from Junot; but I fear from the style of the letter which your husband has written to me that the one
he has sent to the Emperor is calculated to displease
him. Do not be alarmed in anticipation, and, above all,
be perfectly mistress of yourself. You are aware that on
that probably depends the success of your conference?
Do you think it possible that Junot has really tendered
the resignation of all his appointments?"

"I have not the least doubt of it."

"How imprudent! — how precipitate!"

Duroc paced up and down thoughtfully. Excellent
friend! He regretted the imprudence of his brother-
in-arms, of whose glory and good fortune he was never
envious; for envy was not in his nature. He was fearful
that Junot had done what might prove fatal to his interests. With what solicitude I watched his movements may
be easily imagined; for Duroc was, to all who knew the
confidence reposed in him, a sort of mirror, in which the
Emperor was in part reflected. At that moment the clock
struck half-past nine.

"Do you know whether the Emperor is informed you
are here?" said Duroc to me in a whisper.

I answered in the affirmative. The Emperor's bell now
rang, and I was immediately introduced.

Though this was perhaps the twentieth time that I had
had a private interview with the Emperor, yet I had never
felt so agitated on any former occasion. My limbs trembled
under me, my sight failed me, and I had almost lost my
self-possession. I felt that the fate of Junot and of my
children depended almost on a hair.

The Emperor was standing before his desk. When I entered he was coughing violently. But as soon as he recovered he bowed his head gracefully, and an agreeable smile
played upon his countenance.

I now breathed more freely, and advanced with a firm
step.

"Well, Madame Junot," said the Emperor, "what is it
you want with me?"

"I presume your Majesty knows, and I should be glad
to be spared the pain of repeating it."

" No, no. I wish to see how you can make amends for an offense."

" How, Sire ? Surely your Majesty does not think Junot the offender in this case ? He has been much injured!"

" And by whom, pray ? "

" By your Majesty."

" By me! How so ? "

" Do you think, Sire, that it is no injury to wound a heart profoundly devoted to you, which has no wish, no object, but to love and to serve you ? This is an injury, and a deep injury."

" Hem! All this is mere words!"

He paced up and down for a few moments, during which his countenance assumed a serious expression, but without any trace of severity. He sat down in his armchair, made a sign to me to take a seat, and then said in a tone of unusual gravity:

" Madame Junot, observe well what I am going to tell you, for I wish you to write it to Junot. Mark well my words, for I am not in the habit of speaking idly. I wrote to Junot, through the medium of Duroc, informing him that he must choose between the post of my first aid-de-camp and that of Governor of Paris. As there are attached to this last appointment extensive military prerogatives, I do not wish that ANY ONE OF MY SUCCESSORS should take advantage of the example set during my reign, and confer the two appointments on one individual. Do you understand me ? "

" Perfectly, Sire."

" I for some time entertained the design of creating the post of my first aid-de-camp with great privileges and great advantages; but I found impediments in my way. I promised this post to Junot after the Battle of Austerlitz. He reminds me of this in his letter, and he is right. Promises made on a field of battle ought to be sacred. But what I promised was to make his fortune, and I have made it. I promote his interest by giving him the post of Governor of Paris. Let him keep that and resign the other. It is impossible that the man, who may at all hours be summoned to my tent or my palace under the title of my aid-de-camp, should at the same time be Governor of Paris, and have the command of 60 000 men."

6

Then, rising and continuing to speak, as if replying to himself, he added: "No; it cannot be—it is impossible!"

"But your Majesty knows Junot too well to doubt——"

"You do not understand me; I am not speaking of Junot's fidelity. Heaven knows I never doubt that! I have told you that I do not wish to set an example which may serve as an authority to my successors; and, after all, what is this post of first aid-de-camp? A mere empty foolery, to which Junot is sentimental enough to attach importance. He is never on duty at the palace, because that would be neither proper nor possible. Junot is a great officer of the Empire, and because he wears a hussar uniform that is no reason that he is to get himself into scrapes as he did when he was a Colonel, and thought proper to neglect his duty because he was in love with Mademoiselle Louise. Did you know Mademoiselle Louise?"

"No, Sire," replied I; and I burst into an uncontrollable fit of laughter. The Emperor laughed too; but with him gayety was a very fugitive impression, and immediately recovering his gravity, he asked me why I laughed.

"Because, Sire, your Majesty told me just now that you did not talk idly."

He smiled, and, shrugging his shoulders, said: "Ah, you wish me to believe that you are not jealous!"

"Jealous!" I repeated.

"*Ma foi!* why not? You wives are all jealous!" Here he smiled again, and took a pinch of snuff.

"I have explained," resumed he, "my motives for having written to Junot what Duroc communicated to him from me. As a FRIEND, I feel GRATEFUL that he has chosen to keep his post of aid-de-camp. This does not surprise me. But I, as a friend and as a Sovereign, must look to his interests. I shall therefore take no notice of the letter which I received this morning, and he shall still remain Governor of Paris. That post is not transferable. When a man is once Governor of Paris, he is so for life. How inconsiderate Junot is! He is like a youth of twenty. He has written me such a letter! Has he told you what he wrote to me?"

"He would never think of doing that, Sire. But I can perceive by the style of that which I received how much his feelings are wounded."

The Emperor stepped up to his desk, and, after turning over several papers, took up one on which I perceived Junot's writing. He glanced over it, and I perceived by the expression of his countenance that he was moved.

"Here," said he, handing to me Junot's letter, "read that, and tell me whether your husband writes you such letters."

Junot wrote well—I may say remarkably well—as will be seen by the correspondence which is occasionally given in the course of these volumes; but in the letter here referred to there was a talent which emanated, not from the mind, but from the heart, and from a heart imbued with the deepest sensibility. Every line breathed sentiments of honor, generosity, and loyalty. I could not help feeling indignant at the Emperor's treatment of him. Napoleon guessed what was passing in my mind.

"You are displeased, Madame Laurette?" said he, pinching my ear. "Really, Junot is as sentimental as a young German girl! But I do not wish to hurt his feelings. Write to him, and explain what I have said to you. You have not forgotten it?"

"No, Sire; but if your Majesty would permit me to ask a favor, you will render me very happy by granting it."

"What is it?"

"Sire, I will obey your command, and write to Junot. But your Majesty has seen how deeply he was grieved when he wrote that letter? It is not a mere explanation on my part that can repair the wrong he has suffered. You yourself, Sire, must apply the balm to the wound you have inflicted."

The Emperor directed to me a look of ineffable kindness, and, smiling, nodded his head in token of approval.

"Well, well, I will write to him," said he.

"Are you sure, Sire?"

"Quite sure."

"Your Majesty will not forget?"

"I will not," he said emphatically. "I give you my word." Then, after a short pause, he added, in a playful sort of tone:

"Well, and you think poor Junot is sincerely attached to me, after all?"

At this question, put in the manner in which it was, I could not help smiling. I knew well that Napoleon's hobby, if I may be allowed the expression, was to be loved for himself alone. Junot had given him so many proofs of that sort of attachment that he could entertain no doubt on the subject; but possibly he liked to receive new assurances of it, for after the above question he turned the chair which was near him, and, leaning on the back of it, looked at me steadfastly.

"Yes," he added, "I know he is much attached to me —I almost think he loves me better than you."

"Better than me! No, Sire; but certainly better than any mistress."

"How! you certainly are not jealous of me?"

I looked at him significantly; I ventured to revive an old recollection, and uttered the word "Toulon." I observed an expression of satisfaction in his countenance.

"Oh! so he lets you so far into his confidence? Has he told you the history of his adventures when he and I were comrades together? Well, let him speak for himself; but he must not tell tales of me."

All this was said in a tone of pleasantry which made me not in the least fearful of having gone too far. The recollection which I had revived had reference to the following little incident:

When at Toulon, Junot fell in love — so deeply in love that he used to go out at night and sigh and sing under his mistress's window. Napoleon happened to see the object of his attachment, and fell in love with her too. This was enough for Junot, and he immediately relinquished his suit. He never acquainted his friend with this sacrifice, which, however, was not made without a considerable struggle. I knew this little adventure, and as the Emperor's memory was always susceptible of being roused by the slightest hint, I was sure of being understood. However, he did not pursue the subject; but, fixing upon me his clear and penetrating eye, he observed:

"You say he is attached to me, and I believe he is. But, after all, his attachment, like that of all other men, is subordinate to the great chances in the game of life. He is ambitious. He loves glory. He loves all those toys by the aid of which the multitude may be led with a silken thread. He is like all the rest. In short, he is a man."

A frown began to overspread his countenance. He pushed his chair aside, and walked up and down the room with his two hands crossed behind his back. I felt indignant, for TO HIM, at least, Junot had not acted like all the rest, when in '94 and '95 he made him the sharer of his mother's savings.

"Sire," said I, with some degree of impatience, "your Majesty's memory is not faithful; and permit me to observe that your heart especially ought to remind you that to you, at least, Junot always acted the part of a devoted brother. Be pleased to recollect Marseilles. Madame has never forgotten it."

I know not what inspired me with this boldness; but at that moment I felt that I could have said anything. The Emperor darted at me a look by which most people would have been confounded. Then, shrugging his shoulders, he said:

"But even admitting that Junot loves me well, yet I affirm that he does not love me better than the gratification of his ambition. And to that he would sacrifice anything, even you."

"Allow me to assure your Majesty that you do not know Junot's character — that you calumniate his noble heart. He loves you, Sire, better than all the dignities you can heap upon him — better than your crown; better, perhaps, than he loves me (though vanity made me say the contrary just now); better, perhaps, than his children!"

Penetrated with the sincerity of this sentiment, which pervaded Junot's whole existence, and which I conceived was not duly appreciated, I burst into tears.

Napoleon stepped up to me, took me by the hand, and pinching the ends of my fingers, a favor which he had never before conferred on me, he said:

"Come, come, dry up your tears. This is the way with you women, you always resort to tears. This is your infirmity. Yet I am sure your mother was not afflicted with it! She had a perverse spirit; but she was a strongminded woman."

He walked about for a few minutes, during which profound silence prevailed on both sides. The weather was very bad. We were now approaching the equinox, and for the last half-hour a violent storm had been raging. The wind howled mournfully through the long corridors of the palace. My heart was full, my eyes were suffused with tears, and I would have given anything for permission to withdraw. At that moment the clock struck eleven. Napoleon seemed to be roused from his reverie. He stood still and repeated the lines:

> *Il vento sbuffa,*
> *La pioggia precipitasi.*

"What terrible weather this is!" he added; "it is well we are not bivouacking. Poor Junot must have suffered greatly on his marches in Portugal. I understand that the rains there inundate the roads in a single night. Is that true?"

This question led to a multitude of inquiries respecting the climate of Portugal, the character of the inhabitants, the Marquis d'Alora, M. d'Araujo, and the Pope's Nuncio, who, after having very servilely paid his court to the French, and especially to the Duc d'Abrantès, had just then quitted Lisbon as a fugitive. After obtaining all the information he could draw from me respecting the affairs of the Peninsula, he smiled, and said, with a most prepossessing grace:

"Good evening, Madame Junot; I will not say good night, for I am sure you will write to Junot before you retire to bed. Am I not right?"

"Most certainly, Sire," I replied, quite charmed with his kind and gracious manner. "To-morrow's *estafette* shall convey to Junot an accurate account of all the kindness your Majesty has evinced for him to-night. It will make him very happy. But, Sire, your Majesty has promised me a treasure of consolation for your most faithful servant. Certainly he has been wrong in so inconsiderately taking the alarm at Duroc's letter; but he has suffered for it, Sire, and he has suffered long. When my letter shall reach Lisbon, it will be six weeks since Junot received Duroc's. I am sure that a line from your Majesty — that promised line — would go further to console him than whole pages of mine, however tenderly written."

"I have promised to write to him," said the Emperor.

"But, Sire, you will forget!"

"I have given you my word."

After this I could say no more. I made my courtesy, and was about to withdraw, when he detained me by saying:

"Be particular in explaining my reasons for what I have done. Tell him that I never entertained the thought of intrusting the government of Paris to anyone but himself. Hulin is a worthy man, and is very competent for what he has to do, but nothing more. Junot is a young man of talent, but he is too hot-headed. Adieu, Madame Junot. I will tell him that he has an excellent *chargé d'affaires* here. Good evening. Apropos, how is my little godson ? You have but that one boy, I believe ? "

I courtesied.

"But that will not do. You must have many more. I wish to see my throne surrounded by the sons of my friends, and Junot is one of those friends whom I most love and esteem. Tell him this."

As I left the Emperor's closet all who were in waiting outside eyed me with some degree of curiosity. A whole hour and a half's conversation with Napoleon! and at that time too! What could I have had to say to him ? What could he have had to say to me ? All these questions seemed to be written in the countenances of those who now bowed before me — lower, certainly, than they had bowed on my arrival.

On the staircase of the Pavilion of Flora I met Duroc, who was hastening up to ascertain the result of my conference. He had desired the usher of the *salon de service* to inform him as soon as I left the Emperor. He was overjoyed at the account I gave him, but had guessed that all was well from the extraordinary length of the audience.

"Now," observed he, "you will sleep tranquilly; and so shall I, for you must know that that poor fellow Junot has caused me much pain. He wrote me a most unreasonable letter. But without telling him in a direct way what I now say, you may warn him against thoughtlessly giving his friends so much annoyance. Good night, Madame Junot."

Before I retired to rest, I sat down and wrote to Junot a full account of my conversation with the Emperor. With the most scrupulous exactness I set down all that I have above recorded. How shall I describe the happiness of Junot on the receipt of this letter! His answer was full of expressions of the most extravagant joy. It was like the letter of a boy of fifteen.

On the morning which succeeded this interview, I waited
on the Grand-Duchess of Berg to tell her the success of
my mission.   I was bound to make an early visit to her
in return for the kindness she had shown me.   I told her
that M. Prevost was to leave Paris for Lisbon next day,
and requested her to be kind enough to write by him to
Junot and scold him well, as I had already done and as
Duroc had promised also to do.   She was extremely pleased
to hear my account of the conversation I had had with
the Emperor.

"Do you know," said she, "that you are perhaps the
only woman who can say she has been closeted an hour
and a half with the Emperor, unless there were other
reasons for the interview than to talk over a serious matter of business?   Were there any such reasons in your
case?" added she, laughing.

"If there had been," replied I, falling into her vein of
pleasantry, "I should hold my tongue.   Such, I imagine,
is the best way to play one's part on such occasions, and
the Emperor, let me tell you, is not the man to render
the part an easy one."

"What part?" replied the Grand-Duchess, who during
my reply to her question had regarded the expression of
my features with extreme attention, while she bestowed
but little on my words.

"That of a favorite," replied I; "and this I had an
opportunity of observing the other evening at your Imperial Highness's masquerade.   Just when the confusion
occasioned by the presence of Mademoiselle Gu——t suspended the conversation, I happened to be very near
the Emperor — I mean the real Emperor, and not Isabey.
He was engaged in conversation with a lady whom I easily
recognized by her movements.   I did not wish to over-
hear either what she said to him or what the Emperor
said to her, for I have no taste for eavesdropping — but
at a masked ball anything is allowable; and, then, the
Emperor was so satisfied with his disguise, and so persuaded that everyone took Isabey for him, that I was
tempted to punish him for his mistake.   He approached
the place where I was sitting so nearly that I could scarcely
help overhearing his conversation.

"'I have no ambition,' said he to his fair companion,
'to be nicknamed Louis XIV. in miniature; I have no

wish that a woman should expose me to the world as a feeble and heartless being.'

"'Heartless! the heart would be precisely the pleader which would speak in your behalf,' replied the lady with animation.

"The Emperor, to my great satisfaction, rejoined:

"'Pooh! the heart, forsooth! You are like all the rest of your sex — deluded by your silly dreams. The heart! what do you know about the heart? Nothing, but that it is a portion of your body through which passes a large vein where the blood circulates more rapidly when you run than when you walk. Is not this all? But what is the matter here?'

"With these words he rose, offering his arm to the lady, whose stooping figure would have enabled me to recognize the Emperor, even though he had not been recognizable through his own disguise. They moved to the spot where the pretty Mademoiselle Gu——t stood, bathed in tears, and overwhelmed with despair. They, however, soon returned to their seats.

"'There!' said the Emperor; 'there is one of the results of your romantic ideas! That poor girl has reposed faith in the honeyed words of the handsome stripling Murat! She will now probably go and drown herself. How? What is it you say?'

"He inclined his ear, and at the moment I distinctly heard sobs. The Emperor, no doubt, heard them also, for, instantly rising from his seat, he said to the weeping mask:

"'My dear, I do not like to see Josephine weep — she whom I love better than all other women! Therefore, this is nothing but wasting time. Adieu! I come to masked balls to amuse myself.'

"With these words he walked away, and mingled in the crowd, where Rapp and Duroc soon joined him."

The Grand-Duchess was much amazed at the story, and, when it was concluded, asked me:

"Do you happen to know the history of this Mademoiselle Gu——t?"

"No," replied I.

"How!" rejoined her Highness; "did their mother never apply to you to allow them to dance at your parties with tambourines?"

"No," replied I, laughing. "Methinks dancing with tambourines is a little in the gipsy style!"

"And these girls, I assure you," continued the Grand-Duchess, "are little better than gipsies. Their family consists of a mother and three daughters, of whom one, as yet, is quite a child. The other two are grown-up girls. Well, as the fact is now of little consequence, I can tell you that General Junot used to visit these ladies very frequently. You know, they are your neighbors, for they live on the Boulevard de la Madeleine. One of the daughters is excessively pretty; the other is less so, but, then, she is very clever. The young one, as I have told you, is yet a child. Now I have given you the history of this family; and you may perceive that I had MY REASONS for asking you whether you had ever seen Mademoiselle Gu——t dance."

"Will your Imperial Highness," said I, "permit me to inquire how it is that you, who are ever so kind and hospitable to your guests, should have been so severe with Mademoiselle Gu——t?"

The Princess Caroline possessed a countenance in which every feeling of her mind was reflected; and this power of expression was greatly owing to the beautiful transparency of her skin: her cheeks would change from red to pale with wonderful rapidity. At the first mention of Mademoiselle G——t's name, I perceived she changed color slightly twice or thrice; and after some hesitation she told me that the Grand-Duke had bestowed great attention on the young lady, and that therefore she considered her appearance in her house as a great impertinence. For all my pretended ignorance, I knew enough of Mademoiselle Gu——t to be satisfied that I, as well as the Grand-Duchess, had good reason to be offended with her. I may mention that M. de Narbonne, to whom I described the masked ball, burst into an immoderate fit of laughter when I related the little incident in which the Emperor was concerned. I did not at the time understand the cause of his merriment, but some weeks after it was explained to me, when Mademoiselle G——t suddenly returned from Bayonne, whither the Empress had taken her in the character of *lectrice*.

A few days after my interview with the Princess Caroline, the *estafette* from Lisbon, which came regularly every week, brought me the following letter, which had been sent to Junot by his true friend Duroc:

« My Dear Junot: — I presented your letter to the Emperor, but he neither read it to me nor spoke to me on the subject of its contents. Madame Junot, however, who has had the good fortune to see and converse with the Emperor on the business, will tell you that you have imagined, in the letter which I was directed to write to you, unpleasant things which have no existence.

« His Majesty has explained to Madame Junot his reasons for not wishing that one and the same person should hold the two posts of Governor of Paris and Imperial aid-de-camp, and she must be satisfied that he had not the least intention of removing you from the post of Governor of Paris for the purpose of supplanting you by another. So far from that, he even suggested to Madame Junot the propriety of your retaining that post, on account of its being the preferable one of the two, and because, in addition to its other advantages, it includes that confidential trust which you seem to think is attached exclusively to the other. The Emperor's sentiments toward you have not, I assure you, undergone the slightest change, as his conduct on this occasion proves. In a moment of irritation or discontent, you have imagined otherwise; but you must banish that thought and no longer render yourself unhappy.

« A good deal is said about our departure for Spain. Everything has been got ready, but as yet no final orders have been given.

« The carnival is at length over, happily for those who wish to get a comfortable night's rest. During its continuance, balls and entertainments have succeeded each other incessantly. The last was a very superb masquerade at the Grand-Duchess's, which afforded a vast deal of amusement.

« Rely, my dear Junot, on my sincerest attachment.

« Duroc.

« March 3d, 1808. »

Duroc had been greatly hurt by Junot's letter. The fact was that, when Junot was the prey of suspicion, he had no command over himself; and he often said severe things which were apt to wound those to whom they were addressed. Duroc, however, and all who knew him well, were not angry with him, because they were aware that, on these occasions, he himself suffered cruelly. For instance, in the case here alluded to, he had got it into his head that the Emperor wished to punish him for the reports which had gone abroad, in which his name had been coupled with that of the Princess Caroline, and that he wished to deprive him of the post of Governor of Paris — the best in the Empire at that period. It was not the mere loss of the post which vexed him, but he could not endure the idea of a punishment, and in addition to this he had been led to believe that the appointment was to be given to Duroc.

"Of all the men by whom the Emperor is surrounded" (Junot said in a letter to me), "Duroc is most deserving of it; there is only one who can possibly dispute with him the preference, and that is Marmont — Marmont, whom I love at once as my brother and my brother-in-arms! Well, I shall cheerfully see him intrusted with the government of Paris for then I shall at least be sure that the Emperor is defended by a faithful friend. Duroc may be placed in the same category; but he already holds an appointment near the Emperor's person. In short, this affair vexes me to the very bottom of my heart."

I had a very long conversation with Duroc on this subject, and he assured me that Junot's suspicion was as unfounded as unreasonable.

"Junot, and some others," said he, "do not appear to understand me, nor to understand my position. The Emperor would disgrace me were he to create me a Marshal of France. What should I be if removed from his person? I love the Emperor as Junot loves him; and has not Junot made choice of the post of first aid-de-camp in preference to that of Governor of Paris? Why should he judge me differently from himself? Besides, is he not my friend — the friend of my heart? Our fraternity of arms is of too old date to be thus forgotten for a brevet."

Duroc was deeply affected by this affair. I found it very difficult to erase from his mind the painful impression produced by Junot's letter, especially as Junot avoided any explanation with him. Friendship is far more sensitive than love.

CHAPTER IX.

The Emperor at Bayonne — Abdication of Charles IV. — Errors of Napoleon — Abdication of Ferdinand — Junot Created Governor General of Portugal — Embargo on Cotton Repealed — M. Magnien's Proposal — Joseph Bonaparte King of Spain — Ferdinand VII. at Valençay — Charles IV. at Compiègne — Insurrection in Aragon — Massacres at Valencia and Seville — Murat Superseded by Savary — Savary's Absurdity — The Provincial Junta at Seville — Letter from Louis de Bourbon — Murat Made King of Naples — Reception of Joseph at Madrid — He Retires to Vittoria — Affair of Baylen — Capitulation Violated — Commencement of the Revolution in Spain — The Empress at Bordeaux — The Emperor's Return to Paris — The Spanish Junta at Bayonne — Absence of News at Paris — My Interview with Napoleon at Saint Cloud — Fête at the Hôtel de Ville — The Supper — Letter from Spain — New Spanish Catechism.

A T LENGTH the Emperor set out for Bayonne, and then commenced the tragedy which had so important an influence on the destinies of Europe. All the particulars of the interviews which took place in Bayonne between the Sovereign of France and the Sovereigns of Spain are sufficiently known. I say the Sovereigns of Spain, for Spain had then two, and the embarrassment created by the protest of Charles IV. served only, in fact, to give the finishing touch to the work of perdition.

Events now advanced rapidly. Charles IV. proceeded to Bayonne, to appear with his son before the Supreme Tribunal of Napoleon. Ferdinand restored to him his Crown, and the old monarch forthwith abdicated in favor of the Emperor of the French. Here was the commencement of those errors on Napoleon's part which marked the whole course of the Peninsular campaign. The original fault was not merely saving the life of the Prince of the Peace, but employing him at Bayonne as Minister of King Charles IV. The Prince of the Peace had not only fallen from the royal favor, but from his position as a statesman, for Ferdinand VII. had deprived him, one after the other, of all his offices, even to the very lowest, and he was now nothing more than Manuel Godoy. This was

an impolitic proceeding on the part of Napoleon, but it
was not the only one. The next great error was compelling Ferdinand to abdicate.

The Emperor ought rather to have given him a wife
as he desired. He should have seated him on the Spanish throne, controlled all his movements (a thing perfectly
easy), and then all would have been well. I am convinced that Ferdinand acted with good faith toward Napoleon, for I have found, among the papers left by my
husband, Ferdinand's orders transmitted through Felieu,
his Minister of War; and when subsequently the Marquis
del Soccoro (Solano) afforded Junot the opportunity of
disarming his troops, that was nothing more than the result of the bad feeling with which the Spanish people
had been inspired by that multitude of Juntas which
harassed Spain by their endless intrigues and infernal
spirit. The state of things was, however, very different
at Bayonne from the 19th of March, or rather the 4th of
May.

Next came the abdication of Ferdinand and his letter,
couched in such ambiguous terms that it was calculated
to set all Spain in a blaze. But even before the publication of the treaties of Bayonne, many of the towns had
declared their independence; Seville, Badajoz, and Oviedo
rose immediately on the receipt of the intelligence of the
proceedings of the 2d of May.

Palafox, after escorting Godoy to Bayonne, having liberty to depart, availed himself of it to proceed to Saragossa. It is probable, though nothing is known on the
subject, that he went there with the view that Ferdinand
might transmit orders to him. This, however, is of little
consequence; the conduct of Palafox was at all event
judicious. While in Spain the storm was gathering which
was destined to overwhelm us, Junot was fortifying himself at Lisbon, and, to use the Emperor's expression, really
working well.

On his arrival in Lisbon, Junot found two obstacles to
the establishment of any description of government. The
first was the Junta, the other the embargo which the Emperor had laid on cotton, for it may readily be supposed
that Napoleon would not let slip so fine an opportunity of
enforcing the Continental system he had established. The
effect of this measure was that all the cargoes of cotton

were confiscated, and the trade in that article ruined. A complete stagnation ensued in every other branch of trade, and the Exchange in Lisbon, once one of the most busy in Europe, became in a few hours the most deserted.

Of all the valuable qualities which distinguished Junot, none were more remarkable than his clearness and promptitude of conception. This is acknowledged by all who were employed conjointly with him in any undertaking. The Duc de Valmy, Generals Thiébault, Taviel, Fouché, and Boyer, can bear testimony to this fact.

Junot acquainted the Emperor with the obstacles which impeded him. The Emperor immediately comprehended them to their fullest extent, and the next courier conveyed an order for the abolition of the Junta, the establishment of a new and complete Government, with Ministers and all the paraphernalia, and the assumption by Junot of the title of Governor General of Portugal, with emoluments worth six hundred thousand francs a year. He still retained his title and office of Governor of Paris. This, therefore, was the most prosperous period of Junot's life, and the Emperor thus amply indemnified him for the pain which he had suffered a few weeks before.

Junot had no sooner assumed the post of Governor General than he turned his attention to the amelioration of the country. He wrote the most pressing letters to the Emperor to obtain permission to remove the prohibition on cotton goods. This was a measure imperatively called for; for how, thought Junot, are we to raise a tribute from people from whom we take their all?

The magazines of the East India Company at Lisbon were loaded with cotton from North and South America, and they were, by the embargo, interdicted from exporting it, for to say its carriage by land was permitted would be nonsense. At length, however, the permission so much insisted on by Junot was granted. It arrived in the evening, and he immediately summoned M. Fissout, his private secretary (afterward Secretary General to the civil department of the Government of Algiers), and M. Magnien, one of his old college friends. He directed them to write at his dictation the terms of the decree, which next day was to raise the embargo on cotton, and diffuse joy among many thousands of fam-

ilies. While engaged in writing, M. Magnien suddenly
stopped, looked up in the Duke's face, and seemed disposed to say something.

"Well, what do you stop for?" asked Junot.

"I merely stop," replied he, "to see whether an idea
does not occur to you, by which you may secure your
own fortune and that of your children."

"How?" said Junot.

"Thus," replied the other, "and even if you purpose to
take off the embargo to-morrow morning there is yet
time. Cotton now sells for thirty sous per pound; to-
morrow the publication of the decree will make it worth
about five francs on the exchange. Commission me to
purchase five hundred thousand francs' worth, and I venture to say that by to-morrow evening you will be a
gainer of four millions clear profit, without even opening
your purse."

To this proposal Junot at first made no reply. It was a
peculiarity in his character always to observe silence on
receiving any profound impression. But when a few
moments had elapsed he found no want of words to express his feelings. Thus it was in the present instance.
After regarding M. Magnien for some moments with his
frank and candid look, he said:

"But to whom shall we propose to make this purchase?"

"To the first person we find," replied Magnien; "what
matters the seller in such a case?"

"Oh! nothing whatever," replied Junot, his expression
becoming more decided as his anger increased, though
the other could not divine the reason of the change. "It
is a matter of utter indifference whom we rob in the
prosecution of so excellent a scheme."

M. Magnien had very large and round eyes, and as
Junot uttered these last words he opened them very wide.

"Yes!" continued Junot, speaking with increasing energy; "I tell you, sir, it is a matter of indifference whom
we fix on for the purpose of robbery; for I should be a
robber to act in the way you propose. Ay! sir, nothing
but a robber."

"I do not see how that can be," replied Magnien, his
eyes opening wider and wider at each word Junot spoke.

"How, sir! not know that a man from whose coffers I

take three millions is robbed? And then what, pray, am I but a robber?"

"Yet I cannot see how that can happen in the present case," replied M. Magnien.

"In the devil's name," exclaimed Junot, "do you not see that the man from whom I purchase cotton to-night for one franc and fifty centimes will not have it in his magazines to-morrow to sell for five or six francs, as you say he would, and as I am very glad to hear he will? I am sure that when the unfortunate merchant should find he was deprived of the opportunity of selling his cotton at the advanced rate he would vent imprecations on me and my administration."

"But," observed the other, "he need not know who is the purchaser. The secret shall be sacredly kept."

Junot advanced to Magnien, his eyes flashing fire. The college companion thought he was in the presence of his deadliest enemy.

"Magnien," said he, "thank our old friendship, and still more your own stupidity, for your safety; for your stupidity, I am convinced, has inspired you with this fine project. It is therefore beneath me to be angry with you. For, upon reflection, I cannot believe that you, who, for the last two months have been witness to all my anxiety and solicitude for the declining trade of Lisbon, can seriously recommend me to sink it still deeper by such a swindling trick. For I tell you again that what you advise is nothing else. But enough! write on, and say no more about it."

Junot was violently excited. He said no more, but instantly formed a resolution. He dictated the decree to MM. Fissout and Magnien, and then, calling the aid-de-camp on duty, gave him orders to proceed immediately to the Government printer (the aid-de-camp not knowing the contents of the packet), to see it printed before his eyes, and forthwith posted in all quarters of the town, which was immediately done.

By this and similar measures Junot convinced those he governed how intent he was on doing all he could for their benefit. Bandeira, one of the richest and most active merchants in Lisbon, was commissioned by Junot to provide the supplies for the capital. This was a measure of great importance, and as soon as it was accomplished, and

7

Lisbon rendered tranquil on that score, Junot turned his attention to the state of agriculture, and adopted plans which seemed calculated to ameliorate it.

On the successful issue of this undertaking the repose and well-being of a country mainly depend, and Junot was assiduously seconded by the ablest men in Portugal. He directed the marshes to be drained, the land to be cleared, and encouraged the breeding of cattle. These matters being duly attended to, Portugal was sure to be secure from the apprehension of a scarcity of meat and bread — those primary necessaries of life. Nor did he allow the army to remain idle, but rendered its presence in Portugal useful to the country; for he employed the troops in the working of coal mines, some of which were discovered at Coimbra and at Moira.

The ceremony of Junot's installation as Governor General was as solemn as it was unexpected. He had convoked the Junta in the Palace of the Inquisition, a large and imposing edifice, situate in the Roscio Square; and without explaining previously the object of their extraordinary convocation, he arrived on horseback, followed by the whole of his staff, and all the individuals he had selected for his Ministers. He delivered a speech, firm and concise, in which he explained to the Junta the orders he had received, and which he was then about to execute. He then declared the Junta dissolved, and proclaimed the new government and the new Ministry.

He did one thing which was both politic and in good taste. He named two Ministers for each department of the Government; for instance, Hermann and Pedro de Mello for finance; Senhor Lunyt and Sampayo for the Marine. Senhor de Lagard, now Councilor of State, was the Minister of Police; he had just then come from Florence, and was an amiable and excellent individual. The Principal de Castro was Minister of Public Worship and of Justice.

These important changes were effected with the most perfect tranquillity, and Portugal soon began to derive benefit from them. Here Junot found his reward, for he experienced the utmost satisfaction at seeing a whole kingdom regenerated under his auspices. He now possessed the power as well as the will to do good. Unhappily a single day sufficed to destroy all his dreams!

Napoleon was still at Bayonne. He had concluded the two treaties with Ferdinand and Charles IV.* Joseph had been recalled from Naples and placed on the Spanish throne. To Charles IV. was assigned Compiègne, and to Ferdinand the Castle of Navarre. Charles IV. had a civil list of thirty millions of reals; Ferdinand, still under the title of Prince of the Asturias (for it must be borne in mind that the Emperor had never given him any other denomination) had only an annuity allotted him of four hundred thousand francs for himself and his descendants; and in the event of his having no issue, this income was to revert to his brother and his uncle.

However, the Emperor allowed Ferdinand an additional income of six hundred thousand francs from the Treasury of France; which, in the event of his demise, was to revert to the Princess of the Asturias. All this produced a singular effect in Paris. Even the French were amazed at this change of Sovereigns. Already the Prince and Queen of Portugal had set the example, and the Spanish Royal Family followed in the track with incredible celerity. Alas! the time was approaching when downfalls of royalty were to become too familiar to us.

The work of Spain's misfortunes was accomplished. Ferdinand VII. had removed from Bayonne to the prison of Valençay, which he was doomed not to leave until six years after, and Charles IV. repaired to Compiègne, where the Governor of the Palace received him and took him into his safe keeping: this was Comte de Laval-Montmorency. A few days afterward the Emperor received an address from the Supreme Junta sitting at Bayonne, praying that he would send his brother Joseph to reign over Spain. The Council of Castile and the Municipality of Madrid expressed the same wish.

Notwithstanding all that has been said to the contrary, no desire was ever more voluntary or more unanimous; and as the city was not occupied by the French troops the opinions of its inhabitants were freely manifested. Even in the presence of French troops, the silence of the Spaniards was expressive. On the 23d of May, Valencia and Seville were in a state of insurrection, and on the 27th, Saint Ferdinand's Day, the whole of Aragon rose.

* The famous treaty by which Charles abandoned the heritage of his ancestors was signed on the 5th of May, 1808.

The Junta sent the Marquis de Lazan, the brother of Palafox, to recommend the latter to preserve tranquillity; but the mischief had gone too far.   I have good reasons for believing that Palafox had received secret instructions at Bayonne from Ferdinand VII.; and there is also ground to suspect that England strongly instigated the insurrectionary movement in Spain.

Such a proceeding was perfectly consistent with the spirit of the British Cabinet.   When I was conversing, in 1814, with a member of the English Parliament, he expressed himself sorry that the power of Napoleon had not been attacked by a measure which, in his opinion, would inevitably have been triumphant: this was, to have proclaimed Soult King of Portugal when he wished to attain that dignity.   "Imagine," said he, "what would have been the MORAL EFFECT produced in Europe by the defection of one of the first Captains of Napoleon's army!"   He was right.

The magistrates and other public authorities fell sacrifices to the popular fury in various parts of Spain.   The victims selected were those individuals who had been appointed by Charles IV. or the Prince of the Peace, or those whom the Emperor appeared to have acknowledged. Don Francisco de Borja, commander of the Marine Service at Cadiz; Comte de Torre Fresno, Governor of Badajoz; Don Santiago de Guzman, Governor of Tortosa; Lieutenant General Filanghieri, Don Miguel de Cevallos, Don Pedro Truxillo, the Marquis de Laguila, and Baron d'Albala, were ASSASSINATED AND CUT TO PIECES in the insurrections of Valencia and Seville.

The climate of Madrid did not agree with Murat.   He was seized with colic, a disorder which is very prevalent there, and is frequently attended by fatal results.   Savary superseded him at the Spanish capital.   I know not how the latter discharged his duties; but this I know, that he made himself extremely ridiculous.   He used to be served by servants kneeling; I am aware that this may appear incredible; but let those who doubt the fact inquire among the inhabitants of Madrid; the answer will be that General Savary, when at table, had his goblet handed to him by a page on his knees.

About this time the famous provincial Junta was formed at Seville.   Doubtless the Spaniards were not disposed to

receive Joseph; yet, when the Junta of Bayonne named
him as Sovereign, it may be observed that the signatures
of those who approved the new constitution were exceedingly numerous. The list includes the names of the Duke
del Infantado, the Duke del Parque, the Duc de Frias, the
Marquis d'Ariza, the Prince de Castel-Franca, the Comte
de Fuentes, the Archbishop of Burgos, the Marquis de
Santa-Cruz, the Comte de Fernand-Nunez, Fray Augustin,
General de San Juan de Dieu, Fray Miguel d'Acevedo,
etc. But in this long list there appeared another signature which was worth all the rest. I will give it, with
the letter to which it was affixed, and which is addressed
to the Emperor:

« SIRE:— The surrender of the Crown of Spain which has been
made to your Imperial and Royal Majesty by King Charles IV., my
august Sovereign, and which has been ratified by their Highnesses
the Prince of the Asturias and the Infants Don Carlos and Don An-
tonio, imposes upon me the gratifying obligation of laying at the feet
of your Imperial and Royal Majesty the homage of my attachment,
fidelity, and respect. I pray that your Imperial and Royal Majesty
will deign to acknowledge me as your most faithful subject, and
make known to me your sovereign intentions, so that I may give
proof of my eager and cordial submission. Heaven grant long life
to your Imperial and Royal Majesty for the good of the Church and
State!— I am, Sire,

          « Your Imperial and Royal Majesty's most faithful subject,

                              « LOUIS DE BOURBON,
                    « Cardinal de Scala and Archbishop of Toledo.

« TOLEDO, 22d of May, 1808. »

A fine letter, truly, to be written by anyone bearing the
name of Bourbon, even admitting the submission to Napoleon to have been compulsory!
The Emperor was still at Bayonne, busied in making
arrangements for the government of his brother Joseph.
Murat was declared King of Naples. By thus seating a
Prince of his family on every throne in Europe, Napoleon
hoped to consolidate his power. Alas! he soon learned by
cruel experience that among Sovereigns, as among private
individuals, the ties of blood are but a feeble security for
the performance of duty when personal interest inter-
venes.
Murat departed for Naples, accompanied by his wife,
who was at length rendered perfectly happy by the thought
of filling a throne; for the ducal chair which she had
hitherto occupied had been anything but agreeable to her.

Knowing her as I did, I am convinced that her joy at this good fortune must have well-nigh turned her brain. But, after all, this joy was perfectly natural; I do not here mean to convey any reproach to the Princess. On the 9th of July, after the victory of Medina de Rio Seco* had opened to Joseph a road to his capital, he left Bayonne for Madrid, which he entered on the 20th of July. The new Sovereign was received in profound silence. The Spanish people had not yet had the opportunity of appreciating his good qualities, and, above all, his wish to render them happy. He had not been a week in Madrid when the disaster of Baylen, which was felt in all parts of the Peninsula, obliged him to seek a retreat at Vittoria. The ministers, five in number — Mazzaredo, Cabarus, Urquijo, Azanza, and O'Farril — followed him without hesitation; Cevalus and Pinuela remained in Madrid.

On Joseph's entrance an unfortunate circumstance occurred: this was the absolute refusal of the Council of Castile to recognize him. I am enabled to speak with certainty of this fact. It was not known in France, because, as may naturally be supposed, it was not inserted in the *Moniteur*. We were so completely kept in the dark that when King Joseph left Madrid to return to Vittoria, for fear of being carried off by General Castaños, who had just beaten General Dupont at Baylen, the *Moniteur* stated that THE FRENCH ARMY IN SPAIN WAS GOING TO REMOVE ITS QUARTERS TO A PLACE WHERE IT WOULD HAVE THE BENEFIT OF MILDER AIR AND BETTER WATER.

General Vedel has been loudly accused of having abandoned General Dupont. This accusation was probably made only to screen the guilty party. That General Dupont was involuntarily in fault is possible; but, still, he was nevertheless in fault; and the odious affair of Baylen ended with the disgrace of a violated capitulation. It would seem that the Spaniards thought themselves justified in not keeping their faith with men so unmindful of French glory.

While Spain was rising in revolution, while the bonfires of incendiarism were blazing on her hills, and the alarm

---

*This battle was gained by Marshal Bessières on the 4th of July, after a very sanguinary conflict. The Spanish force amounted to 40,000.

bell was sounding from all her steeples, we were living at Paris in the profoundest ignorance of the important events which were developing themselves in that neighboring nation. The Emperor was still at Bayonne, for which place the Empress had set out, taking the road through Bordeaux, as it was the Emperor's pleasure that this part of France, which had sustained so much injury from the war, should at least be soothed by fair words and gracious manners, which Josephine so well knew how to adopt. She received orders to make herself agreeable, and she succeeded in enchanting the Bordelais. This I learned when I passed through that town on my way to the Pyrenees.

While the Empress was there the Emperor was at Bayonne organizing, or rather disorganizing, Spain with an ardor which bordered on infatuation: we poor women who were left at Paris waited impatiently even for a single letter which should quiet the alarms unauthenticated rumors could not fail at such moments to inspire; but there stood Bayonne, like a great gulf, between us and our correspondents, and not a word reached us but what it pleased the Master to make us acquainted with. The result of this capital manœuver, the invention of Louvois, but perfected in our time, spared certainly even greater uneasiness than it inflicted, but kept us in a state of absolute ignorance.

The Emperor returned to Paris early in September. He had remained longer at Bayonne than he intended, but the affairs of Spain had not proceeded quite so passively as he had anticipated. Not only had some impediments arisen within the country, such as the opposition of the Council of Castile, but even the written opinions of those Grandees of Spain who composed that bastard Cortes called the Junta were not adequate to the effect which Napoleon expected from them — the calming and satisfying the public mind.

No tidings arrived of the Army of Portugal, and two months had elapsed without a single letter from that country reaching Paris, when the Emperor arrived from the South to stay only a few days, being about to set out immediately for Erfurth.

My uneasiness about Junot became excessive. I had frequently seen the Arch-Chancellor in the Emperor's absence, and so entirely ignorant did he appear that, unable to believe what was nevertheless a fact, that the Emperor himself had received no letters from Junot, I began to conclude that some great misfortune had occurred. We had then no idea of the nature of the Spanish War, and this total cessation of intelligence appeared impossible. Even an intimate friend of mine, who had means of learning through England what was passing in Portugal, re-received no news; it was distracting.

Immediately, therefore, upon the Emperor's return, I wrote to him to learn if he knew with any certainty that Junot was still living, and supplicating him to send me a single word that might relieve my anxiety. Some days passed before I received an answer, which came at length through the Arch-Chancellor, and with it a lecture upon my presumption in interrogating the Emperor upon matters touching his politics. I thought this remonstrance somewhat singular, but received it with profound submission; and as soon as the Arch-Chancellor left me I dispatched a letter to the Emperor, requesting an audience that same day, as I had a favor to solicit. The Emperor was then at Saint Cloud and I was at Neuilly.

The cause of my request was of some importance. Since Junot had been Governor of Paris, whether he was absent or present, I had always done the honors of the city *fêtes* at the Hôtel de Ville. This time, as usual, though the Emperor had been absent on the 15th of August, the city was desirous of celebrating the Saint Napoleon, and the list of those ladies who were to receive the Empress had been brought to me for presentation to the Grand Marshal. It was perfectly natural to me to preside at these entertainments, when everything was in its right course; but at present matters were very far otherwise. I felt the unpleasantness of my situation and this determined me to request an audience. I received an order to be at Saint Cloud at nine o'clock in the evening.

On my arrival I found the Emperor in his cabinet, looking upon the little private garden reserved for his use; the door was open, and at my entrance, he stood on the step of the door, looking straight before him with the fixed and vacant stare of a person deep in thought. He started at the opening of the door, and, turning sharply toward me, asked with an expression of petulance why I would not believe what he had ordered the Arch-Chancellor to tell me.

"Your husband is perfectly well — what the devil do you mean by these conjugal jeremiads?" "Sire, my mind is relieved since your Majesty has had the goodness to send me word that I might be easy; but in the situation in which I stand at this moment I am come to entreat your Majesty to permit me to decline going to the Hôtel de Ville to-morrow." He was still looking toward the garden door, but on hearing this he turned hastily round, and said in a very singular tone of voice: "Hem! what do you say? — not go to the Hôtel de Ville? And pray, why not?" "Because, Sire, I fear that some misfortune has occurred to Junot. I beg your Majesty's pardon," I continued with firmness, for his bent brow presaged a storm; "but, I repeat, I have no tidings of Junot — NEITHER HAS YOUR MAJESTY ANY — and I am unwilling to expose myself to hear, perhaps, of his death, in a public ball-room." I know not how I acquired so much audacity, but I had it.

The Emperor looked at me angrily, then shrugged his shoulders, but eventually controlled himself. "I have told you that your husband is in good health — why will you not believe me? I cannot prove it, but I give you my word." "It is certainly enough to satisfy me, Sire, but I cannot write a circular to communicate this satisfactory assurance to the four thousand persons who will be present at the city *fête*, and who will think it very extraordinary that I should present myself so publicly when I have such strong cause of uneasiness." "And what should these four thousand persons know about your cause of uneasiness?" he exclaimed in a terrible voice, and advancing toward me with an impetuosity of manner which almost made me afraid of him. "This is the result of your drawing-room councils, letters, and all your gossipings with my enemies. You declaim against me; you attack all my actions. What was that which the Prussian Minister, one of your friends, was lately saying at your house about my tyranny toward his King? Truly I am a very cruel tyrant! If their Great Frederick, that they make so much noise about, had had occasion to punish as much disloyalty as I have, he would have done it more effectually. And, after all, Glogau and Custrin will be much better guarded by my troops than by the Prussians, for they have no great cause to be proud of their defense of them."

This was perhaps the tenth time since my return from Portugal that the Emperor repeated to me what had been said at my house. On the former occasions I was conscious that the truth had been told him; but, in fact, I never heard the Prussian Minister, who certainly visited me frequently, say a word that bore the least analogy to the sentiments which the Emperor imputed to him.

The Baron de Brockhausen was a man of great circumspection, very mild, saying little, and perfectly to be trusted. He stood, moreover, in the difficult position of representing an unfortunate and humiliated nation, and no one was less suited to maintain such an attitude. He consequently shut himself up in absolute silence, and, though he visited me almost daily, we sometimes laughingly remarked after his departure: "The Baron has uttered seven words this evening." He was a truly respectable man — an excellent father, and one of the most estimable Prussians I have ever met with.

This knowledge of his character convinced me at once that the Emperor was only endeavoring (to express myself in his own phrase) TO PUMP ME, and I was also certain that if such a subject of conversation had ever been entertained in my society, M. de Brockhausen was the last person who would have opened his lips upon it. I therefore firmly replied that his Majesty had been misinformed, and I would undertake to say that such words as those he had just repeated had never been uttered in my house.

He stamped with his foot, and, approaching me as quick as lightning, exclaimed: "So I have told an untruth?" "I have the honor to answer," said I very calmly, "that your Majesty is misinformed." "Oh! to be sure — that is what you all say when you are spoken to as on this occasion." "According to your Majesty's observation, it would seem that I am not the only person accused, and I think I may affirm that others are so as unjustly as myself." The word ALL had not escaped me.

The Emperor, when anything nearly affected him, and he did not give vent to his feelings in words, concentrated in the expression of his countenance all the weight of his power. He fixed this look upon me; I looked down, not from fear, as he might observe, but only that it did not become me to dispute in this manner with him. When I again raised my eyes, he was still looking at me, but with a very different, and, to say the truth, very strange expression; and never in the course of my life had I felt less disposed to endure that expression, or the interpretation that might be put upon it.

"What are your Majesty's commands?" said I, receding toward the door; the Emperor did not answer immediately, but presently said: "I forbid you to repeat what has passed here; do you understand me? See that you obey, or I will let you know whom you have to deal with." "I shall obey you, Sire, not for fear of your anger, but that I may not have to blush before conquered foreigners for our family misunderstandings."

I made my obeisance and prepared to go. I was in haste to leave the room; yet I was desirous, before I went, to settle the question which brought me thither, and I told the Emperor that it seemed to me more suitable that I should not make my appearance at the Hôtel de Ville, where my station placed me in the foreground immediately after the Empress, at a moment when reports were current respecting the safety of the Army of Portugal.

He resumed the expression of sovereignty: "And what," said he, in a tone calculated to strike to the heart and make one tremble — "what are those reports?" This time I could not resist a sensation of fear, and replied in a low voice: "They say it is lost — that Junot has been compelled to capitulate like Dupont, and that the English have carried him to Brazil." "It is false! It is false, I tell you!" and he struck his fist upon the table with such violence as to throw down a heap of papers. "It is false!" he exclaimed again, swearing this time like a sub-lieutenant of dragoons. "Junot capitulate like Dupont! it is a tissue of falsehoods; but precisely because it is said, you must go to the Hôtel de Ville. You must go, do you hear? — and even if you were ill, still you ought to go. It is my will — good night."

On returning to my carriage I wept like a child. The Emperor seemed to be very severe toward Junot and me. However, upon reflection I felt assured that nothing unfor-

tunate had occurred to my husband, since he insisted so
pertinaciously upon my going to this ball. On my arrival
at Neuilly I found a friend there waiting to learn the
result of my petition; he took the same view of the subject; and when, after a long stroll under the balmy limes
which bordered the canal, he took leave of me to return
to Paris, I felt reassured, and much more tranquil.

I went to the *fête;* regulated like its predecessors, and
equal in magnificence, I know not why it appeared dull
and melancholy. The Emperor either did not come at all,
or came but for a moment. I was so absorbed in my
own feelings that I cannot now remember whether he
came or not. I do not understand how it happened that
he who usually was so tenacious of his popularity with
his good citizens of Paris should not on this occasion have
made an effort to gratify them.

The *senatus-consultum* authorizing the levy of eighty
thousand conscripts of the classes of 1806, 7, 8, 9, and
10, to be forthwith brought into actual service had just
appeared, and had struck a kind of stupor upon the city.
There was even some talk of calling out eighty thousand
conscripts of the class 1810, as yet scarcely eighteen years
of age; they were to be reserved, it was said, to guard
the coasts. The Emperor knew all the reports that were
circulated, and was certainly not ignorant of what was
said in the shops of Paris. Here, then, was his motive for
insisting on my appearance at this entertainment. Had I
been absent, the most absurd of the suppositions current
concerning the fate of Junot and his army would have
acquired a dangerous consistency.

Thus it is that such men as Napoleon consider private
interests and feelings as perfect nullities in the political
balance. I have since learned that the Battle of Vimiera,
which was fought on the 21st of August, was near destroying Junot and the army! Was the Emperor totally ignorant of this battle on the 4th of September? I think not;
no doubt he would have acquired some confused intelligence of it through the medium of England.

This *fête* was excessively dull, or so at least it appeared
to me. The Empress was present a very short time, and
would not stay to supper. I had a dreadful headache, but
did not like to retire at the same time; it would have
looked absurd. I stayed to supper, and some foreigners

of distinction accompanied me into a separate room, in
which a table of fifty covers was laid.   The ladies only
took their seats around it; the gentlemen stood behind
them.

Comte Frochot, then Prefect of the Seine, was not only
a man of sense, but possessed all the qualifications that
could be required to take the lead with advantage in
such a ceremony.   He was a well-bred man, uniting politeness with dignity, and doing the honors of the civic
feast with as much ease as those of his own house.   In
the connection with which my place in the entertainment
threw me with him, he acted in the most graceful manner possible; but, to say the truth, in Junot's absence I
had no business whatever at the Hôtel de Ville, and matters would have proceeded on this occasion perfectly well
without me.

The Count was thoroughly agreeable; and this qualification, so essential in society, was peculiarly useful to him
in the vast galleries of the Hôtel de Ville, where were
congregated not only the most considerable capitalists of
France, but all the great, the noble, the eminent for birth
or favor, whom Europe deputed as her representatives at
Paris.   There was Metternich, the Austrian Ambassador;
M. de Tolstoi, from Russia; the Baron de Brockhausen,
the Prussian Minister; the Ambassador of Spain, and the
crowd of Envoys from the German Courts, among which
Bavaria, Saxony, and Wirtemberg held the rank of kingdoms.

About this period I received a confidential and very
interesting letter from Madrid, written to me only, by a
Spaniard of position and ability.   I am obliged to withhold his name, and regret that family considerations impose this reserve upon me.   This letter was addressed to
me because its writer was a friend of mine, and because,
knowing my situation in the Imperial Court, he hoped
that I might prove the means of some important truths
reaching the Emperor's ears.   He did not know that Napoleon never listened to a woman.   I regretted, however,
that I had not received this letter before my memorable
audience, as I should certainly have spoken of some of its
contents without giving the whole up to him.

" Spain," the writer says, " is lost; probably you have
no idea of the causes of the evil.   First on the list stand

the disasters of Baylen; Castaños has made great capital
of the signature of one of your great officers of the Empire. He reports that the Captains of Napoleon no
longer hold by him, since Marescot, who had no reason
to sanction Dupont's disgrace (you see I speak as a
Frenchman, because I am a man of honor and a soldier),
was eager to sign the convention. But this is not all;
King Joseph's unfortunate departure from Madrid a week
after his entry,— dear Duchess, you know that distrust
produces distrust,— by proving to the Spaniards that he
had no confidence in them, Joseph pointed out to them
the party they should adopt. Oh, my poor country! may
the virgin and the saints be her protectors, for she is in
great necessity! A Supreme Junta is established at Aranjuez, the beautiful shades of which have witnessed melancholy scenes and bloody tragedies. The waters of the
Tagus have been dyed with Spanish blood. A civil war,
it is true, divided Spain in the cause of Philip V. and
the Archduke. But this is of a totally different nature.
The quarrel between your Emperor and the Pope has
been the mainspring of the mischief. If you did but
know what a catechism is taught the children! All this
would have been spared if the Emperor Napoleon had
put Godoy upon his trial and caused him to be hanged.
Instead of this he treats with him! It is lamentable. I
send you a specimen of the catechism which is dispersed
throughout Andalusia. How important it would be that
the Emperor should see it!»

The following are fragments of the catechism alluded to:

Q. "Child, what art thou?"
A. "A Spaniard, by the grace of God."
Q. "What do you mean by that?"
A. "An honest man."
Q. "Who is our enemy?"
A. "The Emperor of the French."
Q. "What is the Emperor Napoleon?"
A. "A wicked being, the source of all evils, and the focus of all
vices."
Q. "How many natures has he?"
A. "Two: the human and the diabolical."
Q. "How many Emperors of the French are there?"
A. "One actually, in three deceiving persons."
Q. "What are they called?"
A. "Napoleon, Murat, and Manuel Godoy, the Prince of the Peace."
Q. "Which is the most wicked?"

A. "They are all equally so."

Q. "What are the French?"

A. "Apostate Christians, turned heretics."

Q. "What punishment does a Spaniard deserve who fails in his duty?"

A. "The death and infamy of a traitor."

Q. "Is it a sin to kill a Frenchman?"

A. "No, my father; heaven is gained by killing one of these heretical dogs."

These were the principal heads of a catechism which the Spanish priests taught the children, as many great persons very well knew.

CHAPTER X.

News of the Convention of Cintra — Landing of the British Troops — The Miraculous Egg — Patriotism of Comte de Bourmont — Battle of Vimiera — Council of Generals — Admiral Siniavin — General Kellerman Treats with the English Generals — Anecdote — Siniavin's Treachery — The Convention — My Departure for Rochelle — Meeting with Junot — Arrest of M. de Bourmont — Anecdote of the Emperor of Russia — Napoleon and Alexander — The Arch-Chancellor's Fête — Count Metternich and the Duc de Cadore — War with Austria — Defeat of General Moore — Dinner and Breakfast at the Tuileries — The Famous Diamonds.

A T LENGTH tidings from Portugal reached France; they were disastrous for Napoleon, but honorable for Junot and all belonging to him. How noble was his conduct! The glory of the French arms remained untarnished, and to him alone was that due. How often since his terrible death have I wept over that imperishable monument of his victory over England — THE CONVENTION OF CINTRA! Alas! he to whom his whole life was devoted alone disowned its merit.*

* "Junot's movements, on the landing of the English, for the defense of the Capital were in striking contrast to the energy and vigor of his advance upon Abrantès, and his daring seizure of Lisbon when only at the head of an advance guard of a few hundred men.

"With the momentary exception of Junot's threat to burn Lisbon if his terms were not complied with, we look in vain for any traces of that vigor which urged the march from Alcantara; we are astonished to perceive the man who, in the teeth of an English fleet, in contempt of fourteen thousand Portuguese troops, and regardless of a population

In my opinion, the Convention of Cintra, obtained solely by the moral force of the character Junot had acquired, was the counterpart of the Battle of Nazareth in Palestine, fought on the 8th of April, 1799, in which Junot, with three hundred Frenchmen, defeated the advanced guard of the Grand Vizier, killed with his own hand Ayoub-Bey, surnamed Abou-Seff (father of the saber), and produced an incalculable moral effect on the two armies of the East.

One evening when Junot gave a ball at the Government House, an officer belonging to the staff of General Thomières, Commandant of Fort Peniche, arrived with pressing dispatches. The tidings they contained were fearful and certain. The English, to the number of twelve thousand men, had effected a landing with an immense train of artillery and every species of warlike munition. Junot directed the officers about him to increase their attentions to the ladies and the gayety of the ball-room, while he himself retired to his closet and ordered General Laborde immediately to march toward the enemy in order to prevent the whole truth from reaching the city at once. It was at this period that a miraculous hen laid a miraculous egg on the High Altar of the Cathedral bearing in raised characters the words " Death to the French. " In a few minutes the anathematizing egg was conveyed to Headquarters and estimated at its real value as an ill-executed deception on the part of the priests. Junot laughed at the incident, sent for a quantity of eggs, and directed his

of three hundred thousand souls, dared with a few hundred tired grenadiers to seize upon Lisbon, so changed in half a year, so sunk in energy, that, with twenty-five thousand good soldiers, he declined a manly effort, and resorted to a Convention to save an army which was really in very little danger. But such and so variable is the human mind, a momentary slave of every attraction, yet ultimately true to self-interest.

" When Junot entered Portugal, power, honors, fame, even a throne, were within his view; when he proposed the Convention the gorgeous apparition was gone, toil and danger were at hand, fame flitted at a distance, and he easily persuaded himself that prudence and vigor could not be yoked together.

" A saying attributed to Napoleon perfectly describes the Convention in a few words, ' I was going to send Junot before a Council of War, when, fortunately, the English tried their Generals, and saved me the pain of punishing an old friend! ' "—Napier's " History of the Peninsular War," vol. i., p. 269.

aids-de-camp to write on each of them in grease that the former egg was a liar, immersed them in acid, and the next morning sent these eggs with their inscriptions in relief to all the altars in Lisbon, together with a written recipe for the correct performance of the miracle.*

For some days Portugal remained in apparent security; but, nothwithstanding General Laborde's victory over the English at Roliça, another victory gained in Spain, the announcement of the march of twenty thousand French troops through Braganza to succor Lisbon, the entry of Joseph into Madrid, and the *fêtes* in celebration of this event, still the spirit of insurrection raged at Lisbon, and was kept in check only by the presence of Junot. It was nevertheless absolutely necessary to meet the enemy.

On the 15th of August, after celebrating the Emperor's birthday by a grand dinner and a splendid performance at the Opera House, Junot returned at midnight to his private apartments, and assembled there the Ministers and General Travot. He told them he was about to set out to give battle to the English; charged them with their immediate duties; pressed with emotion the hand of General Travot, whose noble character he highly esteemed, and to whose care he was confiding the Capital; and quitted the Government House to seek his death — for at that moment he little expected ever to see again his country, his wife, or his children.

I must not here omit an anecdote of a man often attacked, and whom I always feel desirous of justifying. Comte de Bourmont was at this time among the French refugees at Lisbon; it was in his power to go over to the English or to join the Portuguese insurgents; but, instead of doing either the one or the other, he sought Junot and thus addressed him: " Monsieur le Duc, I have never disowned my country: I am a Frenchman; you are attacked; a resolute heart and two stout arms may be useful to you, and I come to offer them: are you willing to place me upon your staff ? " †

* A slightly different version of this incident will be found in Napier's « History of the Peninsular War, » vol. i.

† Presumably the same M. de Bourmont who volunteered for the campaign in Belgium in 1815, and then betrayed his countrymen in a most treacherous manner when possessed of information to carry over to the enemy.

8

Junot was, perhaps, of all men in the army the most capable of appreciating such conduct; he approached M. de Bourmont, took his hand, which he pressed warmly, and in a tone of emotion replied: "M. de Bourmont, I not only accept your services, but I pledge my honor that no difficulties shall be thrown in the way of your return to France; you have my word, which never fails." And he kept it effectually. M. de Saint Mezard, an officer of the ex-royal bodyguard, M. de Viomesnil, nephew of the Marshal, and many other emigrants, acted in a similar manner; but the example was set by M. de Bourmont.

Junot then proceeded to meet the enemy, who was advancing upon Lisbon by the route of Thomar, numbering above 13,000 effective troops, besides an army of 60,000 Spanish and Portuguese insurgents, the whole country and all the chances of the future in their favor; while Junot's army barely amounted to 9,200 men, destitute of resources. Under these circumstances Junot was eager to engage, and being, above all, desirous of forestalling an attack, he determined to meet the enemy. The battle took place on the 21st of August; the conduct of the army throughout the day, which the oppressive heat of the weather rendered truly laborious, was such as to maintain the glory of our eagles and the purity of our standards, which, thanks to the valor of their defenders and the ability of their chiefs, returned unsullied to France. Notwithstanding all this courage and zeal, the battle was lost; happily our army remained on the field after the fire had ceased, which enabled them to cover the retreat of the wounded, but we lost 1,000 men killed and 800 prisoners, of which number not more than 150 were disabled.

In these almost desperate circumstances Junot assembled Generals Loison, Laborde, Kellerman, and Thiébault, to consult upon the next steps to be taken. To retreat, even by forced marches, across Spain, was impossible; one chance only afforded a ray of hope. I have not yet mentioned the Russian squadron which Junot found in the Tagus on his arrival at Lisbon, and which had ever since been treated by the French army as belonging to a nation whose chief was the brother of our Emperor's heart.

Junot, then, had a right to expect that the co-operation of Admiral Siniavin, who commanded eight vessels, would be of the utmost value to him in this extremity. He had yet to learn that the assistance of an ally is only to be reckoned upon in the time of success. Siniavin was an unsociable animal, and it may be observed that when the Russians are savage it is not by halves. The father of this Admiral was probably one of the number of those who preferred losing their heads to surrendering their beards; at all events he belonged to a barbarous race. In relating the events of this memorable period I have adhered strictly to the papers left by the Duc d'Abrantès, and to the details communicated to me by the Duc de Valmy and Generals Thiébault and de Laborde.

The result of the conference called by the Duke was to send General Kellerman, furnished with full powers, to the English camp, to see what could be done in the way of negotiation. The English General was Sir Hew Dalrymple, and next under him was Sir Arthur Wellesley, afterward Duke of Wellington.

At eleven o'clock in the morning of the 22d, General Kellerman took the road to Vimiera, and was astonished not to meet with any outposts; for a moment he believed the enemy was in retreat, and he has himself related to me a circumstance which proves the accuracy and acuteness of his judgment. "In proportion as I advanced," said he, "without meeting a single English cockade, my confidence revived and became complete when, on my arrival at the English Headquarters, I found myself admitted to treat on terms of perfect equality." It was not till three in the afternoon that General Kellerman found himself in front of the English outposts, which were precisely in their position of the preceding day, and so great was the uneasiness of the English, that, notwithstanding he had attached his white handkerchief to the end of his saber, he had to face about thirty musket shots before he was recognized as a negotiator.

At length he was conducted to Sir Hew Dalrymple, who had arrived that very morning to supersede Sir Arthur Wellesley, just to sign the Convention of Cintra— truly it was hardly worth while! General Kellerman understood the English as perfectly as the French language, but he took care to conceal his knowledge; in war, stratagem is justifiable, and in the existing situation of the French army it was fair to take every possible advantage. The General's *ruse* proved extremely useful to him, for,

after he had opened the basis of his proposition, the two
Generals retired to the embrasure of a window, and he
heard one of them observe in a low tone: "We are not
in a very good position; let us hear what he has to say."
At this moment dinner was announced, and General
Kellerman, having been invited by Sir Hew Dalrymple,
sat down with the English officers. The dinner was gay,
but so extremely frugal as to satisfy the General that
what he had heard of the scarcity of provisions in the
English camp was true. While the party continued at
table an officer returned who had been sent to Figueras.
Nothing having yet transpired to show that the Duc de
Valmy understood English, Sir Arthur and Sir Hew inquired eagerly of the officer in English what news he
brought, to which he replied: "Sir John Moore has not
yet arrived at Figueras." This was the same Sir John
Moore whom the Emperor afterward so effectually drove
into the sea at Corunna. He was to bring an additional
force of fourteen thousand men, the absence or presence
of which was of the utmost importance at this crisis.

In drawing up the preliminary articles the interests of
our allies were stipulated for. "What!" exclaimed Sir Arthur Wellesley; "do you pretend to include the Russian
fleet in your treaty?" "Russia is our ally," replied the
Duc de Valmy, "and it is impossible for us to abandon
her fleet. But I shall not be sorry if you reject this
article, as in that case the Admiral, in his own defense,
will be obliged to disembark his crews, we shall be enabled
to recall our garrisons, and shall thus obtain a reinforcement of ten thousand fresh and veteran troops, which will
enable us to deliver Portugal in three weeks." The two
English Generals again withdrew to the window, and
General Kellerman overheard the words: "That would be
very well, but the ten thousand Russians!" It is manifest that, without intending it, the Russians were very useful to us.

At length the preliminaries were concluded, and General
Kellerman returned to the French Headquarters, accompanied to the outposts by Lord Burghersh, and overwhelmed with civilities by the English officers, who having
previously entertained a high opinion of his military
character, had now received sufficient proof of his diplomatic abilities.

An anecdote related by General Kellerman will prove
how generous and noble in social and private life are those
same Englishmen whom in public affairs we find so little
worthy of esteem. Colonel Taylor, a much esteemed
English officer, possessed a remarkably fine horse; its
color was dark bay, its figure perfect; but its qualities
were even more excellent than its beauty; it obeyed a word
as a sign, and went through all the performances of a
dog. The Colonel was killed at Vimiera in an engagement between the troops under his command and those
of the Duc de Valmy. His horse was taken and brought
to the Duke. As soon as the English learned that it was
in his possession they requested General Kellerman to set
any ransom he pleased upon it, that it might be restored
to his regiment, which was anxious to preserve and take
charge of it in memory of its master. The General refused the ransom, and courteously returned the noble
charger; but the English officers chose a horse of the
finest breed, and presented it to the French General,
through the hands of Sir Arthur Wellesley, with that
peculiar graciousness with which English gentlemen know
so well how to adorn their private transactions.

"Ah," exclaimed Junot, "if this Russian Admiral would
but second us with six thousand additional men, and such
coadjutors as you, I would not quit Portugal!" Nothing
was yet signed. General Kellerman undertook this new
mission; he proceeded to Admiral Siniavin; requested of
him five thousand men from his crews, undertook to
furnish them with arms, and to place them in the forts,
whence he would thus be enabled to withdraw a similar
number of French troops. The Russian was overpersuaded
and promised; but after the lapse of a few hours this
man, whom his Sovereign ought to have exiled to Siberia
for his baseness, retracted, and wrote to Junot that he
could not land a single man; and that, moreover, he
should make his own terms with Sir Charles Cotton, the
English Admiral. This resolution was as injurious to
the Russians as it was to the French, and was, moreover,
disgraceful to the former. Junot has told me that he
suffered more in receiving this letter from Siniavin than
in the loss of the Battle of Vimiera; a hope betrayed is,
in fact, more distressing than the confirmation of an expected misfortune. Then this violation of a pledged word

—this perfidy to an ally! He perceived in the conduct
of Siniavin a sort of presage for the Emperor — perhaps
a warning, for the Czar might have been equally seen in
it. To me it has always been inexplicable that a proceeding, not only so injurious to Junot, but so indefensible in
a military point of view, had not procured for its perpe-
trator the reward of a journey to Tobolsk. Such incon-
sistency in the conduct of Alexander at the very moment
of the conference of Erfurth is perplexing.

Junot, finding himself by the Russian Admiral's proceedings left at liberty to treat separately for himself,
nominated General Kellerman to act for him. Sir George
Murray was the representative of the English General,
and a convention was concluded upon the bases already
agreed upon, although the arrival of Sir John Moore with
the troops under his command had materially changed the
respective positions of the two armies. It is just to acknowledge that honor and good faith characterized the
dealings of the English officers.

Notwithstanding the ability of General Kellerman, many
difficulties arose, upon which Junot observed: "I ask no
favor. If I am refused what I demand for my army, I
retire upon Lisbon, blow up the forts, burn the arsenal
and the fleet, and, master of both banks of the Tagus, I
retreat upon Spain, leaving behind me terrible monuments
of my journey." I have heard him lament that he had
not executed this resolution; and yet he would add: "I
must have starved my army, which would much more certainly have experienced that fate than on its march into
Portugal. Under such circumstances every alternative was
disastrous." General Thiébault considered the plan to be
impracticable; and his opinion as Chief of the Staff, necessarily had great weight in the ultimate decision. With
respect to blowing up the forts, and burning the fleet
and the city, I believe Junot to have been capable of doing it.

At length M. de Grave, aid-de-camp to the Duc d'Abrantès, quitted Lisbon, and arrived in Paris, after a voyage
rendered tedious by dreadful weather, early in October,
bringing to the Emperor the definitive convention which
had been signed by the two Generals-in-Chief on the 30th
of August; upon which Colonel Duncan had been sent as
a hostage to the Duc d'Abrantès, who gave up the Adju-

tant-Commandant Desroches to the English General in the same capacity.

Having opened the letter which the same aid-de-camp brought to me from Junot, I read the copy it inclosed of this glorious convention, the stamp of perhaps the finest military achievements which the annals of our Revolution record. Let its merits be judged of by a comparison with that of Baylen!

Andoche was expected to land at Rochelle or some neighboring port; I therefore set out for that place on the 4th of October, the day after M. de Grave's arrival, taking with me Madame de Grandsaigne, wife of the first aid-de-camp to the Duc d'Abrantès, but leaving my children in Paris, as I concluded my husband would return with me. Alas! I knew not that the Emperor viewed matters through a medium quite at variance with mine.

The French army was landed at Rochelle and various other ports on the coast. Junot arrived in the "Nymph" frigate, Captain Percy, who treated him with great consideration. The fortune of war subsequently afforded me an opportunity of discharging the debt on behalf of my husband toward a relation of Captain Percy (an aid-de-camp, I believe, to the Duke of Wellington), who was prisoner in Spain. Owing to the opinion expressed by the Emperor, our joy on this reunion was overclouded; our intercourse had not its usual freedom; the future dimmed, we talked not of home. When I spoke of the alterations in our Hôtel, Junot answered with bitterness: "What is it to me? I shall never see it."

On our meeting, Junot opened his heart to me, describing all that he had suffered and was suffering. The Emperor had written him some letters, excessively short as usual, and in the last had told him he must never re-enter Paris without victory, to EFFACE THE REMEMBRANCE OF LISBON. The tears stood in his eyes as he repeated this expression. "I believe," said he with bitterness, "that all Europe will judge me differently. What could I do?" Junot then unveiled a part of the intrigues devised to injure him in the Emperor's estimation. It was clear that the same persons who afterward contributed to their master's ruin were already paving the way to it by detaching him from his truest friends. Bessières had been so repeatedly offended that he was almost tempted to retire to his estates. So had Marshal Lannes. Duroc began to be sensible of dependence, and Berthier to feel its full force.

We were one day at table, when we received a letter from Nantes announcing the arrest of M. de Bourmont; upon reading which, with a countenance inflamed with rage, he uttered a terrible oath. "And I had pledged him my word of honor that he might land in perfect safety!" exclaimed he, rising in fury; "this is a trick of M. Fouché. But we will see who gains the day." Accordingly he wrote, and M. de Bourmont was released, but arrested again a few days afterward; on hearing which all my influence with Junot was insufficient to appease him: he immediately set out full speed for Angoulême, through which town he had learned that the Emperor was to pass on his return from Erfurth. I knew that Savary would be there; and though Duroc, Rapp, and Berthier were also of the party, yet, knowing Junot, I feared his violence of character, and dreaded the Emperor.

Nothing could detain him; my entreaties were of no avail. Alas! Napoleon ill understood that strong yet tender spirit, so full of energy, yet as affectionate as that of an enamored woman.

On his return to Rochelle the gloom of his brow had increased, though he had obtained M. de Bourmont's admission into the Military Staff of the Army of Naples with the title of Adjutant General, and also the Comte de Novion's pension of 6,000 francs; the Emperor accorded nearly all he desired.

For instance, M. de Viomesnil, M. de Saint Mezard, and a number of officers of the old régime, who, remembering that they were Frenchmen, refused to bear arms against their country, though they had fled from France when her scaffolds were thirsting for their blood, were indebted to Junot's interposition for the termination of a fifteen years' exile. "Why, then," I asked, "are you sad? Was the Emperor unkind to you?" "No," said he, with a forced smile; "but he was not kind." He was not to enter Paris, the Emperor had repeated to him, but must first return to Lisbon.

The star of Napoleon Bonaparte was at this time shining in the zenith of its splendor. Alas! its radiance blinded him. The interview at Erfurth. in which the Emperor of

Russia gave him so many proofs of fraternal friendship,
was a snare of destiny to lure him to his ruin. One anecdote of this meeting is well known, but is too apposite to
this subject to be omitted here. When Talma, in the part
of Philoctetes, pronounced the line,

« The friendship of a great man is a gift of the gods! »

the Emperor Alexander, rising from his seat, threw himself
into the arms of Napoleon with an emotion so manifest
and sincere that no one could doubt the sentiment which
excited it. I can guarantee the truth of another, and there
are Memoirs in existence which will perhaps one day appear, and will confirm it.

When Count Nicholas Romanzoff came about this time
to Paris, he was assailed on the way, both by Austria and
Prussia, with arguments and inducements to join the famous
alliance, to which Sweden was already pledged; but the
Russians, M. de Romanzoff, and before him M. de Tolstoi,
were inviolable in their fidelity, and turned a deaf ear to all
such remonstrances.

Another fact, apparently indifferent, perhaps eventually
decided the destiny of Napoleon. Being one day in company with the Emperor Alexander at Erfurth, and conversing confidentially with him as with a brother,
Napoleon mentioned Ferdinand VII., spoke of the uneasiness he occasioned him, of the trouble of detaining him
in captivity, and of his intrigues with dairymaids (such
kinds of amours being always odious to Napoleon, he alluded to them in disgust). The Russian Emperor looked
significantly at him for some moments, then, smiling,
turned away his head in a very eloquent silence.
« Do you, then, possess a talisman for mastering this
evil genius ? » said Napoleon, laughing, observing that
Alexander shrugged his shoulders with contemptuous impatience. « Why, really, » replied the other, « when the
captivity of an enemy is as inconvenient to the conqueror
as it must be annoying and wearisome to the conquered,
the best thing that can be done for both is to put an
end to it. » Napoleon stood for a moment motionless, but
made no reply.

It is certain that he did not adopt the counsel; and
that, when in 1815 he had to choose an asylum, this sentence of Alexander's recurred to his memory; and prob-

ably he likewise reverted to it when in 1814 I sent him a message through the Duc de Rovigo, in consequence of a long conversation that I had held with the Emperor of Russia at my Hôtel in the Champs Elysées, which at that time I still occupied. Unfortunately, in 1808 and 1809, Napoleon was too much the dupe of Alexander's friendship, and afterward he had not sufficient confidence in it. But such was the constitution of his mind, that neither his sentiments nor actions could ever accord with those of other men.

After several weeks passed at Erfurth in discussing the destinies and most serious interests of Europe, amid the gayest and most brilliant *fêtes*, Napoleon crossed France, only to march upon Spain, and the Empress returned to Paris to celebrate the commencement of the new year. The Arch-Chancellor gave her a ball in his gloomy mansion of the Carousel, formerly the Hôtel d'Elbœuf. I never knew a *fête* given by Cambacérès to be gay, not even a fancy ball; but the present surpassed all its predecessors in dullness, although D'Aigrefeuille, who acted as Grand Chamberlain and principal Master of Ceremonies, was in himself, with his little sparkling eyes, short, round, and singularly-attired figure, a sufficient provocation to laughter to all who beheld him.

The Arch-Chancellor's coronation robes had been made with a train much longer than the Emperor chose to permit, and it was consequently shortened. Cambacérès, who, as everyone knows, loved economy, and had no objection to distribute the gifts required by his accession to the title of Grand Dignitary without paying too dearly, made D'Aigrefeuille a present of the velvet and ermine clippings from the curtailed mantle. D'Aigrefeuille was enchanted, but as the parings of violet velvet would have required too much seaming for a coat, he laid the fur, which unfortunately, coming from the extremity of the garment, afforded no ermine tails, in numerous bands upon an old Court dress of sky-blue velvet which had belonged to his grandmother.

This grotesque habiliment, with its uniform whiteness, resembled that of a cat or a rabbit, and, with the round, red, and jovial face of the fat little man peering above it, was altogether irresistibly ludicrous. The amusements were somber, the Empress was serious, there was a scarc-

ity of ladies; war with Austria was talked of, and Count
Metternich, lately returned from Vienna, notwithstanding
his habitual courtesy, wore an air of constraint which his
perfect politeness could not entirely subdue.

Count Metternich had made a journey to Vienna toward
the end of November, under pretense (though in reality
on affairs of the utmost importance, announced previously
to leaving Paris) that he should not be more than two or
three weeks absent. The Duc de Cadore, forgetting that
M. de Metternich was no way accountable to him for his
proceedings, thought fit, at this assembly, to rally him in
a half-angry tone on his long procrastinated return. "Do
you know, sir," said he, "that we may reasonably take
exception at this delay; and, indeed, though you still
protest that your intentions are pacific, we may justly con-
strue it as a confirmation of the rumors promulgated by
the English journals."

"I can only repeat to your Excellency," replied M. de
Metternich, "what I have frequently told you on that
head, that the Emperor, my master, desires to continue at
peace with France. As for the delay of my return, I assure you it had no other cause than the obstacle which
the entrance of General Oudinot's corps into Germany
presents to free egress by the way of Bavaria."

The acuteness and fine tact of this reply bears the stamp
of the school of the Prince de Ligne. I afterward asked
M. de Metternich if he had really made it; he laughed,
but gave me no answer. "Did you say so?" I again
asked. "Should I have done amiss if I had?" said he,
still laughing. "Certainly not." "Then probably I said
so, but I do not remember it." The words, however,
were actually his; and the Duc de Cadore had not capacity to contend with this model of all that the high aris-
tocracy can furnish of elegance and exquisite polish, combined with the most perfect and unembarrassed assurance.

M. de Metternich must have stood high in the estimation of the Comte de Stadion, then at the head of the
Austrian counsels to be selected as Ambassador to Napoleon in the critical circumstances of Austria; and already
did the fair-haired Ambassador display symptoms of that
talent which gave him his after-supremacy among the
steersmen of the European state vessel. The Emperor
Napoleon's opinion of him, at first erroneous, was corrected;

but it was then too late, the mischief was irreparably done. He had been treated at Court with a coldness that showed no friendly intentions. As an instance, among others, of the disrespect he experienced, his Countess was once, on a grand Court Day, neither invited to sup with the Empress nor with either of the Princesses; to complete this insult, an article was inserted in the " *Moniteur*," under diplomatic auspices, detailing an imaginary conversation between the Ambassador and the Duc de Cadore, which certainly never occurred, in which the former, in demanding the cause of the slight offered to his lady, was made to appear in a most ridiculous light.

M. de Metternich, thus publicly humiliated, annoyed in his domestic privacy, attacked in his most valuable privileges, deceived in all he had a right to expect from the justice of a Sovereign whom he approached under a title sacred even among savages, wounded in his dearest affections when his wife and children were detained as hostages in Paris, his very life menaced, constrained to fly like a criminal in a carriage with closed blinds, must have been more or less than man could he have excluded resentment from his bosom.

He became the irreconcilable enemy of France; whereas, dazzled by Napoleon's genius, he might have been irresistibly influenced by the same charm which enthralled the Emperor Alexander. Austria declared war against us at that sinister moment when our political horizon was darkening on the side of Italy, and the Emperor was seeking victory in the mountains of the Asturias. Napoleon's parting words to the Legislative Body, when joining his army in eager pursuit of the English, were: " THEY HAVE AT LENGTH INVADED THE CONTINENT."

His anticipations of victory were justified by the event; he saw the leopards of England fly before him the moment he appeared: Moore and his troops were driven out of Spain by his all-conquering legions. Why, then, did he not stay to complete the conquest?

I went to Court in my diamonds on the following day in compliment to Madame de Remusat, and was dressed in a white tulle mantle embroidered in silver llama, the petticoat and train bordered with wreaths of rosebuds, a few similar buds being placed between my diamond wreath and comb.

The Marshals' hall was filled, and supper was laid in the Gallery of Diana. I was among the last arrivals in the Throne Room, and very inconveniently seated — a circumstance, however, to which I was indebted for the choice of a seat in the Concert Room. Madame de Remusat smiled as she recognized me, and the direction of her eye led me to observe that the Empress was giving an order to M. de Beaumont, who, a few moments before the concert concluded, announced to me her Imperial Majesty's invitation to supper.

Scarcely had I paid my respects, on approaching the Empress, when her Majesty motioned me to sit down beside her, and fixed her eyes with an inquisitorial expression upon the rose of yellow diamonds in the center of my wreath. I have since learned that this was at the instigation of the Emperor, who was very curious to know the truth respecting this wonderful rose, FORMED OF A SINGLE BRILLIANT. A smile of intelligence showed that she detected, at the second glance, both the absurdity and malignity of the reports that had reached the Emperor.

The Empress was sometimes thoughtless, but her nature was kind, and in this instance she showed it. Leaning toward me, she whispered:

"Do you know you have been ridiculously misrepresented to the Emperor? and Junot must needs give color to the rumors by talking nonsense! He knows very well diamonds cannot be hollowed; then why should he have said anything so absurd? The consequence is that your courtyard is reported to be paved with gold, that your diamonds are too heavy to be worn, and that you have a Court dress embroidered with brilliants."

Here I could not suppress an exclamation, but the Empress, by a sign, imposed silence, and whispered to me:

"Come and breakfast with me to-morrow; you can then explain all."

The next morning I breakfasted at the Tuileries, and the Empress told me all the absurdities she had heard, among others that Junot had carried off the famous Portugal diamond, that my jewels were much finer than her own, and that my unfortunate rose of yellow brilliants was formed from a single stone, which, if it had been, the Regent, the Czarina, the Portugal, the Sancy and Great

Mogul diamonds must have hidden their diminished heads before the superior splendor of this newly discovered rival.

I have already accounted for the history of the gold rolling about my courtyard, and for the value which rumor thought fit to attach to my jewel case; neither was the reference in these reports to the Portugal diamonds so wholly destitute of foundation, but that it also might be traced to its origin, as in vindication of my husband's honor I feel myself called on to explain.

The principal — or, at least, the most valuable — part of the Prince Regent's baggage, when he quitted Lisbon for Brazil, was composed of all the jewels and other treasures of the Crown. He was desirous also to have taken away the church plate and jewels; this, however, M. d'Araujo, though his influence was declining, found means to prevent; but all the treasure the Prince could obtain possession of, he transported with himself, including the Brazilian ingots of gold.

But the Cabinet of Natural History at Lisbon was furnished with a facsimile of the famous Portugal diamond, as large as an apricot, cut in white wood, and inscribed with the exact weight of the original stone. This Junot brought away; and considering the general renown of the diamond, I thought it might be amusing to the learned of Paris to examine its portrait, or more properly its statue, which I accordingly showed to Millin, and afterward to Devois, my jeweler; not that I made any secret of it, but it never occurred to me as an object of curiosity, except as connected with science. One night, however, I exhibited it openly in my drawing-room, and not a fortnight had elapsed before all Paris, and even the provinces, rang with the news that the Portugal diamond was in my possession; and that the fact was incontrovertible, as I had myself exhibited it.

All this I stated to the Empress, who was easily convinced; but I shall hereafter have occasion to return to the subject in describing a strange interview with the Emperor, which he himself has verified in the "Memorial from Saint Helena."

CHAPTER XI.

The Emperor's Promise to Junot—Berthier's Letters—Junot's Departure for Saragossa—Siege of Saragossa—Its Horrors—Junot's
Wounds—The Emperor's Unkindness—Reduction of Saint Joseph
—Napoleon's Unreasonable Complaint—General Thiébault Summoned to Headquarters—His Remarkable Interview with the Emperor—Napoleon's Return to Paris—Sinister Forebodings—Exile
of Mesdames de Staël and Récamier—Madame Récamier's Refusal
to Be the Emperor's Friend—Fouché's Interposition—Extraordinary Note—Fouché's Ambitious Projects—The Duchesse de Cadaval—Marshal Lannes Ordered to Saragossa—Rescue of Armand
de Fuentès by Junot—Marshal Lannes and the Treasure—Suchet
Replaces Junot.

TO RETURN to Junot. In the momentary opportunity
that he had to converse with the Emperor at Angoulême, he said to him: "Sire, the only favor that
I solicit from your Majesty is to send me again to Lisbon. Let me replace with glory on its walls those eagles
which I brought thence undisgraced. I entreat you, Sire,
suffer me to return to Lisbon." The Emperor promised,
and appointed him to the command of the 8th division,
formed of the same troops which had evacuated Portugal
in consequence of the Convention, and were inflamed with
desire to reconquer their lost title of the "Army of Portugal"; while Junot himself, not humiliated, but sensibly
distressed by his retreat, had never so ardently longed, as
he expressed it, TO DRAW A TRIGGER.

He hastened his departure; and the Prince of Neufchâtel wrote to him on the 16th from the Emperor's headquarters at Chamartin, a league distant from Madrid, an
order to repair to Burgos, there to collect and organize
his forces and supplies with all expedition, and, in case
of need, to support Soult at Saldanha, concluding with:
"You will not, however, M. le Duc, march to the support
of the Marshal unless you yourself consider such a movement absolutely necessary. Your first care will be to dis-
arm the country, and to maintain its tranquillity," etc.
This letter was dispatched in duplicate—a precaution
already rendered necessary by the frequent capture of
couriers by the guerrilla chiefs, Don Julian the Capuchin,
and the elder Mina.

The following is a second letter received by Junot,
dated also from Chamartin the very next day, and beneath
the date is inserted, in the autograph of Berthier the
word "noon."

"Chamartin, 17th of December, 1808.
"*Noon.*

"The Emperor commands, M. le General Duc d'Abrantès, that
you set out personally, immediately on the receipt of this letter, attended only by your aid-de-camp, and repair to Saragossa, where you
will take the chief command of the 3d division, now under the command of the Duke of Conegliano, his Majesty having thought proper
to summon that Marshal to the Imperial Headquarters in order to
appoint him to another destination. The Chief of your staff of the
8th division will remain with that division, and General Harispe will
remain with the third. The Duke of Conegliano has orders to bring
with him only his aids-de-camp; you will, therefore, find the staff,
commissariat, artillery, and engineer department of that army complete. You will leave the provisional command of the 8th division to
the senior General. You will likewise leave all the staff officers, the
engineers, artillery, and commissariat in their present state. BEFORE
YOU ADVANCE TO PORTUGAL, SARAGOSSA MUST FALL. His Majesty, M.
le Duc, confers on you the command of Navarre, Pampeluna, and the
3d division. The Duke of Treviso is at this moment before Saragossa. He is especially instructed to cover the siege of that city on
the side of Barcelona and of Catalonia. You, M. le Duc, are directed
with the 3d division, now placed under your command, to besiege
Saragossa and reduce it. I give you notice that General Guillemont
and Adjutant-General Loucet are marching with four thousand *mique-
lets*, or mountain chasseurs, by the valley of Aragon upon Jaça. This
corps is at your disposal. His Majesty recommends you to leave in
Pampeluna no more than the garrison absolutely requisite for the
defense of the town and citadel, in order to strengthen, as much as
possible, the besieging corps before Saragossa.

"You will find herewith the order to the Duke of Conegliano to
surrender into your hands the command of the 3d division, of which
he is to be informed only by yourself, and in person; you will see
the importance of this necessary disposition to prevent a moment's
lapse or uncertainty in the command.

"Press the siege of Saragossa vigorously. You will find General
Lacoste, the Emperor's aid-de-camp, very useful: he is well acquainted with the country.

"THE PRINCE OF NEUFCHATEL, VICE-CONSTABLE,
"ALEXANDER,
"*Major General to the Emperor.*
"P. S. — You need not take any gens-d'armes of the 8th division;
set out with your aids-de-camp only."

The style of this letter is worthy of remark. It was
dictated by the Emperor himself; he alone could thus
mask his breach of promise under this NECESSITY OF RE-
DUCING SARAGOSSA.

Junot set out for Saragossa with a heavy heart; but I will venture to say the Emperor was in error in not sending him to Portugal with the 8th division: that army was recruited by him and attached to its chief, and every member of it regarded Lisbon as an Eden.

Junot's letters from the siege of Saragossa, if the successive attack of every house can be called a siege, were truly distressing. While the plague which raged within the city extended its ravages also beyond the walls, and continually forced upon the Commander the heartbreaking spectacle of his soldiers perishing at his feet from a disease more mortal than the balls of the enemy, a fresh house was every day assaulted, which the Spaniards defended from room to room; and every foot of ground conquered was the grave of a Frenchman or a Spaniard. " I cannot endure this sight," wrote Junot; " I want a heart of stone, or, rather, I should have no heart."

One of our most intimate friends was a prisoner in Saragossa; and Palafox, to whom he was related, had confined him to shelter him from the popular fury; the melancholy tone of the letter in which Junot informed me that he had acquired this information, showed how much he dreaded the idea of springing a mine under the feet of his friend. He had undertaken this siege against his will, and with a disinclination that pervaded every act and event connected with it, and affected his health; he suffered acutely from his wounds, especially from that which graced his left cheek and those in his head generally.

In the month of January he wrote to me: " There are moments in which I am tempted to blow out my brains. If my hand was not withheld by a remembrance of thee and of my children, one touch of the trigger would terminate my sufferings." This letter terrified me, but I did not yet know all. The Emperor would not endure an hour's delay in the execution of his commands, and he had said: " Go to Saragossa, AND TAKE THE CITY." Saragossa, then, was at any price to be reduced; but it had not yet fallen, and each conquered stone of the fortified houses was purchased with a portion of the best blood of France. The short dry tone of the Emperor's letters speedily intimated his dissatisfaction at the delay; yet Junot had taken the Convent of Saint Joseph, transformed by the Spaniards into a terrible redoubt.

9

Yet did the Emperor, with reports before him addressed directly to himself, detailing the result of every operation, showing that the troops were daily led against houses whence, under safe cover, fell showers of balls, complain that this siege was not at once brought to a close. Oh! it is painful to reflect on the misery thus inconsiderately inflicted on an ardent and affectionate heart like Junot's, which was as much grieved as revolted by such injustice.

After the Emperor had dispatched Junot to Saragossa, he summoned to the Imperial Headquarters all the General officers who had belonged to the Army of Portugal. The following account of General Thiébault's audience was written by himself for these Memoirs:

" Having been ordered to repair to the Headquarters at Valladolid, I arrived there at the moment the Emperor was going to the parade, and followed him thither. General Legendre, ex-chief of General Dupont's staff, was also present, and it was there that the Emperor asked him: ' How is it that your hand did not wither in thus signing the disgrace of France ? ' There seemed to be a fatality in the coincidence of our arrival, since there was an analogy, though no identity, in our situations. I knew I could be reproached with sacrificing nothing to the preservation of wagonloads of stolen gold; but still I was the ex-Chief of the Staff of an army which, in yielding to the enemy a country it was intrusted to defend, had saved only appearances. I congratulated myself, therefore, on receiving no order during this parade, and was walking contentedly to my lodgings, when General Savary overtook me, and said: ' The Emperor orders you to be at his quarters in a quarter of an hour.'

" While preparing to appear before Napoleon, under circumstances of moment, although I had nothing on my own part to justify, it was impossible to wave the question, How am I to act with regard to the Duc d'Abrantès ? I could not deceive myself so far as to deny that in military matters there had been mistakes in Portugal, which, however, could not all be imputed to him; while his devotion to the Emperor and the service was unbounded. He was calumniated and denounced by such men as Loison, Hermann, etc., whom he had loaded with riches. Napoleon, even at Valladolid, was surrounded by the Duke's enemies, among whom Savary must be numbered.

I should have gratified many of them by contributing my
mite of calumny against him, but in so doing I must
have disgraced myself; for it is always dishonorable to
inculpate a Commander in the opinion of the Sovereign.
I loved the Duc d'Abrantès, and was under obligations
to him; but could I have cancelled both these considerations, my resolution would have been the same — to undertake his defense.

« When I entered the great Hall of the Palace of the
Inquisition, of which the Emperor occupied the first floor,
Napoleon was traversing it between the fireplace and the
middle window, and as he paused until I approached him,
and then resumed his promenade, I walked beside him
during the hundred minutes of a conversation of which I
here give some fragments. ' Well,' said he, prefaced only
by GOOD MORNING, SIR, ' so you capitulated to the English, and evacuted Portugal!' ' Sire, the Duc d'Abrantès
yielded only to necessity, and extorted an honorable treaty
from men who, if commanded by him, would not even
have granted us a capitulation.' ' The loss of Lisbon was
the necessary result of the Battle of Vimiera. It was
there, sir, that you should have defeated the enemy, and
not have committed such serious errors.' *

« I comprehended that the Emperor was resolved not to
name the Duc d'Abrantès, and therefore I did not regard
the YOU, when addressed to myself, as anything personal:
on the other hand, aware that the tactics of that battle
could not be defended, I felt it better to be silent than
to enter into discussion with him. He continued: ' And
pray, sir, where did you learn to attack in front an enemy
who occupies a formidable position? You might as well
take a bull by the horns, or knock your head against a
wall. Did Marshal Soult proceed that way at Corunna?
No! he turned the enemy, and drove him out of the Peninsula.' ' Sire, Marshal Soult, at Corunna, was opposed to
an enemy who, incapable of maintaining himself in Spain,
was hastening to embark, and whose forces were continually diminished, while those of the Marshal were increasing by the successive arrival of fresh corps. The Duc
d'Abrantès, on the other hand, unable to retain Portugal,

* Napoleon's delicacy in never mentioning the name of Junot during
the whole course of this conference, and of his reproaches to General
Thiébault, surprises me, and would have sensibly affected my husband.

engaged at Vimiera an enemy who, during the battle [and beyond the possibility of such an event being anticipated], was reinforced by five thousand men, who were disembarked within sight of his camp. And if the Duc d'Abrantès could not force the position of Vimiera, neither did Marshal Soult prevent the embarkation of the English army. As for the manœuver you have done me the honor to point out, Sire, new examples are unnecessary to the demonstration of that great maxim forever established by you Majesty's immortal campaigns — that an enemy may be annihilated by force, but is defeated by skill.' A short silence ensued, the Emperor looking at me.

" ' Besides, sir, is it with fragments of your army that you should meet an enemy? You had twenty-six thousand men, and fought with ten thousand! And that because you had scattered more than twelve thousand men at Peniche, at Almeida, at Elvas, at Santarem, at Lisbon, in the fleet, and on both banks of the Tagus.'*

" ' I am entirely mistaken, Sire, if the separation of nearly the whole of these brigades and garrisons from the main army was not inevitable; and if your Majesty will suffer me to submit a few observations for your consideration, I presume that you will find in them some justification of the Duc d'Abrantès.' His silence authorizing me to proceed, I added: ' The English army that was disembarked on the coast had no place of refuge, and, on the loss of a single battle, would have been under the necessity of abandoning its baggage and wounded. So situated, the acquisition of Peniche was important to General Wellesley, and for the same reason it was incumbent on General Junot to prevent his taking it, more especially as the Peninsula is as easy of defense as difficult of attack; and Peniche lost, Sire, it is evident that all must have been over with us in the North of Portugal. It was to such considerations that the Duc d'Abrantès yielded, in leaving eight hundred Swiss there. Your Majesty had ordered that all vessels in seaworthy condition should be repaired and armed. We had already one of eighty guns, a second ready to join the squadron, two frigates of fifty guns, and a third on the stocks, besides a

---

* General Thiébault declares he was confounded to find that the Emperor knew this report by heart, though contained in more than a hundred pages.

few brigs and corvettes. These vessels, Sire, were necessary not only for defending the mouth of the Tagus, and supporting the Russian fleet against any enterprise of the English blockading squadron, but also to guard the pontoons occupied by the Spanish troops we had disarmed, and to keep Lisbon in check. In such critical circumstances the ships could not be left to their crews; this was the reason for having placed there one thousand men; I will say nothing of the forts.' 'The forts must be defended. But what necessity for pushing two thousand men to the left bank of the Tagus?'

" 'Sire, that measure was suggested by considerations of equal delicacy and importance. Eight Russian vessels, under the command of Admiral Siniavin, were blockaded in the Tagus. The only good anchorage in that road is near the left bank, which was covered with insurgents, increasing daily in numbers and hardihood, who, had that bank been evacuated by us, would soon have been reinforced by detachments from the English vessels; and as they would have lost no time in bringing guns to bear, the situation of the Russian fleet must have been untenable, and the difficulties of our own situation in consequence greatly aggravated. What complaints, Sire, would that Admiral, in such a case, have addressed to his Court! An Admiral, who, moreover, only sought an excuse to make common cause with the English! May he not have speculated on surrendering, and imputing that step to a willful desertion? And how much would the Duc d'Abrantès have been distressed to have furnished him with such a pretext, or to have occasioned any grievance to the Emperor Alexander. Political motives, therefore, decided our military arrangements.'

" To this the Emperor made no reply, and walked for some time in silence.* At length he said: 'And Santarem?' I could find no excuse for the thousand left there, and was silent in my turn, wishing only to defend where I could incontestably convince. 'And Lisbon?' 'Our position, our resources, our security, Sire, all depended on the possession of that city.' 'Capitals, sir, are always guided by events. Conquerors at Vimiera, you would on the field of battle have secured the tranquillity of Lisbon.'

* This openness to conviction, when pressed upon him by the force of truth, was an important trait in the Emperor's character.

'That may be the case, Sire, in regular, but not in popular wars.' (ANOTHER LOOK.) 'In the latter, Sire, the capital is always the most dangerous and most difficult to restrain. And when, like Lisbon, it constitutes an important part of the State, to abandon it is to lose all its resources, and every other dependence with it.' Again he fixed his eyes on me in silence; then advanced a few steps, and at length said: 'But Elvas, sir, and Almeida — what need was there of garrisons there?' 'We expected succor, Sire; General Dupont's division appeared to be marching on Lisbon, either to secure the possession of Portugal, to open a retreat for us, or to command the West of Spain. This division could reach us only through Almeida or Elvas. To abandon these fortresses, therefore, comprised the abandonment of the entire provinces in which they are situated.   So, at least, the Duc d'Abrantès judged.'

« These reasons being admitted, and other questions or subjects furnishing me with an opportunity of enlightening the Emperor with regard to the Duc d'Abrantès, I described the distress he suffered, under the fear of displeasing or grieving his Majesty, and perceived that the Emperor listened with satisfaction; and, as if pleased with the part I had acted, was thenceforward much more unreserved. The new campaign which the Emperor was about to open in Portugal, under the auspices of Marshal Soult, served as a theme for continuing the conversation. In describing the itinerary the Marshal was to follow, his Majesty observed: 'It is substituting the crossing of rivers for that of mountains.' In fact, the line of Galicia embraces the crossing of the Minho, the Douro, the Vouga, and the Mondego. 'Sire,' I answered, 'the passage of the most formidable rivers is preferable to that of the mountains in Beira and the Tras-os-Montes. The difficulties of the passage of rivers, and the means of surmounting those difficulties, are equally well known. But those which these mountains present are incalculable. And let me have the honor to add that Marshal Soult, in following the itinerary your Majesty is pleased to point out, will always march by practicable and beaten tracks; that he will be surrounded by abundance in a country where he has ample room for manœuvring; and, in crossing the three principal rivers, will be supported by three strong cities — Tuy, Oporto, and Coimbra.' He was pleased with a reply so entirely in accordance with the plans he had traced, and, on the whole, appeared satisfied with the interview."

The Emperor once more returned to Paris after having defeated Sir John Moore, taken Madrid, and, as he believed, chastised the Spaniards. The brilliancy of his Court was great, but still more clouded by fears and anxieties than in the preceding year. "War! war!" was the universal text of the Emperor. Cardinal Maury, M. de Cheval, Comte Louis de Narmy, the physician Halley, Millin, all my friends, conversed on coming events with an anxiety that alarmed me. All agreed that the dangers of the Northern war would be increased tenfold by that of Spain. Alas! I knew it but too well, and saw around me nothing but uneasiness and the troubles of many friends.

Junot was at this time interested in the exile of Madame de Staël and Madame Récamier, because, at the request of the former, and convinced that the Emperor might by mildness have converted her into a partisan as useful as her enmity would be dangerous, he had made every effort to soften him in her favor, until Napoleon in a rage, exclaimed: "So! you, too, are going to ally yourself with my enemies." "It is extraordinary," said Junot one day to me, when speaking of the exile, "that the Emperor, who knows enough of my heart to be assured that my blood and life are at his service, will connect you and me with his enemies! His enemies are mine, with only this difference, that I desire no vengeance on my own, while I would exterminate his."

Madame Récamier's exile was shortly after this announced publicly, in consequence of her visit to Coppet, and occasioned sensations to Junot such as he doubtless little expected to have experienced from any of the Emperor's acts; yet such was, at this moment, the delicacy of his situation, that he dared not, or only dared tremblingly, to question so unjust a proceeding.

"Laura," he once wrote to me, "my heart is sick when I think of the exile of Madame Récamier. I told you long ago that I had once passionately loved her: my friendship is now only that of a brother, but united with a sentiment of respectful admiration. She is so superior a being! I thank you for appreciating her. You know she

does you equal justice, and cherishes for you the attachment I should have so much rejoiced in. I had hoped to
bring you together next spring; and how are my wishes
frustrated ? Alas! by a blow which renders desolate the
future existence of an unfortunate woman, who deserves
the homage of all who pronounce her name. My Laura,
I conjure you to see the Empress — see Queen Hortense
— see the Emperor — but no, you must not speak to him.
Alas! how can he who is so just, so great, so remarkable
for goodness — how can he voluntarily oppress a feeble
woman ? "

Madame Récamier deserved all the eulogies Junot
poured upon her: not he only, but Murat, Eugène, Bernadotte, Masséna, and many other brave and loyal French
patriots, regarded her with real friendship, and proclaimed her the best as well as the most beautiful of
women. My own friendship for her is founded on the
conviction that the most noble and generous sentiments
animated her pure heart.

There are circumstances in her history the importance
of which her almost infantine innocence was perhaps incapable of fully discerning. M. Récamier, before his reverse of fortune, wishing his wife to enjoy all the pleasures
natural to her age, gave her a country house at Clichy, to
which the best society of Paris immediately flocked, and
Madame Récamier, in the full blaze of beauty — young,
gay, and happy — thought only of benevolence and amusement. But the serpent found access to this Eden, and
to its pure and beautiful Eve. Fouché presented himself,
and his station insured his admission. He soon invited
her to accept the post of lady of honor to the Empress.
" I have no inclination for it," she replied, in a soft and
insinuating tone, as though fearful by too positive a refusal to provoke the vengeance of covert power; for she
did not suppose the Emperor a stranger to the intrigue.

" That is the answer of a child," rejoined Fouché; " consider the Emperor's situation, — he wants a guide, a female
friend; and where can he find one ? Among the wives of
his Generals ? That is impossible; it would excite scandal." " And why are you so obliging as to imagine that
scandal would spare me ? " " The case is quite different.
You are, to be sure, as young as any of them; but your
marriage, and the station in which it places you, has

established your reputation; it is pure and unblemished. You are privileged to be the Emperor's friend, for it is a friend and not a mistress that he wants;" and so saying, his little twinkling eyes ran over the figure of the young Psyche, while her countenance beamed with native modesty, intelligence, and sweetness.

"I know the cravings of the Emperor's heart," he added; "I know he is unhappy at not being understood, and that he would gladly exchange hours of victory and noisy acclamations which play round the ear without reaching the heart for a few minutes of social and confidential converse. He is weary, too, of daily encountering scenes of jealousy, from which the pure and sacred connection I wish to see established between you and him would be exempt." "But," objected Madame Récamier, quite unconvinced by these profound arguments, "how can I ascertain that it would be agreeable to the Emperor that I should accept this situation? But especially how would it please the Empress, whose establishment is full, that I should displace either her niece, or her friend Madame de La Rochefoucauld? Morever, I tell you, I love my liberty." "I recommend nothing to you that will interfere with your liberty; you are not requested to undertake any burdensome duty. Your post in the Household will be that of the Empress's friend, but particularly the Emperor's. The friend of Napoleon! the friend of the Emperor! consider a little! reflect on my proposition, and I am certain, if you are not prejudiced, your noble and generous soul will accept it with delight."

Madame Récamier was mortal, and it must be acknowledged that the friendship of Napoleon was at that time an *ignis-fatuus* capable of dazzling any being not wholly ethereal even to ruin. The idea of swaying with a kindly influence the destinies of so many millions of men — of sometimes arresting a devastating torrent — might well extort a smile!

While these discussions were pending, Madame Récamier received an invitation from one of the Emperor's sisters to breakfast at her Hôtel. There the conversation turned on friendship, and the charms of such a sentiment between a man and a pure and virtuous woman. "The Emperor is worthy of such happiness," said the Princess, "and fully capable of appreciating it; but he has no such friend. And how is one to be selected for him from among the multitude of our Court ladies ?"

Shortly afterward the Princess inquired whether Madame Récamier liked the theaters, and which she preferred. She was partial, she replied, to the Comédie Française. "Oh, then," said the Princess, "my box is at your service; it is in the lower tier, and therefore requires no ceremony of dress: promise me to make use of it." Madame Récamier promised, and the next morning received the following note:

"The managers of the Comédie Française are informed that her Imperial Highness the Princess —— gives Madame Récamier admission to her box. They are likewise informed that when Madame Récamier uses the box she is at liberty to choose her own company; and that no person is to be admitted, even though a member of the Princess's or the Grand-Duchess's Household, without Madame Récamier's special permission.

"L——PS,
"Secretary to her Imperial Highness the Princess ——."

Madame Récamier's unsuspecting mind received a new light from the perusal of this billet; she returned thanks, but never made use of it. The box faced the Emperor's. Will it now be said that men take no revenge ? I hope, and would fain believe, that the Emperor was not concerned in all this. But Fouché, by promoting her exile, revenged the overthrow of many ambitious projects. He would gladly have restored the halcyon days of Louis XIV., or of Louis XIII., and Mademoiselle de La Fayette; and he himself, by retracing one step only, might have enacted a second Père la Chaise, though I believe the red satin would have been more agreeable to his inclinations.

Reverting to Lisbon, I cannot deny myself the pleasure of relating an interesting trait of the Duchesse de Cadaval, and an ingenious method of awakening the memory of a friendly enemy. The Duchess, whose sweetness and intellectual graces acquired our warm regard, was a Frenchwoman, and daughter of the Duc de Luxembourg. Junot not only offered her personally in Lisbon every proof of friendship within his power, but afterward in writing renewed his assurance of devotedness.

When the Royal Family emigrated to Brazil, the Duchess accompanied them, because a Court equally stupid and suspicious would not leave her two sons behind. Thus compelled to abandon one of the best-ordered houses in

Lisbon, without protection, she was much concerned for its fate, being unable, under such circumstances, to recommend it in writing to Junot's care, or to confide a message for him to anyone.

But an old servant, whom she had left behind, begged to speak with the Duke immediately on his arrival, and requested that he would visit the Hôtel de Cadaval. He complied, and the aged valet led him into a small parlor habitually occupied by the Duchess. Here everything was in the neatest order, and an escritoire purposely left open contained nothing but the very letter in which Junot protested his friendship and desire to prove it. He was thus furnished with the means of testifying his sincerity.

How much must the Duchess now suffer on account of the war which devastates her adopted country! I knew her amiable and excellent son, now the victim of popular odium, when he was the joy and happiness of his mother and family. His sister Adelaide, older than himself, was an invalid, and could not walk; but her two young brothers would lift her by the shoulders and pass whole hours in assisting her to take exercise, never suffering a domestic to relieve them of their fraternal duty.

Junot was long detained before Saragossa; my brother-in-law, who arrived from thence at Paris, gave some dreadful details of the siege, and another letter of Junot's still increased my anxiety.

« When man is in a state of suffering, » he wrote, « he must possess a legitimate power to arrest his suffering, and suicide is his most natural and rational course. »

I mentioned this letter to Duroc, who desired to see it, and having read it, struck his forehead in sorrowful apprehension; for that excellent friend knew that, three days before, Marshal Lannes had been ordered to Saragossa with the Direction-in-Chief of the siege, in which he was to be assisted by the Duc de Treviso and Junot.

I never perfectly understood the Emperor's conduct on this occasion. Perhaps he never formed a clear judgment of the siege of Saragossa, and expected, by deputing Marshal Lannes there, to accomplish by one vigorous effort the capture of the town. But Lannes did no more than Mortier, Junot, or a thousand others might have done without him. THE TOWN WILL BE TAKEN ON SUCH A DAY, THERE ARE SO MANY HOUSES NOW LEFT, was now become a

matter of mere arithmetical calculation; and the arrival of
Lannes to snatch from him the fruits of his long and
barren toils was a severe blow to my husband.

General Rapp, one of the best of created beings, refused
the command of the 6th division in Russia, when, Junot
having offended, Napoleon would have superseded him.
Yet in Russia appearances were against Junot, whereas at
Saragossa they, as well as the reality, were in his favor.
Lannes was indisputably the bravest of all our Generals,
and Junot always did him justice; but in this instance he
performed the part, in the military phrase, of a BAD COM-
RADE. That Junot so regarded the act is evident, because
he told me the following spring:

"I ordered my horses, and was on the point of departing, when I heard the sound of the cannon, and was riveted to the spot. . . . Otherwise . . ."

He had conducted the siege, or rather the reduction of
houses and convents erected into redoubts, from the 20th
of December to the month of February, when Lannes undertook the easy task of overwhelming the ruined rem-
nants. To avoid useless repetition, I will only add that a
final attack was directed against that heroic city through
the Corso; moving batteries were brought to bear; and
at length, utterly exhausted, it fell. Junot courted death
on that sanguinary day, marching through and over fire;
but, strange to say, he, who had been wounded in every
former collision with an enemy, escaped unharmed through
the fury of this struggle.

He wrote to me on the morrow that Marshal Lannes
had contrived to make even success irksome to him, by
taking no more notice of him in the report than if he
had been meanwhile engaged in the siege of Seringapa-
tam, except by merely saying: "At this time the Duc
d'Abrantès was crossing the Corso."

A few days before the final assault Junot learned, by
means of spies, that Armand de Fuentès was in one of
the houses appointed to be undermined, but the particular house could not be ascertained; this information,
therefore, afforded him new anxiety, but no means of dis-
sipating it.

His first care, on the reduction of the city, was to seek
his unhappy friend, and he found him alive. But deliverance after four months' confinement in a damp vault,

without warm clothing, almost without nutriment; deliverance by the hand of a friend, restoration to life, to light and happiness, to the enjoyment of the azure sky and the pure breeze—all these joys were too much for his poor head. He was enjoined strict abstinence, promised compliance, and was at first obedient, but afterward intractable; fell ill, and died at the end of a week, in cruel agonies, at the age of thirty-nine. His brother, Alphonzo Pignatelli, died also far from his home, in the arms of servants at an inn, on his road to the *Eaux-Bonnes*. Both expired amid riches, esteem, affection, happiness, with a lengthened and smiling future in prospect.

Saragossa taken, the fifty thousand infectious corpses which this fatal siege had created thrown into the Ebro or the trenches, and a sort of hollow tranquillity established, the conduct of the monks was inquired into for the purpose of making AN EXAMPLE—a measure deemed necessary, but, necessary as it might be, likely to operate at least as injuriously as beneficially, especially in the manner in which it was effected.

Several monks were tied up in sacks and thrown into the Ebro; but the river cast them on its banks; and the horror and detestation of the French, which the people evinced on discovering their monks strangled and drowned, was beyond all bounds.

The other monks, it is true, were terrified; and one morning a deputation from the Chapter of Saragossa presented themselves on their knees before Marshal Lannes, entreating the favor of his accepting the small present they brought him, a third of the treasure of their Cathedral of our Lady of the Pillar; the other two-thirds they destined for the Ducs d'Abrantès and de Treviso.

The Marshal angrily told the deputed Canons that they should first have offered to the Ducs d'Abrantès and de Treviso the shares intended for them.

In Junot's state of mind his reception of the deputation may be conceived. Demanding whether they meant to make game of him, he drove them out almost by the shoulders.

The Duc de Treviso, who had not the same excuse for ill-humor, was rather more polite, but he also declined acceptance. The Canons restored the jewels to their church, enchanted that Our Lady had protected herself from the misfortune of foregoing a single diamond.

The very same evening, however, the Duc de Montebello sent one of his officers to demand the treasure, and
carried it to Paris.

It is averred on good authority that the treasure of
Our Lady of the Pillar was rare and valuable. Marshal
Lannes, having brought it to Paris, said to the Emperor:
"I have brought from Spain some trumpery jewels of no
real value, which I will place in any hands your Majesty
may appoint. Junot and Mortier were too proud to accept them, as I should have been glad to have done."
The Emperor accordingly gave them to Lannes in ignorance of their value.

All the fatigues of the siege, followed by so many an-
noyances, seriously affected Junot's health. His letters so
alarmed me that I determined to seek an audience of the
Emperor.

"What does she want?" he querulously inquired of
Duroc.

"I believe she wishes to speak to you of Junot, who I
have reason to know from a letter of his which I saw
yesterday is dangerously ill."

The Emperor was thoughtful for a moment, but his
countenance showed more of sadness than displeasure.

"Is not Madame Junot also very ill?" said he, with an
expression of interest which did not escape Duroc, who
mentioned it to me.

"Very ill, Sire. She is to go to a watering place as
soon as the season will permit."

This time the Emperor's gesture showed impatience.

"What ails her?" said he. "These women are always
either ill or quarrelsome! Besides, why does she wear so
many and such large diamonds? IT IS ABSURD!"

Duroc, notwithstanding his excessive attachment to the
Emperor, could not suppress an exclamation, of which
Napoleon took no notice, but continued:

"She wants an audience to talk to me about Junot, and
I have something to say to her. I am very partial to
Madame Junot; I loved her mother much — very much,"
— with emphasis, "and I feel a paternal interest in her.
You often see her, Duroc; you had better tell her from
me that she ought to conduct herself more like a person
attached to me, and not choose her most intimate friends
from among my enemies."

"I do not visit Madame Junot of an evening," replied Duroc; "but when I go there in the morning, I meet no one in any respect deserving of that title. Your Majesty knows me well enough to be assured that otherwise I should not have waited your commands to testify, I dare not say my dissatisfaction, but my regret, to Madame Junot."

"Oh, I know you are not one of those whom I have loaded with favors to be repaid with ingratitude!"

"Your Majesty, I hope, does not include Junot in that number?" said Duroc with warmth.

"HE?—oh no! But let that rest. He asks his recall; he must be recalled—I will not have my old friend aggrieved. Tell Madame Junot her husband shall be replaced in a fortnight. I will send Bessières there; he is conciliating in his manners; he will do his best to reclaim those enraged Aragonese. But, Duroc, you take great interest in Madame Junot! Now, tell me, like an honest fellow, were you ever in love with her?"

Duroc laughed outrageously.

"This is not answering," said the Emperor impatiently; "were you ever in love with Madame Junot?"

Duroc, at length composing himself, replied:

"Never, Sire; I may even say the idea of such a possibility never entered my head. The truth is, neither she nor I ever thought of such a thing."

There was a seriousness in his tone which the Emperor understood; and taking a few pinches of snuff with more than usual celerity, for he was not fond of being obliged to give up his notions, he stepped a few paces, looked over the bridge into the garden, and at last said:

"Well, it is very singular!"

On this subject his own ideas were very singular; and I think he seldom gave women credit for any good qualities.

Duroc repeated to me the whole scene, and his confidence, as I frankly told him, was very ill timed, for my nervous irritation had increased to excess, and I was at the same time suffering from a complaint of the liver and internal inflammation. I thought myself at the point of death. But, alas! both pain and grief are strangers to that assuager of evil—they seem to possess a peculiar tenacity to life.

Junot was no sooner informed that his letter of recall
would be dispatched as soon as he could be replaced than
he wrote to the Emperor, Duroc, and Berthier, that all
Spain could not produce a man more capable of govern-
ing Aragon than General Suchet, for whom he had a
great regard. Suchet amply justified his commendation;
he was eminently brave, and, moreover, was nephew to
the King of Spain, thus being, on many accounts, peculiarly suited to the command Junot requested for him.

Junot received in reply the following letter from the
Count of Huneburg (Clarke), Minister of War, dictated by
the Emperor himself:

"PARIS, 7th of April, 1809.

"MONSIEUR LE DUC: — I have the honor to inform your excellency
that, having received his Majesty's instructions relative to the letter
you addressed to me by a courier the day before yesterday (5th April),
his Majesty has commissioned me to authorize your return to France.
General Suchet will replace you in command of the 3d division of the
Army of Spain.

"His Majesty, however, desires, M. le Duc, that before quitting
Aragon you devote your attention to three important points:

"1st. Determining with the Commandant of Engineers the plan of a
fortress at Tudela, and a redoubt on the heights, with two detached
bastions to defend the communications with the river. These works
are to be originally constructed of earth, but in such a manner as to
be capable of successive completion in a more solid form, and of becoming a strong fortification.

"2dly. To put the fortress of Saragossa into a state of siege, and
plant ten mortars there to command the city.

"3dly. To order the evacuation of all the artillery, and its trans-
portation to France.

"The Commandant of Artillery is charged to take your excellency's
orders for the evacuation of his force, and to submit to you the necessary measures for insuring its safe transport.

"His Majesty likewise wishes the fort of Jaca to be, with all possible
dispatch, put into a state of defense, and enabled to preserve the communications with France by way of Paco, etc.

"Accept, M. le Duc, the assurance of my high consideration.

"The Minister of War,
"COMTE D'HUNEBURG."

Such was the active superintendence of the Emperor.
At the moment of quitting Paris for the campaign of
Wagram, he is giving directions for the erection of a
fortress at Tudela for strengthening those of Jaca and
Saragossa, and furnishing the latter with ten mortars to
command the city.

Junot executed these orders; and while awaiting others he wrote to the Emperor a letter of the highest interest upon the situation of Spain, containing information so much the more valuable that the Emperor was at that time but imperfectly acquainted with the occurrences in Catalonia and Aragon.

Suchet's nomination was expedited, and Junot returned to France with the command of a division in the Grand Army. Thus in a few days joy was again diffused around him, and his letters changed their tone—he no longer talked of dying.

Berthier, however, was then in the tragics—almost to that extremity! He had been but a few weeks married, when M. de Visconti died; and although death and buffoonery have but little sympathy, poor Berthier brought them into curious contact.

"Hem!—hem!—Madame Junot!—Madame Junot!—what do you think of that?—hem!—hem!—I was always unlucky!—always!—the deuce was in the man!—hem!—hem!—to betake himself to dying, what the devil! just as I am married.—If he had died but two months sooner!—what difference did it make to him—I just ask you?"

The pauses in this eloquent oration were filled up by fuming and biting his nails; and it was only interrupted to be repeated to another auditor. The M. de Visconti, be it observed, was known only by Berthier's report. As for the beautiful widow, she married secondly—whom do you think? not Berthier, he was already married, but his wife. An odd compact, it must be confessed!

The prerogatives of rank and favor were here tolerably manifest. The Emperor's corrective rod struck without mercy when young hands were uplifted to supplicate his clemency for an error perhaps venial; but he was all indulgence for arrangements revoltingly scandalous. The widow, without censure, almost inhabited the house of the married man.

Junot at length arrived, and, though himself very ill, was struck by the change in my appearance; for my inflammation had increased to such a degree that I could take no nourishment. The wound in his face was very painful, and affected the optic nerve, and his vertigo was also more frequent. Three weeks' use of the baths of

10

Barèges enabled him to proceed to Germany; but he insisted on first seeing me on the road to the Pyrenees,
where my physicians ordered me. M. Labbat, the physician of Cauterêts, an old friend of my mother, took
charge of me on the journey, and accompanied by two
intimate friends — Madame Lallemand and M. de Cherval
— I accomplished it, lying in my carriage and almost
dying. But I reached Cauterêts, and there, as at the
waters of Caldas da Raynha in Portugal, scarcely had I
drunk the first glass before I was sensible of amendment; at the end of a week I ate as heartily as a la-
borer, and before a fortnight had elapsed was running
about the mountains at the risk of breaking my neck.

CHAPTER XII.

New Campaign in Germany — Bombardment of Vienna — Battle of
Aspern-Essling — Death of Marshal Lannes — The Roman States
Annexed to the French Empire — Bull of Excommunication —
Marshal Soult Determines to Accept the Attributes of Royalty —
New Disasters in Portugal — Captain Schiller and the Countess
W—— g — General Danube — Prince Eugène at Leoben — Mar-
mont's Disappointment — Royal Letters — Peace with Austria —
The Emperor's Return — Opinion at Paris — Inauspicious Omens.

WHILE I was wandering among the lovely valleys of
the Pyrenees, whither I had been ordered by my
physicians, the plains of Germany were again en-
sanguined with war and her lands visited with those
disastrous scourges whose aggravated wounds were reserved with fearful usury for us. Masséna was crossing
the Inn, burning Scharding, and reviving in our memories the hero of Genoa and Rivoli. Napoleon himself sowed the laurel seed before all his generals, leaving
them only the trouble of stretching out their hands to
reap the harvest. The Emperor was a thunderbolt of
war at the commencement of that campaign.

Enraged that the enemy had the audacity, though
trembling, to forestall him, he rushed upon them with the
fury of a lion, and, if I may use the expression, SAWED
the Austrian army asunder, compelling it to retreat pre-

cipitately and in confusion among the defiles of the Bohemian mountains; where, incessantly harassed by the swift succeeding strokes of that ponderous club which the hand of Napoleon so efficiently wielded, they could scarcely for ten days recover breath to fly before him who again commanded the ancient ramparts of Vienna to bow down. This campaign, however, was not like that of Austerlitz, crowned with laurels interspersed with flowers: mourning followed in the train of triumph, and every bulletin plunged a thousand families in tears. For Napoleon's puissant voice could still command the soldier to march ! and he marched — to die ! and he died. The forty-sixth regiment of the line marched from Schard-ing to Ebensberg, a distance of twenty-six leagues, in five-and-thirty hours.

We frequently received letters from headquarters, and the army was still advancing. Vienna resolved on de-fense, and sustained a severe bombardment for thirty hours; but the attention of the Aulic Council was directed less to fortifying than provisioning the capital; for, when taken, she furnished supplies sufficient, as one of our inspectors declared, for a whole campaign. The Arch-duke Charles met Napoleon at the Battle of Essling; and death was rife in both armies; ours lost its bravest chief in Marshal Lannes. The butchery was horrible. The Archduke proclaimed a loss on his own side of 4,300 killed and 12,000 wounded. From this admission of the enemy, generally below the truth, our loss may be esti-mated.

From Vienna was issued the Imperial Decree for an-nexing the Roman States to the French Empire, leaving to the Pope the choice of residing at Rome, and a revenue of two millions of francs. The Emperor had long vehemently declaimed against the danger of a foreign Prince exercising spiritual authority in France. Besides, it was argued that the Roman States were be-stowed by Charlemagne and only resumed by Napoleon.

Pius VII., forgetting that himself had consecrated the head he now devoted to perdition, fulminated a Bull of Excommunication. " Let monarchs once more learn that by the law of Jesus Christ they are subjected to our throne, and owe obedience to our commands; for we also bear sovereign sway, but it is a far more noble

sovereignty," etc.   Alas! the avenging blow which at
last too surely struck him came in a more substantial
shape than this impotent Bull.

It is inexplicable, or to be explained only by the dizzi-
ness which such stupendous and still extending power
produced, that the Emperor, aware of the situation of
Spain, should at such a time have courted new difficulties, by violating the domicile of St. Peter, for the futile
ambition of appointing Prefects of the Tiber and the
Rhine! Policy must not be arrested in its course! True!
Neither could that fatality which swept onward to his
destruction, when in 1814 an unequal struggle against
overwhelming numbers too sadly convinced him how
costly was the sacrifice of 400,000 men to the demon of
fanaticism in Spain.

Meanwhile the French army in Aragon, thanks to the
condition in which Junot had left it, obtained some success.   General Suchet, who fully justified Junot's expectations, completely defeated General Blake at Belchite.
The ADVENTURE of the second expedition to Portugal
happened about the same time; I call it an "adventure,"
because the facts were perfectly romantic. That gleam
of ambition, the undefined shadow of which was thrown
across his path by one of his captains, was one of the
most extraordinary incidents of Napoleon's reign.

A member of the English Parliament justly observed
that it was the policy of the English Government to support, or even to incite the inclinations of Soult — to place
in his hand and on his head the attributes of royalty.
In the English work of Colonel Napier this important
affair is passed over in one line, just declaring that there
is no truth in it.   The Colonel, I am persuaded, drew
his materials from an authentic source; and had he con-
descended to communicate them, they would doubtless
have proved as satisfactory to his readers as to himself;
but he will excuse my objecting that a single line is in-
adequate to such an affair.

There exists a biography of Marshal Soult, published at
Brussels, under the fictitious name Julien, though its real
author is an eminently gifted friend of the Marshal's,
which gives a totally different version of the story, asserting that the Emperor, in delivering his final instructions, told the Marshal: "Monsieur le Maréchal, the

Duc d'Abrantès, by my order, declared that the House of Braganza had ceased to reign. Repeat the proclamation; and if, for the preservation of Portugal, it is necessary to give her a new dynasty, I shall see yours with pleasure." This version may be correct, and is even plausible, but it should either have been suppressed or supported by substantial proof. Those, however, who were about the Emperor at Schönbrunn when Loison arrived and related, with the venom of a serpent, the whole disastrous history of Soult's army, well know the effect the news produced upon him; he turned pale and was seized with one of those nervous affections to which he was occasionally subject.

Subsequently, in the course of the same day, he spoke of the affair in a tone of raillery which he certainly could not have adopted had he been its instigator, and said, laughing, but with that bitter laugh that was far from embellishing his expressive countenance: "Ah! ah! — King of Portugal! Yes, King of Portugal truly! — Nicholas the First. Is not his name Nicholas? Nicholas! — it should rather have been Nicodemus!" Some people have affected to deny this whole scene, because the Emperor could not call Soult Nicholas, when his real name was Jean.* Did he really believe the name to be Nicholas, or did he merely choose to place it in juxtaposition with that of Nicodemus? This question I cannot resolve, but I can positively vouch for the words.

Alas! we had not yet done with that unhappy Portugal; another army was yet to be ingulfed in that all-devouring abyss. When accompanying my husband into Spain, the evidences of my own senses confirmed the frightful disasters of Soult's retreat, which one of my best friends, then Colonel of a cavalry regiment, had painted to me in colors which made me shudder and weep with pity and indignation. This retreat contrasted well with the Convention of Cintra, and showed the relative abilities of our chiefs under their respective circumstances.

It is, indeed, boasted that we did not negotiate the second time; but the alternative is something like that of the Countess W——g in the campaign of Sobieski, who being young and beautiful, the Turks waylaid her on her road to Bavaria with the design of presenting her to the

* The baptismal names of Marshal Soult were Nicolas Jean de Dieu.

Grand Vizier. "But I escaped them," said she triumphantly; "the Turks did not even see me." "And how did
you manage it?" "I encountered Captain Schiller, who
detained me six weeks with him." This famous captain
of pandours made little distinction between friends and
enemies in affairs of gallantry.

The death of Marshal Lannes created a great impression, not only in the army but throughout Europe. But
in France probably this misfortune was less felt than it
would have been had it occurred at any other time.
The Battle of Essling was one of those fatal occasions
in which death strikes with such multiplied and indiscriminate blows that, in the universality of private grief,
a public loss, such as that of Marshal Lannes, makes
less impression.

The Emperor had been warmly attached to Lannes, but
he had also been often offended with him, and now, perhaps, involuntarily showed that his regret was that of
the Sovereign for a man of talent, and that as a friend
he was little affected. He even jested upon the Battle
of Essling, observing that the Austrians had this day
met with an ally they had not reckoned upon, and that
GENERAL DANUBE had proved himself the best officer of
their army. It was to the destruction of the bridges that
the Emperor referred; but I knew not why I never
could accustom myself to his forced laugh; there was no
mirth in it, neither was there anything amusing. I feel
even in the recollection of it, as in an unnatural atmosphere, in which I seem to breathe with difficulty, and
only recover from the oppression by looking up and contemplating him on the summit of that column, forged
from the hostile cannons which he threw so lavishly into
the furnace.

Still victory was faithful to our arms. Prince Eugène
beat Jellachich at Leoben, a place equally memorable to
Austria and Napoleon. The consequence of this victory
was the easy junction of the Armies of Germany and
Italy.

In France great uneasiness was felt respecting the
Grand Army. The Emperor suffered no news to arrive
but what it was his pleasure to send; and everyone knew
that the words of the bulletins were not to be taken for
gospel. I was at the time in the Pyrenees, and had

more authentic information than was generally possessed, because my letters came direct from Germany, and I read no newspaper.

I had regular communications from Junot, who commanded the Saxon and Bavarian troops; but I kept them to myself when they did not agree with the bulletins, as in the case of the Battle of Essling. Prince Eugène's victory over the Archduke John at Raab, in Hungary, is one of the events of this campaign in which the Emperor had the greatest cause to rejoice, but he spoke of it merely as an ordinary affair; its consequences, however, were immense.

Macdonald, who (to the shame, be it spoken, of several marshals who did not very well know to what they owed their bee-besprinkled batons) was not yet reckoned in the list of the great officers of the Empire, took his place among them in recompense of his conduct in this campaign of 1809; as did Marmont, to whose promotion a curious anecdote is attached.

At the formation of the Empire, Marmont received no appointment; Junot was grieved, and so expressed himself to Berthier and Duroc, but found neither of them very well disposed toward his friend. The Emperor had pronounced by his silence, and for Berthier that was sufficient. Duroc had been offended by the assuming manners of Marmont, who, though the most noble, generous, and kind-hearted of men, made himself more enemies by the haughty bearing he adopted than he acquired friends by his excellent qualities. Still, as his manner offered no real offense to anyone, it was childish to be angry about it; and I have often remarked to those who spoke coldly of him for so insufficient a cause, that such testiness was more ridiculous than Marmont's overestimation of his own dignity. In short, he had enemies, and that their prejudices were unjust I may unhesitatingly assert, fearless that even my acknowledged friendship should in this instance lay me open to a charge of partiality.

At the coronation Marmont was nothing. The lesson was bitter; perhaps it was long remembered, for I believe the heart of man will retain the impression of injury. He longed, however, for this distinction, and believed that he had merited it. When on one occasion in this campaign he was fortunate enough to execute at the critical

moment an important evolution, which at present I do not
remember, but of the value of which he was fully conscious, and concluded the Emperor would be so likewise,
he presented himself before him at the close of the
battle to receive the expected meed of approbation.
The Emperor regarded him with bent brows, and abruptly passing him, said: "You have manœuverd like an
oyster."

The sentence was terrible, and the more so as all those
who had had the means of judging of Marmont's
conduct during this day knew that he had particularly
distinguished himself. He returned to his quarters in
despair.

"My friend," said he to his General of Division —
Clausel — to whom he was much attached, "I am lost —
disgraced! Good heavens! what inconceivable ingratitude! When I have made superhuman exertions in his
service — when, by my zeal alone, I have succeeded in
bringing up the troops which in all probability decided
the fate of the battle — after such a sentence, I have
nothing to expect but exile, or at least disgrace." And
this man, usually so cold and calm, strode across the room
with alarming vehemence; it was not the loss of favor
which so affected him — it was the presumed ingratitude
of one whom, like Junot, he loved with all the ardor of
his heart.

General Clausel knew not what to answer; he was confounded by this apostrophe of Napoleon, but endeavored
to console his General by putting the only construction
upon it which, in his opinion, the really successful manœuver of Marmont would allow it to bear. "The Emperor," said he, "is seeking to elude his promise; he has
some destination for the baton more advantageous to his
interests, and you, of whose attachment he is certain,
may wait."

Marmont started — General Clausel had unveiled a mystery which he had himself feared to face. A deception
practiced upon us by a person beloved is more bitter
than if encountered in our ordinary intercourse with the
world. To be unable to depend upon Napoleon! no
longer to recognize in him the General Bonaparte he had
adored and trusted! The idea brought on an attack almost of delirium.

In the midst of this violent agitation, an officer from the Prince of Neufchâtel came to seek the Duke of Ragusa. The Duke looked at General Clausel, who loved him, and after what he had heard, believing his disgrace to be certain, said to him, with a melancholy smile: "Go and support yourself like a man; you have nothing to reproach yourself with — a good conscience is a powerful auxiliary; go, then, with confidence."

General Clausel, who felt that at this moment the consolations of friendship were due to his General, waited his return. He was not absent more than half an hour, and when he reappeared his usually stern and serious countenance was lighted up with such an expression of joy and gayety that the General scarcely thought him in his right mind. His raised hand displayed a paper, but his voice was so stifled with emotion that he could only exclaim: " My friend! my friend! I am a Marshal."

This fact, like many others which relate to his connection with the Emperor, would serve for a text to comment upon, and might furnish a key to the mystery of Marmont's destiny. No doubt he thought himself very happy in holding that parchment, which added not one ray to his glory; but did that moment make amends for the many sleepless nights that preceded it ? — for the disappointments he had felt, and the neglect with which he not unjustly conceived his merits to have been treated ? I believe not.

Again, at this period a great portion of Europe was thrown into mourning by the Battle of Wagram. The news reached me in the Pyrenees, and I own that I felt almost as proud as of the victory of Austerlitz, except that Junot was not there. Masséna, Prince Eugène, Oudinot, and Davoût were chiefly distinguished. This battle was perhaps the most dramatic, and the most sanguinary of our long wars. Death thundering forth at once from the thousand mouths of the artillery presented a magnificent spectacle to the guests invited to this banquet, and who played with their cannons as though their ammunition was as harmless as snowballs. But the horror of that field of carnage, when the excitement of action was over, no pen can describe, nor can imagination conceive it; it is too frightful a subject to be dwelt upon.

While the hostile armies were fighting with such fury
on the borders of Hungary, Junot commanded a division
opposed to Kielmayer; he was in want of troops, which
the King of Westphalia had been directed to bring up.
With a very accurate foresight, Junot wrote to the King
of Wirtemberg to support him. I here transcribe that
Prince's answer, not on account of any special interest
attaching to it, but as a specimen of the zeal with which
at that period the Kings of the Confederation affected to
unite in the views of Napoleon:

"MY COUSIN:—I have received your letter from Amberg, on the
12th, and have already written to you from Ellwangen on the 4th, that
I expected to be obliged to oppose all my disposable troops to the
invasion of the insurgents from the Tyrol and Vorarlberg. You will
consequently understand that the same cause, which prevented my
sending you the reinforcement you wrote to me at Ellwangen to
request, still continuing, and being, moreover, at a distance of forty
leagues from you, it would be very difficult to arrive time enough to
assist you against an enemy who is within a march and a half of you.
According to my official reports, the headquarters of the King of Westphalia are but fourteen leagues distant, consequently he will be in the
rear of Kielmayer's corps; I conceive that, under these circumstances,
there is little room to apprehend that General's advance to any distance
from the frontiers of Bohemia, especially since the brilliant victory of
the 5th and 6th,* the more so as the most recent intelligence from
Nuremberg makes no mention of his approach. With this, I pray God,
my cousin, to take you into his holy and powerful keeping.

"Your good cousin,
                              "FREDERICK.

"Weimgarten, 15th July, 1809."

I do not rightly know what had happened to the King
of Westphalia; but he did not arrive in time — I even
believe he did not arrive at all. Junot would not report
this to the Emperor; but Napoleon heard of it, and was
violently angry with Jerôme. How deeply must the
Emperor have suffered sometimes!

Junot was almost immediately afterward invested with
the military government of Saxony. He had before
been Governor of the Principality of Bayreuth, and commanded the troops of the King of Bavaria; all these
kings, more submissive than the feudatories of our
kings in the Middle Ages, were obsequious even to the
generals of the Emperor. The following will show how
the King of Saxony addressed one of them:

* Wagram.

«My Cousin:— I have learned with satisfaction, by the letter which you addressed to me on the 17th of this month, that his Imperial and Royal Majesty has confided to you the military government of Saxony. I shall have much pleasure in your arrival here, which will afford me an opportunity of renewing my acquaintance with so justly distinguished a General. Be assured that your high reputation has already secured my esteem, and that I shall be happy to prove it to you by the confidence with which I shall promote all your views for the welfare of the service, and of the common cause, to which I am resolved to devote all my resources. With thanks for the obliging sentiments you express toward me, I pray God, my cousin, to take you into his holy and powerful keeping.

«Your affectionate
«FREDERICK AUGUSTUS.

«DRESDEN, 19th August, 1809.»

At length the Emperor made peace with Austria. The treaty was signed by the Duc de Cadore and Prince Metternich, father of the present Chancellor. This peace was a terrible blow to Austria, but she signed it without murmuring; vengeance was not far distant! The Emperor, who only stopped a few days at Munich on his journey, re-entered Paris amid the first burst of joy at the return of peace, yet he might easily perceive a change of sentiment in his capital. The campaign had been so murderous, the victory so obstinately disputed, that France began to consider her laurels too dearly purchased; then, for the first time, a hostile ball found its way to Napoleon's person. It was at Ratisbon; the ball was a spent one, and it struck his heel — but the heel was Napoleon's, and the ball came from the enemy. The whisper arose: WHAT IF THE BALL HAD STRUCK TWO FEET HIGHER? Then the death of Lannes — that of Lasalle by assassination from the hand of a young fanatic. Death thus roaming, under different forms, about the person of the Emperor, seemed, though it dared not touch him, to say: "Take care of thyself!" All these were inauspicious omens.

CHAPTER XIII.

Approaching Divorce — Conversation with the Empress — Her Distress — Fête at the Hôtel de Ville — The Ladies Appointed to Receive the Empress Countermanded — Her Majesty's Sufferings at This Ball — The Emperor and the Queen of Naples — Berthier — The Divorce Pronounced — Affecting Incident — Josephine at Malmaison — The Rhenish Deputation — Mademoiselle Masséna.

A NOTHER interest blended itself with politics, with which it was closely combined: this was the divorce of the Emperor; no one dared speak openly of it, but nevertheless it was a frequent subject of confidential discussion. The drawing-rooms of Paris were then in a singular state of constraint, which men even of thirty years of age cannot now understand; for, as they were of course dismissed to the nursery or to their beds before the hour of assembly, they are not aware that politics were an interdicted subject, except when spoken aside or mysteriously; but so many private interests were bound up in this divorce, that they were too strong for restriction, and it was talked of — in a low voice, it is true — but still it was talked of.

I had an interview with the Empress at Malmaison; I went thither to breakfast by invitation, accompanied by my eldest daughter Josephine, to whom she was much attached. I had sent her a plant from the Pyrenees, and she wished me to see it in the hothouse. But in vain she attempted to employ herself with those objects which pleased her the most; her eyes were frequently suffused with tears; she was pale, and her whole manner showed indisposition.

"It is very cold !" she repeated, drawing her shawl about her; but, alas ! it was the chill of grief creeping about her heart, like the cold hand of Death. I looked at her silently, for respect prevented my opening such a subject of conversation. It was my duty to wait till she spoke first, which she soon did. We were in the hothouse; the child running through its galleries of flowers, and the Empress and I following slowly in silence. She suddenly stopped, gathered some leaves of a shrub near her, and, looking at me with a most melancholy expression of countenance, said:

"Do you know that the Queen of Naples is coming?"
It was now my turn to look pale, but I answered immediately: "No, madame." "She will be here in a week."
Another pause. "And Madame Mère, have you seen her
since your return?" "Certainly, madame; I have already
been in waiting." Upon this the Empress drew closser
to me; she was already very near, and, taking both my
hands, said, in a tone of grief which is still present to
my mind after an interval of four-and-twenty years:
"Madame Junot, I entreat you to tell me all you have
heard relating to me. I ask it as an especial favor—
you know that they all desire to ruin me, and my Hortense, and my Eugène. Madame Junot, I again entreat
as a favor that you will tell me all you know!"

She spoke with the greatest anxiety; her lips trembled,
and her hands were damp and cold. In point of fact
she was right, for there could be no more direct means
of knowing what was passing relative to her than by
learning what was said in the house of Madame Mère.
But it was indiscreet, perhaps, to ask these questions of
me; in the first place, I should not have repeated the
most insignificant sentence which I had heard in Madame's
drawing-room; in the second, I was quite at ease upon
the subject, for since my return from the Pyrenees I
had not heard one single word respecting the Empress
pronounced by Madame.

I gave her this assurance upon my honor; she looked
at me with a doubtful expression: I repeated my assurances, and added that I might positively affirm that since
my return I had not heard the word DIVORCE uttered by
Madame or the Princess. The strength of mind of the
unfortunate wife failed totally on hearing the dreadful
word pronounced; she leaned upon my arm and wept bitterly.
"Madame Junot," she said, "remember what I say to you
this day, here in this hothouse—this place which is now
a paradise, but which may soon become a desert to me
—remember that this separation will be my death, and
it is they who will have killed me!"

She sobbed. My little Josephine, running to her, pulled
her by the shawl to show her some flowers she had
plucked, for the Empress was so fond of her as even to
permit her to gather flowers in her greenhouse. She
took her in her arms, and pressed her to her bosom with

an almost convulsive emotion. The child appeared frightened; but presently, raising her head, and shaking the forest of light silken curls which clustered round her face, she fixed her large blue eyes upon the agitated countenance of her godmother, and said: "I do not like you to cry." The Empress again embraced her tenderly, and, setting her down, said to me:

"You can have little idea how much I have suffered when anyone of you has brought a child to me! Heaven knows that I am not envious, but in this one case I have felt as if a deadly poison were creeping through my veins when I have looked upon the fresh and rosy cheeks of a beautiful child, the joy of its mother, but, above all, the hope of its father! and I, struck with barrenness, shall be driven in disgrace from the bed of him who has given me a crown! Yet God is my witness that I love him more than my life, and much more than that throne, that crown which he has given me!" The Empress may have appeared more beautiful, but never more attractive, than at that moment. If Napoleon had seen her then, surely he could never have divorced her. Ah! in summing up the misfortunes of this fatal year, that divorce must be added to render them complete.

This conversation, of which I have only reported the principal features, made a deep impression upon me. On my return to Paris an hour afterward. I repeated it to Junot, and I still wept while relating to him that deep but gentle grief, so affecting to the feelings. I also told Junot that the Empress desired to see him at the Tuileries at noon the following day.

It was now the 25th of November, and everything was prepared for celebrating the double anniversary of the Coronation and the Battle of Austerlitz. The city of Paris determined to take the lead in the rejoicings, and Comte Frochot had made the most sumptuous preparations for the entertainment at the Hôtel de Ville. The court of the Hôtel was to be as usual transformed into an immense ballroom, to which the old gallery formed a superb avenue. Though indisposed, I prepared to fulfill my duty, and on the 2d of December arrived amid a general sadness which affected the whole Court. The Emperor himself, while he put on a show of gayety, set an example of constraint,— a misfortune was foreseen, and in truth the separation of Napoleon Bonaparte from Josephine must ever be considered a very great one. The Emperor had expressed a wish that the ball should commence early, because it was his desire to see every-one, and especially as few COURT dresses as possible. He repeated: "I see them daily at the Tuileries; the city of Paris gives me a *fête*, and it is the city of Paris I wish to meet." I left home at three o'clock, because I had been told that the Emperor and Empress would dine at the Hôtel de Ville, and, if so, I was to wait upon the Empress.

At the Hôtel de Ville I found everything in the most admirable order, but had not much opportunity of inspect-ing the preparations, as the rooms were already filled with the ladies invited. I proceeded to the small *salon* beside the staircase, where I found the ladies assembled whose names had been sent in to me. They were mostly young, pretty, and very elegant, or at least very polite and pleasing. We remained in the *salon*. I knew that the Queen of Naples had arrived in the morning, but I knew nothing more. Junot, whom I questioned at least ten times, did not know what answer to make; he was in the condition of a man who, having had a very agreeable dream, awakes and wishes to find it reality. I was therefore quite ignorant of any change of plan until M. de Ségur came into the room. Calling me into the recess of one of the windows, which in this ancient building were as deep as a small room, he said in a low voice:

"The face of affairs is changed; your beautiful attend-ants may take their departure to the upper part of the room, and yourself also, my fair *Gouvernante*. You have nothing further to do here. The Empress," he contin-ued in a still lower tone, "is to be received by Frochot only. Do you hear what I have been saying?" He had reason to ask the question, for I stood like a statue. "And why this prohibition?" "I know not; or rather I do know, but I do not choose to say." He laughed, but I could not join in the laugh; this strange command sounded in my ears like a bell tolling the knell of the unfortunate Empress.

Napoleon, while he braved public opinion, was always desirous of ascertaining it, and though he did not suffer

it to control his proceedings, it had its weight in his
decision. He seized the opportunity, therefore, of this
popular *fête* to infuse the idea that the divorce was contemplated; he wished it to be conjectured, to be com-
mented upon in whispers, but not as an authenticated
event admitting of no revocation. Such were the impressions which passed rapidly through my mind, and I
believe they were correct.

I was returning to my companions to explain to them
the necessity of our immediately taking the places
reserved for us in the throne room when Junot and M.
Frochot entered together. "What can be the matter?"
said Frochot, addressing me; "you are perfectly blue;
are you cold?" On the contrary, I was burning hot. I
explained to them the whole affair, and both were thunderstruck; but at the same moment we heard a movement out of doors, and Junot observed:

"You have not a moment to lose; if you should FOLLOW
the Empress into the throne room, although you had not
gone to meet her, the Emperor will consider it the same
thing, and will be angry. You and these ladies must
therefore proceed immediately to your places." I know
not what Frochot said to them, but they were content,
and I was excused interfering. We went up to the
throne room, and had scarcely taken our seats before the
drums announced the Empress's arrival. Never shall I
forget her appearance on that day, or the costume which
so admirably became her. Her countenance, always
gentle, was on that occasion veiled in grief. She had
not expected the solitude she had encountered on the
staircase. Junot, however, met her there at the risk of
displeasing the Emperor, and so, by his contrivance, did
some ladies, who did not know for what purpose they
were there.

The Empress was not deceived, and when she entered
the Grand Salon, when she approached that throne upon
which she was about to take her station in the presence
of the great city, perhaps for the last time, her legs
failed her, her eyes filled with tears, and she seated herself immediately. No wonder that she did so, for after
passing through that long gallery and all the preceding
apartments in the state of mind which everything since
she alighted from her carriage was calculated to produce,

she must have felt ready to sink; yet her face was clothed in smiles! Oh, the tortures of a crown! She was followed by Madame de La Rochefoucauld, her lady of honor, and two ladies of the Palace, whose names I do not remember, for on that day I saw only her.

I sought her eyes the moment she sat down, and would willingly have fallen at her feet to tell her how much I felt for her. She understood, and cast upon me a look of the deepest melancholy, which, perhaps, her eyes had ever expressed since that crown, now robbed of its roses, had been placed upon her head. Junot was beside her. "Were you not afraid" I afterward asked him, "of the wrath of Jupiter?" "No," said he, with an air of gloom that affected me; "I never fear him when he is wrong."

The drums beat again, and in a few moments the Emperor appeared, advancing with a hasty step, and accompanied by the Queen of Naples and the King of Westphalia. I have already said that a change of sentiment respecting the Emperor pervaded the capital. He had conquered, indeed, a hostile monarchy, but tottering and mutilated as that monarchy was, it had risen against us with such tremendous might that France was covered with emblems of mourning. His laurels began to be less verdant. Again, the establishment of eight fortresses which would serve as State prisons was talked of; a divorce was in agitation; Josephine was beloved, and the good citizens of Paris murmured at the proposition. The Emperor's countenance as he entered the Hôtel de Ville very plainly expressed that he was aware of all this.

The Queen of Naples, whose gracious and condescending smile seemed to demand from the Parisians a welcome on her return among them, spoke to everyone with extreme affability. The Emperor, desirous also of being agreeable, walked around the ballroom, conversing, asking questions, and followed by Berthier, who, dangling after his master, filled the office of Chamberlain rather than of Grand Constable. A slight circumstance, in which Berthier was an actor in the course of that evening, contributed to give me pain. The Emperor rose from his chair of State and descended the steps of his throne to make a last visit to the ballroom; at the moment of rising I saw him incline toward the Empress, probably to desire she would follow his example. He stood up

11

first and Berthier, in his hurry to follow him, entangled his foot in the Empress's train as she rose. He narrowly escaped falling himself, and though he caused the Empress to stumble, hurried on to join the Emperor without one word of apology.

Probably Berthier had no intention of being disrespectful to her, but it was carelessly done. He was in the secret, and knew the drama that was about to be enacted; certainly he would have had more consideration a year earlier. The Empress stood for a moment with remarkable dignity, smiling at his awkwardness, while her eyes filled with tears and her lips trembled. Though the weather was bitterly cold the heat in these thronged apartments was excessive. The Emperor made the tour of the Grand Gallery, talking to persons on the one side, while the Empress took the other.

At length the divorce was announced * — and, though expected, the effect which the news produced in France

* "The divorce was, unquestionably, a reverse of fortune for Josephine, which she felt most severely, but she bore it with magnanimity. The particulars of the interview between her and the Emperor are very affecting. When Napoleon mentioned the necessity of a divorce he approached Josephine, gazed on her for a while, and then pronounced the following words: 'Josephine, my excellent Josephine, thou knowest if I have loved thee ! To thee, to thee alone do I owe the only moments of happiness which I have enjoyed in this world. Josephine ! my destiny overmasters my will. My dearest affections must be silent before the interests of France.' 'Say no more,' she replied, 'I was prepared for this; but the blow is not less mortal !'

"Josephine, on hearing from his own lips the determination of the Emperor, fainted and was carried to her chamber.

"On the 15th of December, 1809, the Imperial Council of State was convened, and for the first time officially informed of the intended separation. On the morrow the whole of the family assembled in the Grand Salon at the Tuileries. All were in Court costume. Napoleon's was the only countenance which betrayed emotion, but ill-concealed by the drooping plumes of his hat of ceremony. He stood motionless as a statue, his arms crossed upon his breast; the members of his family were seated around, showing in their expression less of sympathy with so painful a scene than of satisfaction that one was to be removed who had so long held influence, gently exerted as it had been, over their brother. In the center of the apartment was placed an armchair, and before it a small table with a writing apparatus of gold.

"All eyes were directed to that spot, when a door opened, and Josephine, pale but calm, appeared, leaning on the arm of her daugh-

baffles description — among the populace and the middle class especially. It was like their guardian genius deserting them. The upper class were for the most part

ter, whose fast-falling tears showed that she had not attained the resignation of her mother. Both were dressed in the simplest manner. Josephine's dress of white muslin exhibited not a single ornament. She moved slowly and with wonted grace to the seat prepared for her, and there listened to the reading of the act of separation. Behind her chair stood Hortense, whose sobs were audible, and a little further on toward Napoleon, Eugène, trembling as if incapable of supporting himself. Josephine heard in composure the words that placed an eternal barrier between her and greatness, between her and the object of her affection.

"This painful duty over, the Empress appeared to acquire a degree of resolution from the very effort to resign with dignity the formality of power forever. Pressing, for an instant, the handkerchief to her eyes, she rose, and, with a voice which but for a slight tremor might have been called firm, pronounced the oath of acceptance; then sitting down, she took the pen from the hand of the Comte Regnault Saint Jean d'Angely, and signed it. The mother and daughter now left the *salon* followed by Eugène, who appeared to suffer most severely of the three.

"The sad interest of the day had not yet been exhausted. Josephine had remained unseen, sorrowing in her chamber, till Napoleon's usual hour of retiring to rest. He had just placed himself in bed, silent and melancholy, when suddenly the private door opened and the Empress appeared, her hair in disorder, and her face swollen with weeping. Advancing with a tottering step, she stood, as if irresolute, near the bed, clasped her hands, and burst into an agony of tears. Delicacy seemed at first to have arrested her progress, but forgetting everything in the fullness of her grief, she threw herself on the bed, clasped her husband's neck, and sobbed as if her heart would break. Napoleon also wept while he endeavored to console her, and they remained a few minutes locked in each other's arms, silently mingling their tears, until the Emperor, perceiving Constant in the room, dismissed him to the antechamber. After an interview of about an hour, Josephine parted forever from the man whom she so long and so tenderly loved.

"On seeing the Empress retire, which she did in tears, the attendant entered to remove the lights, and found the chamber silent as death, and Napoleon sunk among the bedclothes so as to be invisible. The next morning he still showed the marks of suffering. At eleven, Josephine was to bid adieu to the Tuileries, never to enter the Palace more. The whole household assembled on the stairs in order to obtain a last look of a mistress whom they loved, and who carried with her into exile the hearts of all who had enjoyed the happiness of access to her presence. Josephine was veiled from head to foot, and entering a close carriage with six horses, rapidly drove away, without casting one look backward on the scene of past greatness and departed happiness." — Memes's "Memoirs of the Empress Josephine," p. 337.

indifferent, but still there reigned even here a sentiment of sympathetic melancholy; the ladies of the Court, whose life of ceremony is apt to deaden the affections, were actuated at least by their personal interests, and did not know how these might be affected by the newcomer. Already Josephine's goodness was regretted; her kindness and indulgence none can ever attempt to deny; the only objection to be made against her in this respect being the want of discrimination in her goodness and patronage. The effect of all these varying shades of feeling, whether of affection or self-interest, was to produce a certain degree of stupor in society. I was profoundly afflicted, and went the very next day to Malmaison.

One incident in particular gave a still more dramatic effect to the melancholy close of a career so distinguished by the favors of fortune. Prince Eugène, whose affection for his mother is well known, being at the time in Paris, found himself necessitated by his office of Archchancellor of State to carry to the Senate the message which announced his mother's divorce. " The tears of the Emperor," said that noble young man, " do honor to my mother." And his own, which flowed profusely through this dreadful day, were a consolation in the midst of her sufferings.

The Empress received at Malmaison all who chose to pay their respects to her. The drawing-room, the billiardroom, and the gallery were full of company. The Empress never appeared to greater advantage. She sat at the right of the chimney, beneath Girodet's fine picture, simply dressed, with a large green *capote* upon her head, which served to conceal her tears, which would flow whenever anyone came who particularly reminded her of the happy hours of Malmaison and the Consulate. It was impossible to see without emotion the grief which marked her countenance. She raised her eyes to everyone who approached, even smiled at them; but if the visitor was one of her old associates the tears immediately stole down her cheeks, but quietly and without any of those contractions of the features which make weeping inimical to beauty. No doubt Josephine's despair must have been painful to the Emperor; whether he could have resisted her mute expression of mental agony I know not.

I went again to Malmaison a few days afterward with my little Josephine, whom her godmother had desired me to bring; this time, as I was alone with her, she did not scruple to open all the sorrows of her heart, and she spoke of her grief with an energy of truth quite distressing. She regretted all that she had lost; but it is justice to say that far above all she regretted the Emperor. The attentions of her children in those days of suffering were admirable.

At this time of painful feeling to the Emperor — for he loved Josephine — Napoleon received visits from the whole Rhenish Confederation; the King of Saxony, the King and Queen of Bavaria, the King of Wirtemberg; all, in short, came to Paris to make him a visit, which would scarcely admit of more than one construction — for not only was the divorce in process, but the official authorities had pronounced the marriage void.

The imperial divorce produced some terrible disputes between Cardinal Maury and myself. It had long been the desire, I will not say of his heart, for his heart had no concern with the matter, but of his reason, or rather his ambition; wherefore, I never could imagine. In the whole Court besides, I will undertake to say, though the Empress's partialities, more or less ill founded, and her too extensive good nature, may have afforded ground for some quarrel or complaint, no individual was to be found who wished her removal. On the contrary, regret, when the event did take place, was universal. I did not attempt to conceal mine, though my duty frequently led me to the only place where no such regret was felt, for the family of the Emperor must be excepted from the remark I have just made; there it was viewed with unmixed satisfaction.

Cardinal Maury, as everyone knows, spoke loud and decisively; one day after I had answered him in an undertone as long as possible, I began to grow angry also, for he averred that we should be but too happy if Russia would send us one of her Grand-Duchesses — at the same time that a report was current of the Empress Mother having declared that she would prefer throwing her daughter into the Neva to giving her to Napoleon. I thought it ridiculous to cringe, and go begging, cap in hand, for what might be had at home, and would be given with gratitude; and I expressed this opinion to the Cardinal.

"All that is very well," said he; "but how will you find what we want in France?"

"Close beside you." He looked incredulous. "Let the Emperor," said I, "marry Mademoiselle Masséna; he would have a young wife, pretty, blooming, and perfectly well brought up; he would recompense the glorious services of a veteran soldier; he would unite the army to himself by indissoluble ties; and he would be under no obligations to those kings whom he has three times dethroned, and who will still believe that they do him a favor in giving him a wife — educated in hatred to his name and ours."

When I held this argument, Mademoiselle Masséna was still free: my reasoning was good; would to Heaven the Emperor had followed it in all points! The Cardinal repeated it to him one day; he listened very attentively to the end, and then replied:

"What can Madame Junot mean by meddling with such questions? Recommend her to take care that she do not burn her fingers."

The Cardinal was not a man to give up a subject he had once broached. But the Emperor assumed a serious tone, and said:

"The thing is impossible."

CHAPTER XIV.

The German Kings at Paris — The Queen of Naples at the Tuileries — Her Parties Unsociable — Duets with the Grand-Duke of Wurtzburg — The Kings' Visit to Josephine at Malmaison — The Carnival — The Patrimony of Saint Peter Withdrawn from the Pope — Negotiations Superintended by Lucien Bonaparte — The Pope Carried off from Rome — General Miollis at Rome — Expatriation — A Storm — Port of Cagliari — Lucien and His Family Prisoners to the English — Malta — Palace of the Grand Master — Captain Warren — Arrival at Plymouth — Ludlow Castle — Lucien's Removal to Thorngrove — Domestic Scenes — Lucien's Literary Pursuits — Visit of the Duke of Norfolk.

I KNOW not whether this unlucky divorce influenced our tempers, but Paris was never so dull as at that moment — amid the finest *fêtes* the Empire witnessed, except those of the marriage and the coronation. All those kings who encumbered the avenues of the Palace froze our spirits, without inspiring the distant respect which should be the attribute of royalty. In our ill humor we found fault with all of them. The Court was disunited; there was no central point of union. In vain the Queen of Naples lodged in the Tuileries; the Household of her brother did not like her; and though pre-eminent as flatterers, we make but sorry hypocrites. Queen Hortense was really loved; all was freedom in her society; she set everyone at ease. Music, conversation, drawing, billiards, whatever each person liked best; in short, everyone was amused — which never happened under the auspices of the Queen of Naples, except on occasion of a ball, and except, indeed, when she sang duets with the Grand-Duke of Wurtzburg.

Never in my life have I heard anything so ridiculous as the combination of their voices; neither of them had the smallest notion of diffidence, nor the smallest idea of singing; yet they sang on, both together, as if they really had voices! They were princely voices at best. It was said of La Forest, one of the opera singers, that he must have a wooden voice; this would not have been ill applied to the royal duettists. Oh! those concerts of her Imperial Highness the Princess were odd affairs; yet she had some ladies in her Household who might have taught her what good music was. I have often, for example, wondered how it happened that Madame Lambert did not belong to the establishment of Queen Hortense, where her talents for music and painting, and her love of the arts, would have been justly appreciated.

All the Crowned Heads, Majesties and Highnesses assembled at Paris at the commencement of the year 1810 paid their respects to the ex-Empress at Malmaison, and while consolatory, as indicating the Emperor's will that she should be respected as the wife of his choice, yet these visits were oppressive to her — such, at least, they appeared to me to be. In my visits to Malmaison, the Queen of Naples was always the subject of our conversations. Her conduct since her return to Paris evinced a great desire to please; she made superb presents to all the ladies of the Court. My daughters, though young children, received from her each a suit of coral ornaments, one of which, wrought in relief, was very beautiful. It was in this visit that she presented to the Emperor the well-known superb set of chessmen, in Vesuvian lava and coral.

The carnival approached; the Emperor commanded that it should be gay and brilliant; the authorities of Paris prepared to obey the Imperial mandate, and ball succeeded ball without intermission. But how different was the winter from its predecessor! Mourning was universal, and everyone entered into society to divert the feelings from melancholy retrospection. Nothing was real, and no pleasing remembrances remain of the forced festivities of this spring; almost everyone with whom I have conversed upon the subject agrees in the same recollection of it.

While Napoleon was procuring at Paris the dissolution of his marriage, his affairs went on badly at the Court of Rome. He found there a powerful antagonist in Lucien, who, grateful for the asylum which the Pope had nobly granted him, was indignant at seeing him despoiled of his possessions by the Emperor. He endeavored to infuse a new vigor in the councils of the Vatican. For several months the correspondence between the Cabinet of the Tuileries and that of Rome was active and important; its object was to refuse all further concession

to Napoleon, and to dispute the possession of the Papal
dominions as he had already seized; and when at length
an Imperial decree was launched from Vienna, commanding the Pope to descend from St. Peter's chair—
for to command him to surrender the Roman territory
was much the same thing—Cardinal Consalvi, stimulated
by Lucien, wrote under his dictation a letter calculated
to astonish the Emperor.

Without speaking of the supremacy of the Court of
Rome, which Lucien no more wished than Napoleon to
re-establish in France, it asserted with justice that the
Pope should not be despoiled of his own dominions. But
all this resistance had no effect: the States of the Church
were united to the French Empire, and the situation of
the Pope became critical.

Murat, then at Naples, transmitted to General Radet
at Rome Napoleon's orders for the removal of the Pope
to France; and on the 5th of July, 1809, the General
called upon his Holiness to obey the Emperor's commands. The Pope replied that his double dignity of Sovereign and Chief of the Church placed him beyond the
jurisdiction of the French Emperor. "His predecessors,"
said he to the Envoy, "have saved mine, but this gives
him no claim, except on my gratitude." He shut himself up in the Quirinal, and, clothed in all the Pontifical
ornaments, seated himself in a chair of state, peaceably
to await the coming of General Radet.

The French functionary presented himself in the middle of the night at the principal door of the Palace, and,
finding it closed, forced his way into the apartments of
the Sovereign Pontiff by a window on the ground floor,
took possession of his person, compelled him to enter a
carriage, and instantly drove off on the road to Grenoble,
according to his orders.

Passing the next morning through Viterbo, Radet perceived an alarming degree of agitation in the popular
mind; he hurried the postilions through the necessary
operation of changing horses, and hearing on all sides
cries which threatened an interruption to his important
mission, he called out: "On your knees! the Holy Father
is about to give you his blessing."

The people prostrated themselves in an instant, and
when all their faces were in the dust, Radet, himself

violently applying the whip to the horses, drove off with the rapidity of an arrow, and without the assistance of the postilions, leaving the inhabitants of Viterbo to vent, in harmless maledictions, that rage against us which in another minute would have probably exhibited itself in a more dangerous manner.

Pius VII. remained but a short time at Grenoble; he was soon transferred by the Emperor's orders to Savona, where, kept a close prisoner, almost in sight of his jailers, he was only allowed the liberty of performing mass. General Miollis arrived at Rome to take the command of the city. Lucien then found himself in a strange position. From the commencement of his exile the fine arts, literature, and the education of his children had formed his sole occupations and amusements. The Mæcenas of every man of talent in Rome, he was adored by the artists, whom he employed and understood, for Lucien was never moderately beloved; he was a being of superior worth!

Immediately on the departure of the Holy Father he retired to Tusculum, where he superintended his excavations, and where General Miollis watched him with an inquisitory intrusiveness which Lucien soon found intolerable. With no other title than that of the proscribed brother of the Emperor, for his exclusion from the order of succession threw him, as it were, out of the Family Circle, seeing the Imperial authority crossing the Alps and Apennines to seek him in his studious retreat in the bosom of his numerous family, he determined to quit Europe, and wrote to the Duc de Rovigo, then Minister of Police, to obtain passports for the United States of America.

The Emperor was aware of the demand, without doubt; but he did not appear in the affair, and the answer of the Duc de Rovigo was the transmission of the passports, sanctioning Lucien's expatriation. He then wrote to Naples, requesting Murat to send him an American vessel, released from all embargo. Murat sent the vessel with the most gracious promptitude: Lucien, it seems, frightened them all!

The American ship soon arrived at Civita Vecchia. The entire gallery of Lucien and all the treasures he had found in his researches at Tusculum were carefully packed

up under the inspection of M. de Châtillon, who superintended the department of the arts in Lucien's household.
But the cases were not all put on board; the greater
part was left with Torlonia, the chief banker of Rome.
Lucien carried with him all his numerous family portraits, together with that of Pius VII. "He has been a
hospitable friend to me," said he; "I must not forget
him." At length, in the month of August, 1810, the exiled family quitted Civita Vecchia. It was truly a singular spectacle to see the brother of Napoleon abandoning
Europe to seek an asylum in the New World, carrying thither
a heart devotedly French and a purely patriotic spirit.

The captain set sail in spite of contrary winds, but
had not long cleared the coast before a tremendous storm
arose which threatened the ship with utter destruction.
Lucien, always possessing the calmness of true courage,
required the Captain to put into the port of Cagliari,
which they were approaching. The Princess and children
were ill, assistance and repose were therefore necessary,
and Lucien had letters from the Pope recommending
him to the protection of the Sovereigns on whose territories he might chance to touch in his exile.

On reaching Cagliari, M. de Châtillon landed, and carried to the Sardinian Minister a certificate of the illness
of Lucien's family, requesting permission for him to land
for the purpose of recovery. This affair, which if it had
concerned a French family of unknown name would have
been settled without difficulty, became strangely compli-
cated by the name of Lucien Bonaparte. The Sardinian
Minister humbly replied that such questions concerned
Mr. Hill, the British envoy, and that to him alone its
decision belonged. In vain M. de Châtillon declined the
authority of England; Mr. Hill decreed that M. Lucien
Bonaparte, the American vessel, and all that it contained,
should be captured in the port at Cagliari.

Lucien turned pale on hearing this decision, and exclaimed, with truly French feeling: "I will not submit
to it!" That heart of iron and fire, susceptible also of
all the tender emotions, swelled with unutterable grief
and indignation as he cast his eyes on his proscribed
family and felt that he ought to sway a scepter for their
protection. Notwithstanding the illness of his wife and
children, he would not permit them to land, and thus

passed fourteen days—the most distressing, perhaps, of
his life. "We must go," he said at length, "and let us
see if they will dare to execute their threat."

The American ship sailed out of the port; the two
English frigates, seeing its preparations, had stood out
the preceding evening; and scarcely had the American
advanced a mile, before one of the frigates, the "Po-
mona," Captain Barry, fired a shot, and commanded the
captain to lay to. The American was only a merchant
ship, but the captain's spirit revolted from thus surrendering a passenger who had intrusted his person and
family to his care. "I will not bring to," said he to his
lieutenant.

Captain Barry, receiving no answer, launched his boat,
and came himself with two officers alongside the American ship, which he knew to be incapable of defense.
The captain, however, intended to defend himself; on
perceiving the English captain in his boat he waited till
he was within pistol shot, and then would have fired if
Lucien had not suddenly given him a smart blow on
the arm which compelled him to drop the pistol. With
much difficulty he was persuaded to surrender, and the
English captain announced to his prisoners that he
should convey them to Malta. Captain Barry was then,
what he probably still is, if the cannon, sword, and
tempest have spared his life so long, that perfectly
agreeable character which is natural to an English gentleman; for I may truly affirm that in all my intercourse
with the various nations of Europe I have nowhere
found individuals so perfectly pleasing and polite in
language, manners, and habits as really well-bred Englishmen.

In the interval between their capture and their arrival
at Malta he paid the family every attention that kindness
and respect could suggest, and a voyage in the Mediterranean permit. On reaching Malta they were conducted
to the "Lazaretto"; Lucien solicited permission to remove his wife and children, but was refused by the Governor, General Oakes, with an obstinacy worthy of
Saint Helena. It would seem that the British Government prides itself in being represented by men capable
of every act of cruelty! The object of this policy I
cannot understand.

Lucien was condemned to three days' quarantine, and this useless vexation over, was permitted to take up his residence in the Fort Ricasoli, where he found only damp walls, without an article of furniture, and was obliged at his own expense to procure even chairs and bedding from the town of Valetta. Even the naval officers were indignant at such unworthy treatment; and Lucien, however unwilling to complain, felt it due to the name of a Frenchman to submit his wrongs to the British Government. Its answer arrived at length, ordering that the prisoner should be removed to the castle of Saint Anthony, the residence of the Grand Master in the proud days of the Order, and treated with the utmost consideration, until it was determined in what manner he should be finally disposed of.

In this Gothic castle, which his elevated mind led him to teach his children rather to consider as a retreat than a prison, he and Madame Lucien employed themselves in protecting their young family from *ennui*, and in so doing, defended themselves also from its attacks. Surrounded by a locality full of romance, where every tower had its tale, and every stone seemed the memento of some illustrious name, Lucien compelled new traditions to take their place beside the old, and consoled his wounded spirit by a closer acquaintance with the Muses; here he proceeded with his poem of "Charlemagne"— venting the grief of exile in words of harmony.

Toward the close of the year Captain Warren arrived in the frigate, the "President," to convey Lucien and his family to England. He requested as a favor that he might be allowed to sail for England accompanied by M. de Châtillon, and to leave his wife and children till the spring, hoping that a personal application to the Prince Regent would have the effect of restoring the liberty of which he had been illegally deprived. But again he met with a refusal; in vain he urged the natural fears of a husband and a father in committing the safety of his tender charges to the mercy of the elements at so inclement a season. "I have my orders," was still the reply of Captain Warren.

Everything on board the frigate was arranged with attention to their comfort, and the conduct of the officers was respectful and accommodating; but the cold and

haughty character of Captain Warren increased the dis-
agreeableness of a six weeks' voyage in the midst of
winter and dreadful weather. Its tediousness was caused
by the great round they were compelled to make to avoid
the coast of France, Captain Warren's orders being peremptory to keep out to sea, perfectly armed, and on no
account to surrender his prisoner. They at length reached
the harbor of Plymouth in frightful weather; here again
he encountered inhospitality: the ship was not permitted
to anchor, and rode out through the night in so tremendous a storm that the danger of being wrecked on the
rocks of that dangerous coast was every moment imminent.

How grateful was Lucien for the protection of Heaven,
when, after that tremendous night, he landed in safety
with his children at Plymouth! He here found Mr.
Mackenzie, a State messenger, authorized to offer him an
asylum and the rites of hospitality in their most extended
sense. Lucien, with his usual dignity, returned his
thanks with reserve and coldness, and continued: "I
have been made prisoner illegally, and I protest against
everything which myself and family have undergone
since we quitted the port of Cagliari; I demand to be
allowed to pursue my journey, and beyond that, sir, I
refuse all the offers of your Government, for I can accept nothing from a nation which is the enemy of mine,
nor from a Government that makes war upon my
brother." "Then," replied Mr. Mackenzie, coldly but
politely, "I am obliged to fulfill my commission."

The following day Lucien was conducted to Ludlow
Castle, and placed under the charge of Lord Powis, Lord-
Lieutenant of the county of Salop, and father-in-law of
the Duke of Northumberland. He was recommended by
all means to induce his prisoner to put himself in direct
opposition to the Emperor. His constant refusal produced
a more rigorous captivity, and he was confined to a circuit of two miles round Ludlow, the antique and gloomy
castle of which was of sinister omen, having been the
habitation of the unfortunate children of King Edward.
He obtained, however, at length, permission to quit
Ludlow, and to take up his residence at Thorngrove, on
the road to Worcester, a charming mansion, which he
had himself purchased of M. Lamotte, a Frenchman

established in England, for eighteen thousand guineas; it is surrounded by a park, inclosing a garden and hot-house, and possesses all those exterior and interior comforts so peculiar to the home of an English family.

Having tastefully completed the arrangements of his new habitation and hung the drawing-room with his family portraits, he laid down rules for the domestic life he intended to lead here. His love for the arts and sciences gained strength in this friendly retreat; he had always been fond of astronomy, and now pursued it with ardor. He visited Herschel at Slough, and purchased one of his famous telescopes for fifty thousand francs; he then built an observatory, calculated ephemerides, and announced a new planet in the Milky Way; he was not mistaken, and has the prior right to the merit of this discovery. Thorn-grove became a Lyceum. Lucien composed several comedies, which were acted in his domestic theater, also the tragedy of " Clotaire," a work of real merit, which was performed before an audience of more than two hundred persons, nearly all chosen from the middle classes of the neighborhood; for, considering the Ministry as his enemies, he would have no intercourse with Tories.

As the author, he chose to judge of the effect of the piece, and would therefore take no part in it; M. de Châtillon performed Clotaire; Madame Lucien played well in the becoming costume of Clotilde; the two chil-dren were represented by her young sons, Charles and Paul; the wife of Clotaire by Lucien's eldest daughter, Charlotte, now Princess Gabrielli; and Sigerie, the con-fidant of Clotaire, by Christina, also his daughter by his first wife [and now married to Lord Dudley Stuart], who, in the scarcity of actors in the family, was obliged to take a male part. It seems to me that Ludlow, the first prison of Edward's children, must have suggested to Lucien the plot of this tragedy.

The drama, however, was not the only subject of his muse during his residence at Thorngrove; here he com-pleted his poem of " Charlemagne," and produced that of " Cirneide." The Princess of Canino also, stimulated by his example, composed a poem on the subject of " Ba-thilde, Queen of the Franks"; it is well sustained, in six cantos, with verses of ten syllables in varied rhymes. I shall have occasion to speak of it again with relation to an extraordinary fact, of which I do not believe the Emperor capable, but which proves, at least, the extent to which a base inclination to flatter his supposed wishes was carried by those around him. M. de Châtillon was employed at the same time upon a small poem called the "Odyssey of Lucien; or, The Exile." He also sketched forty-eight designs for the illustration of "Charlemagne" and "Bathilde"; these sketches, which must necessarily embody the intentions of the authors, as they were drawn under their superintendence, were being engraved in London by the celebrated Heath, when the Restoration interrupted the series.

Every member of the family at Thorngrove was actively engaged. Every Sunday the work of the week was brought forward; an examination took place, also a competition for prizes; the day was closed with a concert, in which the young ladies sang, M. de Châtillon played the violin, and Father Maurice the piano.

Thus did Lucien embellish his retreat with everything that could tend to make time pass pleasurably, living like a really wise man, without any false pretensions to philosophy. His style of life excited much curiosity in England, but he studiously retired from observation with a calm and natural dignity which inspired general respect. The Duke of Norfolk, desirous of becoming acquainted with him, visited Thorngrove, where, cheerful, agreeable, and witty, he attracted the affections of the whole family during the three days he passed with them.

CHAPTER XV.

Junot Ordered to Spain — I Accompany Him — Our Journey —
Counter Order to Proceed to Burgos — French Justice — My Fright
— The Horrors of War — Vittoria — Letters from My Children —
Rumored Death of Durosnel — News Conveyed to Madame Duros-
nel — Lavalette Inexpert at Dissimulation — Dreadful Accident at
Prince Schwartzenberg's Ball — The Temporary Ballroom — The
Empress's Courage — The Emperor's Exertions to Render Assist-
ance to the Sufferers — Absence of the Engines — Princess Schwart-
zenberg Burned to Death — Escape of Prince Eugène and the
Vice-Queen — Death of the Princess de la Leyen — Madame de
Br——x — General Solignac — Cleansing of Burgos — Cruelty of
the Soldiers at Arguano — The Spaniard's Sacrifice.

ARLY in the year 1810 Junot received orders to proceed to Spain and there take the command of the 8th
division. This new proof of the Emperor's confidence
gave him no pleasure, for in this profitless Spanish war
all the sentiments of humanity had been outraged, the
glory of our arms had vanished, and victory itself was
unavailing. But it was necessary to obey. I followed
him, and my will alone determined me to take this step,
to which the Emperor reluctantly consented.

Junot's instructions were to reach Bayonne with as
little delay as possible; and we set out on the 2d of
February, when the cold was excessive. "You cannot
accompany me," said he. "Let us set out," I replied;
"you will find my strength greater than you expect."

I equipped myself in a gray cashmere riding habit, a
well-furred Polonese cap, having first had my hair
cropped, fur boots, and a large traveling cloak; and thus
defended I stepped at midnight into a close *calèche* with
Junot, and set out for Bayonne.

We traveled without stopping from Paris to Bordeaux,
and there halted for a few hours to enable me to visit
my aged and venerable friend Madame de Caseaux, who
with her daughter had but a few years before enjoyed
one of the largest fortunes in France; but it was rapidly
vanishing through the trickery of relations; and finding
it nearly dissipated, Laura, resolving to preserve her
mother's gray hairs from the privations of poverty, had

recently came up to Paris to solicit justice. Junot and I received her as a sister, and promoted her suit by every means at our command; but as its object was not yet accomplished we left her the possession of our Hôtel.

Twenty hours more conducted us to Bayonne, and these were partly employed in reading the foreign newspapers given to us by our banker at Bordeaux, and which we examined with avidity, well aware that our own had long published only what suited the Government. The English papers were the most interesting, and already dilated on the approaching marriage of Napoleon, though the Diocesan Court had only annulled his union with Josephine on the 18th of January, which sentence was afterward confirmed by the Metropolitan Court.

During the same journey Junot corrected my opinion of Marshal Soult, assuring me that so superior were his talents that it was a matter of astonishment to him that the Emperor had not intrusted to him the chief command in all Spain.

"But he could not command Marshal Jourdan," said I, with the prejudice of my childhood concerning precedency.

Junot laughed heartily. "Marshal Jourdan!" said he at length; "my dear little Laura, do not you know why he is a Marshal?"

I stared in amazement. "Why, because——"

"You know nothing about it—is not that the truth? Well, neither do I, for the whole army has equal pretensions to the distinction. But Soult! the deuce! he is quite another person! He is, after the Emperor, the most intelligent and capable of all the French generals."

Yet how perversely are men's sentiments and actions sometimes at variance. When Soult was appointed Major General in Spain in the place of Jourdan, Junot, like the others, refused obedience; and I shall presently have occasion to show the deplorable inconvenience resulting from such insubordination among the French chiefs.

Overcome with fatigue on our arrival at Bayonne, I merely disencumbered myself of my riding habit, and, throwing myself on a bed, was presently in a sound sleep, from which Junot awoke me with an embrace and ADIEU.

Starting up, I rubbed my eyes.

"What do you mean? ADIEU!"

"Yes, I here find new orders to enter Spain immediately, and to reach Burgos on the 15th; I have not,
therefore, a minute to lose. You will rejoin me by the
first convoy, and I shall leave you an escort of five hundred men of the battalion of Neufchâtel—men that you
may depend on—so be satisfied."

"Not I, indeed. I did not leave home to travel with
a convoy, or to attend to my personal conveniences. I
shall go with you."

Junot looked at me with mingled astonishment and
emotion.

"You will go with me? and without rest?"

"This instant."

"I will defer my departure, then; lie down again, and
sleep for a few hours."

"Not a single minute."

"Laura, you are unwell."

"No, I am quite well."

"Your hand is burning. I will not allow you to resume
your journey yet—the vanguard of the first division
commenced its march yesterday: a few hours' delay, therefore, will be no breach of duty. We will set out at noon."

"I assure you opposition only annoys me: let us set off
this instant: desire M. Prevôt to have my horse saddled,
and remember that I never intend to cause you a moment's delay: let that be understood between us once
for all—will you?"

I extended my hand to him as to a brother-in-arms;
and, indeed, the adventurous life on which I had entered
placed me on a level with that sex whose courage I was
compelled to assume. I had maturely weighed the enterprise and prepared myself for all emergencies. Junot
was therefore obliged to conform, and we departed, traveling alternately in the *calèche*, on horseback, or on foot,
through the Spanish-looking streets of Bayonne, with its
smiling environs, inhabited by the happiest peasantry
and most beautiful girls in France; the sandy solitudes
of Saint Jean de Luz, where we first inhaled the soft
and aromatic breezes of the South; Alegria, the home of
the Mendizabals; Villa Franca; Villa Real, with its pretty
churches; the picturesque valley of Bergara, with its
Gothic chapel; Mondragon, its sunny vale, and its mines

and mills of bloodstone; and the Salvator Rosa scenery
of Salinas.

But how deplorably were all these landscapes disfigured
by the horrors of war, an evidence of which presented itself
to me one evening, the fourth of my travels in Spain,
under a form that I can never forget. Quite worn out
with walking, I proposed entering the *calèche*, which
always followed us; Junot consented, and fell asleep the
moment we were comfortably seated.

Too much fatigued to follow his example, I sought refreshment at the carriage window, gazing on the steep
and winding road by which we were climbing the side
of a mountain, composed chiefly of brownish granite,
almost covered with moss, but here and there diversified
by groups of stunted oaks; my thoughts, which wandered
far from these surrounding objects, were recalled by my
eyes resting, through the increasing gloom of the twilight, upon the strange appearance of an isolated oak at
a short distance before us, the branches of which seemed
to be broken and swinging heavily in the wind. While
I was seeking my eyeglass to see it more distinctly we
reached the spot, and at the moment I stretched my
head out of the window my forehead encountered the
touch of a human foot!—the foot of a bloody and hor-
ribly mangled corpse, suspended from the tree: a specimen of French justice! nor was it alone: beside it hung
three of its former comrades!

The shriek that escaped me in the first moment of
horror awakened Junot and startled the sleepy postilion;
the latter instantly stopped his mules, leaving us sta-
tionary close to this spectacle, more terrific than imagination can conceive, and on which, in spite of myself, my
eyes would instinctively rest! Oh, how long afterward
did that fearful scene haunt my dreams! The ghastly
countenances, still expressive of demoniac rage, the torn
and clotted limbs, at which even the mules, pinching their
ears and dilating their nostrils, recoiled with an audible
demonstration of terror, made a painful and lasting impression.

"Will you proceed?" cried Junot to the postilion in a
voice of thunder, at the same time smartly striking the
nearest mule with his cane. The *calèche* started with
the celerity of lightning.

"What is the matter with you? It is a necessary evil," said Junot to me, quietly reseating himself in the corner of the carriage, and resuming his nap.

But, oh! I could not sleep; for many a night the balmy soother of our fears and griefs was scared from my pillow.

"Child," said Junot, when I afterward reproached him with his indifference, "you should not have faced war if you cannot endure such sights. What is it you have seen? four rascals who had probably massacerd some sleeping Frenchmen, or some woman, old man, or even child! Take my advice, and reserve your sensibility for other misfortunes."

A few days afterward, amid the tufts of thyme and lavender, and the box and juniper bushes growing among the rocks of Pancorvo, our soldiers discovered the fragments of a body which the assassins had cut to pieces, and on one of the mutilated arms recognized the vestige of a French uniform! Ah! Junot was right; the misfortunes of this war were terrible indeed!

Vittoria would be anywhere remarked as a pretty little town, but its architecture appears to particular advantage in Spain, differing as it does from the prevalent style of the country. The square is large and airy, and the whole aspect of the place indicative of industry and activity. Here I received, with a mother's transport, news from my children, the first which our uninterrupted progress had permitted to reach me.

Ever anxious about that absent portion of myself, which occupied my thoughts every hour in the day, I had written from Bordeaux to my good friend Lavalette, Director-General of the Post, requesting him to forward my letters by *estafette;* he, the best of fathers and of men, understood my maternal feelings, and himself fetched from my Hôtel, before my daughters left it with their aunt for Burgundy, the little packet which I now received by an *estafette* for Madrid. It contained two charming little letters from my girls, and at the foot of Josephine's my little Napoleon had scribbled his name — his hand being of course guided, for he was but two years old. The delicious joy of that moment can be conceived only by those who have been far separated from home, country, friends, and darling children.

Lavalette is another dear friend to whose name the tomb alone responds.

His character was such as Sterne would have delighted to depict — a curious combination of archness with in-genuousness, waggery with veracity and sincerity: at actual dissimulation he was very inexpert, of which I have heard a whimsical instance.

At the Battle of Wagram, Napoleon sent an order to one of the marshals by his favorite equerry and aid-de-camp, General Durosnel, and suddenly uttered a cry as he watched him with his telescope through the field. He had seen Durosnel struck by a bullet and rolling in the dust.

His death was a cause of mourning; he was yet young, and by his intelligent gallantry had acquired the love and esteem of his comrades, as well as of the Emperor, who eulogized him in the bulletin.

But there was one being whose heart was struck by this fatal bullet: the young and loving widow, whose visions of paradise were changed, in a moment, to grief and despair.

Durosnel, as upright as brave, had nothing to leave her: her expectations of provision rested on the Emperor; but, at all events, she could no longer reside in Paris. Her father therefore came from the country to fetch her, and preparations were making for their departure, when, about ten days after the news had reached Paris, the Empress Josephine received a letter from the Emperor in which he said:

« Durosnel is not killed, he is not even wounded; the bullet struck only his horse; LET HIS WIFE KNOW THIS.»

The commission was not easy of execution. So inured is the poor human heart to every variety of suffering that grief in any form cannot surprise it; but joy, a joy that snatches us at once from despair to bliss, oh! that must not be too rudely administered.

The Empress, knowing the effect her news must have on Madame Durosnel, was in great perplexity, and meditated going herself to her, when Lavalette and his wife arrived to breakfast with her Majesty.

"Ah! Heaven has sent you to my aid," she exclaimed.

Then, explaining the whole affair, she imposed the task

on Lavalette, and adding the caution—"Take care what you are about, for you may KILL HER," she pushed him by the shoulders, and sent him to Madame Durosnel. The good-natured Lavalette gladly undertook to carry peace to an afflicted bosom; but just as he reached the door he began to be staggered by the amount of happiness his tidings imported, and to comprehend the delicacy of his mission.

"*Diable!*" thought the AMBASSADOR, as he ascended the stairs; "I almost repent my hasty compliance."

It was barely eleven o'clock, an ill-selected hour for a visit, as the father would probably have hinted; but the Empress's name silenced all objections, and he was immediately introduced into Madame Durosnel's boudoir, where she was seated on a sofa, silent and sorrowful, dressed in weeds, weepers, and all the mournful paraphernalia of early widowhood. As he gazed on her pale and altered countenance, and on the languid eye, raised to meet his, he thought:

"The Empress is right—I shall certainly kill her."

He sat down beside her, but after the first salutation had not a word to offer, while Madame Durosnel, supposing he came to announce some favor from the Emperor, properly waited till he should open the conference. Finding him, however, obstinately silent, she at length began with a trembling voice:

"Her Majesty is doubly gracious in condescending——"

Lavalette started as if suddenly aroused from a dream.

"Madame," said he, "are you beginning to feel consolation?"

"Ah, sir!" was all the wretched mourner could reply, and her face was instantly bathed in tears.

"Deuce take it!" he inwardly ejaculated; "if she reverts to her despair, what can I do?"

And he began turning over every expedient that might put her upon the scent; none appeared more likely than inquiring whether she believed in ghosts.

"Alas! no, sir; would that I could both believe and see them!" and her tears flowed afresh.

In proportion as her grief interested him did the perplexity of her comforter increase; but as something must be done, he at last devised a tale of a woman buried in a trance, and recalled from the tomb by the gravedigger

opening it with a design of plunder. This story he related with all the accompaniments of romance, dwelling
with especial emphasis on the ineffable joy of his heroine's family on recovering their beloved from the jaws
of death. . . .

"Alas!" ejaculated Madame Durosnel, in a voice interrupted by sobs; "they were very happy!"

And she buried her head in the cushions, both to weep
at liberty and to avoid the sight of a man who seemed
to be making a jest of her affliction.

Lavalette began to think his task hopeless, but resolving on a new attempt, he assumed an air of cheerfulness
that contrasted strangely with his anxiety. Putting on
his best smiles, he asked Madame Durosnel whether she
had breakfasted.

"Ah, *Mon Dieu!*" she exclaimed, beginning to suspect
the Empress Josephine's nephew was somewhat crazed.

Lavalette grew impatient, and repeated the inquiry.

"I do not know, sir," she answered, "whether you are
aware that your discourse is very extraordinary. I beg
permission to retire."

"And how is it, Madame," retorted Lavalette, "that
you cannot discover the real object of my mission?"

His expressive countenance conveyed all the rapture
his news imported, and Madame Durosnel, as she surveyed it, fell back on the sofa, exclaiming:

"Ah! what can have happened?"

"Why, nothing at all — nothing has happened! Do you
now understand me, Madame? Will you divest yourself
of those villainous weeds? Your husband is not dead!"
and having uttered the decisive words, he sank down exhausted with the effort. Meanwhile, an alarming shriek
from the overjoyed wife brought her father to her aid,
and Lavalette hastened to escape. The blunt manner in
which, after all his reflections, he had communicated such
joyful tidings had nearly overset Madame Durosnel's reason.

Two years afterward, at Prince Schwartzenberg's ball,
this lady was thrown down and trampled on in the confusion occasioned by the fire; her husband found her in
a state of insensibility, and a man standing over her
occupied in abstracting her earrings from her ears. Her
arms and legs were dreadfully burned, while, strange to
say, her silk stockings were scarcely singed.

This disaster, which gave rise to so many sinister forebodings, took place on Sunday, 1st of July. Prince
Schwartzenberg occupied the old Hôtel Montesson, in the
Rue de Provence; and the apartments not being sufficiently spacious to accommodate the immense concourse
of company, a temporary ballroom was constructed in
the garden. It was like a fairy palace. Flowers, per-
fumes, delicious music, the dazzling splendor of diamonds and rubies, all combined to render it a scene of
Oriental enchantment. The walls of the ballroom were
covered with gold and silver brocade, and ornamented
with draperies of spangled gauze fastened by bouquets
of flowers, while hundreds of crystal girandoles shed
their prismatic luster over the glittering scene.

When the fire was first discovered, the Emperor was
passing round the room and conversing with the ladies.
There was but one door for the ingress and egress of
the company. It was a very large one, opening into
the garden, and fronting the Throne. At the back of
the Throne there was a small wooden gallery, which
made a communication between the ballroom and the
house. It was in the angle of this little gallery that the
fire was first discovered. The ball had just commenced,
and a great part of the company were dancing.

It was at the time remarked as very extraordinary
that nobody thought of ascending the gallery above
mentioned and escaping into the house; but it was certainly natural to fly FROM the flames which issued from
the house, or at least appeared to do so. The Empress
was in conversation with some ladies at a little distance
from the Throne, and when the confusion and alarm
commenced, she, with great *sang-froid*, or perhaps it
may be called courage, ascended the steps of the Throne,
seated herself, and waited till the Emperor went to her.

As to the Emperor, his conduct on this occasion was
beyond all praise. He handed the Empress into the first
carriage which he found standing in the courtyard, and
accompanied her as far as the Place Louis XV. He then
returned alone to Prince Schwartzenberg's Hôtel, where
he actively exerted himself in giving orders and assisting
the persons who had been burned or otherwise hurt.
On the Emperor's return the engines had not yet arrived.
The Austrian Embassy were loud in their praise of the

noble confidence evinced by the Emperor in returning alone to the scene of terror in the middle of the night. He remained on the spot till half-past three on the following morning.

The deeply-lamented victim of this catastrophe, the unfortunate Princess Schwartzenberg, was killed by returning to the ballroom in search of her daughter, who, however, had been saved. A luster fell from the ceiling on the head of the Princess and fractured her skull. She fell into an aperture, caused by the burning of the floor, and her body, with the exception of her bosom and part of one arm, was burned to a cinder. The body was recognizable only by a gold chain round the neck, to which was suspended a locket set round with jewels, whose initial letters formed a motto. The Princess was one of the most charming women of her time: beautiful, amiable, graceful, and accomplished.

Prince Eugène had the good fortune to perceive a small private door behind the Throne, which had been made for the use of the servants who handed round the refreshments. The Prince saved his wife by conducting her through that door to the interior of the house. The Princesse de la Leyen, the niece of the Prince Primate, was burned in a most frightful manner. Like the Princess Schwartzenberg, she had left her daughter dancing, and returned to the ballroom to rescue her. The young lady and her father, after fruitlessly searching for the Princess, concluded that she had returned to Passy, where they resided. On reaching home, however, they found she was not there.

The family then became dreadfully alarmed. The Prince threw off his embroidered coat and decorations, and hastened back to Paris in search of her. Meanwhile a Swedish officer had carried out from the burning ruins of the ballroom the almost lifeless remains of a female. Her countenance was so blackened and disfigured that it was impossible to recognize her features. The silver mounting of her diamond tiara had melted, and penetrated into her head. Hearing a faint groan uttered by what appeared to be merely a mass of cinder, the officer discovered that life was not yet extinct. He conveyed the Princess to a shop in the neighborhood of the Ambassador's Hôtel, where every attention was rendered to her.

After various unintelligible ejaculations, the Princess was heard to utter the word " Passy."

Eager to accomplish his humane task, the officer engaged a *fiacre* and drove the unfortunate lady to Passy, inquiring at every house of respectability whether anyone was missing. At length he reached the abode of the Princesse de la Leyen, whose frightful condition exceeded the worst which the fears of her family had pictured. The unfortunate lady expired on the following day, having lingered four-and-twenty hours in indescribable agony.

A lady of my acquaintance, Madame de Br——x, *dame de compagnie* to Madame Mère, was at Prince Schwartzenberg's *fête*. On the alarm of fire being given, she endeavored to reach the door, but in the confusion she was thrown down and trampled on. With great effort she succeeded in raising herself up, and crawled, as she supposed, to a seat, but the floor appeared to sink under her, and she fell.

She had been unconsciously hurried into the garden, and the hollow into which she fell was a basin, which luckily happened to be dry at the time. By this means her life was saved, but she was dreadfully bruised, and the scars on her arms and neck were indelible memorials of Prince Schwartzenberg's *fête*. This melancholy accident, in addition to its own immediate and fatal consequences, had the effect of creating a sort of superstitious terror. It naturally called to mind a similar catastrophe which occurred on the marriage of Louis XVI. and Marie Antoinette.

To return to Spain. At the miserable little village of Bribiesca we met General Regnier, whom I had not seen since the Egyptian campaign. The animated expression of his astonishment at the *rencontre* formed an agreeable contrast with his habitual reserve. I, however, always admired his calm dignity, and his comrades acknowledged his military talents.

Alas! our next meeting was in a desert yet more wild than Bribiesca.

I rejoiced on arriving at Burgos, where the Duke's headquarter's were fixed, for I was seriously ill, and much in want of repose. Here I enjoyed all its charms, and the consciousness that I was not compelled to raise my head from its pillow at the beat of drum imparted real luxury to the sound of the morning reveille.

General Solignac was under great obligations to Junot for procuring him employment at the recommendation of the Grand-Duchess of Berg, in spite of Napoleon's invincible repugnance to him; and we found him stationed *ad interim* at Burgos, in lieu of General Thiébault, whose generous conduct, talents, and enlightened humanity had converted the anathemas which the Castilians so liberally vented against us into blessings.

He had been invested with the government of Old Castile, on taking possession of which he found that Burgos, although one of the most important posts in Spain, had been for two months unrestrained by the presence of any authority. It is impossible to give an idea of the amount of devastation, pillage, and assassination to which its vicinity was exposed. On our side, the most revolting injustice was daily committed, and atrocities were frequently perpetrated upon us in reprisal; these were again avenged, and a chain of horrors thus established, which afforded no hope of termination. But General Thiébault had the courage to break through it.

Justice, with her tribunals and her judges, had fled as before the sword of the exterminating angel; the few remaining inhabitants were indifferent to life, and wandered like specters through the ill-paved streets of Burgos, without wounding their feet against pointed stones, for the ground was covered with a thick bed of filth, the infected receptacle of more than a hundred human and two hundred animal carcasses. Is it not astonishing that its mephitic exhalations had not added the plague to the catalogue of woes which afflicted the unhappy Peninsula? Another month's delay, and that scourge must have followed.

Thiébault, on his arrival, saw nothing within a circuit of four or five leagues round the city but ruin, despair, and death. The condition of the barracks, the detached depots, and, above all, of the prisons and hospitals was deplorable.

Don Blanco de Salcedo, the Prefect, was a worthy man, but incompetent to remedy this mass of evil. When called upon he seconded General Thiébault with laudable zeal, but with little hope of success; and when the

General proposed to begin by cleansing the city, he shook his head, saying, " Your Excellency might as well attempt to cleanse the Augean stable." But Thiébault had not forgotten Junot's recent achievement of clearing the streets of Lisbon in 1807 of the mines caused by the earthquake of 1755, and of all other obstructions, which was not one of the least considerable benefits conferred by his Government.

The present undertaking was equally successful, and in a few months Burgos put on a new face. The shops were reopened, the markets frequented, justice resumed its course; prisons and barracks were erected, and a promenade planted along the bank of the Arlanzon, to which spot the General, willing to flatter at once the fanaticism and chivalry of the Castilians, removed the St. Peter of Cardena, and the bones of the Cid and Donna Ximena, whose tomb had been violated by our dragoons. The tomb itself he rebuilt, and it still remains, preserved with religious care, in a garden, bordered by the same river, which the Dowager-Marchioness de Villuena has since purchased from the city of Burgos. The Prefect, Corregidor, Intendant — all the authorities, in short, of Burgos, were unanimous in their tribute of praise and gratitude to Thiébault.

His predecessor I will not name: it is unnecessary to add to the pangs of remorse the martyrdom of public censure, but his name was pronounced with abhorrence, and the following is an instance of the terror he inspired:

A regiment was sent from Burgos against a guerrilla party, under the Marquis of Villa Campo, and ordered to treat the Spaniards with the most rigorous severity, especially the inhabitants of Arguano, a little village near the famous forest of Covelleda, whose deep shades, intersected only by narrow footpaths, were the resort of banditti and guerrillas. A principal feature of the whole Spanish war was the celerity with which all our movements were notified to the insurgent leaders, and the difficulty we experienced in procuring a spy or a trustworthy guide.

The battalion had to march through a frightful country, climbing rugged rocks, and crossing frozen torrents, always in dread of unforeseen and sudden dangers. They reached the village, but perceived no movement — heard no noise. Some soldiers advanced, but saw nothing — absolute solitude reigned. The officer in command, suspecting an ambush, ordered the utmost circumspection. The troops entered the street, and arrived at a small opening, where some sheaves of wheat and Indian corn, and a quantity of loaves, were still smoking on the ground, but consumed to a cinder, and swimming in floods of wine, which had streamed from leathern skins that had evidently been purposely broached, as the provisions had been burned to prevent their falling into the hands of the French.

No sooner had the soldiers satisfied themselves that, after all their toils and dangers, no refreshment was to be obtained, than they shouted with rage . . . but no vengeance was within reach! All the inhabitants had fled! — fled into that forest, where they might defy pursuit.

Suddenly cries were heard issuing from one of the deserted cottages among which the soldiers had dispersed themselves, in hopes of discovering some food or booty; they proceeded from a young woman holding a child a year old in her arms, whom the soldiers were dragging before their Lieutenant.

" Stay, Lieutenant," said one of them; " here is a woman we have found sitting beside an old one who is past speaking; question her a little."

She was dressed in the peasant costume of the Soria and Rioja mountains, and was pale but not trembling.

" Why are you alone here ? " asked the Lieutenant.

" I stayed with my grandmother, who is paralytic and could not follow the rest to the forest," replied she haughtily, and as if vexed at being obliged to drop a word in presence of a Frenchman — " I stayed to take care of her."

" Why have your neighbors left the village ? "

The Spaniard's eyes flashed fire; she fixed on the Lieutenant a look of strange import, and answered:

" You know very well; were they not all to be massacred ? "

The Lieutenant shrugged his shoulders.

" But why did you burn the bread and wheat, and empty the wine skins ? "

"That you might find nothing; as they could not carry them off there was no alternative but burning them."

At this moment shouts of joy arose, and the soldiers appeared, carrying a number of hams, some loaves, and, more welcome than all, several skins of wine, all discovered in a vault, the entrance to which was concealed by the straw the old woman was lying on. The young peasant darted on them a glance of fiendish vengeance, while the Lieutenant, who had pondered with anxiety on the destitute condition of his troops, and the sinking sun, rejoiced for a moment in the unexpected supply. But the recent poisoning of several cisterns, and other fearful examples, putting him on his guard, he again interrogated the woman:

"Whence come these provisions?"

"They are the same as those we burned; we concealed them for our friends."

"Is your husband with yonder brigands?"

"My husband is in heaven!" said she, lifting up her eyes; "he died for the good cause — that of God and King Ferdinand!"

"Have you any brothers among them?"

"I have no longer a tie . . . except my poor child" — and she pressed the infant to her heart . . . the poor little creature was thin and sallow, but its large black eyes glistened as they turned to its mother.

"Commander," exclaimed one of the soldiers, "pray order division of the booty, for we are very hungry and thirsty."

"One moment, my man; listen," said he, eyeing the young woman with suspicion; "these provisions are good, I hope?"

"How should they be otherwise?" replied the Spaniard contemptuously; "they were not for you."

"Well! here's to thy health then, demonia," said a young sublieutenant, opening one of the skins and preparing for a draught; but his more prudent commander still restrained him.

"One moment. Since this wine is good, you will not object to a glass."

"Oh dear no! as much as you please."

And, accepting the mess-glass offered by the Lieutenant, she emptied it without hesitation.

"Huzza huzza!" shouted the soldiers, delighted at the prospect of intoxication without danger.

"And your child will drink some also," said the Lieutenant; "he is so pale that it will do him good."

The Spaniard had herself drunk without hesitation, but in holding the cup to her infant's lips her hand trembled; the motion, however, was unperceived, and the child also emptied his glass. Thereupon the provisions speedily disappeared, and all partook both of the food and wine. Suddenly, however, the infant was observed to turn livid, its features contracted, and its mouth, convulsed with agony, gave vent to piteous shrieks. The mother, too, though her fortitude suppressed all complaint, could scarcely stand, and her distorted features betrayed her sufferings.

"Wretch!" exclaimed the Commandant, "thou hast poisoned us!"

"Yes," said she with a ghastly smile, falling to the ground beside her child, already struggling with the death rattle. "Yes, I have poisoned you — I knew you would fetch the skins from their hiding place — was it likely you would leave a dying creature undisturbed on her litter? Yes — yes — you will die, and die in perdition — while I shall go to heaven——"

Her last words were scarcely audible, and the soldiers did not at first comprehend the full horror of their situation; but as the poison operated, the Spaniard's declaration was legibly translated in her convulsed features. No power could longer restrain them; in vain their commander interposed; they repulsed him, and, dragging their expiring victim by the hair to the brink of the torrent, they threw her into it, after lacerating her with more than a hundred saber strokes. She uttered not a groan. As for the child, it was the first victim.

Twenty-two men were destroyed by this exploit — which I cannot call otherwise than great and heroic. The commander himself told me he escaped by miracle. The persuasion that the bed of death would be disturbed in search of booty was indeed holding us as savages; and such was the impression produced by the man who could command: "Let no sanctuary deter your search." By such means were the populace from the beginning exasperated against us, and especially by the

oppressions of General D——. If the inhabitants of Arguano had not received information that they were to
be massacerd, they would not have taken the lead in
massacer.

Such were the people among whom I dwelt. When
this tale was related to me, on the eve of my departure
from Burgos, I shuddered in contemplating the murderous war of people against people! I trembled for the
first time since my entrance into Spain. I became timid.
Alas! it was not on my own account; but I was again
approaching the great crisis of maternity, and amid
what perils, good God! was my child destined to see
the light!

CHAPTER XVI.

Napoleon's Marriage with Maria Louisa—Union of the Papal States
with France—General Kellerman—Junot Quits Valladolid—Siege
of Astorga—Nuptial Festivities in Paris—Maria Louisa's Regret
at Leaving Vienna—Her Favorite Dog—Berthier's Scheme—Arrival of the Empress in France—Her Interview with the Emperor
—A Surprise—The Emperor and Empress Visit Belgium—Abdication of Louis, King of Holland—Projected Treaty with England
—M. Labouchere's Mission to London—Louis Accuses Napoleon
of Bad Faith—Fouché—The Intrigue Unraveled.

I WAS at Burgos when I received the first intelligence
of Napoleon's intended marriage with Maria Louisa.
A friend who wrote to me from Paris spoke of the
disastrous influence which a marriage with an Austrian
Princess was likely to exercise on the destiny of Napoleon. He was, it is true, Emperor of the French, but
he was likewise GENERAL BONAPARTE, who had gained
more than twenty pitched battles over Austria, and who
had twice forced the Imperial Family to fly from their
palace. These were injuries which could not but leave
indelible stains behind them.

The sacrifice which the Emperor Francis was now
about to make bore an odious stamp of selfishness. It
appeared by no means improbable that at some future
time the voice of his daughter, when appealing to him on

13

behalf of her son and her husband, would be no more listened to than when she remonstrated for herself. It was evident that Austria, humbled and mutilated as she was, greeted this marriage only as a temporary balm to her wounds. Napoleon's object was to consolidate his Northern alliances, already well secured on the part of Russia, and to prosecute still further his fatal operations in the Peninsula.

It was likewise during my stay at Burgos that I heard of the union of the Papal States with France. It would be difficult to describe the effect which this intelligence produced in Spain. It was speedily followed by the circulation of thousands of copies of the Bull of Excommunication. Children, even in the tender age of infancy, were taught to lisp the most horrible imprecations on the French. Only those who were witnesses to the reaction which took place in Spain at this period can form a just estimate of the error which Napoleon committed in taking possession of the city of Rome, and making the Pope his captive.

We left Burgos for Valladolid, Junot having received orders to establish there the headquarters of the 8th corps. General Regnier and the 2d corps were near the Tagus, and Marshal Ney, with the 6th corps, was in Salamanca. General Kellerman, Comte de Valmy, was then Governor of Valladolid and of all the kingdom of Leon, as well as of the Asturias and a portion of Spanish Estremadura.

General Kellerman received me with the most marked courtesy. The residence prepared for me was the palace of Charles V., situated in the grand square of the city, and which had formerly been the Hôtel of the Inquisition. The palace is a fine building, and General Kellerman had taken great pains to arrange it for my reception. It did not, it is true, retain the magnificence which it presented when it was the abode of the monarch above mentioned; but such as it was, it appeared to me a paradise after my prison at Burgos.

Junot had received from Paris a letter written by the Prince de Neufchâtel, informing him that the Emperor having directed General Suchet to prosecute actively the sieges of all the towns of Catalonia and Aragon, his Majesty was also anxious that the towns of the west, which still held out, should fall at the same time. Consequently Junot was to take Astorga as speedily as possible.

Junot was overjoyed at the receipt of this letter, and immediately ordered Colonel Valazé and General Boyer, the chief officers of his staff, to make the requisite preparations. He was on the point of departing for Astorga, when he received dispatches from Madrid, directing him to proceed to Salamanca to succeed Ney, who was to be removed to some other place.

I observed that Junot was much ruffled on reading this dispatch. "Why," said I, "should you vex yourself about these contradictory orders? You cannot obey them both. Write to Marshal Ney, and see what his answer will be. His movements must correspond with yours, and yours with his."

Junot followed my advice, and Valladolid not being far from Salamanca, he received an answer in two days. Ney informed Junot that he had received orders from the Commander-in-Chief of the French army, the Prince de Neufchâtel, which orders certainly did not authorize them to fall back on Valladolid. He added that he thought it also the duty of Junot to obey the instructions of Berthier, for that he and the Emperor were their ONLY COMMANDERS.

On learning Ney's resolution, Junot resolved to commence the siege of Astorga. Such was the conduct of the generals whom the Emperor placed under each other's orders in Spain. I shall have to record many examples of the same kind which occurred after the arrival of Masséna.

Junot quitted Valladolid on the 14th of April, and arrived at Astorga on the 17th. As he was passing the bridge of Leon a musket ball fell at the distance of a few paces from his horse, between him and his aid-de-camp. The musket had been fired from a little hill near the bridge. Two officers immediately ascended to the summit of the hill, but no one was to be seen. Junot had a narrow escape, for the assassin had taken his aim well.

On his arrival at Astorga, Junot fixed his headquarters at Castrillo. The digging of the trenches continued for two days, and on the 20th Junot ordered the firing to commence. At seven in the evening the breach was opened. Next day, the 21st, Junot gave orders for an attack. The breach was carried by the *bataillon d'élite*, commanded by M. de Lagrave, one of the Duke's aids-de-camp, a brave and intelligent young officer. At four in the morning of the 22d the town offered to capitulate, and at one in the afternoon the garrison, amounting to 3,500 men, defiled before the Duke and marched in the direction of France.

On the day when the first column of prisoners arrived at Valladolid, M. Magnien asked me to go out in a *calèche* to see them defile. The weather was delightfully fine, and I should have enjoyed an agreeable drive but for a circumstance which filled me with feelings of the most painful kind. I suddenly heard a discharge of musketry at a little distance, and the report of the firing re-echoed amid the hills which rose along the roadside.

"What is that?" said I to M. Magnien. He could not inform me, and he repeated my question to an officer who commanded the convoy of the prisoners.

"Oh, nothing," replied the officer carelessly; "some of those fellows pretend to be lame, and say they cannot march, so I have ordered them to be shot, that's all. Lame indeed! I'll answer for it, that if we were to leave them behind they would soon find the use of their legs to rejoin Don Julian!"

I was horror-struck, and could scarcely believe that I had understood the man rightly. We had by this time arrived at a turn of the road, and I saw two men fall. I felt my blood curdle, and the chill of death seemed to be creeping over me. "Turn back! for heaven's sake, turn back!" I exclaimed to Magnien; "I cannot bear this!"

"And do you imagine, madame," said the officer who had charge of the convoy, "that our prisoners are better treated on board the pontoons of Cadiz? My brother perished there." These words were uttered in a tone and accompanied by a look of revenge which seemed like a sentence of death on the wretched captives.

The musket shot which was fired at Junot on his way from Valladolid to Astorga reminds me of another attempt to assassinate him which occurred at Lisbon. His

aids-de-camp had frequently been troubled by applications
from a man who solicited an audience of the Duke,
under various frivolous pretenses. At length, M. Hersant,
one of Junot's aids-de-camp, arrested the man one evening when he was endeavoring to slip into the interior
apartments unperceived. He was searched, and upon his
person were found a *poignard* and a knife. He did not
deny his murderous design, trusting that the presence
of the English would save him. But, to do them justice,
they showed no disposition to interfere in the affair, except to urge the punishment of the criminal.

Junot himself passed sentence on him. "Go your ways,"
said he; "I will not shed your blood. There are twenty
piasters for you, and tell your comrades that I offer a
hundred to anyone who will come here and follow your
example."

Meanwhile Paris was enlivened by *fêtes* in honor of the
Imperial nuptials. The letters which I received from my
friends were like the descriptions in romances and fairy
tales. As I was not in Paris at that time, I will not enter into a detail of matters which I did not witness; but
I cannot forbear relating the following anecdote connected with Napoleon's marriage:

Berthier, Prince de Neufchâtel, was sent to Vienna to
conduct the Empress to Paris. After she had been married by proxy [to her uncle, Prince Charles], and all the
forms and ceremonies were gone through (which in Vienna is a work of no little time), the day of departure
was fixed. The young Archduchess often shed tears of
regret at her approaching separation from her family.
In the Imperial Family of Austria the bonds of relation-
ship are sacredly revered; and even in the reign of Maria Theresa, and under the cold and artful policy of
Kaunitz, family ties were held dear. Maria Louisa had
been educated in these feelings: she wept to leave
her sisters, her father, and her stepmother, and perhaps also she wept at the thought of being united to a
man who must have been to her almost an object of
terror.

At length the day of departure arrived. The young
Empress bade farewell to all the members of her family,
and then retired to her apartment, where etiquette required that she should wait till Berthier came to conduct

her to her carriage. When Berthier entered the cabinet he found her bathed in tears. With a voice choked by sobs she apologized for appearing so childish. "But," said she, "my grief is excusable. See how I am surrounded here by a thousand things that are dear to me. These are my sister's drawings, that tapestry was wrought by my mother, those paintings are by my Uncle Charles." In this manner she went through the inventory of her cabinet, and there was scarcely a thing, down to the carpet on the floor, which was not the work of some beloved hand. There were her singing birds, her parrot, and, above all, the object which she seemed to value most, and most to regret — a little dog.

It was, of course, known at the Court of Vienna how greatly the Emperor used to be annoyed by Josephine's favorite pet dogs, with Fortuné at their head. Therefore Francis II., like a prudent father, took care that his daughter should leave her pet dog at Vienna. Yet it was a cruel separation, and the Princess and her favorite parted with a tender duo of complaint.

But these regrets, childish as they may appear, Berthier regarded as proofs of a kind and affectionate heart, and when he beheld the tears of the young Archduchess, whom he had expected to find all radiant with smiles, a scheme entered his mind which he tacitly resolved to carry into execution. "I have merely come to acquaint your Majesty," said he, "that you need not depart for two hours to come. I will therefore withdraw until that time." He went immediately to the Emperor and acquainted him with his plan. Francis II., who was the most indulgent of fathers, readily assented to the proposition. Berthier gave his orders, and in less than two hours all was ready.

The Empress left Vienna and soon entered France; she found herself surrounded by festivals and rejoicings, and almost forgot the parrot and the dog. She arrived at Compiègne, and was there met by the Emperor, who stopped her carriage, stepped into it, and seated himself by her side; they proceeded to Saint Cloud and thence to Paris. There Fortune bestowed one of her last smiles on her favorite son, when, leading into the balcony of the Tuileries his young bride, whom he regarded as the pledge of lasting peace and alliance, he presented her to the multitude who were assembled beneath the windows of the Palace.*

On returning from the balcony, he said to her: "Well, Louise, I must give you some little reward for the happiness you have conferred on me;" and leading her into one of the narrow corridors of the Palace, lighted only by one lamp, he hurried on with his beloved Empress, who exclaimed: "Where are we going?" "Come, Louise, come, are you afraid to follow me?" replied the Emperor, who now pressed to his bosom, with much affectionate tenderness, his young bride.

Suddenly they stopped at a closed door, within which they heard a dog that was endeavoring to escape from the apparent prison. The Emperor opened this private door, and desired Louise to enter. She found herself in a room magnificently lighted; the glare of the lamps prevented her for some moments from distinguishing any object; imagine her surprise when she found her favorite dog from Vienna was there to greet her; the apartment was furnished with the same chairs, carpet, the paintings of her sisters, her birds—in short, every object was there, and placed in the room in the same manner as she had left them on quitting her paternal roof.

The Empress, in joy and in gratitude, threw herself in Napoleon's arms, and the moment of a great victory would not have been to the conqueror of the world so sweet as this instant of ecstasy was to the infatuated heart of the adoring bridegroom. After a few minutes had been spent in examining the apartment, the Emperor opened a small door; he beckoned to Berthier, who entered. Napoleon then said: "Louise, it is to him you are indebted for this unexpected joy: I desire you will embrace him, as a just recompense." Berthier took the hand of the Empress, but the Emperor added: "No, no; you must kiss my old and faithful friend."

* "The Empress Maria Louisa was nineteen years of age when she married Napoleon; her hair was of a light color, her eyes blue and expressive, her walk was noble and her figure imposing. Her hands and feet were formed in perfect beauty, and might serve for models. Health, youth, and a florid complexion were joined to much timidity: this latter occasioned the Empress to appear haughty before the ladies of the Court; in private, however, she was amiable, and even affectionate. She appeared to love the Emperor, and was devoted to his will."—*Constant.*

Some weeks after his marriage the Emperor took the Empress with him into Belgium. Maria Louisa received the homage that was paid to her with a certain air of indifference, and there then seemed little reason to expect that she would do the honors of the Court with the grace and amiability which she subsequently displayed.

But an event which caused me more astonishment than all that was going on in Paris was the FORCED abdication of Louis, King of Holland. Louis had been a dear friend of my mother, and his kind and amiable temper made me esteem him very highly. His conduct, which some have blamed and others approved, was in my opinion always that of an honest man. He had a circle of friends devotedly attached to him, and these friends were also mine. I received through them the details of the revolution in Holland — for the abdication of Louis must be termed a revolution.

Louis comprehended his brother's Continental System; but he understood better the interests of the people he had been called upon to govern. These people, who were strangers to customhouse duties, and who were at one period of their history the most flourishing commercial nation in the world, were languishing beneath the terrible system of confiscations and prohibitions. Louis refused to be any longer the instrument of a system of tyranny which was a deathblow to the prosperity of Holland.

Hereupon the Emperor directed an army, commanded by General Oudinot, to advance into Holland. Louis then abdicated, but only in favor of his son. This abdication was rejected. Marshal Oudinot entered Amsterdam, and Europe learned that Holland was incorporated with the French Empire.

When Napoleon found that his brother would not bend to his will, he requested, or rather ordered, his abdication. Louis was of an amiable and pliant disposition; but when he was required to take a step which he could not consent to without injuring his children and his subjects, he displayed a remarkable degree of firmness. He consented to abdicate, but only on certain conditions.

He proposed to his brother that overtures should be made to England, and by rendering the affairs of Holland the basis of a treaty, peace might be obtained, provided France was willing to concede what Louis desired. The Emperor consented to this, and the King of Holland sent M. Labouchere to England to open negotiations. The Marquis of Wellesley was then at the head of the English Ministry. M. Labouchere was well known as one of the first bankers in Europe. His transactions with England were extensive and honorable. Every facility was consequently afforded him for effecting the desired object. The affair proceeded as well as could be wished, when, in an interview which the King of Holland had with his brother, I think at Antwerp, he asked the Emperor why, in an affair which concerned his happiness and the honor of his crown, he behaved with such bad faith, and exposed him to such treatment on the part of England. The Emperor stared at him with astonishment, and knew not what he meant.

"While," continued the King of Holland, "I have in perfect good faith sent to England an honorable man, whose very presence is a sufficient guarantee of my intentions, you have sent an obscure intriguer, for no other would accept such a mission, to treat for you without my concurrence." "It is false!" exclaimed the Emperor, his eyes flashing with rage: "I say it is false!" "And I repeat that it is true," continued his brother. "M. Labouchere has been informed of the fact." "In the devil's name," exclaimed the Emperor, "to whom do you allude? I know nothing of him! . . . I have sent no one!" "But your minister, Fouché, has," said Louis. "I repeat that the individual I allude to is at present in London, negotiating for you, and discussing those very interests which were to form the basis of our treaty. Is this all the confidence I can place in a brother's promise?"

The Emperor was greatly agitated; he turned pale, and pressed his forehead with his hand, threw himself into his chair, and then rose up again. At length, stepping up to his brother, he said: "I perceive there is some plot here; but I know nothing of it. As a Sovereign and a brother, I pledge my word of honor that I am ignorant of it. Do you believe me?" "I do," replied Louis; "but it behooves you to seek out the author of this foul intrigue. It is a duty you owe to me as well as to your own honor. Who could have dared thus to

act in your name?" To this question the Emperor made
no answer, but it was evident that a terrible cloud was
gathering. His brow lowered, his lips were compressed,
and everything betokened a dreadful ebullition of rage.
"You may rely on it, I will discover this tissue of deception," said he to his brother; "I have my suspicion of
the serpent who has been laying his snare."

On his return to Paris the Emperor put the affair into
the hands of Dubois, who speedily discovered that Fouché
sent agents to England much more frequently than the
affairs of the Police required. Having found the thread
of the intrigue, he soon traced out the whole, and the
emissary was arrested and sent to the Temple. This
man proved to be Chevalier Fagan, a returned emigrant.
He confidently believed that he was acting on the part
of the Emperor, and had no idea that he was merely an
agent of Fouché. The result of this affair was Fouché's
disgrace, the cause of which was entirely unknown at
the time.

Other events, equally curious, were going on in the
north of Europe. Bernadotte was chosen King of Sweden
by the States-General assembled at Orebro, and Charles
XIII. adopted him as his son. When he presented himself at the Tuileries to announce to the Emperor his
elevation to the Throne of Sweden, Napoleon did not
appear inclined to allow him to go and reign so far off.
Bernadotte, observing his scruples, said: "Would your
Majesty, then, elevate me above yourself by forcing me
to refuse a crown?" The Emperor looked confused, but
immediately recovering his presence of mind, answered:
"Well! well! be it so! Our destinies must be fulfilled."
Subsequent events proved that the Emperor's fears of
Bernadotte were not unfounded.

CHAPTER XVII.

Fêtes at Valladolid — Arrival of the Prince d'Essling — The Cortége — Masséna's Companion — His Uneasiness — Junot's Conversation with Him — Marshal Ney — Siege of Ciudad-Rodrigo — A Quarrel Threatened — The Emperor's Gloomy Forebodings — Masséna's Retreat — Junot Wounded -- Anecdote of the Duke of Wellington.

WE, TOO, had our amusements at Valladolid. General Kellerman gave a ball, and I gave another. Among the belles who figured at these parties one of the most admired was the Marquise d'Arabacca, the daughter of the Intendant of Valladolid. She was a fine woman, of lively and agreeable manners. When I was talking about her one day with an officer of the Duke's staff, he quoted a couplet of an old French song, and said:

« *Elle aime à rire, elle aime à boire,*
Elle aime à chanter comme nous. »

I learned that the Marchioness had an excellent pianoforte, of which she made no use, and I wrote to request that she would lend it to me. She replied to me by a little note very elegantly written. When I say a little note, I mean three or four lines, but written on a sheet of paper almost as large as that used for official dispatches. This is the custom in the south of Europe. In Italy the ladies never write on note paper. The Marquise d'Arabacca sent me the piano. As soon as it arrived I sat down to try it. I liked the tone very much, but there was an unpleasant jarring in the bass which I could not account for. I opened the instrument, and found lying across the bass strings a little packet of cigars (*cigaritas*). This immediately explained to me the application of the couplet quoted by the officer.

One day after the arrival of an *estafette* from Paris I observed that Junot appeared out of humor. I asked him what was the matter.

" We are to have a new Commander-in-Chief of the Army of Portugal," replied he with a forced smile. " The Emperor does not think Marshal Ney or me fit for the trust. We are to be placed under guardianship."

" Who is appointed ? " inquired I.

" Oh! I cannot complain of the choice that has been made. . . . It is Masséna. . . . He is our senior. . . . I only hope that Ney will accommodate himself to this arrangement as readily as I do."

Next day a letter was received from Vittoria announcing that the Prince d'Essling might be expected at the end of the week. Orders were given for preparing for his reception one-half of the Palace in which we resided; but we had then no idea that he was to be accompanied by a lady.

The day of his expected arrival was exceedingly fine. Junot and General Kellerman, accompanied by their Staffs and principal officers, went on horseback to meet him. The *cortége* amounted to at least two hundred individuals.

When they had advanced about a league from the town they perceived the equipages of the Marshal and his suite. Masséna rode first in a small uncovered *calèche*, and at his side was seated a very boyish officer of dragoons, decorated with the Cross of the Legion of Honor. As this badge of distinction was then very sparingly distributed, its appearance on the breast of so very young an officer attracted general remark.

Masséna's companion seemed anxious to evade notice, and when the Marshal perceived the numerous retinue that was advancing to meet him, he wished to draw up the hood of the *calèche;* but he had not time, for the three Generals-in-Chief set off at full gallop and came up with him in two or three minutes.

They gave him a most cordial reception. Junot was too generous not to relinquish all claims to precedence, whatever he might feel. Ney was sometimes actuated by amiable impulses, and Reignier was too prudent to manifest the least mortification.

However, Masséna appeared ill at ease. From time to time he was observed to cast on his young companion a glance of distress, which was very amusing to some, and was not at all understood by others. As to the young officer of dragoons, he sat with his eyes cast down and riveted on the points of his boots.

" Monsieur le Maréchal," said Junot, " my wife will be delighted to have the honor of receiving you in the Pal-

ace of Charles V. We hope you will be accommodated
to your satisfaction.»

«How,» exclaimed Masséna, with evident confusion; «is
Madame Junot at Valladolid?»

«Certainly,» replied Junot, not a little surprised at the
astonishment expressed by the Marshal.

«Then,» said Masséna, after a little hesitation, «I
cannot think of going to reside in the Palace—that cannot be.»

«If you are afraid of not having sufficient room,»
observed Junot, somewhat piqued, «my wife and I must
turn out—you are my superior in command.»

«*Mon Dieu!* I do not mean that. . . . I do not mean
that,» exclaimed Masséna; «but——»

He did not finish this sentence, and Junot could scarcely
refrain from laughing outright, for at that moment someone whispered in his ear that the Marshal's military companion was a young lady!

The confusion of the veteran Marshal as he drove on
to Valladolid may be easily conceived. As soon as he
reached the foot of the Grand Staircase he requested
Junot to conduct him to my apartments. He advanced
to me with his usual frankness of manner, pressed my
hand, and expressed himself overjoyed to see me. I was
informed that he was very glad Junot's heart was in
safe keeping, for that he was very jealous of Clausel
and Kellerman. As to the lady, she immediately retired
to her own apartment, and during the three months
which the Prince d'Essling passed at Valladolid, I never
caught a glimpse of her but once. She had strict orders
to keep herself concealed.

Masséna was not a Frenchman by birth, but he was
one of the most remarkable men in our Revolution. He
was naturally ill-tempered, and his manners were not
very polished. Being at an early period of his life placed
in a situation in which talent could find its reward, he
rapidly distinguished himself in his military career, and
it was he whom Bonaparte succeeded in the command
of the Army of Italy. Masséna was of a selfish disposition, and was often cruel in conquest. The Emperor
esteemed his military genius very highly, and regretted
that he was sometimes under the necessity of treating
him harshly.

Marshal Ney came to pay a visit to Masséna, but he did it against his inclination. No officer was ever so dissatisfied at being placed under the command of another. Masséna felt Ney's behavior, but he was the better dissembler of the two, and he concealed his ill-humor beneath an air of assumed indifference.

Masséna had as much regard for me as I believe he could have for anyone who could be of no service to him. He used often to come and chat with me in the morning, and these visits were very agreeable to me, as they afforded me some insight into the character of a man who seems to have been but imperfectly known to most of his biographers.

Lieutenant-Colonel Valazé, a young officer of engineers, was a particular favorite of the Duc d'Abrantès. Junot introduced him to Masséna, with the request that he would put him in the way of advancement, by intrusting him with the command of the siege of Ciudad-Rodrigo. Masséna replied that nothing would give him greater pleasure, and Valazé set out for Salamanca as soon as he had received instructions from the General-in-Chief.

Two days after this, Masséna was in my drawing-room playing at some game with Junot, when Valazé suddenly entered. He had returned to Valladolid; Ney would not allow him to be employed. He had no fault to find with him — but he said he had officers of his own; "And the Prince d'Essling," observed he, " Prince as he is, shall not dictate to me how I am to form my Staff."

On the following morning Masséna had a conversation with Junot, in which the latter had great difficulty to pacify him. He was for sending Marshal Ney back again to France.

"You will find," exclaimed he, "that that proud fellow will thwart all our operations by his obstinacy and his vanity."

Junot said nothing, either to defend or blame Ney, though he had been hurt by an observation made by the Marshal, which some person had foolishly repeated to him. Ney had said:

"There is no occasion for the Duc d'Abrantès to trouble me with his *protégés*. If they are so very clever, let him keep them to himself."

These ebullitions of ill-temper often placed Ney in a light which was anything but heroic; yet he was nevertheless a true hero.

Valazé was dispatched a second time to Salamanca. The young man was tossed to and fro like a ball between rackets. Ney flew into a passion, and sent Masséna a very angry letter, in which he told him that he neither regarded his orders nor feared his menaces, when he attempted to disturb the Staff of the army formed by the Prince de Neufchâtel. I cannot attempt to describe Masséna's anger on the perusal of this letter, which he held in his hand when he entered our apartment.

" You see," said he, " how impossible it is to make anything of this man."

This he spoke in a loud and vehement tone, as he paced backward and forward through the room.

I endeavored to calm him, but in vain; and Valazé, who felt his dignity compromised by being thus repulsed, willingly relinquished the honor of commanding the siege. The Prince, however, resolved to go in person to Ciudad-Rodrigo for the express purpose of taking Valazé there. All this boded but indifferently for the success of the approaching campaign.

We now left Valladolid for Salamanca. There was in the Army of Portugal a General of Division commanding the artillery (General Éblé), another commanding the cavalry (General M——), and a third who was chief officer of the Staff (General Fririon). General M—— was a perfect caricature of Murat. He wore on his head a shapska surmounted by feathers, his Polish cloak was lined with fur, and his boots were not unfrequently red. He was not, however, so good looking as Murat. But he was a brave officer, though he rendered himself ridiculous by endeavoring to imitate Murat, with a stature of five feet eight inches. During the campaign of Wagram, he commanded a fortified castle at which M. de Metternich halted under an escort of French *gendarmerie* on his return to his native country. General M—— assumed airs of importance which were the more galling to M. de Metternich, inasmuch as the castle was the property of his wife.

Having exercised his hospitality after a fashion of his own, the General said to the captive Minister:

"Your pardon, Monsieur le Comte; if I were in my own house I would give you a better reception."

At length the siege of Ciudad-Rodrigo commenced. The three Generals-in-Chief left Salamanca to invest a paltry village; for Ciudad-Rodrigo was nothing more. The works were in great part under the direction of Valazé. Masséna was greatly irritated against Ney, and this occasioned a coolness between him and Junot; for the latter defended Ney, who in fact was in the right.

The troops began to defile upon Ciudad-Rodrigo. They were taken from each army corps; and that of Junot, as well as the second and the sixth, furnished its contingent. In the course of these movements some letters passed between Junot and Masséna, at which Junot took offense, and on one occasion a very sharp explanation ensued in consequence. This angry feeling had not subsided before a fresh ground of discord arose respecting a company of artillery belonging to Junot's army corps, which had received orders to defile upon Ciudad-Rodrigo. On learning this fact, the Duke inquired of General Fouché and General Boyer whether they had received and given orders for the departure of the company, and on their answering in the negative, he entered my apartment in a state of irritation, such as I never remember to have seen him in. He did not observe me; but seized his hat and saber, and as he clasped his belt, he said, fortunately loud enough for me to hear:

"There must be an end of this. I am tired of it. A good saber blow will settle all."

I threw myself before him, to prevent his leaving the apartment.

"What are you thinking of?" I exclaimed, in an agony of alarm. He stopped and looked at me with a sort of wild stare; then, seizing me by the arm, he thrust me aside.

"Leave me, Laura," said he, "this affair concerns not you. Leave me. My honor is compromised by this proceeding of the Prince d'Essling. He knows my character. He knows that I will not bear an insult, and surely it is an insult to give orders to the troops in my army corps without consulting me. It is not the first time; I have an old score to settle with him. Leave me, I desire you."

He grasped the hilt of his sword; I plainly saw that he was bent on a duel.

"You shall not leave this room!" said I, for the Prince d'Essling's quarters were so near ours that he would have been there in a few moments, and I was satisfied that, at the first word, Masséna would have been as ready to fight as he himself.

"You shall not leave this room!" I repeated, placing my back to the door; but this was too feeble an obstacle to restrain Junot. He took me up in his arms, in spite of my resistance and, placing me on a chair, opened the door and was going out. The door of the apartment opened into the drawing-room, and there, to his surprise, he found assembled General Boyer, MM. Magnien, Michaud, and Fisson, and Colonel Grandsaigne; in short, with one single exception, he found there none but his friends. The individual who formed this exception, and whom I would name but that he is now suffering under misfortune, was the cause of great mischief both to my husband and to Marshal Ney. I followed Junot into the drawing-room, and addressing myself to those whom I knew to be most devoted to my husband's interests, I conjured them to use all their influence with him. Fortunately there was no need to do so; with Junot the first impulse was always the most to be dreaded. He now felt that he could not, with any shade of propriety, challenge the veteran of the glory of Rivoli, but he nevertheless made some angry remarks about him. These were reported to Masséna with some additions, and the Prince d'Essling, when he afterward told me what he had heard, repeated many expressions which Junot never uttered. Amid these unpleasant feelings, Junot and Masséna left Salamanca to invest Ciudad-Rodrigo. The English with Wellington at their head were advancing from Almeida to relieve the garrison and make a diversion in its favor.

The letters which I received from France brought me a mass of intelligence of divers kinds; for I received all at once letters which had been successively fowarded to me during an interval of months. They exhibited a curious *mélange* of successes, reverses, losses, aggrandizements, disgraces, and favors. First there was the dismissal of Fouché, of which I had not previously

14

heard;* next the taking of the Isle of France by the
English; then the pompous opening of the canal of Saint
Quentin; then the incorporation of the Hanse Towns,
Holland, and several small states with the French Em-
pire. About the same time we took possession of the
Valais in Switzerland, which was merely termed A DE-
PARTMENT. The French Empire then extended from the
54th to the 42d degree of latitude.

All the letters I received concurred on one point—
viz, that the Emperor was greatly changed, in every respect, since his marriage. His position was of a nature
to produce in his mind some degree of inquietude. The
more the Empire increased—the farther it extended—
the more anxiety it was likely to excite in him, who had
created so extraordinary and glorious a power. Affairs
had reached that critical point when even a conquest was
but a triumph mingled with alarm.

For example, when Napoleon took possession of the
Duchy of Oldenburg, he did so for the furtherance of
his Continental System, and his Continental blockade of
all the coast of the North Sea. But the Emperor Alexander could not be satisfied by these motives. The de-
posed Prince was his brother-in-law, and when he heard
of the event he angrily exclaimed: "The Emperor Napoleon is much too selfish!" These words are the more
remarkable, inasmuch as they were uttered in the year
preceding the disasters of Russia.

The letters which I received from my friends in Paris
naturally made mention of the new Empress. The most
various opinions were pronounced upon her. Cardinal
Maury sent me a letter in which he said: "I will not
attempt to describe how much the Emperor is attached to
our charming Empress. This time he may be said to
be really in love; more truly in love than he ever was
with Josephine, for, after all, he never saw her while she
was very young. She was upward of thirty when they
were married. But Maria Louisa is as young and as
blooming as spring. You will be enchanted with her
when you see her."

Maria Louisa's brilliant complexion particularly charmed
the Cardinal. For my own part, I did not see her till
after her accouchement, and even then, though I was told

* I allude here to Fouché's disgrace in 1810.

that she had grown pale, I thought she had too much color, especially when in the least heated. The Cardinal was a great admirer of Maria Louisa, though he had wished the Emperor to marry one of the Russian Grand-Duchesses. "The Empress," added he in the letter above mentioned, "is gay, gracious, and I may even say FAMIL-IAR with those persons whom the Emperor permits her to receive in her intimate circle; her manners are charming to those who are admitted to the *petites soirées* at the Tuileries. Their Majesties join the company at re-versis or billiards. I really wish that you and the Duke could see how happy the Emperor is."

I was informed by other friends that one of the amuse-ments of the Imperial *soirées*, before the Emperor entered the *salon*, was to see the Empress turn her ear round, for, by a movement of the muscles of the jaw, she pos-sessed the singular power of making her ear turn round of itself, almost in a circle. I never heard of anyone except Maria Louisa who could do this.

The Emperor wished to remove, as far as was consist-ent with etiquette, a frequent cause of dissension between him and the Empress Josephine, namely, the numerous visitors received by the latter. Maria Louisa was young, and ignorant of the world, and though accustomed to a great deal of Court etiquette, yet her private circle had been limited to the members of her own family. Thus the rules prescribed by the Emperor neither surprised nor displeased her. One of these rules was that she should receive no male visitors. Paër was the only exception, because he was her music master, and it was ordered that one of the Empress's ladies should be present while she received her lesson.

One day, while the Court was at Saint Cloud, the Emperor unexpectedly presented himself in the Empress's apartments. He perceived a man whose countenance he did not at first recognize. This violation of his rule dis-pleased him, and he expressed himself rather angrily to the *dame de service*, who, I think, was Madame Brignole. She replied that the gentleman was Bennais,* who had come himself to explain the secret spring of a *serre-papier* which he had been making for her Majesty. "No mat-ter," said the Emperor, "he is a man. My orders on

* Bennais was goldsmith to the Emperor.

this subject must not be departed from, or we shall soon have no rules."

During my abode at Salamanca I received intelligence of Junot's wound. It was brought to me by a young officer, a nephew of Casabianca, the Senator. He likewise delivered to me a letter from Junot, but it was scarcely legible; it had been written about two hours before the operation.

"I have been wounded," said Junot in his letter, "in the face by a ball, which broke my nose, and entered my right cheek, where it was stopped by striking against the bone. It is a lucky escape, for had the wound been half an inch higher up, or more in front, I should have been killed. As it is, I shall only have to keep my bed some days, and to suffer a few minutes' pain on the extraction of the ball."

On the 14th of November Masséna began to retire before the Duke of Wellington, but it was not until the month of January that he fully determined on his retreat. He then wished to mislead the English by making hostile demonstrations, and continuing them on the left flank of the enemy's army. The Duke of Wellington was not to be caught in this snare, which, indeed, would scarcely have entrapped a young sublieutenant. Unluckily, he knew too well the precarious and unfortunate condition of the French army.

He opposed to the grand reconnoissance which Junot commanded in person the Brunswick chasseurs, the Hanoverian foot chasseurs, and some squadrons of other troops. Junot, accompanied by General Boyer, his principal Staff officer, was on horseback at a little distance from Rio-Mayor, in front of a very thick forest. He was in his full uniform, and wore his grand cordon. One of the Brunswick chasseurs posted in the forest fired at him with a carbine, and the ball entered exactly in the middle of the nose. Junot did not fall; he merely raised his hand to his face, and said:

"*Parbleu*, Boyer, these fellows are better marksmen than you. They shoot a man better than you can shoot a hare."

He attempted to ride on, but the blood flowed so copiously that in a few moments he felt faint. He was taken from his horse and conveyed to the village of Rio-

Mayor. There he fainted away. There was an inclosed piece of ground near at hand; he was conveyed there and laid on a bank of turf. The chief surgeon of the army arrived and placed a first dressing on the wound. Junot fainted a second time while the bleeding was being stopped. On coming to himself he was observed to shudder. He had been carried into a churchyard, and the bank on which he was reposing was a grave!

The operation of extracting the ball could not be performed till next day. M. Malraison, the chief surgeon of the eighth corps, arrived to perform the operation. To his astonishment, he could not discover where the ball was. At length, after some search, it was discovered to have lodged in the round part of the maxillary bone of the left cheek. The bones of the nose were separated, but not broken. The aim must have been taken with singular precision. The ball had penetrated so deeply into the cheek bone that the incision produced by the pincers on the ball is still discernible.

When M. Malraison had discovered the ball, and was about to commence the operation, he asked Junot whether he would like the ball to be extracted internally or externally; the latter mode, he observed, would leave a scar on the face.

" Never mind," said Junot, when he was informed that there might be some doubt of the healing of the wound in the inside of the mouth. " A scar more or less is no matter to me. I shall even be vain of it."

After all, the wound, though its consequences were serious, left but faint traces externally. Junot was but slightly altered by his two scars; a slight protuberance on his nose was the principal disfigurement.

On the subject of Junot's wound, I must relate an anecdote highly honorable to Lord Wellington, and which shows his disposition in a most favorable point of view.

The French army was in full retreat at the moment when Junot received his wound. Desertions were very frequent among the French, and the nature of the country enabled the enemy to gain abundant information, while we were entirely cut off from it; so that the English perfectly well knew the state of our affairs, while we were ignorant of theirs, and even of our own. Lord

Wellington knew everything.   He was aware of all the misfortunes which had assailed Masséna's army, and a scarcity of provisions was one of these misfortunes.   This knowledge of our miserable condition prompted the Duke of Wellington to show to a man whom he esteemed, and by whom he was in his turn esteemed, a mark of attention which claims my deepest gratitude.   He addressed to the Duc d'Abrantès, whose troops were almost touching his, the following letter:

« Headquarters, *January* 27th, 1811.

« Sir:— I learn with great regret that you have been wounded, and I beg you will let me know whether I can send you anything that may be of use for dressing your wound or accelerating your recovery.

« I do not know whether you have lately heard from the Duchess. At the end of last month she was delivered of a son at Ciudad-Rodrigo. She left that place for Salamanca, and intended to proceed to France at the beginning of this month.» *

« I have the honor to remain, Sir, your very obedient servant,

« WELLINGTON.»

Junot gratefully thanked Lord Wellington for his kindness, but declined availing himself of the offer contained in his letter.   As to what concerned me, he replied that he had heard of my accouchement.   The fact is, he had known it since the 25th of December, the day on which Comte d'Erlon had joined Masséna.

The letter above mentioned is sufficient to explain the marked attention with which I received the Duke of Wellington on his arrival in Paris.   Had Junot then been Governor of the Capital, assuredly the Duke of Wellington would have entered it only after passing over his body; yet before he drew his last breath Junot would have cordially pressed the hand of his noble and generous enemy.

---

* Considerations of safety, which it is unnecessary to detail here, led me to circulate the report that I intended to return to France at the beginning of January.

CHAPTER XVIII.

The Spanish Nun and Marshal Duroc — The Nun's Sister and the Emperor — The Emperor's Altered Appearance — Description of the Young King — Napoleon at Play with His Son — His Conversation with Madame Junot — Rejoicings in Honor of the Birth of the King of Rome — His Christening — Maria Louisa's Accouchement — Madame de Montesquiou — Apathy of Maria Louisa — Anecdote — The Young King's Violent Temper — His Benevolence — The Widow and the Orphan — The Intended Palace.

THE Spanish nuns of the present day afford no idea of what monastic life formerly was. They lead a life of liberty, sometimes even of license. In fact, they enjoy, in too great an extent, the privilege of receiving strangers. With them the *closura* really exists only in name. The visit of a stranger never fails to excite their curiosity in an inordinate degree. As soon as I was installed in my habitation before described, the nuns came two by two and three by three to talk to me, and, as they expressed it, to keep me in good spirits. At first they amused me, but after a time I found their visits tiresome. One of them, who was exceedingly pretty, was less intrusive than her companions, though she appeared very desirous to talk with me. I asked her to come and pay me a visit in my apartment; but when she came I discovered that our conversation was likely to be brief. The pretty sister did not speak a word of French, and I knew only enough of Spanish to be able to give utterance to a few sentences. At first she was very reserved; but one evening when she came to see me, she seemed to pluck up courage, and she pronounced a name which almost made me leap from my chair with astonishment; I could not guess by what chance that name happened to be known in the interior of a convent. I looked at the little nun, who was called Santa Maria da Gracia, a name which she truly deserved, for she was a beautiful and graceful girl. When I fixed my eyes on her, she was as red as a rose, and the blush was the more becoming to her, inasmuch as she, like all the Spanish women, was naturally pale. But still the blush, pretty as it made her look, did not explain her question. I thought I might have misunderstood her, and I asked her what she said. She repeated it, and this time distinctly asked:

"*Donde esta ahora el General Duroc?*" (Where is General Duroc?)

"Why do you ask, sister?" I exclaimed, not a little surprised and amused at the question.

The nun put her finger on her lip, smiled, and showed me thirty-two beautiful pearls. Then she said in a whisper, and with a charming expression of confidence which showed that she saw I had understood her:

"*Esta bien?*" (Is he well?)

"*Oh! muy bien—muy bien*" (Oh, very well—very well!) replied I. And taking her hand I added:

"*Es my amigo el General Duroc.*" (General Duroc is a friend of mine.)

The nun's pretty face was immediately lighted up with a charming expression of joy. Her eyes became more brilliant, and a bright smile played on her lips. She clasped her hands, and, half raising them, came and stood before me as if to get a better view of me. I was another being to her as soon as she learned that I was the friend of the man she loved. And yet for aught she knew I might have been her rival; I might have been Duroc's wife. But in the first moment of her joy, no such thought occurred to the warm-hearted Spaniard.

I learned no more from the little nun, but one of her companions afterward informed me that she made her profession only two months previously. She belonged to a good family in one of the provinces, and from her infancy had been destined for the cloister.

On the following day, when I again saw the nun, I asked whether she was aware that General Duroc was married. She nodded her head affirmatively, and without any appearance of chagrin.

"*Su muger es Espanola*" (His wife is a Spanish lady), added I.

At this information she appeared very much surprised. She several times raised her hands in token of astonishment, but still without any sign of vexation. When I left the convent, she gave me a little relic which I very carefully conveyed to France, and delivered to the person for whom it was intended.

When I mentioned this little adventure to Duroc, it was a long time before he could understand it; and no wonder, for my Santa Maria da Gracia, in her monastic habit, did not bring to his recollection a pretty little Spanish girl dressed in a fringed *basquine*, and a pink bodice embroidered with silver. However, by my description and the mention of her native place, he soon discovered her identity. I was much amused at the embarrassment which this little affair caused him. I promised him that I would be discreet, and I kept my promise.

" It is not for my own sake that I am afraid," said he.

" For whom, then ? " inquired I.

" I will not tell you," said he.

" Well, then, if you will not honestly tell me all, I promise you that I will torment you about the little nun whenever we meet."

" For Heaven's sake, do not," he exclaimed; " I will never forgive you."

" Then tell me what I wish to know."

" I cannot, for it does not concern myself alone."

" Well, but since I have your secret, and have promised to keep it, surely I may be trusted with the secret of another. To a woman two secrets are no heavier than one. When once the effort of discretion is accomplished, one may carry it to any length."

He laughed and bade me farewell. But I executed my threat. Whenever we met, I whispered a word and made a sign which reminded him of Maria da Gracia. He was almost mad. At length he said to me one day: " Madame Junot, how unmerciful you are! What have I done to deserve this persecution at your hands ? . . . But, tell me, did not Maria da Gracia's sister make any inquiry about the Emperor ? "

" Ah ! at length I understand you," said I.

I suspect that the year 1811 was very fertile in events of this kind.

On my return to France I found the Emperor much altered in appearance. His expression had acquired a paternal character. What a beautiful child was the young King of Rome ! How lovely he appeared as he rode through the gardens of the Tuileries in his shell-shaped *calèche*, drawn by two young deer, which had

been trained by Franconi, and which were given him by
his aunt, the Queen of Naples. He resembled one of
those figures of Cupid which have been discovered in
the ruins of Herculaneum. One day I had been visiting the young King; the Emperor was also there, and
he was playing with the child,— as he always played
with those he loved,— that is to say, he was tormenting
him. The Emperor had been riding, and held in his
hand a whip, which attracted the child's notice. He
stretched out his little hand, and when he seized the
whip, burst into a fit of laughter, at the same time embracing his father.

"Is he not a fine boy, Madame Junot?" said the Emperor; "you must confess that he is." I could say so
without flattery, for he was certainly a lovely boy. "You
were not at Paris," continued the Emperor, "when my
son was born. It was on that day I learned how much
the Parisians love me; it is a cruel time for you ladies.
I remember well the day that Junot left his home
when you were going to be confined; I can understand
now why he quitted you. What did the army say on
the birth of the child?" I told him that the soldiers
were enthusiastic during many days; he had already
heard so, but was happy to receive a confirmation of their
joy. He then pinched his son's cheek and his nose; the
child cried.

"Come, come, sir," said the Emperor, "do you suppose you are never to be thwarted; and do Kings cry?"
He then asked if the accounts in the English newspapers relative to my accouchement at Ciudad-Rodrigo
were true. I replied that they were too silly to be so.

As soon as the King of Rome was born, the event was
announced by telegraph* to all the principal towns in
the Empire. At four o'clock the same afternoon, the
marks of rejoicing in the provinces equaled those in Paris.
The Emperor's couriers, pages, and officers were dispatched to the different Foreign Courts with intelligence
of the happy event. The Senate of Italy, and the
municipal bodies of Rome and Milan, had immediate
notice of it. The different fortresses received orders to
fire salutes; the seaports were enlivened by the display of

---

* The semaphore telegraph was invented in 1792 by Claude Chappe.
It was first brought into use for military purposes in the summer of 1794.

colors from the vessels; and everywhere the people
voluntarily illuminated their houses.

Those who regard these popular demonstrations as
expressions of the secret sentiments of a people might
have remarked that in all the faubourgs, as well as in
the lowest and poorest quarters in Paris, the houses were
illuminated to the very uppermost stories. A *fête* was
got up on the occasion by the watermen of the Seine,
which was prolonged until a late hour of the night.
Much of all this was not ordered: it came spontaneously
from the hearts of the people. That same people, who
for thirty-five years previously had experienced so many
emotions, had wept over so many reverses, and had
rejoiced for so many victories, still showed by their
enthusiasm on this occasion that they retained affections
as warm and vivid as in the morning of their greatness.

The King of Rome was baptized on the very day
of his birth — the 20th of March, 1811. The ceremony
was performed at nine in the evening, in the chapel
of the Tuileries. The whole of the Imperial Family
attended, and the Emperor witnessed the ceremony with
the deepest emotion. Napoleon proceeded to the chapel,
followed by the members of the Household, those of
the Empress, of Madame Mère, of the Princesses his
sisters, and of the Kings his brothers. He took his station under a canopy in the center of the chapel, having
before him a stool to kneel on.

A socle of granite had been placed on a carpet of white
velvet embroidered with gold bees, and on this pedestal
stood a gold vase destined for the baptismal font. When
the Emperor approached the font bearing the King of
Rome in his arms, the most profound silence prevailed.
It was a religious silence, unaccompanied by the parade
which might have been expected on such an occasion.
This stillness formed a striking contrast with the joyous
acclamations of the people outside.

Maria Louisa suffered a difficult and protracted accouchement. She was for some time in considerable
danger. Baron Dubois went to acquaint the Emperor
with this circumstance. Napoleon was in a bath, which
he had been ordered to calm the feverish excitement
under which he was suffering. On hearing that the Empress was in danger, he threw on his *robe de chambre*, and

ran downstairs, exclaiming to Dubois: "Save the mother! think only of the mother!" As soon as she was delivered, the Emperor, who was himself indisposed, entered the chamber and ran to embrace her, without at first bestowing a single look upon his son, who indeed might have passed for dead. Nearly ten minutes elapsed before he evinced any signs of life. Every method to produce animation was resorted to. Warm napkins were wrapped round him, and his body was rubbed with the hand; a few drops of brandy were then blown into his mouth, and the royal infant at length uttered a feeble cry.

It is somewhat strange that so much doubt existed at the time of the birth of the King of Rome as to whether he really was a son of Maria Louisa. We have had in later times a similar challenge of the authenticity of the Duc de Bordeaux, Henry V. of France. But such is often the fate of heirs to thrones. Was there anything extraordinary that Maria Louisa at nineteen years of age, fresh and blooming, should become a mother after eleven months of marriage? and that this event should take place in the presence of twenty-two persons, actual eyewitnesses to the birth? I cannot conceive how persons of common sense could at the moment, and even since, allow their imaginations to work so in the face of impossibility!*

When the first gun announced that Maria Louisa was a mother, the most important affairs, as well as the ordinary occupations and duties, were one and all suspended; the people flocked to the Tuileries, hats were thrown up in the air, persons were seen kissing each other, tears were shed, but they were tears of joy. At eleven o'clock Madame Blanchard ascended in a balloon from the square of the École Militaire to announce to the people in the environs of Paris the birth of the son of the Emperor.

A multitude besieged the doors of the Palace for many days to read bulletins of the infant and of the Empress. The Emperor, on learning this, directed that a Chamberlain should be constantly in one of the rooms to pub-

* The marriage of the Emperor and Maria Louisa took place before the civil authorities at Saint Cloud, the 1st of April, 1810, at two o'clock in the afternoon; the following day the religious ceremony was performed in the Great Gallery of the Louvre.

lish the accounts of the Empress's health as soon as they were delivered by the physicians.

I have already mentioned the Emperor's fondness for his son. He used to take the King of Rome in his arms and toss him up in the air. The child would then laugh until the tears stood in his eyes; sometimes the Emperor would take him before a looking-glass, and work his face into all sorts of grimaces; and if the child was frightened and shed tears, Napoleon would say: "What, Sire, do you cry? A King, and cry? Shame, shame!"

The hours at which the young King was taken to the Emperor were not precisely fixed, nor could they be; but his visits were most frequently at the time of *déjeuner*. On these occasions the Emperor would give the child a little claret by dipping his finger in the glass and making him suck it. Sometimes he would daub the young Prince's face with gravy. The child would laugh heartily at seeing his father as much a child as he was himself, and only loved him the more for it. Children invariably love those who play with them. I recollect that once when Napoleon had daubed the young King's face the child was highly amused, and asked the Emperor to do the same to "Maman Quiou," for so he called his governess, Madame de Montesquiou.

The Emperor's selection of that lady for his son's governess was a proof of his excellent judgment. It was the best choice which could have been made. Madame de Montesquiou was young enough to render herself agreeable to a child, while she had sufficient maturity of years to fit her for the high duty which the confidence of her Sovereign had appointed her to fulfill. She was noble in heart as well as in name; and she possessed what the world frequently bestows only on fortune and favor — the esteem of all. She was indeed universally beloved and respected.

The attention she bestowed on the King of Rome during the period of his father's misfortunes would in itself be sufficient to inspire love and respect. Not only had she, from the hour of his birth, lavished on him all the cares of a mother, and a tender mother, but from the day when the unfortunate child was cut off from all his family, and deprived at once of his father and mother, Madame de Montesquiou devoted herself to him, for she alone was left to protect him. To accompany him she deserted country, friends, and family.

Madame de Montesquiou was not liked by the Empress, and the cause has never been satisfactorily ascertained. It has been said, by way of compliment to Maria Louisa, that she never did anyone an injury; yet she possessed an apathy of soul, from the influence of which the governess of her child was not exempt. And what sort of love did she show for her own child? I have seen Maria Louisa, when she was mounting or alighting from her horse, nod her plumed head to him, which never failed to set him crying; for he was frightened by the undulation of her feathers. At other times, when she did not go out, she would repair at four o'clock to his apartment. On these occasions she would take with her a piece of tapestry, with which she would sit down and make a show of working, looking now and then at the little King, and saying, as she nodded her head: "*Bonjour, bonjour.*"

Perhaps, after the lapse of a quarter of an hour, the AUGUST MOTHER would be informed that Isabey or Paër were in attendance in her apartments; the one to give her lessons in drawing, the other in music. It would have been as well had she remained longer every day with her child to take a lesson in maternal feeling from the woman who so admirably supplied her place. But it would have been of little use — feeling is not to be taught.

Every morning at nine o'clock the young King was taken to the Empress. She would sometimes hold him on her lap, caress him, and then commit him to the care of the nurse. And how did she employ herself afterward? She read the papers. When the child grew peevish because he was not amused as his father used to amuse him, and cried at finding himself surrounded by serious and formal faces, his mother ordered him out of the room.

The public christening of the King of Rome took place on the return to Paris of the Emperor and Empress from a tour in the north of France. There have already been so many descriptions of this ceremony that it would be superfluous to enter into a fresh one. I will merely mention that the young Prince received names which show that the alliances formed by Sovereigns, the vows made at the baptismal font, the adoption by every religious formality and the ties of blood, are mere fallacies.

He was christened Napoleon François Charles Joseph! these are the names of his godfathers; they stand upon the register of his baptism, and they also appear on the tomb which closed over him at the early age of twenty-one. Who is there among us who does not recollect those days when he was still gracious and beautiful? There is a print of him which is now very scarce; he is kneeling, his hands joined, and below are the words: "I pray God for my father and for France." To the copy I have, the following are added: "I pray God for France and for my father;" lower down: "We now pray for Thee!"

One of the ushers of the Chamber with whom I was lately conversing wept like a child at his recollections of the young Prince. This man told me that the King of Rome one morning ran to the State Apartments, and reached the door of the Emperor's cabinet alone, for Madame de Montesquiou was unable to keep pace with him. The child raised his eager face to the Usher, and said: "Open the door for me; I wish to see papa."

"Sire," replied the man, "I cannot let your Majesty in." "Why not? I am the little King." "But your Majesty is alone!"

The Emperor had given orders that his son should not be allowed to enter his cabinet unless accompanied by his governess. This order was issued for the purpose of giving the young Prince, whose disposition was somewhat inclined to waywardness, a high idea of his governess's authority.

On receiving this denial from the Usher, the little Prince's eyes became suffused with tears, but he said not a word. He waited till Madame de Montesquiou came up, which was in less than a minute afterward. Then he seized her hand, and, looking proudly at the Usher, he said: "Open the door; the little King desires it." The Usher then opened the door of the cabinet and announced: "His Majesty the King of Rome."

A great deal has been said of the young King's violent temper. It is true he was self-willed, and was easily excited to passion; but this was one of the distinctive characteristics of his cousins; they almost all partook of similar hastiness of temper. I have known Achille Murat so violently overcome by strong passion as to be thrown into convulsions; and this when he was of the same age as the King of Rome. Madame de Montesquiou once corrected the young King for these fits of passion. On another occasion, when he was very violent, she had all the shutters of the windows closed, though it was broad daylight.

The child, astonished to find the light of day excluded and the candles lighted up, inquired of his governess why the shutters were closed. " In order that no one may hear you, Sire," replied she. " The French would never have you for their King if they knew you to be so naughty." " Have I," said he, " cried very loud ? " " You have." " But did they hear me ?" " I fear they did." Then he fell to weeping, but these were tears of repentance. He threw his little arms around his governess's neck, and said: " I will never do so again, Mamma Quiou! pray forgive me."

It happened one day that the King of Rome entered the Emperor's cabinet just as the Council had finished their deliberations. He ran up to his father without taking any notice of anyone in the room. Napoleon, though happy to observe these marks of affection, so natural, and coming so directly from the heart, stopped him, and said: " You have not made your bow, Sire ! Come, make your obedience to these gentlemen." The child turned, and, bowing his head gently, kissed his little hand to the Ministers. The Emperor then raised him in his arms, and addressing them, said: " I hope, gentlemen, it will not be said that I neglect my son's education; he begins to understand infantine civility."

Young Napoleon was an amiable child, and he became more so as he advanced in age. I know many affecting stories of him, which indicate the goodness of his heart. When he was at Saint Cloud he liked to be placed at the window in order that he might see the people passing by. One day he perceived at some distance a young woman in mourning, apparently in great grief, holding by the hand a little boy about his own age. The child held in his hand a paper, which he raised toward the window at which young Napoleon stood. "Why is he dressed in black ?" inquired the young King of his governess. "Because, no doubt, he has lost his father. Do you wish to know what he wants ?"

The Emperor had given orders that his son should always be accessible to those in misfortune who wished to make any application to him by petition. The petitioners were immediately introduced, and they proved to be a young widow and her son. Her husband had died about three months previously of wounds received in Spain, and his widow solicited a pension. Madame de Montesquiou, thinking that this conformity of age between the little orphan and the young King might move the feelings of the latter, placed the petition in his hands. She was not deceived in her expectations. His heart was touched at the sight of the young petitioner. The Emperor was then on a hunting party, and the petition could not be presented to him until next morning at breakfast. Young Napoleon passed the whole of the day in thoughtfulness, and when the appointed hour arrived, he left his apartment to pay his respects to his father. He took care to present the petition apart from all the rest he carried, and this of his own accord.

"Here is a petition, papa," said he, "from a little boy. He is dressed all in black.* His papa has been killed in your service, and his mamma wants a pension, because she is poor and has much to vex her." "Ah! ah!" said the Emperor, taking his son in his arms; "you already grant pensions, do you? *Diable!* you have begun betimes. Come, let us see who this *protégé* of yours is." The widow had sufficient grounds for her claim; but in all probability they would not have been attended to for a year or two, had it not been for the King of Rome's intercession. The brevet of the pension was made out that very day, and a year's arrears added to the order.

Who can have forgotten the day when the Emperor took his son to a review in the Champ de Mars ? How his features brightened with pleasure on hearing the joyous acclamations raised by his veteran bands. "Was he frightened ?" inquired the Empress. "Frightened! no surely," replied Napoleon; "he knew he was surrounded

* It would seem that the mournful habiliments of the child had made a strong impression on the young Prince's mind.

15

by his father's friends." This expression of the Emperor produced an intoxication of joy amid the ranks of the soldiers.

After the review Napoleon conversed some time with the architect, M. Fontaine, on the subject of the Palace intended to be built for the King of Rome, on the elevated ground immediately facing the Military School. The word "Rome" brought to the recollection of the Emperor that he himself had never been in that city. "But," added he, "I shall certainly go there some day, for it is the City of my little King."

CHAPTER XIX.

The Court at Trianon — Madame Ney's Proposition — The Duchesse de Ragusa's Amendment — Our Dinner at M. Ricbourg's — Ney's Court Dress — The Gardens at Trianon — Maria Louisa and Joseph-ine — Madame Mère — Her Household — A Comical Adventure — Madame de Fleurieu — The Prefect of Toulouse — Too Late for Dinner — Dismissal of Fouché — He Is Appointed Governor of Rome — Accusation of Cambacérès — Comte Dubois — His Mission to Fouché — The Emperor's Secret Papers — Fouché's Alarm — Suggestion of Comte Dubois — Louis XVIII. and the Sealed Box.

ON SAINT LOUIS'S DAY the Empress held a grand Court at Trianon. The Empress was very partial to Trianon, and the Emperor, always desirous to please her, ordered that the day of the *fête* should be celebrated there. Consequently, without regarding the inconvenience to which the ladies must be subjected in driving such a distance in full dress, the cards of invitation were issued for Trianon.

Madame Ney, the Duchesse de Ragusa, and myself were together when we heard of the intended *fête*, and the conversation immediately turned upon the difficulty of traveling four leagues and a half in our Court dresses.

"Well!" said Madame Ney, "I propose that we go to Versailles in our morning dresses, and take our Court dresses and our *femmes de chambre* with us. We can set out from Paris time enough to take a drive in the park, and as my husband and General Junot are here, they can escort us to Raimbaud's to dinner, and there we can dress, and afterward go to Trianon without ruffling our dresses or fatiguing ourselves."

This plan was too agreeable not to be approved of. The Duchesse de Ragusa, however, proposed an amendment which was also agreed to unanimously. She had an old friend named Ricbourg, who was formerly *maître d'hôtel* to the King, as well as I recollect, and who was now living at Versailles. He was the friend of the elder M. Perregaux, and had known Madame Marmont from her infancy. The Duchess proposed that we should dine at the house of this old gentleman, there dress, and proceed at once to Trianon. On M. Ricbourg being informed of our intentions he was delighted, for he was acquainted with us all.

Marshal and Madame Ney, Junot and I, the Duchesse de Ragusa, Lavalette, and the Baroness Lallemand all assembled in M. Ricbourg's dining-room on the 25th of August, 1811. We were all in high spirits, and sat down to an excellent dinner.

When we retired from table, Madame Ney told us that she had never been able to prevail on Ney to wear a full dress coat; but hoping that in our joyous party he might be a little less obstinate than usual, she had ordered the dress coat to be brought from Paris, together with the point ruffles and all the other accessories of a full Court costume. However, the difficulty was, not to bring the coat from Paris to Versailles, but to prevail on the Marshal to wear it from Versailles to Trianon.

"My dear," said Madame Ney, in her soft tone of voice, and stepping up to her husband timidly, as if she expected to be repulsed in the attack, "you know we have no time to lose. We ladies are almost ready. Does your dress coat require anything to be done to it?"

"My dress coat!" exclaimed the Marshal, with evident consternation.

"Yes, you know it is the Emperor's wish that you should all appear in Court dresses, and you must——"

"Nonsense!" said Ney; "do not talk to me of that masquerade foolery. I will never put it on to get laughed at, as I laugh at others who wear it."

"But, my dear Ney, it is impossible to go without it. The Emperor——"

"Well, if the Emperor wishes to encourage velvet weaving and embroidery, I am very willing to buy dress coats; but as to wearing them, that is another matter."

Madame Ney, hoping that ocular might be more effectual than oral persuasion, desired her *femme de chambre* to bring in the coat. But when the Marshal saw it, he was more resolutely set against it than before, and appealed to us all for our opinions. I must needs confess that the coat was not likely to be very becoming to Marshal Ney. It was of a light color and was profusely embroidered with flowers; and though in very good taste for a coat of the kind, yet it was perfectly natural that Ney should prefer his General's uniform. In vain did Madame Ney eulogize the coat; her husband was inflexible. At length, tormented by our importunities, for we supported the lady, as was our duty, Ney took the coat from the *femme de chambre*, and, taking hold of her arms, thrust them into the sleeves before the girl knew what he was doing. There stood the poor *femme de chambre*, for all the world like one of those wooden horses on which coats and cloaks are hung in the tailors' shops of the Palais Royal. Ney burst into a fit of laughter, and asked us whether we could seriously advise him to dress himself up like a buffoon on *Mardi Gras*. At this moment, Junot, who had finished dressing, entered in an extremely rich Court costume. On seeing him, Ney, angrily exclaimed:

"How! Is it possible that you submit to wear this harness? . . . Oh, Junot!"

Junot, like all present, was much diverted at this little scene. He told Ney that since 1808 he had frequently worn a Court dress. But nothing could induce Ney to make any concession. He was determined to go in his uniform, and the embroidered coat was folded up and deposited in a portmanteau, to the great satisfaction of the Marshal and the great discomfiture of his lady.

We arrived at Trianon, and shortly after we entered the gallery we were joined by the Comtesse du Chatel. We walked through the beautiful alleys of the gardens, the refreshing coolness of which was delicious, after leaving the crowded gallery. The Empress was making her round of the company, which prevented us from leaving our places. At length she approached our little *coterie*, and addressed a few words to each of us; to me she put her usual question:

"Is it as warm as this in Spain?"

When I had made my reply, and her Majesty had passed us, we withdrew to the fragrant alleys of the gardens, remarking among ourselves the difference between Maria Louisa and Josephine, who always had in readiness some pleasing observation, appropriate to the person to whom it was addressed. Maria Louisa seemed merely to ring the changes of one subject in different keys.

Soon after my return to France, I resumed my attendance on Madame Mère. She received me with the utmost kindness and affability. Her Household was more numerous than it had been when I left her, and the additions made to it were all excellent. Madame Laborde, then a most beautiful woman; Madame de Saint-Sauveur, daughter of the Prince de Masserano; Madame de Rochefort, the mother of Cardinal Bayane, had been appointed ladies-in-waiting to Madame Mère. The post of *Dame pour accompagner Madame Mère* was a most enviable one. She made us all happy.

One day a curious mistake occurred at the residence of Madame Mère, which made us all laugh very heartily at the hero of the adventure.

Madame was engaged to dine with the Queen of Spain. M. de Beaumont, her equerry, had gone to order her carriage, and Madame was sitting in one of the drawing-rooms with Madame de Fleurieu, who was that day lady-in-waiting. It was evening, and the room was but faintly lighted by the embers of the fire, when the two folding doors opened, and the *valet de chambre* ushered in a gentleman dressed in a richly embroidered coat, silk stockings, shoe buckles, having a sword at his side and a *chapeau bras* in his hand. The gentleman advanced into the apartment, bowed slightly to the two ladies, of whom he caught a glimpse in the twilight, then walked up to the fireplace, warmed his feet, hummed a tune, pulled out his watch, compared notes between it and the time-piece, and then said in a voice loud enough to be heard:

"What the devil is the old fool about? . . . Surely, his watch must have stopped."

Madame de Fleurieu knew not what to make of this; she was unable to guess what could have brought a Prefect (for she had descried the prefectorial embroidery on the gentleman's coat) to the residence of Madame Mère at that time of day, and especially when she was going out. The lady-in-waiting was about to ask him what he wanted, when he deliberately advanced to the sofa, and, addressing Madame, asked her whether his Serene Highness would be long making his appearance.

Madame, though generally very affable, was not always able to command herself. She had been surprised and annoyed at the intrusion, and finding herself addressed in this unceremonious way, she lost all patience.

"Monsieur," said she, "I must tell you . . . that——"

"Don't you understand me, madame? I ask you whether you can tell me when the Archchancellor will make his appearance."

The mystery was now more inexplicable than before. Madame de Fleurieu was struck dumb, and gazed in silent amazement at the gentleman. The latter shrugged his shoulders, and returned to his post in front of the fire, put his feet on the fender to warm them, and by turns whistled a tune, and muttered words which sounded very much like the imprecations of a hungry man.

Madame de Fleurieu, who thought it high time to put an end to this singular scene, rose from her seat, and advanced toward the gentleman with that air of courtly dignity which she so well knew how to assume when she placed herself in the first position preparatory to a courtesy.

"Monsieur," said she, "will you be kind enough to inform me where you think you are?"

The gentleman turned round with a careless air, still holding his foot on the fender.

"Where I think I am, madame? . . . I think I am in the house of his Serene Highness the Archchancellor of the Empire, who has done me the honor to invite me to dinner. I am much astonished at not seeing him, for half-past five was the hour appointed."

"Monsieur," gravely replied Madame de Fleurieu, "you are not in the Archchancellor's house. This is the residence of Madame——"

"Madame! . . . Madame who, pray?"

"Madame Mère, the mother of his Majesty the Emperor and King."

On hearing this, the gentleman, without being at all disconcerted, stepped up to Madame, and said: « How happy I am ! how can I express my gratification at thus having the opportunity of becoming acquainted with the mother of the man to whom I owe so many obligations. » He then informed her Imperial Highness that his name was Desmousseaux, and that he was Prefect of Toulouse.

Madame, with her usual affability, received him with the respect due to a public functionary; but the clock struck six, and she said: « Sir, I would advise you to lose no time. Half-past five is the Archchancellor's dinner hour. I cannot compensate you for the loss of your dinner, for I am myself engaged to dine with my daughter-in-law. »

The Prefect took his leave. The mistake was no laughing matter to him. When he descended to the street, he found that the driver of his *voiture de remise*, after having set him down at Madame's door, which he thought was the Archchancellor's, had taken his departure without concerning himself about the fate of the Prefect. It rained, the wind blew violently, and the streets were covered with mud. Now, though the Archchancellor lived in the same street with Madame, yet the two houses were tolerably distant. The poor Prefect arrived, wet and splashed, and, worse than all, almost famished, for it was now half-past six o'clock. The Archchancellor had sat down to dinner, for he made it a rule never to wait, except for ladies or men of very high rank.

When Fouché was disgraced in 1810, the Duc de Rovigo was appointed to the office of Minister of the Police. The Emperor yielded, without being aware of it, to an intrigue which had been planned in the interior of his private cabinet. Cambacérès had vowed the ruin of Fouché, and he denounced him to the Emperor. Napoleon never knew the real facts of the case; he therefore merely dismissed Fouché from his post, and appointed him Governor of Rome. The Archchancellor, however, seemed to think he had not fully accomplished the ruin of Fouché and he returned to the charge. One day after a sitting of the Council of State, the Emperor returned to his cabinet with the Archchancellor, and in a few moments he was heard speaking loudly and in a furious rage.

Comte Dubois, a Councilor of State, who was then
Prefect of Police, was at that moment leaving the Palace,* and about to step into his carriage. He heard someone call him, and on turning round he saw the Emperor
in the balcony which fronted the window of his cabinet,
calling and beckoning him to return.

"Dubois! Dubois!—come back immediately!" said he.

The Prefect was both astonished and alarmed at the
agitated manner of the Emperor, whom he had left perfectly calm only a few moments previously. He of course
instantly returned.

On entering the cabinet he found the Emperor alone
with the Archchancellor. Cambacérès was as usual quite
calm, but Napoleon was in a state of nervous excitement
which rendered him incapable of knowing what he said
or did. On his desk lay a sheet of paper, on which he
had written a few lines which were perfectly illegible.
He walked up and down for a few moments, then suddenly stopping and addressing himself to Comte Dubois,
he said:

"That Fouché is a villain—a treacherous villain! He
wants to treat me as he did his Convention, and his Directory, which he so basely betrayed and sold. . . .
But I am not so short-sighted as Barras, and with me he
will not find it so easy a matter. . . . He has notes
and instructions of MINE, which I desire he will deliver
up."

All this was uttered with great rapidity and violence.

"I know," added Napoleon, still addressing Comte Dubois, "that Fouché and you are not friends; but no matter—you must go to him, and execute an important
mission—important to himself, for it concerns his life."

"Sire," said Comte Dubois, "may I beg to be exempt
from the honor your Majesty is about to confer on me
—you have yourself just now observed that the Duc
d'Otrante is my enemy—consider, then, how painful this
duty will be to me."

"Silence!" said the Emperor; "I am going to intrust
you with a mission which you alone can execute . . .
hear me. . . . Fouché, while in office, received from
me many orders, notes, and confidential letters written

* This happened at Saint Cloud; I here allude to Fouché's first
disgrace.

in my own hand! . . . When I demanded these papers, which he would voluntarily have given up, had he been an honest man, what answer do you think he returned to me? He said he had burned them. He!— Fouché burn papers of importance!—no, no, he is not so simple as that! The fact is, he has now MY PAPERS in his possession, and I insist upon his restoring them. You must go to his *château* at Ferrières, where he now is, and desire him in my name to surrender up these papers. . . . Should he refuse, place him in the custody of a dozen gendarmes, and let him be taken to the Abbaye. *Par Dieu!* I will show him that he should have a speedy trial. . . . Well! why do you hesitate?"

"Sire, what papers am I to ask for? . . . your Majesty should have a list of them . . . suppose he should give me ten, and he should have thirty."

"You are right—sit down." So saying, he pushed Comte Dubois into the chair in which he had been sitting himself, and desired him to write on the scribbled sheet of paper which lay on the desk. He then began to dictate, but with such rapidity that Comte Dubois could not follow him.

At length he threw himself into a chair, and said, "The fact is, I can neither dictate nor write. Take this list, incomplete as it is; it will answer your purpose. Seal the rest of the papers and I will afterward examine them—set off instantly."

Comte Dubois procured post-horses, and started immediately for Ferrières where he arrived before night. He found the vestibule and all the avenues of the house filled with packages and trunks directed to *"Monsieur le Gouverneur de Rome."*

The Governor himself presently appeared, and M. Dubois explained to him in as delicate a way as he could the nature of his visit.

"I give up his notes!" exclaimed Fouché, rising and pacing up and down the room like a madman. "I give up his notes! . . . and where am I to find them? They are all burned . . . I have sworn it, and am ready to swear it again!"

The oath, of course, was not likely to embarrass him; but Comte Dubois had precise and positive orders, and they were not to be eluded by any trifling; the Comte knew that his mission must be executed, and he felt himself under the necessity of pronouncing the word Abbaye.

No sooner had he uttered it than a livid hue overspread the countenance of Fouché, and Comte Dubois feared he would faint. His limbs trembled under him, and he threw himself into his armchair.

"The Abbaye! . . ." he exclaimed, "send me to the Abbaye! What does he mean to do? To bring me to trial?" He was in a painful state of agitation. The Prefect endeavored to calm him, and again spoke of delivering up the papers.

"But I tell you they are all destroyed . . . burned! . . . Do you think I would have kept in my possession papers which would not only have ruined me, but would have ruined my children, and my children's children, to the third and fourth generation?" And he paced about the apartment clasping his hands in a state of agony.

Comte Dubois pitied him, though he had always been the object of Fouché's malevolence. "Listen to me," said he; "I will do for you what I hope you would do for another in similar circumstances. I will tell the Emperor that you would not allow me to see the papers, and that Real has only to come here and break the seals. Real is, I believe, your friend. With the Emperor, it is only the first fit of anger that is to be feared. . . . When once he sleeps on his displeasure, there are seldom any traces of it remaining in the morning. Compose yourself, and all will be well."

He accordingly collected together a parcel of old unimportant papers; for, after all, there appeared to be no others,* and Comte Dubois, having sealed them, took his leave of the disgraced Minister. When he returned to Paris, to report the result of his mission, the Emperor was at first exceedingly angry; but the Prefect at length succeeded in convincing him that the papers had really been burnt. "Fouché's alarm is a sufficient proof

---

* Comte Dubois, when conversing with me on this subject, assured me that he thought the papers had actually been burned. Yet after Fouché's death a sealed box was delivered to Louis XVIII., in compliance with the orders of the deceased Minister.

that they were destroyed," said Comte Dubois. "Send another Councilor of State to Ferrières, for the business of my department will not permit me to go there every day. Your Majesty can send Real or anyone you please."

The Emperor consented to this. Real was sent to Ferrières, where he examined, and made a report upon, the papers sealed up by Comte Dubois. The result of this affair was the appointment of the Duc de Rovigo to the office of Minister of the Police.

The same cabal which had brought about the disgrace of Fouché caused the dismissal of Comte Dubois six months after. As to the Duc d'Otrante, his appointment to the governorship of Rome was almost nominal, and he underwent a sort of exile, until the moment when, for the misfortune of France, he again returned to the Ministry.

CHAPTER XX.

Projected Alliance between Great Britain and Spain — Comte Charles de Châtillon — Napoleon's Ideas Respecting the War in Spain — Taking of Montserrat and Valencia — Napoleon's Recollections at Saint Helena — Probability of French Supremacy in Spain — Confederation of the North — Embassy of the Duc de Vicenza to Saint Petersburg — The Duc de Rovigo — The Affair of the Duc d'Enghien — The Duc de Vicenza Recalled to France — General Lauriston Sent in His Stead — Fancy Quadrilles at Court — The Princess Borghèse and the Queen of Naples.

IN 1811 the English Minister for Foreign Affairs conceived the project of forming an alliance with Spain. This was a bold but excellent plan, but not easy of execution, and Mr. Canning adopted the following scheme to accomplish his object. He employed a Frenchman, who was an emigrant in England, Comte Charles de Châtillon, a man of talent and excellent character. I knew him well, and he has frequently related to me all the particulars of this affair.

He was directed to go to Madrid, and to inform Joseph that England would recognize him as King of Spain on condition of his sending away all the French who were in the Peninsula, to which Great Britain pledged herself

to insure complete inviolability of territory.   Mr. Canning
was the same Minister who had already proposed to
Lucien to form a sort of league against France and the
Emperor.   The disaster of Moscow, however, obviated
the necessity of attempting to execute Mr. Canning's
schemes relative to Spain.   As to Joseph, I think I may
say with confidence that he loved his brother too well,
and prized his own honor too highly, to accede to the
proposition.

The Emperor had conceived singular notions respecting the war in Spain; he had heard the opinions of men
well acquainted with the subject, and yet nothing could
break the delusive spell which the hope of that conquest
had thrown over him.   Thus the mortification he experienced at a check was manifested in the reception which
he gave to Masséna, and the gratification of a triumph
was expressed in the reward given to Suchet.   It was in
allusion to the taking of Tarragona that the Emperor
said: "Suchet — the Marshal's baton is in Tarragona,"
and Suchet gained it!   The Emperor had greatly changed
since the time when he commanded the Army of Italy.
At Lodi, and at Arcola, he threw himself into the midst
of the enemy's fire to induce his soldiers to follow him;
now he threw a baton into the trench, and said: "Go
and fetch it."

The brave Suchet, as an acknowledgment of the Emperor's bounty, immediately took Montserrat, a fortified
mountain of which each hermitage was a redoubt, and
every hermit a stanch partisan.   The kingdom of Valencia next unrolled itself before the Army of Aragon.   The
port of Oropesa and its ancient walls were stained with
the blood of Suchet.   At length he arrived before Valencia and entered it victoriously.   To Suchet the war in
Spain was merely a military tour; and at his resting-
places he planted the national flag on the Moorish or
Roman walls of the ancient cities which are scattered
through the provinces of Spain.

The Emperor conceived a cordial friendship for Marshal Suchet.   Titles, fortune, rank, all were lavishly bestowed upon him.   The title of Duke of Albufera was
accompanied by a majorate producing a rental of 500,000
livres.   This was the richest endowment that Napoleon
ever made.   The war had long kept the Duke of Albu-

fera distant from Paris; he was absent during seven years. At the expiration of that time he returned to France, which he had left with the rank of a General commanding a division; possessing, it is true, a high military reputation, but still merely a General. When he returned he was a Marshal of the Empire, a Duke, a Colonel of the Imperial Guard, and Commander-in-Chief of the two armies of Catalonia and Aragon. Thus, when the Emperor saw him, he said: "Marshal Suchet, you have become a great man since I last saw you."

Napoleon said at Saint Helena, in those hours of captivity the langor of which he tried to divert by his recollections of past happiness: "Suchet was a man the vigor of whose mind and character increased wonderfully." All will admit that words pronounced on a deathbed have so solemn a character that the voice which utters them, however feeble, vibrates forever in the mind. The words I have above quoted were addressed to Dr. O'Meara, and as I conceive that the agonies of death commenced with Napoleon from the day when he set foot on Saint Helena, I regard every word he uttered on his rock of exile as that of a dying man.

Being questioned one day by Dr. O'Meara respecting his (Napoleon's) opinion of the generals whom he had left in France, he replied: "I give the preference to Suchet. Before his time Masséna was the first; but he may be considered as dead. Suchet, Clausel, and Gérard are now in my opinion the best French generals."* The "Memoires" of Madame Campan mention that Napoleon, speaking of Suchet, once said: "It is a pity that sovereigns cannot IMPROVISE men like him. If I had had two marshals such as Suchet, I should not only have conquered Spain, but I should have kept it."

The vigorous efforts made by Napoleon to maintain his position in Spain seemed likely, about the close of the year 1811, to lead to the submission of that country. We were established in Catalonia and Aragon by the victories of Suchet; while advancing to the gates of Cadiz we were completing the conquest of the four kingdoms of Andalusia. The passage of the Sierra Morena — the dispersion of the central Junta — the extraordinary

* Barry O'Meara's "Napoleon at Saint Helena," annotated edition of 1888, Vol. II., p. 45.

Cortes assembled at the Isle of Leon, issuing every day
contradictory decrees — the Council of Regency still dis-
puting with the other authorities — those troubles which
the heads of the new Government had not the power or
perhaps the will to check; all this placed us in an advantageous position. King Joseph must have remarked it
in his visit to Andalusia, the whole of which he jour-
neyed through, and had ample opportunities of convincing himself that everywhere the people were weary of
the war.

The Spaniards disliked the English, and were averse
to any alliance with them. Consequently, in spite of the
victories of Lord Wellington, our precipitate retreat, and
all the misfortunes of the Arapiles,* the probability is
that we might have kept Spain. The Spaniards themselves were of this opinion; hundreds of families returned
to the mother country, and accepted office under the new
Government; and, as was observed by a brave and patriotic Spaniard (Don Gonzalo O'Farrill), applicants multiplied to as great an extent as in the most peaceful days
of the monarchy.

But when threats were uttered by the Emperor of
Russia — when the Emperor Francis forgot that Napoleon
was his son-in-law — when Prussia forgot all her solemn
pledges of friendship and alliance — when, in short, the
formidable league of the North began to count its legions
to ascertain whether it was strong enough to resist France
— then the ill feeling of the Peninsula was revived, and
the little confidence which our troops had recovered was
lost. England, foreseeing our disasters in the north of
Europe, exerted herself, and increased her efforts in the
Peninsula.

One of the columns of his Empire, on the stability of
which Napoleon most confidently relied, was the Confederation of the North. This Confederation, which was
originally conceived by Henri IV. and executed by Napoleon, would have been a glorious work had it been
accomplished for other purposes than those which Napoleon had in view. He committed another grand mistake
in neglecting the German people. He courted the Con-
federated Sovereigns, while their subjects were the real
power which he ought to have conciliated.

* The battle of Salamanca.

The whole of the year 1811 was spent in the inter-
change of fruitless communications. On the 5th of April
the Duc de Bassano was appointed Minister for Foreign
Affairs. On the 6th he addressed a note to Prince Kou-
rakin to demand explanations. In his answer the Prince
again spoke of the Duchy of Oldenburg. He might as
well have talked of the dowry of Queen Mandane.* The
Prince was asked what was meant by the army of 80,000
men who were assembling by order of the Cabinet of
Saint Petersburg. The Ambassador, like a pacific man
as he was, replied that the Duc de Bassano was probably jesting with him; that he knew of no army, and that
such questions were very annoying to the Emperor, his
master.

The cause of several of our misfortunes — I may perhaps say our greatest misfortunes — during the year 1811,
may be traced to the embassy of the Duc de Vicenza to
Saint Petersburg. This will not appear surprising when
I relate the following particulars: Napoleon had sent
the Duc de Rovigo to Saint Petersburg, not in the quality of Ambassador, but as Envoy-Extraordinary. The
attentions which the Emperor Alexander had shown the
Duke at Austerlitz and Erfurth led Napoleon to presume
that he could not make a better choice of an Envoy.
But it was necessary to think of an Ambassador.

The Emperor, who had his caprices like everybody else,
attached great importance to external qualifications in
making a choice of this kind. The Duc de Vicenza was
a man of handsome figure and dignified deportment. His
manners were as elegant as those of any man in France.
He was noble by descent, and he had been ennobled by
Napoleon. These considerations, joined to others which
I do not pretend to know, caused the Duc de Vicenza to
be appointed Ambassador from France to Saint Petersburg.

But no sooner was this appointment known in the
salons of Saint Petersburg than it was unanimously resolved that M. de Caulaincourt should NOT BE RECEIVED
BY ANYBODY. This determination was dictated by no
feelings of hostility to France, for the Duc de Rovigo,
was cordially received in every circle. One day the sub-

* The mother of the elder Cyrus, concerning whom a story will be
found in Herodotus.

ject being alluded to in the presence of the Duc de Rovigo, he inquired what there was objectionable in the new Ambassador, when he was informed that M. de Caulaincourt could not be received in any house of Saint Petersburg on account of the terrible affair of the Duc d'Enghien.

Savary had his faults, but he also had merits, which in some measure counterbalanced them. He was a good Frenchman, and was sincerely attached to the Emperor. On hearing a charge aimed directly at his Master, and which also implicated his comrade, he became irritated, and several warm altercations ensued between him and some individuals at the Court of Saint Petersburg. On one of these occasions he lost all self-command, and addressing himself to a gentleman who had spoken in an offensive way on the subject in question, said: " You are mistaken, sir; the Duc de Vicenza had nothing to do with the affair of the Duc d'Enghien. It was I — I, who now have the honor of addressing you, who ordered the Prince to be shot." The person to whom these words were spoken stood almost petrified, and could not utter a word in reply.

On his return to Paris the Duc de Rovigo found M. de Caulaincourt preparing to set out on his Embassy, and he frankly told him the difficulties he would have to encounter, together with the cause in which they originated. M. de Caulaincourt was alarmed, for though brave on the field of battle, he had not the spirit requisite to face danger in private life. He thought of resigning his appointment; but that was impossible. How could he present himself to the Emperor and say: " Sire, I cannot go to Saint Petersburg, because I am accused of having DELIVERED UP the Duc d'Enghien to you ? "

In his perplexity he hastened to consult Berthier, and, after a long deliberation, the following plan was determined on to relieve the Duc de Vicenza from his embarrassment: A series of instructions were drawn up so as to appear as if they had been given by Berthier in the Emperor's name, at the time of the death of the Duc d'Enghien, and the Duc de Vicenza set out provided with his defense. On his arrival at Saint Petersburg he found, as Savary had announced, a formidable league raised

against him. No visit was paid to him; and when anyone was under the necessity of saluting him it was done
as coldly as possible. The Duc de Vicenza was too high spirited to submit to
this sort of treatment. He appealed to the Czar himself
and demanded justice. The Emperor Alexander expressed such violent displeasure against the offenders that
he seemed ready to send the whole of his Court to
Tobolsk. The Duc de Vicenza thought this was the
proper moment for presenting his justification. "This
accusation is the more painful to me," said he to the Emperor, "inasmuch as I am not guilty, which I can easily
prove."

Thereupon he put his hand in his pocket and drew out
the false document which he carried about with him, and
presenting it to the Emperor, begged he would read it;
but Alexander was more than satisfied. An Ambassador from Napoleon! a Duke of the Empire! a Grand Officer of the Crown of France was kneeling before him,
and praying not only that he would protect him, but
compel his subjects to show honor to him! The Duc de
Vicenza did not comprehend the peculiar positions in
which the Emperor Alexander and he himself stood; but
the Czar was shrewd enough to judge them at a glance.

He profited by his advantage; he raised the Duc de
Vicenza, and thought he could not do better than grant
him his friendship. By securing a claim on the gratitude
of Napoleon's Ambassador, the attitude of that Ambassador became a matter which he had control over. He
therefore spared no efforts to conciliate the feelings of a
man who could never have been induced to become a
traitor. It was, indeed, with the most entire devotedness
to the Emperor Napoleon that M. de Caulaincourt ruined
the interests of his Master.

A person who was an eyewitness to this scene of the
grand drama of 1812 assured me that it was curious to
see the impatience of M. de Caulaincourt, when he was
urged to bring the Cabinet of Saint Petersburg to an
explanation on the subject of the army of 80,000 men
which was now being organized. "No such thing is in
agitation," he wrote to the Duc de Bassano. "It is the
more to be lamented that these reports should be suffered to reach the Emperor Napoleon, since the Emperor

ii

Alexander is much displeased even at the appearance of his distrust." His blindness was inconceivable to those who were ignorant of the plans which had been laid, not to corrupt, but to seduce him. When the Duc de Vicenza presented to Alexander the pretended instructions of Berthier, the Emperor said:

"M. de Caulaincourt, I will not read them. I have long since been acquainted with everything that can be known relative to the unfortunate death of the Duc d'Enghien. The Duke of Baden is my brother-in-law; his Court is, in some degree, a portion of mine. You may therefore be certain that I know the truth of all that concerns you. I know your innocence. I affirm this on my word of honor, and I hope that pledge will be received." So saying, he smiled, and presented his hand to the Duc de Vicenza.

From that moment M. de Caulaincourt was devoted to the Emperor Alexander. The latter was too adroit, and it may be said too generous, to do justice by halves. What he had said in his cabinet he repeated publicly in his Court; and from that moment the affair of the Duc d'Enghien was never alluded to, except for the purpose of affirming the innocence of M. de Caulaincourt.

When the French Minister for Foreign Affairs addressed to the Duc de Vicenza a very urgent note relative to the assembling of the Russian troops, a petulant answer was returned, and these words were used: "I shall make no further reply to inquiries which appear to me to be absurd." Such was the course pursued by our Ambassador when levies of troops were being made in every part of Russia; when the Cabinet of Saint Petersburg was arranging the basis of a treaty with the Porte; when Sweden solicited and obtained the promise of Norway for her treason; when, in short, everything was flagrant and positive!

In spite of his prepossession in favor of M. de Caulaincourt, Napoleon saw that, though his principles were correct, his policy was not so; or rather, it was so far incorrect as to render it advisable to appoint another Ambassador to take his place. M. de Lauriston was therefore sent to Saint Petersburg to supersede him. Lauriston had received special orders from Napoleon to obtain an immediate audience of the Emperor Alexan-

der, and to bring him to an explanation on the subject
of the army. The audience was granted.

" M. de Lauriston," said Alexander, " I am much vexed
to observe that seeds of discord are sown between the
Emperor Napoleon and me; they can produce nothing
but evil fruit. It is strange that I should be suspected
of intentions so perverse as those which are attributed
to me in France. I assemble an army, sir! Where is
it? Eighty thousand men cannot be assembled in secret.
If you will have the goodness to appoint officers who
will serve as guides to mine, they shall go together to
reconnoiter this army, which is said to be entering upon
my territory without my knowledge, without the knowledge of my subjects. You must confess the thing is
absurd!"

Lauriston was greatly perplexed on leaving the cabinet
of the Emperor Alexander, and he wrote a most strange
letter to France. He, too, was under the influence of a
sort of fascination. The tone of irony, mingled with the
confidence of the denial, left no room for doubt. This
delusion was not of long duration; Napoleon had received
positive information respecting the assembling of troops;
but it was not until some time afterward that he was
made acquainted with the treaty between Russia and
Turkey.

The prospect of a new war cast a gloom over society
in general, but particularly around the Court. It was in
vain that the Emperor ordered balls, parties, and quadrilles. Maria Louisa was surrounded by young and
handsome women, who were commanded by Napoleon to
exert every nerve to render her gay; but these ladies
had brothers, fathers, husbands, and lovers, so that the
gayeties of the Court were forced pleasures. About this
time a fancy quadrille was to be danced in the theater
of the Palace, in which the two sisters of the Emperor were
to act the principal parts.

The Princess Borghèse was that evening the most perfect vision of beauty that can be imagined. She represented Italy: on her head she wore a light casque of
burnished gold, surmounted with small ostrich feathers
of spotless white; her bosom was covered with an *ægis*
of golden scales, to which was attached a tunic of Indian
muslin embroidered in gold. The most exquisite part of

her appearance was her arms and her feet: the former were encircled with gold bracelets, in which were set the most beautiful cameos belonging to the house of Borghèse, which is known to possess the richest collection of gems. Her little feet were shod with slender sandals of purple silk, the bands of which were gold; at each point where the latter crossed on the leg was affixed a magnificent cameo; the sash which held the *ægide* on her bosom was of solid gold, and the center was ornamented with that most precious gem of the Borghèse collection — the dying Medusa. To all this splendor and magnificence, was added a short pike highly embossed with gold and precious stones, which she carried in her hand. She seemed a fairy apparition, almost without substance, something celestial.

Her sister, the Queen of Naples, represented France; but she was, indeed, a caricature when beside Pauline. Her figure was naturally inelegant, short, and rather stout; there was no grace in her dress, which was composed of a heavy mantle of purple and a long robe beneath. She wore also a helmet and plume of feathers; but amid all this assemblage of gold, of pearls, and rich ornaments, we still admired her pretty smiling and fresh face, shining in brilliancy, notwithstanding the grotesque confusion with which it was surrounded.

The same evening a second quadrille was danced, which was also extremely brilliant. M. Charles de La-grange, who was a very handsome man, an aid-de-camp to Berthier, was dressed to imitate Apollo; M. de Gals de Malvirade, first page to the Emperor, was a Zephyr; the charming Madame de Mesgrigni represented Flora, or Spring; Madame Legrand was to have personated Love in this quadrille, but her husband, the General, wrote to her on the eve of the gala day that she should not act the wily part of Cupid in the Court quadrilles. Madame Regnault de Saint Jean d'Angely, Madame de Rovigo, Madame Duchâtel, Madame Gazani, Madame de Bassano were very conspicuous among a crowd of elegant women who took part in these brilliant festivities.

CHAPTER XXI.

The Kingdom of Haiti — Coronation of Christophe — State of Europe — Our Allies — Junot Sent to Milan — Bernadotte — He Rejects Napoleon's Overtures of Reconciliation — The Emperor's Departure for Germany — His Interview with Francis II. — War between Great Britain and America — The Emperor Proclaims War with Russia — Removal of the Spanish Royal Family to Rome — Josephine's Altered Appearance — Her Exquisite Taste in Dress — Madame Mère and Maria Louisa — The Queens at Aix — Talma and the Princess Pauline — Conspiracy against the Empress Josephine — Madame Récamier at Lyons — My Interview with Her.

IN THE meanwhile some curious scenes were passing in another quarter of the world. Henri Christophe was crowned King of Haiti, and a capuchin, named Corneille Brell, anointed him with cocoanut oil. In 1804 this same capuchin had anointed the Emperor Dessalines. The grand officers of the crown were entitled Duke of MARMALADE, Count LEMONADE, etc. The constitution of the kingdom of Haiti was copied from the French constitution of 1804. This parody on a great Empire and a great Sovereign gave birth at the time to many amusing pleasantries.

The French portion of Saint Domingo was, by the new arrangement of affairs, divided into two States on the death of Dessalines, the monster of the Antilles. The mulattoes wished to change the form of the government of Saint Domingo, and to establish a Republic with an elective President. Christophe was elected President of the Republic of Haiti for four years, and Petion, another mulatto, denounced him. Christophe then placed a crown upon his woolly head, and made toys of scepters and subjects.

While the pomps and ceremonies of Christophe's coronation occupied the negroes of the Antilles, Europe was threatened with convulsion even to the depths of her ancient foundations. France was preparing for the conflict like a victorious warrior. As to Russia, whose hostile intentions could no longer be concealed, she seemed anxious to give the signal for battle. The other Powers were still timid, for their yet bleeding wounds reminded them that Napoleon would severely punish perjury. The Duc de Bassano had spent the whole of the past year in endeavoring to gain auxiliaries.

Austria, though our ally, seemed unwilling to oppose Russia. Prussia showed herself still less favorably disposed, and M. de Krussmarck, who was then at the head of the Prussian Cabinet, appeared unwilling to make any concession. Yet nothing was more important than to secure the alliance of Prussia; it was necessary that she should act with us or be destroyed. M. de Krussmarck plainly saw that Prussia was lost if France took only a cottage on her frontier. Accordingly, on the 24th of February, 1812, a treaty offensive and defensive was signed between France and the Cabinet of Berlin. With regard to Austria, she was our natural ally, but she was still more our natural enemy. We soon saw the fatal result of that alliance, on which the Emperor so confidently relied. Then Denmark and the Confederation of the Rhine: all were for us when the first trumpet sounded the signal for marching.

Junot had been taking the baths of Berèges, which had greatly improved his health, and he now earnestly solicited the Emperor to give him a military command. Napoleon sent him to Milan to take the command of the troops who were in Italy, and to march them toward the North. Junot was highly satisfied at this appointment, and left Paris at the moment when the treaty offensive and defensive was about to be signed with Austria. That treaty gave us a subsidy of 30,000 men and 60 pieces of cannon. Prince Schwartzenberg was to command the Austrian troops.

On the 26th of March, the same year, Sweden signed a treaty with Russia. A Marshal of France was about to point the cannon of his new kingdom against his own countrymen — against his brother-in-arms — and against the man of whose glory it had so long been alleged that he was jealous. He sold himself for a province. Norway was promised to Sweden, and immediately Sweden unfurled the standard of war against France.

Napoleon made the first advance for a reconciliation with his old brother-in-arms; but his propositions, though presented through the medium of a friendly hand, and one that the Emperor supposed would be agreeable to

King John,* were, however, not accepted. The King of Sweden resolved to lend his aid in pulling down the Colossus. This conduct was not very honorable to him. He alleged in his defense that, on the 26th of January, General Friant had taken possession of Stralsund on the part of France, and had entered Swedish Pomerania by order of the Emperor; but he did not acknowledge that for ten months previously continual conferences had taken place, and that HE, Bernadotte, had rejected every arrangement that was proposed. England, as soon as she learned the defection of Bernadotte, hastened to acknowledge the treaty between Sweden and Russia by a convention which will prove to posterity that though Napoleon might have fallen by the effect of his own faults, yet treason and perfidy hurled him into the abyss on the brink of which he was now standing.

At length Napoleon departed for Germany to give the final orders, and to assemble all the forces which were to march: he clearly saw that this campaign must be decisive, and that nothing could atone for any reverse.† At this time Paris presented a curious but melancholy spectacle. Husbands, sons, brothers, and lovers, were departing to join the army; while wives, mothers, sisters, and mistresses, either remained at home to weep, or sought amusement in Italy, Switzerland, or the various watering places of France.

Before the firing of the first cannon the Emperor wished to make one more endeavor to ascertain the definitive resolution of Russia. M. de Narbonne, in spite of all his courtly experience, had not been able to learn anything in his mission to Wilna. Napoleon entertained greater hope from an interview with the Emperor of Austria, now his father-in-law; and above all, from an interview with M. de Metternich. The Emperor therefore conducted Maria Louisa to Dresden, under the ostensible pretext of paying a visit to her father, who was then in that city, but for the real purpose of discover-

---

* The Queen of Sweden remained in Paris, and she undertook the task of transmitting the Emperor's propositions to the King.

† The population of Europe, according to Humboldt, who is the most correct of calculators, amounted at this period to 182 millions, of which Napoleon had under his domination 85 millions: his control extended over nineteen degrees of latitude and thirty of longitude.

ing the path he had to pursue in the labyrinth which he was about to enter.

The wished-for interview, however, served only to raise new difficulties, and these were increased by the certainty of war between the United States and Great Britain. General Bloomfield, whose Headquarters were at New York, declared, on the part of the American Government, war against England. By a curious coincidence, for there could be no previous understanding in the matter, the Emperor declared war against Russia on the very same day (June 22d, 1812), at his Headquarters of Wilkowsky, near Gumbinen, in Eastern Prussia.

At this period a circumstance took place in France which was but little noticed, because all eyes were directed to the great European Congress; I allude to the removal of the Spanish Royal Family to Rome from Marseilles, where they had resided since they quitted Bayonne. My brother, who was then Lieutenant-General of Police at Marseilles, and who had the illustrious and unfortunate prisoners in some measure under his safe-guard and responsibility, was well pleased at their removal, for Charles IV. had suffered in health from the sedentary life which he was forced to lead at Marseilles; while at Rome he might have the opportunity of renewing his active habits and enjoying his favorite field sports.

The Empress Josephine was a great favorite of the King and Queen of Spain. I have heard from their principal equerry that she was often the tutelary genius of the unfortunate Royal Family, particularly when, in the Emperor's absence, their pecuniary allowances were very tardily paid. She used to exert her influence and make the requisite applications to get these payments settled.

I did not see the Empress Josephine till some time after my return from Spain. When I arrived in Paris she was at Navarre, which place she was forced to leave in the autumn in consequence of the damp. The Empress had already suffered from the humidity of Navarre, the disadvantages of which were only balanced by the beauty of the place during two months of summer; viz, from the end of June to the end of August. I observed that Josephine had grown very stout since the time of my departure for Spain.   This change was at once for the better and the worse.   It imparted a more youthful appearance to her face; but her slender and elegant figure, which had been one of her principal attractions, had entirely disappeared.   She was now decidedly *embonpoint*, and her figure had assumed that matronly air which we find in the statues of Agrippina, Cornelia, etc.

Still, however, she looked uncommonly well, and she wore a dress which became her admirably.   Her judicious taste in these matters contributed to make her appear young much longer than she otherwise would.   The Emperor, who seldom made remarks on female attire, except when a Court dress happened to strike him as having been worn too long, often noticed that of Josephine, of which he seemed proud.   The best proof that can be adduced of the admirable taste of Josephine is the marked absence of elegance displayed by Maria Louisa, though both Empresses employed the same milliners and dress-makers, and Maria Louisa had a large sum allotted for the expenses of her toilet.

I have already mentioned that Madame Mère was very reserved in alluding to the Empress Maria Louisa.   She observed the same rule with respect to her second daughter-in-law as she had observed toward her first; that is to say, she seldom spoke of her, and was always anxious to establish friendly feelings among her numerous children.   In her relations with the latter, Madame Mère admirably maintained the dignity of her own position.

During the first few months of her marriage, the new Empress seemed to imagine that the only individuals of the Imperial Family worthy of her attention were Napoleon and the Queen of Naples.   Madame Mère, whose excellent understanding pointed out to her the impropriety of creating any discord through complaints, which, after all, must be unavailing, determined to depend on herself alone for securing the respect of her young daughter-in-law.   One day Maria Louisa went to visit Napoleon's mother.

" Madame," said she, " I have come to dine with you. But do not disturb yourself, I do not come as the Empress; I wish merely to pay you a friendly visit." Madame, drawing Maria Louisa toward her and kissing her forehead, replied: "Good heavens! I should not dream of anything else. I shall receive you as my daughter, and the Emperor's wife shall share the dinner of the Emperor's mother." The Empress Josephine was less attentive to Madame Mère than Maria Louisa, and in this she was ill advised. The Emperor did not externally show his mother much attention, but he was always deeply offended when he heard that anyone had slighted her.

I departed for Aix, in Savoy, on the 15th of June, 1812, accompanied by my friend Madame Lallemand, my brother-in-law, and my eldest son, the latter then three years of age. Aix was that year exceedingly crowded with company, and it was difficult to obtain a house. I was fortunate enough to find a very good one in the principal square. The Queen of Spain resided opposite to me, and was not so well accommodated. There were here some who had been or hoped to be Queens. The Princess of Sweden was expecting to be Queen; the Queen of Spain was exercising the right and title of Queen; Josephine had been a reigning Empress; while Talma was King of the theaters.

The Queen had but a very limited suite; she seemed anxious to avoid the least appearance of *éclat*. The Empress Josephine, too, had but few attendants. I forget who the ladies were who accompanied her; but I think Madame d'Audenarde was one of them. Madame Mère had brought only one lady of honor with her; this was Madame de Fontanges. I offered to resume my attendance upon Madame, though, in consequence of my ill health, my services had been dispensed with; but Madame would not hear of this.

Talma was among the visitors to Aix this year. He had gone thither by order of his medical attendants to drink the waters and recover his health; but though he seemed likely to grow worse instead of better he was condemned every evening by the Princess Pauline to read scenes from Molière, to divert the Princess and her company. Talma at first could not venture to refuse a request made by the Emperor's sister. It was certainly very amusing to hear him imitate a female voice and repeat almost as well as Mademoiselle Mars : *"Excusez-moi, monsieur, je n'entends pas grec."* Then he would assume a gruff tone of voice and growl like the *Avare*.

This was all very well for a little time, when Talma himself, tired of playing the Emperor, the Prince, and the Grand Turk, seemed to be amused at taking a new line of characters; but he soon grew weary of it. "This will kill me," said he to me one day. "I cannot hold out much longer; she will compel me to leave Aix, which I am sorry for, because I like the place; but I cannot endure the fatigue of those rehearsals every evening, for the Princess is learning the part of Agnes in the '*École des Femmes*,' and that of Angélique in '*Les Femmes Savantes.*'"

The Empress Josephine arrived at Aix before I left, and I had the honor to dine with her. At that time there was a conspiracy formed to oblige her to quit France. An endeavor was made to induce me to join in it; but I would not listen to any suggestion of the kind, and quitted Aix on the 28th of September to return to France. There symptoms of disquietude had already begun to pervade the public mind. Intelligence of brilliant successes was transmitted from Russia, but the tenor of the private letters was of a very different nature.

At this disastrous period women were not exempt from the horrors of persecution. Madame Récamier had been exiled for having paid a visit to Madame de Staël at Coppet. The cause of her exile was too honorable for a woman like Madame Récamier, no less celebrated for the goodness of her heart than for her ravishing beauty, to shrink from its consequences. She repaired to Coppet, notwithstanding the warnings given her by Junot and many other friends. She had scarcely reached her destination when she received notice that the gates of Paris were closed against her.

On the departure of Madame de Staël, Madame Récamier left Switzerland and proceeded to Lyons for the sake of being a little nearer to Paris. Her companion in misfortune was another lady who had excited the Emperor's displeasure, but who was not so much entitled to sympathy, because her object was merely to gain popularity. This was Madame de Chevreuse. In her case her mother-in-law was the true heroine; the conduct of the Duchess of Luynes was admirable in every point of view.

As soon as I arrived at Lyons I proceeded to the Hôtel de l'Europe, for I was aware that Madame Récamier lodged there. I was desirous of being as much with her as possible during my stay at Lyons, and, indeed, my journey thither had been undertaken chiefly for the purpose of seeing her. I cannot describe the painful nature of my feelings on entering a vast chamber, parted into two divisions by a screen. This was the only apartment occupied by Madame Récamier! She whom I had seen in her magnificent Hôtel in the Rue du Mont Blanc, surrounded by all the luxuries that wealth could procure, was now residing in an apartment at an inn, but still as beautiful, as cheerful, and as graceful as ever. She employed herself in acts of benevolence, and received the visits of a few faithful friends, who occasionally left Paris to spend some weeks with her. Among these friends were M. Adrien de Montmorency, the present Duc de Laval, Matthieu de Montmorency, Benjamin Constant, M. de Catelan, and some others.

When I entered, Madame Récamier was sitting at her embroidery frame. "Are you not dull?" said I, as I looked round her solitary abode. "Dull?" replied she, in her soft tone of voice. "I do not know why I should be so. I have various occupations to engage me; but sometimes, indeed, my unfortunate fate presents itself to my mind. Then I feel myself solitary, and I weep; for I will not boast of a stoicism that I do not possess. I could not be happy away from France!" All this she said with so natural an air, and looked so lovely, that I could not help turning to Madame Alexander Doumerc to ascertain what impression it had made on her. The looks we exchanged were expressive of profound admiration at the sight of adversity supported with so much courage.

Madame Récamier had in the apartment a pianoforte, drawing materials, work-frames, books, etc. These alternately occupied her time, but could not entirely exclude melancholy recollections. Madame Doumerc ran her fingers over the keys of the pianoforte and produced those sweet tones which she so well knew how to draw from the instrument. "Ah!" exclaimed Madame Récamier; "revive some of the recollections I share in common with you both! sing me a song; but let it be French, not Italian.» Madame Doumerc requested me to accompany her in one of Boieldieu's romances, the words of which were written by M. de Longchamp when he was banished to America by the Directory. They are expressive of the deepest melancholy, and I could perceive they drew tears from the eyes of the fair exile.

I parted from Madame Récamier with regret. I wished to have stayed longer with her, but I could not. I was anxious to return to Paris to see my children again. My two daughters I had placed at the Abbaye aux Bois before I left Paris, as I could not safely leave them at my Hôtel in the care of their English governess, who was too young for such a charge. I found my family all well. I wrote to Junot to inform him of this; for he loved his children as tenderly as I did.

CHAPTER XXII.

The Russian Campaign — Consequences of the Battle of the Moskowa — Kutuzow — Mallet's Conspiracy and Execution — Maria Louisa — Her Apathy on the Subject of Mallet's Conspiracy — Cambacérès — His Sharp Reply — The King of Rome and the Enfans Trouvés — Napoleon Imitating Haroun-al-Raschid — The Alabaster Shop in the Passage du Panorama — The Emperor's Loose Coats — Maria Louisa's Permission that He Should Dress as He Pleased — Mademoiselle L——— The Medicis Vases — An Invitation to the Elysée Napoléon.

I HAVE already mentioned the fatal credulity of the Duc de Vicenza relative to the troops which the Emperor Alexander was assembling on the Russian frontier. General Lauriston was, fortunately, less credulous; still he became entangled in the inextricable labyrinth into which we were about to enter, and augmented the confusion. Meanwhile the Russian campaign commenced, and the misfortunes of Napoleon obscured his glory and his happy star.

In 1812 the Emperor should have acted more prudently than when, less dazzled by fortune, he found himself in 1806 in the presence of the Russians, who were flying from him to avoid a conflict. Then he halted, took up a formidable position on the Vistula, prepared for the

approaching campaign, established intrenched camps at
Thorn and Praga, as well as bridgeheads on the Vistula,
the Bug, and the Narew, until finally the Battle of Friedland brought about the Treaty of Tilsit. I am aware
that, in answer to these remarks, it may be said that in
1812 the army had nearly reached Moscow at a period of
the year (7th September) when the cold is not severe;
but was it not natural that Moscow, with a population of
400,000 inhabitants, would defend itself?

The victory of the Moskowa, gained by the talent and
courage of Marshal Ney, proved as disastrous in its consequences as a defeat. What a fearful list of killed and
wounded appeared after that battle! The Scythian
Kutuzow, who had the presumption to declare that he
had gained the victory, was rewarded by a title rarely
given in Russia, that of Field-Marshal. Kutuzow, after
all, might reasonably be excused for saying he had conquered an enemy whose loss was so much more disastrous
than his own.

The carnage of that day was incalculable. I have been
assured that more than one hundred and thirty thousand
cannon were fired in the course of the battle. If we
were conquerors, it was only for the vain honor of remaining masters of a field of battle strewed with the
bodies of the dead and saturated with their blood.
" That night," said Junot to me, " was one of the most
horrible I ever passed! We had no provisions — the cold
rain poured incessantly — we had no wood to kindle fires
— and groans and cries of agony resounded on every
side."

We entered Moscow, and in the meantime the Russian
Army of Friedland landed at Riga. The Army of Mol-
davia gained Brese on the Bug. This latter force threatened to cut off our communications with Warsaw. We
now began to awaken from our dream of good fortune.
That waking was terrible. In spite of the precautions
adopted for preventing the disheartening intelligence from
reaching Paris, letters were received. The unauthenticated reports which got into circulation created more
anxiety than bulletins which would have candidly told
the truth — they were even more distressing than the first
bulletin after the retreat from Moscow! — the famous
twenty-ninth bulletin of the Grand Army.

There were at that time in Paris a number of malcon-
tents, as there always are. The police had kept a watch-
ful eye upon them; but for a time its vigilance seemed
to have abated. In truth, since the retirement of Comte
Dubois the police of Paris had been very indifferently
conducted. Of this an event which occurred at the period
here alluded to is an undeniable proof. In after-times it
will scarcely be credited that in Paris one man, by his
own unassisted attempt, was on the point of overthrowing the Government and establishing a new order of
things neither wanted nor sought for, and that that man
HIMSELF placed under arrest the Minister and the Lieutenant of Police. Yet all this really happened on the
23d of October, 1812. *

Mallet's conspiracy produced an agitation which was
felt in the most remote provinces of the Empire. Maria
Louisa was at that time at Saint Cloud. She showed
no signs of alarm, but took her daily rides on horseback in the surrounding woods, which for ought she knew,
might have been the haunt of conspirators. Only General Mallet and his two accomplices had been arrested,
and it was at first believed that they must have con-
federates who would subsequently be discovered. This
was not courage on the part of Maria Louisa; it was her
natural apathy, and a disinclination to trouble herself
about a matter which probably she did not very well
understand.

"What could they have done to ME?" she said, with
an air of *hauteur*, to the Archchancellor when he
went to Saint Cloud to acquaint her with the affair. It

* Of General Mallet's singular conspiracy, to which Madame Junot
here alludes, an interesting and minute account is given by the Duc
de Rovigo. Mallet and his accomplices, Guidal and Lahorie, were
unanimously condemned to death, after a trial which lasted three
days and three nights. The prisoners were sentenced to be shot;
and on the 27th of October, at three in the afternoon, were conducted to the plain of Grenelle. Mallet walked with a firm step
toward the place where the file of soldiers was drawn up. "They are
very young," said he, looking at the conscripts who were to fire at him.
The prisoners were ranged all three abreast, and the detachment
fired at once. After the first discharge General Mallet still remained
standing! He was wounded, but not mortally. On the second discharge he fell, though not quite dead. It has been alleged that the
soldiers struck him with the butt ends of their muskets to extinguish
the lingering spark of life.

seemed as though she meant to say: "I should like to know what they could have done to the daughter of the Emperor of Austria?" But the Archchancellor was not the man to be much overawed by great airs and high-sounding words, for he himself had sat in judgment on a King. And this same Francis II.—this same Emperor of Austria—had been twice compelled to fly before the arms of France.

Cambacérès, departing a little from that cool solemnity which seldom forsook him, replied rather sharply: "Truly, madame, it is fortunate that your Majesty regards these events with so philosophic an eye. You were doubtless aware that General Mallet's intention was to throw the King of Rome upon public charity; that is to say, in the *Enfans Trouvés;* and as to your Majesty, you were to be disposed of afterward." *

It is well known that Napoleon was fond of going about Paris early in the morning, accompanied only by the Duke of Friouli, and was always greatly pleased when he escaped being recognized.

About six o'clock one morning, in the month of March or April, he left the Elysée in company with Duroc. They bent their course toward the Boulevards, and on arriving there the Emperor observed that they had got out very soon, as all the shops were yet closed. "I must not play the Haroun-al-Raschid so early," said he; "besides, I believe it was always at night that he wandered forth with his faithful Giaffar."

When they arrived at the Passage du Panorama some of the shops were already opened. One of them particularly attracted the Emperor's attention. It was the celebrated *magazin* of Florence alabaster, which was kept then, as it is now, by M. L—— and his sister, natives of Switzerland. There was at that moment nobody in the shop but a servant girl, who was sweeping it, and whose movements were much constrained by the fear of breaking any of the brittle but valuable articles around her. The Emperor was amused at the cautious way in which she per-

---

* In the pocket of Mallet a plan was found settling what was to be done with the members of the Imperial Family. The King of Rome was to be disposed of in the manner mentioned above. Maria Louisa was never informed what was to be her fate; it was by no means flattering to the pride of the daughter of the Cæsars.

formed her task, and after he had stood looking at her
for some time, he said: "*Ah ça!* who keeps this shop?
Is there neither master nor mistress here?"
"Do you want to buy anything?" said the girl, sus-
pending her labor. Then, leaning on her broom, she
rested her chin on her two hands, and stared the Emperor full in the face, apparently half inclined to laugh
at his eccentric appearance. Certainly it would be difficult to imagine a more comical figure than Napoleon
presented in his Haroun-al-Raschid costume, as he used
to call it. He wore the famous gray frock coat;* but it
was not the coat itself, it was the make of it which rendered it so singular. The Emperor would never allow
his clothes to be in the least degree tight, and consequently his tailors made his coats as if they had measured them upon a sentry box.

When he married Maria Louisa, the King of Naples
prevailed on him to have his clothes made by his tailor.
The Emperor wore them most courageously for a short
time, but he could endure the torture no longer, and he
begged for mercy. He submitted the question to the decision of the Empress, who, as long as she could ride on
horseback, and take four or five meals a day, was always
good humored and willing to agree to anything. She
therefore granted Napoleon full power to dress according to his own fancy, saying that she liked the Emperor
AS WELL ONE WAY AS ANOTHER. Perhaps she would have
spoken more correctly had she said SHE DID NOT LIKE
HIM ANY BETTER ONE WAY THAN ANOTHER.

With the loose frock coat above described the Emperor
wore a round hat, slouched over his forehead to prevent
his being recognized. His unfashionable appearance,
joined to his abrupt and unceremonious manner, led the
servant girl to conclude, at the first glance, that he
wished only to purchase some trifle worth about ten or
fifteen francs, and that it was certainly not worth while
to call her young and pretty mistress for so paltry a
customer.

But the Emperor thought differently, and after looking
about him for a few minutes he asked in an authorita.
tive tone whether there was anyone to whom he could
speak. Mademoiselle L——, who had just risen, at that

* Latterly he frequently wore a blue one.

17

moment came downstairs. On seeing her the Emperor
was struck by her beauty and her elegant appearance; and,
in truth, she might well have vied with the finest woman
of the Imperial Court. "*Parbleu*, madame," said the
Emperor, touching the brim of his hat (for he could not
venture to take it off, lest he should be known), "it
would appear that you are not very early folks here. A
good shopkeeper should look after her business better."
"That would be very true, sir," replied Mademoiselle
L——, "if business were going on well. But as it is, it
matters very little whether we are in our shops or not."
"Is trade, then, so very bad?" said Napoleon, examining various things on the counter. "Ruined, sir, totally
ruined. I know not what will become of us." "Indeed!
I had no idea that France was in so pitiable a condition.
I am a foreigner. I wish to make a few purchases, and
at the same time I should like to learn from so agreeable a person as yourself some particulars respecting the
state of business in Paris. What sort of vases do you
call these?" "Those are the Medicis form," replied
Mademoiselle L——. "They are very beautiful. What
is the price of them?" Mademoiselle L—— opened at
once her ears and her eyes. The vases were marked at
three thousand francs. She told Napoleon the price of
them, but he merely nodded his head, and then said:
"Pray what is the reason that trade is so bad?" "Oh,
sir, as long as that LITTLE MAN, our Emperor, is so madly
intent on war, how can we hope to enjoy either prosperity or happiness?" As she spoke these words Mademoiselle L—— threw herself into a chair, and the Emperor stood looking at her with the admiration which
her beauty was calculated to excite. "Is your husband
with the army?" inquired the Emperor. "I am not
married, sir; I live here with my brother, whom I assist
in carrying on his business. We are not French, we are
Swiss." "Ah, ah,! said the Emperor; and he uttered
these exclamations with as much indifference as if he
had been yawning. "Well, I will purchase these two
Medicis vases. I will send for them at eleven o'clock.
Take care to have them ready."

With these words, which were delivered in a truly
Imperial tone of authority, he touched the brim of his
hat, and darted out of the shop, beckoning the Duke of

Friouli to follow him. "That girl is very interesting," said he to Duroc, as they left the Passage du Panorama. "When she told me she was a Swiss, I fancied I beheld before me one of the wives or sisters of the heroes of the Reutly.* Do you think she knew me?" "I am confident she did not, Sire. Her manner was too calm and too self-possessed. She had no suspicion in whose presence she was."

The Emperor remained silent and thoughtful for a few moments, then, as if suddenly recovering from his abstraction, he looked around him with an air of calm dignity. Duroc, who described the whole of this scene to me, said he was certain that some unworthy thought had for a moment crossed the Emperor's mind, but that he had immediately banished it.

At eleven o'clock two porters, accompanied by a footman in Imperial livery, arrived at the shop of Mademoiselle L——. The footman was the bearer of a little billet, requesting that the lady would herself accompany the vases and receive the payment for them.

"And where am I to go?" said Mademoiselle L——, trembling, for on seeing the Imperial livery she began to regret the freedom with which she had spoken to her customer in the morning. "To the Elysée Napoléon, mademoiselle," said the footman. The vases were carefully packed and delivered to the porters, and Mademoiselle L——, accompanied by her brother, followed them, trembling like an aspen leaf; yet she was far from suspecting the whole truth. On arriving at the Elysée Napoléon, they were immediately ushered into the Emperor's cabinet. He took three bills of a thousand francs from his desk, and, presenting them to Mademoiselle L——, said with a smile: "Another time, mademoiselle, do not be so ready to murmur at the stagnation of trade." Then, wishing her good-morning, he retired into his interior apartment.

The brother and sister were both sensibly alive to this generosity. Mademoiselle L—— used to relate the adventure with the most charming simplicity and feeling. It had taught her a lesson, and since that morning she readily admitted that depression of trade may exist with-

* The field in which William Tell, Walther, Furst, and Stauffacher took the oath.

out any fault being chargeable to the head of a Government. The LITTLE MAN, too, had grown wonderfully large in her estimation, not because he had purchased from her a pair of vases worth three thousand francs, but because he had forgotten a remark which many others in his exalted station would have regarded as an unpardonable offense.

CHAPTER XXIII.

A Chapter of Anecdotes — M. Hervé's Conspiracy — The Ladies of Honor and Their Diamonds — The Archchancellor — The Country House at Belleville — The Plot Discovered — Exile of M. Hervé — A Mystification — A Journey to Fontainebleau — The Emperor's Displeasure — The Imperial Writing Paper — Examination of Handwriting — M. Arbusson — M. Lavalette — The Real Offenders Discovered — Prince and Princess Louis.

HAVING in my last chapter said so much about the Minister and the Prefect of the Police, I will here relate an anecdote connected with the police which I omitted to insert at its proper date (1809), during the campaign of Wagram.

The Empress Josephine was at Malmaison, and the Emperor at Vienna. The Empress had with her a great retinue of attendants and visitors, and, with her accustomed amiability, she wished to see all around her cheerful and happy. One day she thought she observed the Comtesse de Thalouet looking very uneasy and low-spirited. She inquired what was the matter, and the Countess replied "that she had something important to tell her, but that it must be communicated to her Majesty ALONE." The Empress was alarmed, and desired the Countess to follow her to a private apartment. There Madame de Thalouet informed her that she had learned, through a channel which admitted of no doubt, that a frightful conspiracy was on foot, and on the point of breaking out. "The blow," said she, "is to be struck at all the Imperial Family at once." The poor Comtesse de Thalouet, on being asked from whom she had received this information, replied that it had been communicated to her by M. Hervé de Morlaix, a man of worth and respectability, who was happy in thus being enabled to save his Sovereigns from the danger that threatened them. The Comtesse de Thalouet introduced M. Hervé to the Empress Josephine, who, being naturally timid, lent a ready ear to the story, and was so greatly alarmed that she resolved to communicate the matter privately to the Archchancellor, since M. Hervé had made his disclosure on condition that it should not be made known to the police.

"If," said he, "the Minister and the Prefect of the Police should be made acquainted with this affair by your Majesty, they will never forgive me for having been more vigilant than they in watching over the welfare of the Imperial Family; and they will take care to thwart the discovery which I am about to bring to light. But the man, or rather the MONSTER, who contemplates this dreadful crime, has some confidence in me, because I have promised him the money requisite for carrying his plot into effect. Your Majesty is of course aware that I shall advance this money only for the purpose of catching him in the trap. But to do this, I must have disposable funds, and though I am rich, yet all my capital is invested, and I cannot positively lay my hands on ten thousand francs, while it is necessary to command at least three hundred thousand."

The Empress might as well have hoped to find the wealth of India, as three hundred thousand francs in her treasury in the month of July. Besides, she had no means of procuring money, for the Emperor had placed every obstacle in the way of her raising loans. She held a council with her ladies of honor, and the result was that they presented their diamonds to the Empress, and begged she would dispose of them as she pleased. She was touched by this proof of their devotedness; and reflecting that it was necessary to be cautious in the employment of property, which was doubly valuable because it had been given from feelings of attachment, she determined to make the Archchancellor acquainted with the affair. Cambacérès was greatly astonished, and though not friendly to Fouché, he nevertheless acquitted him of the charge of negligence, and expressed his doubts of the existence of the plot. When he was informed that the disclosure had been made by M. Hervé, he knew not

what to think. He resolved to go himself to M. Hervé's
house at Belleville, which was represented to be the
place of rendezvous of the assassin who was to annihi-
late the whole Imperial Family. M. Hervé, far from being
disconcerted, expressed himself pleased at the Archchancellor's intention of making himself personally acquainted
with the facts of the case. The Archchancellor, however, obtained no information by his visit. He was
shown into a garden, at the end of which was a small
door leading out to some fields, through which it was
said the conspirator entered. M. Hervé explained the
affair very cleverly, but the person to whom he explained
it was more clever than he. Cambacérès thought the
story suspicious. Moreover, it was an awkward affair,
in whatever way it might be viewed. If true, it was necessary that the Government should immediately take
cognizance of it; and if false, the dignity of the Empress
was compromised. The Archchancellor said nothing to
M. Hervé, but on his return to Paris he disclosed the
whole matter to Comte Dubois. Hervé's house was surrounded, and he himself put under surveillance. It was
speedily discovered that he had speculated to a vast ex-
tend in the funds, and had lost such large sums of money
that he was on the verge of ruin. In short, M. Hervé
was a second Latude, and he had speculated on the
alarm he might excite in the Empress's mind; first for
the Emperor, who was most dear to her, and next for
herself and all the Imperial Family. The Comtesse de
Thalouet, on whose fears Hervé had successfully worked,
thought herself happy in being able to render the Empress so important a service as to make her acquainted
with the supposed plot. All was going on well, when
Josephine took it into her head to consult the Archchancellor. This was fortunate for herself. It saved
her a severe remonstrance on the part of the Emperor,
who merely laughed at her when he heard the story on
his return from Wagram. The Prefect of the Police
made a descent upon M. Hervé, who had imprudently
kept drafts in his own handwriting of the letters written
by the CONSPIRATOR. These letters were copied by a
young secretary who had no idea he was doing any harm.
In M. Hervé's desk other papers were found which
amply proved his guilt, and in addition to this he made

a full confession. He was sent to prison, where he remained until the return of the Emperor, who treated the
affair very lightly, and merely called it a hoax upon the
gravity of the Archchancellor. M. Hervé was liberated;
but he was exiled to Morlaix, and forbidden to return to
Paris.

Another adventure, which happened at a later period,
shows with what caution evidence, even apparently the
most positive, should be received, in a question which
involves the punishment of any individual.

Comte R. de S—— and M. Carion de Nisas one day
received letters from the Emperor's Chamberlain on duty,
directing them to proceed immediately to Fontainebleau,
where the Court then was. Comte de S—— was at his
country seat. He immediately set off in a *calèche* with
six horses, and proceeded to Fontainebleau with the utmost speed. But in spite of all his haste, he did not get
there until after the arrival of Carion de Nisas, who, as
soon as he had alighted from his *calèche*, related to him
an adventure which was not a little mortifying.

Carion de Nisas being in Paris when he received his
letter, was enabled to reach Fontainebleau sooner than
Comte R. He arrived at nine o'clock in the evening,
greatly fatigued by his journey, and having largely paid
his postilions for the speed with which they had driven
him. He hastened to the *salon de service* the more
eagerly as he observed an unusual bustle about the
palace. The Chamberlain on duty, to whom he first
addressed himself, stared at him as if he had been
speaking Greek, and at length seriously asked him what
he wanted.

" *Parbleu!* " exclaimed M. de Nisas, " I want to see
the Emperor."

" You have told me so already; but, I repeat, it is
impossible."

" But his Majesty wishes to see me."

" The Emperor wishes to see you! . . . That is
equally impossible; for you are not on the list."

" But you wrote to me."

" Surely you are dreaming! "

" Here is your letter."

He showed the Chamberlain the letter he had received
that morning, and in consequence of which he had hur-

ried to Fontainebleau. The Chamberlain, after glancing
at the writing, said:

" M. de Nisas, this is all a hoax. This letter is not my
writing."

At that moment Comte R. de S—— arrived, and, far
from clearing up the mystery, only helped to render it
the more obscure.

" But, at any rate, I will pay my respects to his Majesty," said he; "that is a privilege which I am always
happy to exercise."

" No doubt of that," said the Chamberlain (M. de
Tournou); "but unluckily there is a little obstacle in the
way of your doing so now. The Emperor set off this
morning at four o'clock."

" Set off!" exclaimed the two mystified visitors with
one voice; "and pray where is he gone?"

" To Italy," replied the Chamberlain. They had now
no alternative but to return to Paris, and some days
elapsed before they heard any more of the matter.

In the meanwhile, the Emperor, who daily received by
estafette intelligence of all that was doing at Court, heard
of the hoax, and was greatly displeased at it. The Prefect of the Police received strict orders to discover the
individual who had dared to use the name of a great
civil officer of the Crown, and also to inquire among the
individuals of the Imperial Household how it happened
that the writing paper appropriated to the Emperor's private use should have been procured for the purpose of
playing a trick.

It happened that the paper on which the forged letters
had been written was of a peculiar manufacture; it had
a cipher different from that of any other paper. This
matter demanded investigation. The natural conclusion
was that it had been abstracted from the Emperor's cabinet, or from the *salon de service*, and it could have been
taken only by some of the officers of the Household, or
the servants.

The Emperor's paper maker was summoned to appear
before the Prefect of Police. He acknowledged that the
paper on which the letters were written was of his manufacture. He was ordered to deliver up all the letters
which he had received from Court containing orders for
paper. The police then summoned five examiners of

handwriting, employed by the Criminal Court, and laid before them the letters produced by the paper maker, together with the two letters which had been sent to Comte de S—— and M. Carion de Nisas. The result of the examination was that, of the letters produced by the paper manufacturer, there was one the handwriting of which corresponded with that of the two hoaxing letters. The letter in question was from M. Arbusson, a member of the Council of State.

M. Arbusson was a steady, respectable old gentleman, whose appearance was truly patriarchal. On finding himself arrested, he was perfectly dismayed, and on learning the offense with which he was charged his astonishment was mingled with indignation. He pointed to his gray hairs, and asked whether at his time of life he was likely to be playing tricks which would scarcely be pardonable in a young page. He was shown the hoaxing letters, together with his own, and was informed that on a careful examination of the handwriting he was declared to be the culprit, and that the Emperor had sent a formal order for his arrest. M. Arbusson was confounded; but as he knew himself to be innocent, he made up his mind to endure the annoyance, and wait till the mystery should be cleared up.

Meanwhile M. Arbusson's arrest, and the extraordinary cause assigned for it, created a considerable sensation in Paris. He had many friends who went immediately to see him, and who felt great interest in the affair. Among the number was Lavalette, who was ever ready to exert himself to serve his friends. After a vast deal of troublesome investigation, he succeeded in tracing out the real offenders.

"Give me two hours," said he; "I think I can convince you of your mistake; but at this moment I am not at liberty to disclose the secret." At the expiration of two hours, Comte Lavalette named the real offenders to Comte Dubois.

The authors of the hoax proved to be Prince and Princess Louis. They were one evening in their box at the Comédie Française. Opposite to them sat Comte R. de S—— and M. Carion de Nisas, who were laughing very heartily. The Prince and Princess determined to laugh too, but at their expense, by sending them on a fool's errand to Fontainebleau. As the Emperor was gone, they hoped to keep the joke entirely among themselves, for they expected to arrive at Fontainebleau in time to desire the Chamberlain on duty not to show the letters, but to burn them. The affair, however, turned out more seriously than they anticipated; for poor M. Arbusson was conveyed to the office of the Prefect of Police, and they themselves incurred the deep displeasure of the Emperor. M. Arbusson was immediately conducted home, and M. de Lavalette suspended his report to the Emperor until the Prince and Princess had time to frame an excuse for themselves. Napoleon did not very readily forgive tricks of this sort, particularly when his name was mixed up with them.

CHAPTER XXIV.

Burning of Moscow — Discouragement of the French Army — The Retreat — Napoleon on His Return to France — His Narrow Escape from a Party of Cossacks — His Arrival at Warsaw — The Abbé de Pradt — Napoleon's Interview with the King of Saxony at Dresden — His Arrival at the Tuileries — The Emperor's Peculiarities of Feeling — General Kutuzow and General Morosow — Bravery of Marshal Ney — Horrors of the Retreat — Junot's Wounds — General Duroc's Sympathy — Berthier Plays the Sovereign Prince — Junot and Prince Eugène — Correspondence between Berthier and Junot.

THE news which reached us from the Army of Russia was as scarce as it was discouraging. No letters passed; we were deprived even of that consolation which is so soothing to absent friends. Such was our painful situation in the years 1812 and 1813. At that time the first rumors reached Paris of the burning of Moscow * — that horrible catastrophe which the blind rage of Napoleon's enemies led them to characterize as an heroic deed, and which would have been furiously anathematized had the deed been perpetrated by his order. When the deadly cold succeeded the flames of Moscow — those flames whose devouring tongues spread through

* See the « Memoirs » of the Comte de Ségur, who gives the most ample details of this campaign, and also the terrible account of Labaume.

the Holy City with her forty times forty cupolas; when the greater part of that army, surprised in the midst of security, saw that a return home was almost impracticable, then a fatal discouragement took possession of those brave men who had so often faced the most formidable dangers. Too soon our reverses began to assume a more decided aspect. In vain did the Emperor endeavor to conceal the real state of affairs by pretended confidence, and by issuing decrees respecting the theaters, dated from Moscow. Nothing could prevent the truth reaching the army; and nothing could prevent its coming to us, notwithstanding our distance from the scene of the terrible drama.

Kutuzow, wishing to prevent the junction of Marshal Victor, attacked the King of Naples at Winskowo, and defeated him in spite of his obstinate and courageous defense. Napoleon then determined on his retreat. Thus, the whole of Europe in arms — more than a million of men slaying each other — a capital burned and ravaged — widows and orphans weeping — graves opening to receive those who fell, even as they set foot on their native soil — all this tragedy was at length terminated by a calamitous retreat. After forty days' occupation Napoleon abandoned Moscow — Moscow which he expected to see in all her Muscovite and Gothic glory, with her Oriental wealth, her gardens, her cupolas, and her roofs of gold, her palaces, and her bazaars: all these he found buried beneath a heap of ashes.

Napoleon had determined on his return to France amid all the disasters of the retreat. He first mentioned his intention to Duroc. "If you had heard him," said the Duke of Frioul when relating this conversation to me, "you would have admired him more in this than in any other circumstance of his life." Napoleon next intimated his intended return to the Duke of Vicenza, who had lost his brother in the general mortality, and who was desirous of returning to France to console his mother. Napoleon told him that he should travel under his name. The matter was also communicated to Berthier, who with the Dukes of Frioul and Vicenza, were the only persons to whom the Emperor imparted his secret. On the 5th of December he set off for Smorgony, after a long conference with General Hogendorp, the Governor of Wilna, whom he ordered to make every possible exertion to collect provisions and ammunition in the last-mentioned town. "I SHALL HAVE MORE WEIGHT on my throne at the Tuileries than at the head of the army," said he to the few persons who were near him at the moment of his departure; and he was right.

On the following night he had a narrow escape at Ochsmiana. This was a small town, half fortified, and occupied by a body of Königsberg troops. On the Emperor's arrival a party of Cossacks, who entered the town by surprise, had just been repulsed. It was by a mere chance that the Emperor was not taken.* On his arrival at Wilna, Napoleon stopped a short time to see the Duke of Bassano, for whom he entertained a most sincere friendship and esteem. He asked the Duke some questions respecting the condition of Wilna, then a point of the utmost importance to the army. At Warsaw, where he arrived at one in the afternoon, he would not alight at any private house. He went to the Hôtel d'Angleterre, and immediately sent for M. de Pradt, who had been dispatched to Warsaw to collect information and draw up reports on the state of the country. M. de Pradt remained for some time with the Emperor in a little parlor on the ground floor of the Hôtel d'Angleterre, for Napoleon would not allow any other apartment to be prepared for him.†

Nine days after his departure from Smorgony, Napoleon was at Dresden, where he had a short interview with the King of Saxony. From Dresden he proceeded to Erfurth. There he left his sledge, and got into the traveling carriage of M. de Saint Aignan, the Minister from France to the Duke of Weimar, and brother-in-law

---

* This was a most unpardonable instance of neglect on the part of the officer who had the command of the town. The great Condé said: "The most able general may have the misfortune to be beaten, but never to be surprised."

† It is a curious fact that in this same parlor in which the Emperor dined on the day of his arrival at Warsaw, the dead body of Moreau was for a moment deposited, when the traitor's remains were conveyed into the country for which his perfidious hand had pointed cannon against his countrymen and his brothers-in-arms. The funeral convoy passed through Warsaw, and rested at the Hôtel d'Angleterre, and the coffin was placed in the little parlor in which Napoleon had dined a few months previously.

of the Duke of Vicenza. He afterward passed through all the towns on the frontiers; and on the 19th of December, a quarter of an hour after midnight, he arrived before the front gate of the Tuileries. Since Mallet's conspiracy unusual vigilance had been observed by the police of Paris and the sentinels of the Palace. The Empress was about to retire to bed when the Emperor's *calèche* stopped at the gate.

The Guard did not at first recognize him in the little vehicle in which he was seated with the Duke of Vicenza, who after a fortnight's *tête-à-tête* escorted the Emperor to the door of Maria Louisa's chamber, and then hastened to take that repose of which he stood so greatly in need. Before daybreak on the following morning (the 20th of December) the cannon of the Invalides announced to the City of Paris that the Emperor had returned. I was then too unwell to go to the Tuileries, but I dispatched my brother thither, as I was very anxious to have intelligence of Junot. Albert on his return informed me that the Emperor's levee had never been so splendid nor so numerous. As to Napoleon himself, he was perfect, sympathizing in all the anxiety which prevailed, and in the most touching manner soothing the fears of fathers and brothers who came to obtain intelligence of their relatives.

Napoleon, like all sovereigns, felt a pride in being beloved. Yet it is strange that in general he never thought of conferring any but worldly recompenses on the men who were most sincerely devoted to him; as if a single kind word, coming from the heart, would not have repaid such men better than a rich principality such as he conferred on Davoût, who was not on that account the more attached to him. On these subjects the Emperor had singular ideas; and yet, at the time to which I refer, he must well have known what it was to suffer uneasiness of mind. The state of Paris caused him to feel a degree of inquietude which, in spite of all his fortitude and self-command, he could not conceal from those who knew him well. When the Empress Josephine shared with him that thorny seat called a throne, he could make her the CONFIDANTE of his vexations, and that confidence relieved him. With Maria Louisa, on the contrary, he was always obliged to keep up a sort of mask and to conceal from her the cloud which would sometimes gather on his brow; "for," thought he, "she may write to her father; and the Austrian family, who hate me, would rejoice to learn that I have my turn of uneasiness and fear."

While Napoleon was dejected by the first frowns with which fortune had visited him, the Russians were triumphantly chanting their songs of victory. Overjoyed at an event which they had no reason to look for, and which was indeed almost the effect of chance, they did not even see the sacrifice at which their success had been purchased, nor the fragile base on which it stood. Muscovite vanity was reluctant to acknowledge that THE WEATHER had had a large share in their victory; though it was a general remark among the common people in Russia that it was not General Kutuzow, but General Morosow, * who had destroyed the French army.

Junot was deeply affected whenever he spoke of the disasters of the Russian campaign, and he never liked any person to question him on the subject. When we were alone together he allowed himself to give way to the profound melancholy which took possession of him — and then he spoke to me in confidence of what he had seen. One day, at breakfast, he read a long paragraph in the "*Moniteur,*" describing the return to France of part of the troops from Russia. He threw the journal from him with a bitter smile, accompanied by a sort of imprecation.

"Is it not unworthy of the Emperor," said he to me, "to endeavor to conceal from the nation the extent of her loss; and, after all, how is the truth to be concealed? Here is this journal speaking of troops arriving at Mayence on their return from Russia!" At this he shrugged his shoulders. "Of the four hundred thousand men who passed the Niemen," added he despondingly, "not fifty thousand have returned."

He used to tell me that it was at the passage of the Niemen that Ney's bravery and talent were most conspicuously displayed. As to the passage of the Beresina, he could scarcely ever bring himself to speak of it; but one evening he described to us the horrors of the disastrous night on which the army passed that river. He

* General Frost.

made us tremble. Women and children were driven by the lances of the Cossacks into the freezing water of the river; the bodies of the slain were crushed beneath the wheels of the *fourgons* in which useless riches had been stowed; females were captured by the Cossacks and exposed to every sort of outrage; children stripped and thrown naked upon the snow — shrieks and groans mingled with roaring of the cannon; and while the wrecks of the army hurried across the bridges, thousands fell into the river without the possibility of being rescued! Twenty thousand prisoners were taken — the treasures of Moscow were wrested from us, and we lost one hundred and fifty pieces of cannon. In short, we were in our turn plundered — and ignominiously, like vile brigands!

Junot said that if General Kutuzow had not allowed the French to gain two marches upon him, and if General Wittgenstein had not committed some egregious faults, our army must have been utterly destroyed, either at the passage of the Beresina, or more especially at the affair of Kowno, or at the passage of the Niemen. In the retreat from Russia, Ney distinguished himself as he had previously done in the famous retreat in Portugal. He was always the last to retire, and the foremost to face the enemy, and to animate the drooping courage of his troops; in short, he himself was worth more than ten battalions. But in the waters of the Niemen were ingulfed, in spite of the supernatural efforts of the hero, the wreck of the finest army that France ever arrayed against her enemies.

Junot suffered dreadfully from his wounds after his return from Russia. The last wound in particular, which he had received in Spain in the winter of 1811, had given him a severe shock. To this was added a return of pain from another wound which he had received in Italy (at Lonato), which had laid the skull open, and had left a furrow so deep that one's finger might be laid in it. This last wound had probably affected the fibers of the brain, and had deranged the whole cerebral functions. Without having lost anything of his intellectual powers, Junot was in a singular state. During the day he was often exceedingly drowsy, and could enjoy no sleep at night. It was most grievous to see him. One day he was sitting beside my sofa, in company with my brother,

Duroc, and General Valence. I had observed that the latter showed a very sincere regard for Junot, especially since his return from Russia. I felt grateful to him for this, and I was much gratified by the circumstance on which his friendship was grounded. I learned it from Duroc. On the day when we were all assembled together, as I have mentioned above, M. de Narbonne was announced. He had arrived only a few hours before, and hastened immediately to visit one of his dearest friends. Junot flew to him, embraced him, and then, conducting him to me, said:

" Here is not only a friend, but a noble brother-in-arms!" and he shook him cordially by the hand.

M. de Narbonne expressed his concern for the state of health in which he saw me, and observing that we had none but friends with us, he again pressed Junot's hand, and appeared to question him by his looks, not knowing whether I had been made acquainted with what had passed between the Emperor and Junot.

" It is just the same, my dear friend," said Junot, his countenance at the same time changing* " Yes, I suffer here as I suffered when I was there, and perhaps even more acutely."

He laid his head upon my shoulder, and dropped a tear. Oh, what were my feelings at that moment! Never since we had been married had I seen Junot shed a tear but once, and that was under the most distressing circumstances. I therefore knew well how much he was suffering.

" Junot, Junot!" said Duroc, in a loud tone of voice, " you are unjust to the Emperor. He loves you. I can swear that he loves you as steadfastly as he has ever loved you! Ask Madame Junot, who has seen him not long since. Tell him then that he is in the wrong," added Duroc, evidently impatient at my silence.

" I have already told him so," I replied to the Grand Marshal, " and what more can I do ? He will not believe me."

" Because you do not tell me so with the accent of truth, my dear. You would wish to convince me without being convinced yourself." Then, raising himself, he added: " But I know WELL what I do know!"

* He had confided everything to M. de Narbonne in Russia.

"Junot!" exclaimed M. de Narbonne, "I must say with Duroc that you are unjust. The Emperor loves you. In the name of Heaven, whom does he love if he does not love you — you, the oldest of his friends? I say you are unjust to him."

"And do you tell me this?" rejoined Junot, "you who have been witness of what he did for Rapp, when he wished to give him my army corps? If he did not give it, it was because Rapp was too noble-minded to accept the spoil of a friend. But the Emperor wished to take from me those soldiers whom I had led to the cannon's mouth at the battle of the Moskowa. He would have deprived me of the means of acquiring glory. And who could have dared to attempt this, but he who can attempt all? No, no, I am not unjust! Napoleon no longer loves me, and if I may venture to tell you so, he no longer loves us."

Junot was greatly excited as he uttered these words. His handsome countenance expressed the wounded feelings of a generous heart. His friends remained silent, but it was evident that they all sympathized with the old friend who had been looked coldly on in the moment of affliction, and repelled as troublesome when he sought, not for places, cordons, or favors, but for one kind word.*

"My dear Andoche," I at length said, "it is your duty to speak to the Emperor. I have already told you so often, and I again repeat it. I believe that if the Emperor were aware of all that you suffer, he would not only eagerly repair the injury he has done you, but that he would do so in a marked way."

Duroc said nothing; but Albert, M. de Narbonne, and General de Valence, all declared that I was right, and that Junot ought to do as I advised him. At that moment, M. de Valence, hearing five o'clock strike, took up his hat and departed. As soon as he had gone, Junot drew his chair close to Comte de Narbonne, and said to him:

* I love and revere the memory of the Emperor too highly to render it possible that any misconstruction can be attached to my words. I am not making an accusation, but merely stating a fact when I say that the reverses of the Russian campaign had greatly altered Napoleon.

18

"Do you imagine that I have not done what you suggest? Do you think, then, that I have been thus stricken to the heart without at least defending myself? Duroc well knows that I have written; he also knows what answer I have received."

Junot's features here assumed a fearful expression — an expression which, alas! I could afterward easily account for. Duroc advanced to him, and took his hand, which he pressed.

"You distress me greatly, Junot," he said. "Be comforted. Compose yourself for her sake;" and he pointed to me.

"She shall see what I have done," resumed Junot. "I wish also that my brother and Comte de Narbonne should know it."

He went to his own apartment, and speedily returned with a portfolio, containing many letters. Some of these letters were from the Emperor. I recognized the handwriting. This astonished me, because I knew that Junot kept all the Emperor's letters in a small box of sandalwood richly mounted in gold. This box had belonged to Mourad Bey. Junot brought it from Egypt, and from the moment he became possessed of it, he appropriated it to the purpose of containing Napoleon's letters, of which he had at that period a great number. I therefore never thought of asking him for this box, although I much wished for it. The box itself was, moreover, inclosed in a beautiful case made for it by Jacob, and it was kept in Junot's bedchamber.*

Junot then seated himself by my sofa, and taking several of the papers from his portfolio, he said:

"A few months before the bulletins appeared I had some explanations with Berthier, relative to a matter which then concerned me. It was on the subject of the Fourth Corps which I commanded, and which I had led from Italy to Germany, and even to the frontiers of Poland. Some difficulties were raised on the arrival of the Viceroy; I also raised some in my turn — not that I had any repugnance to serve under Eugène, a loyal and brave fellow whom I loved as my brother; but this new

* When the Duc de Rovigo came some months afterward to seize the correspondence of the Emperor, he carried away the little box above mentioned, and I have never seen it since.

arrangement did not suit me, and I protested against it. The answers which I received betrayed a change in the sentiments of the Emperor. I wrote to Duroc on the subject. You recollect it,» said he, addressing himself directly to Duroc.

The latter nodded his head affirmatively, and Junot continued:

«The Emperor was then at Dresden. Here is Berthier's letter; it is official in every word. Berthier sometimes plays the sovereign prince to his old comrades.» Here Junot shrugged his shoulders; Comte de Narbonne and Duroc smiled.

« *To the Duc d'Abrantès.*

«DRESDEN, 28th May, 1812.
«MONSIEUR LE DUC:

«I have to acquaint you that the Emperor has received your letter. I have also received that which you had addressed to me through M. de Contréglise. You are mistaken in supposing that the Emperor has shown you any slight. His Majesty KNOWS TOO WELL YOUR DEVOTION TO HIM, AND HOW VERY USEFUL YOUR BRAVERY IS ON THE FIELD OF BATTLE. You have misunderstood the order which has been given, for I informed you that you would remain under the orders of the Viceroy to command several divisions. But, that the matter may not be left in any uncertainty, I will make you acquainted with the intentions of his Majesty. You will retain the rank of second in command of the 4th corps, under the orders of the Prince Viceroy, who commands several corps of the center. But the 4th corps being a part of the Army of Italy, and formed by the Viceroy, it is the Emperor's wish that the Staff of that corps should be at the same time the Staff of his Imperial and Royal Highness, as Commander of several central corps of the Grand Army. You are therefore, in fact, the Commander of the 4th corps, under the orders of the Viceroy. The Emperor reposes every confidence in you. His Majesty loves you — and for myself, I know enough of you to feel persuaded that this assurance will dispel the uneasiness under which you appear to have labored.

«ALEXANDRE,
« Prince de Neufchâtel.»

« This letter made a great impression upon me,» observed Junot. « I acknowledged the receipt of it immediately; and though my answer was expressed in a single line, it sufficiently told how much I was mortified at this formal and official style of correspondence from an old friend, even though it were a matter of business. Berthier no sooner received my letter, than he wrote me the following answer with his own hand:

"DRESDEN, 28th May, 1812.

"MY DEAR DUC D'ABRANTÈS:

"Why do you make yourself unhappy without reason? The Emperor's attachment to you is unabated. You are now on the field of battle, where he will be enabled to appreciate his true friends. We are of that number. The Emperor has no wish to offend you.— You remain with the 4th corps, as Commander of that corps, under the orders of the Viceroy. It is the Emperor's desire that the Staff of that corps shall be the Staff of the Viceroy, who is the Commander of several corps. You have, then, that which is preferable, viz, the military command of the 4th corps. This arrangement is made only with a view to economy by making one Staff less. The 4th corps has come from Italy, and was formed by the Viceroy — and it is natural that the Staff of that corps should be his Staff rather than that of the Bavarians — that is to say, the Chief General Staff.

Set your mind at rest: the Emperor, in the conversation which he has had with me, has more than ever convinced me of the confidence he reposes in you. GENERAL JUNOT LIVES IN HIS HEART — HE BEARS IN MIND HIS FORMER SERVICES — HE HOPES TO HAVE THEM RENEWED.

"A thousand compliments, my dear Duke,

"From yours,

"ALEXANDRE."

In spite of the assurances contained in the above letter, Junot still entertained some unpleasant feelings on the affair of Prince Eugène, and he again wrote to Berthier on the subject. Notwithstanding the friendship which Junot cherished for Prince Eugène, he could not forget that ten years previously he had seen him a young Colonel in his father-in-law's Guard. Prior to that time, Junot had entertained for Eugène a sort of patronizing friendship, such as might naturally be extended to a promising young officer, by a man of Junot's high military rank and reputation. All this was matter of such recent date that it could scarcely be expected that Junot should bow his scarred forehead to the young Viceroy. The truth is, that the illusion of sovereignty and power never consecrated any of the members of the Imperial Family, except Napoleon himself. This truth, evident as it was, the Emperor could never be convinced of, and many misfortunes may be traced to his blindness on this head.

In answer to the letter which Junot wrote to Berthier, and to which I have above alluded, he received the following, written entirely in Berthier's hand:

"WILNA, 6th July, 1812.

"MY DEAR DUC D'ABRANTÈS:

"I have spoken of you to the Emperor, who considers it useless for you to come here. His Majesty expects to depart hence every moment, and your corps will move to-morrow morning.

"Continue to command the 4th corps. The Emperor does not wish to form a new Staff for the Viceroy, but desires that he should have the Staff of the 4th corps. The EMPEROR ESTEEMS YOU. DO NOT TORMENT YOURSELF. BE PATIENT. HIS MAJESTY KNOWS YOUR SITUATION — HE WILL TAKE IT KINDLY OF YOU TO RETAIN IT. You will fight at the head of the 4th corps. Is not that the principal consideration ? — Is not that being really the Commander ? — Accept my remembrances, my dear Junot. The Emperor will soon take this matter into consideration, and everything will be arranged to your satisfaction,

"Accept every assurance of my friendship.
                                          "ALEXANDRE."

CHAPTER XXV.

Junot's Letter to Me — The Battle of the Moskowa — The Wounded — Marmont — The Bear in a Pie — Junot's Bad State of Health — He Applies for Leave of Absence — Loss of His Baggage — Junot and Bonaparte at Marseilles — The Bulletins — Junot Solicits Leave to Go to the Emperor at Moscow — Receives Orders to Proceed to Moladitchno — His Answer to Berthier — His Letter to the Emperor — The Report of the King of Naples — The Battle of Smolensko — Duroc — His Forebodings — Blamable Conduct of Murat.

A
FTER Berthier's letter dated from Wilna, Junot became more easy in his mind. I received a letter from him dated from Mojaisk; it was written in a cheerful tone, and he spoke almost jokingly of the climate and the cannon balls of the Russians. I subjoin this letter. It is curious, inasmuch as it shows how easily Junot was impressed with anything which came from the Emperor. An assurance of regard rendered him happy — an unkind word reduced him to despair.

"MOJAISK, September 13th, 1812.

"I wrote you a few lines, my dear Laura, after the great battle of the 7th, just to show you that I was not killed, and I now confirm the good news by these presents. I have to tell you, moreover, that though we have had to contend with most deadly weather, and a biting frost and wind which has swept to their graves vast numbers of those who were debilitated by fatigue and privation, yet I am

very well, I may even say better than ever. This morning I made
a breakfast that might have served for four. I was with Desgenettes,
who was dying of hunger, and with whom I drank your health. He
is very well, and I beg you will inform his wife of this.

"The advanced guard of the Russian army is at most ten leagues
from Moscow. It is said that the Russians wish to give us battle
once more. Be it so. We are ready for them whenever they please.

"The Emperor was very well pleased with the conduct of my
army corps at the great battle. The troops, certainly, performed
miracles. I never in my life witnessed such a storm of bullets,
grapeshot, bombs, etc. All my staff officers who were round me
have been, without exception, killed or wounded. Poor Lagrave is
killed!* Alexander has had two horses wounded by cannon balls.
As to me, I remained unharmed in the midst of all these dangers;
I never even had occasion to move or dismount from my horse:
and here I am well.

"You are, of course, in Paris at present, in the midst of your
children, and I am here surrounded by upward of three thousand
wounded men, Russians, French, or Allies. It is a frightful spectacle. Rapp, Grouchy, Nansouty, Friant, Gratien, are among the
number.

"Kiss the children for me; and pray, my dear Laura, for my
return as sincerely as I desire to be near you, whom I love with
all my heart.

"I have written to the unfortunate Duchesse de Ragusa† and to
the Marshal. Ask her if she has received my letter, and send me
news of the Marshal, if indeed he yet survives."

In another letter, dated Mojaisk, October 6th, 1812,
Junot said:

"For the last two days the weather has been superb. I shall
perhaps go to a bear hunt; if I kill one I shall send it to you
in a pie."

A third letter, which I received from Junot, dated
Mojaisk, November 15th, is too important to be omitted.
I transcribe it at length because it is necessary for the
explanation of some things to which I shall presently
refer:

"Mojaisk, November 15th, 1812.

"I have received, my dear Laura, your first letter from Paris dated
September 12th. If you imagine that I let you enjoy so much happiness without jealousy, you are much mistaken. I envy you during the

* It was at first supposed that he had been killed; but it was
afterward discovered that he had only been made prisoner and sent
to Russia.

† I have already mentioned that the Duc de Ragusa was wounded at
the battle of the Arapiles [Salamanca]. The Duchess had gone to
Bayonne to meet him, and had not then returned.

day when you see and caress your children; I envy you during the night, when you repose among them. I hope it will not now be very long before I share this happiness with you; it is the only happiness I shall henceforth care for. I am sorry to perceive that the slightest vexation of mind has an unfavorable effect on your health. You are not yet well; but I entreat you not to torment yourself about the bulletin of the 23d. You are well aware that many innocent victims have felt the FURY OF VESUVIUS. It is a dangerous volcano, and woe to him who is out of favor and within reach of the irruption. But Jupiter may be merciful and may save those whom, but a moment before, he had abandoned to the fury of the volcano. I will tell you all some time or other. I can only tell you now that if the Emperor had seen me that day, I should have been praised; highly praised, etc.»

The following is from Essling, and is dated December 22d, 1812:

«Well, my dear Laura, many days have again passed over without any letters from you, or without your receiving any from me; the fact is I have not been able to write to you. Yesterday your presents arrived at Königsberg; I thank you for them; and I hope I shall be able to go and fetch them myself. I have written to inform the Emperor of the state of my health, the urgency of my affairs, and your illness, which is augmented by my absence, and your knowledge of what I suffer. I have solicited a *congé* which is indispensable to me; for without it I cannot hope to recover my health, so as to be enabled to make another campaign. Request an audience of the Emperor, and urge him to grant me the *congé*. He surely cannot refuse it. I may yet serve him, but if I do not recover, I shall be disabled for life.

« This letter, my dear Laura, will I know, give you pain; but I must write it. I could deceive you when our condition was worse than it is; but now the truth must be told. I cannot walk without the help of a stick, and I am unable to mount my horse.* This climate is killing me, I have lived so long in warm countries, that I feel more than others the rigorous severity of this atmosphere, which, indeed, has spared no one.

« I am going to Thorn, where I hope to hear that my *congé* is granted. The Emperor cannot refuse it. I do not seek it merely from the desire of returning to Paris; but the state of my health, yours, and pecuniary considerations, urge me. I cannot enter upon another campaign without an entire renewal of my baggage; † I must go myself to Paris, and make one more sacrifice. It is only for your sake that I look forward to the future; for myself, I need but little. A man who, like me, has served through this campaign without complaining, may defy

---

* Junot was at that time only forty-one years of age.
† He had lost the whole of his baggage, etc., amounting in value to upward of 200,000 francs. It included his campaign plate, his *fourgons*, his horses and carriages. He saved only a *dormeuse calèche*, and one box of plate.

anyone to imagine the possibility of a change in his sentiments. My
mind, which has been long resolved, is now more firmly made up than
ever, and whatsoever may happen, my attachment to the Emperor is
unalterable.

"Adieu, my beloved Laura. Kiss your children for me. Love me,
and pray that you may speedily see me again.

"I shall set off immediately to Thorn. The cold is dreadfully
severe.

"Yours,

"Junot."

I will now proceed to explain the circumstances which
led Junot to the conviction that Napoleon was to him
no longer the General Bonaparte of Toulon. This change
was perhaps perfectly natural, but it was nevertheless
revolting to Junot's ardent and impassioned soul. He
required a reciprocity of friendly feeling, the more im-
periously inasmuch as he knew how completely he himself remained unchanged. He was attached to the man,
and not to the Emperor. He loved him as sincerely as
when at Marseilles he determined to share the captivity
of General Bonaparte, when the prison was but a step-
ping-stone to the scaffold. It may therefore be imagined
what was the state of his feelings, when he beheld the
first bulletin in which his name was marked by the
finger of malevolence and injustice. Scarcely had he
recovered from his first mortifying surprise, than a second bulletin, still more unjust than the first, overwhelmed him.

He wished to see the Emperor, and asked permission
to leave Mojaisk to go to Moscow. He hoped that a few
moments' conversation would place his conduct, which
had ever been noble, disinterested, and chivalrous, in its
proper point of view. But Berthier still continued to
send him letters like those from Wilna, which I have
above quoted, and Junot was lulled into treacherous
security.

Then came the disasters of Moscow; and for the first
time Junot learned that there was a greater misfortune
than to suffer by Napoleon, viz, to suffer with him.
What would he not have given to have had an empire to
lay at his feet? No one so well as I can know the
anguish he suffered.

He received orders from the Prince de Neufchâtel to
proceed to Moladitchno. The following is his answer to

the Prince de Neufchâtel, and I subjoin to it his letter
to the Emperor:

« MOLADITCHNO, December 3d, 1812.
« MONSEIGNEUR:

« I have received orders from your Serene Highness to proceed
hither. I have been here since yesterday evening, for there was not
a village on the road, and not a drop of water to be procured. More
than a third of the cavalry has been left behind and dismounted.
Some went in search of villages on the roads opening into the highroad; others have proceeded to Wislieka, and it is said that some
portion of the troops have taken the road to Minsk.

« Your Serene Highness's first letter directs me to proceed to Moladitchno, and there to assemble this cavalry, whence I must conclude
that you think it may be assembled to-day. But some time is necessary. I will review them, count their arms and report their condition
to your Serene Highness. You will see what share of glory I may
hope to gain from the command which has been given me for concluding the campaign. Never was a commander of my rank sent on
such a mission; and I can affirm, upon my honor, that I am not in a
condition to resist fifty — I will not say Cossacks — but armed and
mounted peasants. I will obey the orders I have received; but, Monseigneur, if I am doomed to end my life in a way so unworthy of my
past career, I beg you will inform his Majesty of this last proof of my
devotedness. Let him know that I have lived his most faithful and
most attached subject, that I shall never change to the latest moment of
my existence, and that I confidently consign to him the fate of my beloved and unfortunate family.
                                            « I have the honor to be, etc. »

                    « *To the Emperor.*

                             « MOLADITCHNO, December 3d, 1812.
« SIRE:

« This memorable campaign is on the point of terminating. I
began it with a command calculated to procure me glory, and I end it
with one quite unworthy of my rank, and which can bring me nothing
but dishonor. Two bulletins, Sire, have overwhelmed me with grief
and astonishment. If public approbation is not the object most dear to
me, the good opinion of your Majesty is that which I prize more highly
than my life.

« The bulletin which mentions the march of the army on Smolensko
says that I LOST MYSELF, AND THAT I MADE A FALSE MOVEMENT. The fact
is, Sire, I did not LOSE MYSELF; I only made on the second day a march of
six leagues instead of eight, which I intended to have accomplished;
but this matter was easily repaired on the succeeding days. General
Tharreau lost himself through disobedience, though I had left posts of
cavalry to enable him to advance on Boullianou. At ten at night,
when I summoned my generals in order to arrange our march, General Tharreau was not to be found at the post which I had assigned to
him. I concluded that he had remained behind, and sent in search of
him. The officer whom I sent returned to the camp at three o'clock

in the morning without having found him. I then recollected the opinion he had expressed on the preceding day, respecting the direction of our march; and knowing his headstrong character, I did not doubt but that he had determined to proceed to the right to reach the Mitislaw road. I dispatched in pursuit of him Colonel Revest, the chief officer of my Staff, and he found him more than four leagues distant from us. He did not return to the camp until four in the afternoon. I heard that your Majesty had reason to be dissatisfied with General Tharreau, and I hoped by dint of marching to repair the fault he had committed. In my endeavor to screen him, I have brought upon myself the punishment due to his misconduct.* The whole of the 8th corps can bear witness to this fact. But I am only anxious that your Majesty should know the truth: this act of self-justification costs me dear.

« The bulletin detailing the battle of the 19th of August before Smolensko, accuses me of not having acted with sufficient firmness, consequently I betrayed fear. Well, Sire, your Majesty may satisfy yourself of my conduct; it was that day witnessed by General Valence, General Sebastiani, General Bruyères, and several others. I received orders to go and defend the construction of the bridges over the Boristhenes. I did so, and we crossed that river very slowly, on account of our artillery, the bridges being in a very bad state. The roads, which we were obliged to make, also retarded us considerably. I could not debouch from the wood until two o'clock, and I took up my position. I had received no orders to engage. I did not even know, Sire, what troops were fighting on my left; but after the lapse of half an hour, and when Gudin's division arrived, the firing having recommenced much more vigorously I mounted my horse and crossed a wide ravine with two battalions of light infantry and my cavalry. I arrived on a superb position in the enemy's rear. The plain, or rather the plateau which separated us from the position of the Russian rear guard, was covered with sharpshooters and cavalry. Nevertheless, being convinced that we might be useful in the attack of the front, I sent forward my little advance guard, who discovered that the artillery would have to reconstruct a bridge in a village on the right before it could pass. While this was doing, I sent to order the 8th corps to come and rejoin me as speedily as possible. »†

The idea of Junot wanting firmness to enter upon an engagement was pronounced to be absurd, even by his enemies, and his high favor had created him many. It

---

* It would be absurd to say that Junot voluntarily incurred the Emperor's displeasure for the sake of General Tharreau. The fact is, that Tharreau was already in disgrace, and Junot knew what must be the inevitable consequence of bringing him to a court martial. Junot thought that he himself could more easily obtain pardon. This was another of his illusions.

† A few lines appear to be wanting in the above copy of Junot's letter to the Emperor. But they are of little importance. The two affairs are sufficiently explained.

was the King of Naples who had made that report to the Emperor. He alleged that he had addressed the following words to Junot:

"Come, Junot—march!—forward!—the Marshal's baton is there!"

Such was the account of the affair given by the King of Naples. But Junot told a different story, and he corroborated it by proof. It was the affair with the VESUVIUS, which he had explained to me in his letter from Mojaisk, dated the 15th of November. In the first place Junot, conscious of having acted rightly, expected that the cloud which had arisen between him and the Emperor would soon disperse. He knew that the Battle of Smolensko had not been attended by the result which the Emperor wished, and this disappointment sufficiently accounted to Junot for his not obtaining justice immediately. Junot waited long—perhaps too long. He at length perceived that though the Emperor must have been acquainted with everything relating to the Battle of Smolensko, yet he nevertheless observed silence. The King of Naples was to be at the head of the army on the Emperor's return to France. Whether it was that Napoleon did not wish to offend him by a formal contradiction of his misstatement, I cannot pretend to say. But whatever might be the reason, Junot never received a word of reparation for the injuries cast upon his reputation, and a thick veil will ever conceal the first causes of the intrigue hatched against him. The army was then in full retreat. Junot received the order from the Prince of Neufchâtel, which he answered by the letter I have above quoted, and he wrote to the Emperor to explain matters, which Napoleon must have known as well as he did. The Emperor read Junot's letter, and he read it with considerable attention:

"It is vexatious," said he; "but the bulletins are published."

This requires no comment, and I will not attempt to guess the motives which could have urged the Emperor to make an answer so devoid of all justice. I was long in ignorance of all these facts, and I thank Heaven that I did not become acquainted with them sooner. Had I known them on the day when I had the interview with the Emperor, there would, probably, have arisen a more

stormy explanation than that in which, according to the
"Memorial" of Saint Helena, he said "he had allowed me
to scold him AS IF HE HAD BEEN A LITTLE BOY."

After showing us all these papers, Junot said:
"You know now all that has happened during this fatal
year. This is the truth. Must it be by the mouth of
Napoleon that my name is to be transmitted, under a
false coloring, so positively! This thought kills me."

"But surely," said I to Duroc, "something may be
done in this affair. Formerly we might have spoken to
the Empress Josephine. But how is it possible to reach
the Emperor's ear through the medium of such a person
as Maria Louisa?"

The disclosures which Junot had made to me and his
friends tended greatly to relieve his mind. He could
now freely speak on the subject which distressed him to
me and Duroc, when the latter escaped from his prison,
of which he was already beginning to feel the restraint.

One day Junot took him by the hand, and said:
"My dear Duroc, you have cause to complain as well
as I. Indeed, as I said the other day, we have ALL
reason to complain."

I had observed that since his return from Russia, Duroc
had become much more thoughtful and serious than ever
he had been in his life before. I knew him well enough to
be assured that his thoughtfulness was not caused by
anything personally concerning himself. I was not mistaken. He mentioned to us numerous circumstances calculated to create the most gloomy forebodings for the
future.

The news which we received from Russia was not of a
nature to banish these discouraging anticipations.
Murat had abandoned the army which the Emperor had
consigned to him. The more it was disorganized, the
more it behooved him to have remained with it till the
last moment. But he said the affairs of HIS KINGDOM
called him home.

Universal blame seemed to be attached to the King
of Naples. The general officers, by whom my *salon* was
almost constantly thronged since the return of Junot,
expressed the most decided condemnation of Murat's
conduct, in thus abandoning the army at the moment
when new danger was impending. That danger was the

more to be dreaded since its counterstroke would be felt even in Paris. A little reflection might have convinced Murat of another fact, viz, that the blow would shake Naples and his precarious throne more violently than an eruption of his VESUVIUS.

CHAPTER XXVI.

The European Tocsin — Proclamation of the Emperor Alexander — Napoleon's Speech to the Legislative Body — Alexander as Pacificator of Europe — Sixth Coalition against France — Defection of Prussia — Marshal Soult in Spain — Bernadotte's Letter to the Emperor — War Declared against Prussia — Amount of the French Army — Supplies Granted by the Senate — The Guards of Honor — Death of Lagrange — Forebodings of Junot — Duroc Endeavors to Console Him — Napoleon and the Old Soldier — Enthusiasm of France — Marshal Macdonald Abandoned — The King of Naples — Misunderstanding between Murat and Napoleon — Quarrels of the King and Queen of Naples — Murat's Demand — Napoleon's Decree — Letters from the Emperor to His Sister and Murat — Injudicious Articles in the "Moniteur" — Maria Louisa's Indifference to the Critical Nature of Affairs — King Joseph Falls Back on France — Battle of Vittoria.

WARNED of his danger by the tocsin which the Powers of Europe sounded on all sides, Napoleon once more summoned the resources of France, whose blood and treasure were never exhausted when either was required in the defense of her glory and honor. To the occupation of Warsaw by the Russians,* the Emperor answered by a *senatus consultum*,† which nominated the Regency during the minority of the King of Rome. To the first step which was advanced to attack him he opposed the assurance of the perpetuation of his dynasty. To the proclamation of Alexander,‡ which invited the Germans to shake off the yoke of France, he replied by his speech to the Legislative Body. "I wish for peace," said Napoleon in that speech. "It is necessary to the world. Four times since the rupture of the Treaty of Amiens I have made formal

* On the 8th of February, 1813.
† See the "*Moniteur*" of the 5th of February, 1813.
‡ This was dated from Warsaw, 10th of February, 1813.

propositions for it. But I will never conclude any but
an honorable peace, and one that is suitable to the greatness of my Empire.»

The Emperor Alexander soon undertook to play the
part of pacificator of Europe. A manifesto from Warsaw
dated the 22d of February, followed the proclamation
of the 10th from the same city. It called upon all the
nations of Germany to declare their independence, as if
it would have been less honorable to them to answer
the appeal of Napoleon than to bend before the lance
of a Cossack! Finally, on the 1st of March, the sixth
coalition against France was proclaimed throughout
Europe, and for the sixth time she proudly defied her
enemies.

On the same day Prussia, following up her old system
of defection, deserted her falling friend, to form an alliance with one whose fortune was rising. The treaty of
alliance between Russia and Prussia was signed at
Kalisch. At the same time England and Sweden also
signed a treaty for overthrowing the common enemy. A
man who was his natural ally — the brother-in-law of his
brother, signed the treaty which was to create another
enemy to France and to Napoleon; for the Prince Royal
of Sweden* did all, and Charles XIII. was merely the
shadow of a King.

This new treaty of 1813 was only a confirmation of
preceding treaties (24th of March and 3d of May, 1812);
but on this occasion Sweden was bought. The price of
her treachery was twenty-five millions of francs, and the
cession of Guadaloupe, which had been abandoned to the
English by General Ernouf. A revolting degree of baseness characterized all these treaties and capitulations.

Every day the most disastrous news arrived from
Spain. Every letter that reached us brought intelligence
of the loss of a friend, a battle, or a province. Marshal
Soult, who by superhuman efforts had struggled with his
position, which had now been rendered worse by the
removal of the best portion of his troops to Russia, was
obliged to retire to Valladolid in the north of Spain.
This measure, which was indispensable, and which had
been delayed but too long, had a serious moral influence
both on the enemy and on our troops. It discouraged

* Formerly Marshal Bernadotte, Prince of Ponte Corvo.

the latter in proportion as it gave confidence to the
former; and our sojourn in Spain became more than
ever precarious. I think it must have been about this
time that Bernadotte wrote to the Emperor, recommending him, AS A FRIEND, to lay aside his ambition, to moderate that THIRST OF CONQUEST which was fatal to Europe.
"I am disinterested" added he, "in this question, and
you may believe that nothing but my profound attachment to my country and to you prompts this recommendation."

Can anything be conceived more preposterous than
this!—Bernadotte, Prince of Sweden, telling Napoleon,
Emperor of the French, that he ought to sheathe his
sword when he, Bernadotte, draws his. Bernadotte was
now allied to all those antiquated sovereigns which his
Republican pride had so long spurned; but among them
there was not one whose talent could cope with his. In
this respect all, except himself, were null.

While these preparations were making for the *dénouement* of the grand drama, Napoleon was actively organizing his means of defense. The Guards of Honor at
once furnished these means, and became, as it were,
hostages for the security of the internal provinces.
France, which had been unceasingly insulted by Prussia,
at length took a decided step; not traitorously, and in
the dark, but openly, in the Senate of the Empire. In
that assembly the declaration of war against Prussia was
read.

This was a painful moment to those who, like Junot
and his brothers-in-arms, were acquainted with the resources of France. They knew, for example that the
French army in Germany, at the very time when war was
declared against Prussia, consisted of only 30,000 veteran
troops. Its headquarters were at Statsfurts, near Halberstadt. It was commanded by Prince Eugène, who had
taken up a position on the Elbe and the Saale, the scene
of our former glory. We were in possession of Magdeburg, Wittemberg, and Torgau.

The Senate granted the Emperor the supplies he demanded for repelling the meditated aggression against
France. One hundred and eighty thousand men were
ordered to be raised by the *senatus consultum* of the 3d
of April, 1813. Among these were the 10,000 Guards of

Honor who were the occasion of so much outcry being raised against the Emperor. In this, as in many other cases, the Emperor was too well served. He asked the Minister of the Interior for only 2,000 Guards of Honor, and it was thought to be the most flattering compliment that could be paid to him to send 10,000. Thus 8,000 families vented their reproaches against the Emperor, and cursed instead of blessing him. In addition to the above supplies, 37 civic cohorts were created for the defense of the maritime fortresses.

About this time an occurrence took place which deeply affected the Emperor's spirits. It was the death of M. Lagrange, the celebrated mathematician. Napoleon was much attached to Lagrange, and was deeply affected by his death; indeed, the event made an impression on his mind which appeared almost like a presentiment.

"I cannot master my grief," said he to Duroc; "I cannot account for the melancholy effect produced upon me by the death of Lagrange. There seems to be a sort of presentiment in my affliction." Duroc endeavored to dissipate these gloomy forebodings, though he himself could not always escape their influence.

Junot had again fallen into a state of melancholy inquietude, from which all my endeavors could not rouse him. His mental dejection manifested itself in a strange way. He used frequently to shed tears. He who had always been so perfectly master of himself would now sometimes weep like a child.

I was at that time *enceinte*. One day, when we were alone together, he said to me in a tone and manner which I shall never forget :

"Laura, if our child should be a boy, promise, swear to me that you will bring him up to love and fear the Emperor. Promise me that you will spare no pains to inspire him with the same attachment to the Emperor which I cherish, for I still love him!" Here his voice faltered with emotion. "Why do you not reply?" continued he, seeing that I answered only with tears; for I confess that at that moment no power on earth could have made me promise what he asked of me, when I saw his fidelity and attachment so ill requited.

"Laura," resumed Junot, "your silence pains me more than you can conceive. Do you mean me to understand, my love, that my son (if it should be a son) will not receive from you the same lessons which I myself would give him ? »

"But, my dear Junot, you will give him those lessons yourself."

" I! no — no. That would require me to live for years; and my life is measured only by days."

"And can you wish me to reply to such words as these ? Dear Andoche, you do not consider that you are wounding the heart of one who loves you better than all the world. It is unkind to speak to me thus. However, I readily promise that the child shall be brought up as you wish; and when I make a promise, you know I will keep it. But Andoche, the state of your health requires attention. Do not think of returning to the army. To remain at home is a duty which you now owe to yourself and your family. Do not leave me; do not leave your children and your friends, whom you love, and by whom you are so fondly beloved."

Though I should live for a hundred years to come, and other recollections may vanish from my mind, I shall never forget the glance which Junot then cast upon me. His eyes flashed fire, and his whole frame was convulsed with emotion as he exclaimed:

"Laura, you do not understand me! How, when you know the injuries I have received from that plumed coxcomb *—when you know all that his vengeance has contrived to ruin me—you cannot see that I have but one answer to make to all this ?

"And what is it?" inquired I tremblingly, for I was much alarmed by his excited manner.

"To die," answered he. "When I am pierced by a Russian or Austrian saber, when a Prussian or English cannon ball shall hurl me beneath my horse's feet; then I will ask them with my dying breath whether I want resolution."

[That unfortunate phrase of the bulletin was incessantly present in his mind.†]

In the evening he was more composed. It was always after such storms that he seemed to conclude an armistice with his sufferings. M. de Flahaut and General Valence

* He here alluded to the King of Naples.
† The bulletin of the Russian campaign already alluded to.

19

dined with us that day. After dinner we withdrew to the billiard room; for Junot, who was anxious to divert his uneasy thoughts, proposed that we should play at billiards. " I will play against Valence," said he, "and you, Laura, against M. de Flahaut. Valence," he exclaimed, running with the vivacity of a young man to snatch up his cue, "Valence, I will stake twenty-five louis against a hundred bottles of your best Sillery. Will you strike the bargain ? "

"Oh, with all my heart," said Valence, "especially if the Duchess will join us. But she has not said she will."

"Oh, my wife always does as I wish. Do you not, Laura ? " said Junot, who appeared to be in unusually good spirits.

"I can have no objection," replied I, "to be your second in a duel in which the only blood that will be shed is a bottle of champagne. It would be well if all duels ended no worse.

As I finished speaking, Junot stepped up to me, and, embracing me, whispered in my ear:

"Hear me, Laura — you are a good player, and I enjoin you now to play your best. I have a thought in my head — a foolish one, perhaps — but no matter. He raised his eyes, and I was struck by their radiant expression. "If I win," continued he, "I shall regard my success as a token of Heaven's will respecting the cause of my sufferings. There stands my comrade (pointing to General Valence). He knows me; he was beside me when Murat wished to give me orders, though he was not authorized to give me any. And because I did only my duty, he —— "

"Yes, yes," said I, anxious to break off the unpleasant train of thought, "he has acted basely. But come, let us commence our game. Rely on it, I will do my best."

He smiled, and we ranged ourselves in the order of battle.

"But what are Madame d'Abrantès and I to play for ? " inquired M. de Flahaut.

We had quite forgotten to fix our stake, and in truth it was no easy matter to determine on what it was to be, for I made it a rule never to play for money, and as I never drank anything but water, General Valence's stake would have been but little incitement for me to win.

"Well," said I to M. de Flahaut, "if you please, I will play for a bottle — mind, it must be as large as these gentlemen's wine bottles — filled with *eau de Portugal* instead of champagne. Do you agree to this?"

"Willingly! and if you should lose, as you are an invalid, I will add to it a bottle of ether."

We laughed, and commenced our game. Junot and I won. He had his hundred bottles of Sillery, and I my *eau de Portugal* and ether.

"Well, my dear Laura, we have won," said Junot very joyfully.

I looked at him with surprise, for in general he was very indifferent about either winning or losing.

"Do you know," said he to me, after our friends had taken leave of us, "I had connected in my mind with that game at billiards a thought which lies very near to my heart. I played it to ascertain whether the Emperor is still attached to me."

On hearing these words uttered by a man who had for months pined in the agony of doubting whether the man for whom he lived, and for whom he died, returned or acknowledged his devotedness — on hearing Junot avow a weakness which he himself would have laughed at in another, I confess I was moved to tears.

"Well, then," said I, embracing him, "you see that he is still attached to you. Make yourself happy, then, and let me see you as cheerful as you used to be two years ago."

One or two mornings after this he entered my chamber about nine o'clock. He was pale. His eyes were red and swollen, and he appeared deeply dejected.

"Laura," said he, "I must leave you. I am about to depart. See what a GREAT FAVOR the Emperor has conferred on me."

So saying, he threw down upon my bed two brevets, one of which appointed him Governor of Venice, and the other Governor-General of the Illyrian provinces.

"Here," continued he, "is the answer which has been returned to the request I addressed to him eight days ago. I asked leave to serve in this new campaign.* I

* The campaign of Dresden was just then about to open.

solicited as a favor that he would give me the chance of being killed. This is all I now wish for.»

I said everything that appeared to me calculated to console him, and I at length succeeded in convincing him that the appointments offered to him were really posts of high confidence and importance. The Illyrian provinces were an object of envy to Austria; but that motive, perhaps the most powerful of all those, which induced the Emperor of Austria to abandon his son-in-law, was not then so obvious as it afterward appeared. Junot became more calm and seemed convinced of the reasonableness of what I said. At that moment he was informed that Duroc wished to see him. Our excellent friend, foreseeing that the hardest struggle would be at the first moment, had come with the kind intention of saying what he could to calm his irritation. Though I had not risen, I desired that Duroc might be shown into my chamber. Duroc was in plain clothes, and had just been making a morning round with the Emperor, which he frequently did after his return from Russia.

"If he is anxious for popularity," said the Duc de Frioul, "he has reason to be satisfied. Our stroll this morning was through the Faubourg Saint Antoine. I did not myself think that he was so much in favor as he is. You cannot form an idea, Junot, of the enthusiasm of the people. He stopped before some houses that are being built in the Rue Charonne. His hat was slouched over his forehead as usual; but in spite of that, it is so easy to recognize him that I am always afraid of something unpleasant occurring in these expeditions, in which I play the Giaffar. This morning we were surrounded by two hundred workmen, who were all laboring with their pickaxes and shovels. The Emperor was as calm as if he had been surrounded by his Old Guard. While he was observing the men at work, he fixed his eyes particularly on one, who moved his arm with difficulty, and appeared to be less active than his comrades.

" 'It is singular,' said the Emperor, 'but I think I know that man's face.' The workman, observing that the LITTLE MAN looked at him so steadfastly, looked very hard at him in his turn. The scrutiny was not long, and the workman, who was an old soldier, recognized his General.

His pickaxe fell from his hand, and his limbs seemed to tremble under him.

"'General!' exclaimed the man in a voice faltering with emotion.

"'Well, well, my brave fellow!' said the Emperor, 'so you know me, do you? *Par Dieu!* and I recollect you. I said to Duroc, as soon as I saw you, "That is a face I know." Now I recollect you perfectly — you were a corporal in the 32d, and you were wounded at the Bridge of Arcola. *Par Dieu!*'

"To every word uttered by the Emperor the man replied by bowing his head, and saying, 'Yes, General.'

"'But why have you betaken yourself to this work?' inquired the Emperor. 'If you can lift a spade, you can shoulder a musket.'

"'No,' replied the man with an oath expressive of his vexation; 'no, I cannot carry a musket.' And he showed us the difficulty he had in raising his arm.

"'But you were in the Guards at Austerlitz,' continued the Emperor. 'Your name is Bernard, if I mistake not.'

"'It is, General.'

"'And why are you not in the Invalides?'

"'I am entitled to be there, General — but ——'

"'Oh yes; I remember now what you allude to;' and a cloud gathered on his brow. 'Marshal Serrurier did not give me a good report of you. How happens this? If you entertain opinions unfavorable to the Government, you may leave France and go and build houses in America.'

"'But, General, in that case, I must not only leave my country, but you — whom I love even more than my country.'

"'Me!' said the Emperor, laughing. '*Par Dieu*, this is strange enough. How do you reconcile your attachment to me with your hatred of the Empire?'

"'Because, General, my attachment is to you personally — to you alone.'

"I am certain," pursued the Duc de Frioul, "that the man had no idea of the force of meaning conveyed in these simple words, TO YOU ALONE, though they evidently came sincerely from his heart. The Emperor felt them, and understood at once the noble mind of the man who uttered them. Even the title of GENERAL, with which he constantly addressed the Emperor, had its bright side in this little story; for it was not dictated by any feeling of insolence, but was merely the effect of habit in the old soldier. The Emperor looked at him with some little expression of dissatisfaction, but more of kindness. The old soldier stood there before him, hat in hand, and with as respectful an air as if he had been under arms on a parade day at the Tuileries.

" '*Ah ça!*' exclaimed the Emperor, 'have you not the cross ?'

" Bernard half opened his jacket and showed the cross on his bosom. 'You see, General, it is in its right place. You gave it me at the Battle of Wagram for a ball which the Austrians fired at me. You were passing at the moment when they were raising me up, and seeing me wounded, like a brave man, you gave me the cross. It has been a healing plaster to my wound. I never take it from my breast. I sleep with it, and when I come to work I put it within my jacket.'

" 'Why so ?' said the Emperor. 'Do you think that your work would disgrace the cross ? Your labor is honorable, and you should not blush to perform it. What would your comrades think of you ?—those comrades to whom you preach republicanism ? They must laugh at you, my poor Bernard; for, surely, this is nothing but pride.'

" Bernard knew not what reply to make. He recollected that some of his comrades had laughed at him, and others had been offended with him. He cast down his eyes.

" 'Have you not the pension attached to your cross ?' resumed the Emperor after a short pause. 'I am sorry that the Marshal did not ask me what was to be done before he turned you out of the old soldiers' retreat. Was there not some other reason besides that which I have just alluded to ? Come, tell the truth.'

" 'To be candid, General, there was another reason. The truth is, I was a little unsteady on the *décadis*. That is to say — I mean, the Sundays — I was punished several times — and then came that affair.* You know

* The affair, as he termed it, was that he got tipsy one day and called out " *Vive la République !*"

what I allude to, General. "Well," thought I, "since they have turned me out, I must try and get my bread elsewhere;" and so I tried my hand at the spade and pickaxe. But, still, I am sorry at being out of the Invalides; and if you can, General, I wish you would get me sent back again.'

"He raised his head to look at the Emperor, and his expressive countenance was at that moment irresistibly persuasive, for the big tears which overflowed his eyes ran down a furrow formed by a deep scar in his left cheek. The Emperor made no reply, but stood looking at him for some moments, then, turning to me, he asked me for my purse, and taking out three napoleons, he presented them to Bernard.

"'There is something for you and your comrades to drink my health. Now go to breakfast. But do not get tipsy, for then I shall be obliged to pay your master for the loss of your day's work. Adieu.'

"The workmen all threw down their spades, shouted ' Vive l Empereur / ' and thronged round Napoleon to kiss his hands. Bernard alone was silent, and he kept back from the rest; but there was more real affection expressed in his silence than in the shouts of his companions, which were raised for a gift of money. The Emperor, stepping up to him, said:

"' Bernard, you must call on General Sougis or Marshal Bessières; or, if you prefer it, come to the castle and ask for this young man' (striking me on the shoulder). ' He will have a message for you from me.' So saying, he took off his hat, and bade adieu to the workmen, who continued crying, ' Vive l'Empereur / ' long after he was out of sight."

I listened to this story with great interest when Duroc related it to us. As to Duroc, it did not make so great an impression on him, for he witnessed similar occurrences almost every day. However, he agreed with me that this was something out of the common. There was a spice of the ancient Roman in Bernard's character. The Emperor felt this, for he did not converse with him in his character of Sovereign. The monarch would have been displeased — the General not only pardoned, but appreciated the old soldier's greatness of mind. Bernard obtained a situation in the service of the Palace, and he soon accustomed himself to say 'his Majesty,' when he spoke of the Emperor. But the drollest part of the story is that, after the restoration of the Bourbons, he became a furious Imperialist, and would have knocked anyone down who should have dared to speak of the Emperor in his hearing without using the title "His Majesty the Emperor and King."

Bernard had been a stanch Republican before he entered the guards; but he was sincerely devoted to the Emperor. He had served at the siege of Toulon, and in the campaigns of Italy and Egypt, and he regarded General Bonaparte with a sort of religious veneration. He could imagine nothing more exalted than his title of General, immortalized as it was by so many brilliant victories; but on the establishment of the Empire, when the signatures were being collected, he went to Marshal Davoût and told him that he would not sign for the Empire. The Marshal, or some one who officiated for him, mentioned this to the Emperor. Napoleon, who wished that all the votes should be perfectly free, directed that Bernard should sign as he pleased. He accordingly gave his signature for the negative; but it was accompanied by every good wish for the welfare of his General, and the offer of his blood and his life to serve him. When he was wounded at Wagram, the Emperor, who was always anxious to preserve good soldiers and good Frenchmen, gave him the cross, and ordered that he should be attended to as carefully as if he had been one of the officers of his staff. Napoleon was pleased with the originality of his character. It is astonishing that this man never rose higher than the rank of corporal, for he was clever, and had received some little education. The Emperor forgot him for two or three years. Then came the affair of the Invalides, when Bernard had not only spoken with great license, but had several times shouted "*Vive la République!*" In short, General Serrurier had found it necessary to show him the door.

"The recollection of the siege of Toulon," said the Duc de Frioul, addressing Junot, "reminded the Emperor of you; and, I assure you, he spoke of you as the friend he loved best, with Marmont and myself. I affirm this, Junot, on the honor of your old brother-in-arms."

Junot pressed Duroc's hand and said:

" Do you swear this ? "

" Upon my honor. "

" Enough, Duroc. Then I am convinced he is unchanged. I will therefore set off. I will serve him
wherever he may desire me to go; and, after all, what
matters whether my blood be shed in the North or the
South ? But I should wish that the Emperor would grant
me, as he did when I was in Portugal, the privilege of
corresponding with him directly. Do you think he
will ? "

" I am sure of it. "

" How can you be sure of it ? "

" Because he told me so. "

" Duroc, " said Junot joyfully, " ask him to give me an
audience to-morrow morning. "

On the following morning Junot saw the Emperor.
Napoleon was as kind to him as he could possibly wish.
He set off for Illyria, where it was arranged I should
join him as soon as the state of my health would enable
me to undertake the journey. Junot was to go first to
Trent, and then to prepare my residence at Venice.*

France has been reproached with having abandoned the
cause of Napoleon in 1814. Perhaps there really was at
that time a depression of spirit, which had its influence
on the conduct of the French people. But I can confidently affirm that in the preceding year (1813) the public
enthusiasm was very great. The country was once more
in danger. Napoleon openly proclaimed this, and France
heard him. The disasters of the retreat from Russia
were frightful; but such was the affection which that
man inspired that the mass of the people breathed not a
syllable of reproach. Some few voices might be raised,
and occasionally foolish or even clever things might be
said; but what of that ? France faithfully pursued her
glory; and the recollection of twenty years of victory was
not to be effaced by a defeat which might still be excused by the confidence Napoleon reposed in his allies.
But he did not seek this justification, he contented himself with calling his people to arms; and 250,000 men
rallied round the national banners whenever the words

---

* Laybach was the chief town of the Illyrian Government; but as
Junot was at the same time Governor of Venice, I chose the latter
as my place of residence.

FOREIGN INVASION were pronounced. These words were electrical.

Prussia, who was the first, as she ever has been, to give the signal of defection, then perpetrated the odious affair of Taurogen. General York abandoned Marshal Macdonald, who had penetrated victoriously into Samogitia, attacked Livonia, and threatened Riga. He was then constrained to abandon his success, and not only to fall back, but to see his unworthy ally sign a convention with the Russians. Macdonald was obliged to retire as far as Lawartz and the Oder, instead of establishing himself in the enemy's territory. But this treachery excited only a louder cry to arms. France became a camp, and every town an arsenal.

I have already mentioned that the King of Naples departed for his kingdom, consigning to Prince Eugène the command of the army which Napoleon had intrusted to him (Murat). The Emperor had placed a sacred trust in his hands, but he could not appreciate it. He abandoned the precious remains of our brave legions, and cast upon the Viceroy of Italy the whole weight of that responsibility which Napoleon had given as a mark of preference to one whom he thought the bravest and most worthy. He ran away from the responsibility, in short; for the truth must be told. He forsook the army at Posen and returned to Naples.

I will here relate a few particulars which throw some light on the obscurity of this part of his life. A rancorous feeling had superseded the sentiments which once united the two brothers-in-law; these sentiments, however, had never been of the most cordial description. Napoleon's partiality for Murat was grounded solely on his courage, and the useful account to which it might be turned. I do not say this from my own personal impression; I state the fact from positive information, divested of all partiality.

The Emperor did not cherish for Murat the sincere friendship which he entertained for the other officers of the Army of Italy. He used frequently to make him the subject of derision; and many of us have heard him laugh at the King of Naples, whom he used to called a *Franconi King*. This unfriendly feeling was of old date, and its cause was well known to his intimate friends.

The circumstance which rendered King Joachim almost inimical to his brother-in-law had its rise in what took place at the time of his expedition against Sicily (1809). Murat saw himself braved by the Anglo-Sicilian fleet, and with an impulse of courage which was peculiar to him, he exclaimed "*En avant!*" without even knowing that he would be followed. He proposed a descent on Sicily. The course was arranged, and one division, that of General Cavaignac, started on the campaign. The other division did not follow — why, I cannot pretend to say.

But the King of Naples explained the matter in a way which reflected great blame on his brother-in-law. He attributed its nonsuccess to the Emperor, who, he alleged had given secret orders. He returned to Naples mortified by his defeat, and with revenge rankling in his heart. From that time ill feeling was apparent between Murat and Napoleon, and a bitter correspondence was carried on between the Court of the Tuileries and that of Naples.

Queen Caroline, who had been carrying on a sort of opposition to her husband, through circumstances of a purely domestic nature, seeing a fair pretext for war, took part against the King; and the Palace of Naples presented the scandalous spectacle of a conjugal rupture. These dissensions extended to the individuals of the Court. Every trifle afforded the King and Queen a pretext for annoying each other.

There was a physician or surgeon named Paborde, who was a great favorite of the King, and was consequently detested by the Queen; Paborde was on the eve of marriage with a very beautiful young lady (Mademoiselle Saint Même). This affair, which nobody would have cared about if the King and Queen had not meddled with it, became a subject of deadly feud. Joachim, like all henpecked husbands, declared loudly that he would not be controlled by his wife, and that he would not be a SECOND BACCIOCHI. He regarded the French army as a sort of auxiliary for seconding the Queen; the consequence was that he demanded the recall of the French troops. The Emperor frowned, and answered by a dry negative. Murat then manifested feelings of the most absurd distrust. The Queen and he became implacable enemies,

and the interior of the Palace of Naples was a scene of
discord.

A second demand, equally maladroit and ill timed,
completed the misunderstanding between the two Crowned
Heads. Murat required that all the French in his service should be naturalized as Neapolitans. The thing
was ill judged in every way. "Ah!" said the Emperor,
"then it would appear that our brother no longer regards himself as a Frenchman." In his indignation at
this proposition of Murat, Napoleon immediately issued
the following decree, which Joachim did not easily
forget:

"Considering that the Kingdom of Naples forms A
PORTION OF THE GRAND EMPIRE; that the Prince who
reigns in that country has RISEN FROM THE RANKS OF THE
FRENCH ARMY; that he was raised to the Throne BY THE
EFFORTS AND THE BLOOD OF FRENCHMEN, Napoleon declares
that French citizens are BY RIGHT citizens of the Two
Sicilies."

I had at that time a great number of friends in
Naples, several of whom held appointments at the Court.
All concurred in assuring me that nothing could be
more absurd than the conduct of Murat on this occasion. He sulked like a child, tore off his Cross of the
Legion of Honor, and the Grand Cordons of the Order.
He repaired to Capo-di-Monte, and there the most disagreeable altercations ensued between him and the
Queen. Murat devoted himself to low private intrigues,
and frequently passed a great part of the night in reading police reports, which were the more calculated to
alarm him, inasmuch as those who drew them up knew
his weak side. To gratify his taste for espionage he
lost sight of what was due to himself; for he would receive and converse with the lowest and most degraded
of informers.

Still, in spite of all his weakness, Murat had some good
points in his character. In 1812, when the drums beat
to arms, he seemed anxious that the Emperor should
summon him. When the summons was given, though he
appeared to hesitate, he was nevertheless resolved. He set
off for Russia, but it was with a sore heart; and he
manifested his grievances at an ill-chosen moment. As
the Emperor said of him, he was always brave on the

field of battle; and in the campaign of Russia he showed the greatest valor and determination. He gained battles over the Russians, and added to the glory of our eagles. In the dreadful retreat from Moscow the Emperor was surrounded by a battalion which might justly have been called his IMPERIAL BATTALION. In it colonels discharged the duty of sub-officers, and generals that of captains and lieutenants. Murat was Colonel of this battalion.

There was something chivalrous in this body of men, decorated with gold epaulets, thus constituting themselves the Guard of their beloved chief; for such Napoleon was to them at that time, though he thought proper to tell me, in the audience I had with him after his return from Russia, that he experienced nothing but ingratitude.

It has been alleged that when Murat received the command from the Emperor he consented only to lead the army into the Prussian territory, and that as soon as it should reach Königsberg he was to return to Naples. Those who knew anything of the Emperor must be convinced of the inaccuracy of this statement. Is it to be supposed that at a moment when he had serious reason to be displeased with Murat he would have allowed the latter to dictate terms to him — he who would never submit to dictation from any of the Powers of Europe?

The idea is absurd; besides an article in the "*Moniteur*" of the 8th of February (that is, after he learned that Murat had abandoned the command) proves quite the contrary. The following is the article alluded to:

"The King of Naples being indisposed, has been obliged to resign the command of the army, which he has transferred to the Prince Viceroy. The latter is more accustomed to the management of important trusts, and he has the entire confidence of the Emperor."

On the 24th and the 26th of the preceding January, Napoleon had written the following letter to his sister Caroline: "The King of Naples has left the army. Your husband is very brave ON THE FIELD OF BATTLE, but he is weaker than a WOMAN or a MONK when he is not in the presence of the enemy. He has no moral courage."

In February or March following he wrote to Murat thus: "I will not say anything here of my dissatisfaction with your conduct since I left the army; for that is owing to the weakness of your character. You are a good soldier. You fight bravely on the field of battle; but out of it you have neither character nor energy. However, I presume you are not of the number of those who believe that the lion is dead, and that they may, etc. If you make this calculation you are completely deceived. You have done me all the harm that you possibly could do since my departure from Wilna. But I will say no more of that. The title of King has turned your head. If you wish to preserve that title you must look to your conduct."

This letter, which was addressed to Murat in 1813, gave the finishing stroke to his wounded vanity, which had been not a little mortified by the article in the "*Moniteur.*" He now became the enemy of Napoleon.

I may here observe that it was singularly injudicious in Napoleon to sanction the insertion of offensive personalties in the "*Moniteur.*" He perhaps created more enemies by that unfortunate journal than by his cannon. The article on the Queen of Prussia, for example, which was at once false and unjust; those on the Prince Royal of Sweden, M. de Stadion, M. de Metternich, etc., together with all that appeared from 1803 to 1814 against the Prince of Wales, afterward George IV. Truly it is inconceivable that so great a man as Napoleon should have resorted to such petty means of punishing those who had incurred his displeasure.

Meanwhile the clouds gathered more and more thickly, and the storm seemed ready to break. At this critical moment how was Maria Louisa employed — she who, of all others, might be supposed to tremble when the Austrian cannon were about to roar on the heights of Montmartre ? The Empress occupied herself in working embroidery and playing on the piano. She visited her son, or had him brought to her at certain hours of the day; and the child, who knew his nurse better than his mother, could sometimes with difficulty be prevailed on to hold up his little rosy face to let the Empress kiss him.

Maria Louisa was not a general favorite with the frequenters of the Court. This may be easily accounted for. She associated solely with her own little interior circle, and the Duchesse de Montebello was almost the only individual admitted to any familiarity. This choice was doubtless a good one; but still she might have made herself more agreeable at those little *soirées* to which only about forty or fifty ladies were admitted. These ladies were alternately invited, so that about ten or twelve were present every evening. They were the *dames du palais*, and the ladies of honor to the Imperial Princesses.

Spain had felt the effects of our disasters in the North. King Joseph, after having exerted every human effort, was compelled to retire upon France. At this juncture it was especially requisite that our force in Spain should have been headed by such men as Marshal Soult or Marshal Suchet. But the former was still in Saxony and the latter was occupied in driving Sir George Murray from Tarragona, who at length fled and left us all his artillery.

But what signified this victory? Jourdan, who commanded King Joseph's army, was unluckily at the head of it at the fatal Battle of Vittoria. All was lost — baggage, artillery, everything fell into the hands of the enemy. The road to France was impracticable; it was necessary to proceed by way of Pampeluna, and even in that direction the road was covered with guerrillas. It was there that General Foy, with twenty thousand men, stopped almost the whole right wing of the English army at the Battle of Tolosa in Biscay.

On hearing of the disastrous Battle of Vittoria, the Emperor sent for Marshal Soult. "You must depart for Spain," said he, "in an hour. All has been lost by the strangest mismanagement. Depart, and serve me — serve your country, as I know you can serve her, and my gratitude will be boundless!" Marshal Soult departed from Dresden possessed of no other information than the total destruction of the Army of Spain. He arrived on the frontier just as the expiring wrecks of that superb army had touched their native soil. He rallied them, and attacked the enemy at Roncesvalles. The battle was obstinately contested; but what availed even the talent of Soult, it could not recall the dead to life. After the Battle of Vittoria the army had ceased to exist. Its miserable remains retired into France, after leaving upward of eight thousand men among the mountains of Roncesvalles.

CHAPTER XXVII.

The Continental Coalition — The Tugend-Bund — Prussia Declares War against France — Military Position of Europe — Napoleon's Departure from Paris — The Imperial Family at Dresden — Erfurth — Battle of Weissenfels — Defiles of Poserna — Death of Marshal Bessières — Battle of Lutzen — Napoleon at the Tomb of Gustavus Adolphus — The King of Saxony and Prince Eugène — Scene Between the Emperor and M. Metternich — Battle of Bautzen — Bernadotte Joins the Allies — Visit from Lavalette — Death of Duroc — The King of Naples — His Alarm Respecting the English — He Rejoins Napoleon — Treaties of Reichenbach and Peterswalden — Junot at Gorizia — General Moreau's Arrival in Europe — His Interview with the Allied Sovereigns at Prague — The Emperor Alexander — General Jomini — The Two Renegades — Moreau's Death — His Remains Conveyed to St. Petersburg.

THE Sixth Continental Coalition, as I have said, was now formed against France. The Emperor had, perhaps, provoked the total defection of Prussia by his ill-judged rejection of the propositions addressed, on the 6th of February, by M. Hardenberg to Comte de Saint Marsan, our Minister at Berlin. These propositions had for their object to make the King of Prussia a pacificator between the two Emperors. The Court of Berlin, and especially the King, were perfectly sincere when, in February, 1813, they offered their mediation. Two circumstances of little importance prevented its being accepted, and induced Napoleon to place but little faith in this friendly proposition, the protecting air of which was certainly ill calculated to please him. It is well known that after the Battle of Jena the Emperor Napoleon received overtures from the famous association called the *Tugend-Bund* (the Union of Virtue). This association, which had already assumed a formidable character, invited Napoleon to emancipate Germany, and to confer on her representative and liberal institutions. The Emperor committed the impolitic error of refusing, and his refusal was attended by two fatal results to himself and to France. The first was to convert into an implacable and powerful enemy a force which, in his hands, might have become the lever of the north of Europe, by placing at his disposal all the youth of Germany. The *Tugend-Bund* had greatly augmented its power since the Battle of Jena. The cabinet of Berlin was under the influence of that association, and was its organ in important circumstances; it had been instrumental in determining King William to depart for Breslau, where other interests were to come under discussion. The *Tugend-Bund* thus became the enemy of Napoleon through his refusal to espouse its cause.

On learning that the King of Prussia was at Breslau, Napoleon smiled, with an expression which enabled those who observed him to guess what was passing in his mind. The note communicated to M. de Saint Marsan was refused, with some offensive remark. There were two causes which at that time urged the Emperor to a sort of half-revealed hostility toward Prussia: the certainty he supposed he possessed of the treason of the Cabinet of Berlin, and, on the other hand, the extreme confidence he reposed in the Cabinet of Vienna.

As soon as Prussia declared war against France, and proclaimed her accession to the treaty of Continental alliance, we were in a terrible position. The army commanded by Prince Eugène, which constituted our principal force, did not amount to two thousand men — veteran troops! The Viceroy performed prodigies during the time he remained without aid and almost without hope, surrounded only by dissatisfied troops, and by allies ready to desert our cause. We were still in possession of Magdeburg, and the Viceroy's headquarters were at Stassfurth, near Halberstadt, while Rapp, who was shut up in Dantzic, maintained himself like a hero. Junot had departed for the Illyrian Provinces and Venice, for the English threatened the coast of the South, and the Emperor saw, in the hour of danger, the advantage of sending thither a man devoted to him like his old friend. Berlin was occupied by the Cossacks. The new city of Dresden was taken by the Prussians. Hamburg was evacuated, and the forces of the French army, though formidable in appearance, were not calculated to inspire confidence in men capable of appreciating them.

The Emperor's departure, in April, 1813, caused a deep sensation in the city of Paris. On all previous occasions his departure had never given rise to apprehension. Victory had ever been faithful to him; but Fortune had

20

ceased to smile, and alarm had now taken the place of confidence. News was looked for with a mingled feeling of impatience and fear. It was known that negotiations were opened — but what would be the result ?

The Imperial Family assembled at Dresden. The Emperor of Austria, the best of men, and most affectionate of fathers was happy to see his daughter again, and, above all, to see her happy, for so she certainly was At that time the Emperor Francis was not inclined to go to war. Austria was no doubt eager to repair her losses, and especially to make amends for the vast misfortunes which had surrounded her since 1805. Thus, in 1808, the Cabinet of Vienna proposed to that of St. Petersburg the triple alliance of Austria, Prussia, and Russia, which proposition was rejected. But, in 1813, if Napoleon had consented to restore the Illyrian Provinces, and some other conquests useless to France but important to Austria, the latter power would have been what natural and political laws had ordained she should be — our faithful ally.

Napoleon, having left Paris on the 15th of April, arrived at Mayence on the 17th, and on the 25th reached Erfurth. Here he remained a few days and then proceeded to his headquarters. The Battle of Weissenfels was fought on the 29th of April. Our advanced guard, composed entirely of infantry, for we had no cavalry since the disasters of Moscow, defeated the Russian advanced guard, which was composed entirely of cavalry. Alas! this partial triumph was the precursor of a sad reverse of fortune. The ground was disputed foot by foot.

Napoleon was well aware that the issue of the campaign depended on its opening. The conflict was obstinate on both sides and every little skirmish was attended with vast bloodshed. General Wittgenstein commanded a numerous force of infantry and cavalry, with which he was instructed to defend the defile, or, rather, the defiles of Poserna. A formidable artillery force augmented the strength of this position, which, nevertheless, Napoleon resolved to carry. This was on the eve of the Battle of Lutzen, and Napoleon made choice of Bessières for the dangerous enterprise.

On the 1st of May the Marshal, seeing the defiles of Poserna so formidably defended, and knowing how important it was for the French army to gain possession of them, entered the defile of Rippach, which was more strongly defended than the rest, and advanced sword in hand at the head of the *tirailleurs*, whom he encouraged at once by his words and his example. The heights were carried, the enemy was routed, and we were in possession of the defile. At this moment Bessières, who was always the first in the face of danger, received a fatal wound. A ball entered his breast, and he breathed his last before he could be fully aware of the glory that attended his death.

His aids-de-camp and those immediately about him for a time concealed the event from the knowledge of the army. A cloak was thrown over the body, and the Emperor was the only person made acquainted with the misfortune. The intelligence overwhelmed him. Bessières's death was an immense loss to Napoleon; he felt it both as a Sovereign and a friend. That same night the Emperor wrote these few lines to the Duchess of Istria: "Your husband has perished for his country — and he closed without pain his glorious life."

After this first disastrous loss, a triumph, though won with blood-stained laurels, was ostentatiously announced by the French journals. This was the Battle of Lutzen. Napoleon probably wished to revive the recollection of Gustavus Adolphus, who died and was interred at Lutzen. The Emperor arrived at the latter place on the night of the 1st of May. His spirits were greatly depressed.* The death of Bessières, which had happened only a few hours before, and which he was constrained at the moment to conceal — the critical circumstances in which he was placed — all tended to cast a gloom over every surrounding object. Napoleon was not usually influenced by external circumstances, but the very weight of his misfortunes produced a reaction.

---

* The day following the Battle of Lutzen the Emperor slowly traversed the ranks of a regiment of the Guard, his head down, his hands crossed behind his back, and his attitude evincing lassitude and preoccupation. A grenadier wished to avail himself of the occasion to present a petition for his notice, but was checked by one of his comrades possessed of the rough but kindly tact of a soldier. "Leave him alone to-day," said the Vieille Moustache; "see how cut up he is. He has lost one of his sons!" — *Madame Junot.*

He visited the tomb of Gustavus Adolphus,* and there, in the silence of night, during the interval between the loss of a beloved friend and the gaining of a victory, Napoleon experienced impressions which, by his own acknowledgment, appeared to him a revelation. Be this as it may, the Battle of Lutzen was won by a phenomenon, or an inspiration of the Emperor's genius, which a mind like his might naturally attribute to a sort of predestination. "This is like one of our Egyptian battles," said he, as he surveyed the ground; "we have infantry and artillery, but no cavalry; gentlemen, we must not spare ourselves here!" He afterward remarked: "I have gained the Battle of Lutzen like the General-in-Chief of the Army of Italy and the Army of Egypt!" In the utmost heat of the action Napoleon alighted from his horse, and, to use his own words, he DID NOT SPARE HIMSELF. Whole batteries were carried by bayonet charges.

Meanwhile Prince Eugène, by a skillful and well-executed march, had opened the gates of Dresden to the aged King of Saxony. This was the last exploit of the Viceroy's brilliant campaign. Unfortunately Napoleon required his services in Italy, whither he returned on the 12th of May, the very day on which the King of Saxony re-entered his capital. On the 18th of May, Eugène was in Milan. By his intelligence and activity he raised a new army, and that army was fighting in Germany in the month of August following. It consisted of 45,000 infantry and 2,000 cavalry. All this partakes of the miraculous. Within the space of eleven months the Army of Italy furnished nearly 90,000 troops — 40,000 at the beginning of 1812, 20,000 in the autumn, and 28,000 at the end of March, 1813.

These latter, commanded by General Bertrand, joined the Army of Germany on the very day of the Battle of Lutzen. The departure of Prince Eugène made a deep impression on Austria. His journey was regarded, though perhaps unjustly, as a proof of distrust; and at that moment, when Austria openly assumed the character of armed mediator, her dignity felt wounded.

Napoleon had a conference with Count Metternich, for at that time he had not been elevated to the rank of

* There is an obelisk erected on the spot near the roadside from Weissenfels to Leipsic, where Gustavus fell.

Prince. The conversation was warmly maintained, and there appeared reason to apprehend that something unpleasant might ensue. The Emperor began to lose all self-command. He advanced toward M. de Metternich, speaking in an elevated tone of voice, and by a sudden motion of his arm he struck the hat which M. de Metternich held in his hand, and it fell to the ground. Napoleon saw this, and appeared a little disconcerted at the accident.

The interlocutors continued walking about; M. de Metternich maintained his *sang-froid*, and took no notice of the hat. This circumstance, so trivial in itself, had its influence on the mind of Napoleon; he became preoccupied, and looked at the unfortunate hat every time he passed it in a way that showed he was not a little vexed at his own warmth. " What will he do ? " thought M. de Metternich, who was resolved to go away without his hat rather than stoop to take it up.

After two or three turns up and down the room the Emperor, by an artful manœuver, managed to pass quite close to the hat, so that it came precisely in his way. He then gently gave it a kick with his foot, PICKED IT UP, and carefully laid it on a chair which stood near him. In this little affair, so insignificant in itself, Napoleon showed all the address and presence of mind which he so well knew how to exercise in matters of great importance.

While the Army of Italy was engaged in opposing the Russians, the most active communications were maintained between France and Austria. Comte Louis de Narbonne and M. de Caulaincourt, both of whom were very anxious to bring about peace, to which they were likewise convinced Russia was not averse, were appointed to negotiate on the part of France. The Battle of Bautzen was fought on the 21st of May. On the 2d of May, the day on which the Battle of Lutzen was gained, Napoleon had remarked: " We shall conquer about three o'clock this afternoon. " A similar prediction preceded the victory of Bautzen. But what torrents of blood sullied our laurels! Our loss was considerable, though inferior to that of the Russians and the Prussians. The Emperor, on his part, acknowledged the loss of 20,000 men. Nevertheless, the advantage attending the victory was immense.

It rendered us masters of all the roads leading to Silesia, and thus opened to us the heart of Prussia. The news, circulated about this time, of the junction of the Prince Royal of Sweden with the coalition of the Allies, added to the public disquiet. On the 18th of May he had landed at Stralsund with 30,000 Swedes. This, on the part of Bernadotte, was an absolute treason to his country, which nothing can ever obliterate. At Stralsund he assembled, under his own command, an army of 140,000 men, consisting of Russians, Prussians, and Swedes. This was the army which, after having beaten Marshal Ney at Dennewitz, as well as the brave Oudinot, saved Berlin, by preventing Napoleon from profiting by the advantage gained at Dresden.

Paris was deserted. Those ladies whose husbands were absent with the army had set off to their country seats, or to the different watering places, and none remained in the capital except those who, like myself, had peremptory reasons for not leaving it. A little circle of friends assembled at my house every evening. Lavalette came to see me on one of these occasions, and I observed that he looked gloomy and chagrined, he who was always so cheerful and good-humored.

" Heavens ! " exclaimed I; " what is the matter ? You look as melancholy as if you had come from a funeral ! " Lavalette changed color. He put his hand into his bosom and drew out a letter. It was from the Grand Army, and was in the handwriting of Duroc. " Ah ! " said I; " a thousand thanks for this. I have not had news for so long a time ! "

I broke open the letter; it had been written at two separate times, and so rapidly that it was scarcely legible. He had begun to write to me on the eve of the Battle of Bautzen, and had finished the letter next day — so at least I imagined.

Duroc's letter ran as follows :

" It is ten o'clock at night. Though I am worn out with fatigue, I am unwilling that a courier should leave without bearing some tidings from me, as I have not had an opportunity for a long time of writing to you. But you will not reproach me, because you know full well my friendship for you.

" I received yesterday a letter from Junot, to which I will reply as soon as I have an instant; in the meantime tell him that the Emperor is content with him, and '*qu'il l'aime toujours*.' Poor Junot ! it is with him as with me; the friendship of the Emperor is the breath of our life; indeed, I could not support the sight of his displeasure.

"The death of Bessières is terrible. He is fortunate in the tribute of universal regret that has been paid to him.

"Yet another victory ! It seems that a happy presentiment made me hasten to close my letter. This victory is the result of one of the finest pieces of generalship in the whole military career of the Emperor. You can indeed be proud of his talents. Good-bye. Send me word how you are. I am anxious about you.

"DUROC."

Next morning, before ten o'clock, M. de Lavalette again called on me. On recollecting his agitated manner the night before, a sinister idea crossed my mind; I thought of Illyria, and hurrying to meet him as soon as he entered, I exclaimed: "What has happened to Junot?" "Nothing," he replied; and, seating himself beside me, he took both my hands in his, and said in that feeling manner so peculiarly his own:

"My dearest friend, we have sustained a great misfortune, for it is a misfortune common to us all." Then, after a pause, as if fearful to utter the fatal words, he added: "Duroc is dead! He was killed at the Battle of Ripenbach, or, rather, by one of those fatalities which Providence is pleased to inflict upon us—it was after the battle was ended!"

He then informed me that Duroc, standing behind the Emperor in conversation with General Kirschner, was killed by the ricochet of a ball, which was fired from so great a distance that it was inconceivable how it should have taken effect. It did so, however, and too fatally; for the second rebound inflicted Duroc's deathblow. This event deeply affected the Emperor. He followed the Duke of Friouli to a cottage, to which he was conveyed, in the village of Marksdorff, at the entrance of which the fatal occurrence took place. Duroc, who was scarcely able to breathe, was laid on a bed, and a sheet was thrown over him. On seeing the Emperor so deeply moved, he said: "Sire, leave this scene, I entreat you; it is too much for your feelings. I consign my family to your care."

Duroc was one of those rare men who are but sparingly sent into the world. He was universally beloved and esteemed, and the favor which the Emperor bestowed on him never excited envy. His death was an irreparable loss to Napoleon.*

I had many friends at Naples attached to the Court of the Queen and King Joachim, and I received from them, about this time, letters which surprised me strangely. The King, I was informed, had received from the Emperor orders to rejoin him in Germany, and it was reported, even in the interior of the Palace, that Joachim refused to go. I may here briefly relate the circumstances which followed the inexplicable departure of the King of Naples, when he abandoned the French at Posen on the 17th of January, 1813.

Murat, doubtless, behaved badly to the Emperor; but it is a fact of which I have proofs in my possession, that a conspiracy formed in the bosom of his family was the sole cause of his first faults. It was likewise a very artfully-contrived scheme which occasioned his precipitate departure from Posen on the 17th of January. Unfounded alarms were raised in the mind of Joachim relative to the designs of the English on his dominions. Urgent messages were dispatched to him, with the intelligence that an English fleet was in sight off the coast of Calabria, and that preparations were making for a landing.

This intelligence, together with letters from the Queen, induced him suddenly to leave his headquarters at Posen. He set off, accompanied by his aid-de-camp, General Rosetti, and hurried to Naples in a state of anxiety which almost deprived him of the power of sleeping or taking food. Sometimes he would rub his head, and wildly exclaim: "The English! The English! Rosetti, you will see that when we get to Florence we shall find they have landed, and that they are masters of Calabria!"

Instead of repairing to Naples, he proceeded to Caserta, where the Queen and her family then were. The lady who furnished me with these particulars was at that time at Caserta in the exercise of her Court duty. She assured me that the first interview between Joachim and Caroline was exceedingly cold and constrained, and that violent scenes ensued after the King's return. Murat rejoined the Emperor during the armistice of Pleswitz.

* And one not forgotten by him. See in his will made at Saint Helena mention made of Duroc's daughter. [Duroc had married a Spanish lady, Mademoiselle Hervas d'Alménara.]

Napoleon gave him the command of the right wing of the army on the day of the Battle of Dresden.

From that time to the moment of his departure for Italy, which was after the Battle of Leipsic, his conduct was worthy of what he had shown himself to be when with the Army of Italy and in Egypt. He seemed anxious to prove that he had no wish to spare his blood in the service of the Emperor.

Our ill fortune in Spain produced a fatal influence in the North in spite of the presence of Napoleon. The combined disasters of Russia and the Peninsula inspired our adversaries with renewed confidence. Alliances were signed against us in all quarters. The treaties of Reichenbach and Peterswalden gave to the coalition an army of two hundred and fifty thousand men; and yet, at the commencement of the campaign, England was so destitute of financial resources that she could not grant subsidies.

About this time I received a letter from Junot dated Gorizia. He had set out on a long journey along the shore of the Adriatic; but the information he received led him to apprehend that the English would effect a landing at Fiume. He immediately returned to Gorizia; and on the 5th of July the English really presented themselves before Fiume with a small squadron, consisting of an eighty-gun ship and several smaller vessels filled with English troops. The ships fired on the city, and after a short resistance, which was materially abridged by the defection of some Croatian troops, the English effected a landing.

General Moreau, who had resided for some time in America, embarked on the 21st of June for Europe, accompanied by his wife and M. de Swinine, a person attached to the Russian embassy. Moreau returned to Europe with revenge in his heart, and a determination to wreak it at any price, even that of honor. He landed, I think, at Gothenberg on the 24th of July, and from thence proceeded to Prague to see the Allied Sovereigns, who awaited him with a degree of impatience which seemed to say: WE COUNT ON YOU TO AID US IN OUR DESIGNS ON FRANCE.

He agreed to direct the operations of the campaign. No doubt he must have felt many bitter pangs of remorse when he beheld those national colors and those uniforms which he himself had so often led against the Austrians and Prussians. On the eve of the Battle of Dresden the Emperor Alexander came to him and said: "I have come to receive your commands; I am your aid-de-camp." A Russian officer who was present on this occasion assured me that when the Emperor Alexander uttered the above words Moreau became deadly pale, and trembled so violently that it was easy to discern the painful state of his feelings. One day he met General Jomini, who, owing to some cause of dissatisfaction, had left the French army, in which he had long served. Moreau, though but slightly acquainted with him, was so happy to find someone situated like himself that he stepped up to him and took him cordially by the hand. General Jomini, however, withdrew his hand, and replied coolly to the greeting of Moreau.

"It is somewhat strange," said the latter to his fellow-renegade, but with a certain degree of reserve, for he saw the other was not inclined to meet his advances— "it is strange that we should meet here under circumstances so similar." "It is one of the whimsical decrees of fate," replied General Jomini; "but, after all, our cases are not so very similar, for you must know I am not a Frenchman." Moreau heaved a deep sigh, and, covering his face with his hand, turned away and said no more. This circumstance took place three or four days before his death.*

* Moreau was killed in the following manner: — Accompanied by the Emperor Alexander, he was making a reconnaissance before Dresden on the 27th of August, 1813. The Czar, following up his declaration of being Moreau's aid-de-camp, obliged him to pass first along a bridge which was rather narrow. A ball fired from the French army struck Moreau and shattered his right knee, then, after passing through the body of his horse, it carried away a part of his left leg. Consternation prevailed throughout the Russian camp. The Czar was deeply affected. As to Moreau, he suffered a martyrdom of agony. A litter was formed, which was supported on the Cossacks' pikes, and in this manner Moreau was borne from the field of battle. He was conveyed to a house, where the Emperor Alexander's chief surgeon amputated his right leg. He bore the operation courageously, and when it was over he said to the surgeon: "But the left, sir, what is to be done with that?" The surgeon looked at him with surprise. "Yes," pursued Moreau, "what is to be done with this fragment of a limb? It is perfectly

CHAPTER XXVIII.

The Duke of Rovigo — Junot's Illness and Death — State of Spain — Treaty of Alliance with Denmark — Congress of Prague — Propositions to Austria — Rupture of the Armistice — Prince Schwartzenberg — Battle of Dresden — French Reverses Elsewhere — Surrender of Saint Sebastian — Wellington Enters France — Battle of Leipsic — Death of Prince Poniatowski — Napoleon's Visit to the King of Saxony — The French Army Cross the Rhine — The Emperor's Arrival at Mayence — Surrender of Pampeluna — The French Driven from Spain — The Typhus Fever — Treachery of Prince Schwartzenberg and the Prince of Wirtemberg — Evacuation of Holland — Restoration of the House of Orange — Napoleon's Arrival at Saint Cloud — Murat — Intrigues of England — Admiral Bentinck and the Duc de Vauguyon — The Emperor's Laconic Letter to Murat — The Duchesse de Narbonne — Napoleon's Benevolence — Bourbon Ingratitude.

THE severe shock I had sustained by the death of my two valued friends, Bessières and Duroc, had produced a serious effect upon my health; but, alas! a still more dreadful blow awaited me. One day, as I was reclining on my sofa after a sleepless night and much suffering, I was startled by the voice of my brother, who was speaking loudly in the adjoining room. In his interlocutor I fancied I recognized the voice of the Duke of Rovigo. In a moment the door was opened, and the Duke, though kept back by my brother, pushed his way into the room.

"I come by command of the Emperor," cried the Duke, "and in his name I must have free access everywhere."

useless." The surgeon replied that he feared it would be impossible to save it. "Then cut it off," said General Moreau coolly; and he extended his leg with a stoicism which would have been truly sublime had he received the wound FOR his country. He suffered the most terrible agony. The Emperor Alexander was deeply afflicted at the terrible death of the man whom he had called his friend and taken as his counselor. He shed tears upon his death-bed. The whole Allied army might be said to have received a wound in the person of General Moreau. The army was beaten at every point, and completely routed. The torments endured by General Moreau might almost be regarded as a retributive punishment. An aid-de-camp of the Emperor Alexander informed me

At these words Albert ceased to dispute his entrance, and he advanced into the room. Albert stepped up to me, and taking both my hands in his, said in a voice faltering with agitation: "My beloved sister — summon all your resolution, I implore you. The Duke brings you sad tidings — Junot has been attacked with a serious illness." *

These words pierced me to the heart; I uttered a stifled scream, but could not articulate a single word. Albert, perceiving the thought that crossed my mind, embraced me, and said: "No, on my honor, nothing has happened worse than what I tell you. My dear sister, compose yourself; for the sake of your children, for the sake of Junot, I entreat you."

He threw on my knee a letter which he had brought with him, and which inclosed another one from my husband. It was one which Junot had written in the first

---

that he was assailed by an intolerable thirst, and that he suffered the torture of a death in the desert. He expired on the night of the 1st of September. His body was embalmed at Prague, and conveyed to St. Petersburg, where the Czar caused it to be buried in the Catholic church of that city.

On the 28th of August the curiosity of the wayfarers in one of the streets of Dresden was attracted by the piteous howling of a dog. He was one of those English terriers so remarkable for attachment to their masters. The dog wandered about evidently seeking someone he loved; at length, when exhausted by fatigue, he lay down at the threshold of a door. One of the passers-by, who had been struck by the poor animal's evident distress, observed a silver collar which he wore round his neck, and on examining it closer found inscribed upon it the words, "*J'appartiens au Général Moreau.*"

* Immediately on receiving the intelligence mentioned above, I, though in a delicate condition of health, set out for the frontier, and proceeded as far as Chamouni, where I awaited with impatience the arrival of Junot. The General, however, had been brought to Lyons, and thence was conveyed to my father-in-law's residence at Montbard.

When the news of Junot's death reached the Emperor, he was at the Marcolini Palace at Dresden. He had there an apartment where he transacted business, a very favorite one of his, as it opened immediately upon the garden, and also had a private exit, so that he was not obliged to run the gauntlet of the Chamberlains and Court officials.

When my brother's letter was given to him he hastily tore it open, holding it in his left hand. After he had read the first few lines he violently hit the letter with his right hand, striking it out of his grasp, and then, recovering his hold with the rapidity of a flash of lightning, exclaimed: "Junot! . . . Junot! . . . Great God! . . ." clasping his hands together so tightly that the letter was completely crushed.

moments of his madness, and he had sent it off by a special courier to the Emperor, who now forwarded it to me, accompanied by a few words in his own handwriting:

«Madame Junot:— Look at the inclosed letter which your husband has written to me. I have been greatly distressed in reading it. It will give you a terrible insight as to his condition, and you should take immediate measures to remedy it. Leave without losing an instant. Junot must now be on the French frontier, according to the news given to me by the Viceroy. «N.»

I let the letter of the Emperor fall to the ground, and gazed half stupefied at my brother and at the Duke of Rovigo. Indeed, I was myself almost bereft of reason at that moment.

The suddenness of the intelligence completely overpowered me. I had received, only four days previously, a long letter from Junot, which bore not the slightest trace of the terrible mental illness that was now so unexpectedly disclosed to me. The Emperor would not allow Junot to be brought to Paris for medical aid, but directed that he should be taken to his family at Montbard. Alas! my most dreadful anticipations were realized. The most unfortunate scene had ensued on the arrival of my husband in his paternal home.

Junot's father, who was naturally of a melancholy temperament, sank into a state of helpless stupor on witnessing the afflicting malady of his son. Junot's sisters could do nothing but weep and lament, and his nephew, Charles Maldan, was a perfect nullity. Junot was, however, surrounded by the affection of the inhabitants of his native town, who seemed to vie with each other in showing him the most considerate attention.

There are events which the mind cannot endure to dwell on, in spite of any effort to summon resolution. I can scarcely ever bring myself to think or speak of the melancholy scenes which ensued at Montbard after the arrival of Junot, who breathed his last on the 29th of July, at four in the afternoon.

* * * * * * *

Now, after the lapse of a long interval of time, I can pardon, though I cannot forget, the culpable stupidity of Junot's family, who suffered the man whose safety they should have watched over from pride, if not from affection, to do what he did in the delirium of a brain fever.

My own convalescence was long retarded. Though still
at the early age of twenty-seven, I had been struck down
by two of the most cruel blows a woman could undergo
— the simultaneous loss of a husband and a child.

Indeed, for a long time my brother Albert could not
look at me without the tears standing in his eyes, as he
regarded my excessive paleness as being the precursor
of my death.

One morning a post chaise entered the court of Sech-
eron, and, to my surprise, my brother-in-law, M. Geouffre,
got out of it. "My children, my children! What has
happened to them?" I cried. "Nothing at all," he said.
"I have come to bring you a letter from the Minister of
State, in which he has officially demanded all the private
correspondence of the Emperor with Junot." Junot possessed more than 500 letters in Napoleon's own handwriting, and these were kept in a secret drawer. Albert
sprang up from his chair, and exclaimed in a voice of
thunder: "It is false! The Emperor cannot have commanded such an insult!" The Duke of Rovigo had presented himself at my Hôtel, and had requested the
presence of one of the guardians of my husband's property
in order that he might obtain possession of the Emperor's
letters. My brother-in-law attended, and informed him
that the usual official seals after death had been placed
on all the drawers in the absence of the owner. General
Savary only laughed at this reply, and said: "Bah! I
have my orders. You must give me the letters of the
Emperor, and I must take them." My brother told him
of an obstacle in the way — namely, a golden word-lock
placed upon the secret coffer. "The Duchess is the only
person who knows the word now my poor brother no
longer exists; and the key which the Duke always carried
about with him was lost during his illness." "I beg your
pardon," said the Duke of Rovigo, holding out his hand,
"here is your brother's gold key."

This was a circumstance I could never understand.
Albert had seen the key recently at Montbard. How,
then, could Savary have got possession of it?

The coffer was opened, for the Duke had also discovered
the password (which was my own name misspelled —
"LORE"), and he took out all the letters of the Emperor,
and also those of another member of his family, my

brother-in-law protesting at the same time against the violation of the seals which had been placed upon my property by the Juge de la Paix.

The intelligence from Spain received in private letters was very alarming. Napoleon still maintained the war in the Peninsula, and contented himself with sending back Marshal Soult, whose forces he diminished by taking 12,000 of the Guard, and nearly 40,000 of the old troops. This was depopulating the Army of Spain. The result of this measure was that Marshal Suchet was obliged to abandon Valencia, and march on the Ebro. In the meantime we signed a Treaty of Alliance with Denmark, and the Congress of Prague was opened.

At that Congress were decided the destinies of Europe, and Napoleon lost the game he was playing against the Sovereigns solely by his own fault. One of the causes which chiefly contributed to his error was the mistaken opinion he had formed of M. Metternich. I have heard him express this opinion in conversation. Subsequently, perhaps, he corrected it; but at that time M. Metternich's dignity was wounded.

On the 8th of August, Napoleon sent new propositions to the Emperor Francis. New discussions ensued. The 10th of August arrived; the armistice was broken, and the Sovereigns of Sweden, Russia, and Prussia signified to France their intention of resuming hostilities. There then appeared reason to believe that Napoleon's principal object had been merely to gain the time necessary for the arrival of his troops.

As to the Confederation of the Rhine, it was first proposed to break it up — then continue it. The whole of Italy was to remain under the direct or indirect domination of France. We therefore became a dangerous rival to England with our ports, and those of Italy, Belgium, and Holland. The war commenced. Napoleon had now to depend upon the resources of his genius. The Allied forces amounted to 600,000 men, while those of France did not exceed 350,000, two-thirds of which consisted of young conscripts scarcely arrived at manhood. To the numerical advantage of the Allies must be added the immense advantage they possessed in fighting on friendly territories, with the facility of obtaining provisions, etc.

On the 20th of August, Napoleon was informed of the junction of the Austrian troops with the Allies. Prince Schwartzenberg was appointed Generalissimo of all the forces of the Coalition. Napoleon was still himself, and his presence at the head of his army had not lost its magic power. On the 20th of August he learned that Austria had abandoned him; and on the 21st he resumed the offensive, and defeated Blucher. Amid the triumph of Goldberg,* he was warned of the march of the Allies on Dresden,† advised by Moreau. He resigned the Army of Silesia to Macdonald, and hastened with his Guard to succor Dresden,‡ where he arrived at nine on the morning of the 26th.

Some skirmishing was going on in the suburbs. Napoleon then gave an example of that luminous intelligence which elevated him to the highest rank among military commanders. His eagle eye scanned the battle at a glance. He immediately saw the course on which depended victory or defeat. Instead of waiting for the attack, he ordered it. The Prussians and Russians, apparently bewildered by the impetuosity of the movement, were repulsed to a great distance, leaving 40,000 slain on the ground which they had been masters of in the morning.

On the evening of that day Napoleon entered Dresden with the 2d and 6th corps. Throughout the whole of the battle he had himself fought like a sub-lieutenant, sword in hand; he was always the foremost, leading the way with equal indifference to death or glory. During the battle he had only 65,000 men to contend with 185,000. Next day the Emperor arose before daylight, having had only two hours' sleep. He took his station in the center, with the King of Naples on his right and the Prince of the Moskowa on his left. In this manner he attacked the enemy, whose forces amounted to 180,000.

Napoleon's plan was not, and could not have been, arranged beforehand. He took his glass, and examined

---

* A strong position, carried by our army on the 23d of August, 1813.

† The combined forces had debouched from Bohemia on Dresden by the left bank of the Elbe, while Napoleon repulsed Blucher in the direction of the Oder.

‡ The troops marched forty leagues in seventy-two hours without receiving rations; and they fought for ten days without rest.

the field of battle. He discerned a great void. This was to be filled up by the corps of Kleinau, but it could not be brought up until two o'clock, and it was now only six. Napoleon at once conceived his plan of victory. The attack was arranged, executed, and proved victorious. The enemy lost 17,000 prisoners, and 14,000 killed or wounded. Such were the results of this brilliant and ably-planned battle.*

He was now master of Dresden. Alexander was flying, and Fortune had resumed her smiles. But, in the meanwhile, Marshal Macdonald had sustained a terrible reverse. Blucher was driving him from Silesia. Marshal Davoût also was evacuating Schwerin. General Vandamme was made prisoner in the mountains of Bohemia with 12,000 men. Marshal Oudinot was defeated by his old comrade Bernadotte.

This event saved Berlin, which the Emperor had so confidently counted on entering that decrees had been prepared dated from that city. The disasters of the campaign were in a great measure attributed, and perhaps justly, to General Jomini, who carried over to the enemy documents which he had surreptitiously obtained from Marshal Ney. The intelligence thus conveyed saved Berlin, as it made known Napoleon's intention of proceeding thither.

Not only in the North, and under his own eyes, did reverses crowd upon each other; Spain was torn from him, province by province, village by village. Our troops bravely defended every inch of ground; but resistance only served to prove our weakness. Marshal Suchet, however, once more sounded the trumpet of victory. Lord William Bentinck, who had brought fresh troops from Sicily, landed them on the coast of Catalonia.

A battle was fought at Villafranca de Panada, eight leagues from Barcelona, and the Anglo-Sicilian army, which was defeated by Generals Suchet and Decaen, lost an immense number of troops. But such was our position that we could not afford to lose a single man, even though his loss might be compensated by slaying ten of the enemy. The victory of Villafranca de Panada did

* It is well known that Napoleon very often spoke of his lucky star. At the conclusion of this important day he exclaimed: « I cannot be beaten! »

21

not prevent the surrender of Saint Sebastian. The English took that fortress after a protracted and inglorious siege; and they committed all the horrors which we read of in the history of the Middle Ages on the occasion of the sacking of cities by the bands of *condottieri* or free troops. Wellington now crossed the Bidassoa and entered France.

Hostilities had recommenced on the 28th of September by a combined movement of three of the Allied armies. The Emperor at first beat Blucher, and obliged him to retire on the Saale. Napoleon seemed now to flatter himself with the idea of renewing on the line of the Elbe, the glory of Frederick in his wars with Austria. It is strange that in such a position he should have allowed empty visions to engross his mind. His most important object was to secure the fidelity of Bavaria and Wirtemberg; and these two Allies forsook him.

He learned at Duben the defection of both from the King of Wirtemberg himself. The Emperor entered Leipsic on the 15th of October. We now possessed only 600 pieces of artillery, and the Allies had more than 1,000. All the veteran and most efficient portion of our army were shut up in garrisons, and the Emperor, by some inexplicable infatuation, awaited 350,000 men before Leipsic, with a feeble and dispirited force scarcely amounting to 140,000. The day after his arrival at Leipsic, Napoleon gave the enemy battle before a village called Wachau, and was victorious. He now proposed an armistice to the Allied Sovereigns, and offered to evacuate Germany as far as the Rhine. But it was too late. They refused the proposed armistice.

Dismay pervaded the minds of all the Generals-in-Chief who surrounded Napoleon. A council was held by them, to which Berthier and M. Daru were summoned. They all agreed that he should do anything rather than come to an engagement. The conference being ended, Comte Daru and the Prince of Neufchâtel solicited an audience. Berthier represented the immense disadvantage of fighting with such an inferiority of force. He added that the Generals themselves were so disheartened that they were unable to animate the sinking courage of their troops; and he closed his picture by representing the terrible chance of a defeat opening to our enemies the road to Paris.

Encouraged by the silence of the Emperor, M. Daru spoke in his turn. He pointed out the destitute condition of the army, without a hospital in its rear, a circumstance which operated as a powerful discouragement to the troops. "Your Majesty is aware," pursued the Count, "that it is not my fault if we have not our accustomed resources. It is therefore necessary that we should come to a determination which, however mortifying it may be, is nevertheless urgent in present circumstances."

Napoleon looked for some moments at Comte Daru and the Prince of Neufchâtel, and then said: "Have you anything more to tell me?" They bowed, and made no reply. "Well, then, hear my answer. As to you, Berthier, you ought to know very well that your opinion on such a question has not the weight of a straw against my determination. You might therefore have spared yourself the trouble of speaking. You, Daru, should confine yourself to your pen, and not interfere with military matters. You are not qualified to judge in this affair. As to those who sent you, let them obey. This is my answer." He then dismissed them.

The next day the Battle of Leipsic was fought. What must have been Napoleon's feelings when he beheld a quarter of his troops pass over to the enemy, and point against their comrades the guns which had dealt death among the enemy's ranks only an hour before! In this manner the Battle of Leipsic may be said to have been both lost and gained by our army. The center* and the right were victorious. The left was abandoned by the Saxons in the middle of the battle, and delivered up to the enemy. The Battle of Leipsic, instead of being a defeat, may be said to have been one of Napoleon's most brilliant military achievements. At all events, the day was as glorious to him as it was disgraceful to those who so basely betrayed him; and, I may add, to those who so basely bought over the traitors.

The retreat was ordered, and it commenced in the

---

* The center was commanded by the Emperor in person, and the right by the King of Naples. For the space of seven hours they resisted upward of 270,000 men with a force of 9,500. The Prince of Sweden overpowered Marshal Ney on the left. The Marshal, nevertheless, defended himself for a considerable time with 40,000 men against 150,000.

most perfect order. Night was then drawing in. Before daylight the bridges were crossed, and all was proceeding without confusion, when an event, which has never yet been clearly explained, spread terror through the ranks of the French army. I allude to the blowing up of the bridge across the Elster. The subofficer by whom this act was committed, either from want of judgment, or, what is not improbable, being bribed by the enemy, was the sole author of the misfortune by which the rear of our army was sacrificed.

This officer, who was directed to blow up the bridge across the Elster, stated that he was deceived by a party of Cossacks who had advanced and crossed the river; and the bridge was destroyed while ten thousand men were still engaged in defending the barriers of the suburbs to afford time to the reserve and the parks of artillery to pass, supposing the enemy to be still in possession of the city. This event, which separated the troops who had crossed the bridge from all the reserve, was a fatal blow to the French army. The rear guard, having no means of retreating, was at the mercy of the enemy. A frightful scene then ensued. The troops hurried in disorder to the western outlets of the plain, to reach the different passages of the arms of the river with which the road to France is intersected.

Whole battalions were made prisoners, and others were drowned. Marshal Macdonald saved himself by swimming. The Polish hero, Prince Poniatowski, perished here. He had been wounded in a charge made in the streets of the city, at the head of the Polish lancers, and arriving, feeble from loss of blood, on the banks of the Elster, and still anxious to protect the retreat of those who will always be proud to call him their brother-in-arms, he plunged into the river and was drowned.

An admirable trait in the life of Napoleon was the visit he made to the King of Saxony in passing through Leipsic. The venerable Sovereign was sinking under the weight of his grief for the treason of his countrymen. Napoleon knew him too well to attribute to him any share of the odium of that disgraceful defection. He said all he could to console the Nestor of Germany. But this visit, which the King prided himself on having received, brought upon him a cruel revenge. He was overwhelmed with every species of insult, and was even punished as a traitor for no other reason than that he had not been guilty of treason.

The unfortunate old monarch was made prisoner by the Allied Sovereigns, and condemned like a criminal to forfeit one-half of his States. This sentence was executed. The Prince Royal of Sweden was one of the most severe at that council of Kings who now began to strike indiscriminately those whom they had acknowledged and addressed as " Brother."

The French army, the amount of which at Leipsic was between 140,000 and 150,000 men, scarcely numbered 90,000 on its arrival at Erfurth. Fresh supplies of provisions and ammunition helped to revive the drooping spirits of the troops, and they continued their march toward France. On the 2d of November the army crossed the Rhine. This at least was a strong barrier. But alas! it had not been respected by our ambition, could we then hope that vengeance would respect it?

On the 3d of November the Emperor arrived at Mayence. This was the second time that he had entered his Empire as a fugitive. But in the previous year his situation was very different from what it was at present. Then he had still great resources in his power which might enable him to command immense results. Now all was lost!

I received from Mayence a letter which assured me that he was profoundly dejected. While at Mayence he received intelligence of the surrender of Pampeluna. The fall of that fortress secured the liberation of Western Spain. The surrender was caused by want of provisions. This event augmented Napoleon's melancholy. He immediately left Mayence, and pursued his journey to Saint Cloud. There news of a still more mortifying nature awaited him. The lines of Saint Jean de Luz, commanded by Marshal Soult, had been forced by Wellington. The French were now entirely driven out of Spain.

At this moment Heaven visited us with another disaster! The typhus fever swept away, in the space of six weeks, upward of 40,000 men, who were crowded together in the hospitals on the banks of the Rhine. The malady prevailed not only on the Rhine; it likewise extended its deadly ravages along the Elbe. Marshal Saint Cyr, who was shut up in Dresden with 30,000 men, had 6,000 sick.* He was obliged to capitulate.

And what was the consequence? The capitulation, concluded by Generals Tolstoi and Klemann, was not ratified by the Generalissimo, Prince Schwartzenberg, who, abusing his title as Commander-in-Chief, did not scruple to make his lieutenants perjure themselves. The treacherous conduct of Prince Schwartzenberg soon found imitators. On the 1st of January, 1814, the Prince of Wirtemberg signed a capitulation with Rapp, at Dantzic, and afterward refused to execute it.

Holland was now evacuated. General Mollitor, with 14,000 men, could no longer resist General Bulow, who had 60,000. The House of Orange was recalled. Dantzic — Dresden — all had capitulated, and all had been betrayed. There remained not a single friend to France on the other side of the Rhine. Denmark herself, so long faithful to us, the friend of the Committee of Public Safety, and the ally of Robespierre — Denmark had not courage to adhere to Napoleon in his misfortune.

The Emperor arrived at Saint Cloud on the 9th of November, and lost not a moment in adopting the necessary steps for the defense of France. He saw the necessity of organizing a system of security in Paris. To extreme dangers he determined to apply extreme remedies. On the 15th of December the Senate had placed 300,000 conscripts at Napoleon's disposal. On the 2d of December the Emperor had notified to Count Metternich his willingness to accept the conditions of Frankfort. As a guarantee of his intentions he liberated Ferdinand VII., and on the 11th of December he signed the Treaty of Valençay. On the 19th of December the Legislative Body was opened by the Emperor in person.

For a long time previously the conduct of Murat had been such as to excite the suspicion that he meditated defection. England, ever ready to seize at anything which might accelerate the fall of Napoleon, eagerly strove to bring to maturity this new germ of misfortune. Agents were sent to Italy: the condition of its different provinces was

---

* Marshal Saint Cyr was taken with 23,000 men, 13 generals of division, 20 generals of brigade, and 1,700 officers. To these must be added 6,000 invalids in the hospitals of Dresden.

easily revealed, especially at the moment when the typhus fever had swept away almost the whole of that
army which Prince Eugène had sent to Germany in the
spring of the same year. A deep-laid plan was then
conceived; and to render the blow more severe to Napoleon, it was intended that the hand of Murat should inflict
it.

Lord Castlereagh, like an able Minister as he was,
perfectly understood the importance not only of gaining
over Murat, but of maintaining him where he was.
Murat had entered into some negotiations with England,
and the preliminaries of a treaty had been exchanged.
Of this treaty the following were the bases:

England was to acknowledge Joachim Murat as King
of Naples, and to pledge herself to obtain a similar
acknowledgment from Ferdinand, who was to abandon
the Neapolitan States, and retire to Sicily. The Kingdom of Naples was to be augmented by the whole of the
Marshes of Ancona. Italy was to be declared independent,
and all the little sovereignties restored as they were
before the conquest. To aid the fulfillment of this latter
clause, England was to advance twenty millions to Murat
for the expenses of the war which he would probably
have to enter upon, and to place an army of twenty-five
thousand men at his disposal.

Admiral Bentinck, Commander-in-Chief of the British
forces in the Mediterranean, was instructed to pursue
this negotiation, in which England evinced a deep interest. M. de la Vauguyon, who was then master of Rome,
where he had succeeded General Miollis in the command
of the Papal States, used all his efforts to bring Murat
to a decision. But his courier repeatedly returned without any satisfactory answer. Nothing seemed to indicate
any assurance that King Joachim would adopt the course
which he (Vauguyon) regarded as the only one fitting
for him to follow. Mention was even made of a treaty
with Austria. M. von Mire, the Austrian Minister at
Naples, had acquired an ascendency over the Queen which
he turned to the disadvantage of his own Sovereign; and
Murat's weakness ruined him in this most important
juncture of his life.

M. de la Vauguyon remained in Rome, anxiously waiting until it should please Murat to come to a decision.

Receiving no intelligence, he began to be uneasy, when one day his *valet de chambre* announced that there were two strangers waiting, who earnestly requested to see him immediately. "Have you told them I am dressing?" said the Duke. "Yes," replied the valet; "but they say they will wait."

M. de la Vauguyon continued dressing, without hurrying himself the least, when a second message, somewhat more peremptory, was sent to him. He then stepped into his cabinet, and desired his valet to usher in the two visitors. He beheld before him two men of very common appearance; one of them, who was of short stature, thus addressed him in an accent which betrayed him to be an Englishman:

"I have requested this interview, Duke, with some degree of urgency, because I have but a very short time to remain here; but it is necessary that I should speak to you, since I cannot obtain any intelligence from King Joachim. I am Admiral Bentinck." The Duc de la Vauguyon made every apology for the delay, but in truth his astonishment almost overwhelmed him.

"General," continued Admiral Bentinck, "King Joachim does not behave well to my Government. He knows what he may expect from England, and he ought to act with more candor and energy. In the crisis in which Europe at present stands, it is urgent that the affairs of Italy should be promptly decided. We offer twenty-five millions in money, and twenty-five thousand troops. Will your King accept these propositions, and with them the friendship of the English Government? He ought to be aware that the alliance of Great Britain will secure to him the assistance of all the other Sovereigns of Europe. From whom would he wish to derive his power? From England or from Austria? He must promptly decide. The step I have now taken proves my personal esteem for your character by thus trusting to your honor; and it likewise shows the interest I feel for the success of what has been so happily begun."

The Duc de la Vauguyon assured Admiral Bentinck that he had spared no endeavor to bring the King of Naples to the wished-for decision. Bentinck was probably aware of this. It was his confidence in the noble character of the Duke, and his personal desire to see the

business settled, which induced him to hazard a step
which might have led to his imprisonment. But the
Admiral had placed confidence in the honor of M. de la
Vauguyon, and that shield was sacred.

The Admiral's boat was waiting for him at Civita
Vecchia, and he departed, recommending the Duke to
spare no endeavors to secure the INTERESTS OF ITALY.
But what was the Duke's disappointment, when, after
having dispatched a letter to Joachim, more urgent than
the rest, there arrived in Rome one of the King's aids-
de-camp, who merely passed through the city, and was
carrying to the Austrian advanced posts the ratification
of the treaty which Murat had signed with Austria!
Amid this conflict of intrigues Murat had written to the
Emperor Napoleon a letter, to which he received the
following laconic answer:

«Direct your course to Pavia, and there WAIT FOR ORDERS.»

Murat, naturally irritated by this haughty treatment,
determined to occupy the Papal States. Hitherto M. de
la Vauguyon had been in Rome only as Commander of
the Neapolitan division; the King now ordered him to
take the title of Governor-General of the Roman States.
Murat set out for Naples to join the Viceroy with his
army, and to advance on the Po; but it was with a
tardiness which showed how little his fidelity was to be
trusted.

About this time Comte Louis de Narbonne died. He
was just recovering from an attack of typhus fever,
when he met with a fall from his horse which led to a
fatal result.

The Comte was survived by his mother, the Duchesse
de Narbonne, who was a woman of extraordinary energy
of character. She had returned to France after the death
of the Princesses, to whom she was devotedly attached.
Her son treated her with the most unremitting and affectionate attention. She detested the Emperor, and, in
spite of her fondness for her son, she could never pardon him for having attached himself to the Imperial
Family. Napoleon knew this, and he used often to jest
with Comte Louis at the old Duchess's prejudice.

The death of the Comte de Narbonne was more deeply
felt by Napoleon, inasmuch as he thought it had been

hastened by his appointment at Torgau. He wished, if
possible, to mitigate the shock which he knew the intelligence would occasion to the venerable Duchess, who
was then in her eightieth year. He inquired who would
be the fittest person to convey to her intimation of her
melancholy loss. He was told that she had already been
informed of it. He then sent for General Flahaut, and
directed him to go immediately to pay a visit to the
Duchess, and to give her every assurance of his (Napoleon's) condolence for the misfortune that had befallen her.

M. de Flahaut acquitted himself of his mission, though
he undertook it with a degree of repugnance that might
easily be accounted for. He knew the spirit of the
Duchesse de Narbonne, and he feared that she might reply to the Emperor's message in a way that would be
painful for him to hear, and which he could not repeat
to the Emperor.

When the Duchess saw M. de Flahaut, she betrayed
considerable emotion. She advanced a few steps toward
him, but was obliged to support herself by resting her
hand on a table.

" Madame," said General de Flahaut, when he had conducted her to her chair, " I am sent hither by the
Emperor to express to you his sincere sympathy for the
melancholy loss you have sustained."

The Duchess bowed her head, and uttered some words
which M. de Flahaut did not distinctly hear. After the
lapse of a few moments, when she appeared more composed, he added:

" His Majesty desires, madame, that you will inform
him how he can serve you — in short, what he can do
for you ? "

The Duchess turned red, then pale, and was evidently
struggling to conceal the agitation of her feelings.

" I can only return thanks," said she, cautiously avoid-
ing to pronounce the name of the Emperor. " I do not,
and I never will, ask for anything; but," added she, with
admirable dignity, " my circumstances enjoin me to refuse nothing."

The Emperor immediately granted her a pension of
2,000 francs.

This is not a solitary example of Napoleon's benevolence. He was one day informed that the widow of a

French marshal was living in Paris in circumstances of extreme indigence. This was Madame de Mailly. He immediately ordered the War Minister to place her name on the pension list of widows of the great officers of the Empire. This gave her an annuity of 20,000 francs.

When Louis XVIII. returned to France, Madame de Narbonne, whose attachment to the exiled family had never been abated, and who had given repeated proofs of the most disinterested devotedness, went to pay her court to the King with the certainty of being received with distinguished attention. His Majesty, indeed, said many gracious things to her; and, taking her by the hand, assured her that he would do something to ameliorate her circumstances. Two days afterward he sent her 1,000 francs. This was precisely the interest at five per cent of the salary which the Comte de Narbonne had received as aid-de-camp to the Emperor. This recollection was anything but pleasing to the Duchess, and I have been assured that she sent the money back.

I must relate one more anecdote of the Duchesse de Narbonne and Napoleon. On the 21st of March, 1815, the streets of Paris still re-echoed the shouts of a joyous population. It was half-past six in the evening. The Duchesse de Narbonne had just risen from dinner, having no company with her but Dr. Kappeler. The Doctor offered her his arm, and conducted her to her great armchair, which was wheeled to the window. She then resided in the Rue Ferme-des-Mathurins. The Doctor took his seat beside her, and listened, as he always did, with renewed interest to those stories of past times which she, as well as her son, related so delightfully. Once or twice the Doctor adverted to the Emperor's return, which, of course, was the engrossing topic of conversation everywhere; but whenever he alluded to the subject the Duchess frowned, and, in the peremptory tone of a woman of eighty-three, said:

" Doctor, let us talk of something else."

Suddenly a carriage drove up to the door, and in a few moments the *valet de chambre* announced the Grand-Marshal. General Bertrand then filled that post. He is one of the most well-bred and kind-hearted of men. He advanced to the Duchess with all the respectful gallantry of a courtier of Versailles, and told her he had been sent by HIS MAJESTY THE EMPEROR to inquire how she was, and to know whether she had been taken care of in his absence. He also begged her to inform him whether he could do anything for her.

The interview was short; but it made a profound impression on the Duchesse de Narbonne. As soon as the Grand-Marshal was gone, she summoned Doctor Kappeler, who had retired into an adjoining room.

"Do you know, Doctor, that THAT man is not so very bad? What do you think? He arrived only yesterday evening, and amid all his occupations and embarrassments he has thought of me — of one who he knows dislikes him! That is really very generous."

But the Hundred Days passed away, and there was another return; and perhaps General Bertrand's visit to Madame de Narbonne was recollected with displeasure by the restored Court. Such, at least, may be presumed to have been the fact, from the sort of refusal which was given to an application for 30,000 francs due to the Duchesse de Narbonne; and due to her the more justly, because her conduct at the death of Madame Adelaide had been truly noble. She had sent to Mittau, where Louis XVIII. and the Duchesse d'Angoulême then were, the property which she became possessed of in virtue of her office, and which she was the better entitled to, inasmuch as she had lost all her own fortune by following her royal mistress in exile.

She counted confidently on the receipt of the 30,000 francs due to her, and when she was informed that the payment was indefinitely delayed, the intelligence proved a fatal disappointment to her. In the morning, when the Doctor went out after breakfast, he left her well. On his return at five o'clock he found her stricken with the hand of death. He loved her with the affection of a son, and he employed all the resources of his art to restore that energy which was the essence of her existence; but it was extinguished. All that he could do was to prolong her life for the space of two months. She then expired, at the age of eighty-four, possessing all her faculties as perfectly as if she had been but thirty.

CHAPTER XXIX.

Blucher Crosses the Rhine — Comparative Force of the French Army
and That of the Allies — Assemblage at the Court of Napoleon —
Committees of the Senate and the Legislative Body — Napoleon's
Speech — The Russians Take Possession of Dantzic — Broken Treaties — Our Last Resource — Liberation of the Pope and of Ferdinand VII.— Napoleon's Farewell to the National Guard — The Duke
of Vicenza's Mission to the Headquarters of the Allies — Madame
Récamier Proceeds to Italy — Her Arrival at Naples — Her First
Visit to the King and Queen — The Lazzaroni del Carmine — Caroline's Captivating Manners — Madame Récamier's Second Visit at
Court — Murat's Despair — Caroline's Energy — English Ships in
the Bay of Naples.

I WAS now in the sixth month of my widowhood, and
since Junot's death I had lived in perfect seclusion.
I did not even occupy those apartments of my Hôtel
which looked toward the street; but my friends called
upon me every day and brought me intelligence of what
was going on. I was regularly informed of our progress-
ive degrees of misfortune, and the information was
truly appalling. One day Lavalette called on me and
said, in a tone of despair, that all was lost. I was astonished to see him so dejected, for he was generally in
good spirits.

"Blucher," continued he, "has crossed the Rhine at
the head of a formidable army — the Army of Silesia!
It appears that nothing has opposed him, and that he
has effected the passage from Mannheim to Coblentz
without encountering the slightest obstacle." "Heavens!"
exclaimed I; "is France no longer France! Are we not
the same people who, in 1792, forced the Prussians to
recross the frontier?"

Blucher's army amounted to 160,000 men; yet it was
only the second in force. Among the hosts who were
pouring down upon us with all the fury of vengeance,
the Grand Army, commanded by Prince Schwartzenberg,
amounted to 190,000 men; the Army of the North, commanded by Bernadotte, counted 130,000; then there were
100,000 troops headed by Generals Beningsen and Taeun-
zien; General Bellegarde had 80,000 men in Italy; and

the German, Polish, Dutch, and Russian reserves presented altogether about 800,000 troops. To this astonishing army may be added 200,000 Spaniards, Portuguese,
and English, commanded by Wellington, who were thirsting for vengeance at the barrier of the Pyrenees, as
Blucher was on that of the Rhine.

To this menacing invasion what forces had we to oppose? No more than 350,000 men! And how were they
disposed? One hundred thousand were shut up in the
fortresses of Hamburg and Dantzic, beyond the Oder,
the Elbe, and the Rhine. Prince Eugène had a feeble
army in Italy to oppose to Murat and Bellegarde. Soult
and Suchet had scarcely 80,000 men to encounter the
formidable army of Wellington. The Emperor had under
his direct command the corps of Marshals Ney, Marmont,
Macdonald, Mortier, Victor, and Augereau. But what
was the force of these army corps?

Marshal Ney's scarcely amounted to 14,000 men,
Marshal Augereau's did not amount to 3,000, and the
Imperial Guard was included in these numbers. Thus,
to resist all Europe in arms against us, we had only an
army in which each man counted four adversaries.
Patriotism, it is true, might still do much; but personal
misfortunes had unnerved us. We were no longer ourselves. Amid all these troubles and terrors, amid the
distant roar of Russian and Prussian cannon, arrived the
last day of the year 1813.

On the first day of January, 1814, Napoleon for the
last time received the New Year's homage of his Court.
There was a pretty numerous attendance at the Tuileries.
When all the company had arrived, the Emperor entered
from the inner apartments. His manner was calm and
grave, but on his brow there sat a cloud which denoted
an approaching storm. Napoleon had appointed two
Committees to draw up a report on the state of France.
These Committees were formed from members of the
Senate and the Legislative Body.

The Committee for the Senate was composed of MM.
de Talleyrand, Fontanes, Saint Marsan, Barbé Marbois,
and Beurnonville, and was presided over by M. de Lacépède. The Committee for the Legislative Body consisted
of MM. Raynouard, Lainé, Gallois, Flauguergues, and
Maine de Biran, and the President was the Duc de

Masso. M. Raynouard was the orator of the Legislative Body, and he spoke with a degree of candor and energy which was calculated to produce a fatal impression on the rest of France. The Emperor immediately felt this. The report of M. Raynouard likewise contained expressions disrespectful to the Emperor, the effect of which could not fail to be like a tocsin summoning the the people to revolt.

The Emperor said nothing the first day on learning what had passed in the Legislative Body; but on the 1st of January, when all the authorities of the Empire were assembled in the *Salle du Trône*, he delivered a speech, the violence of which filled the offenders with dismay:

"I have suppressed the printing of your address," said he; "it was of an incendiary nature. Eleven-twelfths of the Legislative Body are, I know, composed of good citizens, and I attach no blame to them; but the other twelfth is a factious party, and your Committee was selected from that number. That man named Lainé is in correspondence with the Prince Regent through the medium of the Advocate de Sêze. I have proofs of this fact. The report of the Committee has hurt me exceedingly. I would rather have lost two battles. What does it tend to? To strengthen the pretensions of the enemy. If I were to be guided by it I should concede more than the enemy demands. Because he asks for the province of Champagne would you have me surrender that of Brie? Would you make remonstrances in the presence of the enemy? Your object was to humiliate me! My life may be sacrificed, but never my honor. I was not born in the rank of Kings; I do not depend on the Throne. What is a throne? A few deal boards covered with velvet. Four months hence, and I will publish the odious report of your Committee. The vengeance of the enemy is directed against my person, more than against the French people. But, for that reason, should I be justified in dismembering the State? Must I sacrifice my pride to obtain peace? I am proud, because I am brave. I am proud, because I have done great things for France. In a word, France has more need of me than I have need of her. In three months we shall have peace, or I shall be dead. Go to your homes;—it was not thus you should have rebuked me."*

The Legislative Body, though mute that day, was nevertheless the organ of the nation. The Committee had been maladroit in speaking as it did; but Napoleon was no less so in his reply, which, though it did not appear in the " *Moniteur* " as it was delivered, was nevertheless known throughout Europe eight days afterward. It was like issuing a manifesto against France, while he ought to have held out to her a friendly hand in the hour of her distress, when both mutually required support. The Emperor's reply, which was speedily circulated throughout Paris, gave rise to a multitude of commentaries. It was like the signal of discord.

To the honor of Napoleon, it must be mentioned that though he has been held up as a tyrant, ever ready to punish, and as a despot exercising the most arbitrary self-will, yet this incident was followed by no measures of severity. Among the members of the Committee there were men who might justly have incurred punishment. M. Lainé had been actively engaged at Bordeaux, at the head of a Royalist faction, and was about to resume his exertions. The Emperor knew this, and perhaps he did wrong not to detain him in Paris.

But I say again that the Emperor's disposition was not naturally tyrannical. He no doubt frequently adopted the most arbitrary measures, but in those instances it will be found that he was usually influenced by reports which obscured the truth and biased his judgment. When left to himself to make a decision, it was almost invariably noble and generous.

On the 1st of January the brave General Rapp was obliged to allow the Russians to enter Dantzic after a most heroic resistance. The besieged were allowed to return to France with the honors of war, taking with them their arms and baggage. None of these conditions were observed; all were violated, and the garrison was sent to Siberia! It is curious to note the three flagrant violations of treaties which took place during the time that Europe waged war against us.

* See also Bourrienne's "Memoirs of Napoleon Bonaparte" (edition of 1885), Vol. III., pp. 83, 84.

The first instance occurred in Egypt, at the treaty of El-Arish, by Admiral Keith, and the brave Klèber. The second was the violation of the treaty by Prince Schwartzenberg at Dresden. The third, and perhaps the most dishonorable, if there can be any difference in a breach of faith, was the violation of the Convention of Dantzic. It is honorable to the character of the French, as a nation, that during the twenty-two years in which we warred against the whole of Europe, our enemies cannot accuse us of a similar breach of faith. Our generals maintained their pride, even amid perils and reverses; for true honor will never appeal to necessity as an apology for a dereliction from duty.

Every day we learned the progress of the Allies from private letters, for the "*Moniteur*" still drew a veil over the truth. The line of hostile lances and bayonets was hourly more and more closely drawn, and we beheld the danger without seeing how it could be averted. Napoleon organized one hundred and twenty thousand of the National Guards to cover Lyons and Paris, and to form a reserve. This was our last resource! The enemy had been for some time in possession of Langres, Dijon, Chalons, Nancy, and Vaucouleurs, and threatened immediately to march on Paris. Blucher had established his forces at Saint Dizier and Joinville.

On learning that the Austrians were in possession of Bar-sur-Aube, the Emperor determined to quit Paris. He had already liberated the King of Spain and the Pope; Ferdinand VII. had left Valençay, and Pius VII. had departed from Fontainebleau. By this measure Napoleon hoped to secure the friendship of a man who had been guilty of deposing his own father. Ferdinand, however, remained his enemy.

Nothing is more curious than to observe the sudden coldness of feeling which some persons betrayed toward Napoleon the moment his happy star began to grow dim. In one day I heard ten different versions of the manner in which he took leave of the National Guard, and confided his wife and child to their protection. Many, who had witnessed the scene, returned from it with tears in their eyes; while others regarded as affectation the burst of sensibility which he had evinced when he presented his son to the National Guard.

22

If I had seen him I could have guessed whether his feelings were genuine or not, for I knew him too well to be deceived. But from all that I heard, I should be inclined to say that he was really animated by the sentiments he manifested. He was a father, and he doted on his child. His heart must have been moved when he gazed on the lovely boy who had been destined at his birth to wear twenty crowns, but who had been dispossessed of his inheritance by those who were his natural protectors. Whatever may now be said of Napoleon's farewell to the National Guard, there can be no doubt that the enthusiasm of the Parisians was that day at its height.

No person who was then in the capital can forget the prolonged shouts of *Vive l'Empereur! Vive le Roi de Rome!* The Place du Carrousel resounded with the oaths of fidelity taken by the officers of the National Guard; and yet, before a few weeks elapsed, these oaths, so solemnly pledged, were betrayed and forgotten.

Napoleon was anxious to make one more attempt to bring the Allied Sovereigns to something like reasonable conditions: and he accordingly sent the Duke of Vicenza to the headquarters of the Allied army. The Duke was a favorite of the Emperor Alexander, and Napoleon was perfectly aware of the importance of regaining the friendship of the Sovereign of Russia. Alas! why did he ever lose it ? Alexander loved him as a brother. Be this as it may, the Duke of Vicenza was on such a footing with the Emperor Alexander as enabled him to make propositions of peace and friendship with some probability of success. Napoleon, with the view of giving more dignity to the Duke, appointed him his Minister for Foreign Affairs.

It now became necessary that the Emperor should have near him a Minister to correspond with the Plenipotentiary. The Duke of Vicenza could scarcely expect that the Emperor could himself maintain the diplomatic correspondence amid the rapid operations of the prodigious campaign. The Duke of Bassano was nominated to this duty.

About the time when Murat leagued with the enemies of France, a curious scene took place in the interior of the Palace of Naples. Of this scene I here present to the reader an accurate description, derived from one of the actors in it, and there were but three. I allude to Madame Récamier, who during her exile, having no hope of seeing Madame de Staël at Coppet, determined to proceed to Italy — to visit Naples with its beautiful bay — and to see Vesuvius. On her arrival at Naples, Madame Récamier fixed her abode at the *Hôtel de l'Europe*, on the Chiaia.

On the morning after her arrival, she was visited by the Neapolitan Minister for Foreign Affairs, who waited upon her by order of the King and Queen, to invite her to the Palace. Madame Récamier, was more annoyed than flattered by this mark of royal graciousness. She had known Murat, but he had never been one of her intimate friends. Indeed, Murat's elevation to royalty had been so sudden that he had been speedily removed from the sphere of all his early connections. He had at one period of his life admired Madame Récamier, and had even made love to her, as he did to every attractive woman of his acquaintance; but she gave him to understand that his attentions were not acceptable, and he took the hint with a good grace.

It was now very long since Madame Récamier had seen him. As to the Queen, she had scarcely any personal acquaintance with her, and she could not be expected to entertain any very strong predilection for the sister of the man who had persecuted her and all her friends. It was therefore with feelings rather painful than gratifying that she repaired to the Palace. She accepted the invitation because she would not treat with incivility a mark of courtesy shown to her in a foreign land during her exile.

The Queen of Naples was a woman of considerable shrewdness, energy of character, and talent. I use this latter term in reference to her political life only. That excepted, she was as ignorant as a woman can well be, or, I ought rather to say, as women were a hundred years ago. Though wanting in the most ordinary education, yet, if a grave political question came under discussion, she could speak like a well-informed statesman.

Queen Caroline had a peculiarity of manner and temper which was very far from agreeable. I allude to her habit of ridiculing and teasing her acquaintances.

For my own part, I can truly say that I was always nervous for a week after we had any of our rehearsals of plays or quadrilles. This disposition, which she indulged to a most disagreeable extent, created for her more enemies than her beauty. One may accommodate one's self to a rivalry, especially if there be nothing very superior in it; but to be continually reminded of that superiority is insufferable, particularly when one has not altogether a contemptible opinion of one's self.

Caroline received Madame Récamier with transport. Madame Récamier was touched by the kind reception she experienced, and expressed her heartfelt gratitude to the Queen of Naples. "Ah!" said Caroline; "I shall perhaps soon have to solicit a proof of your friendship; I hope you will not withhold it. I shall be much in need of it."

This was on the 16th of January. Everything that was said in the Palace was a subject of conversation in Naples, and all the gossip in the city was faithfully reported in the Palace. "He must abandon the Emperor," exclaimed the populace. "We will no longer be dragged from our homes to fight at the other end of the world. We must have peace."

These shouts for peace were, by a curious anomaly, raised by men armed with stilettos, which they brandished with threatening attitudes in front of the Palace of Joachim, the popular King — the King of Feathers — who was a great favorite with the *Lazzaroni del Carmine*. His smiling, good-humored countenance, his fantastic costume — in short, all his peculiarities — recommended him strongly to that class of his subjects above mentioned.

Besides, Murat was a man of amiable disposition; he was a good husband and a good father. But, after all, the love of his subjects was ephemeral, and it was chilled by the fear of war and the English invasion. Murmurs increased ever day, and Murat could not go out of his Palace without encountering dissatisfied groups. Such was the state of things when Madame Récamier arrived at Naples.

In compliance with the invitation she had received, she proceeded to the Palace about noon. She found the Queen as amiable and as gracious as before. Nobody better understood the art of captivating those whom she

wished to gain over to her interests than the Queen of
Naples. She possessed this great charm in common with
her brother Napoleon. Her apartments in the Palace
were fitted up with luxurious taste. Her bedchamber,
which commanded a view of the bay, was hung with
white satin, the rich soft folds of which harmonized admirably with the brilliant complexion of the mistress of
the apartment. She frequently received visitors while in
bed, as she had been in the habit of doing in Paris.
Her bed-curtains were of richly worked tulle, lined with
pink satin.

On receiving Madame Récamier, Caroline expressed
her regret at seeing her in exile, but assured her that
the hardships of that exile would be considerably miti-
gated by her residence in Naples. Murat, too, who was
present at the interview, gave her every assurance of the
interest he felt in her behalf. When Madame Récamier
took her leave, the King and Queen invited her to visit
them again on the following day. She could easily perceive that very uneasy feelings prevailed in the interior
of the Palace. Public report, indeed, had Madame Récamier lent ear to it, would have informed her that happiness was not an inmate of the royal abode, splendid
as it was.

On the following day, as she proceeded to the Palace,
everything presented a strange aspect, from the quay of
the Chiaia to the steps of the throne. Being a stranger
in the country, and unacquainted with the turbulent habits of the people, she was half inclined to return home
when she beheld the agitation which prevailed. She
passed through several apartments of the Palace without
seeing a chamberlain.

At length she reached the door of the Queen's chamber; she tapped gently, and Caroline herself, who anxiously expected her, opened the door. As soon as she
entered she was struck with the extraordinary picture
that presented itself. The King and Queen were alone.
Murat was pale, his hair disordered, his eyes rolling
wildly, and to all appearance he was under the influence
of some overpowering excitement. The Queen, on her
part, was very pale, and much agitated, but her superior
fortitude was evident in every glance which she darted
on her husband—that man to whom Napoleon justly

said: "You are brave only on the field of battle—in any other situation you have not the courage of a woman or monk."

"In the name of Heaven! for the sake of your own glory! remain here, I implore you; and do not show yourself in this state!" exclaimed Caroline to her husband, on the entrance of Madame Récamier. "Would you wish to convince the Neapolitans that they have a King who is not worthy of the name? Stay where you are, I conjure you." These words, I CONJURE YOU, were uttered in the authoritative tone of I DESIRE YOU. "Pray stay with him for a few moments," said the Queen to Madame Récamier; "I am going to give a few orders, and will return immediately."

No sooner had Caroline left the room than Murat flew to Madame Récamier, and, taking her by the two hands, said, with the deepest emotion: "Tell me—tell me the truth—it is certain that you must think I have behaved very basely. Is it not so?" "Be composed," said Madame Récamier; "why this agitation? What has happened?" "Alas!" continued the unfortunate Murat, sinking into a chair, "does not all France vent anathemas on my head! Am I not called Murat the traitor—Murat the renegade?" He hid his face in his hands and burst into tears.

On seeing this violent agitation, Madame Récamier immediately suspected that he had not determined to sign the treaty with Austria and England, a treaty which was calculated to alienate him and his children from France; for it would require more than the interval of a generation to wipe away such a stain. With her accustomed good sense, she immediately perceived that a little calm advice offered by a friend, who, like herself, had no personal interest in the question at issue, might give a fixed direction to his wavering sentiments.

"Do you ask me for my opinion?" said she with a serious air. "Ah! give it me," he exclaimed eagerly, "draw me from the gulf that yawns before me. On all sides I see nothing but misfortune and disaster." "Hear me, then," resumed Madame Récamier; "you know that I do not like the Emperor! I am myself an exile, and my friends are proscribed. All who are dear to me have been plunged into misery by Napoleon. But still, in

spite of these considerations, I will give you the same
advice which I would give to my own brother in the like
circumstances—you ought not to forsake the Emperor.
No, I say again you ought not to forsake him!"
As she uttered these words Murat became more and
more pale. He looked at her for some moments without
making any reply. Then, rising with impetuosity, he
took her hand, and led her to the balcony before the
window, and, pointing to the Bay of Naples, already
filled with English ships, he exclaimed in a voice half
stifled with emotion: "Behold! look yonder! and now tell
me whether this is the moment when France should
address to me the title of TRAITOR!"
Madame Récamier was astounded at what she heard,
for, judging from all that she had had an opportunity of
observing within the past hour, she confidently believed
that Murat had not yet come to any decision; and yet
the English ships hoisted their flags in the very port of
his capital. She said nothing. What, indeed, could she
have said—she who never spoke but in sincerity and
candor?
Murat seemed perfectly bewildered with despair and
grief, when the Queen suddenly entered. She also was
deadly pale. On perceiving the King in the pitiable
state in which he was she trembled, and, running up to
him, exclaimed: "In the name of Heaven, Joachim, be
silent, or at least speak lower! In the adjoining room
there are a hundred ears listening to you. Be silent!
Have you lost all self-command?"
Finding she could produce no effect upon him, she ran
to a table on which was some water, sugar, and orange-
flower water. She herself mixed a portion, and, pouring
into it some drops of ether, she brought it to him:
"Drink this and compose yourself," said she. "The
crisis has now arrived. Murat, recollect what you are.
You are King of Naples. Do not lose sight of the duty
you owe to your subjects and to your family. Hear
me! In six weeks, perhaps, the Emperor may himself be
in Italy." At this sharp apostrophe Murat again trembled. "What ails you?" resumed Caroline. "What are
you afraid of? Reflect on your situation. View it as it
really is. The worst you have to fear is to find yourself
face to face with the Emperor. Well, then! Suppose

he were now only fifty leagues from Naples, and that you are going to mount your horse to meet him.» Murat hid his face in his hands. "How! You dare not face him?» said Caroline, with a gesture of contempt. "Then I will do so for you! Yes, I will mount my horse. I will place myself at the head of the army, and I will go to the Emperor and ask him by WHAT RIGHT he takes from me that which he gave as a reward for the blood you have shed for his glory!» Madame Récamier gazed at her with painful astonishment, and could not help exclaiming: "Oh, Madame!» The Queen understood the reproach conveyed in these words. She paced two or three times up and down the apartment, and then, as if in reply to Madame Récamier, she said: "Doubtless I am his sister. I know it but too well. Yet why did he give me a Crown? If I am his sister I am likewise Queen of Naples!»

Then, as if overcome by the weight of so many distressing sensations, she threw herself on a sofa and was silent. Presently a sort of murmur was heard on the quay. Caroline rose suddenly, ran to Murat, and, looking at him steadfastly, said: "Now you may show yourself. Go, my dear Joachim—and recollect who you are!» Murat rose, passed his hand through his hair, and stepped up to a mirror to adjust the deranged appearance of his cravat. He then embraced the Queen, and, taking Madame Récamier's hand, he said to her with a tone of sincere kindness: "You will return and dine with us. We shall be alone; do not refuse.»

Madame Récamier promised, and Murat then took leave of her and the Queen. When he had passed the folds of the satin curtains which were drawn over the door, the Queen rushed into the arms of Madame Récamier, and shed a torrent of tears. "You see," said she, "I am obliged to have courage for him as well as myself! At a time, too, when my own fortitude is scarcely borne up even by my affection for my children—when I am hourly distracted by thinking of my brother, who believes me to be guilty of treason to him. Oh, pity me! I have need of pity, and I deserve it. If you could search my heart, you would see what torture I am doomed to bear!»

On returning to her Hôtel, Madame Récamier was

absorbed in agitating reflections. Suddenly her attention was roused by a noise in the street. She ran to the window, and saw the whole population of the Carmine * and Santa Lucia assembled round Murat, who was parading the city on horseback. The intelligence of the treaty of alliance, confirmed by the presence of the English ships in the port, had excited the populace, and their enthusiasm for Murat and the Queen was at its height. The King was still pale, but he appeared in good spirits; as he passed the balcony of Madame Réca· mier, he looked up and gracefully saluted her.

CHAPTER XXX.

Solitude of the Tuileries — Advance of the Allied Armies — Napoleon in Champagne — Intrigues of M. de Talleyrand — His Interview with the Emperor — The Coup de Poing — The Battle of Brienne — College Recollections — The Congress of Châtillon — The Emperor Alexander and the Duc de Vicenza — Battles of Champaubert and Montmirail — Napoleon's Refusal to Sign the Powers for the Duc de Vicenza — The Campaign of France — Comte d'Artois at Vesoul — M. Wildermetz — His Message to the Emperor Alexander — Horrors Committed by the Cossacks — Buffon's Country House — Suppression of News in the Journals — First Performance of the Oriflamme — Bernardin St. Pierre, and Jean Jacques Rousseau.

WE ARE now on the eve of the most heart-rending period of the brilliant career of the Emperor. No more balls at the Imperial Palace, the silence and the solitude of whose walls were now disturbed only by the voice of that beautiful child, which was also to be stifled in exile. The fatal cordon of hostile forces by which we were surrounded approached us more and more. One day we learned that the Wirtemberg troops had entered Epinal; another time that the Prussians were masters of Nancy, of Chalons-sur-Saône, and that the Austrians were in Chambéry. The Army of Silesia, commanded by Blucher, established itself in the vicinity of Paris, for

---

* Il Carmine is that part of Naples inhabited by fishermen and lazzaroni. Santa Lucia is the district occupied by merchants and bankers. The Chiaia is the fashionable part of the city.

so we may term Saint Dizier and Joinville. The enemy was at length on the Marne. Then the Emperor quitted Paris!

He had long hesitated before he adopted this course, either because he was waiting to see the effect of the negotiations opened at Frankfort, or because he hoped that there would be a general rising in France at the sight of the foreign invaders. Doubtless this was naturally to be expected from the bravery and energy of the French people. But he himself had worn out all their springs of action — they had lost their elasticity. The most determined and the most active required repose; a general desire for it prevailed from the cottage of the soldier to the palace of the Marshal. Napoleon never could be brought to understand the law of necessity. He endeavored to make everything yield to him, while he himself would never bend to circumstances.

At this time Parisian society presented an extraordinary aspect. Grief and alarm now prevailed in those houses which had but recently been the scenes of uninterrupted festivity. The numerous families arrayed in mourning cast a gloom over the streets and public promenades, and it was particularly melancholy to observe the many young females who wore widow's weeds. This last circumstance struck the Emperor of Russia, as he himself informed me. While the Emperor was in Champagne, exhibiting a last proof of that talent and energy which had raised him to one of the first thrones in the world, M. de Talleyrand remained in Paris, and his intrigues gave the finishing stroke to Napoleon's misfortunes.

It is said that the Emperor, on the eve of his departure to join the army, summoned M. de Talleyrand to the Tuileries, and there spoke to him, in a tone that might be called more than firm, of the affairs of Spain. It would appear that the Emperor was not at that time very well acquainted with the style of conversation which was maintained in the coterie of M. de Talleyrand when the affairs of Spain came under discussion.

"Well, Monsieur de Talleyrand," said the Emperor, walking straight up to him, "I think it is somewhat strange that you should allege I made you the gaoler of Ferdinand, when you yourself made the proposition to me!" Talleyrand assumed one of his inscrutable looks;

PRINCE TALLEYRAND

Photogravure after Gerard

half closing his little eyes, and screwing up his lips, he stood with one hand resting upon the back of a chair, and the other in his waist-coat pocket. Nothing increases anger so much as coolness. The Emperor was violently irritated at Talleyrand's immovability of countenance and coolness of manner, and he exclaimed in a voice of thunder, and stamping his foot, "Why do you not answer me?" The same silence was maintained. Napoleon's eyes flashed fire. Talleyrand became alarmed, not without reason, and then he stammered out the following words, which were certainly anything but satisfactory: "I am at a loss to understand what your Majesty means."

Napoleon attempted to speak, but rage choked his utterance. He advanced first one step, then a second, then a third, until at length he came close up to the Prince of Benevento. He then raised his hand to the height of the Prince's chin, and continuing to advance, he forced Talleyrand to recede, which was no easy matter, owing to the defect in one of his feet. However, it was more advisable to recede than advance, for the Emperor's little hand was still held up, and was clenched in the form necessary for giving what is vulgarly called a *coup de poing*. However, it was not given. The Emperor merely drove the Prince of Benevento, half walking, half hobbling, along the whole length of the large cabinet of the *Pavillon de Flore*. At length the Prince reached the wall of the apartment, and Napoleon repeated: "So you presume to say that you did not advise the captivity of the Princes?"

Here the scene ended. It had already been too long, and, at the same time, not long enough. Since the Emperor had gone so far, he ought to have gone a little farther, and sent the Prince of Benevento to Vincennes, consigning him to the hands of General Daumesnil, with the recommendation to treat him with all possible respect, but to keep him rigidly *au secret*. Machiavelli truly says, "One should never make an enemy by halves."

On the evening of the day on which this scene was acted, the Prince of Benevento had company. The Chamberlain on duty at the Tuileries had overheard everything, and had repeated all he knew; for the truth is, though I am sorry to say it, the SERVANTS OF HONOR who dance attendance upon royalty differ but little from servants of any other kind. As I was myself lady of honor to a Princess, I may attack this class of people without the fear of being thought unjust or prejudiced; and I have often thought, when we were assembled in the *salon de service*, gossiping about what did not concern us, that we very much resembled those who were amusing themselves in a similar way in the story below us.

However this may be, it is nevertheless certain that the Chamberlain on duty at the Tuileries, whose name I need not mention, reported that the Prince of Benevento had received a *coup de poing* from the Emperor. M. de Talleyrand, as I have already observed, had a party that same evening, and one of the visitors, who was on familiar terms with the Prince, stepped up to him, saying, " Ah, Monseigneur, what have I heard ? " " What ? " inquired the Prince, with one of his cool, impenetrable looks. " I have been informed that the Emperor treated you——" " Oh," interrupted the Prince, " that is a thing that happens every day — every day." The Prince had heard no mention of the *coup de poing*, of which he flattered himself nobody knew; and when he said " every day," he merely meant that the Emperor was out of temper and unreasonable every day.

M. de Talleyrand's friend, however, who had no very refined notions of etiquette, as may be readily imagined from his address to the Prince, took it into his head that Talleyrand was in the daily habit of receiving a box on the ear from the Emperor. This mistake gave rise to a fund of merriment when it came to be reported that the Prince of Benevento daily submitted to the Emperor's correction with that indifference which might be inferred from the negligent shrug of the shoulders that accompanied the words, " Every day! — *Mon Dieu !* — Every day! "

I am not competent to judge of the merits of the military movements made by the Emperor in Champagne, but I have heard it alleged that his genius never was so brilliantly displayed as in that campaign. He drove the Prussians from Saint Dizier, and this triumph was almost immediately followed by the Battle of Brienne. What painful feelings must have arisen in his mind while he was fighting to preserve his Crown under the walls of the old college where, in his boyhood, he had passed so many happy hours! At Brienne he had also fought battles, but they were followed by no pangs of grief or remorse. His soldiers were his college companions, his ammunition snowballs, and the ransom of the prisoners some fruit, a book, or a print. I have frequently heard the Emperor describe his amusements at Brienne. I recollect in particular, one day, when Madame de Brienne paid a visit to Madame Mère, accompanied by her niece, Madame de Loménie. The Emperor, who was present, conversed with her for a considerable time with almost filial affection. The respect he showed to Madame de Brienne was unmixed with any trace of affectation; his behavior to her was perfectly easy and natural. I am certain that Napoleon must have suffered cruelly on the day of the Battle of Brienne. I am sure of it, from the complacency with which I have so often heard him dwell on the happiness he enjoyed at college. It was there that he first became acquainted with Bourrienne.

The Battle of Brienne was followed by several others. In the midst of these conflicts, when cannons were roaring and blood flowing in every part of France, from the banks of the Rhine to those of the Mincio, a Congress was opened, as if in derision of the impotence of human will. This Congress held its sittings at Châtillon, in the heart of one of our provinces. Its members were Count Stadion, for Austria; Baron Humboldt, for Prussia; Count Razumowsky, for Russia; while Lord Aberdeen, Lord Cathcart, and Lord Castlereagh, the English Minister for Foreign Affairs, represented the interests of Great Britain.

This latter circumstance might have enabled Napoleon to see that his fate was decreed. England being represented by three members at the Congress sufficiently indicated the degree of influence she was about to claim over the destiny of Napoleon; while at the same time, the other Powers showed their submission to England by each sending only one Plenipotentiary. As to France, she sent only one individual to the Congress at Châtillon, and that was General Caulaincourt, the Duke of Vicenza.*

* The Emperor, who highly and justly esteemed the Duke of Bassano had withdrawn him from the post of Minister for Foreign Affairs,

He was then, nobody knows why, Minister for Foreign Affairs. I know very well the private motive which induced the Emperor to send him to Châtillon; but one thing which I cannot comprehend is, how Napoleon should imagine that that reason could have any weight in the scale of general interests.

The reason to which I allude is the cordial friendship with which the Emperor Alexander honored the Duke of Vicenza. It was one of those friendships, almost fraternal, which are so rare in the world, and, above all, rare among Sovereigns. But in the circumstances in which Alexander stood, being called to the head of the gigantic coalition of Europe, he appeared in the face of the whole world as the opponent of Napoleon, and therefore the latter was wrong in flattering himself that any private interest could have weight with him in opposition to the general interests. Sovereigns have two natures. Napoleon well knew this.

While the Congress was sitting the Allied armies were advancing on Paris and inclosing us within their ranks. The Emperor fought and gained several battles, and seemed to surpass himself in energy and talent. But what availed this? France was overrun with enemies, who were marching in all directions upon the capital.

The victory of Champaubert revived a faint ray of hope. Alsuvieff, the Russian General, was taken, with a corps of 6,000 men and 45 officers. This was succeeded by the Battle of Montmirail. General Sacken, with a part of the Army of Silesia, commanded by Blucher, was attacked and beaten by the Emperor. Twenty-five pieces of artillery, 3,000 killed, 2,000 wounded, and 1,000 prisoners, were the result of this battle, which, as well as the engagement of the preceding day, proved the inferiority of Blucher, and, indeed, of all who were opposed to the Emperor.

Two days before the battles of Montmirail and Cham·paubert, the Duke of Bassano, who had been daily urging the Emperor to send more extended powers to the Duke of Vicenza, had at length prevailed on Napoleon to draw

merely to satisfy petty passions, which he had not time to contend with. He gave the Duke of Bassano full powers to correspond with Châtillon. But to have done any good it would have been requisite for him to have been on the spot.

up the instructions and to sign them, in order that they
might be forwarded to Châtillon. On the eve of the
Battle of Champaubert, the Duke said to the Emperor:
" Sire, the powers are ready." " I will sign them to-
morrow," replied Napoleon. " If I should be killed they
will not be wanted; if I should conquer we shall then be
able to treat with better advantage."

Next day the Duke of Bassano, who, it is well known,
was with the Emperor in all his battles, went to him after
the victory, and presented to him the powers which he
had promised to sign. The Emperor made the same reply as that which he had given on the preceding day.
The Duke of Bassano withdrew much disappointed. On
the evening of the Battle of Montmirail he again urged
the Emperor to sign the powers. But some strange
visions had entered the Emperor's brain. He smiled,
and, looking at the maps of France and Europe which
lay before him: " I now stand in such a situation that
I need not yield an inch of ground," said he to the Duke,
" and I will sign nothing."

The campaign in France is a sublime effort of Napoleon's genius, and places him in the rank of the most
celebrated captains, if not at their head. But what result did he anticipate? What conclusion could be expected from partial victories like those of Montmirail
and Champaubert, while innumerable legions covered
our plains on the North and South. The Congress of
Châtillon, it is true, held out some hope, but, as I have
before observed, the presence of three envoys from England might have opened the eyes of the Emperor, even
though he had been blinded by the blaze of his ancient
glory. The following anecdote, the correctness of which
I can vouch for, I had from the party concerned:

When the Comte d'Artois arrived at Vesoul he was
accompanied by several persons attached to the Bourbon
cause, while a crowd of persons, who came to meet him,
were awaiting his arrival to pay homage to him such as
never was rendered to Napoleon. The Prince had met
with an old Swiss officer, named Wildermetz. This person was dispatched to the Russian Headquarters to request that the Emperor Alexander would authorize the
Comte d'Artois, and I believe the Duc de Berry, to proceed to the Headquarters of the Allied Sovereigns, and

enter themselves as volunteers during the campaign of
RECONQUERING France. M. de Wildermetz was charged
with a similar message to Count Stadion for the Emperor of Austria. He likewise had a letter accrediting
him to Prince Metternich.

On his arrival at the Russian Headquarters he saw the
Emperor Alexander, who addressed him thus: "M. de
Wildermetz, you will tell the Comte d'Artois that I am
extremely sorry to be obliged to refuse his request, but
we are just now engaged in conferences of a serious and
important nature. They may terminate in MAINTAINING
THE EMPEROR NAPOLEON ON THE THRONE OF FRANCE.
Under these circumstances their Royal Highnesses would
be placed here in an awkward position, and, in every
respect, it is better that they should remain some time
longer on the frontier." M. de Wildermetz returned to
Franche-Comté to report this answer, but the Princes
had left the place before he arrived.

Napoleon hoped to draw the whole of the hostile army
after him, when he fell back upon Saint Dizier. This
was a bold resolution, and one the generosity of which
the Parisians ought to have felt. But he was pursued by
only a corps of ten thousand men, and the entire mass
of the Allied Force fell upon Paris with all the fury of
a tempest. The Emperor of Russia waited only to direct
the attack on La Fère-Champenoise, and then proceeded
to Paris, as if he had been making a journey from Moscow to St. Petersburg. The enemy was at the gates of
Paris, and yet no measures had been taken for the defense of the Capital.

The Russians had the courage to burn their palaces,
why did we not fire our *faubourgs* for their reception ?
We had not even arms wherewith to equip our men.
Ammunition, too, was wanting. Was this from want of
foresight, or was it the result of treason ? Alas! it is too
true that we had among us at that period many who
were unworthy of the name of Frenchmen.

The Cossacks committed atrocious horrors in the department of the Aisne. They then marched upon Sens.
Dijon was laid under a contribution of two millions.
Saumur was subjected to their insults, not only in the
persons of its inhabitants but in those of its municipal
body, and Montbard, which now contained the grave of

one who would have valiantly defended it—that of Junot—Montbard, which was likewise the cradle of a man
whose fame belonged to all Europe, was delivered up to
the pillage of the Allied troops.

Montbard was the favorite retreat of Buffon; he had
fitted up a house there with exquisite taste. The gardens were superb, and the greenhouses and plantations
were objects of curiosity to travelers. All was now laid
waste. My father-in-law's house was visited with a similar fate by the exterminating hand of the invaders. The
unfortunate old man was unable to bear up against this
new calamity, following so closely on the death of his
much-beloved son. He died a few weeks after the invasion, without ever recovering his speech, which he lost
by a paralytic attack occasioned by the sight of the Russian and German uniforms.

Our fertile provinces were now inundated with battalions of barbarians, and every day their destroying lines
drew closer. The Government, acting on its secret principles, prohibited the journals from publishing the truth.
Whether this measure was wise or unwise I do not pretend to determine. But this, however, I can say, that
the intelligence most cautiously concealed was generally
well known; and that, perhaps, it would at this time
have been better policy to have allowed a perfectly free
expression of opinion.

Throughout the whole of this crisis the Emperor's
conduct was certainly admirable; but yet all he did led
to no effective result. The Battle of Montereau was
doubtless one of the most brilliant conceptions of his
genius, and one of the most remarkable examples of the
valor of our troops and the skill of our generals. But
what we then wanted was peace—with peace all might
have been saved.

An *opéra de circonstance*, entitled the "*Oriflamme*," was
brought out in Paris at the very time when the Comte
d'Artois was at Vesoul. At such a time the title might
well have appeared ominous, but a sort of general vertigo
seemed to prevail. I well remember the first performance of the "*Oriflamme*." It was like a national convention
of the *beau monde*. Every box was filled. The Faubourg
Saint Germain saw with enthusiasm the title of the
"*Oriflamme*," and prepared to bestow on the piece the

23

most extravagant applause. I was then in the habit of seeing many of the residents of the royal Faubourg, and their joy knew no bounds.

The success of the "*Oriflamme*" was extraordinary. The authors certainly could not be accused of Royalist opinions. I can answer for one of them at least, that is M. Étienne. The other was M Baour Lormian.

Joseph Bonaparte had settled upon Bernardin de Saint-Pierre a pension of 6,ooo francs, which, together with some other property he possessed, afforded him sufficient means of subsistence.

It was extremely interesting to hear Bernardin de Saint-Pierre converse about Jean Jacques Rousseau. He had been his pupil, and he was much attached to his master. I one day advised him to write his conversations with J. J. Rousseau, and to publish them.

"No," said he, "I cannot prevail on myself to do that." "Why?" inquired I.

"Because I should feel as though I were putting my friend's noble thoughts up to sale; and I could not tolerate that idea."

He told me that one day he and Rousseau went to dine together in the country — I think to Belleville or Menilmontant. Rousseau was profoundly melancholy that day. He was suffering from that nervous state of feeling which rendered him unhappy beyond the power of consolation, and made him see misery where he might often have found happiness. Bernardin respected those moments when Rousseau's mind seemed to retire within itself. He walked silently beside his friend, speaking only in reply to the observations made to him, leaving him undisturbed to his reveries, for he knew by experience that solitude and silence are the best friends of grief. As they walked in this manner, side by side, Rousseau sometimes stooped to gather a flower, which he placed in his herbal that he might afterward compare it with a corresponding one in the Flora of Linnæus. He had with him a book, in which he noted down his observations. At that moment the bell of a distant convent announced the hour of vespers. Rousseau started, then, throwing himself on his knees, he ejaculated a fervent prayer, and in joining his hands he let fall some flowers which he had just gathered. His prayer being ended, he rose, and the two friends continued their promenade. After a few moments' silence, Rousseau said to Bernardin de Saint-Pierre:

"I have often felt inclined in moments like this, to become a Catholic. Do you know why? That I might turn monk."

His friend looked at him with astonishment.

"Yes," pursued Rousseau, "I firmly believe that a solitude like a monastery, peopled by men serving God, must be a foretaste of heaven."

Bernardin shook his head with an air of doubt, and said:

"Then why not enter our communion? You will found a PARACLETE, in which you soon will have more disciples than Abélard."

"The reason why I do not put that design into execution," said Rousseau, with a melancholy smile, "is because if I were to quit the world I must relinquish love; and how is it possible to live without love?"

When Cardinal Maury announced to me the death of Bernadin de Saint-Pierre, the reader may readily imagine, from all that I have related of my former acquaintance with this celebrated man, that I was much shocked at the intelligence.

"It is curious," said I to Cardinal Maury, "that within a very short time you have been the first to acquaint me with the deaths of two very celebrated men — viz, the Abbé Delille and Bernardin de Saint-Pierre."

"True," said the Cardinal, pausing and looking thoughtful. Then, taking my hand, he said:

"I wonder who will be the first person to tell you of my death! Let us see. It will be Millin! no — Cherval! no — Talleyrand! Yes, it will be Talleyrand!"

"Nonsense!" said I. "Judging from your looks, your Excellency bids fair to outlive me."

He shook his head sorrowfully. He was depressed in spirits, for he foresaw the *dénouement* of the drama that was passing before us. He had a presentiment that the Empire would not long survive and he told me so with painful emotion, for he was much attached to the Emperor.

"Well," said he again, "I should like to guess who will tell you of my death!"

It was a postilion of Viterbo.

CHAPTER XXXI.

The Austrians before Grenoble — Paris in the Winter of 1814 — False Reports of the Enemy's Progress — Saint Dizier — Review on the Place du Carrousel — Cardinal Maury Predicts the Return of the Bourbons — The Duc d'Angoulême Enters Bordeaux — The Treaty of Chaumont — Ferdinand VII. Re-enters Spain — Talleyrand's Influence in the Restoration of the Bourbons — The Empress and the King of Rome Leave Paris — The Attack on Paris — Rovigo and Talleyrand — Capitulation of Paris.

THE Austrians were now before Grenoble, maintaining a heavy cannonade. Affairs every day assumed a more somber aspect. The invaders were advancing upon us with such terrible speed and regularity that nothing seemed likely to check their progress. The Germans were penetrating into Dauphiné; the English and Spaniards were advancing by the Pyrenees. Hitherto our attention had been exclusively directed toward the North, but now the torrent was gaining upon us on all sides.

One of the singularities of that period was the gay aspect of Paris during the winter of 1814. Masked balls and private balls were given without intermission, and yet the disastrous intelligence that was daily received put dozens of families into mourning. Meanwhile the Emperor acquired some partial advantages over the Allied armies. But what did they avail? Only to show the more convincingly that all was lost. Treason, too, had made rapid progress. In many towns the White Flag was concealed in some of the houses in anticipation of the favorable moment for raising the cry of *Vive le Roi.* How was it that the Duke of Rovigo, who was sincerely attached to the Emperor, did not make himself acquainted with the real state of France at that time? The truth is that the Duke was a most incompetent Minister of the Police. Toulouse, Bordeaux, and a great part of the South, where trade had suffered greatly by the War, ardently prayed for peace apart from any wish for the return of the Bourbons.

Will it be believed that Napoleon's evil star now so completely ruled his destiny that he allowed himself to be misled by false reports of the march of the enemy's forces, which reports, however, caused the loss of Paris? After the affair of Saint Dizier, the Emperor's object was to make a diversion, to draw together all the enemy's forces, and to give a decisive battle, which should deliver Paris.

Information, which was subsequently ascertained to be false, induced Napoleon to march to meet the corps of Winzingerode with a force amounting only to ten thousand men, all cavalry. In his rear there was no infantry; in short, no army. The marches and countermarches requisite for this operation caused Napoleon to lose four days. This loss was irreparable.

Now that I have arrived at the period when we bade adieu to our days of glory, I must mention an occurrence which I think sufficiently important to claim a place in these " Memoirs;" I allude to the presentation to the city of Paris of the last colors taken by the Emperor from the enemy. It was a most imposing ceremony, and the recollection of it must still be vivid in the minds of many of my own age. I shall never forget what I felt on that occasion.

It was on a Sunday; the weather was superb for that season of the year, for it was then the end of February. An immense concourse of people thronged the quays of the Louvre, the Place du Carrousel, and the Rue de Rivoli. The Minister at War (Clarke), who already in his heart had pronounced against the colors which he bore in triumph, took a conspicuous part in the ceremony. The *cortége* passed along the Quay, the Place du Carrousel, and the Pont Royal, in admirable order. First came General Hulin and all his Staff, preceded by a numerous military band; then followed the Staff of the Gendarmery of Paris, the National Guard, and finally the ten flags, two of which were borne by officers of the Imperial Guard. I could not help remarking the expression which was imprinted on the countenances of these two men. It partook at once of the pride of triumph and the dejection which necessarily followed the reflection: THESE FLAGS WERE TAKEN FROM THE ENEMY ONLY TWENTY LEAGUES FROM PARIS ! The other eight flags were borne by four officers of the Line and four officers of the National Guard.

Next came the Minister at War in his carriage, followed and preceded by his aids-de-camp, likewise in carriages, which, by the way, I may observe, had rather a ludicrous effect. The procession was closed by the Imperial Guard and troops of the Line. It entered the Court of the Tuileries by the triumphal arch of the Carrousel, and the Minister at War, having halted under the Vestibule de l'Horloge, received there the trophies which he was afterward to present to the Empress.

King Joseph, whom the Emperor had left in Paris as his Lieutenant-General, that day reviewed the National Guards. The Place du Carrousel and the Court of the Tuileries were filled with troops. I saw King Joseph at a distance, riding along the ranks of the National Guard and troops of the Line. His striking resemblance to the Emperor might have made me fancy myself transported back to the glorious days of the Consulate and the Empire.

When the flags were carried through the Court of the Tuileries, the drums beat and the National Guard presented arms; that movement was electrifying, and a general shout of "*Vive l'Empereur!*" was once more re-echoed by the walls of the Tuileries. The Minister at War first proceeded to the Hall of the Council of State, where he was received by a Master of the Ceremonies. He was afterward conducted to the *Salon de la Paix*, where the Comte de Ségur, as Grand Master of Ceremonies, awaited him. The Comte de Ségur introduced him to the *Salle du Trône*, where the Empress, surrounded by her Ladies and Gentlemen in waiting, the Princes, Grand Dignitaries, Ministers, and Grand Officers of the Empire, received the flags presented to her by the Minister at War (the Duc de Feltre). A formal speech was delivered by the Duke, to which the Empress replied very briefly.

After this solemn ceremony the flags were conveyed to the Invalides and consigned to the care of that same Marshal Serrurier to whom Napoleon gave such a good-natured reproof, when, a year afterward, he found the *Hôtel des Invalides* deserted by his old brothers-in-arms who had fought with him in Egypt and Italy. Of the ten flags, one was Austrian, four were Prussian, and five Russian. They were brought to Paris by Baron Mortemart, one of the Emperor's orderly officers.

One evening Cardinal Maury came to visit me. When he entered I observed that he looked particularly dull. I had two or three friends with me, and he asked me to favor him with a few minutes' conversation in my cabinet. As soon as we entered he closed the door, threw himself on a sofa, and, folding his arms with an air of despondency, he said: "All is lost! Heaven alone can save us by a miracle! We must now invoke that miracle, for I have ordered prayers of forty hours." I shuddered! Prayers of forty hours! It seemed like the preparation for death. It was the precursor of the death of our country.

"Heavens!" I exclaimed, "surely we may hope that the genius of the Emperor——" The Cardinal shook his head mournfully. "He is dragging us into the abyss into which he has plunged himself! His obstinacy banishes all hope. Oh that we lived in the days in which ecclesiastics bore the halberd and the sword! Old as I am, I would mount my horse. I would go to the Emperor and say, 'Sire, if those who are about you have not courage to let you hear the truth, I will tell you that you are hurling yourself and France to destruction. I have come to lend my feeble aid in her defense.'"

"No, Cardinal," said I, "do not regret your mission of peace and conciliation. Remain with us, and pray for the success of our arms."

The most disastrous news had succeeded the delusive hope which for a moment cheered us. In the space of five days the Emperor had beaten all the corps of the Army of Silesia, and driven them between the Aisne and the Marne. The five corps of the Army of Silesia lost more than twenty thousand men in the space of five days. The genius of the Army of Italy once more favored Napoleon; yet her smiles were but transient. The Emperor's able and rapidly-conceived plans were all defeated by whom? By Blucher, the fugitive of Jena, the prisoner of Lübeck!

In the meanwhile the party of the old *noblesse* was gaining strength. The Cardinal told me many remarkable particulars on this subject. "The Emperor," said he, "does not attach sufficient importance to old recollections. Even the defects of the *régime* of the Bourbons, when contrasted with those of his, were converted into bless-

ings.   The pusillanimity of Louis XVI. and all the
abuses of his reign vanished, in comparison with the
absolutism of Napoleon.»   "Do you, then, think it possible," said I, "that the Bourbons will ever return to
France?"   At first he made no reply.   This subject did
not please him.   The Bourbons would certainly not receive him on their arrival in France.

"Yes," said the Cardinal, after a pause, "they will
return; and the Emigrants who have been continually
blundering, will, for once, probably see their way rightly,
and will manœuver by instinct, if not by talent.   If this
result do not arrive, it must be owing to a renewal of
the same faults which they committed at Coblentz at the
time of the Emigration.   The Emperor has loaded them
with favors.   He will see their gratitude."

The Cardinal was right.   The greatest fault Napoleon
ever committed was to surround himself with men who,
while they kissed his hand, were plotting treason against
him.   He who so often followed the maxims of Machiavelli
ought to have borne in mind the following precept:
"Never restore to men the half of what they have lost,
for they will use it against you."

Bordeaux soon opened its gates to the Duc d'Angoulême.
The Prince was preceded by an Anglo-Spanish advanced
guard.

I received from Châtillon, where I had many friends,
intelligence of the rupture of the negotiations.   Napoleon, after long insisting on the bases of the treaty proposed at Frankfort, presented, through the medium of
the Duke of Vicenza, a counter-project, declaring that
he, Napoleon, would consent to remain Sovereign of
France circumscribed within its old limits, with only the
additions of Savoy, Nice, and the Isle of Elba.*   The
Allies rejected all these propositions, and faithfully adhered to the declarations of the treaty, offensive and
defensive, signed at Chaumont on the 1st of March —
the situation of Napoleon had changed since the Treaty
of Frankfort!

The definitive reply was given on the 19th of March.
Napoleon resolved that, if he fell, his fall should be

* He also wished to retain a portion of Italy for Prince Eugène,
the Grand-Duchy of Berg, and the Principality of Neufchâtel. The
latter was for Berthier. A clause for Berthier!

without a parallel. On the 20th and 21st of March he fought the Battles of Arcis-sur-Aube. On these two days he exposed himself to danger like a common soldier, giving proofs of the rarest courage and presence of mind at a time when he must have been a prey to the most harassing anxiety. The enemy's artillery kept up a terrible fire! The balls bounded through the air without intermission.

In the very heat of the engagement there came up a corps of that sacred phalanx, composed of men whose courage had been tried in a hundred battles — I mean the Old Guard. At the moment when the corps arrived on the field, the Emperor saw that the danger was imminent. He formed the troops into squares. The enemy's fire redoubled, and a bomb fell close to the foremost rank of one of the squares. In spite of the long-tried courage of the veterans, this occurrence caused a movement in the ranks. Napoleon immediately saw how important was the result of that moment.

He spurred his horse and galloped up close to the bombshell, and, turning to the troops, said with a smile, "Well, what is the matter? surely you are not frightened at this?" In another instant the shell burst; and not only did Napoleon and his horse escape unhurt, but it happened that no injury was sustained by anyone. This was the way in which Napoleon led his troops to victory!

Ferdinand VII. had now returned to his kingdom. On his arrival at La Flania, near Figuieres, he was delivered up by Marshal Suchet, in the presence of the two combined armies. Thus did the long Peninsular War terminate just at the point at which it began, and, to complete the mortification, Spain, whose soil had been drenched with the blood of so many martyrs of liberty, was a few months afterward again made subject to the stupid and tyrannical yoke of divine right.

I have now arrived at the crises of our misfortunes. The Emperor was forsaken by all his Allies. Murat had totally abandoned him. He occupied Tuscany, and had become, as it were, the ally of Ferdinand IV., his enemy, the man who regarded him as a usurper. Both now marched together against the French. I have already mentioned that the Emperor Napoleon was misled by a false report, either through treachery or accident. This error was fatal to Paris, which was abandoned with no other defenders than Clarke, the War Minister, and King Joseph — the latter abandoned us. Though I entertain a profound respect for General Clarke, I must confess that I do not think he was equal to the important trust reposed in him.

But the mainspring which set the machinery in motion was M. de Talleyrand, whom the Emperor would have done well to have lodged in Vincennes. It was not the unassisted efforts of the Faubourg Saint Germain that brought about the Restoration: it is a great error to suppose so. No doubt the Royalists had in Paris very active *coteries* of intriguing priests and women; but these obscure arsenals merely prepared the arms which were directed against the Emperor. M. de Talleyrand was not the sole author of the Restoration; he merely fixed the cockades which were already prepared. To this he will owe all his celebrity, and not to a political career which is not signalized by any incident important to his country.

In spite of the Hosanna at that time chanted by a chorus of old women in honor of the genius of M. de Talleyrand, it might fairly be asked what he had ever done either FOR or AGAINST France. He was a man of wit, and his *bonmots* were excellent. But wit was his only qualification. It was a finely-painted curtain, behind which there was absolutely NOTHING till the 30th of March. On the 30th of March, M. de Talleyrand distinguished himself by doing something important AGAINST France. I will briefly trace his course during that memorable period.

The danger became daily more and more pressing. The Emperor momentarily received intelligence of new defections. The conscripts were refractory and discontented; treason multiplied in the departments, and rendered more frightful the disasters caused by the presence of the Allied troops. There was no recruiting; contributions could no longer be levied, and money was scarce. Our most fertile provinces were desolated by the requisitions of the enemy.

This disastrous state of things was aggravated by Napoleon himself, by his fatal distrust of the population of Paris. He was afraid to arm that population too long before the hour of danger really arrived, and then perfidy in the hour of need had neutralized our means of defense. He was deceived, as I have said, at Saint Dizier by Winzingerode's corps of cavalry, which he took for the enemy's advanced guard; and having repulsed it, he discovered that the main army was not in its rear. What an error! He now found that he had been betrayed. He saw before him his own ruin, and that of France. He determined on a retrograde movement behind the Forest of Fontainebleau.

The inhabitants of Paris were in a state of the most painful anxiety. What was to be their fate? We concealed all that we could conceal of our valuables, and prepared for flight; but in which direction were we to go? The English were advancing by the way of Guienne; the Austrians by the Lyonnais, the Bourbonnais, and Burgundy. Champagne was the theater of war, as well as the provinces toward Flanders. On all sides there were disasters and ruin, towns and villages burned, and the earth deluged with blood.

On the 28th of March a Council of Regency was held, and it was resolved that the Empress and the King of Rome should quit Paris. Who could have advised a measure so impolitic, and so little productive of advantage to the Empress herself? Was it expected that the English would show her more respect than the Austrians if she had encountered them? Maria Louisa was our shield, and we would have been her defense.

The departure of the Empress and the King of Rome is still involved in mystery. They proceeded to Blois, accompanied by an escort of two thousand six hundred picked troops, leaving Paris to be defended by King Joseph and the National Guard without arms. Doubtless Napoleon ordered their departure, but he must have been deceived. Maria Louisa was followed by all the Ministers and all the Great Dignitaries, except M. de Talleyrand, Savary, and Clarke, who were not to depart until the 30th.

The approaches to Paris were defended by Marshals Marmont and Mortier, the former having with him only two thousand four hundred seasoned infantry and eight hundred cavalry. Marmont defended the heights of

Belleville and Romainville. The Duke of Treviso had
to defend the intervening space from the canal to the
Seine, and Marmont from the canal to the Marne. On
the day of the attack, the 30th of March, universal terror prevailed. The interior of every house was the
abode of mourning and despair. Paris seemed like a
city struck by the malediction of Heaven. The Duke of
Rovigo had received instructions not to quit the capital
before the Prince of Benevento.

This was strange, and it may serve as an answer to
those who allege that the Emperor never respected social
liberty where his interests were concerned. M. de Talleyrand was free to depart; it was only the Emperor's
Minister who was detained captive, for his departure depended on that of the Prince of Benevento. But to quit
Paris at that particular moment would not have suited
the Prince's purpose. It was necessary to invent an excuse, and the following was thought of. I know not why
the Duke of Rovigo has not related the circumstance as
it really happened. Perhaps he wished to disguise, under
the veil of silence, the sort of mystification that was
played upon him.

Prince Talleyrand still remained in Paris, for his absence was not wished by the party who had been busily
preparing white flags and cockades. That party wished
to get rid of the Duke of Rovigo. He was devoted to
the Emperor. I must render him this justice, if I have
been severe to him on other points. What was wanted
was to get him to depart, and to allow the Prince of
Benevento to stay.

This object was effected by the clever management of
Madame de Remusat. That lady repaired to the Prefecture of the Police. She was on terms of intimate
friendship with M Étienne Pasquier, then Prefect. " My
dear Baron," said she, as she entered his cabinet, " I have
come to request that you will do me a service." " What
is it?" " M. de Talleyrand must not quit Paris."

Accustomed as M. Pasquier was to extraordinary revo-
lutions of opinions and parties, he could not repress a
very significant expression of surprise while he listened
to Madame de Remusat. It was some time before he
made any reply. At length he said: " What can I do,
madame? M. de Talleyrand must quit Paris like all the

rest of the Great Dignitaries. You would not have me disobey the Emperor's order; for he is still Emperor, and may be back again to-morrow." Madame de Remusat shrugged her shoulders with an air of contempt: "Come, come, Baron, surely you are not one of those who think he has power to work miracles! He has no longer any army, no Empire."

Baron Pasquier shook his head. "But that is nothing to the purpose," said he; "you propose a thing that cannot be done. It is perfectly impossible to do what you wish. Where is M. de Talleyrand?" "At your door, in my carriage." "Is not your husband at the Barrière du Maine with his company?" "He is." "Well, I should imagine that he is the best person to detain M. de Talleyrand in Paris. Let him set out in his own carriage, with his own liveries, so as to let it be seen that he does set out. On his arrival at the Barrière, your husband may detain him if he pleases. I have no need to appear in the business. This is my advice; and if you think fit you may follow it."

Madame de Remusat left the cabinet of the Prefect perfectly satisfied. As soon as the Duke of Rovigo was informed, by his spies, that the Prince of Benevento had left his Hôtel, he left his, and quitted Paris without seeking any further information, and without knowing whether the enemy was not practicing some artful scheme. I beg his pardon for speaking of him thus candidly; but his conduct was worse than MALADROIT — it was stupid.

When M. de Talleyrand learned that the Duke of Rovigo had thus left the field open to him, he said nothing, but he smiled with that satirical expression so customary with him. He returned to Paris, and his conduct there is so well known that I need scarcely describe it. He, without any reserve, placed himself in hostility to the falling party, and joined the party that was triumphing. There certainly is, in M. de Talleyrand's nature, some quality which attracts him toward those who are gaining power, and repels him from those who are losing that same power. We saw proofs of this on the 18th Brumaire, in 1814, and in 1830.

Thus it was that M. de Talleyrand remained in Paris after all the members of the Government had joined the Empress at Blois. The poor Duke of Rovigo was so ill served by his spies that they gave him false reports, and the account of the above affair, as given in his "Memoirs," is wholly incorrect. The story is as I have related it. Several of the actors who took part in the drama are still living. My account may possibly displease them; but they can only deny my statements, they cannot prove them to be untrue.

While all these incidents were passing, the inhabitants of Paris were in a dreadful state of alarm. I had concealed most of my diamonds in a girdle which I wore over my corset. My pearls, and some other jewels of minor value, were concealed in a similar manner by Mademoiselle Poidevin, the governess of my daughters. Toward evening my drawing-room began to fill.

Madame Juste de Noailles was among my visitors. She was very uneasy at the aspect of affairs, though not alarmed for the safety of herself and her family. In the event of a return of the Bourbons the Noailles were sure of standing on a favorable footing. But her husband was at the Headquarters of the Emperor Alexander, and she was anxious to see what turn affairs would take.

At length eleven o'clock struck. The fatal morning was approaching, and I had as yet formed no settled determination. I sat down and wrote to the Duke of Ragusa. The friendship which had united him to the Duke of Abrantès induced me to appeal to him for advice, and I felt assured that he would direct me to the most prudent course. I therefore wrote to him that, being ALONE in my house with my four young children, I was greatly perplexed, and did not know whether it would be most advisable to depart or to remain where I was.

I sent my letter to the Hôtel de Raguse, where the Marshal happened to be at that very moment engaged in drawing up the capitulation, or rather in receiving the conditions. Occupied as he must have been, he seized his first moment of leisure to answer me. The following is a copy of his letter:

"I thank you, madame, for the proof of confidence you have given me. Since you ask for my advice, I would recommend you not to quit Paris, which to-morrow will certainly be more tranquil than any place within twenty leagues round. After having done all in my power for the honor of France and the French arms, I am forced to sign a capitulation which will permit foreign troops to enter our capital to-morrow! All my efforts have been unavailing. I have been compelled to yield to numbers, whatever regret I may have felt in doing so. But it was my duty to spare the blood of the soldiers confided to my charge. I could not do otherwise than I have done; and I hope that my country will judge me as I deserve. My conscience expects this justice.»

I received this letter at two o'clock in the morning. I read it to the friends who had assembled at my house. It, of course, decided us not to leave Paris; but at the same time it profoundly grieved us. A capitulation! — and before the very Barriers of Paris!

It is false that Napoleon sent M. de Girardin to Paris, with orders that the powder magazines of Grenelle should be blown up before the arrival of the Allies. The Emperor, on the contrary, was destitute of ammunition, and desired that the powder should be conveyed, if possible, to Fontainebleau. He loved his Parisians better than to sacrifice them wantonly, without any prospect of ulterior good.

CHAPTER XXXII.

The Allies Enter Paris — First Appearance of the White Cockade — The Allied Troops and Their White Scarfs — The Emperor Alexander at the Hôtel of M. de Talleyrand — The Council — Napoleon at Fontainebleau — A Conspiracy — Berthier Deserts the Emperor — The Duke of Ragusa and General Souham — Deputation of the Marshals — The Emperor of Russia — His Answer to the Marshals —Napoleon's Conversation on Suicide — He Takes Poison — His Recovery.

THE Allies had now actually entered Paris. The Duke of Ragusa had retired to Essonne, together with Generals Souham, Compans, and several others. At two o'clock on the morning of the 31st of March, that day so important in the history of France, the capitulation of Paris was signed. The Bourbons would consequently have been proclaimed at daybreak by their party, had the assent of the Allied Powers been positive and unreserved; but even at eleven o'clock in the fore--

noon nothing betokened the intended restoration.   It was
not until twelve o'clock that some white cockades and
flags became visible in the Place Louis XV.   These
demonstrations of royalty were paraded along the Place
by about forty persons on horseback, who waved the
flags and shouted *"Vive le Roi! Vivent les Bourbons!"*
But the people were mournful and silent, and did not
join in these cries.   This is an unquestionable fact.

The Archbishop of Malines himself declared that however desirous he was to see the fall of Bonaparte, he
neither heard nor saw anything on the 31st of March that
could lead him to expect the return of the old Dynasty.
The Duke Dalberg, who was at a window in the Hôtel
of M. de Talleyrand, exclaimed: "They are mounting
the white cockade!"   Then some of the party assembled
at M. de Talleyrand's went out merely TO SEE, as one of
them expressed it, what had caused the uproar.   Ten
men on horseback, with white flags, proceeded in the
direction of the Boulevard de la Madeleine.   As they
passed through the Rue Royale the shouts became
louder.   Windows were opened, white cockades were
thrown out, and ladies waved white handkerchiefs.

The group of persons described above were on the
Boulevard de la Madeleine when they met M. Tourton,
a General Officer of the National Guard.   He was on
horseback, and was accompanied by an aid-de-camp of
the Emperor of Russia.   Both were stopped by the
group, who continued to shout " *Vive le Roi! Vivent les
Bourbons !* "

M. Tourton said he could not grant them the protection they required until he had orders from the Government; and the Emperor of Russia's aid-de-camp seemed
very much embarrassed.   These two gentlemen proceeded
to the Barrière de Belleville, leaving the group on the
Boulevard.   The fact is that all this movement was only
partial, and that if a squadron of the Imperial Guard
had galloped through Paris the little party of Bourbonites
would speedily have been dispersed.

On the 31st of March the Allied Sovereigns entered
Paris.   As they advanced into the capital the demonstrations in favor of the Bourbons became more positive,
either because the fear of Napoleon had hitherto repressed
the real sentiments of the populace, or because that

populace merely followed the inclination natural to mankind, to salute the rising and to turn from the setting
sun.

A circumstance, trivial in itself, had a singular influence at this crisis; it was observed that the Allied
troops had all white scarfs tied round their arms: they
were worn as the sign of victory, and not as the badge
of French Royalism. Most people, however, regarded
them in the latter point of view, and the Royalists, art-
fully profiting by the mistake, reported that Louis XVIII.
was acknowledged by the Emperor of Russia, and even
by the Emperor of Austria, that Prince Schwartzenberg
wore the white scarf, and that the King's arrival might
be looked for next day.

It is a positive fact that no pledge for the Restoration had been given by the Allies. No doubt the Emperor Alexander might cherish a feeling more or less
favorable to the Bourbons; but as yet that feeling had
not been manifested. The Emperor of Russia arrived at
M. de Talleyrand's on foot, having alighted from his
horse after seeing the troops defile. He was received by
M. de Talleyrand, having as *aides des cérémonies* M. de
Pradt on the one hand and the Abbé Louis on the
other. Both were eagerly craving for the good things of
office, and they humbly bowed before the conqueror in
the hope of sharing the spoil of the conquered. M. de
Talleyrand did not reflect that these two gentlemen
were of his own cloth; if he had, he would probably
have shaken off the Archbishop of Malines at least.

I ought, however, to mention that, previously to the
arrival of the Emperor of Russia, M. de Nesselrode had
been closeted for two hours with M. de Talleyrand; and
there is reason to believe that in that *tête-à-tête* were
DETERMINED the matters which were subsequently DIS-
CUSSED in the Council: whether this was with the cognizance of the Emperor of Russia I know not.

On his way to the house of M. de Talleyrand the Emperor Alexander was accosted by Vicomte Sosthènes de
La Rochefoucauld who earnestly implored him to restore
to France her legitimate Sovereign. This step on the
part of M. de La Rochefoucauld was as honorable as the
conduct of the persons to whom I have just alluded was
base. M. de La Rochefoucauld never served Napoleon in

24

any way, whether in the army or the Imperial Household. His sentiments were always consistent.
When he mounted the white cockade he merely manifested a feeling which had long been cherished by himself and his family. The reply of Alexander to the
petition of M. de La Rochefoucauld was singularly cir-
cumspect. He held out to him no hope; and, indeed,
his reply might without difficulty have been construed
into a refusal.

This indecision arose out of a cause which was not, at
the time generally understood in Paris. The Emperor
of Russia was not convinced that the whole nation shared
the enthusiasm of a few hundred individuals whom M.
de Talleyrand presented to him as the KINGDOM. At the
recent engagement at Fère-Champenoise, the Russians
had seen a few thousand men allow themselves to be cut
to pieces rather than yield to the enemy; and these men
had been taken from the plow only a few days before.
What, then, was to be expected from the army — the
marshals and the generals?

This question occupied the attention of the Emperor
Alexander — I know this from a source of unquestionable
authority. Thus far M. de Talleyrand may be said to
have aided the Restoration, for between him and M. de
Nesselrode the plans were previously arranged. The
Emperor Alexander was induced to adopt them, and one
strong argument employed to effect this object was the
defection of Marmont. Marmont! the brother-in-arms,
the aid-de-camp, the dearest bosom friend of Napoleon,
since the death of Junot, Lannes, Duroc, Bessières; yes,
even he had abandoned him! It was evident, then, that
France wished to depose him. Another fatal circumstance was Napoleon's separation from Maria Louisa.*

Nevertheless the Emperor of Russia firmly resisted the
suggested restoration on the grounds proposed by M. de
Talleyrand. "What means would you employ?" inquired the Emperor Alexander. "The constituted authorities," confidently replied M. de Talleyrand. The
Emperor appeared astonished. "What authorities? they
are all dispersed." "I ask your Majesty's pardon. The
members of the Senate are in sufficient number. (This
was not true.) So are those of the Legislative Body.

* The Empress and her son were still at Blois.

The Senate having once pronounced, France will obey its dictates."* Alexander still hesitated.

"Will your Majesty be pleased to hear two witnesses in confirmation of my testimony?" With these words M. de Talleyrand sent for the Baron Louis and the Archbishop of Malines. On the evidence of these two men the Emperor of Russia formed his opinion on the state of France! In truth, I am almost inclined to believe that his mind was made up beforehand.

The Council was held immediately afterward. It consisted of the Emperor Alexander and the King of Prussia, the Duke Dalberg, M. Nesselrode, M. Pozzo di Borgo, Prince Schwartzenberg, Prince Lichtenstein, M. de Talleyrand, Baron Louis, and the Archbishop of Malines. These individuals were ranged on the right and left of the large table which stood in the middle of the apartment.

The Emperor Alexander did not sit down, but alternately stood and walked about; his mind seemed quite absorbed in the great interests which were under consideration. He expatiated largely on the misfortunes of war, and ended by observing that Napoleon, having merited to be deprived of a power which he had abused, France should be allowed to choose another Sovereign, and that the Allies should aid that important object by assisting to repress the efforts of persons striving to maintain an order of things which it was necessary totally to abolish.

Having said this much, he turned to the King of Prussia, and to Prince Schwartzenberg, who represented the Emperor of Austria, and asked them whether they concurred in his opinion. Alexander then made several noble and generous remarks, and betrayed considerable emotion. It is but justice to acknowledge that in his intervention in the affairs of France he was at the outset actuated by the most magnanimous feeling.

The conduct of the Archbishop of Malines was curious on this occasion. It will be best painted in colors borrowed from his own palette. "When the Emperor asked

---

*This remark of M. de Talleyrand is a terrible condemnation on the Senate. It would lead to the inference that if the Senate had protested against the arbitrary commands of Napoleon, it would have been seconded by France.

me my opinion," said he, in his description of the above
scene, "I eagerly declared we were all Royalists—that
ALL France was of the same opinion—that we had only
observed silence on account of the Congress of Châtillon"
(that is to say, through fear). To this the Abbé added
a thousand fine things of the same sort. Thus the business of the Council was settled. I have neither added
nor invented. The affair was reported in the journals;
but not with the above details, for the authenticity of
which I am enabled to vouch.

The Senate was convoked on the 1st of April. On the
2d the Act of Abdication was declared, and on the 3d
the wreck of the Legislative Body declared its concurrence
in the abdication. Napoleon was at Fontainebleau with
Berthier, Maret, Caulaincourt, Bertrand, and the majority
of the marshals.

Few persons are aware that Napoleon was doomed to
death during the few days which preceded his abdication,
by a band of conspirators composed of the most distinguished Chiefs of the army. "But," said one of them in
the Council in which these demons discussed their
atrocious project, "what are we to do with him? There
are two or three among us who, like Antony,* would
exhibit their blood-stained robes to the people, and make
us play the parts of Cassius and Brutus. I have no wish
to see my house burned, and to be sent into exile."
"Well," said another, "we must leave no trace of him.
He must be sent to heaven like Romulus." The others
applauded, and then a most horrible discussion commenced.

It is not in my power to relate the details. Suffice it
to say that the Emperor's death was proposed and discussed for the space of an hour, with a degree of coolness which might be expected among Indian savages
armed with tomahawks. "But," said he who had spoken
first, "we must come to some determination. The Emperor of Russia is impatient. The month of April is
advancing, and nothing has been done. Now, for the
last time, we will speak to him of his abdication. He
must sign it definitely—or——" A horrible gesture
followed this last word.

* They alluded to the Duke of Bassano, Caulaincourt, Bertrand, and
some others.

Yes, the life of Napoleon was threatened by those very men whom he had loaded with wealth, honors, and favors, to whom he had given luster from the reflection of his own glory. Napoleon was warned of the conspiracy, and it must have been the most agonizing event of his whole life. The torments of Saint Helena were nothing in comparison with what he must have suffered when a pen was presented to him by a man who presumed to say, " Sign — if you wish to live." If these last words were not articulated, the look, the gesture, the inflection of the voice, expressed more than the tongue could have uttered.

The Emperor of Russia wished to ascertain the feeling of the army before he adopted a final resolution. Napoleon made choice of Marshal Macdonald, Marshal Lefebvre, Marshal Oudinot, the Duke of Vicenza, Marshal Ney, and the Duke of Bassano, to bear to the Emperor Alexander the propositions which he had to make to the Allied Powers. Some time previous to this occurred a scene the remembrance of which fills me with indignation against the man whom it almost exclusively concerns. I allude to Berthier.

The Prince of Neufchâtel was with the Emperor, and he invented an excuse for leaving him, alleging that his presence was required in Paris, for the purpose of securing some papers which were of importance to the Emperor himself. While he spoke, Napoleon looked at him with melancholy surprise, which, however, Berthier did not or would not observe. " Berthier," said Napoleon, taking his hand, " you see that I have need of consolation — and how much I require at this moment to be surrounded by my true friends." He pronounced these last words emphatically. Berthier made no reply. Napoleon continued: " You will be back to-morrow, Berthier ? " " Certainly, Sire," replied the Prince of Neufchâtel. And he left the Emperor's cabinet with treason in his heart.

After his departure, Napoleon remained for some time silent. He followed him with his eyes, and when Berthier was out of sight, he cast them down toward the ground, on which he looked thoughtfully for several minutes. At length he advanced to the Duke of Bassano, and laying his hand on his arm he pressed it forcibly, and said:

"Maret, he will not come back." He then threw himself dejectedly into a chair. He was right. Berthier did not return.

The Duke of Ragusa had left his army corps under the command of General Souham. This corps was in the neighborhood of Essonne. Marshal Marmont was still undetermined as to what course he should adopt. The Convention which, on the 5th of April, had been · concluded at Chevilly between him and Prince Schwartzenberg had been disavowed. But there was one thing very unpardonable in the Duke of Ragusa, which was his having sent a copy of the Act of Abdication, which was not yet known, to the army; and the remarks which accompanied the document sufficiently explained what were his motives for sending it.

General Souham then thought that if the Emperor should return to power they had gone too far to retract — that they were lost; and in the absence of the Duke of Ragusa he determined for himself as to what course he should adopt. He told the troops that they were to march against the enemy. The soldiers joyfully flew to arms; but they continued their march to a considerable distance without, as they expected, coming up with the enemy. At length, when they reached the neighborhood of Versailles, they discovered they had been deceived.

They then turned furiously against their generals, who were well-nigh being sacrificed to their anger and disappointment. Cries of "*Vive l'Empereur! Mort aux étrangers! Mort aux Prussiens! Mort aux Russes!*" resounded on every side. This news speedily reached Paris, but not soon enough to enlighten the Emperor Alexander. But did he wish it? This is a secret which it is impossible to divine. And yet I think he was sincere on his first arrival in Paris.

The particulars of the deputation of the marshals to the Emperor of Russia have been detailed in so many publications that I think it unnecessary to repeat them here. I may merely mention that the number of marshals being complete, the Emperor wished to add Marshal Macdonald, and he said to the Duke of Bassano: "I wish to include the Duke of Tarentum. He is not attached to me; but I know him to be an honest man, and for that reason his voice will have more weight with the Emperor of Russia than any other. Write to him, Maret.»

Then, after a moment's reflection, he added: "But poor Marmont! He will be grieved that I do not include him in the deputation. Well, Maret, we must have his name in it too. Set down Macdonald's name. But do not erase Marmont's." I know not whether the Duke of Ragusa was ever made acquainted with this fact. If so, I think it must have caused him a pang of regret.

The marshals, after a long conference with Napoleon, set out for Paris. They stopped at Petit-Bourg, at the Headquarters of the Prince of Wirtemberg to take fresh escorts. Marshal Marmont did not alight from his carriage, which was remarked as extraordinary. On their arrival in Paris they immediately waited on the Emperor of Russia. There Marmont evinced signs of great agitation. It was doubtless caused by grief — for he was not a traitor. No, he was incapable of that; but he was unhappy, and no wonder, if he knew the extent of the mischief he had done. When the marshals entered the apartment in which the Emperor of Russia was in readiness to receive them, Marmont did not accompany them. Was he at that time aware of the step which Souham had taken?

The Emperor of Russia gave the marshals an attentive hearing. Doubtless his determination was formed; but he would not even in appearance, put any restraint upon the nation. The abdication in favor of Napoleon II., by his father, was one of the three measures proposed to the Council, the rejection of which had been brought about by M. de Talleyrand.

The Emperor of Russia spoke on the question with considerable warmth. The arguments brought forward in favor of the son of Napoleon appeared to produce an impression on him. Above all things, civil war was in his opinion most to be dreaded. At the moment when he appeared to be ready to yield the point in question, one of his officers delivered to him a packet. He opened it, and his countenance suddenly changed.

"How is this, gentlemen," said he to the marshals, in a tone of reproach. "You are treating with me in the name of the army. You give me assurance of its sentiments, and at the same moment I receive intelligence that the army corps of the Duke of Ragusa has adhered to the Act of Abdication as proclaimed by the Senate!» He exhibited to them the declaration of adherence, signed by all the generals and superior officers of the 5th corps. From that moment all was at an end. The Emperor declared that everything had been unalterably settled.

Such was the answer conveyed to Napoleon. On receiving it he was more deeply afflicted at finding himself abandoned by the men whom he had created than by the loss of his Crown. The Duke of Bassano assured me that the Emperor never appeared to him so truly great as at that moment. Throughout the whole day his conversation turned on subjects of the most gloomy kind, and he dwelt much on suicide. He spoke so frequently on this subject that Marchand, his first *valet de chambre*, and Constant were struck with it. They consulted together, and both with common consent removed from the Emperor's chamber an Arabian poniard and the balls from his pistol case.*

The Duke of Bassano had also remarked this continued allusion to suicide, notwithstanding his efforts to divert Napoleon's thoughts from it. The Duke spoke to Marchand, after he had taken leave of the Emperor previous to retiring to rest, and he expressed himself satisfied with the precautions which had been taken.

The Duke had been in bed some time, when he was awoke by Constant, who came to him pale and trembling. "M. le Duc," he exclaimed, "come immediately to the Emperor! His Majesty has been taken very ill!» The Duke of Bassano immediately hurried to the bedside of the Emperor, whom he found pale and cold as a marble statue. He had taken poison!

When Napoleon departed for his second campaign in Russia, Corvisart gave him some poison of so subtle a nature that in a few minutes, even in a few seconds, it would produce death. This poison was the same as that treated of by Cabanis, and consisted of the prussic acid

---

* Marchand, as is well known, accompanied Napoleon to the Isle of Elba, and subsequently to Saint Helena. Constant, who imagined that he had been ill treated by the Emperor, quitted his service at Fontainebleau, after having received 50,000 francs from the funds of his royal master to repair his house.

which has subsequently been ascertained to be so fatal in its effects. It was with this same poison that Condorcet terminated his existence.

Napoleon constantly carried it about him. It was inclosed in a little bag hermetically sealed, and suspended round his neck. As he always wore a flannel waistcoat next to his skin, the little bag had for a long time escaped the observation of Marchand, and he had forgotten it. Napoleon was confident in the efficacy of this poison, and regarded it as the means of being master of himself. He swallowed it on the night above mentioned, after having put his affairs in order and written some letters. He had tacitly bidden farewell to the Duke of Bassano and some of his other friends, but without giving them cause for the slightest suspicion. The poison was, as I have already observed, extremely violent in its nature; but, by reason of its subtlety, it was the more liable to lose its power by being kept for any length of time. This happened in the present instance. It caused the Emperor dreadful pain, but it did not prove fatal.

When the Duke of Bassano perceived him in a condition closely resembling death, he knelt down at his bedside and burst into tears. "Ah, Sire!" he exclaimed; "what have you done?" The Emperor raised his eyes and looked at the Duke with an expression of affection; then, stretching to him his cold, damp hand, he said: "You see, God has decreed that I shall not die! He, too, condemns me to suffer!"

The Duke of Bassano could never relate this scene without the most painful emotion. The affair was but little known at the time of its occurrence, notwithstanding the importance which was attached to the most trivial act of Napoleon. But it was deemed prudent to conceal from the knowledge of the multitude everything calculated to excite sympathy for the victim and indignation against his persecutors.

CHAPTER XXXIII.

Marmont and the Convention of Chevilly — Indignation of the Troops against Marmont — The 4th of April at Fontainebleau — The Abdication — Napoleon's Forbearance — Carnot and Napoleon — M. Czernicheff — M. Platow's Appetite — How Madame Junot's Servants Proposed to Get Rid of Him — The Effect of the Drug — M. Volinski — Grand Ceremony of Expiation — A Te Deum.

WHEN the Provisional Government saw that the army, which was described as being in a state of subjection, was, on the contrary, in open revolt, an order was sent to the Duke of Ragusa directing him to depart immediately and restore order. When it was understood that the Marshal was in the neighborhood of Versailles, a plan was laid to assassinate him. I could myself name several officers who were fully resolved to strike the blow. A fault in the unfortunate Convention of Chevilly had exasperated not only the officers, but the soldiers — this was the stipulation of a place of secure retirement for the Emperor and his family.

There was, it must be confessed, in Marmont's conduct in this affair, a touch of IMPUDENCE. I am sorry to employ this word, but it comes naturally to the point of my pen. Did he mean to tell the French people that the safety of Napoleon — of that Colossus whose powerful hands had controlled the two hemispheres — depended upon him? On his arrival at Versailles, Marmont dared not venture to present himself to his troops. He acquainted the General Officers with his arrival, and retired to a farm at Grand Montreuil. The General Officers did not choose to take the responsibility on their own heads, and they took with them a number of officers of every rank. The unfortunate Marmont was thus surrounded by an accusing circle, who raised cries of vengeance which might well have excited terror in a man less inured to danger than the Duke of Ragusa. "But what would you have done in my place?" he exclaimed, in a moment of despair.

All were appeased by the abdication of the Emperor! That act may be regarded as the noblest of Napoleon's life. It was not duly appreciated by a nation like the French, who consider everything with levity. He might have returned to Paris in disguise and have excited an insurrection: the Allied Sovereigns might have been massacred, and the streets deluged with blood. But he chose to descend from the Throne rather than to continue on it by such means.

On the 4th of April the Emperor reviewed at Fontainebleau his Guard and the troops who still remained faithful to him. Marshal Ney, Marshal Lefebvre, and Marshal Oudinot were present at this review. The Emperor had very properly forbidden any of the journals from being circulated among the military. He still cherished hope. The review passed off very quietly. When it was ended, Marshal Lefebvre entered the cabinet. "Sire," said he, in a voice faltering with emotion, "you would not listen to your faithful servants! You are lost! The Senate has declared the abdication!" Marshal Lefebvre had advised Napoleon to defend himself in Paris.

The Guard still continued faithful, but the troops of the Line had been tampered with. The Duke of Bassano was still at Fontainebleau. He would not leave the Emperor, and spared no effort to sustain his fortitude. The Duke of Reggio was likewise at Fontainebleau. After the parade on the 5th, the Emperor sent for him, and asked whether he thought the troops would follow him to Italy. "No, Sire," replied the Marshal; "your Majesty has abdicated!" "Yes, but on certain conditions!" "Soldiers cannot discern these nice distinctions," observed the Marshal. The Emperor made no reply.

At one in the morning Marshals Ney and Macdonald returned from Paris. Marshal Ney, who entered first, said: "Sire, we have succeeded only in part." And he related how the defection of the 5th corps had prevented them from settling the question of the abdication by securing the succession of his son. Napoleon was deeply wounded by the conduct of the troops confided to the command of Marmont. Marmont certainly was not a traitor; and yet no traitor could have done greater mischief.

"To what place am I to retire with my family?" inquired Napoleon. "Wherever your Majesty may please. To the Isle of Elba, for example, with a revenue of six millions." "Six millions! that is a large allowance, considering that I am only a soldier." At that moment Napoleon had with him at Fontainebleau the troops of Macdonald, Mortier, Lefebvre, and Marmont. These different corps amounted altogether to 45,000 men. Deducting 12,000 as the number of Marmont's corps, there remained 33,000, with which Napoleon might have commenced civil war. Before the expiration of a fortnight he would have doubled his forces. His forbearance, in this particular, has never been fully acknowledged. It has even been pronounced want of firmness! His abdication was prompted by a noble impulse of his generous nature. He abdicated to save France from the horrors of civil war.

It has been frequently alleged that Napoleon was a tyrant, who punished with imprisonment or exile all who ventured to utter a word in opposition to his will. It would be easy to quote a thousand examples in refutation of these assertions; but it will suffice to mention the cases of Carnot and Lafayette. Carnot refused to sanction the Consulate for life — the Empire, and its hereditary succession. He was firm and honest in his opinions, and he never expressed a sentiment in opposition to his conscience. He was a truly noble-minded man. The Emperor, who knew and esteemed his integrity, never reproached him for the line of conduct he had adopted; but, at the same time, he never bestowed upon him any favor — this was perfectly natural.

In 1809, Carnot, after having governed provinces and had mountains of gold at his disposal, was reduced to very straitened circumstances. A severe loss which he sustained left him no alternative but a prison, or to appeal to the generosity of a friend. He required eighty thousand francs to extricate him from his embarrassment. Where could he find a friend who would go such a length to serve him?

After several days of bitter inquietude (for a prison is a fearful prospect to a man of spirit, whatever may be the cause that drives him into it), Carnot came to the conclusion that there was but one man in Paris to whom he could address himself without humiliation, and that man was his enemy — it was the Emperor!

Carnot wrote to Napoleon. His letter was what might

be expected from such a man. On receiving it the Emperor was deeply moved. He had a heart formed to understand the noble spirit of the writer. He mentioned the affair to the Duke of Bassano; in him, too, Carnot found a responsive hearer.

"Carnot must be extricated from this difficulty," said Napoleon; "but how can we manage it? One cannot offer money to such a man. Maret, you must draw up a memorial in which you will propose to me to allow him the arrears of his pay as a Lieutenant-General during the time he held that rank previous to the formation of the Empire, and send him an order for the amount. You must also send him a brevet for a pension of 12,-000 francs, the arrears of which will likewise be due to him, for he shall have a Senatorship. In this manner he will be under no obligation, except to his country, of which I am merely the organ."

Carnot received the brevets above mentioned, and was thus enabled to fulfill his engagements without incurring the insupportable burden of a favor. He felt and acknowledged Napoleon's generosity, and he stood nobly by him in the hour of adversity.

With the Emperor Alexander there arrived in Paris a number of Russians who had been our visitors on former occasions. Among them was M. Czernicheff. He was the most agreeable of all. I have several times had occasion to mention him in the course of these "Memoirs." As soon as he arrived he came to pay me a visit.

M. Czernicheff spoke about the position of France with admirable judgment and shrewdness. He was remarkable for the readiness with which he took a mental *coup d'œil* of things, and his opinions were always unbiased by prejudice. The conversation turned on various persons who had played a distinguished part during the Empire, and I was much surprised to learn that the Emperor Alexander entertained toward some of them not merely a prejudice, but a sort of dislike, which caused him to refuse seeing them. One of these persons was the Duke of Rovigo. I was amazed at hearing this. Czernicheff did not tell me the cause of this dislike, but I afterward learned it.

"And how have you been treated amid all these changes?" inquired M. Czernicheff.

"But indifferently," I replied. "I have a person quartered in my house who, disagreeable as he is, might be endured. But his followers are absolutely insufferable. They give my servants no rest."

"Whom do you allude to?" inquired M. Czernicheff.

"To Platow."

"Platow! he is lodged at Madame de Remusat's."

"That is the father, but the son is here, as my cook can testify, for he regularly dispatches twelve different dishes at his *déjeuner*, exclusive of the dessert, which is equally copious, as my *maître d'hôtel* well knows."

This was nothing more than the truth. Never did any animal walking on two legs exhibit such an example of gluttony.

Then I had the most bitter complaints from my *femme de charge*. She came to me one day and said she could no longer bear to see such destruction. She was every day obliged to give out a pair of sheets for M. Platow, because he thought proper to go to bed in his boots. Consequently, the sheets were not only covered with mud, but were slit in enormous rents by the spurs of the young DAUPHIN of the banks of the Don. Poor Blanche was exceedingly careful of my household linen, which was very fine, and she was not sparing of her imprecations on the RUSSIAN SAVAGES. At length, after a day or two, I observed that her anger was somewhat appeased, and I inquired whether our guest was behaving better.

"By no means, madame," said she; "but I now give him the coarse sheets belonging to the stablemen. They are far too good for a savage like him," she added in a contemptuous tone.

Another incident of a similar nature occurred among my servants. They were so disgusted at the gluttonous appetite of young Platow that they determined to give him a little wholesome correction. For this purpose they resorted to a scheme which I should certainly have prohibited had I been informed of it in time.

They procured a small quantity of an emetic drug, and mixed it not only in the dishes which were served for the Cossack's *déjeuner*, but also in his wine and the bottle of brandy which he regularly swallowed after EVERY MEAL. They might have killed him; but they had no

idea they were incurring any such danger, and were
merely intent on amusing themselves with what they
conceived to be a most admirable joke.

Platow that day ate with more than his usual appetite,
which was remarked with great satisfaction by the *valet
de chambre* whom I had appointed to attend upon him.
Joseph was an old confidential servant who had accompanied me in all my travels. The disorder and destruction which he witnessed in the house of his mistress
irritated him, and inspired him with a bitterness of feeling which did not belong to his nature.

Platow dispatched his usual hearty *déjeuner*, after which
he swallowed a large basin of *café à la crème* and the
remains of his bottle of brandy. Being somewhat exhausted by this exertion, he yawned, stretched out his
arms, and finally threw himself on the bed, where he
soon began to snore so loudly that Joseph feared he would
shatter the panes of glass in the windows.

Joseph was at first surprised, but at length he became
uneasy. He removed the dishes from the table without
disturbing Platow. He went in and out of the room,
purposely making a noise to endeavor to awaken the
Cossack, but without effect. At length he approached
the bedside and looked at him. He looked, as he always
did, very ugly; but he was perfectly calm, and his res-
piration, though heavy, was very regular.

Joseph left him. Several hours elapsed, and the Cossack continued sleeping, apparently in a state of the
most perfect beatitude. At five o'clock in the afternoon
. he awoke, and expressed himself much astonished at
his long nap. Joseph, who had been the first to think of
the emetic scheme, was carefully watching the result of
what he termed his *espièglerie*. As soon as he heard the
Cossack begin to yawn and swear, which were always
his first signs of waking existence, Joseph entered the
chamber and asked him in German how he was.

"Wonderfully well," replied he; "I have never felt
myself better since I have been in Paris; it is strange,
too, for I have taken no exercise, and yet I have a most
keen appetite. Desire the cook to hurry the dinner!"

Joseph was petrified with astonishment.

"Say I want dinner as soon as possible," continued
young Platow, without noticing the surprise of Joseph,

who proceeded to the kitchen with such an air of consternation that the *maître d'hôtel* exclaimed with alarm:
"*Mon Dieu!* is he dead?"

"Dead truly!" said Joseph, with two or three determined oaths; "dead indeed! There is no such good luck.
He wants his dinner!"

"His dinner!" exclaimed the other servants.

"Impossible!" said the *maître d'hôtel*. "Well, in that
case we must give him another dose."

Joseph opposed the proposition.

"No, no," said he, "we have already gone far enough
in this business without the knowledge of madame. I
shall go and tell her all."

Accordingly he came to me, and told me how they
had dosed the Cossack, and that the medicine had only
had the effect of giving him a better appetite. I could
scarcely refrain from laughter, but nevertheless I preserved my gravity. I told him that I considered his
conduct very blamable, and desired it might not be repeated under pain of my great displeasure. I told the
story to Czernicheff, who enjoyed a hearty laugh at it.

"I must let the Emperor know it," said he; "for you,
madame, must be freed from this troublesome guest.
To-morrow I will take care to get him removed, and I
will send you, in his stead, an officer attached to the
Emperor's Staff, who I think will be a protection rather
than an annoyance to you."

Platow left my house next day, and I received in his
place M. Volinski, Gentleman of the Chamber to the
Emperor of Russia. His conduct was perfectly gentlemanly, and until the arrival of Lord Cathcart my house
maintained its usual regularity.

The Emperor of Russia stopped but a short time at the
house of M. de Talleyrand. He subsequently took up
his residence in the Elysée Napoléon, in the suite of
apartments usually occupied by the Emperor. This removal was said to have been dictated by the apprehension of meeting with mined apartments, or some other
hidden danger. I know very well that the Elysée was
examined by two Russian engineers, accompanied by one
of the Emperor Alexander's officers. The cellars and
closets were all explored with the most scrupulous care.
As to the Tuileries, it being well known that the Comte

d'Artois was expected to arrive, no one could, in conscience, take his place.

This was the real origin of this selection, while many
people imagined it to have a very profound significance.
The Emperor of Russia and the King of Prussia, in spite
of their apparent confidence, were guarded with the most
scrupulous vigilance. The posts of Cossacks of the Russian Imperial Guard were not limited to the Palace of
the Elysée or its environs, they extended to the Boulevard from the Avenue of Marigny; and I saw Cossacks
coming as far as the Champs-Elysées in their sentinel
walks.

About this time a ceremony took place in Paris, at
which I was present, because there was nothing in it
that could be mortifying to a French heart. The death
of Louis XVI. had long been admitted to be one of the
most serious misfortunes of the Revolution. The Emperor Napoleon never spoke of that Sovereign but in
terms of the highest respect, and always prefixed the
epithet UNFORTUNATE to his name. The ceremony to
which I have alluded was proposed by the Emperor of
Russia and the King of Prussia.

It consisted of a kind of expiation and purification of
the spot on which Louis XVI. and the Queen were be-
headed. I went to see this ceremony, and I had a place
at a window in the Hôtel of Madame de Remusat, next
to the Hôtel de Crillon, and what was termed the Hôtel
de Courlande. The ceremony took place on the 10th of
April. The weather was extremely fine, and warm for
the season. The Emperor of Russia and King of Prussia, accompanied by Prince Schwartzenberg, took their
station at the entrance of the Rue Royale, the King of
Prussia being on the right of the Emperor Alexander,
and Prince Schwartzenberg on his left. There was a
long parade, during which the Russian, Prussian, and
Austrian military bands vied with each other in playing
the air *Vive Henri Quatre.* The cavalry defiled, and
then withdrew into the Champs-Elysées; but the infantry
ranged themselves round an altar which was raised in
the middle of the Place, and which was elevated on a
platform having twelve or fifteen steps.

The Emperor of Russia alighted from his horse, and,
followed by the King of Prussia, the Grand-Duke Con-

25

stantine, Lord Cathcart, and Prince Schwartzenberg, advanced to the altar. When the Emperor had nearly reached the altar, the *Te Deum* commenced. At the moment of the benediction, the Sovereigns and persons who accompanied them, as well as the twenty-five thousand troops who covered the Place, all knelt down. On rising, the Grand-Duke Constantine took off his hat, and immediately salvos of artillery were heard. The Greek priest presented the cross to the Emperor Alexander, who kissed it; his example was followed by the individuals who accompanied him, though they were not of the Greek faith.*

CHAPTER XXXIV.

Dispersion of the Imperial Family—Judas and Saint Peter—The Emperor of Austria's Arrival in Paris—Napoleon's Act of Abdication Signed—Forfeiture of Majorats—M. Metternich's Advice—Visit to Me from the Emperor of Russia—The Bronze Figure of Napoleon—Alexander's Opinion of the Duke of Rovigo—The Duke of Bassano—Junot's Portrait—The Emperor's Departure—His Majesty's Second Visit—His Conversation on the Duke of Vicenza—His Admiration of Paris—Promises His Influence in Favor of My Son's Majorats—Lord Cathcart.

THE Empress Maria Louisa was now at Rambouillet, and was preparing to set out for Germany. Napoleon's brothers and sisters were all scattered about in various places. Queen Hortense was in Paris; the Empress Josephine was at Malmaison; the Princess Pauline was in Provence, residing at a country house near Orgon; Madame Mère and Cardinal Fesch were on their way from Lyons to Rome; Jérôme and Joseph were about to depart to America, and Lucien was in England. The different members of the Imperial Family were all separated and dispersed, while the other proscribed family were returning to the land of their fathers. The Comte d'Artois re-entered Paris after an exile of twenty-two years.

Every day the journals were filled with the names of generals who seemed to fancy that their adherence to

* The King of Prussia was a Protestant, Prince Schwartzenberg a Catholic, and the Emperor Alexander belonged to the Greek communion.

the new Government could not be declared speedily
enough, or in terms sufficiently servile. This was most
indecent conduct in persons who had all their lives enjoyed the favors of the man toward whom some of them
now acted the part of Judas, and others that of Saint
Peter. And yet the Emperor's Act of Abdication, though
signed, or at least assented to by him, had not appeared.
It was not published till the 12th.

M. de Metternich came to Paris with the Emperor of
Austria. They arrived, I think, on the 14th or 15th of
April. Though honored with the friendship of M. de
Metternich, yet I never conversed with him on the political affairs of the time. I may, therefore, without reserve state what I presume to have been his sentiments,
as if he were a stranger to me.

I have reason to believe that both he and the Emperor of Austria were much disappointed at not having
reached Paris in time to secure the Regency for Maria
Louisa, and to make Russia declare in favor of the Imperial Orphan. The Emperor of Austria experienced,
on his entry into Paris, a truly Imperial reception. This
was not intended as a mark of honor to the House of
Hapsburg: it was an artful political contrivance for dazzling the Emperor Francis, and stifling any regrets
which might have led him to say: "If my daughter had
been Regent here!" But while he was lingering on the
road from Dijon, Maria Louisa, the Empress of the
French, became Grand-Duchess of Parma and Placentia!

The reception given to the Emperor Francis was superb. The passage of carriages or any other vehicles
was prohibited through a great portion of the capital.
The streets were lined with troops and bands of music.
In short, it was a perfect *fête*.

At length the Emperor Napoleon's Act of Abdication
was made public.* It is simple and noble, and worthy
of him in his most glorious days:

"The Allied Powers having proclaimed the Emperor Napoleon to
be the only obstacle to the re-establishment of peace in Europe, the

* An interesting facsimile of this document, which was entirely in
the autograph of Napoleon, will be found in Bourrienne's "Memoirs."
It is blotted, and nearly illegible, and bears tokens of the manner in
which an unwelcome duty is hurried over.

Emperor Napoleon, faithful to his oath, declares that he renounces for himself and his heirs the Thrones of France and Italy, and that there is no sacrifice, even that of life, which he is not ready to make for the interests of France.

« Given at the Palace of Fontainebleau, April 11, 1814.

« NAPOLEON.»

Berthier, Prince of Neufchâtel, sent in his adherence to the new Government, dated the 11th of April. For some time the Emperor had observed him biting his nails and absorbed in reverie. He guessed his intention. When the Emperor's abdication was made public — when our allegiance was annulled — I, in common with many others, began to turn our thoughts to the fate that awaited our families. M. de Metternich, whom I had seen the day after his arrival, told me that the majorats would be forfeited, with the exception of those in Illyria and the kingdom of Italy, — those, in short, under the dominion of Austria.

"Mine," observed I, "are in Westphalia, Prussia, and Hanover." M. de Metternich shook his head, and said: "I am much afraid that you will lose them all." But when I showed him the titles of a portion of them, producing a revenue of about fifty thousand francs, he said that they might possibly be restored to me in virtue of my claims, which had been confirmed by the King of Prussia himself. He referred to the territories and castle of Acken, which had been the personal property of the King of Prussia, but ceded by him in three different treaties, and which he had a right, if he chose, to relinquish.

"Assert your claim," said M. de Metternich; "I will use all my influence to support it; but if you would take my advice, you would first of all appeal for the protection of the Emperor Alexander. He has great influence over the King of Prussia."

I mentioned the business to M. Czernicheff, and expressed my wish to obtain an audience of the Emperor of Russia. "I will mention your wish," replied M. Czernicheff; "but I doubt whether he will grant it," added he, laughing. "Why not ?" "I don't know; but I could lay a wager he will not," he said, still laughing. "His Majesty's refusal cannot be caused by any very serious fault of mine, since it appears to afford you so much amusement.» Next day M. Czernicheff brought the answer. "I told you how it would be," said he; "the Emperor will not receive you at the Elysée." "Good heavens!" I exclaimed, quite surprised and mortified, "what have I done to displease him?"

M. Czernicheff continued speaking as though he did not hear me. "He will not receive you at the Elysée, because he says he wishes to DO HIMSELF THE HONOR of coming to see you. These were his own words; what do you think of them?" "This kind condescension touches me to the very heart," I replied. "Yes," added M. Czernicheff; "his Majesty wishes to pay a visit to the widow of the man of whom he has so frequently heard and read." He further added that the Emperor of Russia would be with me next day between twelve and one o'clock, if that time WOULD BE CONVENIENT TO ME.

I must confess that I was totally unprepared for this excess of Imperial courtesy; and notwithstanding all I had heard the Duke of Vicenza say of the Emperor Alexander, I scarcely believed that he would have carried his condescension so far. Next day about one o'clock the Emperor arrived. I then resided in my Hôtel in the Rue des Champs-Elysées. He was alone, in an open carriage, and had but one servant with him. I hurried to the head of the staircase to receive him, leading by the hand my little son, scarcely three years of age. As soon as the Emperor saw me he bowed in recognition of the mistress of the house; then, taking my hand, he conducted me into the apartment with an air of kindness and affability. When we had reached the inner drawing-room, preceding the billiard-room, I stopped, and after thanking the Emperor for having come to visit a widow and her young family, I presented my children to him, who made their obeisance to his Majesty and withdrew.

I then remained alone with the Emperor of Russia. I found myself quite in a new character—that of a petitioner to a foreign Sovereign! I who had never but once solicited anything, even from the Emperor Napoleon. But I was a mother! That consideration prompted my suit.

"Sire," said I, "those children whom your Majesty has just seen have lost their father at a very early age. In losing him they lost everything. They are reduced to beggary if they forfeit their majorats; they were the price of their unfortunate father's blood." While I said this we walked up and down the billiard-room and the *salon*. The Emperor led me to an armchair at the side of the fireplace; he then drew a small chair in front of me, and seated himself on it.

"Sire," said I, rising, "I cannot possibly suffer your Majesty to sit on that chair." "Pray resume your seat, madame," said he, with a charming smile; "I prefer sitting here in order to hear you the more distinctly. You know I am deaf in one ear." He then again seated himself before me, and our conversation commenced; I noted it down as soon as the Emperor left me.

"First of all," said Alexander, "let me know what is the boon you have to solicit from me. Explain the affair to me that I may understand it." I stated my case to him. "The matter appears to me to be beyond a doubt," said he. "Draw up an explanatory note of the business, and I will MYSELF give it to the King of Prussia. Czernicheff shall take charge of this affair by my order, and shall report to you the result. He is a friend of yours, I believe?"

I replied in the affirmative, and added that I thought him an excellent man, possessing more merit than most persons were for a long time willing to give him credit for, because he was a man of fashion and agreeable manners. "But," said the Emperor, laughing, "I should have imagined that in France those were additional claims to favor." "Sometimes, Sire."

At that moment Alexander directed his eye toward a console on which stood a small bronze figure of the Emperor Napoleon, about two feet and a half high, and clothed in the Imperial robes. The Emperor of Russia looked at it for some moments, then turning from it he remained silent. This silence was embarrassing to us both. At length Alexander broke it, saying: "One thing which particularly struck me on my entrance into Paris was the vast number of persons, especially women and children, in mourning."

"Sire," returned I, "your Majesty would have seen a great many more if all the widows and orphans in Paris had gone to meet you. As for my family and myself,

I can only say that your Majesty neither saw my widow's weeds nor the mourning of my children." Alexander took my hand, and pressing it in a friendly manner, he said: "I know it, I know it."

Then again, turning to look at the figure of Napoleon, he said, as if speaking to himself: "I do assure you, Duchess, that I loved that man as much — perhaps I may say more — than any one of my brothers, and when he betrayed me I suffered more by his treachery than by the war he brought upon me. Would you believe, madame, that the officer who brought me the first intelligence that the Emperor Napoleon had crossed the Vistula was imprisoned and put into irons? Yes, had Napoleon been willing to maintain the fraternity of arms and of hearts which subsisted between us at Erfurth, I confidently believe that we should have rendered Europe the finest part of the universe." As he uttered these last words he rose and began to walk rapidly up and down the room.

"But Napoleon was surrounded by a set of men who have ruined him. One of them in particular — one of them is to me the object of an aversion which I can never overcome!" He paused — I could not venture to question him. "That man," resumed Alexander, "has committed thousands of iniquities in the name of Napoleon for which his unfortunate master is now called to account. I allude to the Duke of Rovigo!" I knew he did, and I was in no way astonished to hear him mention the name.

Alexander, who had been walking about, now came and resumed his seat on the chair near me: "One might almost suppose that you had guessed to whom I alluded?" I smiled. "Has he, then, behaved equally ill to his comrades?" "Not to all of 'them, Sire; my husband had serious cause to complain of him; but still I am of opinion that your Majesty has been prepossessed against the Duke of Rovigo. He has his faults; but he cannot be accused of willfully behaving ill to the Emperor, to whom he is devotedly attached. Your Majesty has, perhaps, been misinformed, and——" "No, no," resumed he hastily, "not at all misinformed. I know the truth. That man had the insolence to attempt to introduce his police system into my Palace at St. Petersburg — to

place spies about me. It exceeds all belief; and
then —— » He stopped, and appeared to be struggling
to repress his rage.

" Since my arrival in Paris," continued the Emperor,
" he has twenty times solicited an audience of me; but I
have constantly refused to receive him. I understand he
intends to ask the Comte d'Artois to see him. Truly
the Duke of Rovigo would do well to recollect Vincennes.
He ought also to screen an innocent man from the odium
which belongs to himself; for poor Caulaincourt was at
that time at Strasburg, and not at Vincennes, so that he
could have had nothing to do with ordering the death of
the Duc d'Enghien."

The conversation was now becoming more and more
interesting. I listened with a degree of attention and
interest which must doubtless have been visibly depicted
in my countenance, for the Emperor's politeness became
more marked. He once more sat down beside me, for
he rose and sat down by turns. " The Duke of Bassano," *
continued he, " is another person who has done the Emperor a great deal of harm." " I am sorry to differ from
your Majesty," observed I. " There is no man in France
who would more readily lay down his life for the Emperor
than M. de Bassano." " What matters that, if he has
not served him dutifully ? "

" Sire, is it not possible that unjust, perhaps even ma-
lignant, reports may have reached your Majesty's ear,
and influenced you against the Duke of Bassano ? He is
an able statesman, a man of talent and incorruptible integrity. He has been a martyr to the cause which he
served in his youth. He has never forsaken his principles, and has always been devoted to his country. These
sentiments are innate in him. When M. de Bassano sent
in his adherence to the Provisional Government, it was
because he thought France could now only be saved by
the union of her children."

I stopped short, and felt quite astonished at having
said so much. But I could not refrain from speaking
the truth in defense of my friend, and then the affability of the Emperor of Russia divested me of all fear. His
Majesty listened to me attentively, and when I had
ended, he said: " Was the Duke of Abrantès on very
* Maret.

cordial terms of friendship with the Duke of Bassano?"
"He was, Sire; and, besides, my husband was from the
same province as M. de Bassano. They were both natives
of Burgundy, and I may almost add that they were
brothers-in-arms!" "How?" "Because M. de Bassano
was never absent from a single battle in which the
Emperor was engaged. He is a brave man, and has exposed himself to all the dangers of a soldier's life without the hope of a soldier's recompense; for the only
reward he would have gained by having a leg or an arm
shot off would be NOT to have the benefit of the *Invalides.*"
Alexander smiled.

"Ah!" resumed he; "I did not know he was so brave
a man: and General Savary? What sort of a reputation
for courage does he enjoy?" "He is a very brave man,
Sire; I have always heard that admitted even by my
husband, who was not easily pleased on that score."
"General Junot had a glorious military reputation. The
Sovereign is happy who is surrounded by such men.
But how happens it, madame, that you have not your
husband's portrait among your collection of pictures?"
And he looked round with an air of curiosity. "If your
Majesty wishes to see a portrait of Junot, and a striking
likeness of him, I can show you one. But I must re-
quest your Majesty to take the trouble to step into
another apartment."

I shall never forget the rapid and gracious manner in
which the Emperor rose and offered me his arm. "Will
you be kind enough to show me the way?" said he. I
led him through the billiard-room, the library, the large
cabinet fitted up in the style of an antique apartment,
then through my bedchamber into another cabinet, and
finally into my little *boudoir*, in which was the portrait
of Junot.*

This portrait, the work of Baron Gros, is a mere sketch,
but a hundred times more valuable than many finished
pictures. The Duke of Abrantès is represented in the
picturesque military costume of the generals of the Republic. At the time it was painted, Junot was scarcely
twenty-seven years of age, and yet he was a Brigadier-
General in the deserts of Syria, and with only three
hundred French troops he defeated and destroyed four

* See Vol. II., p. 238.

thousand Turks. Junot's reward consisted of the order of the day, and a picture painted at the expense of the Government by one of our most able artists. There was a competition, and Junot gave the prize to Gros. The sketch of Junot's head was made by Gros for the purpose of being copied into the large picture to be called "The Battle of Nazareth."

"Did not Napoleon treat the Duke of Abrantès very unjustly?" resumed the Emperor, as if sorry for having so far disclosed his feelings.

"Yes, Sire; but he was nevertheless much attached to Junot, and I know that he was deeply grieved by his death."

"Have you seen him since that event?"

"No, Sire."

"How happens that?"

"Because he has always been absent from Paris, and I have been in the country."

"Is that the only reason?"

I made no reply.

"Tell me, did you not write to the Emperor, when you were at Geneva or Lausanne?"

I raised my eyes to the Emperor Alexander with great astonishment. He continued:

"Your letter fell into my hands, together with several others, which were captured with an *estafette*, after the Battle of Dresden. I believe, too, an Auditor of the Council of State, bearing dispatches to the Emperor Napoleon, was also made prisoner by my Cossacks. To the best of my recollection, this happened on the day after the death of Moreau. In your letter to Napoleon, you addressed him with the courage and candor of a noble heart, and I formed a high idea of the woman who could write so. From some passages in that letter, I observed that your feelings had been wounded to the quick by the Duke of Rovigo, who is truly like an evil genius to the good and the unfortunate. However, I know not whether you will be pleased or displeased, when I tell you, that the Emperor never received your letter.* Are you sorry for this?"

---

* The Czar was very proud of the rôle of amateur detective, and another instance is given of his boasting of the violation of private correspondence in the "Memoirs of Marshal Macdonald" (1893 edition, p. 334)

"Perhaps not, Sire. My first impulse may have carried me too far. However, I have no very distinct recollection of what I wrote."

"You wrote like a noble-minded woman; and without having the honor to know you, I conceived for you a very high esteem."

"But, Sire, permit me to say that your Majesty judges me wrongly if you suppose me to be the enemy of Napoleon. He has doubtless caused me much pain; but still, I cherish for his name, for his glory, a profound veneration amounting to a sort of worship."

On his departure the Emperor bowed to me with the easy grace of a polished gentleman, free from anything approaching to royal *hauteur*. I followed him out of the room, when, suddenly turning round and perceiving me, he said: "Why do you leave the room, madame?" We were by this time at the head of the staircase. "Sire," said I, "your Majesty will permit me——" "I will permit nothing of the kind. How! would you wish to see me to my carriage?" "Certainly, Sire," replied I, smiling, for I was amused at the astonishment with which he appeared to regard a thing which appeared to me perfectly a matter of course. "See me to my carriage!" said the Emperor, smiling in his turn. "*Mon Dieu!* What would be said of me in St. Petersburg if I allowed myself to be escorted by a lady?"

"But we are not in St. Petersburg, Sire," said I; "and I entreat that you will permit me to do what I conceive to be the duty of the mistress of a house toward a Sovereign visitor." "Nay, nay," said the Emperor, taking my hand, and conducting me back to the door of the drawing-room, "the conquered must submit to the conqueror"; and then he added, with a charming grace: "Suppose I COMMAND you to stay where you are?" "I am not your Majesty's subject, Sire." "Well, then, you will prevent my paying you another visit. Surely you will not punish me so far as that?" "That fear, Sire, insures my ready obedience. I will not stir another step." He then descended the staircase, running as if to prevent my following him.

Some days after this visit of the Emperor Alexander, he called on me again one morning. He had given me no intimation of this intended honor. He came on foot, and quite unattended, and was dressed in plain clothes, wearing a round hat and a green coat. If Joseph, my *valet de chambre*, had not happened to recognize him, he would have been upstairs and into my *boudoir* before I was aware of his being in the house.

On this second visit he was even more gracious and communicative than on the first. Everyone must acknowledge the charm of this sort of affability in a Sovereign; it carries with it a PRESTIGE, the influence of which must be felt by persons of the coldest temperament.* Besides, in 1814, Alexander was really great. Yes, the term GREAT may truly be applied to the man who, having the cup of revenge within his reach, averts his lips from the delicious beverage. This is being something superior to human nature! On this occasion Alexander spoke to me of Napoleon. He had abdicated, and his fate was sealed.

"Have you seen the Duke of Vicenza?"† inquired Alexander, with an expression which I could not but remark. "I have, Sire." "I am glad to hear it. But how had you the courage to do so? It would have been all very well a month ago, but within the last fortnight——" "Because I had heard him less talked about within the last fortnight. I therefore called on the old friend of my childhood—him whom I so long called my brother." The Emperor Alexander approached me, took my hand, and pressed it; then, after a pause, he said: "You did right—very right. I assure you again, on my word of honor as a Sovereign, that the Duke of Vicenza is perfectly innocent of the crime with which he is charged!" This was the second time the Emperor Alexander had spoken to me with great warmth on the same subject.

Our conversation next turned on Paris, and the persons who had been most conspicuous in the Imperial Court, especially the ladies. He spoke of Madame Ney and the Empress Josephine. He seemed very curious to hear what I had to say of the latter; and frequently brought the conversation back to her, though I constantly endeavored to let it drop. At length he said, with a good-humored smile: "I almost think you are afraid of me."

* Madame de Sévigné gives a proof of this feeling in the letter in which she mentions having danced with the King.

† General Caulaincourt.

" By no means, Sire! your Majesty's kindness renders that quite impossible. But you must be aware that on such a subject I feel myself bound to be silent." He appeared to reflect for a few moments, and then he said: " You are right! This is the second lesson you have given me. I thank you."

Our conversation then changed to another subject. The Emperor spoke of our theaters, our museums, with which he was highly delighted; and he declared that the magnificent city of Paris had not its equal in the whole world. " My stony city (*ma ville de pierre*)," said he, " will also be a splendid place one day or other. You must come and see it; say you will; I am sure you would like St. Petersburg; and we will give you a wel-come. Then you can testify on your return that we are not quite such savages as we are said to be." I was deeply touched by these words, which he uttered with the most unaffected kindness of manner.

He next spoke of the state of my affairs, and asked me in what circumstances Junot had left his family. I replied: " Without any fortune." " How! and Napoleon ——" " It was not in his power to do anything, Sire. He was in Champagne at the time of Junot's death, and his attention was engrossed by matters of greater import than making a provision for us." " But your majorats? Prince Metternich is your friend." He paused for a mo-ment, and then continued: " It is his duty to protect you and your family." " Our majorats, Sire, are in Prus-sia and in Hanover, consequently M. de Metternich can do nothing in the business. He is my friend, and I will not be so unjust as to accuse him of indifference. I will not myself solicit his intervention with Prussia; it is yours I should wish to have, Sire."

The Emperor smiled. " Mine? Well, so be it. Czer-nicheff has begun the business, and he shall follow it up." I courtesied; and he added with charming grace: " Let it be understood. He shall arrange the business with the King of Prussia IN MY NAME. Will that satisfy you?" " The widow of Junot can wish for nothing more when she has such an advocate for her children."

A flood of tears prevented me from saying more. Al-exander took my hand (an English custom which he had contracted, and which I at first thought very strange), and said: "Would it be inconvenient or unpleasant to you to have another LODGER in your house ? In the hotels near the Elysée, which have extensive suites of apartments, there is none but yours that has the ground floor unoccupied. I wish you could receive Lord Cathcart, the English Ambassador to me; and allow me to mention that you are to provide nothing but lodging room either for Lord Cathcart or his attendants. His lordship is a man of agreeable and gentlemanly manners, and his presence here will be a protection to you. Besides, as I shall sometimes have occasion to call on him, I may at the same time take the opportunity of visiting his hostess, so that I shall hear whether he gives her any reason to complain.

CHAPTER XXXV.

The Staff Officer of the Prince Royal of Sweden — Motives of Bernadotte's Visit to Paris — His Proposition to the Comte d'Artois — Visit from the Duke of Wellington — General and Lady Cole — Miss E. Bathurst — The Monster Prince — His Love Adventures.

I HAD gone out one day to take an airing. On my return home I found my servants in a state of great alarm and consternation. My *valet de chambre* informed me that an officer of the Staff of the Prince Royal of Sweden, accompanied by some others, had called about an hour before my return. They had taken a survey of the house from the cellar to the very uppermost rooms.

On being informed that one of the Emperor of Russia's officers lodged in the apartments overlooking the garden, the Swedish officer said, with an insolent air: "Well, he must remove." "But," said Joseph, "where are we to put him if you dislodge him?" "Is there not an apartment adjoining the billiard-room which we just passed through?" That is my mistress's apartment," said Joseph indignantly. "And, pray, who is your mistress?" said the officer, in a jeering, impertinent tone.

Joseph was greatly irritated. He had been with Junot in the campaigns of Egypt and Italy. To see our enemies in France deeply mortified him; to see them in Paris nearly broke his heart; but to be insulted by them in his master's house was more than he could possibly endure. Directing a look of the most consummate contempt at the Swedish officer, he replied: "The mistress of this house is the widow of a man at the mention of whose name Frenchmen and foreigners should raise their hats and bow with respect." (The officer had kept on his hat.) "He was General Junot, Duke of Abrantès. If he were now living, and Governor of Paris, you would not have been allowed to enter it." The officer replied to this only by a shrug of the shoulders, and continued to make out his list of quarters, marking the different rooms, as is customary in a conquered city. This chamber was for the Colonel, that for the General, etc. "I tell you once more," said my *valet de chambre*, "that this is my mistress's apartment." "I must obey my orders." "And who ordered you to come here?" "His Royal Highness the Prince of Sweden." The officers took their departure. I returned home shortly after, and my *valet de chambre* related to me what had occurred. My first impulse is always impetuous; and I flew to my desk and wrote the following note:

"MONSEIGNEUR:—The Allied troops occupy Paris. I have received no offense from the officers or their inferiors of any rank whatever. I must confess that it appears to me as strange as it is vexatious that I should have experienced the first insult just at the time your Royal Highness arrived in Paris. Feeling assured that it cannot be by your orders that my house (hitherto respected by all parties) should be violated by any of your officers, I complain of what has taken place to-day in the hope that you will make me a suitable apology."

About an hour after my letter had been delivered at the Hôtel of the Prince Royal of Sweden, in the Rue d'Anjou Saint Honoré, I received a visit from his first aid-de-camp, Count Brahé. He made me a very handsome apology on the part of the Prince of Sweden, and assured me that his Royal Highness and the persons of his Household were totally ignorant of the intrusion and annoyance to which I had been exposed in his name. I was charmed with the politeness and elegant manners of Count Brahé, who seemed to have been brought up in the same school of good breeding as M. de Metternich. Few persons could comprehend what was Bernadotte's object in coming to Paris at that time; still less could they understand his eagerness to hurl Napoleon from his throne. There was then no chance of a Republic, as on the 18th Brumaire. But though General Bernadotte had forsaken France he still loved her. His rank, as Prince Royal, had only made him change his opinions. Being no longer a Republican he had become a Royalist. The Princess of Sweden used to complain bitterly of the *ennui* of the frigid and gloomy Court of Sweden, which was never excited except when they shot kings at masked balls.

On hearing the Princess make these complaints, M. de Talleyrand used to say: "But really, madame, this is very well for a beginning." Bernadotte thought so, too. But the BEGINNING had unfortunately become the END, since the downfall of the great European Colossus, and Bernadotte looked fondly back to his native country. He offered to his Royal Highness, Monsieur, who had just arrived in Paris, his services in putting down the different factions which might still exist in the army, over which his name might yet have some influence.

To effect this object, he conceived it would be requisite to be invested with some imposing title, such as Generalissimo of the Forces or Lieutenant-General of the Kingdom: the latter, it is true, was the title which Monsieur himself held; but he thought it might be rendered more practically useful when possessed by Bernadotte. The latter, therefore, consented to abandon the government of his own States, and to remain a year in France if necessary.

The proposition of the Prince Royal of Sweden was made to Comte d'Artois; but after a very brief consideration his Royal Highness was informed that the sooner he returned to his own army the better. This was the reason of that sudden departure which left the Princess unprotected and a prey to the unfortunate attachment which she conceived for a man who was certainly the very last person in the world who might have been expected to play the part of a romantic lover.

At this time I was in the habit of seeing Prince Metternich every day. He frequently called on me in the morning, and almost always took tea with me in the evening. He was extremely fearful of being suspected of interfering in the affairs of France.

In reference to this subject I may relate a circumstance which took place before my departure from Paris, at the time when Louis XVIII. was forming his Ministry. Lord Wellington had been in Paris for some days before he learned that I also was there, and that I was residing very near him. He called on me, and I was much pleased and interested by his conversation. I have already mentioned that Lord Wellington was highly esteemed by the Duke of Abrantès, who had imbued me with the same favorable opinion of him, so I was the friend of Lord Wellington though the enemy of the English General. His lordship resided at the Hôtel de la Reynière, which belonged to Ouvrard.

"I have come to beg your kind reception of a new lodger," said Lord Wellington to me one day. "I allude to Lord Cathcart." "He cannot fail to be welcome, my lord," said I, "since the Emperor Alexander has introduced him."

Lord Cathcart came that same morning. As soon as he arrived he sent to say he wished to pay his respects to me. When he entered, he requested, in the most polite terms, that I would permit him to reside in my house. His manners were those of a polished man of rank, and I saw at once that I should have every reason to congratulate myself on having him quartered beneath my roof. Next morning he took possession of the suite of apartments on the ground floor. They consisted of four drawing-rooms, a spacious gallery, two small billiard-rooms, and a large cabinet, which might easily be converted into a bedchamber. This was the suite of apartments in which I used to receive company. They overlooked the gardens. There was also a bathroom attached to them

I devoted to Lord Cathcart's use a great portion of my stables. They had become useless to me since the death of my husband; for I kept only four carriage horses and a saddle horse. Lord Cathcart assured me that he would be answerable for his servants committing no depredations, and I must in justice say that they were extremely well behaved and quiet.

My house was soon entirely filled. The apartments on the first floor, overlooking the garden, were occupied by General and Lady Cole. They occasioned no incon-

26

venience to me; but there was a great difference between them and Lord Cathcart. This difference extended even to their servants, which I discovered to my cost.* Lady Cole was a very pleasing woman, and the General was a true model of an English country gentleman. Lady Cole often came to take tea with me in the evening. On one of these occasions she told me that she had a favor to ask of me.

"A young lady, an intimate friend of mine," said she, "is very anxious to see Paris. Her relations will intrust her to my care; but if I take charge of her she must reside with me. How can I manage this unless you grant me permission?" I assured her that I was most ready to do everything in my power to oblige her, but that I could not render the walls of my house elastic. It was already completely filled by Lord Cathcart, the General and herself, my household, my brother, and my uncles the Prince and the Abbé Comnena.

"But she can sleep in the great divan, in the *boudoir*," said Lady Cole, "if you have no objection." I gave my consent, though I was certain that my divan would be destroyed. But how could I refuse? "Well, since I have your consent, my young friend shall come to-morrow. Her brother is aid-de-camp to Lord Wellington, and he will himself thank you for your hospitality to his sister."

The young lady had been in Paris since the previous day; but Lady Cole had very politely declined bringing her until she had obtained my consent. When she introduced me to her I was struck with her beauty. Her fine fresh complexion, her beautiful fair hair, and her soft blue eyes, produced altogether that youthful appearance which is found only among English women. It is the same with the English children; they are always prettier than any others. A child may have a white and red complexion, and fair curly hair; it may be dressed in a white frock with a pink or blue sash—all this

---

* There were in my *boudoir*, which adjoined my bedchamber, four small landscapes painted on vellum, given to me by my brother-in-law, M. de Geouffre, and valued on account of their beauty as well as a pledge of friendship. I presume that some of the servants of Lady Cole had taken a fancy to them; for the day after her departure, when the apartments were being put in order, they were nowhere to be found.

makes a pretty child, but still it is not like an English child. It is the same with young English girls.

Lady Cole's young friend pleased me at first sight, and the hospitality which I had granted as a favor to Lady Cole became a source of gratification to myself. This young lady was Miss Eliza Bathurst, a relation of the English Secretary of the War Department. She was not only pretty and agreeable, but she possessed considerable talents and accomplishments. Alas! I little thought that the lovely flower with which I was so highly charmed would be so early blighted! Some time after her visit to Paris she accompanied her mother to Rome. It was at the time the Duc de Laval was our Ambassador there.

One day Miss Bathurst, with a party of friends, was riding on horseback along the banks of the Tiber. The weather was delightful. They were admiring the clear blue sky and the brilliant sun, which spreads a sort of magical glory over the Campagna di Roma. Suddenly Miss Bathurst's horse took fright; she endeavored to rein him in. The animal darted off, and plunged, with his rider, into the Tiber, where the young lady perished. I was deeply shocked on hearing this event, when I recollected the many attractive and amiable qualities of Miss Bathurst. Her brother, Lord Wellington's aid-de-camp, was a very fine young man. In person he resembled his sister. I do not know what became of him.

One day M. de Metternich called on me and said: "Will you promise not to laugh at a gentleman whom I wish to introduce to you?" "That must depend on what sort of person he is. You know I am very apt to laugh. But tell me who he is." "He is a friend of mine. He is not at all handsome; I tell you that beforehand. And to convince you of that fact, I may inform you that he goes by the name of the MONSTER PRINCE." "Surely you are joking!" "I am not, indeed. He has another name, it is true. His real name is Wenzel Lichtenstein. His brother, Prince Moritz Lichtenstein, has also requested me to introduce him to you, which, with your permission, I will do. The two brothers are very unlike each other. Pray behave well when you see Wenzel."

Prince Wenzel Lichtenstein was certainly the most ugly man I ever beheld in my life. He was the very perfection of ugliness. One might imagine he was endowed with this perfection by a fairy, as others are said to have been endowed with beauty. Nothing was wanting to complete it. Even his voice was the strangest that can well be imagined. I must confess that when I first saw him I was perfectly petrified.

"Well," said Metternich, the next time he called on me, "what do you think of him?" "That he is by no means handsome. That is very certain. Poor fellow! He must be very unhappy if he is tender-hearted." I made the same remark to another friend who happened to call upon me that same day. "I beg your pardon," said he, "you are quite mistaken. Prince Wenzel, ugly as he is, has made his conquests." "Impossible!" I exclaimed; "unless he happened to meet with a woman as frightful as himself." "By no means. The lady whose affections he won was very pretty. The affair made some noise not long since at Vienna."

The gentleman who gave me these particulars mentioned Princess ——. I was confounded. I was assured that Prince Wenzel had had several such adventures, and that he had now become so confident that he never doubted his success with any woman. "Have a care of yourself," said my friend, who had made me thus far acquainted with the secret biography of the MONSTER PRINCE. "Upon my word," replied I, "you are right to put me on my guard, for he must possess infinite powers of seduction to have rendered himself agreeable to any woman."

————

CHAPTER XXXVI.

Letter from Fontainebleau — M. Corvisart — Visit to Malmaison — Josephine's Sorrow — My Opinion of Maria Louisa — Josephine's Projects — Future Duchess of Navarre — Approaching Departure of Napoleon for Elba — Augereau's Proclamation — The Emperor Leaves France — Commissioners Who Accompanied Him — General Bertrand.

I RECEIVED a letter from Fontainebleau, written in a strain of unreserved confidence. The Emperor was very ill. The poison he had taken had not been productive of the effect he expected from it, but had

proved highly injurious to his health. It is worthy of
remark, as illustrative of the dishonesty of the newspapers of the period, that not one of them made the
slightest allusion to this poisoning. The "*Gazette de
France*" of the 14th of April, 1814, says : "The day on
which Napoleon was to sign his abdication he found on
his table a packet containing the conditions of the abdication, and likewise a pistol." "Ah," said the Emperor,
"they wish to counsel me; but they shall learn that I
follow no advice but my own."

Be this as it may, he was now seriously ill, and M.
Corvisart's attentions stood him in the utmost stead.
The care with which he watched over him was only
equaled by his skill. I saw Corvisart at this period:
the tears were starting from the eyes of a man whose
firmness of character was never known to falter! He
never dwelt but with sorrow on what was taking place
at Fontainebleau. I loved Corvisart as a man who had
saved my life; but since 1814 I have loved him for the
exalted qualities which he then displayed.

The letter I received from Fontainebleau entered into
much detail respecting the preparations for the Emperor's departure. When I heard of it, though never
expecting he would accept the plan which I had proposed for his adoption,* I relied at least on a verbal
answer. The Duke of Rovigo afterward told me that he
had not delivered my letter. I am unable to vouch for
the truth of this assertion. I went to Malmaison the day
after receiving the letter from Fontainebleau.

I knew the Empress Josephine to be extremely uneasy
respecting the passing occurrences, and she could not

* This plan was somewhat singular, and is believed to have arisen
solely in the ardent mind of Madame d'Abrantès. She told Savary,
Duke of Rovigo, that she should write a letter to Napoleon, who
was yet at Fontainebleau, proposing to him to come to her house
incognito; and that at the expected second visit to her of the Emperor Alexander, he should suddenly present himself to the Autocrat
and demand of him protection for his son Napoleon II.; that she
knew the high opinion and affection Alexander entertained for the
Emperor, and she was sure that he would listen to him, and exert
his powerful interest with the other Sovereigns to secure the nomination of a Regency to act for the son. Savary undertook to deliver
this letter; but, as appears by the sequel, he did not carry out the
trust imposed upon him.

fail to set a high value on any intelligence derived from
the spot. It was early when I arrived, and the Empress
was still in her bedroom. I repaired to Madame d'Audenarde's apartment, and begged she would inquire of
her Majesty whether I might see her before breakfast.
My name was no sooner mentioned to the Empress than
she desired I should be admitted. She was still in bed,
and stretching out her arms as soon as she saw me, she
burst into tears, and exclaimed: "Alas! Madame Junot,
Madame Junot!"

I was deeply affected at the meeting. I knew how
sincerely she was attached to the Emperor; and at this
moment every reproach she had to make was cast into
shade by the heavy misfortune which oppressed him. I
could read her feelings, and this burst of deep affliction
found in my heart the most congenial sympathy. I wept
with the afflicted Princess, and my tears were more
bitter than her own, for they flowed over a sorrow which
death had occasioned, whereas she had still hope. The
hundred days have proved how reasonably she could
indulge it.

When I told her of my having received a letter from
Fontainebleau she said to me, with an eagerness she had
never displayed on any former occasion: "Oh ! I beseech
you, do read me that letter; read THE WHOLE of it; I desire
to know EVERYTHING." The contents were very painful for
Josephine's heart, as many passages related to the King
of Rome and to Maria Louisa.

"What do you think of that woman ?" said the Empress Josephine, looking at me with a remarkable expression. "I, Madame ! What I have always thought —
that such a woman should never have crossed the
frontiers of France; I say so from the bottom of my
heart." "Indeed !" said Josephine, fixing on me her eyes
bathed in tears, but smiling at the idea that I shared
her opinion.

I repeated the expression, adding that I did so not to
gratify the Empress Josephine, but because such was my
belief. And I think so still, at the present day, after
the lapse of twenty-two years. "Madame Junot," said
the Empress Josephine, "I have a great mind to write
to Napoleon. Would you know the reason ? I wish he
would permit my accompanying him to the island of

Elba, if Maria Louisa should keep away. Do you think she will follow him?" "Quite the contrary; she is incapable of doing so." "But if the Emperor of Austria should send to Napoleon his wife and child, as indeed he ought to do?" [Josephine, it may be seen, was not much skilled in politics.] "I am very anxious to know whether that will be the case; and you, Madame Junot," she always called me thus, "may be useful to me in this emergency." "How so, Madame?" "By putting the question to M. de Metternich; he is a friend of yours; you often see him; nothing can be more easy than to ask him."

"Your Majesty is quite mistaken. M. de Metternich is no doubt a great friend of mine; I often see him; but when he arrived at Paris he told me that if he called to take in my society a short relaxation from the fatigue of his occupations, he entreated that I would never speak to him again upon matters respecting which he could not even give me a reply. In a word, he made me promise I should never talk politics with him."

The Empress did not seem displeased at my refusal; she was kind-hearted, and knew how incapable I was of refusing her through any unkind motive. She merely shed tears, and said that my grounds of objection were a fresh source of sorrow to her. "I am beset with misfortunes," added she, bursting again into tears. I then observed to her that the Emperor's consent that she should go to the island of Elba was more than doubtful. She seemed astonished. "Why should he refuse it?"

"Because his sisters will assuredly go there, as well as Madame Mère. Let your Majesty recollect all you have suffered when seated on the Throne of France, in the Imperial Palace of the Tuileries, when strong in the title of the Emperor's consort; if, when you were Sovereign, Madame, the Emperor's sisters could disturb your repose, what might they not do at the present day?"

The Empress fell into deep meditation, a circumstance of rare occurrence. "I think you are in the right," she at last said to me — "I think you are in the right." She remained for some time with her head resting upon her hand. On a sudden she raised it, and said to me: "Have you seen the Comte d'Artois?" "No, Madame." "You have, then, never heard anything said respecting me?"

"Absolutely nothing." "Madame Junot, you are deceiving me." "I assure your Majesty, on my word of honor, that I am not." "I hear that it is intended to deprive me of the title of Majesty, and to compel me to assume the name and title of Duchesse de Navarre." I repeated my assertion that I knew nothing whatever.

The ruling desire in Josephine's mind at this moment was to retain the title of MAJESTY; I even think she had already made this request to the Emperor of Russia, though she assured me she had not yet mentioned the subject to him. She was greatly agitated; her face was scarlet, and I could perceive that the various recent occurrences had made a deep impression upon her.

It is well known that she had become very corpulent; she had lost her slender figure; her features were altered; she was divested of that elegance which had once made her the most fascinating woman of Paris and of her Court. All that was left to her was a dignified deportment and great elegance of manners, and especially of dress. The last was always an important point with her.

It was very late when I left Malmaison for Paris, and I did not reach home until nearly six o'clock. I found another letter, which announced Napoleon's departure as fixed for the following day; but a circumstance which would have been painful to the Empress Josephine had she known it was that, on the same day on which she delighted in recalling to her mind the visit of the Emperor of Russia, he had gone with the Emperor of Austria to dine with Maria Louisa at Rambouillet. I learned this on my return. Maria Louisa appeared resigned and indifferent to her fate; Madame de Montesquieu was to accompany her in order not to quit her pupil — happily, as we hoped, for the future prospects of France.

What were Napoleon's feelings on reading the act of adhesion, the proclamation of Marshal Augereau? of a man who had never forgiven him the Bridge of Arcola, and who now in his proclamation to his soldiers had the audacity to pen and to commit to the press — to his eternal shame — a phrase so insulting to the nation itself?

After admitting that Louis XVIII. was the beloved Sovereign wished for in the secret aspirations of AUGEREAU himself, he added: "Soldiers, you are released from your oaths by the very abdication of a man who, after having sacrificed millions of victims to his cruel ambition, had not the courage to die the death of a soldier."

What must Napoleon not have felt on learning that Ney had given a magnificent breakfast to the Emperor of Russia, and that he wept at the kindness of his Royal guest!

All was anxiety at the Tuileries until the Emperor should have quitted France. It was not enough that he should have fallen — he must be crushed; his removal was no security — they longed for his death. At last he took his departure. The immortal picture of Horace Vernet, which represents Napoleon quitting his faithful Guards in the Court of the Palace, renders superfluous all description of this scene.*

The Emperor quitted Fontainebleau on the 20th of April, escorted, like a prisoner, by Commissioners from all the Allied Powers. England was represented by Colonel Campbell, Russia by General Schuwaloff, Austria by General Köller, Prussia by M. de Schack, and France by I know not whom; the escort of foreign troops amounted to fifteen hundred men.

The 20th of April, then, was the day that the Emperor quitted Fontainebleau, which he was to revisit on the 20th of March following. The suite of the Emperor was too considerable, and the escort too numerous, to allow of rapid traveling; he had only reached Montargis late on the same day. General Bertrand was alone with the Emperor in his carriage. On that morning *piquets* of cavalry and escorts had reconnoitered the road. Well-founded fears were entertained of a rescue. Had the Emperor uttered a word a civil war would have been kindled, and perhaps not twenty thousand of the Allied troops would have escaped out of France.

Napoleon's carriage was drawn by six horses; it was immediately followed by a special troop of cavalry, con-

---

*When the Emperor passed in review, in the great Court of the Palace, the troops that had been faithful, and whose headquarters were at Fontainebleau, he was, as may be supposed, very much affected. He said to the officer who carried the colors: "As I cannot take leave personally of all my friends who surround me at this moment, I embrace these colors, and bid them an eternal adieu."

sisting of twenty-five men; then came the generals, the
French, Prussian, Austrian, Russian, and English commissioners, with their long train of carriages, also drawn
by six horses. The Emperor's baggage followed, but
not sufficient to fill SIXTY carriages, as it has been asserted
in many newspapers. They amounted to twenty at most
—a remarkable circumstance was that a part of the Guard
was cantoned in the country, and under arms; but they
had been enjoined, many days before, not to give the
slightest indication of pity toward their fallen master.
The least movement might have occasioned his death!
The Guard maintained a profound silence; it was dejected and broken in spirits.

The Emperor was calm and serene. He bowed with
that smile so peculiar to him, and which so brightened
his countenance. He perhaps showed himself a greater
man on that day than at moments when he stood before
the admiring world. He was then surrounded by a devoted body of men,—the least wave of his hand, and
thousands of swords would have been drawn from their
scabbards. But he suppressed every feeling. On the
night of Napoleon's passing Montargis he slept at the
Castle of Briare; this was the 23d of April. He then
continued his journey toward Saint Tropez and Orgon.

CHAPTER XXXVII.

Arrival of the Duc de Berri—Reception of Louis XVIII. in London
—The Comte d'Artois—Madame de Lawestine—The Duc de
Berri—Louis XVIII.—Dangerous Excess of Joy—The Duc de
Berri at Bayeux.

BUT I must now bestow attention on the events which
were taking place at Paris under my own eyes,
and engrossing the public mind. The day on which
Napoleon quitted the Castle of Fontainebleau as a prisoner, the Duc de Berri arrived at Paris, and Louis XVIII.
made that royal entrance into London which he had
assuredly never meditated in his most sanguine dreams.

Louis XVIII. at his return to France was only known
to us by a doubtful tradition, and there was nothing to

his advantage in the accounts we received of him. The Comte d'Artois was also, to France, a new personage. "The Comte d'Artois," said the Duc de Mouchy, M. de Laigle, and a crowd of our fashionables of the period intervening before the Revolution of 1814, "is a delightful man; he is elegance itself; a charming prince, and will be the very oracle of fashion!" Next followed a long account of all the hearts which the Comte d'Artois had immolated, a detail of overpowering interest respecting the importance of Madame de Polignac, the despair of Madame de Gontaut. In short, there was really something to expect from a prince who, while breaking every heart, could spread so much happiness.

It was in the midst of a conversation which chanced to dwell on the friendships of the Comte d'Artois that two persons who knew him well gave me an insight into his true character. The illusion immediately vanished — nothing was left to admire in him except his good nature; we might add to it the most accomplished manners, and even a species of worldly wit which might be worthy of admiration in 1780, but which in 1814, and especially in 1830, nearly caused the ruin of France.

The Duc de Berri was called the descendant of Henri IV. Poor Henri IV.! he is ever at hand to be used as a comparison. This adulation was distributed with due reference to the peculiarity of disposition. The Duc d'Angoulême descended from Saint Louis because of his devotion; the Duc de Berri from Henri IV. because of his worldly passions; and the Comte d'Artois from Francis I. because he had been a man of consummate gallantry five-and-twenty years before. How amusing!

With respect to Louis XVIII., he was really a superior man. His ideas, when he first arrived in France, were framed upon a comprehensive scale, and rested upon a broad foundation — witness the constitutional charter. In Louis XVIII. I found a man of capacity, of profound wisdom, and of a deep knowledge of men. I have often been closeted with him in a private audience. On one occasion, in particular, I remained with him for three-quarters of an hour, and have assuredly never repented paying close attention to his words. Nothing was to be lost of his conversation. He spoke with consummate talent, and could read the characters of men.

He was devoid of every kind feeling, if we are to judge from the opinions of those who were about him, and to believe in the sincerity of such a circle. Louis XVIII. was deeply learned. Like all princes, he was gifted with an extraordinary memory; to AFFECTION he was not insensible; but he was a stranger to any deep, settled friendship.

When Louis XVIII. heard the news that the Crown of France was DECREED to him he was well-nigh yielding it up. He felt such a revolution within him that he fainted away, and was for a short time seriously ill from excess of joy. This particular was made known to me by a person who had long resided near Hartwell. It was perhaps deemed conducive to the dignity of Louis XVIII. to conceal this fact, which is nevertheless incontrovertible.

The new position of the King of France no sooner became known than the deportment of the Prince Regent of England toward him altered on a sudden; for, in spite of all that has been said to the contrary, his royal demeanor in his intercourse with a brother Sovereign was more than familiar, a circumstance which I learned from those who had assuredly no interest in perverting the truth.

A singular coincidence appeared in the following circumstance: The same day on which Napoleon quitted Fontainebleau to commence his exile, Louis XVIII. made his entry into London as King of France, namely, on the 20th of April. I had then many friends in London, and they apprised me of all that passed at that epoch.

The reception of the King was not one of the least curious circumstances of the day. I received the following details:

Louis XVIII. left Hartwell on the morning of the 20th of April, 1814, and breakfasted at Stanmore, where the Prince Regent met him. From thence to London the road was crowded, the English all wearing white ribbons and laurel wreaths. One can understand the former as complimentary to the Bourbons; but the laurels, were they worn in token of having vanquished the French? Louis XVIII. wore on this occasion the uniform of a French marshal, which, with his velvet boots, could not have looked quite consistent. The Prince Regent wore a

Court suit, and, in common with all his followers, a white cockade. At a quarter before six P. M. the cavalcade reached Albemarle Street, where everything was prepared for the reception of his Majesty at Grillon's Hotel. Next day the King received almost all the city of London. Doubtless, the genuine enthusiasm was very great; but all who know the English character are aware that *éclat* is the MODE with them. It is sufficient to TALK of anyone, and everybody thinks himself bound to run to see the wonder. The number of carriages that thronged Albemarle Street during the whole of the 21st of April is almost incredible. In the evening the King followed the Duchesse d'Angoulême, who had gone to visit the Queen of England. His carriage was drawn by six horses, decorated with numerous bows of white ribbon. The English are, in general, extremely fond of using gewgaws to testify their joy.

At half-past six o'clock the King of France entered the court of Carlton House. The guard was commanded by Colonel Mercer, a distinguished officer, whom I knew indirectly, being intimately connected with one of his relations. The music struck up "God Save the King," which was followed by poor "Henri Quatre," who thus made a prelude in London to his long and brilliant career in France during 1814 and 1815. The Prince de Condé and the Duc de Bourbon accompanied his Majesty. On his approach the guard presented arms, and the Regent hastened to receive the guest, who, from his pensioner, had become his ally. The monarchs shook hands, and forthwith the air resounded with huzzas. Giving his arm to the King, his Royal Highness, although, now grown corpulent, and no longer entitled to the merited appellation of the finest man in England,— where fine men are so numerous,— still presented, I am told, an air and figure of striking elegance. The King having been conducted into a suitable apartment, a Chapter was held of the Order of the Garter, at which His Majesty was proposed as a knight. Being duly elected, the Dukes of York and Kent introduced the novice. He entered the hall of the Chapter with a step sufficiently firm for a King who could not walk. Kneeling on a velvet cushion, the Regent gave him the customary accolade, and tied on the Garter with his own hands.

In exchange for the Garter, Louis XVIII. gave his
blue *cordon* to the Duke of York. One thing was odd
enough — namely, that Louis XVIII. had not already
possessed the Order of the Garter, for he had been King
of France a long time; but, then, he had been a fugitive
and unhappy King.

On the 22d the Lord Mayor and the sheriffs of the
city of London waited on the King to offer their con-
gratulations; and then followed a crowd of deputations
from French towns, each of which was fearful of arriving too late. The town of Dunkirk, among others, was
desirous of first engrossing Louis XVIII.; and, instead
of awaiting him quietly in its corner, dispatched its good
citizens to seek their King in a foreign land.

The Prince Regent accompanied his royal ally to Do-
ver, where the latter embarked on board a vessel commanded by the Duke of Clarence. General Girard had
been dispatched to Hartwell to receive the orders of the
King. The different marshals awaited him on the sea-
shore, or I know not where else. In short, fifteen days
only after the departure of Napoleon for Elba that great
man was almost wholly forgotten by those who should
religiously have treasured his memory.

The delight of the people of England at these events
amounted to a delirium. Posterity, who will coolly judge
of all that passed, will understand the full extent of the
danger of Great Britain as developed by the Saturnalian
manifestations of joy universal throughout the capital.
"They must have been in great fear," says some writer
or other, "to have made a vow to erect such a wonder
as the Escurial;" and, in like manner, I say that the
English must have been in dire peril to evince so much
exultation at the fall of their enemy. The whole Metropolis was illuminated; and at Carlton House a transparency was exhibited, representing the arms and crown
of France, supported by Victory and Renown. Under-
neath was inscribed: "*Louis XVIII.! Vive les Bourbons!*"

A regiment was in garrison in the environs of Bayeux.
The Duc de Berri, passing through that city, was told
that this regiment was very ill affected toward the House
of Bourbon, and felt desirous of personally ascertaining
the fact. The Prince played a showy part in this affair;

his conduct was brave, and loyal, and worthy, for the occasion, of Henri Quatre. Arrived near the regiment, he demanded the Colonel's horses, under what pretext I know not. The Colonel hastened to send them, and appeared himself before the adventurous Prince, who asked him:

"Where is your regiment?"

The Colonel offered to conduct his Highness, if he were desirous to see the soldiers. The Duke accepted the offer. The troop was under arms.

"Soldiers," said the Prince, "you know me not yet; but we shall soon grow acquainted. I am the Duc de Berri, nephew of Louis XVIII., the King whom France has recognized. Will you join with me? Come, then; cry '*Vive le Roi!*'"

The entire regiment joined in this exclamation, one voice alone shouting "*Vive l'Empereur!*"—ONE voice alone. And Napoleon had abdicated but ten days.

Hearing this single cry, the Duke smiled, and said: "It is but the remains of an old custom — once more!"

And the man cried: "*Vive le Roi!*"

The papers of the day (and all of them repeated the story) said that the second time the cry was unanimous.

The Duke, who, as we hinted, played the principal part in the piece, ordered an extraordinary distribution to the troop. He did well in giving; did they do so in receiving this bounty?

"Upon THIS," continued the journals, "the acclamations were enthusiastic, and the whole regiment requested permission to take the name of Berri."

The Duke was, in fact, a man, who, had he lived, would have been of great service in supporting the Bourbon family. His assassin, in striking HIM, knew well what he did; he attacked the tree at its roots.

CHAPTER XXXVIII.

Cardinal Maury's Mysterious Visit — Scene in the Archiepiscopal
Chapel.

CARDINAL MAURY wrote one day requesting to see me,
but expressed a great wish for secrecy. "I entreat," said he in his letter, "that nobody may
know of your visit. This is the reason why I do not
come to you." I was astonished at this air of mystery.
Nevertheless, I complied with the Cardinal's desire;
and arriving at the great gate of Nôtre Dame, I went
into the church, and after performing my devotions went
out by the little red door, and entered the Archiepiscopal precincts, where the Cardinal lodged before his departure for Italy. His Eminence awaited me in the
chapel, whither I was conducted by his *valet de chambre.*
I confess that this mystery and these precautions amused
me infinitely.

The Archiepiscopal chapel, which had been constructed
by Cardinal Fesch during his short Episcopacy, was very
peculiar in form; its situation in the garden, surrounded
by flowers, gave it an aspect always very touching to
me when I have attended divine service therein. I
knelt down on entering and said a prayer; I then advanced toward the Cardinal, who, seated on one of the
armchairs which stood before the balustrade, seemed
either praying or reflecting. His countenance was peculiar: he gazed on me, but made no motion even for me
to advance; I felt some trepidation. I, however, went to
him.

"Your Eminence has desired to see me," said I; "I attend
your orders." He started, gazed on me anew, and then
said: "You are kind to come. But I knew you would.
You know how to be the friend of those who are no
longer fortunate. Is it not so?" His large forehead
contracted, while his little eyes glared in their orbits,
and his voice became tremulous. "Will you serve me?"
said he at length, fixing on me an earnest glance. "Undoubtedly, if I can. But my influence is very slight.
In what can I be of use to you?" "You might save

me!" said he in a low voice, looking meanwhile round the chapel like a man who dreads to encounter a spy. "Save you, Monseigneur?" "Yes; listen to me. I am certain that at Rome they want to impose on me a severe penance. They will perhaps seek to shut me up in a cloister; but I will not go there. No! by all the fiends," cried he, forgetting his caution, "they shall not have me living! I will fear Consalvi no more than I did that silly Duc d'Aiguillon." He was red as his cassock, and appeared beside himself. I regarded him with astonishment, and did not see in what way I could be useful to him. He soon told me.

"This Court of Rome, which imagines itself of some consequence because the Pope is recognized by schismatical and Protestant Sovereigns, fancies it can still act as it did at the time when the IMBECILES condemned Galileo. But they are deceived; and I will adopt the guise of a schismatic in order to laugh at them. You must obtain me an audience of the Emperor of Russia." I stood aghast. "You will not?" "I did not say that, Monseigneur. But your Eminence should reflect a moment ere you invoke the aid of a Prince who is not of the Catholic communion. I do not think it can be done with proper dignity." The Cardinal regarded me with concentrated rage. He would have crushed me if he had dared. He rose, traversed the chapel for some time, and then again approached me.

"You censure me, then?" said he. "No, sir; but I confess I should grieve at taking a message from you to the Emperor of Russia." "*Diable! diable!*" repeated he, pacing the floor again, and occasionally taking a large pinch of Spanish snuff from the pocket of his undervest. Suddenly he stopped; then coming up to me once more, he said, with that voice of thunder known to belong to him: "But, nevertheless, you are my friend. How can you see me depart for Rome without having fears for my life?" "Oh, Monseigneur!"

"I know well that they will not poison me like Zizim. I know well that they will not roast me before a slow fire; but they will probably incarcerate me in the monastery of Albano, or in a convent situated in the most savage mountains of the Apennines. And once there,

27

what would become of me? And all because I have obeyed him whom Pius VII. consecrated, anointed, crowned with his own hand! And this Consalvi!"

He smote his forehead with his hand, powdering his face in the most whimsical-looking manner imaginable with his snuff.

"Monseigneur, your fears are, I am sure, without foundation. But, even admitting them, what can I do in the matter?" "Well, speak to Metternich! He is Catholic, apostolic, and Roman, and, I think, would not willingly see me ill treated." "That I will do with pleasure," answered I. "I am confident M. de Metternich will do his utmost to serve your Eminence, and I will speak to him this very day. But, after all, what am I to say? for I cannot tell him that the Holy Father means to kill your Eminence, or transform you into a lay brother, for he would not listen to me." "And why not?" demanded he, in an eager tone.

"Why, Monseigneur? Because the Pope is the most perfect human being in Rome. He is an angel and a saint. Your Eminence is misinformed if you have fears of him; neither is Cardinal Consalvi capable of so much treachery." "Really!" rejoined he, with an expression I had never witnessed in him before. "Ah! you pretend to know all the gang better than I? Well, be it so. But meanwhile, I take care of my skin." (I quote the Cardinal's own phrase.) "If you object to introducing me to your friends from the fear of compromising yourself, you are at liberty not to do so."

Hearing the Cardinal's last speech I became offended, rose, and walked toward the door. "I have the honor," said I, "to observe to your Eminence that I am disposed to execute every commission you may give me; but I cannot suffer friendship to carry me so far as to become ridiculous. When you can make use of my services, I am at your command." I was about to retire, when he came to me, took me by the hand, and seated me in an arm-chair.

"The Emperor," said he, "might well say that you had a head of iron." "He might have added," returned I, "that with this head of iron I have a woman's heart to serve those I love. This is perhaps better than where

there is a head more pliable and a less feeling heart."
"Hem! I know that you are right, and perhaps it is as
you say: I know that Metternich must not be told that
the Pope and Consalvi mean to act falsely; but he may
be led to understand as much." "I cannot speak of Cardinal Consalvi in this matter without evil, and I esteem
him too much to——"
"Ah! you were going to tell me that you also esteem
La Somaglia, Spada, and Pacca! Oh, that Cardinal
Pacca!" "But, Monseigneur, I know nothing against
Consalvi; why, therefore, should I speak ill of him?"
"But I know, and I direct you to speak." "That will
not suffice, Monseigneur. Your Eminence is irritated,
and not master of yourself. At this moment I must not
hear you." The Cardinal looked as if he could beat me;
but he perhaps thought better of it. He ascended or
rather jumped up the two steps of the sanctuary, disappeared through the little door which was to the left of
the altar, and gained the private staircase which led to
his apartment.

After his departure I remained some time expecting he
would return. I pitied his folly, but was resolved not to
cede my point. He came not, nor did he send anyone.
After waiting a quarter of an hour, I went to my carriage and drove home.

The same evening I related the conversation to my
uncle, the Abbé Comnena, whose virtues and intelligence
were to me the surest guide. He applauded my conduct,
assuring me he would have done the same in my place.
From this moment I felt at ease, particularly as Albert,
to whom I also mentioned the affair, coincided in opinion with my uncle. I thus felt that I had not erred in
apparently refusing to serve a friend, but in reality declining to second a vengeance ill conceived, even in the
interest of the person who desired to consummate it.

The next day the Cardinal wrote me a strange letter,
wherein he begged pardon for the conversation of the
previous day, asking me to forget, and, above all, not to
mention it. He told me likewise that he was about to
depart for Italy, and would come to bid me farewell. I
replied that I should be delighted to see him; that I
advised him to write to Metternich, and place entire confidence in him. With respect to mentioning our inter-

view, I frankly said that I had disclosed it to my uncle and my brother, who were both too dear to me to conceal from them my thoughts, and more particularly my conduct in a matter bearing upon politics.

CHAPTER XXXIX.

The Joy of Paris — Conversation of the Emperor with the Postmaster at Montélimart — The Inhabitants of Avignon Always Violent — Fury of the Populace at Orgon — Meaning of « Nicholas » — The Emperor Arrives at Avignon — Precautions — Devotion of an Officer — A Harangue — Proposals for Assassination — Vincent, the Butcher of Avignon, and One of the Assassins of La Glacière — Recrimination — The Female Servant at the Inn — « O Richard! O mon Roi! » — The Priest — The Emperor's Alms — The Princess Pauline — Monsieur de Montbreton — A Disguise — « O Napoleon, What Have You Done ? » — The Emperor in the Midst of Five Hundred Peasants — Jacques Dumont — Recollections of Egypt — Two Hundred Messengers to Carry One Letter — Departure for Porto Ferrajo — Embarkation.

WHILE Louis XVIII. was advancing toward the throne of Clovis, Paris testified the same joy which it had before then exhibited on so many opposite occasions. At this time Napoleon, still in the midst of his enemies, received a short but most extraordinary letter, which was put into his hands at Montélimart. He immediately entered into conversation with the postmaster, and asked him if he was the master of the house. "Yes, Sire." "How far do you reckon it from hence to Avignon?" "Eight hours' journey, if your Majesty be well driven, but the roads are bad."

Napoleon walked about musing. "Eight hours!" at length he said, "and now it is ——" "Twenty minutes to seven, Sire," replied General Bertrand; "your Majesty should set out again at ten." "Let the horses be put to at nine," said Napoleon; and, continuing his walk, he appeared to be calculating how long his journey would take him. "I shall arrive at six o'clock in the morning," continued he; "these natives of Avignon were always hotheaded. Well," pursued he, "we must warn the commissioners of the Allied Powers. We will change horses outside the town."

At this time several of the public officers of the commune of Montélimart were introduced to the Emperor. He conversed with them for some moments with a calmness most remarkable at such a time, when the question of his own life or death was being agitated around him. When these officers spoke to him of their regrets, he replied in these words, replete with wisdom and firmness,* "Gentlemen, act like me: be resigned."

The troops in the city, when they saw him getting into the carriage, cried out enthusiastically, " *Vive l'Empereur!* " Two stages further on, at Donzène, he was met by cries of vengeance. The inhabitants were celebrating a *fête* for the arrival of the King in Paris, and the sight of the Emperor roused their indignation. He looked out upon the women, who, like furies, were shouting and uttering invectives against him: it was a shocking spectacle.

On his arrival at Orgon he was convinced that his fears were well founded.† In proportion as he removed from Paris and entered Provence, Napoleon observed gloomy countenances and armed hands. Mothers demanded their children, and widows their husbands. There was a terrible eloquence in these cries, wrung from the wretched people; but was it right to overwhelm him who was as wretched as they ?

At Avignon the danger which had been secretly threatening the travelers since leaving Valence broke out with a fury which alarmed the commissioners of the Allies. Napoleon was always calm and remarkably unconcerned, while all around him were inspired with an ardor which perhaps had not him alone for its object.‡ Already for

* Would it be believed that the spirit of party has endeavored to cast a censure upon this affecting reply ?

† At Orgon the Emperor ran a risk of his life, and only owed his safety to the lucky thought of passing for one of the suite of the commissioners. He was to stop at the Hôtel Royale, to which there were two entrances; and while the Emperor was conversing with the master of the house, preparations were made for his departure by one of these.

‡ As Napoleon approached Avignon he found the populace ripe for disorder; and as he advanced more toward the south of France violence and danger increased. Everyone knows that this part of the French Empire is of all others the most blind instrument in all great movements and political reactions. Religious and revolu-

some days, since the arrival of Napoleon had been announced, the tumult in the city had been terrible, and
the National Guard was wholly occupied in quieting the
people.

On Sunday, the 23d of April, couriers, and carriages
with the Imperial arms, arrived at the posthouse — that
same house which was shortly afterward to serve as the
scaffold of a virtuous man.* A popular disturbance
ensued, and was only allayed by the Emperor's suite
who were in these carriages assuming the white cockade.
The riot lasted during the greater part of the day; but
at last, weary of waiting, the crowd separated.

On Monday, the 24th of April, Colonel Campbell, the
commissioner of England, arrived at Avignon at four
o'clock in the morning. The officer at the gate through
which Napoleon was to enter anxiously inquired of
Colonel Campbell if the Emperor's escort were sufficient
to make a strong resistance in the event of an attack.

tionary madness have both successively been idolized there. The
people of that lovely country have danced round the scaffold of
terror, and a year later they massacred the Terrorists confined in
the fortress of Saint Jean. After having assassinated Marshal Brune
at Avignon, the people saluted with outrage and with menace their
beloved Emperor. The most ignoble epithets were hurled at him,
accompanied with ribald verses, in which his name appeared in
every line. A single fact that occurred at this moment will speak
more volumes than the historian can write. On leaving a small
inn where he had passed the night, he was walking toward his
carriage to proceed to Fréjus, when a lady, who was mixed in the
mob that was vociferating "DOWN WITH NICHOLAS!" addressed herself to Napoleon, believing him to be one of the suite, and begged
him to point out NICHOLAS to her. "I am Nicholas," replied he
with dignity. "You are jesting," said the lady; "Nicholas has not
so benevolent a countenance as you have; and, besides, he is a
greater man than you." "Oh!" rejoined the Emperor, "I understand: you suppose that Nicholas has the stature of a giant
and the face of an ogre." Napoleon drew from his pocket several
pieces of gold, and desired her to compare the likeness. The lady
examined the profile with confusion and surprise, while the Emperor told her to distribute the money among the mob of the place,
as a gift on the part of NICHOLAS. It may not be generally known
that the name "Nicholas" in the French language is an opprobri-
ous term, and is often applied to those who, either from want of
reason, common sense, or reflection, hope to succeed in some rash
or mad-brained exploit. (Compare also Napoleon's use of this name
in reference to Soult when in Portugal.)

* The dastardly murder of Marshal Brune is alluded to.

"Do you really fear any attempt?" asked the Colonel. The officer replied in the affirmative. The Colonel then appeared uneasy, and in consequence of this intelligence, and from what he himself witnessed, he ordered the post-horses to be taken to the city gate opposite to that through which the Emperor was to enter, and sent an express that the escort should direct its course thither.

But he could not give his orders so secretly as to escape the notice of the townspeople, and a furious crowd surrounded the Imperial carriage as soon as it appeared. The officer, whose conduct was so honorable to him, and whose name I regret much to be unable to give, was unavoidably absent from this newly-appointed place when Napoleon arrived there, and when he came up the carriage was entirely surrounded by an angry mob, and a drunken man, brandishing an old saber, had already his hand on the door of the Emperor's carriage, uttering frightful imprecations.

On a movement that indicated the design on the part of the ruffian, a footman of the Emperor, named François, who was seated on the outside, drew his sword. " Remain quiet," exclaimed the officer, and at the same instant the Emperor rapidly let down the front glass and said in a loud and commanding tone, " François, remain still, I command you." By this time the horses were put to, and the carriage started. As soon as he felt himself in motion the Emperor bowed to the officer, and, smiling, thanked him very cordially.

General Schuwaloff, the commissioner from Russia, General Köller, and Colonel Campbell, behaved admirably in this affair. There were two others of whom I cannot say the same — I will not name them. It has been said that the Prussian commissioner harangued the people, exhorting them " to let the tyrant live that he might be punished by repentance and regrets, which would inflict upon him a thousand deaths." This bad taste in the foreign commissioner did not escape Napoleon, who, smiling ironically, said, " In truth, General, you speak French admirably."

Much has been said of several proposals made to the King and to Monsieur to assassinate Napoleon, and of the constant refusal of the King. I will believe this, as also the innocence of M. de Talleyrand in this affair. I nevertheless recollect that, under Louis XIV., the Marquis de Louville wrote to the Duc de Beauvilliers and to M. de Torcy, all three considered among the most virtuous men of their age: "Let the handsome Amirant of Castile be pursued, and let him be killed wherever he may be, and no matter in what way." However chivalrous the loyalty and piety of M. de Blacas may be, it is not more so than that of M. de Louville; and therefore I have a right to suspect that a blow, the most important in its results, was intended to have been struck at Orgon. Emissaries were sent into this town; the Emperor was expected there. The famous Vincent, the town butcher, and one of the murderers of La Glacière, was at the head of two hundred wretches who were shouting that they would have the blood of the Emperor, of the Tyrant, of the *Corsican.*

Napoleon was aware, from the time of his arrival at Montélimart, of the danger which he would run at Orgon and at Fréjus. Life had now become a burden to him; but to lose it by the dagger of the assassin, yet streaming with the blood of women and aged priests, was abhorrent to his feelings. General Köller and the other commissioners were informed by him of what was about to take place. They received the communication as honorable men might be expected to do.

The Emperor arrived at Orgon in the first carriage; he was with General Köller. But how was he to escape recognition from eyes that found his portrait on the smallest coin? The posthouse at Orgon had a courtyard with a gate at each extremity. Between these the carriage of the Emperor halted; a figure clothed like him was suspended to a rope and swung about in the air, accompanied by the shouts of the whole crowd thirsting for his blood.

The postmaster and mistress of Orgon wished to protect the travelers, whoever they might be, from the dangers which threatened them. They therefore closed the gate toward the disturbed portion of the town, and hastened the postilions. It is known how this gate was shattered beneath the blows of this butcher himself, encouraged by a gentleman, said to be of the neighborhood, who, from the preceding day, had been profusely scattering money among the people.

An excitement was thus kept up among them, and the hatred of the women especially was aroused by the recollection of the losses they had sustained in the Emperor's wars. " I lost two of my sons at Mojaisk," cried one. " I lost my husband and my father at Wagram," said her companion. " And I," exclaimed a man with a wooden leg, " have been thus mutilated since I was twenty." " And the taxes," cried another, " are they not disgraceful — and a jug of wine to cost threepence, and all to support his BUTCHERIES, which he calls wars — death to the tyrant! "

These cries assumed every moment a more serious character. What happened a few weeks later at Avignon has shown the horrors that might have been committed at Orgon. The Emperor appears to have escaped this extreme danger by disguising himself in a traveling coat of General Köller.

Other accounts attribute his preservation to a female servant at the inn. This woman had resolved to strike the first blow at the Emperor, but when she saw him before her, stripped of his power and overwhelmed by misfortune, her feeling toward him relented, and she exerted herself for his preservation. She cried out to the mob with a loud voice: " Stand by and let the commissioners pass who are going to embark the tyrant."

The following anecdote of the Emperor on his way to Elba also ought not to be omitted: A little on the north of Lyons, at La Tour, the Emperor supped alone (he was not in the habit of supping with the Allied Commissioners); his meal was soon over, and, as the night was fine, he went out and walked in the road. A respectable ecclesiastic followed at the same time to speak with him.

Napoleon was singing in a low tone (he is known to have had a very bad voice), and the air that the priest recognized was, *O Richard! O mon Roi!* He sang for some time; at length he stopped, leaned against a tree, and looked up to heaven. He remained some time contemplating a star, and then resumed his lonely walk. The priest now placed himself opposite to him, and Napoleon started on seeing a man so near.

"Who are you?" he asked. "I am an ecclesiastic, Sire, and rector of this commune." "Have you been so long?" "Since its formation — since your Majesty restored religion to France" (and the worthy priest bowed to the Emperor. All are not ungrateful!). Napoleon walked on for some time in silence: "Has this village suffered much?" "Greatly, Sire; its burdens were too heavy."

The Emperor pursued his way; at length, stopping suddenly, he looked up to the sky, and inquired the name of a certain star. The priest being unable to inform him, he said: "Once I knew the names of all these stars — and of my own; but now——" He was silent for a short space, and then resumed: "Yes, now I forget everything." They were now approaching the house; the Emperor took some gold from his pocket, and, giving it to the priest, said: "I cannot do more; but the humble are great in the eyes of God. Pray for me, and mine alms will bring forth fruit." "Sire!"

The mode of uttering this single word probably expressed much, for the Emperor started when he heard it, and replied: "Yes, perhaps you are right — perhaps I was too fond of war; but it is too serious a question," said he, smiling, "to be discussed on the highway. Once more adieu! Pray for me!"

I have already remarked that Lyons was on the point of rising in his favor, and that he was hurried through that city by night. It is certain that he was for a long time in fear of his life, and that it was only when in sight of the Mediterranean that his spirits recovered their wonted elasticity.

One consolation was afforded to him under these painful circumstances. His sister, the Princess Pauline, after having passed the winter at Nice and Hyères, had hired a small country house, where she was awaiting the final issue of events in the greatest anxiety. She was informed that her brother was approaching, and that his life was threatened. She knew the disposition of the country; and when she heard that the Emperor was but a few leagues distant she was in the greatest alarm. The mad cries of the populace were heard even beneath the windows of the house in which the Princess was living with no other attendants than Madame la Marquise de

Saluces, one of her ladies, and M. le Comte de Montbreton, her principal equerry.

At two in the afternoon of the 26th of April the Emperor's arrival was announced. M. de Montbreton hastened into the hall to meet him, when a person unknown
to the Count leaped hastily from the carriage and inquired
for the Princess. It was the Emperor, but so disguised
that it was impossible to recognize him. He knew M.
de Montbreton well, and said: "These poor wretches
would have murdered me — I have escaped only by
means of this disguise." "Your Majesty has done well,"
replied the Count.

At this moment they entered the chamber of the Princess. She extended her arms to him and burst into
tears. All at once her attention was arrested by the
Austrian uniform which he wore, and she turned pale.
"How is this?" she asked. "Why this uniform?"
"Pauline," replied Napoleon, "do you wish me dead?"
The Princess, looking at him steadfastly, replied: "I cannot embrace you in that dress — O Napoleon, what have
you done?"

The Emperor immediately retired, and having substituted for the Austrian the uniform of one of the Old
Guard, entered the chamber of his sister, who ran to him
and embraced him with a tenderness which drew tears
from the eyes of all present. Napoleon himself was
much affected. These emotions, however, were but of
short duration. He approached the window and looked
into the little court beneath, which was filled with a
crowd of persons, for the most part as much exasperated against him as those of Orgon, or Fréjus, and of
Avignon.

Napoleon, profiting by a momentary calm which appeared to have fallen upon them, descended into this
very small courtyard, in which were four or five hundred
persons. He had on his three-cornered hat, and the
coat of the Imperial Guard, the rest of his dress being
the same as that in which the soldiers had always seen
him.

The commissioners, when they saw him in the midst
of these peasants, became alarmed, and General Köller
respectfully reminded him that until his arrival at Porto
Ferrajo they were answerable for his safety. "To

whom ? " said the Emperor sarcastically. "To the whole
world, Sire," replied the General. In spite of these rep-
resentations, Napoleon resolved to trust himself in the
crowd, which soon became still more dense around him.
A confused buzz was heard, and the commissioners,
greatly alarmed, entreated him to return into the house;
but this was the sort of danger that delighted him.

While he was in the crowd he noticed in a corner of
the courtyard a man about fifty years old, with a gash
across his nose and a red ribbon in his buttonhole.
The Emperor perceived that this man was looking at
him, and, returning his gaze, appeared to be endeavoring to recollect his name. All at once he smiled, and,
approaching him, said: "Are you not Jacques Dumont ? "
The man could not immediately reply, but at length he
said: "Yes, my lord — yes, General — yes, yes, Sire! "
"You were in Egypt with me ? " "Yes, Sire! " and the
old soldier drew himself up, and put his hand to his
forehead as if to give the military salute.

"You were wounded, but that seems to me very long
ago." "At the Battle of Trebbia, Sire, with the brave
General Suchet; I was unable to serve any longer.
Yet now, whenever the drum beats, I feel like a de-
serter. Under your ensign, Sire, I could still serve
wherever your Majesty should command." And the brave
old man shed tears as he said: "My name! to recollect
my name at the end of fifteen years." The Emperor on
dismissing him presented him with a cross.

Napoleon having expressed a desire to communicate
with Marshal Masséna, at that time in command at Toulon,
the greatest eagerness was displayed among the crowd
to convey his letter. "I will go! " exclaimed two hundred voices at once, in a delirium of enthusiasm. "Let
it be I," cried a woman, "for the Emperor knew my
husband — 'twas he who gave him his horse that he
might better pursue those Austrians in Italy."

At this moment General Köller approached M. de
Montbreton. "How shall we induce his Majesty to return into the house ? said the General; "I would not say
anything unpleasant, nevertheless ——" The Count understood the General's meaning, and ten minutes afterward the Princess Borghèse sent for her brother.
Napoleon, restored to a sense of his situation by these

simple words, "Sire, the Princess would speak to you
without witnesses," hastened to OBEY.

The Emperor remained a day and a half with his
sister, and then took the road to Porto Ferrajo, to reign
over fruits and fields, which subsequently were changed
to fetters and a barren rock.

The Russian, English, and Prussian commissioners
left him at Saint Euphemia, where he embarked for
Porto Ferrajo. General Köller was the only one who
accompanied him to Elba (unless Colonel Campbell was
also with him).

_____

CHAPTER XL.

Anglomania — A Stroke of the Pen — Fête of Prince Schwartzenberg
at Saint Cloud — The Comédie Française — The Polonaise — Œdipe
— Maubrueil and Talleyrand, and the Robbery of the Diamonds
of the Queen of Westphalia — Maria Louisa — The Ices of the Duc
de Berri — The Grenadier.

WHILE the Exile was thus traveling toward his prison,
the new King of France made his entry into
Paris. He arrived from London in an English
dress, with an English hat, and an ENGLISH white cockade that the Prince Regent himself had fastened in; and
nature decreed that the change should be complete; the
new King was unable to walk, as he then labored under
a fit of the gout; he wore velvet boots, and appeared in
powder; he was the representative of the good old men
of 1789.

The Charter was granted, and we ought to have been
satisfied with it. Indeed, it was an excellent one, and
had it been adhered to we should have had no reason to
complain. When Napoleon read it he exclaimed: "This
one stroke of the pen has done in an instant what I have
been endeavoring to do for the last twenty years." This
was very complimentary, and I believe he felt it to be
true.

Prince Schwartzenberg gave a splendid _fête_ at the
Palace of Saint Cloud, in which he was then living. The
period of my mourning had not yet expired, and that

served me as a pretext for my absence. The Emperor
of Russia and the Grand-Dukes Michael and Nicholas;
the King of Prussia and the Princess; the Duc de Berri
and an immense and elegant assemblage of nobility, were
present.

The company of the Comédie Française were in attendance at this *fête*. Mademoiselle Mars played in "*Le
Legs*" (the Legacy) most exquisitely, as she always does.
This was succeeded by "*La Suite d'un Bal Masqué*," a
pretty lively comedy, by Madame de Bawr, formerly the
wife of M. de Saint Simon, who has given his name to a
religious sect lately much in vogue: his wife composed
plays perhaps better than her husband knew how to introduce a new religion. The temporary theater was
erected in the gallery painted by Mignard. The effect
was most complete, and the Emperor Alexander told me
the next day that he had no idea of a play being performed in such perfection.

A slight accident cast a gloom over one portion of the
company — a garland of flowers, cut in paper, which
decorated the gallery, caught fire. The terrible misfortune which had happened to the same Prince Schwartzenberg at the marriage of Maria Louisa immediately
occurred to them, and a feeling of superstition, which
was perhaps excusable, threw a shade over that portion
of the assembly by whom the facts were known. The
supper was served in a room adjoining the orangery, in
which was a great profusion of flowers. The dancing
was continued until daylight, and the whole *fête* was very
well arranged. The Prince must have felt perfectly satisfied if no recollection of the past disturbed him.

The next day "*Œdipe*" was performed at the Grand
Opera, at which were present his Majesty and the
Duchesse d'Angoulême. The interior of the theater presented a most extraordinary appearance — none of the
women had diamonds; all were in white, and all their
ornaments consisted of plumes of feathers, of lilies, and
of bunches or garlands of white lilac.

There was in the whole scene an elegance for which I
could not at first account; I, however, afterward attributed it to the agreeable color that prevailed, and to the
scent of the spring flowers which spread itself in every
direction. The opera of "*Œdipe*" was ill chosen on this

occasion, as it contained passages that would bear a disagreeable interpretation.

Between the acts the orchestra played *Vive Henri Quatre* which air was introduced three times more in the course of the ballet.

The Duchesse d'Angoulême was condescending, but appeared melancholy — melancholy, however, in a being who sacrifices on the altar of the living God all resentment, every painful thought, and all recollection of injury, is a feeling which should indeed be permitted to her who has wept for twenty years over those whom she lost by a death more frightful in its manner than in itself.

The theft of the Queen of Westphalia's diamonds by Maubreuil was of a very extraordinary character, and one of which M. de Talleyrand can furnish the particulars. The Queen was returning leisurely to her residence in Germany, when she was surrounded, stopped, and then robbed, by persons under the direction of a man whom the Princess Catharine herself recollected. This man showed her an order, signed by Louis XVIII., and then set to work with a quickness and regularity that showed, as the Princess said, that this was not the first time that he had been thus employed. M. de Maubreuil, before this adventure, was wholly unknown; but since, according to custom, we have spoken of nothing but him. This man, the bearer, as I have said, of an order signed by Louis XVIII., stopped the Queen of Westphalia on the 21st of April, at seven o'clock in the morning, between Sens and Weimans. He took from her a hundred thousand francs in gold, and her diamonds, estimated at about five million francs. He was accompanied by twenty persons, and had with him as an OSTENSIBLE accomplice a fellow of the name of Desies.

M. de Talleyrand was, as is well known, greatly compromised in this affair. What may have been the origin of it, it is not necessary to inquire; it was highly impolitic, and the event has since justified what I then asserted — M. de Talleyrand is not free from blame. Beyond this, until we have more positive evidence, we must be silent.

One of the most disgraceful characteristics of the journals of this time was the spontaneous servility which they exhibited toward the newcomers, and the indifference, and even impertinence, which marked their conduct toward those who were no longer in power. They never gave, for instance, to Maria Louisa any other title than her Imperial Highness the Archduchess.

The Duc de Berri possessed, in 1814, qualities likely to render him more popular than most men. His countenance was open and his manner frank. Anecdotes were told of him which amused the people; and, besides, he possessed qualities that reminded them of Henri IV.

He was in the habit of taking two ices every night before he went to bed. On one occasion he returned home later than usual; it was five o'clock, and the day was beginning to break. The servant who had charge of the ices, finding that the Prince did not return, looked wistfully at them, now fast dissolving, and, that they might not be lost, determined to swallow both. Scarcely had he finished them, when the Prince entered, and called for his ices. The unlucky fellow had hidden himself; for at this time the Prince made everyone tremble by his violence of temper. The Duke, being appeased, desired to see the culprit, that he might judge whether he deserved his pardon. The servant approached trembling. "Well, rascal," said the Duke, "what induced you to eat my ices? Take care another time to leave ONE for me."

On another occasion, at a review, a grenadier called out very loud, "Vive l'Empereur!" The Prince went up to him, and said: "How is it that you are so fond of a man who did not pay you, and who led you, without recompense, from one end of Europe to the other?" The grenadier raised his eyes, and looked at the Duke with a gloomy air; then dropped his eyes upon his firelock and replied: "What is it to you if WE chose to give him credit?" The grenadier certainly had the best of this interview.

CHAPTER XLI.

I Make My Court — Presentation — Louis XVIII. — Junot and the
Lisbon Bible.

THE day on which the ladies had received notice to go
to the Tuileries I consulted my uncle and Albert,
and determined to pay what is called MY COURT.
But there was one point of embarrassment. We all
recollected the luxury of the Imperial Court: I still had
my jewels, but I did not make use of them. I had a
garland of diamonds, but I would not put it on; neither
did I wear any of my most valuable diamonds. I selected
a set of emeralds surrounded by small diamonds; it was
termed a morning full dress, but even this seemed to me
too brilliant.

As for my robes, I could not dream of wearing one of
my Imperial Court dresses, and therefore had one made
for the occasion of white satin, covered with white crape,
and decorated with blonde. I put a few simple ornaments in my hair, and thus completed the Court toilet
for my presentation to Louis XVIII. I give the details
as being characteristic of the period I am describing.

I was introduced to the Duchesse d'Angoulême on
the first day She received all the ladies standing, having beside her the Duchesse de Seran, who knew none
of us, and was obliged to ask three-fourths of the names.
The Dauphiness inclined her head, and we passed on
after having made our reverence to the Princess. I was
between Madame Juste de Noailles and the Duchess of
Hamilton (the latter accompanying us as the Duchesse
d'Aubigné).

I arrived in front of the Princess; I courtesied as they
named me, and was about to pass on, when the Dauphiness, repeating my name, fixed on me that kind look
which secured her the love of all by whom she was surrounded. That glance directed me to stop — I stopped.
"You are Madame Junot?" "Yes, Madame." "You
suffered much, I think, in your last expedition to
Spain?" The Princess said this in an accent of such
great interest that I could not avoid raising my eyes to

2ɒ

her, though with the greatest respect. "Have you saved
your son?" she continued. "Yes, Madame." I had very
nearly added: "That child lives, and I will educate him
for you — to defend you!" It struck me, however, that
such a boast might be considered somewhat *mal à propos*.
My looks meanwhile spoke for me, and I comprehended
her reply. "You no longer suffer from your hardships,
then?" pursued she. I answered that I had returned
three years ago. She appeared to calculate, and then
said: "Ah, that is true."

Making a movement of the head, she indicated that I
might pass on. My life, since the age of fifteen, had
been passed in familiar intercourse not only with the
Princes of Germany (and it is known that everything
connected with etiquette is of much importance to them),
but with almost all the Crowned Heads of Europe. I
was touched with the kindness and the fascination of the
Dauphiness. Tears came into my eyes, and I described
my feelings vividly to Madame de Noailles, who knew
well how to appreciate them.

On speaking the same evening to my uncle and
brother of the goodness of the Princess, the latter told
me I should be to blame if I did not go to the Tuileries with my son, and request from Louis XVIII. the 200,-
000 francs entered on the State Ledger for my eldest
son. It seemed evident that Madame d'Angoulême, rigid
and severe to the world generally, had been particularly
kind to me; I therefore wrote next day for my first
audience. I was answered by the Duc de Chartres without delay, that the King would receive me the following
day between three and four o'clock.

I framed the requisite answers to such questions as I
thought might be put to me; and felt no trepidation
when I entered the cabinet of the King.

It should be recollected that Louis XVIII. had a very
kind and even soft address: he was extremely polite after
the manner of kings, which seemed to impose silence
upon you. Notwithstanding his black velvet boots and
absurd general appearance, I found myself at once as
much at ease with his Majesty as if we had been acquainted for ten years. He made me sit down near him,
entered himself upon the subject of my audience, and
asked if my request was within scope of the law. He

added, with much grace: "The Duc d'Abrantès did not die in my service; but such a man does honor to his country, which should therefore render her acknowledgments: I will take charge of it."

The King then entered upon the subject which I most dreaded — that of the Emperor. He spoke to me of my mother and of him. As my "Memoirs" had not then been published, I could not imagine how the King had become so well acquainted with Napoleon's earliest years. But, upon reflection, it appeared perfectly natural. He talked a long time, asking questions as princes asked them, and received laconic answers as became a subject.

He spoke, among other things, of my Uncle Demetrius, whom he had not only known in exile, but who, continuing faithful, had been charged by Louis XVIII., then Monsieur and Regent of France, with several delicate and even dangerous missions to the King of Naples (father to Queen Amelia). He talked of my uncle with much complacency, saying that he had known him when young and gay. "One day," continued the King, "he supped with me at Brunois. We made a comparison which had the longer memory. I believe I beat him; and can you imagine how? By enumerating the *curés* of Meudon in chronological order."

I could not help laughing at this anecdote in a degree not quite respectful; but when one laughs at what they say, and not in derision, kings excuse us. However, I gained my purpose in the audience, for with my customary freedom I said to his Majesty: "True, Sire, that was a droll idea, but the list must have been very long, and not a little tiresome to your Majesty to repeat." "You mean tiresome for him to hear?"

I laughed again, and the King seemed glad to see me so joyous. It was a happy moment for my purpose. I presented him my petition, and invoked his goodness for my son, relating to him the Prussian history, which I had not then communicated to anyone. In listening to it Louis XVIII. colored slightly; in fact, he perceived the humiliation of the proposal. It was at this audience that I offered his Majesty my Hôtel for the depository of the Crown wardrobe, and that he pledged his word that, at the end of the year, the purchase should be concluded. I spoke to him also of my brother, and he granted every request, leaving me, on my withdrawing, as satisfied and content with Louis XVIII. as it was possible to be with a king.

I will now relate a curious story, which is necessary to the epoch under review:

When Junot was sent to Lisbon, the Emperor ordered him to forward to France all the *chef-d'œuvres* of art. These were not very numerous, Lisbon being only a commercial city, badly paved and smelling worse. However, there was the famous Lisbon Bible, a MS. of the thirteenth century, and the minatures of Lulio Clavio. Junot transmitted to France the twelve large volumes bound in black, with huge clasps; and he told the Emperor that, having in the library the two most celebrated Bibles in the world, and possessing himself the Bibliomania, he should be extremely grateful if his Majesty would bestow on him this Lisbon Bible. The Emperor consented, and the book became our personal property. At Junot's death, when his affairs were discovered to be in so deplorable a condition, it became necessary to be active. By the advice of my friend, M. Millin, I applied to the Emperor, requesting him to purchase for the Imperial Library this same Bible, which, from the nature of the gift, could not be included in the catalogue of effects. His Majesty replied that he was willing to do so, and referred me to Messrs. Millin and Anglès for them to fix the price. This was settled at 144,000 francs; but at the moment when the money was about to be paid arrived all the political troubles.

Scarcely had the Allies been six weeks in Paris, ere I received a billet — an order — I scarce know what, for my rage dulled my perceptions, from the Marquis of Pal-. mella, couched in such terms as might be used to a *femme de chambre* who had stolen her mistress's shawl. I did not answer it; I was too much irritated. I satisfied myself with stating the facts to the King, who was touched with the circumstance, and said he knew his brother of Portugal wished to recover the Bible; but since it had become private property, the most sacred of all things, in order to avoid any disagreement with the Portuguese King, and at the same time to do as much as possible for me, he wished to know what price I myself set upon the work. Ultimately, he sent the Duke of

Ragusa to treat upon the subject, and M. de Blacas interested himself in it likewise. Of M. de Palmella's behavior throughout the affair, I cannot speak with any degree of commendation.

The King afterward said with a good deal of heartiness:

" Madame d'Abrantès is a widow. I have thought proper to undertake her defense. But if the least CLAIM is revived, it will have no effect. »

Such was the affair of the Bible, altogether honorable to Louis XVIII. That Prince, if he had some bad qualities, was not without his good ones to redeem them.

The Duke of Rovigo, that complete meddler in all things, having learned that I had had a private audience of the King, came in a great hurry to inquire if Louis XVIII. had mentioned the Duc d'Enghien. I replied with the simple word, No!

CHAPTER XLII.

Lord Wellington—Embarrassment—The Riding Coat and Dusty Shoes — Fêtes at Vienna—Napoleon.

THE horizon gradually darkened, and heavy clouds portended a coming storm. Vienna was at this moment resplendent with all the rank and luxury of Europe concentrated upon one single point; everyone went to Vienna to be present at the Congress. The wealthiest and most beautiful women of the Continent were there, and England contributed her full share of nobility and loveliness.

M. de Metternich was both Chancellor of the Court and of the State, with an influence extending throughout Europe, to which he formulated laws, although Lord Castlereagh, Mr. Canning, and perhaps Capo d'Istria, were there as the originators of them. I had seen Lord Wellington immediately after his arrival from Toulouse. The frequent relations he had been in with my husband had established a sort of intimacy between us, which, on my part, was heightened by a knowledge of the admirable arrangements he had made in Spain for my safety. I asked him one day to dine with me.

Several ladies of my acquaintance had been desirous of knowing him — among others, the Comtesse de Lucay, lady of the wardrobe to the Empress Maria Louisa. "Ah !" said Lord Wellington to me, "would you show me as something marvelous ?" "No, certainly. Whom would you have ?" "Whom you please: Metternich — he is amiable, and so witty." I agreed with him, but etiquette induced me to pause. Which of the two should I place on my right ? To which of the two should I give my hand in going to table ? These petty considerations prevented me from asking them at the same time.

I invited Englishmen and Frenchmen; I would have asked Cardinal Maury, who was to leave in a day or two for Italy, but by virtue of his office he would claim precedence over all. It was necessary to omit him. I invited Sir George Murray, the Duke's Quartermaster-General, a French Lieutenant-General, and the Comte de Lucay. The day arrived, and with it one of those mishaps so disagreeable to the mistress of a house.

I had intimated to the Lieutenant-General that it was to be a dinner of ceremony, but not in uniform — no one but men of elegant manners. The Marquis de Balincourt, and two or three similar persons; Prince Wenzel de Lichtenstein, and his brother Prince Maurice. All were suitable to each other. The Duke of Wellington, who had then just assumed that rank, came in the full dress of a gentleman, with the Order of the Garter, looking as well as private attire would permit him to do. The ladies present consisted of Madame Duchâtel, Madame Lallemand, the Baroness Thomières, the Comtesse de Lucay, Madame Doumerc, and myself.

We were all as elegant as we could be, and in those days this was saying something. My house, always excellently furnished, was on this occasion ornamented with peculiar care, and seemed to join in our female coquetry. There were flowers everywhere, and flowers in the month of May — a month redolent of roses ! "It seems," says the Duke, "that you have adopted our fashion of dining late. Is it not a delightful one ?"

I dared not tell him that I was waiting for General Comte de C——; but as he had desired to dine with one of our generals, I had selected a man who belonged both to the old and the new *noblesse;* and, in fact, my choice struck me as excellent. However, as time passed on, I ordered dinner, and two minutes after my expected guest arrived. But how? Heavens! in a riding coat, with nankeen trousers and dusty shoes. I cannot tell what I felt at this moment. It was a great act of rudeness to me, but still greater to the Duke of Wellington. "He did not intend to do anything that might be disagreeable to me, and trusted I would excuse his want of ceremony?" *Mon Dieu!* As for the Duke, he was inclined to laugh, but said nothing. With regard to the rest, all went well. My self-love, as hostess, might even have been flattered. But that unfortunate surtout — those miserable nankeen trousers!

Wellington was very complaisant — friendly even — and stopped to hear Madame Emilie Doumerc sing; she was a particular friend of mine, and one of the most exquisite sirens ever created.

M. de Metternich, to whom I related my embarrassment respecting the place and the arm, excused me, and came after dinner.

When Lord Wellington was gone, I said to the General: "*Ah, ça!* Now, will you explain to me the trousers and the riding coat? You, whom I have known in the country dress for our society alone!" "So I would again," replied he. "But do you imagine that I would pay the least compliment to a personage who draws us along in chains after him, like Lord Wellington?"

I stood astonished. "We are all of the same mind," continued he. I confess I knew not what to say. He was so honest — so far from showing a disposition to offend ME. I have set down the above anecdote to show the spirit of the army at this epoch.

When the Allied Sovereigns were in London, I received intelligence of all the sumptuous entertainments, first by letter from Prince Metternich, and afterward by verbal description from that Minister during his brief residence at Paris. I parted from him with regret, for I loved him tenderly, and felt confident of finding in him a faithful friend.

He wrote me from Vienna in November: "I have been passing a month at Baden. But my furlough has been very short, and already the political world is assembling

at Vienna; as if life consisted but in attending to the requisitions of others. You will hear anon of a grand ball
which I purpose giving in a charming house that I have
in the Faubourg of Vienna." And this *fête* was given
and described in all the newspapers of the day. The
Prince de Ligne observed: "*Par Dieu !* if the Congress
moves slowly, at least it dances well."

In the midst of this gayety the news of Napoleon's return from Elba seemed as startling as a thunderbolt on
a serene day. When the first news reached Paris of
Napoleon's disembarkation, we regarded each other with
almost stupid astonishment, and gazed around to ascertain if it were not a dream. Louis XVIII. was well
advised not to quit France; had he only gone to Brussels, which was no longer ours, France would not again
have received him. But all counsels offered to him were
not equally wise, and this period was fatal in its results.
He believed like his advisers, that severity was necessary, but they inflicted punishment with as little judgment
as they bestowed rewards.

CHAPTER XLIII.

M. Dumoulin of Grenoble at Porto Ferrajo — An Audience — The
Emperor's Opinion on Dauphiné — M. Fourrier, Prefect of Gren-
oble — Departure of M. Dumoulin — Resolution of the Congress —
The Landing — Orders for Grenoble — M. Gavin — Proclamation —
Charles de Labédoyère — Dauphiné — The Nobility Offer Their
Services — Projects for Defense — Café Tortoni — Caricatures — M.
Jacqueminot (now General) the Principal Actor in This Scene —
Madame de Vaudé — Conferences — The Duc de Feltre, Minister
of War — Alarm of the Congress — Order of March — M. Barginet
of Grenoble — Recollections of the Château of Vizille — Successive
Desertions from the King — Orders are Given Twice to Fire upon
the Emperor — "I Have Seen the Lord."

IN A stormy evening of the month of September, 1814,
a young man, calling himself a merchant, traveling
for a house at Genoa, arrived at Porto Ferrajo, and
put up at the inn of the port. He, immediately on landing, inquired for M. Emery, Chief Surgeon of the Guard,
the same person who followed Napoleon to Saint Helena,
and to whom the Emperor left in his will 100,000 francs.

This young man was M. Dumoulin, the son of a rich merchant at Grenoble, and the early friend of M. Emery. "Here I am," said Dumoulin, "but what are you doing here? Why is not the Emperor in France? If his foot were once again on the shores of France, in three days he would be at the Tuileries. The enthusiasm in his favor has been increased by his humiliation. The Emperor must return, I say. Can I be presented to him?" "You shall see him this very night."

M. Dumoulin only took time to change his coat, when he was conducted to the wretched dwelling of Napoleon, who started on the entrance of a stranger, but immediately recovered himself on hearing his name. He conversed with him for some time on the state of Dauphiné, and then entered, at length, on the condition of the south of France and of France itself; he afterward listened with evident satisfaction to Dumoulin's suggestions as to his return. There were several maps in his room, and while he spoke he traced his purposed route upon them.

"But, Sire," said M. Dumoulin, "the roads that your Majesty is tracing are impracticable, especially for cavalry." "Resolution will overcome everything," said Napoleon. "Cannon can be CARRIED; and infantry can march twenty leagues a day. Do you not know the power of a firm resolve in important conjunctures?" These were the Emperor's own words, which I received from M. Dumoulin himself, who took them down the same evening that they were uttered at Porto Ferrajo. "And then," continued the Emperor, "Dauphiné is for us; they do not like the Royal Family — they and Brittany were the first who proclaimed their liberty at the Castle of Vizille, now belonging to M. Perrier."

Napoleon then questioned M. Dumoulin respecting the TRIUMPHAL journey of the Comte d'Artois through the South, and laughed heartily at the narrative which he received: his gayety, however, was checked on learning the conduct of M. Fourrier, Prefect of Grenoble, a man of some talent, who wrote the preface to the excellent work on Egypt, whither the Emperor had taken him, and who owed everything to Napoleon.

He was the son of a tailor of Auxerre, and should have been a Liberal, but was, on the contrary, so anxious for the favor of the Royal party, that, like St. Peter, he denied his master, asserting in exculpation that he had FORGOTTEN him—an excuse which would not certainly have occurred to everyone. The Emperor, in speaking of him on this occasion, said: "I know him; he will not succeed; he would do better to remain a writer, for he will never make a courtier."

The conference lasted for some time; when Napoleon dismissed M. Dumoulin he started for France, having remained on the island about thirty-six hours. On his departure the Emperor said to him: "Write frequently to Emery; be prudent; be faithful. I am not now rich, but I have still sufficient to assist those who may devote themselves to me."

I have spoken of this interview to show that the Emperor was aware of the feelings which existed in his favor throughout Dauphiné. As soon, therefore, as he learned the resolution of the Congress to shut him up in a fortress, or to send him to the Azores or to Saint Helena, he no longer hesitated to embark for France.

The details of his departure and arrival are well known; and as I have but little room to spare I shall devote my remaining space to particulars interesting although but little known. As soon as his foot touched the soil of France, Napoleon said to Dr. Emery: "Start for Grenoble; travel night and day until you arrive at the house of Dumoulin, who must set out immediately to join me." He intrusted him also with dispatches to be forwarded by some safe and trustworthy person to the Duke of Bassano, and to the Colonel of the 7th Regiment of the Line, then at Chambéry.

When the doctor was about to set out, the Emperor called him back, and having pointed out to him on a map his route, said: "You will take the road by Grasse, Digne, and Gap. When you arrive at Grenoble be sure to send me an account of each day's journey; and, above all, of the disposition of the people."

Dr. Emery was high-minded and ardent, and well fitted for such a mission. He only stopped at Digne and Gap to change horses; so much did he fear an arrest, not for his own sake, but for the cause in which he was engaged. On the morning of the 4th of March, Emery entered Grenoble, where everyone was as yet in ignorance of the landing of the Emperor, but which was known at Paris by telegraph. He hastened to Dumoulin, and his first words were: "The Emperor has landed; let us thank God."

He was so overcome by fatigue that they were obliged to cut off his boots; but this had to be done with great caution, as important papers were concealed within them. These documents were to be printed, and Dumoulin placed them in the hands of M. Gavin, a printer, as determined a partisan as himself, who finished them the same evening in the chamber of Dumoulin. While thus engaged they fancied themselves betrayed; they stopped to listen, then resumed their work, saying: "If they will only allow us to finish it!"

About the same time letters arrived from Paris inclos-ing manuscript proclamations. These were to invite the patriots to unite in this one endeavor to cast off the for-eign yoke, and once more become Frenchmen. "On the 1st of March," said this proclamation, "France again be-came free; and she must take her rank as the first of nations," etc.

Some asserted that this attempt was in favor of the Emperor; others, of Napoleon II. The style of the proc-lamation was not very hostile to the Bourbons. At the same time the Imperial Guard was reassembled under the command of Generals Lefebvre-Desnouettes and Lalle-mand, and of Colonel Briche. They wished to possess themselves of La Fère, but the desertion of General Lyons frustrated this well-concerted project.

There was a report, which I consider altogether false, although it gained great credit at the time: It was said that this movement arose from a party belonging neither to the Emperor nor to the Bourbons. I do not believe it. The fact is that neither M. Emery nor M. Dumoulin knew by whom the proclamations were issued, nor have they ever been able to discover; nevertheless, a month later, when the Emperor was at the Tuileries, persons came to claim a reward.

When Dumoulin knew that the Emperor's letter to M. de Labédoyère was of great importance, he resolved to be the bearer of it himself; and immediately hastened, or rather flew, to Chambéry, where, incredible to relate, he arrived at nine on the same evening.

Labédoyère read the letter with considerable emotion, and exclaimed: "Yes, indeed, the Emperor may reckon on me. I must wait till the news of his arrival be officially known before I can act. You may, sir, return to his Majesty, and assure him that I am his FOR LIFE OR DEATH!" Alas! the unfortunate young man knew not that he was so truly foretelling his destiny!

Dumoulin again started, after a few moments' rest, for Grenoble, where he arrived at five in the morning. Positive intelligence of the landing of the Emperor had now spread through Grenoble, and official notice of it had reached the Prefect. General Marchand (by whom precautions were taken for the protection of the city) and a company of soldiers were ordered to occupy a defile through which the Emperor would have to pass on his approach.

On the morning of the 5th an extraordinary procession of old gentlemen appeared before General Marchand, and OFFERED HIM THE SERVICES OF THE NOBILITY OF DAUPHINÉ. The General thanked them, and they went their way. At this time printed proclamations were scattered about in abundance, and appeared to be well received among the garrison. Murmurs were heard in the ranks, and General Marchand was even threatened with death should he attempt resistance. "We will do no harm to the Bourbons," exclaimed some; "but let them restore his throne to the Emperor, and return as they came."

Uneasy at the disposition of the town and troops, the General and Prefect convoked the principal inhabitants, and it was determined in this council that Grenoble should hold out to the last extremity. Another meeting took place on the same day, composed of officers of the 5th regiment, and of a company of engineers, who all solemnly engaged not to act in any way against the Emperor or those who accompanied him, three hundred of whom were of the battalion of his Guard at Elba.

The situation of Marchand was critical; the soldiers declared that they would not oppose the Emperor; everything seemed to threaten a rising, and the murmurs of a discontented population were already heard. M. Fourrier (the Prefect) put forth an official proclamation, announcing the arrival of Bonaparte, which the people received with cries of contempt; it produced, indeed, a very droll effect, for it occasioned the mass to declare in favor of the Emperor. What completed the destruction of the Royalist party was the call made to the GENTLEMEN; for among such as could bear arms there were not two who were not devoted to the Emperor, having served in the army since 1792.

A few weeks after the arrival of Louis XVII. Paris is said to have been inundated by a crowd of the old nobility, who filled the approaches of the Palace, and greatly injured the cause of the Bourbons. One morning five persons entered Tortoni's in a very stately manner, and placed themselves at the same table. They were all habited alike, in the complete costume of the old times.

They inquired for the bill of fare, and, looking disdainfully around them, appeared to pay no attention to the crowd, who were amusing themselves with the peculiarity of their dress and appearance; a conversation in the same spirit as their manners and dress accompanied their scanty meal, which was terminated by a characteristic song. The police, however, will not allow a jest at the expense of those in power, however ridiculous that power may be; and the five persons who had ventured on this burlesque were conducted to prison, where they remained many weeks — I believe I may say many months.

On leaving the prison of l'Abbaye they were ordered to ask pardon of the Duc d'Angoulême and the Duc de Berri, which they did. As they were leaving the Tuileries, M. Jacqueminot, one of the five offenders, and who is at present a General officer, met on the stairs a personage dressed precisely as he had been at the famous breakfast. He stopped him, and, taking him by the hand, said: "May I ask you if you have worn this dress long?"

"Yes, sir, very long," replied the other with an air of indignant surprise. "And has no mischief ever happened to you from wearing it?" said Jacqueminot, with a plaintive expression.

"Sir! sir! do you mean to insult me? No, certainly not — no mischief." "Ah, sir, you are very fortunate; I wore it but for two hours, and I have spent three months in prison for my frolic." These were so many blows leveled at the Royal authority.

A barrister of Grenoble offered to assassinate the Emperor; this was one scheme among many. Madame de Vaudé herself tells us, in her "Reminiscences," that she wished to go, like a new Judith, and slay this Holophernes. For this purpose she asked for neither dagger, nor pistol, nor cannon; she only required a post-chaise. But the person to whom she addressed herself was a man of honor and good sense; he looked upon her as insane, or as acting from other motives than those which she professed. The result of both these proposals was the same.

During this time the partisans of Napoleon were busily employed. Conferences were held at the house of M. Dumoulin; and, on the night of the 5th or 6th, Dr. Fournier, a rich hemp merchant of the Faubourg Saint Joseph, M. Risson, and many others, determined that every sacrifice both of person and property should be risked. On perceiving these decided manifestations the authorities fortified the gate of Beaune, at the entrance of the Faubourg Saint Joseph, through which the Emperor would have to pass, and thirty pieces of cannon were placed upon the ramparts; the soldiers of the 4th Regiment of Artillery received orders to stand in readiness on the batteries; they did so, and often did the inhabitants approach and shake them by the hand.

"He is coming," said they; "but what will you do? you will not oppose him; it is not in your nature." "We know what we have to do." In the meantime the Comte d'Artois and the Duc d'Orléans arrived at Lyons. They were entreated to hasten to Grenoble, and were assured that no engagement should take place with the troops of the USURPER before their arrival. Immediately after, orders were given to the artillery to fire on the Emperor as soon as he should appear on the road leading to the gate of Beaune. At this time Generals Marchand and Mouton-Duvernet were making careful search for Dr. Emery; but although he remained within the city he was undiscovered. Grenoble was a point of considerable importance for the Emperor, on account of its large depot of artillery.

While all was in agitation in the South, the King convoked the Chambers, dismissed Marshal Soult, the Minister of War; and substituted for him the Duc de Feltre, a man wholly unfit for this office. The Congress of Vienna, too, felt extreme alarm on hearing of Napoleon's journey. The discussions with which they were now fully occupied ceased at the voice which proclaimed the approach of Napoleon. Austria, France, and England were already leagued against Russia and Prussia. Talleyrand felt assured of the success of his intrigue. Had the Emperor been willing or able to wait for the dissolution of the Congress he might then have mounted his Throne.

Napoleon would then have had to contend only against internal enemies, whose numbers in a few months would have been greatly diminished.

Grenoble, while these deliberations were passing in it, presented a most extraordinary spectacle. All authority was at an end, for the people would acknowledge none. The troops kept within their barracks, while the whole population filled the square and streets through which Napoleon was expected to pass on the following day. In six days he had marched seventy-two leagues across a rough and mountainous country!

On the morning of the 7th of March a squadron of the 4th Hussars entered Grenoble from Vienne, and at noon the 7th Regiment of the Line, commanded by Labédoyère. This morning, at daybreak, Dumoulin quitted Grenoble. He started on horseback at a gallop, and passed behind some *gendarmes*, whose duty it was to prevent anyone from leaving the city. He rejoined the Emperor as he was leaving Lamure, a large town on the road from Grenoble to Marseilles. " *Vive l'Empereur!* " cried Dumoulin as he galloped past the advanced guard. " *Vive l'Empereur!* " they replied, and he leaped from his horse and ran to Napoleon.

" Who are you, young man ? " said the Emperor. " I am Dumoulin, Sire, coming to offer you my arm and fortune. It was I who last autumn ——» " Oh, I recollect; mount your horse again, and let us converse." Dumoulin was again in the saddle, when, after many questions, the Emperor inquired what effect his proclamations had had upon the people and soldiers. " That which your Majesty might expect," said Dumoulin; "they have produced the greatest enthusiasm." " The battalion sent out from Grenoble," said the Emperor, "joined me

as soon as they saw me. I had only to show myself;
my old soldiers soon recollected me."

The line of march was arranged in this manner. The
Emperor was preceded by four mounted chasseurs of his
Guard, and four Polish Lancers, who cleared the way.
Then came Napoleon, some paces before his attendants,
and having at his side only Generals Bertrand, Drouot,
and Cambronne.

At five or six paces distant were several officers, among
whom could be distinguished General Count Germanouski, Colonel of the Polish Lancers. A dozen chasseurs
and lancers followed, then the Emperor's Guard, a body
of a hundred horsemen, Poles and chasseurs; behind these
came the body of the army — a force of six hundred
men, increased by a battalion of the 5th and a company
of engineers.

Napoleon appeared absorbed in thought, for at Grenoble was to be determined his success or failure. They
were on the road from Lamure to Vizille. The Emperor
had advanced before his companions, and was slowly de-
scending the side of Laffray; he was in deep meditation. All at once he was struck by the appearance of a
group of young men who were advancing toward him.
He stopped his horse, and, smiling, said: " Who are
you, my children; and what would you say to me ? "

The young men looked at each other; then one of them,
chosen by his companions, advanced to the Emperor; the
expression of his countenance was amiable, and full of
intelligence. Napoleon extended his hand toward him; he
seized it, and kissed it with a sentiment of respect and delight; he wished to speak, but could only utter uncon-
nected words: " General! — Citizen! — Sire! "

This was Barginet himself, then a pupil at the Imperial
College at Grenoble. He was an estimable young man,
and possessed a heart truly French. He related this anecdote with a feeling which will be shared by all his countrymen. " You have something to say to me, my friend,"
said the Emperor; " speak without fear. Where do you
come from, and what would you have ? "

" We come from Grenoble, Sire; we are pupils of the Imperial School, and, hearing of your return, my companions
and myself wished to see you one day sooner, and to assure
you, Sire, that we are ready to die for you."

Napoleon was deeply affected by conduct so noble and so enthusiastic. " In devoting yourselves to me," said he, " you devote yourselves to France. But you are young to become soldiers. Do your parents know of your resolution ? " M. Barginet answered, a little embarrassed: " Sire, we set out without informing anyone." " That is not right — our first duty in society is to obey our parents — never forget that; at least," he added, smiling, " you will never again fail in this duty on a similar occasion. But come, fear nothing; tell me what they say of me in Grenoble ? "

This unexpected question produced on the young student, as he has since informed me, the effect of an electric shock. He answered that Grenoble and its neighborhood looked for him with the utmost anxiety and love; but that the people also expected from him liberal institutions, peace, and the total repeal of certain taxes, which were held in utter detestation. Louis XVIII. promised to abolish them, and his neglect of this promise was highly injurious to him.

Napoleon turned away, and did not immediately reply; at length he said: " The people are right to reckon upon me. I love them, and wish them to be happy. Their rights have been outraged for the last year; I will repair this evil. France has been the most splendid Empire of the world; it shall become the seat of liberty."

At this moment, on a sudden turn of the road, a pile of buildings presented themselves to his view, and Napoleon inquired what they were. " It is the Castle of Vizille, Sire, where in 1788 the States-General of Dauphiné proclaimed liberty." The Emperor then inquired particularly into the history of Dauphiné. This was a characteristic trait in Napoleon; he always conversed with those whom he met on subjects on which they were best informed.

And as this young student might have been expected to be better acquainted with the history of his own province than with any other subject, the Emperor led him to speak of it. He seemed much surprised on learning that Hannibal had passed over the same road where he now was two thousand years before. Hannibal was his hero, as is well known.

29

"I will stop at Vizille and pass the night there," said the Emperor, after a moment's hesitation. "No, Sire," said the youth. "Why so?" said Napoleon, astonished at his decided tone. "Grenoble is but three leagues distant, Sire; you have enemies there, and should face them tonight." "Who are my enemies at Grenoble?" said the Emperor, looking kindly on him. "I cannot name them, Sire; I can only put you on your guard." "How old are you, and where have you been educated?" "I am sixteen, Sire, and my education is one of the benefits that I have received from you. I am a public pupil of the school of Grenoble." "Do you understand mathematics?" "No, Sire." "What, then, do you know?" "I have studied literature and history." "Pooh; literature will not make a General officer. You must follow me to Paris, and you shall enter at Saint Cyr or Fontainebleau." "My parents are too poor to defray my expenses there." "I will take care of that. I am your father also; so that is settled. Adieu; when WE reach Paris you must remind the Minister of War of the promise that I have just made you." This promise was fulfilled: a decree of the 10th of April, 1815, named him as a public pupil at Saint Cyr or Fontainebleau, and a decision, dated a few days after, freed him from the payment of the fees required by the regulations.

I have mentioned the defection of the troops sent against the Emperor; I shall now give some particulars of this event. On the night of the 6th of March a battalion of the 5th Regiment of the Line, and a company of sappers, marched out toward Lamure. They were commanded by an aid-de-camp of General Marchand, and the most violent measures were enjoined on them. These troops met about forty or fifty grenadiers who had set out from Lamure for the purpose of clearing the road. The officers, not seeing Napoleon, would not allow the two bodies to approach. The grenadiers fell back to join the Emperor, and the others took up a position on a rising ground between Lamure and the lakes of Laffray.

On learning the resistance that his soldiers had met with, the Emperor felt uneasy; his fate was to be decided at Grenoble, or by the troops at that station. Of this he was well aware. The inhabitants of Lamure and the neighboring villages received the Emperor as he passed with every demonstration of joy; they did not even appear uneasy as to the issue of the struggle that was about to take place.

The Emperor rode a very small and spirited mountain pony, from which he rarely dismounted; but on seeing the troops that occupied the plain of Lamure he quitted his horse and advanced quickly toward them. The valley in which this important scene took place is wild and picturesque; it is, I think, called the Vale of Beaumont. Napoleon stood on a little hill which overlooked the plain filled with the troops sent against him. He had his grenadiers with him, but they carried their pieces under their left arms. When he appeared, a feeble voice ordered an advance — the soldiers stood still.

Then the Emperor, approaching them and unbuttoning his greatcoat, said in a loud voice: "Soldiers, I am your Emperor; do you not recollect me? If there is one among you who wishes to kill his General, here I am." "Vive l'Empereur!" shouted the soldiers, suddenly throwing down their muskets and running to him. The young aid-de-camp twice gave the order to fire upon the Emperor, but at the second time he was obliged to fly, for the soldiers would have fired upon him.

The Emperor was at this time superior to himself. He would not be the head of a party, the chief of a turbulent faction. He refused the services of the officers who came to join him, and who proposed returning to Grenoble and obliging the authorities to open the gates to him. The inhabitants of Mateline also offered to rise en masse in his favor; but he refused both. He wished to be a SOVEREIGN, only depending upon the love of his people and of the army.

Shortly after this memorable event, Napoleon, finding himself thirsty, as he passed through the village of Laffray, entered the dwelling of an old woman, who, not recognizing him, spoke of him with the greatest affection. "Could I but see him," said she, "before I die, to kiss his hand and entreat him to relieve us from the droits réunis."

On going away the Emperor discovered himself to her, and gave her two or three Napoleons. "Now," said the old woman, "like Simeon, I can die, for I HAVE SEEN THE LORD."

Thus was he beloved by France, and these good and simple-minded peasants saw in him the glory of their country, and this glory was their own.

CHAPTER XLIV.

Arrival of the Emperor at Vizille—"What Have You There, Sir Priest?"—The White Riband—The Marseillaise and the Chant du Départ—The Approach of the Troops—7th Regiment of the Line —Labédoyère Embraced by the Emperor—History of the 7th—The Eagle Concealed in a Drum—Triumphal March—The Aid-de-Camp Always for Firing—New Obstruction—Dr. Emery—Gates of Grenoble Burst Open—Novel Species of Homage to be Offered at the Feet of an Emperor—Inn Kept by One of the Veterans of Egypt —Knight of the Legion of Honor and Brevet Officer—M. Dumoulin in 1830—Lafayette Twice Fatal to the Imperial Dynasty and the Destinies of France—M. Champollion Figeac—Plan for Reaching Paris without Firing a Gun—Diplomacy—Presentation of the Bishop and Curés of the Four Parishes of Grenoble—The Imperial Court —Rejoicings—Kiss on Both Cheeks—A Makeshift Tricolor— Speech of a Free and Brave Man—Departure from Grenoble.

THE Emperor was still at some distance from Vizille when the sound of the bells, blended with the confused murmur of its whole population coming out to meet him, told him of his welcome. Scarcely, indeed, had he reached the bridge than he was surrounded by a crowd, wild with joy, who strewed on his path a shower of violets and mountain hyacinths.

"Long live the Emperor!" was the universal shout. "Down with the *calotte!*" "What's that they say?" he asked. "They cry: 'Down with the priests!'" was Dumoulin's answer. "But this is not the fitting spot, my friends, to show our love to his Majesty; wait till we reach Grenoble!" "Grenoble!" exclaimed the troop; "on to Grenoble!"

In this manner Napoleon passed through Vizille in the midst of a crowd intoxicated with zeal for him. When in front of the church he perceived a man dressed in black, who was vociferating like a madman, and crying: "Long live the Emperor! long live the great Napoleon!"

This was the *Curé*. The Emperor stopped before him.
"Good-day, sir," he said; "I am obliged to you. But,
pray, M. l'Abbé, what have you there?" and pointed to
a small white ribbon. "Ah, Sire, your pardon; IT IS
NOTHING," replied the *Curé*, quite confused, and thrusting
his lily-white ribbon in his pocket. However, there arose
from the crowd that fierce buzz which is, as it were, the
voice of the people. The poor priest turned pale and
looked at Napoleon. The Emperor held out his hand,
which the *Curè* kissed with transport, exclaiming: "*Vive
l'Empereur!*"

The whole population of Vizille followed the Emperor,
and at this moment there were more than six thousand
of the country people around him. Almost all the young
men of this town, in particular, wore tricolored ribbons
in their hats, and preceded the Emperor singing the
Marseillaise and the *Chant du Départ*. Every house was
thrown open, and the soldiers, who were overcome with
fatigue, entered to refresh themselves, if but for a moment. There was something antique and beautiful, like
the traditions of the olden times, in these popular rejoicings and this universal demonstration of the love of
a free nation.

In this mode they reached the little village of Brié.
between Grenoble and Vizille, about five in the evening,
when suddenly the Emperor stopped, and, looking through
his glass, exclaimed: "I am not mistaken; here are the
troops. Ha! ha! it looks at if they were coming to give
us battle!"

Dumoulin, who, from residing at Grenoble, was well
acquainted with the country and the troops of the garrison, spurred on his horse to reconnoiter. After some
minutes he returned with the news of his having encountered M. de Launay, Adjutant-Major of the 7th Regiment, who had been sent forward by Labédoyère to
apprise the Emperor that he was on his march to join
him.

At that moment the soldiers of the 7th came up, running, and in the greatest disorder. It had been impossible to keep them in their ranks—they shouted, they
wept! The Emperor was much affected. "Where is the
Colonel?" he said. "Ah, Sire, do I see you once more?"
exclaimed the noble young man, taking hold of Napoleon's

stirrup; his fine face was radiant with joy, and his eyes filled with tears. "Come to my arms, *mon cher enfant*," cried the Emperor, who embraced him like a brother. "But my eagle?" Labédoyère presented it to him. Napoleon took it, gazed upon it, twice kissed it; two tears fell upon this emblem of our glory, thus sanctified by this noble baptism.

Here it becomes necessary to relate the remarkable events which had preceded this arrival of the 7th Regiment of the Line. I have spoken of the agitation which prevailed at Grenoble, and of the ill will of the Prefect, of General Marchand, and even of M. Renauldon, the Mayor of the town, who controlled nothing, and therefore was good for nothing.

Everything displayed a sinister aspect, as soon as the soldiers appeared although with sadness, to prepare for the execution of their orders. Nevertheless, they feared, at the Prefecture, that the troops would not fire, and, above all, there was a dread of civil war and its terrible scenes. In the midst of this agitation, the beat of a drum was heard on Monday, March 7th, about noon, and directly after a regiment was seen to march through the town, and draw up in order of battle on the *Grande Place*.

This was the 7th which had come from Chambéry; it was the finest regiment in France, whose Colonel was one of the bravest and most singularly handsome men in the army. Labédoyère at this epoch was scarcely thirty years of age, and as handsome as Renaud. His fair hair hung in clusters over his head, and gave an imposing effect to his ample and commanding brow; his eyes were blue, yet brilliant and full of fire; he was elegantly made, tall, active, and of the noblest presence. His devotion to the Emperor was a worship.

On reaching the *Grande Place*, Labédoyère perceived that General de Villiers, Commander of the Department, had followed him; he was the bearer of orders from General Marchand. Labédoyère listened to them, and at first did not answer a word. While the General was speaking, murmurs arose from the ranks, and already everything presaged the scene about to follow. Suddenly their Colonel commanded silence, and cried with a loud voice:

"Soldiers, I am ordered to lead you to battle against your Emperor. Soldiers, I resign my command, and am no longer your Colonel. I never will conduct you on the road of dishonor!" Cries immediately rose on every side of "No! no!" "Long live our Colonel!" "*Vive l'Empereur!*" "Lead on, Colonel!" "You have my thanks," exclaimed Labédoyère; "but I cannot command you. The Emperor received my first oath; he claims me, and I must repair to him. Soldiers, my dear comrades, you can remain under your flag; for me, I return to him under whom I have always fought. Adieu! I hasten to the national flag — adieu!"

The cries of "*Vive l'Empereur!*" became enthusiastic; the ranks were broken, the Colonel surrounded. "Colonel," exclaimed an officer, "you cannot forsake men who love you — lead them to the Emperor!" "Yes, yes!" was the cry — "to the Emperor! to the Emperor! *Vive notre Colonel!*"

Labédoyère looked at them with emotion. Unfortunate young man! Heaven owed him these few hours of happiness as a counterpoise for the misfortunes in store for him. "Then, you will have it so, my friends!" he exclaimed; "well, forward! LET HIM WHO LOVES ME FOLLOW ME!" "We will all go!" cried an old soldier; "and had you led us against the Emperor, we would not have followed you. Colonel, look here! — Drummer!"

Instantly the drummer tore open his drum, and drew from it the eagle of the 7th, which had been thus preserved. He placed it in the hands of the Colonel, who took it and kissed it with respectful joy. At the same moment the white flag was torn and trampled under foot, both by townsmen and soldiers; and immediately, as if by the stroke of an enchanter's wand, each soldier had a tricolored cockade in his cap. The regiment forthwith began its march, drums beating, the band in front, and in quick time. More than six thousand persons left the town with them; it was a general madness.

Napoleon arrived before Grenoble on March 7th, at six in the evening. He had about fifteen thousand persons with him. The gates were closed, and the greatest confusion prevailed in the town. After the departure of the 7th, General Marchand held a review, harangued the soldiers, and endeavored to raise the shout "*Vive le Roi!*" The soldiers had remained dull and gloomy, and had not even lifted their eyes toward their leaders.

General Marchand called a Council of War, but no resolution was agreed upon, and the confusion increased at the approach of evening with the news of the Emperor's marching upon Grenoble. At the same time word was brought that the soldiers and officers of the 5th, who were confined to their barracks, were escaping through the windows, and hurrying along the ramparts to join the Emperor.

It was at this moment that Napoleon entered the Faubourg Saint Joseph, and arrived at the entrance called the Beaune Gate, which is separated from the road by a ditch twenty-five feet in width. The guard had just been withdrawn, and as the inhabitants were thronging over the wooden bridge it could not be destroyed. Dr. Emery, who had until now remained actively employed, though concealed in Grenoble, came forth and made himself known to the Emperor, who pulled him by the ear to testify his joy at seeing him.

"We have waited for you with impatience, Sire," said M. Emery. "Well," exclaimed one of the Emperor's suite, "we must force the gate." "No, no!" cried Napoleon, who discovered no uneasiness at the delay, but walked with folded arms and tranquil looks in the midst of the admiring multitudes who had followed him so far from their homes. It was night; the soldiers and others lighted a quantity of torches they had purchased in the Faubourg. A cry was heard from the ramparts: "They are going to fire!" and, indeed, the young aid-de-camp of General Marchand was on the ramparts endeavoring to excite the soldiers. At last, exasperated at the inactivity of the troops, he seized a match, and was about to fire a gun, when a woman threw herself upon him, and, wresting the match from him, exclaimed:

"Wretch, what are you about to do? Know ye not that our husbands and sons are with the Emperor? Besides, we will have the Emperor — *Vive l'Empereur!*" On this cry the name of the Emperor burst from a thousand tongues. However, so close was the Emperor to the battery, that M. Emery besought him to withdraw. "Come, come," said Napoleon, "what do you suppose will

happen to me? A BULLET MAY KILL, BUT DOES NOT HURT."
(His very words, which have been religiously preserved.)

At last it was known that General Marchand had
quitted Grenoble and taken away the keys of the town —
a poor revenge in so great a conjuncture. Immediately
the inhabitants dashed open the gate of Beaune and saw
a glorious spectacle. Thirty thousand persons lined the
streets and the *Grande Place;* every house was illuminated, and the Emperor never experienced such a reception, even when at the height of his power.

Each of the townsmen gave a billet to a soldier, for
they would not allow anyone to invite two; all wished
to share in what they called the festival of their city.
The Emperor refused to repair to the Prefecture; but,
recollecting that one of his veterans of Egypt kept an
inn at Grenoble, he insisted on going to the Three Dolphins, and scarcely was he there than a deputation from
the people was introduced.

"Sire," said the spokesman, "we obeyed you when you
ordered us not to burst open the gates of our city, but
if you will deign to turn to the window, your Majesty
will perceive those very gates which we now lay at your
feet, to prove that we did not take any part in the unworthy resistance that has been offered you." And,
throwing open the window, he pointed to the two gates,
which were lying before the inn.

The Emperor smiled at these testimonies of profound
affection, when more violent cries than ever of *"Vive
l'Empereur!"* seeming to proceed from twenty thousand
men, were heard. This was from a battalion of the 5th
which had forcibly returned to the city, led by Captain
Pelaprat, and crying: *"Vive l'Empereur!* DOWN WITH
THE BOURBONS!"

Dumoulin and Emery, who had hitherto taken no
rest, had just thrown themselves on a bed, when a friend
came to summon the former to the Emperor. He rose,
and repaired to the Three Dolphins. He was introduced
by the Grand-Marshal, and the Emperor said, on seeing
him: "I wish to testify to you, M. Dumoulin, my satisfaction at your noble conduct; you are a member of the
Legion of Honor — you will follow me to Paris." "Ah,
Sire, how can I acknowledge your kindness; and in what
quality?"

"Brevet officer.   Come with me; my fortune will be yours; I attach you to my person." And, tapping him on the shoulder as he was taking leave, "Wait," he said (opening a writing desk, he took a cross out of it); "take this, and to-morrow, early, begin your office near my person.   Grand-Marshal, here is a new officer of my Household," he said, pulling the ear of the newly-made knight of the Legion of Honor.   Thus did this man create his *séides*, and make himself adored.

On leaving the room where the Emperor was, M. Dumoulin met M. Champollion Figeac, afterward keeper of the manuscripts in the Royal Library at Paris, and brother of the famous Champollion.   He was the second of the friends to whom the secret of the voyage from Elba had been intrusted.   He was going to undertake the office of secretary — a post which he filled during the eight-and-forty hours the Emperor sojourned at Grenoble.

The Emperor knew nothing of him, but, having asked Dumoulin for a SURE man, the latter had recommended M. Champollion, who was devoted.   I adduce this circumstance merely for the sake of still showing Napoleon in a new light.   After thanking M. Champollion, he spoke to him of Egypt, and seemed to forget Grenoble, the island of Elba, and even Paris; he talked of his beloved Egypt, of the fourteen dynasties of the Lagides shut up in the Pyramids, of the Arab people, of the Isthmus of Suez.

"What say they of the great works which I have directed respecting the translation of the Chinese dictionary, and the new French translation of Strabo? When I shall arrive at Paris I will require an account of these literary labors." The conversation was thus prolonged until one o'clock in the morning.   "Go to bed," said the Emperor to M. Champollion, "and return to-morrow as early as you can."

Next day, the 8th of March, at six o'clock in the morning, M. Champollion was in the bedchamber of the Emperor.   He had risen an hour previously, and awaited him.   "To work," said he.   At half-past eight an officer arrived, who came from Lyons in the name of General Brayer.   He belonged to the General's Staff, was named Molien de Saint Yon, and came to assure the Emperor of the devotion of General Brayer.

"Return immediately," said Napoleon, "and assure Brayer of my friendship." M. Molien assured the Emperor of the enthusiasm of the Lyonnais. Napoleon kept him a short time, and gave him a number of instructions. "Above all things," said he on parting, "tell Brayer that I will reach Paris without firing a shot."

From the morning of the 8th the Emperor was longed for and expected by the whole city; but he occupied himself meanwhile with important cares. "M. Fourrier has done justice to himself," said Napoleon, "in quitting Grenoble. But whom can I nominate Prefect?" A voice named M. Savoie Rollin, formerly Prefect of Rouen. "Is Savoie Rollin here?" cried the Emperor. "And your National Guard — it should be numerous. But he who commanded it yesterday for the Comte de Lille cannot command it now. Mention the most worthy citizen of your town," added he, turning toward the inhabitants of Grenoble.

On seeking M. Savoie Rollin, he was found to be in the country. They offered to M. Alphonse Perrier or M. Adolphe (I am not sure which but it was a brother of the Minister) the command of the National Guard; but, as he was a friend of the Comte de Montal, he objected to supersede him.

They offered to M. Didier, Sub-Prefect of the Isère, the vacant post of Prefect: he was a timid man, and refused. "Well," said the Emperor, "a Councilor of the Prefecture can perform the functions of Prefect." And to command the National Guard he named an old major of the Imperial army.

It was at Grenoble also, on the 8th of March, that Napoleon dictated to M. Champollion his letter to the Emperor of Austria. As soon as the Emperor was visible, M. Simon, the Bishop, presented himself at the head of his Chapter and of the four *Curés* of the city of Grenoble. He had, in fact, all his clergy, with the exception of his Vicar-General, M. Bouchard. A curious incident took place at this audience.

As the Bishop presented the *Curés* to the Emperor, designating them by their proper names, at the moment when he said: "I have the honor to present to your Majesty M. de la Grez——" "Ah! it is you, M. le Curé," said Napoleon, "who spoke so injuriously of me every Sunday in your sermons to the cookmaids." "Ah! *Mon Dieu!*" answered the troubled ecclesiastic, "I assure you, Sire——" "Oh, I know you are a good priest! go on, if it amuses you. I permit liberty of worship." The poor *Curé* remained stupefied. Napoleon, seeing him so unhappy, said: "Come, think no more of it. Only be kind and charitable toward all. That is the true law of Jesus Christ."

The judges were also announced. The Emperor was marvelously great in this audience. He talked jurisprudence like the most skillful among them, and, above all, mentioned the necessity of reforming several ill-constructed laws. "I have long discussed in the Council of State," said he, "the necessity of repairing the civil code as well as the criminal. But what could I do? I had always to struggle against men who spoke only of giving power to the strong arm." His ideas were lucid, powerful, just, and precise.

"We shall, I trust," pursued he, "find ourselves in more peaceable circumstances, and, working together, we shall do good work." But the most touching thing was to see the Emperor approached by the different officers. They seemed as if they had recovered a brother; they wept tears of joy, and trembled in speaking to him. "The Bourbons repudiated your glories," said Napoleon. "In so doing they not only committed a fault, but inflicted an insult on France."

After giving these audiences the Emperor descended at length to pass in review the garrison, consisting of the 5th and 7th Regiments of the Line, some squadrons of the 4th Hussars, some engineers, and two companies of Artillery, all in good order, together with 1,500 of the National Guard. He was carried on the shoulders of the people. A young girl approached him with a laurel branch in her hand, reciting some verses.

"What can I do for you, my pretty girl?" said the Emperor. The maiden blushed; then, lifting her eyes to Napoleon, answered: "I have nothing to ask of your Majesty; but you would render me very happy by embracing me." The Emperor kissed her. "I embrace in you all the ladies of Grenoble," said he aloud, turning his head to either side with a charming smile.

As he was advancing toward the place of the review, it was discovered that there was no tricolored flag. On the instant Dumoulin ran into a linen draper's shop and selecting the proper colors — white, red, and blue — he stitched them together, and in a few minutes the flag was ready. Enthusiastic plaudits followed, and nothing could describe the delirium spread over the whole assembly when the military music struck up the *Marseillaise* hymn. After the review, a deputation of respectable citizens presented themselves bearing an address to be offered to the Emperor. It was in the first instance received by Marshal Bertrand, who, having looked over it, observed that there was one line too strongly put, which it would be necessary to suppress.

" The Emperor," said he, " with all his goodness, could not accord so much as you would here have him promise." " Monsieur," replied M. Boissonet, an advocate and a man of talent and energy, " if we drive away these Bourbons, whom foreigners have imposed on us, it is liberty that we ask. We doubt not of possessing it with the Emperor; but we intend also to have it WITHOUT him: we await, sir, your announcing us to his Majesty." This language, from a man of liberal opinions and strong feelings, should have made Napoleon aware that liberty had been only compromised by him; and his reflections might have still further impressed on him the proper course to take on his return to the country.

On the 8th of March, at four o'clock in the evening, Napoleon quitted Grenoble with all his staff, and slept at Bourgoin, a large town ten leagues distant. From the Gulf of San Juan to Grenoble, he had constantly traveled either on horseback or on foot. At the latter place he purchased a carriage. Next morning, on approaching Lyons, the Emperor ordered Colonel Germanouski to take with him six men and push a reconnaissance on to La Guillotière.

Scarcely had they perceived the Polish Lancers, when the entire population hastened to present themselves before the Emperor. The enthusiasm that prevailed during two days, was, indeed, greater than that at Grenoble. At Saint Denis de Brou, two stages before Lyons, Napoleon encountered the population of that city. Marshal

Soult had not forescen this when he said to the King on the 5th of March: "Bonaparte will remain this year in Dauphiné, and next year he will attempt to take Bourgoin."

CHAPTER XLV.

Approach to Lyons — The Old Farrier, Mayor, and Orator — Appearance of Resistance — Marshal Macdonald — The Comte d'Artois at Lyons — Napoleon Enters Lyons — His Address to the National Guard, and to the Lyonnais — The Duc d'Orléans Defeated by the Emperor's Troops at Bourgoin — M. de Blacas — Sitting of the Chamber of Deputies — Oath of the Princes to the Constitutional Charter — M. Dandre — Departure of Louis XVIII. — Melancholy Impressions — Arrival of the Emperor in Paris — His Reception by the People — Secret Influence of Fouché — Sinister Presentiments — The French Marshals of 1815 — Waterloo — Conclusion.

NAPOLEON disembarked in the Gulf of San Juan on the 1st of March with nine hundred men. It was on the 9th of the same month that he entered Lyons with eight thousand men and thirty pieces of cannon. The road from Grenoble to Lyons is studded with villages, or rather small wealthy towns, the entire population of which surrounded the open carriage in which the Emperor traveled, and formed an enthusiastic *cortége*.

It was during the journey from Grenoble to Lyons, and not on his road from Cannes to Grenoble, that he was accosted by a respectable old man, who was at once the farrier, Mayor, and orator of his village. He and all the inhabitants of his district descended from their mountains, and presented themselves to the Emperor. On seeing this old man, his head covered with snowy hair, and his loins bound with a tricolored sash,* while his leather apron had not been laid aside, Napoleon stopped his carriage, and beckoned him to approach.

"Sire," said the aged spokesman, "you have re-entered France, and are proceeding to Paris! When you shall arrive there, forget not those who have opened to you

* The Mayors in France wear a sash as the insignia of office; the color designates the Government in power.

the road. They are freemen, and determined to be so.
We will have neither priests nor foreigners for our masters. We are ready to give you all you ask; but you
must preserve our rights in their full integrity; recollect
that we are poor, and are your children. Adieu, Sire!
May God guide and protect you! Remember that you
represent the people." This was an harangue very different from that of M. de Fontanes. Napoleon was silent
at first; but after awhile he replied:
"Yes, I will never forget you, people of Dauphiné.
You have recalled to my mind all those grand and noble
sentiments which, twenty years ago, made me designate
France as the GREAT NATION. She is so still, and will
always be so. As to you, Mr. Mayor," said he to the old
farrier, "you have spoken to my soul! Give me your
hand." Then, suddenly, he leaped from his carriage, and
embraced the old farrier heartily. I give this fact from
the testimony of an eyewitness, who told me that when
the Emperor re-entered his carriage he spoke to no one,
but remained in a profound reverie.

At Bourgoin the Emperor perceived the first marks
of serious resistance he would have to encounter. The
Comte d'Artois had arrived at Lyons, the second city in
the kingdom. Macdonald, who commanded the troops,
loved not the Emperor, and therefore nothing was to be
expected from him. He was of the class of those Republican generals who, for a single warlike act, had acquired a reputation which they had failed to maintain.
He was not, in fact, worthy to be the brother-in-arms of
Napoleon, and he cherished a sentiment of fierce revenge
against the Emperor because he had been only made a
marshal in 1809.

I have heard that when this officer returned from his
audience of Louis XVIII. he expressed regret at going
to fight the Emperor. I would believe this, but cannot.
His influence with the troops was but slight. His name
had, indeed, a little éclat, but it was of no avail in opposition to that of Napoleon. This was evident at a review which took place in presence of the Comte d'Artois.
The 13th Regiment of Dragoons, at that period recently
returned from Spain, was composed of old soldiers. The
Colonel, interrogated first by the Marshal and then by
the Prince, replied: "Monseigneur, I will shed my

blood for the cause of your Royal Highness;" and, drawing his saber, he shouted: *"Vive le Roi!"* No voice echoed him. The regiment remained dull and stern.

The Prince then made a last effort; he approached a subaltern whose breast was adorned with the eagle. "Give me your hand, my brave comrade," said the Comte d'Artois, "and shout with me *'Vive le Roi!'*" "No, Monseigneur," firmly but respectfully answered the veteran; "I honor your Royal Highness, but I cannot join in your cry. Mine is: *'Vive l'Empereur!'*" And at the same instant the whole regiment repeated this name, so cherished, so beloved. The Prince at once retreated, and throwing himself into his carriage, exclaimed: "All is lost!"

And the chariot of the King's brother was not escorted to the gates of the town even by one of the yeomanry of the National Guard of Lyons. The 13th Regiment, although it had refused to join the Comte d'Artois, was very indignant at this conduct, and furnished a small escort, which was joined by a single mounted National Guard; and I was assured at the time — I know not with what truth — that the Emperor bestowed on this young man the cross of the Legion of Honor.

While the unfortunate Prince fled before the Emperor, Marshal Macdonald occupied the bridge of La Guillotière; and there, with two battalions of infantry, made preparations to dispute the Emperor's passage; but as soon as his men perceived the red cloaks of the 4th Hussar Regiment, they raised one unanimous cry of *"Vive l'Empereur!"*

I own I should like to have seen the Marshal's physiognomy on hearing these cries, and when, a few minutes after, the Emperor himself traversed this bridge. He awaited his Majesty's approach, and they conversed together for a few minutes.* Napoleon then bade him a

---

*We have it, however, upon the authority of the Duke of Tarentum himself that no interview took place with Napoleon either at Lyons or in Paris in 1815. After 1814 he never saw the Emperor again.

After describing the disorganized and disaffected condition of Lyons in 1815, Marshal Macdonald says that as he and his staff approached the Guillotière bridge, Napoleon's Advance Guard appeared at the other end: "At this sight officers and soldiers mingled their cheers with the shouts of the populace; shakos were waved on bayonets in friendly adieu. The Marshal immediately took the road to Paris, and Napoleon entered Lyons without any obstacle.

What he said to the mounted National Guard of Lyons is well known. When they presented themselves, he addressed them as follows: " The original institution of the National Guard does not permit it to become cavalry. You have, besides, behaved ill to the Comte d'Artois: in his misfortune you have abandoned him. I will not accept your services." *

But it is not thus he spoke to his good city of Lyons at large. The address he uttered on quitting it was almost wholly written by himself, and merits to be exactly copied. It shows the Ossianic turn of his mind, and affords good materials for estimating him. " Lyonnais! at the moment of quitting your town to repair to my capital I feel that it behooves me to make known to you the sentiments with which you have inspired me. You have always occupied a first place in my affections. Upon the throne, and in exile, you have always shown toward me the same sentiments. The elevated character by which you are distinguished, merits, indeed, all my esteem. In more tranquil moments I shall return and occupy myself respecting your city and its manufactures. People of Lyons, I love you!"

In this last simple phrase, placed as the termination of a speech equally simple, might be recognized a seal of affection between the Sovereign and his people. The Lyonnais were in a delirium of joy the day the speech was delivered.

I confess I cannot comprehend what the Ministry of M. de Blacas proposed by making an officer of the *guard-du-corps* appear at the balcony of the Tuileries, and announce officially that the Duc d'Orléans had completely defeated the Emperor in the environs of Bour-

token of delight; the feeble barricades were thrown down; everyone pressed forward to welcome the new arrivals to the town. From that instant all was lost. We made our way back and remounted our horses; there was no time to lose." He then relates the difficulties he experienced in regaining the Bourbonnais highroad, and makes no allusion to having even seen Napoleon. "Recollections of Marshal Macdonald," pp. 378-381 (Bentley, 1893).

* Napoleon, it has often been observed, had a very peculiar faculty of replying in energetic terms, and was seldom known to hesitate.

30

goin. I might amuse myself here by relating the
several conversations, full of boasting, which some persons of the Royal cause held with me after the publication of this verbal bulletin. But those events were too
serious and grave. Alas! the enchantment was likewise
too short! Next day came couriers from Monsieur, stating the real condition of things.

Louis XVIII. was not without talents for government;
but he was unequal to these circumstances; and undoubtedly, but for the Allied Powers, would have lost
his throne once more, never to regain it. His infatuation
in employing M. de Blacas, a country squire, turned into
a First Gentleman of the Court, was excessive. The impertinence of this man weighed on France as a plague,
despised as he was by all the Allied Sovereigns, who
saw in him nothing but a pernicious favorite of the Court.
He had no idea of the direction of public opinion in
this crisis, and had conducted the monarchy to the brink
of a precipice, while his creatures plied him with incense and flattery, which effectually turned his weak head.
Had Louis XVIII. but known what the Allied Princes
said of him, or even seen them shrug their shoulders in
pity ! M. de Blacas was no doubt very learned in some
points; but what availed all his knowledge of the history
of the Lower Empire, since he was ignorant of that of
yesterday as regarded his own country ? In the twelve
months which preceded Napoleon's return I can trace
nothing but an odious system of fraud and deception.

Truth was never made manifest to the King until
Napoleon arrived at Fontainebleau. Neither had any
measures been taken to insure the escape of the Royal
Family although from the 15th of March the authorities
were aware of the rapid advance of the Emperor. Was
this the result of heedlessness or of treason ? In truth,
one knows not what name to give it.

I must here describe the scene, the memory of which
will never fade from the minds of those who witnessed
it. I allude to the sitting of the Chamber of Deputies
on the 18th and 19th of March. The King made a
speech, a good one, doubtless; but nothing took effect
like the exclamation of the Comte d'Artois: " Sire," cried
he, " permit that I unite my voice, and that of all your
family, with your own. Yes, Sire, it is in the name of

honor that we swear fidelity to your Majesty and to the Constitutional Charter, which secures the happiness of the French!» The Duc de Berri, the Duc d'Orléans, and the Prince de Condé, all exclaimed: "We swear it!" It is difficult for anyone but a witness of this remarkable scene to have a just idea of it.

They had talked of defending Paris with a *corps d' armée* commanded by the Duc de Berri; but this was a silly thought. In fact, if one could have laughed at all just then, it would have been at the men who surrounded Louis XVIII. The most absurd was M. Dandre, Prefect of Police, who was altogether a most singular personage. When he was at length convinced of what everybody else had known long before, namely, that Bonaparte had disembarked in France, he did nothing but repeat the fact. "How!" said he, rubbing his hands, "has he DARED to come here? But so much the better; they will shoot him!"

The Court was in 1815, as it had been in 1791, wrapped in complete blindness. M. de Blacas sought to persuade the King that Bonaparte's disembarkation was to his great advantage. Louis XVIII. said himself to an individual of my family who was greatly in his confidence: "This poor Blacas brought to my mind Olivarès announcing to Philip IV. the loss of Portugal, when he spoke to me of the good I should derive from the arrival of Bonaparte."

About midnight, on the 19th of March, Louis XVIII. quitted the *château* of the Tuileries, which he now inhabited after an exile of twenty-three years. He perhaps suffered at this moment more than formerly, for he was about to recommence a life of misfortune, and courage is exhausted by grief. He knew also the extent of the evil that his departure might occasion — the melancholy result of emigration was evident in 1791 — of that court spirit which had already produced such profound misfortunes, and was now in action again.

The staircases, the courts, the avenues of the *château* were crowded with persons, all silent and in consternation. At the moment when his carriage, drawn by eight horses, drew up, every eye was turned toward the top of the grand staircase. The King descended slowly, for his infirmities pressed the more heavily on him in this agonizing hour. This departure of a decrepit Prince in the middle of the night, quitting his capital as a fugitive, could not be otherwise than affecting.*

Twenty-four hours had not intervened ere this Palace witnessed a scene of a very different nature — the return of the Emperor. He had arrived on the eve at Fontainebleau with his brave grenadiers; and, upon hearing of the departure of the Bourbons, he rightly perceived that there must be no interregnum. He therefore hastened forward, desirous of reaching the Capital without any delay; but the crowd assembled on the road impeded him at every step, and it was not till nine o'clock P. M. that he entered Paris.

What must have been his emotions on passing under the triumphal arch of the Tuileries — on finding himself borne thither by that faithful army which now conducted him, through the shades of night, to this Royal residence so long his own?

But on arriving at Paris, Napoleon found, as has been remarked, a great difference as contrasted with the enthusiasm of Lyons and Dauphiné. The metropolis was, in fact, surprised. Paris is not like another city; it contains a swarming population, who know not how to direct their own emotions. And although its population thronged to behold Napoleon, the city presented on the evening of the 20th of March a *triste* and sullen aspect.

The theaters were shut; and when the Emperor reached the gates of the Tuileries he found, indeed, an immense crowd; but the absence of many faces he expected to see was remarked by him with the greater bitterness, as the enthusiasm of the provinces had led him to anticipate very different things. The fact is that Paris was secretly influenced by the faction at whose head was Fouché.

I have mentioned the strange circumstance that from fifty to sixty letters arrived at Grenoble on the morning of the 5th of March with the Paris postmark. The Em-

* The Court Newsman had a difficult task to perform in drawing up his chronicle at this time. The "*Moniteur*" contains on the same day the following announcement:

"The King and the Princes left in the night.

"His Majesty the Emperor arrived this evening at eight o'clock at his Palace of the Tuileries."

The different tone of respect with which the DEPARTING monarch is treated will be noticed.

peror declared he had no knowledge of these letters. Who was at work, then ? It has been said that the Duke of Otranto was an agent for the Duc d'Orléans. I believe this to be probable enough; but it matters not. The vicinity of Murat, who came within twenty leagues: of Paris, also excites in me strange suspicions. The Duke of Otranto stood well with the Queen of Naples — an intriguing woman, to whom France was always a point of aim and hope; she had then lost all.

However this might be, the state of Paris was throughout forced and unnatural. The very spirit of change seemed attached to the walls of the Tuileries; and Napoleon was subject to its influence when, on the 20th of March, he again crossed the threshold of the Palace — on the 20th of March, that day which had, in the same mansion, witnessed Fortune's last smile upon him at the birth of the King of Rome. He desired to consecrate that event by a miraculous return. But by what thoughts was that return accompanied!

He perceived on the instant, unhappy man! that fate had reversed his chances; for that infant which had spread peace and hope throughout his immense capital — the joy of whose population reverberated round his throne, and seemed calculated to sustain it — that infant was no longer in his power. Who can divine what were the reflections which occupied the great soul of Napoleon when he placed his hand on the marble balustrade of that staircase which, but a few months before, so many Kings had ascended and descended simply as his courtiers? Doubtless he imagined he should again see them crouch before him. His mistake was in forgetting that it was the people alone who had borne him on their arms to the Tuileries.

What were the marshals doing all this time ? One of them (Marshal Ney) said to Louis XVIII.: "Sire, I will bring him to you like a wild beast in an iron cage." Another (Marshal Soult) issued a proclamation in which he designated Bonaparte a VILLAIN; while a third (either Macdonald or Mortier) made an arrangement to invest his property in an enemy's country; and these were the men who should have made for him a rampart with their bodies.

It was then that Napoleon, destitute of all the aid he should have received from these individuals (brave, doubtless, in themselves, but ILLUSTRIOUS only through him), re-entered on the 20th of March the *château* of the Tuileries, while the fire lighted on the previous evening for the use of Louis XVIII. still burned in the principal kitchen. Napoleon did not well comprehend his position; it was new to him, and he should therefore have employed new assistants. He believed the marshals less fickle, and regretted HIS OWN MEN, as he termed them. But these men were no longer HIS—they acted for THEMSELVES—and his error concerning them ruined him.*

The 20th of March was perhaps the most important day in the life of Napoleon. It MIGHT have been a day of regeneration both for him and France; it WAS a day fatal to both. Thus I regard the 20th of March, 1815, as the termination of the grand military and political existence of Napoleon Bonaparte. Here we must stop, for his last great day was accomplished! WATERLOO was the tomb of all that had escaped the saber of the Cossacks and the cannon of the Austrians and Russians.

The 20th of March, then, is the day whereon, in these "Memoirs," I quit Napoleon. I have conducted him, as it were, almost from his cradle to mature age, through the world, which rang with his marvelous deeds, and unto this day, when, more surprising than ever, he re-entered alone, at the head of a few brave men, the palace conquered by his sword, whence he issued to confront entire Europe armed against him.

Let us pause awhile on the recollection of so many great actions—so many brilliant achievements. Even yet we may bow before a destiny unlike any other. Napoleon was to France, from 1795 to 1814, a tutelary Providence—a light which will shine during ages to come. Under gilded ceilings or roofs of thatch this truth will always be proclaimed and recognized; and I am happy that my name should be attached to this relation of events designed to perpetuate the memory of that epoch.

*For a narrative of the "Hundred Days," and of the subsequent events of Napoleon's life, a reference can be made to the fourth volume of Bourrienne's "Memoirs of Bonaparte."

THE END.

APPENDIX

APPENDIX

CONTEMPORARY RULERS

FRANCE.—1774, Louis XVI. 1793, Louis XVII.—The Republic. 1802, The Consulate. 1804, Napoleon I. 1814, Louis XVIII. 1815, Napoleon. 1815, Louis XVIII.

MONACO.—1814, Honorius V.

ENGLAND.—1760, George III. (1812, Prince of Wales Regent.) 1820, George IV.

SPAIN.—1788, Charles IV. 1808, Ferdinand VII. 1808, Joseph (Bonaparte). 1814, Ferdinand VII.

PORTUGAL.—1777, Maria and Peter III. (1786, Maria only.) 1791, John Prince Regent (Retirement to the Brazils). 1816, John VI.

ITALY (Pope).—1775, Pius VI. 1800, Pius VII. 1823, Leo XII.

NAPLES (AND SICILY).—1759, Ferdinand IV. 1806, Joseph (Bonaparte). 1808, Joachim (Murat). 1815, Ferdinand I. (and IV.).

SARDINIA.—1773, Victor Amadeus II. 1796, Charles Emmanuel II. 1802, Victor Emmanuel I. (until 1805). 1814, the same restored.

ITALY (King of). Napoleon I., 1805 to 1814.

ROME (King of). Napoleon II., 1811 to 1814.

ETRURIA (established 1801).—Louis I. 1803, Louis II.

TUSCANY (Grand-Duke).—1790, Ferdinand III. 1808, (Grand-Duchess) Eliza (Bonaparte-Bacchiochi). 1814, Ferdinand III.

TURKEY.—1789, Selim III. 1807, Mustapha IV. 1808, Mahmoud VI.

EGYPT.—Mehemet Ali.

ALGIERS.

PRUSSIA.—1786, Frederick William II. 1797, Frederick William III.

GERMANY (Austria).— 1790, Leopold II. 1792, Francis II. 1806, Francis I.

HOLLAND (Netherlands).— 1757, William IV. (to 1795). 1806, Louis (Bonaparte) to 1810. 1814, William Frederick.

POLAND.— 1764, Stanislaus II. (Partition of Poland, 1795).

RUSSIA.— 1762, Peter III., Catherine II. 1796, Paul I. 1801, Alexander I. 1828, Nicholas I.

SWEDEN.— 1792, Gustavus IV. 1809, Charles XIII. 1818, Charles XIV.

NORWAY (with Denmark to 1814; with Sweden after 1814).

DENMARK.— 1766, Christian VII. (1784, Frederick Prince Regent.) 1808, Frederick VI.

BAVARIA.— (Elector) Charles Maximilian, (King) Maximilian I.

HANOVER.— George III. (of England), George IV. (of England), William IV. (of England), Ernest (King of Hanover), 1837.

SAXONY.— (Elector until 1806) Frederick Augustus III. (and I.). 1827, Antony Clement.

WESTPHALIA.— 1807, Jérôme (to 1813).

WIRTEMBERG.— (Elector 1803, King 1805) Frederick II. (and I.). 1816, William I.

PERSIA.— 1795, Aga Mohammed. 1797, Fatah Ali. 1835, Mohammed.

INDIA.— 1772, Warren Hastings. 1785, Sir John Macpherson. 1786, Lord Cornwallis. 1793, Lord Teignmouth — (Lord Cornwallis, for a short time, followed by Sir Alured Clarke for a few weeks). 1798, the Marquess of Wellesley. 1805, Lord Cornwallis— (Sir George Barlow). 1807, Lord Minto. 1813, Earl of Moira. 1823, Lord Amherst.

CHINA.

JAPAN.

UNITED STATES.— 1789, George Washington. 1797, John Adams. 1801, Thomas Jefferson. 1809, James Madison. 1817, James Monroe.

HAYTI AND SAINT DOMINGO.— 1794, Toussaint. 1804, Dessalines. 1807, Christophe (Hayti). 1807, Petion (St. Domingo.)

BRAZIL.—Pedro I.

MEXICO (see Spain).

CURIOUS COINCIDENCE

Some curious instances of the especial connection of the letter M with the two Napoleons, First and Third, may perhaps be noted. Marbœuf was one of the first to recognize the talent of Napoleon at the École Militaire. Montenotte was one of his earliest, Marengo one of his greatest, battles; Mantua his principal siege, and Melas opened to him the way into Italy. He fought at Montmirail, Montereau, and Mont Saint Jean; Paris was lost for him at the Battle of Montmartre, and his troops were defeated at Maida. Other battles took place at Malojaroslowitz, Medina de la Rio Seco, Millessimo, the Mincio, Mohilow, Mohrungen, Mojaisk, Montebello, etc., and General Mack surrendered to Napoleon at Ulm, while both Malta and the Mauritius were lost to the French. Milan was the first, Madrid the middle, and Moscow the last capital of the enemy to be entered. Josephine was born at Martinique, and Maria Louisa partook of his highest destinies; Moreau and Murat betrayed him. Six of his Marshals (Macdonald, Marmont, Masséna, Moncey, Mortier, and Murat) and twenty-six of his Generals of Division had names beginning with the letter M. Maret, Mollien, Miot, Molé, Montalivet, and Melzi served him well in their diplomatic or civil capacities. Cardinal Maury represented the Church, and Mdlle. Mars the stage. His first Chamberlain was Montesquieu; his last sojourn Malmaison. He lost Egypt through the blunders of Menou, employed Miollis to arrest the Pope, and created Ney Prince of the Moskowa, and Regnier Duke of Massa. Malet conspired against him, and Metternich overcame him ultimately in the field of diplomacy. He gave himself up to Captain Maitland, was sent to Saint Helena, where he had the company of Count Montholon and Sir Pulteney Malcolm, and the services of his valet Marchand. Two of his brothers took the titles of Montfort and Musignano, and his

Mother had the official title of **Madame Mère** bestowed upon her by the Emperor. We leave it to the reader to trace out the coincidence farther in regard to Napoleon III. The words **M**ontijo, **M**orny, **M**agenta, **M**ac**M**ahon, **M**alakoff, **M**exico, **M**aximilian, **M**ontauban, **M**etz, **M**oltke, etc., will at once occur to him.

THE PRINCESSE DE LAMBALLE

"THE Princesse de Lamballe having been spared on the night of the 2d, flung herself on her bed oppressed with every species of anxiety and horror. She closed her eyes, but only to open them in an instant, startled with frightful dreams. About eight o'clock next morning two national guards entered her room to inform her that she was going to be removed to the Abbaye. She slipped on her gown, and went down stairs into the Sessions Room. When she entered this frightful court, the sight of weapons stained with blood, and of executioners whose hands, faces, and clothes were smeared over with the same red dye, gave her such a shock that she fainted several times. At length she was subjected to a mock examination, after which, just as she was stepping across the threshold of the door, she received on the back of her head a blow with a hanger, which made the blood spout. Two men then laid fast hold of her, and obliged her to walk over dead bodies, while she was fainting every instant. They then completed her murder by running her through with their spears on a heap of corpses. She was afterward stripped, and her naked body exposed to the insults of the populace. In this state it remained more than two hours. When any blood gushing from its wounds stained the skin, some men, placed there for the purpose, immediately washed it off, to make the spectators take more particular notice of its whiteness. I must not venture to describe the excesses of barbarity and lustful indecency with which this corpse was defiled. I shall only say that a cannon was charged with one of the legs! Toward noon the murderers determined to cut off her head, and carry it in triumph round Paris. Her other scattered limbs were also given to troops of cannibals who trailed them along the streets. The pike that supported the head was planted under the very windows of the Duke of Orléans. He was sitting down to dinner at the time, but rose from his chair and gazed at the ghastly spectacle without discovering the least symptom of uneasiness, terror, or satisfaction."—*Peltier*.

"It is sometimes not uninstructive to follow the career of the wretches who perpetrate such crimes to their latter end. In a remote situation on the seacoast lived a middle-aged man, in a solitary cottage, unattended by any human being. The police had strict orders from the First Consul to watch him with peculiar care. He died of suffocation produced by an accident which had befallen him when eating, uttering the most horrid blasphemies, and in the midst of frightful tortures. He had been the principal actor in the murder of the Princesse de Lamballe."—*Duchesse d'Abrantès*.

"Madame de Lamballe's sincere attachment to the Queen was her only crime. In the midst of our commotions she had played no part; nothing could render her suspected by the people, to whom she was only known by repeated acts of beneficence. When summoned to the bar of La Force, many among the crowd besought pardon from her, and the assassins for a moment stood doubtful, but soon murdered her. Immediately they cut off her head and her breasts; her body was opened, her heart torn out; and the tigers who had so mangled her took a barbarous pleasure in going to show her head and heart to Louis XVI. and his family at the Temple. Madame de Lamballe was beautiful, gentle, obliging, and moderate."—*Mercier*.

"Marshal Brune is said to have been present at the time of the Princess's murder, which has given rise to an insinuation that he was partially responsible for it."—See, for instance, Sir William Fraser's "*Hic et Ubique*," p. 129.

"Marie Thérèse Louise de Savoie Carignan Lamballe, widow of Louis Alexander Joseph Stanislas de Bourbon Penthièvre, Prince de Lamballe, was born in September, 1749, and was Mistress of the Household to the Queen of France, to whom she was united by bonds of the tenderest affection."—"*Biographie Moderne*."